DH
18t
us
fam
12—

The Unearthly

By
ROBERT HICHENS

Author of "THE GARDEN OF ALLAH,"
"BELLADONNA," ETC.

COSMOPOLITAN BOOK CORPORATION
NEW YORK   MCMXXVI

Printed in the United States of America by
J. J. LITTLE AND IVES COMPANY, NEW YORK

Contents

The Unearthly

The Unearthly

Book One—The Jew

CHAPTER I

It was a Saturday afternoon in the month of November, the last Saturday of the month. Swathes of pale gray mist melting into pearly white marked the course of the small river Rythe towards the cathedral city of Drearney. The river flowed through meadows, terribly damp in this season of the year, under an occasional archway of brick, by the small station of Eastley on the main line from London to the sea, and finally through the heart of the city, between old, leaning houses on the south side of the precincts, and out into the flat green marshes, where some of the finest sheep in the country found pasturage thoroughly to their liking. And it sang as it went, but in a voice so low as to be almost inaudible. And few in Drearney heard it. For the winter twilight was falling. Afternoon service in the cathedral was ending. There was a great bustle of shoppers in the High Street, and in many of the houses kettles were being put on fires to boil. For this was England, and one of the most thoroughly English places in the whole island, and on Saturday afternoons there were always many cozy gatherings in cozy, for the most part unpretentious, drawing-rooms round well-spread tea tables, gatherings of women, with sometimes a clergyman or two, a young doctor, or schoolmaster, or lawyer, or two or three of those retired, elderly men, soldiers, former civil servants, or members of the Stock Exchange, whose presence is valued in country towns, and who are the very life-blood of committees.

Miss Creswell had been "to cathedral," and on coming out

into the darkening afternoon she paused for a moment in the
shadow of the twin towers, which made her well-wrapped-up
figure look tiny despite its quite decent size, and considered
what she should do. She meant to go to tea somewhere. The
question was where? There were several pleasant houses
where she knew she would be welcome. The lovely power of
choice was surely hers. (For she continued to believe in free
will.) Which of these pleasant houses was she "in the mood"
for?

For some reason or other—perhaps she was a little vague
after hearing a very modern setting of "Lead, Kindly Light"
—she couldn't make up her mind on the matter at once, and
after standing for a moment on the gravel in front of the west
door of the cathedral she crossed it slowly till she was close to
two shops which displayed their wares actually within the majestic shelter of the precincts. In the windows of these dignified little shops, bow-windows which somehow looked conscious
of their apartness from all the other shops of Drearney, were
displayed wares connected with the cathedral, books about it,
small reproductions of statues within it, and photographs of
those who ministered in it in various capacities. Here were
to be seen cabinet photographs of Dean Brand, thin and erect
in a very ecclesiastical-looking chair which suggested a throne;
of Canon Hobson, merry and suave; of Canon Armytage with
his beautiful curly gray head carried slightly on one side; of
Canon Jackton, tiny and saturnine, with a mouth like a little
purse, the strings of which had just been drawn tight; of Canon
Blunt, also Archdeacon of Morburton, wearing the very wiggy
wig which made him conspicuous among his ecclesiastical
brethren and holding a pince-nez delicately between the thumb
and long forefinger of his right hand. Here were also to be
seen honorary and minor canons of various types; the head-
master of the famous Queen's School of Drearney, a gentleman
with an impressive black beard and fixed dark eyes, which
seemed to be engaged in looking through a stone wall not
shown in the photograph; a charming group of cherubs forming part of the cathedral choir; a much less charming selection
of lay vicars, most of them with walrus mustaches and fat
hands; and finally—to crown the attractions—a full-length of
Mr. Swarpes, the head verger of the cathedral, a sanguine
personage in a processional attitude, who wore his robes with
an air, and held one arm akimbo, and looked quite ready to

lead on the Archbishop of Canterbury himself to St. Augustine's chair.

Now all these people without exception Miss Creswell knew personally. She saw them very often indeed in the flesh. She was familiar with their faces, and thought that she was familiar with their characters. There was therefore no reason why she should be interested in looking at their photographs. Yet now she stood looking at them in the fading daylight, and an odd thought went through her mind. It was this: "How much of spirituality is distributed among all these people whose lives are spent mainly in the so-called service of God? How much of soul is there in all these different-sized and differently proportioned bodies? How much of the Gleam from afar is in these many eyes of dean, archdeacon, canons, honorary and minor canons, choir-boys, lay vicars and vergers?"

And then, just after she happened to make this inquiry of herself—or of them—her eyes fell on another photograph of a thin man of perhaps thirty-four or thirty-five with extraordinarily rough hair, which seemed to be sprouting violently from his head in all directions—"quarreling hair" someone had called it—steady eyes, an eager, slightly turned-up nose and lips firmly pressed together: Mr. Hendry, the organist of the cathedral. It was rumored that though, as everybody allowed, Mr. Hendry was a very clever man and an exceptionally accomplished musician, he didn't "really" believe in God. Nobody had ever heard him make that statement. Nobody even claimed to have ever heard him say such a dreadful thing. But somehow it had "got about" that Mr. Hendry's belief in God was very shaky, to say the least of it.

Certainly since he had come to Drearney the singing had immensely improved, had become far more sensitive, even far more religious than it had been. Instead of merely bawling their way through too familiar music, the choir now really sang. And often the music which they sang was new and highly original. For Mr. Hendry had somehow managed to "get over" the precentor, Mr. Prowse. But people seemed to think that the organist took such trouble about the music simply because he happened to be intensely musical, not at all because he had any devout Protestant feeling in him, that it was the artist who was at work in him, not the deeply religious man.

Miss Creswell remembered all this as she stood and looked

at his photograph. Nevertheless a still small voice within her said, "There's more spirituality in his face than in all the other faces put together."

And she remembered an episode in her life when she had been in Athens. (For she was one of those English spinsters who travel.) On a Sunday in Athens she had meant to go to the English Protestant Church, and she had set out to find it. But she had not found it. And, hearing a sound of music in a Byzantine church among some cypresses, she had gone in there, and had heard there the most wonderfully mystical singing that had ever fallen on her ears. It had been a revelation to her of what religious singing can be, and she had never forgotten it. The singers had been Russians, the church the Russian Church in Athens. Now she seemed to see in the face of the organist, Mr. Hendry, something of the mystery she had heard in those Russian voices.

A movement roused her from her unusual contemplation of the familiar faces in the bow-windows. She looked and saw that a man, who must surely have come up noiselessly, was standing beside her, apparently gazing at the photographs as she had just been gazing. Startled at finding him there, she glanced at him with sharp inquiry, and immediately she had the feeling that he had been there for some time, and that the unusual thoughts which had been passing through her mind had been sent to her by him, or had come to her from him, perhaps without any deliberate intention on his part.

"I thought all that because he was thinking all that." So she expressed it to herself as she looked at the man.

He turned slowly and looked at her. The cathedral clock began to strike the half-hour. And immediately Miss Creswell moved away from the window and from the stranger, who did not follow her, but remained standing still in front of the shops.

Miss Creswell was still undecided about her destination, but she walked away with decision and briskly, not towards the archway and narrow lane which led to the High Street, but towards the larger loneliness of the precincts, about whose lawns were dotted the comfortable homes of the cathedral dignitaries. She would go to one of the canons' houses for tea. But—to which?

Not all the canons attached to the cathedral foundation were in Drearney just then. Canon Armytage was at Oxford giving lectures. Canon Jackton was at Menton reposing, and Canon Hobson was somewhere up in the North holding a mission. But the archdeacon was at home. Miss Creswell could see two or three lights beaming from the windows of his large Gothic house with the very modern porch which Mrs. Blunt, for some unknown reason, had insisted on having "built on." And Canon Barrimore would certainly be at home too. He was canon in residence just now. (Miss Creswell was thankful for that.) And she had just heard him reading the lessons in cathedral in his deep, sonorous voice with the wonderful inflections that gave you a thrill at moments. Of all the canons who were in residence from time to time at Drearney, Canon Barrimore was the most popular as a "draw." He filled the cathedral whenever he preached, and he was a really brilliant man, modern, daring in his sermons if not in his life, and extremely fond of society—though perhaps not specially fond of the society of Drearney. He got people down from London to entertain his mind and sharpen his wits on, clever people, famous people even, sometimes. Such a man was a godsend in Drearney, Miss Creswell thought. And the Barrimores were always very nice to her. They liked her. She knew that. And she and the canon discussed poetry together. For she was one of the very few people in Drearney who were really fond of poetry, and she knew all about Masefield, and De la Mare, and W. H. Davies, and Yeats, and Lascelles Abercrombie.

After a moment's hesitation Miss Creswell decided to go to the Barrimores' to tea.

Their house, red brick and Georgian, with lots of laurel bushes in its garden, was in a comparatively remote part of the precincts, set right back at the very end of a long lawn where the choristers sometimes played games discreetly. To reach it Miss Creswell had to turn a corner to the right beyond Mr. Hendry's small house. Just before she turned this corner some impulse made her look back into the gathering twilight which was softly enfolding the cathedral and its environs.

In the distance she saw the solitary figure of a man walking slowly, yet she thought purposefully, towards her on the narrow path between the grass plots. No other being was in sight. She stood quite still for a moment with her eyes fixed on this figure. A cawing of rooks came to her from some hidden place, probably from Dean's Yard. There was an almost biting coldness in the damp air, and suddenly she was aware of it. Not a time for standing about—or strolling about! Her hands met inside her fur muff and she moved briskly towards the house beyond the laurel bushes.

Mrs. Barrimore was at home, and Miss Creswell stepped into the house with a pleasant feeling of anticipation, and also a slight and unusual feeling of relief. It was rather dismal outside in the November weather, what with so much fog about and the day going so early. The light and warmth of the house made an agreeable contrast. It was a great mercy to be comfortable and to have cheerful people about you. She would forget the dreary cawing of the rooks and the cold of the coming night.

The well-known sound of the canon's deep, ringing voice came out to her from the big drawing-room on the ground floor as the man servant opened the door. And she heard the sound of another voice, unknown to her, a woman's voice. And then she was walking in, and seeing the log fire, and the tea table, and being greeted.

Canon Barrimore and Mrs. Barrimore apparently were a very contented couple, but physically they were ill-assorted, for Mrs. Barrimore was very tall and large-boned and pale and angular, and her husband was very firm and small-boned and red. His face with the slightly tucked-in chin was red all over, and was crowned with snow-white, rather thin hair. His blue eyes looked fiery and intelligent, and he bore himself with a very complete self-possession that had perhaps at times just the faintest hint of self-complacency in it. Mrs. Barrimore looked like something large that was inclined to fade away. The canon looked like something small which had every intention of persisting. With them Miss Creswell saw a woman who was a stranger to her, and who, she felt positive at once, lived in London and had come down to Drearney for the week-end, a vivid, plain, flat-cheeked, small-eyed, energetic creature, with a kind and willing yet at the same time not uncritical expression. After being greeted Miss Creswell was introduced to this woman, who was Mrs. Sotheby, well known in London and elsewhere as a social worker, a writer in the reviews, an occasional speaker on social questions, and an objector to prohibition in any form.

"Miss Creswell is one of our stand-bys when we are down here," said the canon to Mrs. Sotheby, as Miss Creswell sat down by the fire. "She knows about all that's going on—and

chicle ingeniously constructed to be used by Powers
er. And more, she seemed to know that she was
to know it with painful, with alarmed conviction.
was the anthem by?" she heard Mrs. Sotheby saying.
. Barrimore gave her another cup of tea.

hem was written by our organist, Hendry," said
"A very clever musician, he is."

ote that anthem he's a mystic at heart," said Mrs.
I'm sure Evelyn Underhill would have felt that if
it. There was a fundamental mysticism in the
must be an interesting man."

him to dine tonight, then you can find out. What
about Hendry, Miss Creswell? Do you find him
.

is. But I know him very little. And I always
ensely reserved."

at home here," said the canon, "except with me.
t on well. I understand his agnosticism."

torious in London that most of the clever agnostics,
m scientists and celebrated doctors, went from time
St. John's, Arundel Street, Mayfair, Canon Barri-
ch, to hear him preach. His sermons were like
ays and were much appreciated by "my agnostics"
mes playfully called his flock.

dded the canon, with a touch of probably uncon-
rbity, "he at any rate can understand the sermons
ach here during my three months of residence."

this he looked across the tea table at Miss Cres-
seemed to her that his blue eyes commanded her
had so often been, to express her joy in his preach-
ght each year when the time of his residence came

couldn't. Something seemed to inhibit her. She
im, and saw in his eyes the question, "Why are
ke yourself today?" So plainly was it written in
t she felt as if she saw the words appear mysteri-
the background of the room. She read them, and
rd herself saying:

remember reading during the war that eventually
r would come to mankind out of the North?"

n looked surprised, startled almost. She saw Mrs.
nd Mrs. Sotheby, who had just begun a new con-

the others don't. It's extraordinary what people don't know.
How many miles are we from London, dear?" He turned to
his wife, who was bending from the height with tea-cake to
Miss Creswell.

"About forty miles, I should think," said she in a thin voice.

"Well, at any rate not much more. And the dear souls in
this place have managed not to hear about almost everything
that is going on and interesting London people. My pulpit
allusions must mean very little to them. I often wonder"—
he tucked in his chin and his voice took on an added sonority
—"why they come to hear me. But they do come—aha!"

The final exclamation was a sort of deep bass chuckle, which
seemed to drop down and disappear between the canon's stiff
white collar and his throat.

"The dean of course is altogether beyond them," he continued, after an instant of apparently humorous reverie. "I'm
sure that many of them consider him to be a son of Belial!"

A rather startling faint laugh came unexpectedly from Mrs.
Barrimore.

"My wife enjoys the idea of that, but Mrs. Dean thinks a
Very Reverend has certain obligations which her Ambrose forgets the existence of."

"Does she?" said Mrs. Sotheby. "I think if I married a dean
my husband's intellectual misbehavior would be very precious
in my sight. Dean Brand is a perpetual joy—to me at any
rate."

"And what do you say?" asked the canon of Miss Creswell.

He knew Miss Creswell delighted in his sermons, and had a
tremendous, but not silly, admiration for his intellect. As he
considered her a very well-informed and sensible woman this
pleased him very much. He was frankly fond of Miss Creswell,
and knowing that she enjoyed clever talk and never made a
fool of herself, he often got his wife to invite her to his Saturday dinners, when big guns from London or elsewhere were
staying with him. The brilliant Dean of Drearney was a star
which shone outside ecclesiastical circles. He was indeed
known as a writer and public speaker to almost everyone with
any pretension to intelligence. But somehow he seldom quite
"came off" in the pulpit. Now Canon Barrimore always came
off. This fact gave him a distinct advantage over the dean
in Drearney. Nevertheless, with such a famous man established in the deanery, the canon could not consider himself

completely cock of the walk in the precincts. And in his question to Miss Creswell, as she realized, there was just a hint of the faintest uneasiness.

Such an uneasiness, on any other day, she would almost certainly not have felt critical about. Indeed she was so fond of the canon, and admired him so much, that she never criticized him. But this evening, somehow, she did not seem to be quite her usual self. Something sharp, something clear, something penetrating, was surely alert within her.

She found herself thinking, "He would like me to run down the dean." The thought was followed by a slight feeling of distaste. A little more and it might have been a feeling of disgust.

Wondering at herself Miss Creswell made some non-committal rejoinder. But that didn't satisfy Canon Barrimore. He needed his compliment before Mrs. Sotheby, and he pressed for it.

"Come now, Miss Creswell! I know you've always got your opinion on everything, and a very clear and sensible opinion too. Don't you think we are very fortunate in having such a dean to speak to us from the cathedral pulpit?"

Now Miss Creswell preferred Canon Barrimore's sermons to the dean's, and so did everyone else in Drearney. And Canon Barrimore knew it. No one better. He had therefore given her a very good opening for a compliment to him at the dean's expense. On any other day she would surely have taken advantage of it. But today she felt that she couldn't, that she must stand up for the dean in order to avoid feeding the vanity of the canon, which she realized for the first time to be opposed to spirituality. So she said:

"Yes, indeed I do. But I'm afraid his sermons are almost wasted here." (She turned towards Mrs. Sotheby.) "We aren't a very intellectual set in Drearney," she added, "and if we are given hard intellectual nuts we aren't always able to crack them. The dean's nuts are hard, but the kernels are always well worth getting at."

Again there came the startling faint laugh from Mrs. Barrimore.

"You're amused, my dear?" said the canon, rather sharply.

"I was imagining Drearney trying to feed on a diet composed exclusively of the dean's nuts," she replied.

And she leaned her long body to one side, let her pale head

drop slightly, and faintly
joined in and began talking
economy and his opinions
She said he was at heart
agree to that and declared
sort of man who had an it
who was always unpleasan

"If you agree with hi
intellect."

"Like Bernard Shaw,"
do what he tells you shoul
mous length what an excep

"They both remind me
Barrimore. *"He ought to*

"And Bernard Shaw
"Imagine his sermons!"

And then, having arrive
mons, he again, as Miss
gave her carefully prepared
understood, as never before,
as the singer needs it, the a
she was oddly oppressed by
creeping vanity in men. W
and talked again, she wond
amazement, why she had ne
for praise. But she could
struck by it. He was a d
good-hearted. Yes! But no
praises like the mouth of a
she couldn't, she just simply
the gaping became patheti
couldn't.

And why couldn't she? S
of the two dignified little s
beginning of this odd develo
silently progressing. And s
tion of the precision and ter
esses. A cancer begins. Ar
in each case isn't there a vic
by a feeling that was like a
came out of a realization o
seemed a sudden knowledge

she was a
outside of
being used,

"Whom
And Mr

"The an
the canon.

"If he w
Sotheby.
she'd heard
music. H

"I'll ask
do you say
interesting

"I feel
find him i

"He's n
He and I

It was
many of th
to time to
more's ch
brilliant e
as he som

"And,"
querable
which I p

As he s
well, and
to be as s
ing, her
round.

But—s
looked at
you so u
his eyes
ously up
then she

"Do y
a new Sa

The c
Barrimo

versation between themselves, looking at her inquiringly. And she wondered what she was doing and what she was going to do. She didn't understand what had prompted her to ask that curiously abrupt question. And she glanced round on them all.

"Surely," she said, "either during, or soon after the war, there was some prophecy to the effect that a new Savior would come to mankind out of the North."

There was a moment of silence. Then Mrs. Sotheby said, "Aren't you thinking of a dream Tolstoy is supposed to have had long before the war, a great dream which he wrote down, and which was published after his death?"

"Perhaps I am. Do you think such a dream could come true?" She saw Mrs. Sotheby's small, eager eyes fixed upon her with the intensity of one deeply interested in the minds of her neighbors. The canon meanwhile was exchanging a glance with his wife.

"I suppose it might," said Mrs. Sotheby. "But I don't see why it should. One thing, however, I will say. I've traveled a great deal, and I think if a new Savior ever is destined to come to mankind he is far more likely to come out of the North than out of the South. All *strangeness* of brain"—she laid a strong emphasis on the word "strangeness"—"in Europe at any rate seems to me to be up in the North."

"Religious fanatics abound in the East," observed the canon.

"Yes," said Mrs. Sotheby, "but I don't think a fanatic could ever save anyone."

"The world has had its Savior," said the canon, in his most sonorous voice. "Curiously enough I'm preaching on mankind's outrageous expectation of being saved over and over again tomorrow evening in the cathedral. We've got a missioner tomorrow morning.

"I shall come in the evening," said Miss Creswell.

It was a bun at last and the gaping mouth shut on it with decisive avidity.

And then Miss Creswell got up to go.

The canon—it was his cordial custom—accompanied his departing guest to the front door. As he opened it he saw her look quickly, questioningly he thought, out into the darkness of the precincts. "Are you expecting anyone to fetch you?"

"Oh no! Thank you so much for my pleasant hour. I always feel true hospitality in your house."

The canon looked pleased. His bun had done him good, and he was ready for more. He pressed his guest's hand.

"It was strange your speaking—and so abruptly, if you'll forgive me for saying so—about a Savior just now. What do you think prompted you to ask that question?"

"It was abrupt, I know," she said.

And she stopped.

"I think it was a striking case of telepathy," he said.

She looked startled.

"My mind was full of the sermon I have just finished writing. I told you its subject—the cry of mankind for repeated Salvation."

"Yes."

"You spoke out of my mind."

"You think so?"

"Don't you?"

She wanted to say "No," but she didn't. For she liked him very much, and he had always been very kind to her. And so she only said, "How strange!"

"Yes—the power of one mind over another."

He meant of course the power of his mind over hers. A last thrust of vanity! And yet he was really a dear man.

"Good-by!"

The yellow light vanished as he shut the door behind her. The precincts looked very dark and lonely in the cold November evening. She went forward slowly.

Meanwhile Canon Barrimore had returned to the warm and brightly lit drawing-room, where he found Mrs. Sotheby and his wife talking about the visitor who had just left them. As he came in he caught the words, "One of the best of our neighbors here," spoken in his wife's thin voice.

"You're speaking about Miss Creswell, of course," he said.

"Yes," said Mrs. Sotheby, "I liked her. A thoroughly straightforward woman with no nonsense about her and plenty of sense."

"Exactly. We like her immensely too. But she was not quite at her best today."

"Wasn't she?"

"No—no. Didn't it strike you that she was decidedly *décousue?* She went from one thing to another without any apparent purpose that I at any rate was able to divine. To use an expression of the stage, she didn't join her flats. Something had certainly upset her before she came to the house. I wonder what it was."

"I didn't notice. But of course I don't know her," said Mrs. Sotheby.

"I'm sure you agree with me, dear?" said the canon to his wife.

"Yes. Instead of gliding as usual, she rather plunged."

"Certainly she was a bit abrupt about the Savior from the North," said Mrs. Sotheby, like one wishing if possible to find some point of agreement.

The canon smiled.

"I think I've pitched upon the reason for that."

"Yes?"

"Yes. That, I think, was a clear case of telepathy, of the influence of one mind over another subject mind." He explained, alluding to his sermon. "She thought so too. We spoke about it at the hall door. But there was something wrong—something wrong. However, that's neither here nor there. D'you know her niece in London?"

"Who is that?"

"Imogen Lowrie."

"Imogen! Of course I do!"

"Lady Lowrie is Miss Creswell's sister."

"And that pretty bit of modern insolence is coming down tonight by the late train to stay with her aunt," said Mrs. Barrimore.

"She'll be in the cathedral tomorrow night," said the canon, tucking in his chin. "She hates church-going, but she comes to hear me. I'm sure I don't know why—aha!" Once again the bass chuckle seemed to drop down between his collar and his throat. "And now, if you'll forgive me, I must go and give the last polish to my sermon for tomorrow night."

"He's as particular about his sermons as Anatole France used to be about his smallest stories," said Mrs. Barrimore, as her husband, very upright, went out of the room. "I always call him the conscious artist."

And then again there sounded by the fire her faint unexpected laugh.

CHAPTER II

THE way through the precincts that evening seemed to Miss
Creswell very long, and the winter darkness exceptional.
Usually when she was in the precincts she was companioned
by a delightful sense of intimate safety. Within the ancient gray
walls, where still by night a watchman walked and cried the
hours, all possibility of danger seemed blotted out. The ugly
voices of the world were hushed by those green lawns. There
one never met a beggar, a tramp, or any hostile or even enigmatic figure. Nobody whom you encountered "in the pre-
cints" needed any explanation. And Miss Creswell had often
wished that her house stood in that tranquil enclosure.

That evening, however, the usual feeling of pleasant intimacy and safety had left her, and as she walked briskly
forward, peering into the dimness that brooded over the wet
grass and about the houses withdrawn in their gardens, she
found herself longing for the lights and the vulgar bustle of
the High Street.

As she turned the corner by the organist's house she hesitated. She saw a light in one of the lower windows and
wondered if Mr. Hendry were in his study. He was unmarried and lived alone, except for a couple of servants. The
blind of the lighted window was up, but she could not see
anyone in the room. It was strange how that light held her.
She did not want to get away from it, to lose it in the darkness. Such a reluctance was entirely unreasonable and quite
unworthy of her, a strong, healthy, middle-aged and, she hoped,
sensible woman, who had traveled in many out-of-the-way and
in some perhaps even dangerous places alone. She realized it
and walked on towards the archway, not far from the twin
towers, the main exit from the precincts to the town. But as
she walked she looked furtively about her and was always
listening for the sound of footfalls. And presently she heard
footfalls approaching her from a distance. Then she was conscious of a leaping of her heart and of a desire to turn back.
But she resisted the desire, pulled herself together, walked on
resolutely and in a moment met Honorary Canon Smale, nick-
named in the town "Mr. Pomposity," proceeding homewards
majestically, wearing woolen gloves and holding a stout
umbrella.

Though pompous Canon Smale was sociable, and he insisted on escorting Miss Creswell as far as the High Street, where he left her amid the blaze of lights and the bustle of crowds. Miss Creswell didn't really like Canon Smale. He was too self-important and too narrow-minded to please her type of nature. But she felt grateful to him that evening, and her good-by and her expression of thanks for his company were so cordial that he retreated in high good humor, and with an even more pronounced suggestion of "Here we go! Here we go!" in his gait than usual.

Miss Creswell lived in a fairly large country house—it really was that—on the north side of the city. The back of it and the main door were on Ewenden Road opposite to a long line of uninteresting villas. But her house stood alone, and had been built long before the town had encroached towards the railway which ran in a deep cutting beyond the end of her spacious garden.

Ewenden Road had only been in existence for some twenty years. Miss Creswell frankly regretted its existence. But as all the chief rooms of her abode looked out on the garden she was often able to forget the existence of suburbia. And it was certainly an advantage being as it were alone and at the same time in a city and in the country. Beyond the hidden railway were fields and copses. Low hills and woods closed in the distance. There was nothing striking about the view, but it was pleasant and green and calm, and the large garden was a perpetual delight to its owner. For Miss Creswell was one of those innumerable spinster ladies in England who take an active interest in gardening, and who may be seen out of doors in all weathers "doing things" in garden gloves, and shady hats, and covering aprons with a touch of blue in them.

She lived alone and was fairly satisfied to live alone as she had so many friends about her. But she very often had a guest or two with her, and, as Mrs. Barrimore was aware, that night she was expecting "that pretty bit of modern insolence," her niece, Imogen Lowrie.

When she got home she felt glad of that. She felt that she wanted company. For she wasn't feeling so cheerful and normal as usual. A certain uneasiness which she couldn't get rid of and which even verged on apprehension, companioned her. Her niece was coming down very late. She wouldn't arrive till past ten, when the last train from London got in.

Miss Creswell would have to dine alone. But that didn't matter. She would read some interesting book at dinner. What did matter was that she would have gay and careless youth in the house with her that night.

Imogen was preposterously unlike her aunt, and often laughed at her and flouted her with the careless impudence which was part of her birthright. Nevertheless, she and her aunt "got on," and Miss Creswell often felt that something—she didn't know really just what it was—deep down in Imogen, hidden and seldom manifesting its presence even surreptitiously, had hold of something in her. Whether Imogen felt this too her aunt didn't know.

Soon after ten o'clock had chimed from the great center tower of the cathedral Miss Creswell's modest landau car drew up to Ewenden House with Imogen in it.

"Hullo!" called a clear young voice, as Miss Creswell showed in the lighted hall. "Surely the train's damned late, isn't it?"

"Is it? I don't think so. How are you, dear?"

"Tired. I was hunting today. I trained down and got back late. Hugo was with me and had the deuce of a spill."

"Good evening, Harriet. You know the way, don't you? It's the usual room next to mine." (This to Imogen's maid.)

"Yes, ma'am, thank you."

"Don't you want something to eat, Im?"

"No, thanks. I gobbled some food before starting. But I should be glad of a drink. Whisky, please. Scotch of course. Where shall we have it?"

"In the library. I am sitting there."

"The good old library! It's a genuine piece too. No pretense about it."

And this was true, for Miss Creswell loved books and had not only inherited many from her father, but had added to them considerably from time to time when she had had some spare money. As they came into the large book-lined room Imogen had a good look at her aunt, whom by the way she never called "aunt" but always "Towser" for some unknown reason. And "Towser" had a good look at her.

Imogen was tall, very slim and long limbed, with dark hair (which of course entirely concealed her very pretty ears), large irresponsible hazel eyes, that sometimes looked green, sometimes yellow, and a small full-lipped mouth that never gaped. She had a charming nose of the straight, short type often seen in England, level, thin dark eyebrows, a lovely neck where youth showed in all its enchanting graciousness, long hands with slight fingers, narrow ankles and small feet. She was in fact really what many people would have called a beautiful girl. But she was so heavily "made up" that one scarcely knew what she was. With Imogen it was not a case of a touch of rouge here and there, or a powdered nose. No. The whole surface of her young face—she was only just twenty-one—was covered with something white which gave her skin an arum-lily hue. The same mystery covered the whole of her neck that was seen. Her eyebrows were darkened. Under her careless, often impudent, eyes shadows of deep blue-black were painted. And on her almost childish cheeks there were sharp touches of a sort of orange-red which suggested a face lit up by the glare of a conflagration. Her naturally pouting lips were a bright sealing-wax red and looked sticky. Her figure, which at this moment was clothed in a very perfect tailor-made coat and skirt, was quite lovely.

The net effect of her was of an aristocratic girl with an intellect who, for some mysterious reason, had decided to become a street-walker, and whose "beat" was probably not far from Piccadilly Circus.

The contrast between her and her aunt was striking. For Miss Creswell had a fresh, countrified complexion, never used even powder, but actually had the temerity to soap her face every morning with "old brown Windsor," wore her brown hair liberally sprinkled with gray parted in the middle, was daring enough to show her ears to the world, and looked exactly like what she was, a comfortably-off, healthy, sensible, energetic Englishwoman of middle age, kind, intelligent and prepared to be friendly. Only in one way was she, perhaps, slightly deceptive. She didn't look specially like a spinster. She might indeed very well have passed for a married woman, though she had not the face of a mother.

Over the Scotch whisky—and of course Imogen smoked—they had one of those talks which ought surely to be difficult, but which somehow are not, given two hearts between which there is a hidden and mysterious link. Imogen was all that her aunt was not, and never could have been, even had she been born thirty years later than she had been. Imogen was vain, and Miss Creswell was quite without vanity. Imogen was full of careless, youthful selfishness, intellectual pride, hardy self-assurance. Miss Creswell thought a great deal for others, had never been puffed up about her brains, though she didn't consider herself by any means a fool, and had only the self-assurance that comes from being quite sensible and quite natural.

Imogen had unbounded physical courage, amounting even to physical recklessness. Miss Creswell was no coward, but she had sufficient imagination to be aware of the dangers of this mortal life, and sufficient care for herself to guard against them when needful. Imogen was a sportswoman. Miss Creswell was a traveler but not a sportswoman. She painted in water-colors. Imogen painted her face and neck. Miss Creswell gardened. Imogen hunted, played all manner of games, drove a motor, rode in amateur steeplechases, and occasionally shot. Imogen was what is called modern. Miss Creswell, even in her youth, had never felt herself to be modern. Nor—and here her good sense showed—did she now consider herself to be "old-fashioned." She didn't struggle to keep up with any so-called movement, or to force her mind into any mold because it was the fashionable mold. She just went on her way, the way that was natural to her, and avoided being shocked by the demonstrations of the absurdly named "new" world, and Imogen never tried to shock Towser, nor to avoid shocking her. She was Imogen, painted, powdered, arum-lily white, orange and sealing-wax red, because she chose to be so. And Towser was Towser with the dear old brown Windsor face because Towser chose to be so. And that was all right.

Presently the clock in the library struck twelve, and Imogen remembered that she was supposed to be tired.

"Well, Towser, I suppose you want to turn in," she said. She got up and looked into a mirror. "We had quite a good run today. That new Irish mare Hugo picked up for me carried me well. But Hugo was damned unlucky. He's the best man on a horse I ever laid eyes on and yet he's always having spills. There are precious few bones in that beautiful body of his that he hasn't broken, and he'll break those few for a certainty before he's done with it. Poor old Hugo!"

"Do you mean to marry him?"

"I don't believe I shall. Somehow I'm not sure he's the man for me. Of course if it didn't do I could get rid of him. He'd always let me divorce him if I wanted to. He's sworn that over and over again. And Hugo's a man of his word. So I shouldn't run any real risk in marrying him. But I don't believe I shall do it." All this time she had been looking, staring into the mirror. Now she turned round. "D'you think he's the man for me, Towser?"

"I scarcely know him. He'd suit the hunting side of you very well."

"Oh, Lord, yes! But I've got a brain and he hasn't, not a real brain. But I might find another man for that. Hugo would let me do what I liked."

"Are you sure?"

"He'd have to, or I should give him the chuck."

"But suppose he wouldn't take it?"

"He'd take it all right. He'd jolly well have to take it. My will's at least twice as strong as his."

"It may seem to be while he's desperately in love with you. But are you sure it would prove to be in marriage?"

Imogen smiled, and in that smile there was the enormous conceit of successful youth. "Now, Towser! Can you see a man ordering me about?"

After a slight pause Miss Creswell said, "Yes."

Imogen put one hand on her hip and shook her dark head. "Now, Towser—Towser!" she said, exactly in the voice considered by most people appropriate for the addressing of a dog. "Down, boy, down!"

"Oh, I'm quite serious," said Miss Creswell with unruffled calm. "You've probably never come up against a really tremendous will yet. You've probably never realized at all what a really tremendous will is like."

Imogen took her hand from her hip, and an intent look banished the conceited smile that was half ironic from her painted face. She came away from the mirror, suddenly crumpled up in the soft flowery manner of supple youth on a chair close to her aunt, stared into her face, and said, "Who's the man?"

Miss Creswell, to her own astonishment, blushed. She felt herself blushing, tried to stop, failed utterly and finally had to let the thing go—as Imogen would have said in her slangy way. "What nonsense, Im! I was speaking about Hugo."

"Now, Towser, now!"

"Hugo, as you yourself said, isn't specially strong in the will, though of course he's a wonderful horseman and all that sort of thing. But his character and brain——"

"Never mind about Hugo's character and brain, Towser! Tell me—who's the man?"

And she stretched out a long, beautiful hand, and laid it imperatively on Miss Creswell's knee.

"This is really foolish, Im."

"Very foolish, I'm afraid, Towser! But we know what women are. Where did you meet him? Surely not in Drearney! Don't tell me he's a minor canon, for if you do I simply shan't swallow it. No, little Towser, I shan't!"

"Now, Im, this is really too absurd! Merely because I say that you have never yet——"

"I'm awfully tired. I've been hunting. I've had three train journeys, and a row with Hugo, and a scrambled dinner practically eaten off a tray. I ought to be in bed with my head on a bolster and an "eidy" up to my chin. But here I sit till I know who's the man. And I'll prove to you what a really tremendous will is, Towser, unless you come out of all this maze of prevarication and give me a bit of honest truth. Now up with your paws and let's hear your bow-wow."

Miss Creswell began to laugh, but the long, beautiful hand tightened on her knee.

"Now, no hysteria, Towser!" said the soft, impudent voice. "Or I shall slap your paws. I shall indeed! Gently, now, gently!"

"Im, you really are an impossible niece. And the absurd way you jump at conclusions——"

"I don't need to jump. You present me with them, you dear innocent thing. Now—is he a minor canon? Because if he is I shall give you up. I simply won't possess an aunt who thinks a minor canon has a really tremendous will."

"Well, he isn't a minor canon."

"Where did you meet him?"

Miss Creswell seemed to hesitate, but she knew Imogen thoroughly, and it was past twelve o'clock, and now, all of a sudden, she felt that she wanted to speak.

"I met him in front of a photograph shop."

"Towser! Towser! I'm surprised at you getting off with a stranger in front of a photograph shop! This is worse than what we are all doing in London."

"Im dear, if you can't stop being absurd I shan't say another word."

Miss Creswell spoke without the least touch of temper, but with a genuine seriousness which snuffed out for the moment the volubility of her niece.

"But I can stop being absurd." And she drew her chair nearer and looked earnest beneath her paint. "What photograph shop?"

"The one—or rather the two; for there are two of them—in the precincts."

"In the precincts!" Imogen was evidently about to say something flippant, but she checked herself. "And when?"

"Today. After the second service. I had been to cathedral."

"Good girl!"

"When I came out I thought I would go and pay a visit somewhere. But I couldn't immediately make up my mind where. And while I was hesitating I found myself before the photograph shops. You know them?"

"Of course, full of deans, and canons, and choir-boys, and pretty-pretty vergers with silver pokers in their hands."

"I was standing there and looking at them. Of course I know them all very well."

"I should think so!"

"Yes. But just then I seemed to look at them in quite a new way. I seemed to consider them critically, as a stranger might have done who was judging their characters only by their faces. And the thought came to me: 'How much spirituality is there in all these people whose lives are spent in the so-called service of God?' Something like that! And I thought about spirituality and the Gleam from afar."

"The Gleam from afar?"

"Yes. Those very words came into my mind. And then I looked at a photograph of Mr. Hendry, the organist. You know they say in the town that he's an atheist."

"Do they really?"

"Or at any rate an agnostic."

"But that's different."

"Of course. Anyhow, they say he's very shaky in what they call his beliefs. But while I was looking at his photograph, I thought, 'There's more spirituality in that face than in all the others put together.' And then I remembered some singing I'd heard in the Russian church in Athens. Im, it was marvelous. It was mysticism going unclothed in music. It was the soul of man singing unveiled by the body. And I thought, 'In that face—of Mr. Hendry—there is something of the mystery I heard in those Russian voices in Greece.' Just then, exactly at that moment, someone moved close by me. Till then I had supposed I was entirely alone. I hadn't felt that anyone was near me. I hadn't heard anyone come. I looked and there was a man standing beside me, apparently looking at the photographs too."

Miss Creswell stopped speaking. Her usually calm face looked oddly excited, almost agitated.

"What was he like?" asked Imogen. She was quite serious now, and still kept her hand on Miss Creswell's knee.

"He was tall."

"How tall?"

"He looked to me quite six feet high and he was broad."

"A gentleman?"

"Oh no! I mean—I don't know! He may have been. But I never thought about such a thing as that. One couldn't. It would have been absurd."

"That's good!" said Imogen.

"Why—good?"

"It means that he must have been a *man*."

"It didn't matter whether he was born what's called a gentleman or not."

"I feel he had long hair and a tremendous beard. Am I right?"

"No. He was clean shaven, and his hair wasn't long. Nor particularly short either."

The sealing-wax lips drew together in a pout that was slightly disdainful. "A voluminous cloak?"

"Oh no. He was dressed in a perfectly ordinary way. He had on a long dark overcoat, a soft hat."

"Umbrella? Gloves?"

"He wasn't carrying anything. I don't know whether he had gloves. Anyhow if he had he wasn't wearing them. He may have been carrying them."

"Go ahead!"

"Directly I saw this man I had an odd feeling about him. I seemed to realize, to know absolutely, that the thoughts which had just been passing through my mind about the photographed people in the window and Mr. Hendry had come from this man, that they had not been my own thoughts, the thoughts absolutely natural to me, but merely a direct echo of his. He had been thinking that, and so I had had to think that. You understand, Im?"

"Yes."

"Have you ever had a feeling like that?"

"That I was merely echoing the thoughts that had just been in another's mind because they had been there?"

"Yes."

"Not I, Towser! My thoughts are ordinary enough at times, God knows! But at least they're my own, as far as I know. Drive on!"

"The man had been standing sideways to me. But as this realization—it seemed like that—came to me he turned round and looked at me."

"What was he like?"

"I thought he had the most remarkable face I had ever seen. I told you it was clean shaven. It reminded me very much of a lion's face. You know it's said that everybody resembles some animal or bird. Well, this man had a face like a lion, I thought. His forehead seemed to me—I only looked at him for an instant—broad and low. His features, I think, were blunt and tremendously powerful. His mouth was rather large and firm, but very sensitive. I specially noticed that. He had dark, not black, hair, with a little gray in it, very thick hair as far as I could see. Of course he had on a hat. His eyes were extraordinary. They looked to me large and sleepy, and somehow veiled, under long, thick eyebrows. Then he seemed to open them more, and they looked then enormous. They had a peculiar expression of intense power and remoteness, as if the man had abnormal force and could project it to vast distances. That's how it struck me. Of course I only looked at him for a second. But I seemed able to gather up an immense amount about him nevertheless."

"And then?"

"I walked away and went to tea at the Barrimores'."

"Oh!"

"What else did you expect?"

"Well, Towser, if any man had made such a colossal impression on me as that man evidently made on you I should have spoken to him right away. Or I should have waited till he spoke to me. By the way, was he going to speak to you?"

"How can I know?"

"Of course you know! A woman can always tell such a thing. Was he?"

"I don't know; honestly, Im, I don't know. But I was

so confused by the whole thing—his personality seemed to throw me into sudden awful confusion—that I think I lost the use of some of my faculties just then. There's something I haven't told you that I feel sure of about him. He certainly was not English, and I'm pretty sure he was a Jew."

"A Jew—oh, Lord! Why did you tell me that?"

"Why shouldn't I tell you it?"

"You know I can't stand Jews. And since the war they seem to have multiplied like locusts. Wherever one goes it's nothing but Jews, Jews, Jews. Everybody seems to be a Jew. The most unlikely people turn out to be Jews. Whenever I'm mad about a singer I find out he's, or she's, a Jew or a Jewess. Whenever I throw up my hat over a picture I find it was painted by a Jew. Whenever I'm crazy about a new book they tell me at Hatchard's, 'Oh, a young Jew wrote that!' I went with Hugo to the new dance club; the 'a little lower than the angels' we all call it. It's in Mayfair, the house old Lady Randon had to sell after she lost her last bib and tucker at baccarat. There was a dancer from the Argentine there, a real beauty, and a nose as straight as a ruler. Corraso, he calls himself. I danced with him. Never knew anything like it. Sheer perfection. Now I find he's a Jew. I'm sick of it, Towser! And, besides, if I'm afraid of anything I believe I'm afraid of Israel."

"Why?"

"Couldn't tell you. But Israel's in the air—in the air! And it means something. It means too much."

"I can't help that, can I? I feel convinced that man was a Jew."

"A Jew with a face like a lion and blunt features!"

"Yes."

"And it all ended in tea with the Barrimores?"

"It seemed to end."

"Seemed? Have you met him again?"

"It isn't that. When I was just going to turn the corner by Mr. Hendry's house, in going to the Barrimores, I looked back and saw the man, I believe, coming towards me in the distance."

"Following you up!" said Imogen with a twist of her bright red lips that suggested satire, not unkind, but light-hearted—a laugh dropping down as it were to age from the fortifications of youth.

"That was the last I saw of him, probably the last I shall ever see of him. But his mind followed me, Im."

"His mind—like a hound on the trail, eh?"

"That's just it—how I felt it. And all the time I was at the Barrimores' I felt that I was thinking thoughts that would have been his had he been there, that I was looking at people—there were only the canon and Mrs. Barrimore and Mrs. Sotheby——"

"Old Anne Sotheby! I know the old volcano."

"Yes, she said she knew you. I felt that I was looking at accustomed things and people with new eyes to a certain extent —with his eyes. I can't easily explain. There were things I should have said on any other day. Today I just couldn't say them. *He* wouldn't let me. That man's got some exceptional power. And it was upon me at the Barrimores'. Since I saw him, felt his personality, there's been a loss of independence in me. And I don't like it, Im. I've never known anything of this sort before."

"A bit fussed by it all, aren't you, Towser?"

Miss Creswell looked at the painted face close to her and wished that it were not painted. The blue shadows beneath her niece's careless eyes bothered her tonight, though she was thoroughly accustomed to them. For Imogen had begun making her face up when she was only sixteen.

"I don't feel free any more," she said, and her voice sounded cold with depression.

"Because you've stood with an unknown Jew in front of a photograph shop! Damned odd, to be sure!"

"I suppose as usual you are laughing at me!" said Miss Creswell with a touch of wholly unwonted irritation.

"Well, Towser, I'll be quite frank——"

"Oh do, dear, by all means—do!"

"Thanks. Then, since you ask me for it, I'm afraid you've fallen in love at first sight."

"In love!" exclaimed Miss Creswell. And this time the satire was all on her side. "In love! We aren't discussing a hunting Adonis who's broken nearly every bone in his beautiful body."

"Noli me tangere!" murmured Imogen, as if to herself.

"But you don't understand, and probably nobody else would. Come, let's go to bed."

"Towser—you aren't angry? You aren't going to bite?"

"No, no. But how can I expect you to understand?"

"But you did."

"Yes. That's true. Because I must say for you that you have a very quick gift of understanding."

"Well then—give me a real clue."

"I don't know whether I can. Wait a minute!"

Imogen waited in silence and stillness, always with her hand on her aunt's knee. And she looked downwards, no longer at Miss Creswell with intentness.

"Is this a clue?" at last said Miss Creswell. "When I was at the Barrimores' today, and we were talking about—let me see! I think it was about Canon Barrimore's sermons."

"I'm quite sure it was!"

"I was suddenly moved to say a thing which had nothing whatever to do with the conversation. My saying it startled them all, I believe. And it startled me too. I asked them whether they remembered reading during the war that eventually a new Savior would come to mankind out of the North. The reason I had to ask that—I realize it now—was because I had just seen that man."

"Is that your clue?"

"Perhaps."

"And a Jew!"

"That doesn't matter."

"Then was it a tremendous spiritual influence you seemed to feel emanating from that man?"

"It must have been. But I felt it as mental, overpoweringly mental. I'm sure, Im, that that man, whoever he is, whether Jew or Gentile, is an extraordinary being."

"Wonder what he's doing here!"

"So do I!"

"On the trail of souls, perhaps."

Miss Creswell didn't say anything.

"I'm bound to say I should like to run across him," said Imogen. "And if I do—if I do—I shall speak to him right away, Jew or no Jew. I've spoken to men before now without an introduction. I'd speak to a man in a London street if I felt like it—or let him speak to me."

The clock struck one.

"Didn't I tell you I was tired, Towser? And you keep me up till all hours telling me about your adventures with Jews in front of photograph shops! Come along!"

She put her arm through her aunt's.

As they went out of the room she added, "A Savior out of the North! How cold it sounds!" And she shivered.

CHAPTER III

CANON BARRIMORE usually preached at the morning service in the cathedral when he was in residence in Drearney. When he preached in the evening it was an event. As Miss Prowse, the precentor's elderly sister, had once said in her final way— summing-up, verdict and black-cap way—"*All* sermons sound best in the evening." Now Canon Barrimore's sermons sounded brilliant in the morning, even at the end of the portentously long service which preceded them. The effect of them in the evening, therefore, when electric lights outlined the screens and shone like stars behind the distant altar, and when everybody was "worked up"—again Miss Prowse's expression—by the beauty of the illuminated cathedral, and by the emotionalism which religion, when connected with a magnificent church and with really good music, engenders in the hours of darkness—the effect of them in the evening was invariably prodigious.

Not that Canon Barrimore was a rhetorical orator. Not at all! In the first place he never preached extempore. All his sermons were brilliant, well considered, and consummately polished essays, written out, typed out and then splendidly read aloud. As a rule he gave a week to one sermon. He was a stylist. He was a wit. He wrought with the patient pains of a true artist. And his sermons—each of them lasted exactly half an hour—were full of culture, showed wide reading and usually contained allusions to all sorts of literature both English and foreign, and frequent quotations from the poets, but seldom familiar quotations. For Canon Barrimore had a hatred of the usual thing, and never, if he could help it, said in the pulpit anything that the average man would be likely to say. And the strange thing was that in spite of all this, in spite of the care, and the polish, and the wit, and the culture, and the sometimes obscure literary allusions, Drearney adored his way of preaching and his sermons. To the whole of educated Drearney, to the whole of Drearney which considered itself cultivated and intelligent, Canon Barrimore stood for intellect.

His was indeed a triumph. For it was not a mere facile victory over the emotions, but a victory over the brains of the community.

"I don't want to make them cry," he had been heard to say. "I want to make them think. And that's ten times harder."

As a matter of fact he did both, when he wished to do both. For he was a master of the pathetic stop when he chose. But he scorned easy emotion, though he reveled in epigram and loved to make people smile to the verge—but not beyond it—of laughter.

On the Sunday after Imogen's arrival at Ewenden House the cathedral bells began ringing at six o'clock, and as the hour of half past six drew near, dark throngs of citizens were to be seen streaming through the November darkness down the narrow lane that led to the precincts archway. Women, as almost everywhere in England, were in the majority, but there were plenty of men too. For in Drearney, as in London, it was the fashion for "free-thinking" men to make a boast of going to church when Canon Barrimore preached. Even Mr. Barker, the clever ecclesiastical lawyer, who hated parsons, never missed a service when the canon was going to preach; even Lady Bateford, the owner of Bateford Castle five miles outside the city, was always to be seen in the stalls when he mounted into the pulpit, although she was an ardent, though confused, Christian Scientist, and smiled with a pale and elusive satire when the poor old Church of England was mentioned.

And—perhaps greatest triumph of all—even the painted Imogen, who as a rule genuinely detested going to church, enjoyed hearing Canon Barrimore preach. For though Imogen knocked about a great deal with young men of the sporting type, and danced incessantly, she had a secret reverence for intellect and was the pet of many of the clever men of the day, who even wrote her long letters, and frequently sat in her pocket at tea time when she was in the mood to be serious.

Playfully, as is the way of such youth as hers, she seemed to patronize them, to take their learning lightly, sometimes to be laughing at their serious or profound outlook on life. Nevertheless she knew their measure, could gage their value, could even find moments now and then to worship with hidden enthusiasm at their altars. For Imogen had the faculty of the diviner who holds the rod. She seemed always to know instinctively where there were water-springs.

On this Sunday evening she and her aunt walked to cathedral. The intimate talk of the evening before had not been renewed between them. The Jew with the face of a lion had not been mentioned by either of them again. Imogen, who for once had really seemed rather tired and much less restless than usual, had spent the greater part of the day in the library browsing among the books there, and scribbling. Miss Creswell had been to morning church. Some Drearney people had looked in at tea time, and Imogen had taken a short walk in the twilight alone.

She called these brief visits to her aunt—she was leaving on the Monday morning—"going into retreat." She seemed to enjoy them mildly. But Miss Creswell was certain that her niece would find it very trying if she were forced to prolong her retreat until Tuesday. For Imogen was almost furiously restless in her manner of life, and one quiet day was usually as much as she could put up with.

"Church bells at night make me feel damnably melancholy," she said in her high clear voice, as she and her aunt turned out of High Street into Cathedral Lane.

Some of the moving church-goers, who pressed round them in the narrow alley, hearing the word "damnably," peered eagerly to see who had spoken it.

"Why is it," continued the insouciant girl, still in the same clear and penetrating voice, "that an evening service in England seems to put the lid down on life, and knock in the tin tacks?"

"D'you think it does?"

"Don't you, Towser?"

The word "Towser," following close on the heels of "damnably," caused more peering in Cathedral Lane, and subdued whisperings among would-be worshipers semi-shrouded under the eaves of the old houses by the night.

"Doesn't evening service in England make you feel infernally sorry for yourself?"

"No, I don't think it does."

"I often wonder, Towser, how much imagination you have."

"Not more than the average, I dare say," said Miss Creswell, with the utmost equanimity.

"If it wasn't for old Barrimore," continued Imogen, from the midst of a high collar of fur which framed her arum-lily face, "I shouldn't have come. I do wish those bells would stop. They make me want to throw up my head and howl."

"There's the five-minutes bell."

"That's better, though it sounds like a call to a funeral. Oh—why must life end?"

"What's the matter with you, Im?"

"When there's a pause in the noise of life the silence is fearful, I think. I know why jazz has been the rage since the war. We products of catastrophe—we want jazz. Jazz stamps on the under-things. 'Down, down, you devils, down!' That's what jazz says. Jazz isn't music. It's a machine for crushing things. I need jazz tonight. I need it now." She spoke half tragically, half whimsically.

They passed under the archway into the precincts.

Imogen took hold of Miss Creswell's arm. "Your photograph shops!" she said in a lower voice. "I wonder if *he'll* be here tonight."

"In cathedral?"

"Yes."

"Most unlikely, I should think. He didn't look at all like a church-going man."

"If he doesn't like churches why should he come to Drearney? It's all churches and clergymen here. And why should he stand and gaze at photographs of canons and choir-boys?"

And then they went in by the west door and were in the reverberating nave.

The vast nave was not strongly lighted; the service was going to take place not in it, as sometimes happened, but on the other side of the elaborately carved screen of stone which divided it from the choir. Far off there was a glow of greater light which seemed to beckon onward and to give a promise of hidden glories. There were people lingering in the nave, and some had already taken their places in the rows of straw-bottomed chairs with short wooden legs which made a big patch of ugliness at the foot of the steps leading to the screen. These loiterers loved not sermons, even when preached by a Barrimore, but liked to hear sweet music echoing through arches from the distance. They were not very many, however, and the crowd passed them by with hurrying footsteps, eager to find good places not too far from the pulpit.

Miss Creswell and Imogen had no need to hurry, for the former could always have two stalls among the wives and families of the cathedral dignitaries when she wanted them.

And her friend, Mr. Swarpes, was well aware that she did want them whenever Canon Barrimore was preaching. And now, as they passed through the archway into the choir, after slowly mounting the steps, there was the great Swarpes himself in his ample robe of office swimming with urbane dignity to the encounter, and bending his pomaded head, covered with jet-black hair, in gracious greeting and reassurance, as who should say, "Have no fear! *I* will provide!" Throwing his wings wide he preceded them with lordly gait to two excellent stalls opposite the organ on the pulpit side, and having stood still in a majestic pose while they entered them, he then bent his head slightly and withdrew. Mrs. Dean was looming up in the distance.

"Isn't he killing, Towser?" whispered Imogen to her aunt before she kneeled down. "What it must be like to have the verger-feeling inside one!"

And then she buried her painted face in her hands and pressed it against her white kid gloves. She remained thus for some time, not praying, however. She was trying to withdraw into herself and to find her own secret. Where was the real Imogen? In the darkness she heard footsteps passing on the cathedral pavement, the rustle of women's clothes, the click of a swinging door. Far up above them all, faintly in the distance of the dark evening, the five-minutes bell was ringing as if in another world. It stopped. There was a sound like a faint wind stealing through the cathedral and then a hushed murmur from the organ. With a sensation of reluctance Imogen got up from her knees, sat down in her deep stall and looked around.

The great choir was crowded. Not one of the many chairs and pews between the choir stalls and the altar steps, between the painted tombs of dead princes and warriors, was empty. Extra chairs had been brought in and grouped round the base of the high pulpit and round the archbishop's throne. These too were full. Yet more people kept anxiously pouring in through the opening on the left, opposite to the throne, by which the procession would enter in a moment. On the other side of the choir, Imogen and her aunt were faced by solemn batches of important people, or rather of people important in Drearney. They sat under the long row of lights which outlined the screen behind them with still bodies and grave faces, and about them swept waves of sound from the organ, now gathering strength and volume. As Imogen looked at them and at the less important crowd in the ordinary seats, the crowd of people who didn't matter in the sight of the men who carried the pokers, the thought came to her, "All these people have come here this evening not for God but for old Barrimore!" And that was a triumph for the canon, and no doubt it would warm him when in a moment he walked in, the last figure in the long procession which was already on the way from the hidden regions of ecclesiasticism. "These have all come for *me!*" A warming thought indeed—the creature taking precedence of the Creator! And suddenly Imogen had to look at her aunt, and she remembered the thoughts of her aunt in the twilight before the photograph shops, the thoughts sent, as her aunt believed, to her by the Jew with the lion face.

"What is it, Im?" Miss Creswell whispered.

Imogen leaned nearer to her.

"I've just had a thought which perhaps came from *him!*"

"From him?"

"From your Jew! Do you see him here?"

"No."

"Have you looked for him?"

"Yes."

"Have you the feeling that he is here?"

"I wouldn't trust myself. We so often suggestion ourselves."

"Somehow I think he *is* here."

And then the organ was louder, and there was a curious flat even sound in the distance, a little cold, somehow, and stagnant, combined of the feet of men and boys moving very slowly over pavement. People stirred in their seats preparing to get up. And Imogen was astonished at herself. Usually she considered the sayings of other people much less than her own. She had little respect for authority, though secret respect for what her brains told her was intellect. An aunt as such would certainly—she loved the expression—"cut no ice" with her. But evidently for once her aunt had impressed her, and very strongly, more strongly than she had known till now. Or—was it her aunt who had made this strangely strong impression? A human being can surely become a mere vehicle for conveyance. Imogen's walk that day in the twilight alone had had a purpose; she had gone out with expectation. She had returned with disappointment. What did it all mean? How Hugo would laugh if he knew! He would stretch his long arms, show his rows of superb white teeth, and laugh! But fools laughed in their folly! And for all his beautiful body, Hugo was a bit of a fool, a fool with a perfect seat on a horse. There was old Barrimore, at last, moving along with his tucked-in chin, intensely aware of the crowd, and of the fact that it had gathered for him. The silver pokers went before majestically. It was all very nice. Oh—there was the dean! So Canon Barrimore did not come last.

Imogen only just knew the dean. She thought him a brilliant iconoclast who ought to have been anywhere rather than in a Deanery, despite his undoubted mysticism. But mysticism, combined with an intellect so sharp and biting, and with so much sardonic humor, was merely confusing, she thought. Mysticism ought to be all of a piece, and the dean's mysticism wasn't! Still he was very rare and refreshing.

And then she kneeled down again.

Imogen had a strong taste for literature and a feeling for prose. In consequence she invariably enjoyed hearing a sermon by Canon Barrimore. She admired his work, much as she admired the work of certain favorite authors, not because it was edifying to the soul, but because it was beautifully proportioned, finely laid out, thoughtful, amusing, striking. She thought of Canon Barrimore as an artist rather than as a clergyman. She did not bother about his theology, or care very much what were his beliefs. What rejoiced her was his way of putting things, the perfection of his language, his wit, his humor, and the delicious form of his sermons. So when presently he mounted into the pulpit, spread out the typed copy of his half-an-hour sermon, tucked in his chin, gave out his text—he called it "my motto for this evening"—and then began, "I wonder how many of my hearers have read John Masefield's poem, 'The Everlasting Mercy',", she turned sideways in her stall, and, with a feeling of pleasantly keen interest, which was certainly a tribute to Canon Barrimore—for Imogen being modern and very young was of course enormously critical —she fixed her eyes on the trim, red man with the magnificently sonorous voice perched high above her.

"Old Barrimore!" She knew him well. He was one of the clever men who made a pet of her when she found time to allow them to. He had visited her in that long room on the

third floor in Lowndes Square in which no one was allowed
to set foot without a special invitation. Imogen's "cheek" was
so consummate that she had succeeded in creating the impression that it was a privilege to be allowed into that deep-blue
room. Quite celebrated men boasted of having been to tea
or supper up there. Other men of parts wanted to be invited there—and weren't. "Old Barrimore" had been there
twice, and had tucked in his chin over the privilege accorded
to him, "I'm sure I don't know why—aha!" And now, up
there in the pulpit, he was very much aware of the pretty,
painted girl down below him. He had seen her, without seeming to, when he walked in before the dean in the procession.
And he congratulated himself on having that clever creature
from London there to hear a sermon which was really far
too brilliant a piece of art for Drearney.

"Old Barrimore!" He was delightfully clever and delightfully vain. Imogen knew just how vain, because she was
able to measure his by her own vanity. Hitherto, she had enjoyed his vanity, as she enjoyed her own though less consciously.
It had entertained her as part of him, and an important part.
But this evening, as she sat sideways in her stall looking up
at the figure in the pulpit, she began to feel sorry about it.
Why were clever men vain when they would be so much more
charming, so much nearer to greatness, in simplicity? Puppies were simple, and because of that everyone loved puppies.
Imogen thought now that it would be difficult to love a clever
man. And, while she listened, she ran over mentally the long
list of clever men whom she knew: politicians, financiers,
painters, writers, diplomats, musicians, actors. Few of them,
very few, she thought, were lovable. But Hugo, a bit of a
fool—he was lovable though she couldn't exactly love him.
But anyhow with him cleverness didn't stand in the way, for
he wasn't clever. And she wondered how old Barrimore would
be if his brilliance were withdrawn from him, and his vanity
went with it.

How fine his voice was and how finely he used it! The
matter of his sermon was excellent as usual and prompted
thought. The expression of the matter was very near perfection. Often he had his huge audience smiling over some delicious bit of satire, or some sly epigram. There were moments
of eloquence, too, when the voice became more sonorous. This
was one of his very best sermons.

And he knew it! Imogen felt that. Somehow, in some almost mysterious way, he told it to her, by something in his self-possessed manner, by something in his fine voice, by something in his look and in the carriage of his head, as he turned this way and that in the pulpit, raking the congregation with his fiery blue eyes. (For although he read his sermons, evidently, before going into the pulpit, he got them almost by heart.) He knew it and was gloating over the fact as a greedy man gloats over a favorite dish.

A feeling of faint disgust and of immeasurable detachment came to Imogen just then. She was certainly not spiritual. On the contrary she was a girl of the world and far more worldly even than she knew herself to be. But, at any rate, with her brain she could apprehend spirituality, with her brain could mark its absence. And she said to herself now:

"God and religion are only the peg on which old Barrimore hangs up his cleverness so that it shall be seen and admired of men!"

As the words went through her mind she looked away from the preacher and began to consider the congregation, though she was still listening to the sermon so attentively that not a word of it escaped her. She could see a great many people. But she could not see them clearly. For when Canon Barrimore had gone into the pulpit all the lights, except those which threw him into relief, had been lowered. In consequence of this she saw masses of faces vaguely, and the more distant ones as a blur. She was struck by their expression of absorbed attention. The canon had magnetism as well as cleverness. These faces were surely not critical. They were rather, she thought, the faces of worshipers—of the canon of course. Perhaps just a few were critical, faces of some of those immediately opposite to her in the stalls. For there sat wives and daughters of other canons. And how could they not be critical? Mrs. Dean, too, was there, a woman steeped for long years in the prickly stream of thought which flowed from her husband's peculiar brain. She could not easily accept any mental food, and one saw that in her rather severe, pale face.

But those other people crowding round the archbishop's throne and up beyond the gilded and painted tombs to the altar steps—how absorbed, how uncritical they surely were. Some perhaps were understanding. Others were straining in the effort to understand, realizing that the sonorous voice was telling them things worth hearing and worthy of being comprehended.

Her eyes traveled slowly over the crowding faces towards the altar steps. Now she was looking at the blur—humanity mingled, fading off, en masse, but still full of meaning, full of mysterious significance—full, very full, of mysterious significance.

For a moment she lost some words of the sermon. It seemed as if the canon's big voice faded for an instant out of her ears. That was a strange sensation. The voice died away—from her, as life seems to die away from the human being suddenly seized with an attack of vertigo. She felt as if a strange and altogether unusual stillness held her body. Of course she had been sitting still before, but surely not like this. This was like a mystic stillness, such as a world in snow seems to have. The sensation only lasted for a moment. Then—it seemed to her as if with the bang of a big sound abruptly released—the voice of the canon was again powerfully in her ears, and her mind was able once more to be attentive, and the odd stillness seemed to glide away from her body, releasing it.

She was no longer looking toward the blur of human faces which were crowded together near the foot of the altar steps. But she wished that she were out of her stall, that she were sitting among them. All the interestingness, all the fascination of the crowd seemed to her now to be concentrated up there. She longed to get up and to go there.

Canon Barrimore was drawing towards the end of his masterly essay on humanity's impudent cry for a Savior when a Savior, the only Savior, had long ago been sent, and had dwelt among men in Palestine. Imogen, so admirable was the form of his sermon, felt the appointed end close upon her and knew that intellectually it was going to be absolutely satisfying. The old boy was really a master of his job. She had the feeling that he was going to end with some exquisite quotation, something that would grip the heart as a conclusion to something which had gripped the brain. And so it was. With a singularly final gesture Canon Barrimore closed the typed manuscript which lay on the desk of the pulpit, and, lifting up his voice, he almost chanted the closing lines of "The Everlasting Mercy."

"O lovely lily clean,
O lily springing green,
O lily bursting white,
Dear lily of delight,
Spring in my heart agen
That I may flower to men."

Imogen felt tears spring into the eyes that looked out above the heavily painted shadows. There rang the true impulse; there a great heart was beating. And there, too, was a great simplicity.

A wide rustle went through the crowded choir. Everybody was instinctively moving. Everybody was mentally sighing and preparing to get up. The spell was over. Reaction was already manifest.

But then a strange thing happened. Canon Barrimore, after a moment of what seemed like almost confused hesitation, raised his right hand, and said in a less strong, less confident voice than usual. "One moment! I have not quite finished. There are, as we know, two sides to almost every question."

"A bromide!" murmured Imogen, startled. "A complete bromide! What's the matter?"

And then, to her amazement, and to the amazement probably of the greater part of his congregation, Canon Barrimore proceeded practically to annul the effect of his own sermon. His theme having been that mankind had had its Savior, did not need, and was impious in demanding, or even in desiring another, he now—in a very extempore manner, which proved that all this was a mere after-thought—dwelt on the changing difficulties of changing epochs in the world's history, said that one must guard against being too drastic, that possibly new times needed new teachers, that perhaps not every soul could be saved by the same means, etc., etc.

"But he's hedging, he's hedging in the most barefaced manner!" said Imogen to herself, bewildered.

And then she looked at her aunt. And in a moment she seemed to understand something.

"*He* is here!" she whispered.

And Miss Creswell whispered back:

"Yes, *he* must be here."

CHAPTER IV

WHEN the last prayers had been spoken, and the "Dresden Amen" had been sung softly by the choir, there was a moment as usual for silent prayer. And again Imogen, though kneeling with her painted face in her hands, did not pray. She had no desire to pray. She felt bristling with an unusual excitement and alertness. The preliminary sigh, as of wind, went through the great church, and the organ sounded faintly while people rose from their knees and stood to see the procession go out. Canon Barrimore rose with the rest, and stood upright in the pulpit with a verger below him by the pulpit steps, waiting to take his place in the procession when it had advanced up the chancel, and was turning to go out by the opening in the wrought-iron screen. Imogen gazed up at him with intentness, with such intentness that almost immediately he glanced down at her. When he did that she saw in his face an expression of confusion and almost of distress, in his blue eyes a look as of shame or even of guilt.

"He hates having spoiled the effect of that sermon of his," she thought. "And he's wondering why he did it."

And then the procession came up, and the canon descended the pulpit steps, and went out in front of the dean, still flushed and oddly confused, and Mr. Hendry finished his prelude and blazed out in some big and jubilant piece of music unknown to Imogen. And the congregation began to disperse.

Miss Creswell was devoted to music and loved the organ, and usually she stayed in her stall till Mr. Hendry had played his last note. But tonight, perhaps feeling the sudden restlessness of Imogen, she got up and they came down into the choir, and joined the crowd that was going slowly towards the archway in the screen which divided the choir from the nave. Many of those who had been sitting in what were often called in Drearney "the popular seats" went out by the opening near the pulpit following the procession, and the two crowds mingled together on the long flight of steps leading down from the great center screen to the level of the nave.

Mr. Hendry was playing a brilliant and powerful thing, modern evidently but fine, and when Miss Creswell had passed beyond the screen she stood still for a moment to listen. The music was sounding fiercely in her ears. Her mind was full

of the sermon she had just heard and its strange and totally
unexpected conclusion. She felt surprised, oddly moved and
strung up. Below her in the nave, mingling with the music,
she heard the noise of multitudinous feet faintly; she saw
masses of human forms moving slowly towards the night.
And these masses of people just then seemed to her negligible.
The meaning of them seemed diminished to her, as if something had caused them to become less important as individuals,
and therefore also as a mass, than they usually were. Something had surely intruded itself among them, something so
much more powerful and remarkable than they were, or could
ever be, that it had taken the color out of them, as intensely
strong sunshine takes the color out of a landscape.

"Well, and what did you think of the sermon, Miss
Creswell?"

Miss Creswell started, turned round and saw the pale face
of the dean's wife close to hers.

"Very clever and brilliantly written, wasn't it?" said Mrs.
Brand. "But what was the matter at the end?"

"The matter?"

"Yes. Canon Barrimore turned round on himself, attacked
his own argument, and practically gave the *coup de grâce* to
his own assertions. What can have induced him to put in that
disastrous *post scriptum?*"

"Some sudden impulse, I suppose," said Miss Creswell
slowly, like one carefully choosing her words.

"But Canon Barrimore is the least impulsive preacher I
know. With him everything is prepared. Nothing is ever left
to chance."

"No, that's true."

"One might really suppose that the thoughts of another mind
had been suddenly injected into him and that he had been
forced to give utterance to them."

"It *was* very like that," said Miss Creswell, turning eyes
that began to look astonished on the speaker. "Do you think
that——"

But at this moment some obsequious person cringed into
social relations with the dean's wife, and Miss Creswell turned
round to find Imogen.

But no Imogen was there. People were still streaming out
of the choir through the archway. Many more were gathered
on the steps listening to the voluntary. Quickly Miss Creswell

looked from one to another seeking her niece. Imogen
knew a good many people in Drearney. No doubt she had
seen one of them, had gone away to enter into a conversation,
to exchange a few words with some friend or acquaintance.
Miss Creswell looked about, waited, but she did not catch
sight of her niece, whose tall figure would be surely discernible
even in the midst of the gathering of people on the steps. This
gathering began to grow less. The voluntary was drawing to
its close. The lingering congregation felt that instinctively
and—for few are genuinely musical though so many are "fond
of music"—began to go down into the nave and make their
way towards the west door. From above came the slow boom
of the cathedral clock striking eight. Miss Creswell looked
at her watch. Eight already! Where could Imogen be?
She searched again, looking at everyone still left in her neighborhood carefully, searching with method. Mr. Hendry in
the organ loft struck the last great chords of the fantasia he
had been playing. With the sudden cessation of the music
night seemed to close about the cathedral, and Miss Creswell
realized that Imogen had deliberately left her and gone away,
no doubt with someone whom she knew and had met by chance
on the steps. She must be waiting by the west door. Miss
Creswell went down the steps, almost the last to go, and
walked quickly along the nave. But when she reached the
west door Imogen was not there. She saw only Miss Prowse,
the precentor's sister, in confabulation with another elderly
lady just outside the great porch.

"Good night, Miss Creswell," said Miss Prowse, looking
round with her bead-like eyes.

"Good night!" said Miss Creswell.

"Your niece has gone on. She came out quite five minutes
ago. She seemed in a hurry, I thought."

"I was talking on the steps. I will catch her up. Good
night."

"Good night. Is she staying long?"

"No, she leaves me tomorrow." And then Miss Creswell
walked on alone into the darkness of the precincts.

"How very extraordinary the ways of the modern young
woman are!" said Miss Prowse, to her friend, Mrs. Witney,
wife of Mr. Witney, rector of St. James-cum-St. Ambrose.
"Just think of a niece leaving her aunt to walk home in the dark
alone while she—well—well, really!"

"While she what?" asked Mrs. Witney.

"Well, she gave *me* the impression that she was on the chase after somebody."

"Perhaps she was trying to catch up a friend."

"Let's hope he *was* a friend," said Miss Prowse charitably.

"Do you mean it was a man?"

"Well, it looked very like it. But we mustn't say anything. Precincts most certainly have ears, as I discovered five and thirty years ago. Pity she covers her face with paint, isn't it? But even the shop-girls paint nowadays. I suppose the servants will begin next. Well, good night, dear. Henry hates being kept waiting for his supper. And he's always so cross on a Sunday evening. All the services, you know!"

"My poor husband's the same. But I quite understand it. Good night."

Meanwhile Miss Creswell was traversing Cathedral Lane, which, in striking contrast to the neighboring High Street, was badly lit and really almost dangerously dark. As she walked along in the somber shadows of the overhanging houses, which were, most of them, some hundreds of years old, she felt excited and angry. It was very rarely that she felt either the one or the other. And she could not remember any occasion when she had felt the full force of both these ugly feelings as she felt it now. She was quite accustomed to being treated casually by Imogen. Imogen had always been thoroughly spoiled, and had responded to the spoiling in the usual manner of the human being by becoming thoroughly selfish. From her childhood she had been "out" to have a good time, and as unselfishness, in her code, stood usually for a bad time she had had as little to do with it as possible. Nevertheless, though taking her own way ruthlessly enough, she had hitherto always showed the conventional decent manners to her aunt in all the small ways. She had certainly seldom been solicitous. But she had never been vulgarly rude.

As she walked along the lane, however, Miss Creswell told herself that tonight Imogen had been vulgarly rude. She had had no right to go off without a word of explanation, leaving her aunt and hostess to wait and search for her and then to make her way home in the dark alone. Not that there was the slightest danger! Not that Miss Creswell hadn't taken that walk in the dark by herself dozens of times! But Imogen, though of course she was proud of being unconventional, and indeed made a point of unconventionality, ought to have shown a little more care for the feelings of an older woman with whom she was staying.

Miss Creswell came into the High Street. Drearney was not only a cathedral city but a military city. There was a big cavalry barracks just outside the town which contained also an infantry depot. On Sunday evenings soldiers swarmed in the streets, surrounded by ardent maidens, whose enthusiasm for the protectors of the body evidently far outweighed their admiration for the supervisors of the soul. As Miss Creswell emerged into the brightly lit thoroughfare she was jostled by a stream of saucy young men in uniform and amorous, giggling girls. At the corner of the lane stood a group of very young girls waiting to "get off" with the soldiers, and shrieking with laughter at the impertinent remarks addressed to them by lounging dragoons and "Buffs." The roadway was nearly full of animated throngs of men and girls talking, laughing, and pulling each other about. "Sauce" was in the air. Everyone was being, or was trying to be, jocose. Sheer animal spirits and sex prompted to horse-play. And as Miss Creswell crossed the road she was more than once knocked up against, more than once greeted with "Beg pardon, I'm sure!" followed by shrilling laughter.

All this devil of youth, all this sexual exuberance, coming upon her and, as it were, engulfing her, just after the cathedral service and the mysterious disappearance of Imogen, had a painful and unusual effect upon her nerves. She felt old and deserted and dreadfully out of things. By temperament a contented and cheerful woman she was quite unaccustomed to any of the ugly feelings of the typical old maid. It was seldom indeed that she was afflicted with bitter envy of youth, or was gnawed by the tooth of jealousy. But tonight she was all on edge and painfully sensitive, and as she made her way towards the outskirts of the town and Ewenden Road, a deep melancholy descended upon her. It was combined with a strong sensation of anger which she felt growing within her.

As she drew near to her house it occurred to her that Imogen might be already there waiting for her. The girl had an impatient spirit. She might have said to herself, when she saw her aunt talking to the dean's wife, "Oh, bother all these old fogeys! I'm not going to hang about and talk to them!" And she might have made her way home, and be now in the library by the fire, deep in a book. It was quite possible. In that case anger and touchiness were really not called for. And Miss Creswell pulled herself together and resolved, if indeed she found Imogen there, to say nothing, and to conceal the fact that she had been angry.

She drew out her latch-key presently, and put it into her hall door. As she did this she was aware of a desire to find Imogen in the house so strong that it startled her. She turned the key, opened the door, and stood in the lighted hall. She shut the hall door and directly it was shut called out, "Imogen! Im! Im!" No answer came to her call. She put down her umbrella and prayer-book on the hall table and immediately went into the library. The large room was lit only by a log fire which was sending out blue flames on the open hearth. Miss Creswell turned on the electric light. No Imogen!

She now felt quite certain that the girl was not in the house. And as she stood by the fire for a moment she knew that she had not really expected her to be in the house. She had only tried to expect that.

After standing for a moment she rang the bell. Jonson, her butler, came.

"Miss Lowrie hasn't come in yet, has she, Jonson?"

"No, ma'am. I thought she was with you, ma'am."

"Yes. But after the service she went off to see some of her friends. She may be a little late." Miss Creswell paused; then she added, "In case she is, I won't wait for her. Supper at half past eight as usual."

"Yes, ma'am."

Miss Creswell went upstairs to take off her hat and her fur coat. As she came down again the clock in the hall was striking the half-hour.

"Supper is ready, ma'am," said Jonson, appearing at the dining-room door.

Without making any reply Miss Creswell went into the dining-room and sat down alone to supper. She didn't want to eat. Her feeling of anger had returned. She felt too angry to eat or even to sit still. But she forced herself to do both and to drink her usual glass of claret. And all the time she was eating and looking very calm under the eyes of Jonson she was listening for the sound of the hall door-bell. But she didn't hear it, and presently she had finished and she got up from the table.

"Shall I keep the supper for Miss Lowrie, ma'am?"

"Yes, you had better. She may have supper with her friends, but in case she doesn't you'd better keep some. I'll have my coffee now, please, in the library."

"Yes, ma'am."

Miss Creswell went into the library. It was now after nine o'clock. Above the hearth there was a fine Venetian mirror which she had picked up long ago in a side street in Venice at a little-known antiquary's shop. She went to this mirror and looked at her reflection. She had what is generally called a "fresh" complexion, but tonight—not a doubt of it—her face was flushed. There was no calm in her brown eyes. They bore witness, she thought, to the evil spirit within her, the evil spirit which, since she had been in the house, and even before, when she was in the midst of the roistering soldiers and their girls in the High Street, had been telling her something. She remembered Imogen's words when they had spoken together about "the Jew." (So Miss Creswell called the stranger she had seen before the photograph shops to herself.) Imogen had said, "I'm bound to say I should like to run across him. And if I do I shall speak to him right away." And that had happened. Miss Creswell felt sure of it. He had been in the cathedral that evening. Imogen had caught sight of him going out, had recognized him, and had followed him. She had spoken to him. She was with him now.

It was outrageous—from the point of view of convention. But that wasn't really why Miss Creswell was so excited, so angry, so almost wildly uneasy and restless. What Imogen did no longer shocked her. The girl possessed the advantage of her who is openly a law unto herself. She was forgiven more easily than the less daring are forgiven. Miss Creswell was accustomed to Imogen doing all sorts of unexpected and wholly unconventional things. One more or less wouldn't normally have upset her. She was upset tonight because she felt personally concerned in the matter. For it was she who had awakened Imogen's interest in the strange man, who had set it going; and now Imogen, with the insolence and daring of youth, had "cut her out."

Miss Creswell felt dreadfully vulgar and full of an intimate humiliation as she thought just that, in just those words. She hadn't known, hadn't even suspected, that it was in her to feel as she did at her age. And as she looked at herself in the mirror she asked herself, "How can you feel as you do? How can you have such ugly things in you? How is it possible that you are jealous of Imogen because she has done what you would never have dreamed of doing, what you would never have thought it decent to do?" But it was that which almost made her hate Imogen—the possibilities open to Imogen and closed to herself. What Imogen's life was, and what hers had been! Till today she had never bothered about all that, had never been troubled by it. She had not thought that her type of nature wanted what Imogen's type of nature snatched at perpetually. But now suddenly she felt that she did want what Imogen had coolly taken that night. And it seemed to her monstrous that Imogen had taken advantage of her kindly confidence to embark on an adventure without one word to her. It was not fair. It was not at all fair! The girl had behaved badly, abominably.

She heard the door open and turned round. Jonson was there with her coffee on a silver tray. It seemed to her that he looked rather anxious and surprised. Probably he was wondering where Miss Lowrie was. As she took the coffee cup she said, trying to manage a careless voice, "Don't sit up after ten if you want to go to bed, Jonson. I shall be here and can let Miss Imogen in. I dare say she'll be a little late."

"Thank you, ma'am."

"Leave the tray. I may take another cup."

"Certainly, ma'am."

And when Jonson had gone she did drink two cups of coffee, though one was her usual allowance. Then she sat down by the fire, took up a book and tried to force herself to read, and to read with interest.

But that was impossible. Though she fixed her eyes on the print and read words she could not concentrate on their meaning. Her mind was full of the insolence of youth and of the freedom that insolence took as its birthright. In her day youth had been less insolent and far less free. Her father and mother had not been specially strait-laced, but if she had attempted to lead a life such as Imogen habitually led she would certainly have been met with uncompromising opposition. But it had never occurred to her to run wild. It had never occurred to her to knock about alone with any man who took a fancy to her at night, to go from one dance club to another with him, to drive about with him till three or four in the morning. What Imogen did perpetually, and as a matter of course, she had never done at all. And as to following a total stranger in the street, getting into conversation with him, and staying out with him till—she glanced at the clock—till ten o'clock at night, such conduct could never have seemed a possibility to her. Nor could she have supposed that any girl, even in these days, with any pretension to be what is called "a lady" could behave as Imogen had behaved, must be behaving now. And she, Annie Creswell, had brought it about.

She realized now the strength of the impression she must have made on Imogen by her narrative. Certainly the girl had seemed to take the narrative lightly, even to laugh over the impression made on her aunt. But nevertheless that impression had been conveyed to her, and at second hand, without losing any of its force. She had not seen and yet she must have believed. That was remarkable, because Imogen was skeptical, satirical, old already in worldly knowledge and in knowledge of men. And her dislike of Jews was genuine. Miss Creswell knew that. She had even remonstrated with her niece about it, condemning it as bigoted and unreasonable.

But this Jew was surely not as other Jews.

At this point Miss Creswell dropped all pretense with herself. She wasn't really reading the book she was holding. She couldn't possibly read it. And now she laid it down. Sitting in an armchair suggested calmness, repose. She wasn't calm. As to repose—she was all tingling and thrilling with an angry excitement. She got up from the low chair and walked about the long room between the bookcases.

She felt at that moment terribly jealous and she knew it, recognized her feeling for what it was, but she also knew that this was no ordinary jealousy. It was, she believed,. not physical. No; it was a keen, even fierce, mental jealousy, almost an intellectual jealousy. Imogen was out there in the darkness, tasting a mind that she longed to taste, having contact with a nature, mysterious, powerful, extraordinary even, that she longed to have contact with. That was why she was jealous. She had an odd sensation of being intimate in a strange way, a strange new way, with this unknown Jew. He had planted thoughts in her. When she left him, like a hound he had pursued her—by means of thought-power. Through her, using her as a vehicle, he had approached Imogen's mind, had set it quivering, on the alert.

And lastly—she could not doubt it—he had got on the trail of Canon Barrimore. That episode in the cathedral had been astonishing. She had been so preoccupied that she had not dwelt on it, had not fully savored the amazingness of it. Now she did dwell on it, did savor it.

That man, so artistic, so vain of his artistry, such a stickler for form, for completeness, for the supreme value of the final sentence rounding the whole; that man, the slave of preparation, the declared enemy of utterances delivered extempore and on the spur of the moment; that man had been induced, forced —it must have been that—to fall on his own week's work and publicly to bring it to nought! The quotation from Masefield had been final. It had been the perfect end to a perfect piece of prose, and had lifted up the arguments brought forward in the sermon to the feet of the one and only Savior as it were. Never had any quotation, Miss Creswell thought, fallen more beautifully into place.

And then the dust and the ruins!

The cause of them! The cause of them! She seemed to know it was the Jew, her Jew—till Imogen had done the outrageous thing, prompted by the insolence of her youth.

"Be self-possessed. That's the whole art of living!"

Who had said that? Wasn't it Mephistopheles? Anyhow it was abominably true. And Imogen from her childhood had been enameled with self-possession. And so the art of living was hers.

"And not mine!" Miss Creswell said to herself bitterly. "Not mine!"

Past ten o'clock now! Just how long was the outrage going to last?

The library door opened softly. "Do you really wish me to go to bed, ma'am?" said Jonson's alto voice. "I can easily sit up."

"Certainly not, Jonson! I don't wish it. I will let Miss Lowrie in."

"Thank you, ma'am. Good night, ma'am."

"Good night, Jonson."

Jonson went out closing the door softly behind him, and Miss Creswell was once more alone.

Although she knew what the time was she looked once more at the clock. Between ten and eleven now! What could be happening? Where were they? Was it possible that

Imogen had actually gone with the Jew to wherever he was staying for the moment? Miss Creswell was positive he did not live
in Drearney, that he was a newcomer to the place. He was
probably in one of the few hotels—in the County Hotel, or in
"The Rose and Crown." Those were the two chief houses,
and both of them were in the High Street. There were two
or three others; but they were mere inns, pot-houses almost.
If Imogen had gone to a hotel she would certainly be recognized. And what would people think? What must they
think? Miss Creswell felt hot all over. She took a step
or two towards the library door. Her jealousy was prompting
her to what seemed to her a desperate action. She felt inclined to put on her things and go out in search of Imogen.
She might have done this. At that moment she was capable
of doing it, so insufferable did she feel her situation to be,
so impossible did it seem to her to stay quietly where she was,
alone, deserted, abandoned and—so she felt it—insulted.

But just as she laid her hand on the door, and was beginning
to open it, she heard the tingle of the electric bell of the hall
door. The eager noise ceased. So—Imogen had come back
at last! Miss Creswell felt a wave of angry heat go up to
her forehead, to the roots of her smooth hair. She stood where
she was. Her anger kept her there. The bell sounded again.
It was quite evident that the servants had all gone up to bed.
She was alone down there in command of the situation.
Imogen could not get into the house unless she, the outraged
one, chose. Miss Creswell's lips set hard. She had a ridiculous inclination, absolutely childish, absolutely indefensible—
and she knew that—to switch off the light, to creep across the
hall and up the staircase, and to go to bed leaving her niece
outside in the night. It would serve her right. It would teach
her a lesson. It would show her that she could not play fast
and loose with the conventions, that she could not forever take
her own selfish and insolent way without sometimes paying a
price.

Again the vibration of the eager, determined sound, again
the pause and then again the bell! But this time the sound
went on and on with a sort of bitter obstinacy.

"I *will* get in!" That was what the bell was saying, "You
shall let me in!"

And "Shall I?" was Miss Creswell's silent response.

What exactly would have happened if there had not been

an intervention she never knew, nor could determine. But at this moment she heard a hurried sound somewhere above, and then a heavy step coming downstairs. Instantly she went out into the hall and saw Jonson, with a startled expression on his face, hurrying down the front stairs.

"Oh, I beg pardon, ma'am," he began on seeing her. "It seemed to me that I——"

"It's all right, Jonson, I was just going to open the door." All this time the bell was sounding—sounding.

"You can go. I will open the door."

"Excuse my coming down the front stairs, ma'am. But I happened to be——"

"It's all right. You can go."

"Thank you, ma'am."

As he turned and went away Miss Creswell walked to the hall door and opened it.

"Damn it, Towser! Had you all gone to bed? I thought I was locked out for the night." Imogen stepped into the hall, with her fur collar drawn high up and partially hiding her painted face.

Miss Creswell shut the hall door. "I forbid you to call me Towser!" she managed to say in a shaking voice. For some reason the use by her niece of the familiar name tonight seemed to take from her the last shred of dignity and self-control. She had been accustomed to that name for years. Preposterous though it was she had never minded its use and application to her. But now, for the first time, it enraged her. "I forbid you to call me by that name, and I forbid you to swear in my house!" she said, trying to steady her voice.

And then she put up the chain on the hall door, walked into the library and shut the door behind her, leaving her niece in the hall.

When she had opened the door she had not intended to do this, and when she had done it she was astonished and disconcerted. But she was not her own mistress tonight. She felt raw, as if the skin had been stripped from her soul leaving it exposed like a horrible red wound. And she was hating Imogen with a deadly hatred, she who had never hated anyone before.

"I will not bear it!" she was saying to herself now with trembling lips. "I will not bear to be treated like this, spoken to like this, by an insolent girl, whether she is my niece or not!"

And she remembered the shrilling laughter of the girls in the High Street that night. They had been jeering at her as they clung to the arms of their soldiers. Youth jeers at age. Yes. But she would at least be properly treated by her own niece in her own house.

The library door opened and Imogen appeared, without her coat but still wearing her hat. "I say, Tow—I say what's the matter?" she asked, seriously.

"Nothing's the matter. But I'm tired of hearing that stupid name, and I'm very tired of hearing you swear. That's all. You'll find some supper left for you in the dining-room. I allowed Jonson to go to bed, and now I'm going up to bed too."

"Come, Aunt Annie—if I must—do drop it!"

"Please don't talk about it. Now I'm going to bed."

"But don't you want to know where I've been at this time of night?"

"That doesn't interest me. As I crossed the High Street this evening it was full of giggling girls running after soldiers. That seems to be the principal occupation of girls since the war."

"Oh, it was just the same before the war. I'm certain of that. But you surely don't think I have been in the High Street running after privates from the cavalry barracks?"

"I don't know what you've been doing. Nor do I care. All I care for is that while you are staying in my house with me you treat me with ordinary decency and politeness."

"I know I've been rather casual this evening. But I hadn't time to let you know."

"Let me know what?"

"When we were at the top of the steps coming out I saw *him* down below in the nave. I recognized him directly by your description. He turned round and looked back, and so I saw his face. You were talking to the dean's wife and I couldn't interrupt you. *That* would have been rude!"

"You could perfectly well have——"

"What?"

"Stayed where you were."

"Oh no, I couldn't. I had to follow him—your Jew."

"I forbid you to call him my Jew!" said Miss Creswell, with acute exasperation. "I don't know the man. I've never spoken to him, and I never wish to. Now go and have your supper—if you haven't had supper already."

"Of course I haven't."

"Then go—go. And I'll go to bed."

"No, you won't! Indeed you won't! What is the matter? Why are you so frightfully angry? It can't be merely because I left you and stayed away for a little while."

"A little while! It's getting on for eleven."

"But it isn't that. You had your chance."

"My chance? What do you mean?"

"You met him first. You could have spoken to him. And you wouldn't. You hurried away. Then why be furious with me for doing what you didn't want to do?"

"I did want to do it. I wanted to do it terribly. But I didn't think—I didn't consider that——" And at that point Miss Creswell had to stop. If she had gone on she knew that she would have lost the last shred of self-control and begun to cry.

Imogen quite understood now. Perhaps she had quite understood before. But she didn't laugh. A gentle look came into her eyes. She didn't let it degenerate into a look of pity. She knew such a look would be cruel at such a moment, and she had no wish to be cruel. Besides just then she realized how very much those miss in life who are deprived of the faculty to dare, who long for the interestingness life has to offer in superabundant measure but who are held back from hunting it and possessing it by a thousand scruples and fears.

"What a mercy I'm free from all that sort of thing!" she thought, as she looked at her aunt's flushed face and tear-filmed eyes.

And, as only a woman can, she understood the hatred she was encountering just then. But she was resolved not to let it last, and she put her arm round Miss Creswell's shoulder.

"Perhaps I've been a beast. But don't hate me for it, Towser," she said. (And she used the old name by accident, without being aware that she used it.) "Let me explain. Let me tell you! I'm hungry now. I must eat. All this time I've been walking. Come in with me and let me tell you about him."

Somehow, when Miss Creswell knew that Imogen had not been in any house during her absence, she felt better.

"You must come!"

The soft pressure on her shoulder—that, and perhaps something else—governed Miss Creswell then. Suddenly she felt weak. The hardness went out of her. She gave a deep, trembling sigh and allowed Imogen to lead her out of the room.

CHAPTER V

IMOGEN sat down at the table and helped herself very deliberately to some mayonnaise of chicken which Jonson had left in front of her plate. "I'm hungry," she said. "He's taken it out of me." She spoke the last words with a touch of forced flippancy, but her painted face was unusually grave.

"I must have something to drink," she added. "What would I give for a cocktail!" She stretched out her hand to a decanter of whisky, then drew it back. "No, I don't know that I will just yet. It's a rotten habit always wanting a drink, but once you get into the cocktail frame of body——" She looked up. "How you're hating me, Aunt Annie!"

"Nonsense!"

"I can't eat while you stand."

"I'm going to bed."

"You won't sleep a wink if you don't let me tell you."

Miss Creswell sat down by the table with a pitiful attempt at cool dignity which something within her seemed laughing and crying at.

"I knew *he* was in the cathedral."

"How could you know?"

"But you knew. You said so after old Barrimore made a fool of himself."

"I didn't really know. That was impossible."

"Oh yes, you did. The strange thing is that, when you first told me about him, although I laughed at you I was impressed. Somehow you conveyed him to me. He came to me first through you. When we were on the steps I was watching for him. I looked down at the crowd going out, and presently, when you were speaking to Mrs. Brand, I saw him in the nave. He turned his head and I saw his face. He seemed to be looking straight at me, but I don't know whether he was. Then I went after him. You remember I told you that if I ran across that man I should speak to him right away? You remember?"

"Yes," said Miss Creswell, reluctantly.

"You can't say I didn't warn you."

She waited, but her aunt didn't speak, only sat still looking unusually rigid.

"In the porch I saw that dreadful little Prowse creature pouncing for gossip. He passed close to her, and I was behind him. But I didn't speak to him then. I followed him out of the precincts till we were at the beginning of Cathedral Lane. Then he turned to the left up Dangate Street by the precincts wall. That was my chance. Everyone seemed to go away by Cathedral Lane. Dangate Street was deserted. He was walking slowly. I could catch him up easily. (You know how fast I can walk.) But I kept behind him for some time, and I noticed that he looked tremendously solitary."

"What d'you mean? You said he was alone!"

"Yes, but not everyone who is alone is solitary. There was an extraordinary detachment about him, and I felt that his spirit was alone as well as his body, was much more alone than his body. And I actually hesitated. For a minute I wasn't sure whether I would speak to him or not. The scales were almost even for an instant. But then—he looked round. And I knew my hesitation had made him do that."

Miss Creswell had reddened and she felt again that the evil spirit was in her eyes. "Do you mean that he knew you were dogging him and wanted you to speak to him?" she asked, in a hard voice.

Imogen smiled. "D'you remember when I accused you of having fallen in love at first sight how satirical you felt? Well, I feel like that now. Aunt Annie, that man isn't like other men. How right you were about not knowing, or caring, whether he was a gentleman or not. One could never think of him as being either a gentleman or not a gentleman. He is just a being. Yes, that's what he is!"

She pushed away her plate, then got up and helped herself to something else. Then again she stretched her hand to the decanter of whisky. "I feel reaction," she said. "I must!" She poured out a little whisky and some soda-water, and sat down again.

"When he turned round, I knew I must speak to him at once, and I came up with him. You're right. He is a Jew. Directly I was able to look really at him, to examine his face, I knew it. Not the hook-nosed Jew—the other type, the blunt-featured type. But there's the unmistakable look of

Israel. You know how I have always hated it. I don't even
know why. I love what Jews can do in a thousand ways, but
I've always disliked them. I revel in what flows from them
but can't bear the source. It's hopelessly unreasonable, but
I've never been able to help it. I've been like Hugo. He never
says 'Jew.' He always says 'Damned Jew.' That's what
I've been. But with *him* I didn't feel any of that repulsion.
I said to myself, 'He's a Jew—yes.' But it didn't matter.
It even seemed right, as if he *had* to be a Jew. I don't know
quite how to explain. His being a Jew seemed inevitable
to me."

Miss Creswell nodded. The flush had died out of her face.
The evil spirit had gone from her eyes which were fixed on
her niece.

"When I came up to him I said, 'I've been following you.
I want to speak to you.' He stopped. He wasn't at all surprised. There are so many things he isn't. For instance he
isn't the least bit sexual, and yet he isn't the least bit emascu-
late, effeminate, a-sexual. He seems to me like a big man
free, freed from it all quietly, away from it all in freedom.
With some very big men a girl like me often feels, 'In the
alcove behind the curtains how different he could be! How
weak, how greedy, how undignified, and what an animal!'
Well, you know, in these days we're out of the cotton-wool,
Aunt Annie!"

"Oh, I know—I know!"

"With him I couldn't even think of alcoves and curtains
and animalism. No."

She paused, and looked across the room at the drawn curtains over the dining-room windows.

"We looked at each other, and all the time I was looking
I was examining him. He is quite six feet high, but not more
I should say. And he's about forty, and looks a little older
because his thoughts have been so large and so intense. I feel
as if his thoughts were sometimes so forcible that they must
surely split his body asunder. He's not handsome—as Hugo
is handsome for instance—but he's got a wonderful face—wonderful in its impressiveness and its power of changing. And
his eyes are what you said they were. They are veiled and
then illuminated, as if strong lights were set behind them and
glowed through them. And they are very large when they
are wide open, and have a good deal of the remoteness one

sees in the eyes of certain animals. Cats can look like that—but in a small, petty sort of way. His eyes aren't animal in the ugly sense, only full of far-away detachment very often. His hair is tremendously thick and close. It seems to grow in slabs almost. And his forehead is low and covered with very curious lines, some large and some very small, almost invisible, feathery lines sloping down by the temples."

"Do you mean to say that you could see all this in Dangate Street?"

"No. But we didn't stay in Dangate Street all the time. When I said I wanted to speak to him—I said it again after that instant when we had looked at each other—he said, with a strong foreign accent, not a pretty one, not French or Italian, 'Yes, certainly you can speak to me. Why not?' And then we walked on together in the dark. I felt absolutely at home."

"When don't you?"

"Oh, of course I'm not shy. What's the good of shyness? It's merely a stone you throw in your own path if you're a fool. What I mean is that with him I felt at home as one might feel at home with a great view, or the sea. Can you understand, Aunt Annie?"

"I don't know." Again the burning jealousy, a jealousy that seemed intellectual, was flaming up in Miss Creswell. She tried to overcome it, for it was making her suffer intensely. But it showed in the hardness of her voice, in the rigidity of her unusual manner, and in the expression of her usually kind and cheerful eyes.

"Try to understand. I want you to understand."

"Why?"

"He's in you too."

"Please don't say that. And now if you have finished——"
She was seeing those two walking on together in the dark, at home with each other. And there was something mysteriously intolerable to her in that mental vision.

"But I haven't nearly finished." And she helped herself again from the dish she had drawn in front of her. "Do have a little drink for once!" she pleaded.

"No, thank you."

"But you must! I'm going to make you, just for company and good fellowship." And she poured out a whisky and soda.

"Now you must!"

She leaned over to her aunt, at the same time pushing the glass towards her, put an arm round her neck, in a rather offhand boyish way, and then gave her a kiss.

"I won't let you hate me, I simply won't! I may be a beast sometimes, but I'm less of a beast with you than with almost anyone else I know. And if *you* had gone off after church and met him I shouldn't have minded, I shouldn't really. I should only have wished you luck and thought you deserved it for your cheek."

And then something in Miss Creswell seemed to break, with a little crash, quite subdued but still a crash, and she began to laugh and nearly to cry at the same time in a very human way, and she drank some whisky and soda, and let Im hug her and said, "I don't know what it all means. But I'm not like myself tonight. I'm like something that's broken away from an anchor. I'm adrift."

"He's cut your painter," said Imogen seriously. "Last night directly we began to talk I saw you were different, that something had happened to you."

"Not directly!"

"Well, very soon. And look at how he affected old Barrimore. It was like a miracle. Your Savior from the North!"

Miss Creswell started. "D'you mean—did he seem to you——"

"No—because he's so absolutely different from all the conventional ideas of a Savior. Has it never struck you, Towser, how terribly conventional we are in our ideas? Directly the word 'Savior' is uttered, I'm positive five people out of six think of long fair hair, white robes, white hands, slow movements, conventional gestures of blessing, emaciation, vegetarianism and beards. Don't think I want to be irreverent. I don't. But isn't it true?"

"I dare say it is."

"I know it is. Even I do. And he isn't like that, he isn't like anyone else I have ever seen. But he's got just a touch of what I imagine Walt Whitman may have been—possibly, and a touch of a great actor."

"An actor!"

"Yes, who has never acted. Can you understand?"

"It's rather complicated."

"So is he; tremendously complicated in simplicity. It's a

plain frame without any ornaments. It isn't even gilded. But the picture inside is extraordinary. D'you know the name I've given to him?"

"You have given him a name?"

"Yes; but he doesn't know it."

"What is it?"

"I call him 'The Unearthly.'"

Miss Creswell felt as if her face lost some of its healthy color. "The Unearthly!" she repeated. "What an extraordinary——"

She broke off, and looked about the familiar room which she knew to be part of the familiar house. And it seemed to her that ever since that encounter in front of the photograph shops after cathedral, Drearney had been changed, and she changed in it. While she looked at the room, with its well-known bits of furniture, its walls covered with old leather, its apricot-colored curtains, a curious thing happened. The room, though of course it didn't really change, suggested to her darkness for an instant, and in that darkness she realized a lighted window.

"Wait a moment!" she said, turning to Imogen. "I know one thing. He went to see Mr. Hendry yesterday evening. He was with Mr. Hendry when I passed in front of the house going home. He was in the room with the lighted window."

"I don't know where he was, but he did go to see Mr. Hendry yesterday after the cathedral service you were at."

"That's why I stopped and wanted to go in."

"Did you?"

"Yes—but go on. Why do you call him by such an extraordinary name?"

"It came to me while I was with him, not because he was spiritual, mystic, anything of that kind exactly. I scarcely know how to put it. But—wait a moment! Once when I was traveling with mother in Italy we went on an excursion in the mountains from Lake Como towards the Swiss frontier. And high up in a very lonely place, we came to a house where a sculptor was living. He had an atelier there. We went in, and he showed us some of his work. (He was a German-Swiss, I remember—yes, really!) One of his things struck me very much. It was an imaginative work, not a portrait, and he called it, 'Pure thought divorced from emotion.' It was a man's head brooding, plunged in thought, drowned in it.

There were greater depths of thought in it than even in
Rodin's 'Penseur.' It was in wood."

"In wood?"

"Yes—a wonderful thing. I wanted to buy it, but he
wouldn't sell. So we came away. The man was a genius,
I think. But I've even forgotten his name. He was one
of the lonely ones who live for work. Well, this bust reminded me in a way of him, though the features were different.
Most people think too little, or scarcely at all really. But
he must think too much. And how I wonder what about!
I've never wanted so much to be able to be in another's mind
as I want to be in his—right in, coiled up in it, immersed,
imprisoned."

"Im!" said Miss Creswell. She stretched out her hand.
All through her she felt what seemed to her like a strong
movement of the blood, wavelike, coming up and retreating.

"Yes?"

"That's it. You've expressed it, my feeling about him. I
had it. I have it. It's that extraordinary wish—its instinctive, or seems so—to get into his mind, as one might get into
a great mysterious nest, and coil up there. And then?"

"Then? God knows what would happen then."

Miss Creswell got up impulsively. "How strange that you
should say that! And now I know, now I can tell you! I
was angry, very angry with you, because I thought you had
gone to do what I had longed to do—you had gone to get
close to that mind. I felt mental jealousy. That was it!"

"Don't you feel it now?"

"Not as I did now I've spoken of it, and you've told me.
But what is it? What's the meaning of it? You're young.
But I'm not young. And I've never had any feeling of this
kind before."

"Nor I—never!"

"But then——"

"He's not like other men. He has a force they haven't got."

"You've finished. Do let's go into the library."

"I'll carry the drinks!" And with an odd sudden smile
she picked up the two glasses.

"I'll smoke too. I seem to want things greedily after
being with him. And yet, though he's a Jew, I don't believe
he could be greedy for anything except things that feed the
mind. His mind is voracious, I should think."

She followed her aunt softly, balancing the glasses with out-stretched arms, to the door.

"Go on, dear!" said Miss Creswell, staying to turn out the light.

"Where did you go after Dangate Street?"

They were by the blue-flamed fire now, and the library door was shut.

"We walked up Dangate Street till we came to the turning that leads by Market Street to the crossing, the Cattle Market and the Dane."

"I know where you have been. You have been in the Dane."

"Yes."

"On the city wall?"

"And in the gardens." Imogen lighted a cigarette and stretched out her thin, strong legs.

Miss Creswell felt a twinge of intimate, terribly intimate mental pain. "You talk of being together, walking. Did you do all this in silence?" she asked. And she strove hard to keep pain out of her voice, to speak naturally and pleasantly.

"At first we didn't say anything. We just walked quietly side by side. I've done plenty of what people call odd things in my life, but this was one of the oddest. To be walking at night with a total stranger here in Drearney, and not to be even talking. Such silences are for intimacy. But I felt intimate with him."

"How could you possibly?"

"I don't know. But I just did. You don't want to talk to a big view. That's rather how I felt. It seemed perfectly natural—just to keep along by his side in silence. When we got to the Cattle Market I said, 'Where are we going?' We had come among people and lights, and I felt more ordinary then. We stood under a lamp and I saw him plainly, very distinctly for the first time. 'Where are we going?' I asked.

"Of course any ordinary man, in fact almost any man, whether ordinary or not, must have thought—well, you can imagine what. I'm young, and I'm not particularly respect-able-looking, I hope. And then my question! But he didn't think anything of that kind. He said, 'Wherever you please!' with his rather ugly accent. And I said, 'Let's go and walk on the Dane.' And then he said, 'Yes, certainly.' I'm sure he hadn't the faintest idea what the Dane was. We went by

the Cattle Market and came into the Dane, and I led him
up the steep path to the old city wall. I was afraid we
might find some soldiers there with their girls. But we didn't.
There wasn't a soul.

"When we were on the top I stood still. I felt the time
had come to say something. We couldn't go on in perpetual
silence. I stood still, and so did he. And then I said, 'You
interest me most tremendously. I don't know why. Who
are you and what are you doing in Drearney?' I was abrupt—
but I knew he wouldn't mind. And, after all, my joining him
had been abrupt. It was no use trying to play propriety and
hang on to convention after what I'd done. Was it?"

"No."

"Besides I like to go for things. It's the best way, in fact
the only way in this damned obstructive world."

"What did he say?"

"He looked at me, and then he said—by the way I forgot
to tell you he has a splendid speaking voice, much finer than
old Barrimore's even; and he doesn't plump it out into sonority
as Barrimore does, but just let's it be as it is—he said, 'I'm
a Russian Jew. My name is Peter Kharkoff. I have spent
many years in America, and I'm an American citizen. I'm
living in Switzerland and I'm going back there.'

"Ordinary enough, wasn't it? I don't know what I had
expected, but it certainly wasn't that. America—Switzerland!
No, it certainly wasn't that. Now if he had said, 'I come
from Palestine. I was born in the wilderness of Judea'—or,
'My home is in Morocco. When I was a child I ran barefoot
in the Ghetto of Fez'—something of that kind, I should have
felt, 'Yes, I suppose you were!' Or 'Yes, I suppose you did.'

"But America—Switzerland! I thought of Fifth Avenue
and then I thought of Lucerne, and I said, 'I don't seem to
see you as an American citizen in Switzerland somehow. Have
you been in Russia?' He said, 'Yes, I was born there. But
I haven't been there since I was a child.' Then I thought of
something"—she looked significantly at her aunt—"and I
said, 'Were you born in the south of Russia?' And he told
me, 'No, in the north.' And then he turned and looked down.

"It was dark where we were, but we could see lights from
the town, and it was silent round about us, but we could hear
distant noises. I couldn't have told what they were exactly,
but I could just hear them. The sound of life—that was

what we heard. And then he began to talk. Russians are tremendous talkers, I've found. He talked slowly and without any excitement, in the most natural way you can imagine."

"What did he talk about?"

"Life. He spoke about it as if he wasn't immersed in it, but looked at it, contemplated it, as I might contemplate a vast picture which interested me. I've heard clever men try to do that. But it has always seemed to me like a pose. There's always been something pharisaical about it. You know what I mean; the 'I'm not as other men' tone, critical, condemnatory, or assuming astonishment. 'How can they, the wretched creatures?' Or 'What pleasure can they possibly find in such follies?' Whenever I've heard clever men talking about life I have always ended up with the impression that what they said might be summed up like this: 'A precious mess you're all making of it! Now, if you'd only listen to me!' . . ."

"Yes, I know that! And when they write——"

"When they write about life it's even worse. It's a red-faced judge with the black-cap drawn down over his beastly bushy eyebrows. But he wasn't like that. He talked about life as if it interested him profoundly, as a phenomenon of which he was not a part, but he talked entirely without conceit. Presently, I said to him, 'Have you ever been ill?' "

"Why did you say that?"

"I suppose I wanted to see if I could bring him right down among all the ordinary people who have colds, and stomach-ache, and rheumatism, and neuralgia. He told me, 'No, never.' The extraordinary thing is that I felt it was true. That man gives me the impression that he is always speaking the truth. I asked him, 'Do you ever tell lies?' He said, 'Lies are dull. Truth is never dull. I prefer truth.' I said I had told hundreds of lies. Then he said, 'I am sure you have. Even your face is meant to be a lie.' That was one straight from the shoulder, wasn't it, Tow—Aunt Annie?"

"You can call me Towser if you like. What does it matter? I suppose he meant your make-up?"

"Yes. I asked him why he said 'meant.' And he told me because the reality of my face couldn't be hidden by paint and powder. The truth of a face lies in the expression, he declared, and he added that painting emphasizes expression. He said that a sad face unpainted is less sad to the beholder's eyes than a painted sad face." •

"I expect that's true."

"Of course. He said it. We went down into the Dane Garden and walked up and down the narrow paths under the damp trees. I asked him what he was doing in Drearney, and he told me he had read a good deal about it and supposed it to be typical and therefore worth visiting. Wasn't it now the cradle of English Protestantism? I thought of Miss Prowse and a few others, and I said I considered it to be a cats' cradle."

"Really, Im!"

"Oh, it was all right. He had no idea what I meant by that. Then I asked him what he thought of Drearney. He said it seemed to him to be the comfortable home of routine. The canons were creatures of habit and slept on the breast of tradition, sucking peacefully at the well-filled bottle of milky Mother Church. I couldn't help laughing. But he didn't laugh. He said he had been to the afternoon service on Saturday."

"I didn't see him there."

"He was there. He is very much interested in statistics."

"Statistics!" exclaimed Miss Creswell in a rather dismal voice.

"Yes. He had counted the number of times the choir-boys and men and the clergy had yawned during the service. How many times do you think, Towser?"

"My dear Im! I haven't the slightest idea."

"He said that between them they yawned seventy-two times."

"What an extraordinary conversation!"

"It didn't seem so to me. I asked him what he had done when the service was over."

Miss Creswell leaned forward, her eyes fixed on Imogen's.

"He told me he had gone to look into some shops where there were photographs of all the cathedral people. I should think he's a student of heaps of things, physiognomy among them."

"Yes? Yes?"

"Among the photographs he found one face that was not traditional but entirely individual. He called it the face of a seeker in the dark, who wasn't fumbling for a box of stinking matches, or crying out, 'Where's a candle?' but who was going steadily forward in the hope of reaching a great flood of light."

"Mr. Hendry! Of course he meant Mr. Hendry!"

"Yes, he did."

"But how did he get to know Mr. Hendry? How was it he went to Mr. Hendry's house?"

"Ah, that's where you come in!"

"I? Did he say anything about me?"

"Yes. He said there was a woman standing beside him in front of the shop windows. Presently she went away into the precincts—he called it into the garden of the cathedral—and he followed at a distance."

"But why did he follow me?"

"I asked him, and he said, 'She had been thinking about me and about that man'—he meant Mr. Hendry—'and her thought called me.' When he reached Mr. Hendry's house he saw one of the windows lighted up."

"The study window on the ground floor."

"He realized who lived there——"

"How could he?"

"Well—you knew! He went to the lighted window, looked in, saw Mr. Hendry, and knocked on the glass."

"How extraordinary!"

"It didn't seem so when he told it. Mr. Hendry came out and asked him into the house and he went in. Hendry's thoroughly unconventional, isn't he?"

"I believe he is. He certainly looks so. I wonder what they talked about."

"So do I—but he didn't tell me. All he said was that Mr. Hendry wanted truth, and that was a thing very few men knew they wanted. But Mr. Hendry did know it."

Imogen paused and threw the end of her cigarette into the fire. When the pause came Miss Creswell was aware of a creeping sense of depression, perhaps of disappointment. "Is that all?" she asked, after waiting for a minute or two.

"No. He spoke of old Barrimore, and I told Peter——"

"Peter!"

"Kharkoff—that it was he who had made old Barrimore ruin the effect of his own sermon. He didn't deny it."

"Did he acknowledge it?"

"No. He just looked at me and said, 'Do you think Christ did succeed in his purpose? Do you think He did save the world?' I couldn't say anything. I stood on the path—we were still in the Dane—and looked at him and remembered he was a Jew. But remembering that didn't seem to help things. At last he said, 'Good night.' He took off his hat. I said, 'But when am I going to see you again?' He said, 'I am leaving tomorrow. I'm going back to Switzerland.' I said, 'I must have your address.' He gave it to me. It's in my bag."

"Do get it, Im."

Imogen got up, went out into the hall, and returned with a card. On it was printed, Peter Kharkoff. 7, Rue les Bergues, Genève. Miss Creswell took it and stared at it.

"And that's all?" she said at last.

"That's all—up to now," said Imogen.

CHAPTER VI

ONLY after Imogen had gone back to London and she was once more alone did Miss Creswell recall a small incident which had happened when she was at tea at the Barrimores' on the memorable evening of the encounter in front of the photograph shops. Canon Barrimore had told Mrs. Sotheby that he would invite Mr. Hendry to dinner that evening. Miss Creswell wished to know whether he had done so, and whether Mr. Hendry had accepted the invitation. If he had, and had spent an evening in the canon's company immediately after the Jew's visit to him, the curious incident of the spoiled sermon might be accounted for by something else than Peter Kharkoff's presence in the cathedral on the night when it was preached. As she had been a vehicle for the conveyance of Kharkoff's peculiar power—so she thought of it—to Imogen, so might Mr. Hendry have been the vehicle of its conveyance to the canon.

If it were not so, if no vehicle had been required, then Peter Kharkoff must have been able to act directly upon Canon Barrimore's mind from a distance and, out of the midst of the concentrated crowd, have been able to force his mind through the crowd of minds to that clever, artistic and self-satisfied man, and to impose it, like a tyrant, overturning the canon's mind from its throne. She wished intensely to know whether such a feat had really been performed, or whether Mr. Hendry had perhaps prepared the way innocently for what had happened by talking at dinner about his remarkable visitor, and possibly conveying to his host some of that visitor's views. If Mr. Hendry had done that, the canon might have been turning those views over in his acquisitive brain for hours before he went into the pulpit; but if he had not, what had happened seemed to Miss Creswell to partake of the nature of a miracle. Secretly she was longing to be convinced of the possibility of the miraculous in connection with the mysterious Jew. But she didn't want to be ridiculous. She didn't want to be one of the credulous, silly women who are forever catching at absurdities and turning them into marvels in order to add a trimming of the fantastic to the monotony of life. Rather than to imagine, she wanted to know. But she hoped eagerly that the knowledge would be what something within her yearned for.

After Imogen's departure on the Monday morning Miss Creswell felt very flat and unusually depressed. She was the victim of a sharp and very unpleasant reaction. Quite suddenly she looked at her life, looked at it in the face fully as it seemed to her for the first time, and found it drab, empty, singularly featureless. Was this indeed the life with which hitherto she had believed herself satisfied? What was there in it to satisfy? The long succession of the little things now seemed to her intolerable; the getting up in the morning and going down to coffee and toast and eggs and bacon, to the Morning Post, to the orders in the kitchen, the directions to the gardener, the letter and note writing, the little stroll round the garden, the walk into the town to "do some shopping," the visit to the library to return and take out books. In the High Street friends and acquaintances would be encountered, and there would be greetings, smiles, scraps of conversation, hopes of better weather and so forth. And then home to lunch—the usual sort of lunch. After lunch a little rest in the library, with some work or a book. Then the afternoon with a drive in the car, or a walk, visits to friends, talks with this one and that one, a working party, perhaps, or a committee meeting at the deanery or elsewhere, possibly service at the cathedral followed by tea somewhere with someone, or at home with friends. More reading or writing in the library, then dinner at home or out with more friends. An hour or two talking, musing, reading, playing patience if alone, bridge if in company. And so to bed . . . to that recumbent posture in silence and darkness which is like a nightly rehearsal for the grave.

Had all this contented her? Really it had. But she could scarcely believe that now. For her life had had a tremendous shake, and she was just beginning to realize in some degree the effect upon her of what had happened. Again the thought came to her, "A cancer begins and a mental process begins. And in each case isn't there a victim?" But was she really going to allow herself to be made a victim? And she tried to pull herself together, to call up in herself a force of defiance. What had happened after all? She had seen a stranger who had seemed to her unusual and remarkable. She had, or thought she had, felt a force coming from him to her and affecting her. She had seemed to note that force acting upon others, and had fancied that she had, in one case, served as a vehicle for its conveyance. She had received report of the stranger from Imogen. And—she had suffered. Now Imogen was gone and the stranger was gone. She had sent Imogen away in her own car and knew of her departure. But she felt that she knew with equal certainty of the departure of the stranger. How was that? The emptiness of Ewenden House and of the city at whose edge it was set told her that he had gone. She could not have felt this dreadful dulness, this aimless depression, if he had still been in Drearney. She knew that quite positively, and the knowledge alarmed her. His presence had affected her powerfully. It was dreadful to be equally affected by his absence. Never before had she come face to face with the fact that one human being can populate or make empty and totally void a place for another human being. She faced that fact now. Drearney had been marvelously full. Now it was empty. Life had been removed—to Geneva.

She, who had traveled much, had naturally been to Geneva. She knew that city of still and of rushing waters, deep blue and silky green, fairly well. But she had never been beset by any longing to return there. Now such a longing beset her. The thought of Geneva attracted her intensely. She saw the swans floating above the weirs. She saw white sails gleaming in sunshine on the lake. She saw Mont Blanc with its snows touched to rose color by the setting sun. And the city was full of life, pulsing with thought, thrilling with interest. And Drearney was cold and dull and dead.

The last of November in Drearney! How dreadful! How bloodless! And December to follow!

But she might go abroad.

Usually, following an English custom, Miss Creswell, if she went abroad, started towards the end of January, and as a rule she was back by the middle of April, or thereabouts. But there was nothing to prevent her from starting earlier if she chose. She was not bound to be in England for Christmas. A great many people went to Switzerland for Christmas. She might do the same. Christmas in Drearney no longer held any attraction for her.

She had several stupid little engagements for the Monday. She duly kept them all. In the evening of that day she dined at the house of some friends in the country, about three miles out from Drearney. The dinner was good, the company agreeable, even lively. And she had all the luck of the cards at bridge. But she came home in the car alarmed at the boredom of which she had been the victim. So might be bored a woman who was in love with someone far away. But she was not in love, not the least bit in love. And it was that which made her condition alarming to herself. For any woman may be in love. She may regret it. She may even contemn it. But it doesn't, it cannot, completely puzzle her. But Miss Creswell, it seemed, was a victim not to her heart, but to her mind. A man had stretched out and gripped hold of the fibers of her mind. She felt the strain of the tug like something physical within her. Her freedom was gone. She was alarmed, miserable, excited.

On the following day she resolved to try to see Mr. Hendry. She did not know him well. Few people in Drearney did. But he had been to her house three or four times, and she had sometimes had little talks with him at the deanery or elsewhere. He had always interested her, but it had seemed to her that he was difficult to know, and it had been in her mind that a woman of her type could not appeal to his violently active intelligence and reserved, though enthusiastic, unconventionality. Without intention—she was quite sure of that—he had made her feel more than once that, in his sight, she was a very long way from being a modern. Probably he numbered her among the many "cathedral ladies" to whom the practices of religion in an important and beautiful building served as a distraction from the black monotony of humdrum life. She did not number herself among them naturally, each of us being different in his, or her, own eyes from all the others. But she had a shrewd suspicion that in Mr. Hendry's consideration she was just a "cathedral lady."

She turned over in her mind various possible ways of "getting at" him. She might send him an invitation to lunch or dinner. Somehow she felt that she couldn't ask him to tea. Something so spinstery about that! But a tête-à-tête lunch or dinner would be unusual. And Mr. Hendry was extremely intelligent. If she broached the subject which was pushing her towards him he might guess why she was hospitable to him. That wouldn't do. Finally she decided that she must meet him casually without attempting to make an appointment, and she went that afternoon to service in the cathedral intending to stay till the outgoing voluntary was over, and to meet Mr. Hendry as he came out with some perfectly natural questions about the music which would lead to further and more important conversation. But Mr. Hendry wasn't at the organ that day. A deputy—one of his pupils—took his place, and Miss Creswell's design was frustrated.

She was severely disappointed, and came out of the cathedral into the darkening evening feeling melancholy and deprived. Instinctively, as once before, she crossed the gravel space in front of the west door and stood before the dignified little shops.

Why wasn't *he* there? If he stood beside her now she would certainly speak to him, following the example of Imogen. It was useless and foolish to be bound by the shackles of convention. There was nothing wrong in being attracted to a mind. She wished she had spoken to him on that Saturday evening. If she had she would not now be feeling sore. She would not now be filled with irritation against Imogen and Mr. Hendry.

Mr. Hendry! Her eyes fell again on his photograph, and suddenly she came to a resolve. She would go to his house and ask for him. He would be surprised, no doubt. He would expect an explanation. (For she had never called on him yet.) She would have to give some reason for her visit. What reason could she give? As she walked towards his house she debated about that. But she had come to no conclusion when she entered his garden, stood in front of his hall door and had rung his bell.

An elderly maid servant, with flat feet which she turned out very much as she walked slowly, came to answer the bell, and in response to Miss Creswell's inquiry said that Mr. Hendry was in but that she believed he was "simpony writin'" at the moment. This sounded repellent, but Miss Creswell, driven on by something imperious within her, begged the elderly maid to take in her card and to ask whether she could be received.

"Certainly, mum. Will you kindly step in the drawin'-room?"

A door was opened on the left, opposite to the room of the lighted window—so Miss Creswell thought of the room on whose window-pane *he* had knocked—and she was left alone for a moment in a severe, fireless chamber which was evidently little used by the owner of the house.

Then a quick step was audible outside, the door was sharply opened, and a rather high-pitched, nervous, energetic voice said, "How d'you do, Miss Creswell! What can I do for you? But please come into a room with a fire. This is like a well. I never use it—hate drawing-rooms. It's only my inherent conventionality, come down to me, I suppose, from conventional forebears, which makes me have one. This will be better."

And then the door of the room of the lighted window was opened quickly, and they were both by a fire among books, and manuscripts, and pipes, and piles of letters, and a clever man's muddle of the things he likes best.

"May I offer you some——"

"No, thank you. I am having tea at home today."

"Do sit down. This is the best chair. That's why I fill it up with the Mass in B Minor, I suppose." And with a quick laugh, that sounded the least bit shy, he cleared an armchair by the fire and drew it a little nearer to the flames. "Do sit down!" he repeated, with an evidently strong attempt at cordiality.

"Thank you very much."

Miss Creswell sat down, and he stood by the fire near to her, looking at her with his too observant brown eyes. A peculiarity of Mr. Hendry was that though he was decidedly a shy man, under all his energy and enthusiasm and lack of conventionality and mental hardihood, he couldn't, simply couldn't, talk to people without looking them straight in the face. He had to keep his eyes on them, and they were eyes which disconcerted many people. They disconcerted Miss Creswell now. For they were, she thought, obviously asking her, "Well, why are you here? What is it? What's brought you to me this November evening?" And what was she to answer?

"Do forgive me for interrupting you in your work," she began tentatively. "I'm afraid you were composing. Weren't you?"

"Having a shot at a symphony that'll probably never be heard," he said, with another short laugh.

She saw the blaze of work in his eyes. She felt the gleam of it, hot and fierce, in his manner.

"I'm really ashamed to interrupt you," she said, "but I wanted to know——"

"Yes?"

She had intended to say, "I wanted to know what music you played on Sunday after the evening service." But under his eyes she somehow couldn't. And instead she actually blurted out her real reason for calling on him. She told him about the encounter by the photograph shops, about her interest in the Jew, and about her pause on her way home from the Barrimores' before his lighted window.

"I understand he called on you after I had seen him," she said. And then she was silent, for she did not care to mention Imogen.

All the time she had been speaking, Mr. Hendry had kept his eyes fixed upon her. She saw a strong expression of surprise come into his face. Then it seemed to die out, as if he had changed his mind about something and was no longer astonished at her strange visit and strange frankness. But still in his eyes she seemed to read the question, "What is it? What exactly has brought you to me on this November evening?"

She felt she must say something more. But before she could say it he jerked out, "You're right; he did call. I was in here smoking a pipe after cathedral when I felt there was someone in the garden. Then I heard a rap on the glass there, threw up the window, and there he stood. I asked him in, and he came and stayed a good bit."

"One thing! Please do forgive me for seeming so curious. I know it must seem very strange——"

"Not at all!"

"Oh yes, it must! But did you dine with the Barrimores on that evening—Saturday?"

"No, I didn't. They kindly sent to ask me but I didn't feel like going. Fact is that man—well, I didn't feel I could chance breaking his visit, cutting it short, you know. And the Barrimores' invitation came while he was still with me."

"I quite understand. So you didn't go!"

"No!" he said; and the look of surprise reappeared on his face.

"I was only wondering," she said, rather falteringly. "I was at the Barrimores' when the canon said he was going to ask you."

"Ah!"

"Well? Well?" said his eyes, impatiently, she thought.

"You must think—I'm afraid really I must seem almost impertinent!" She felt her face flushing.

"My dear Miss Creswell! As if you could possibly——"

"The fact is," she said, now with a sort of desperation, "and I may as well acknowledge it since I've come here—that man has made such a strange impression upon me, has filled me with such—I scarcely know what to call it. Curiosity seems such a poor weak word in connection with him. I want to know more about him. I want to know him. And when I knew he had been to see you I felt—I felt obliged to come here and ask you to tell me something about him!"

"So that's it!" said his intent eyes. And he tapped a thin, long-fingered and very intellectual-looking hand on the mantel-piece. "May I venture to ask you a question?" he then said, after a moment of hesitation.

"Surely—considering that I have asked you so many! At least I'm afraid I have."

"How came you to know that this Peter Kharkoff called on me last Saturday evening?"

"I guessed it."

"Really?"

"That is—in a way! But only afterwards, not until Sunday. And my guess was confirmed by someone. I'm afraid I can't say by whom."

He was silent. He had begun, she thought, to look rather abstracted, rather remote, as if involved in a cloud of thought. His eyes still looked at her, but the almost prying intentness had gone out of them. She wondered very much what he was thinking about just then. His tall, thin and rather angular figure, clad in a pair of loose gray trousers—he was never seen in any other pair except in the evening sometimes—a dark jacket and waistcoat topped by a low collar and skimpy blue necktie spotted with white, leaned against the high mantelpiece in a careless, negligent attitude. But his right hand was now clutched tight into a fist. And his narrow pale face, beneath the sprouting, violent hair, dust-brown and apparently always full of excitement, seemed alive with a still intensity. Miss Creswell felt that she ought to go. He had not responded to her plainly put statement. He had not told her anything about Peter Kharkoff. Apparently then he did not wish or intend to tell her anything. She felt that it was entirely impossible for her to make any more demands upon him. She had interrupted him in the midst of his work, and such work, the composing of a symphony. Now she simply must go. She moved in her seat, put her hands on its arms.

"Well, really I mustn't——"

Mr. Hendry started. "Oh, but you said you wanted me to tell you something about my visitor of Saturday!"

"But you're working. I really mustn't take up your time."

"But you asked to see me when you knew I was working, didn't you?"

Miss Creswell reddened again. "I oughtn't to have done that, but I was carried away."

"Well, but now it's done, why not let yourself have the benefit of it, if benefit there is? Do you know anything of this Peter Kharkoff?"

"Just a little, a very little. I know he's a Russian Jew, has been in America and lives in Geneva at present."

"Yes—in Geneva. I shall go there when I next get a holiday. I've got his address—rue les Bergues. I shall go there and look him up. That man——" He broke off and suddenly thrust his long hands into the pockets of the gray trousers and slightly lifted his shoulders, frowning.

"Yes?" said Miss Creswell eagerly.

Mr. Hendry bent down towards her. "What's the curse of our age?" he asked abruptly.

"The curse of—I don't know."

"I do. It's lies. Men have always eaten lies now and then. But our age simply feeds upon them. Lies are our daily bread. The making of lies the daily bread of man, his main sustenance, began in the war. Lies were no new thing of course, God knows! But the definite and deliberate substituting of lies for truth on an enormous scale, day after day, month after month, year in year out—that started in the war under the cursed egis of authority. And I say, 'Damn the men who fed and feed the people on lies.' But look here now—who among all the people you know even tries to cling to the rock of truth?"

She looked up at him. She was astonished by this abrupt outburst which seemed to have nothing to do with the subject they had been speaking about. "Surely," she began, "most decent people try to stick to the truth."

"D'you think so?" he said. "Well, I don't. I suppose we are most of us what are called decent here in Drearney, but I hear lies told every day. And how can one expect anything else when our politicians are liars, and our priests are liars, and our journalists are the biggest liars of all. D'you take in a daily paper?"

"Yes."

"Then you start the day with a full diet of lies, some carefully calculated, some just thrown in by chance as it were, out of sheer heedlessness or rank carelessness. 'Influencing public opinion'! You know the phrase?"

"Yes."

"What does it mean? It means stuffing the public with the selected lies which certain ruffians in high places think are calculated to bring about the current of opinion most surely favorable to their own ends—generally beastly. That's what it means. As to religion it's full up with lies. We suck in plenty of them here in cathedral. I'm shocking you. Forgive me!"

He suddenly seemed to be aware of his auditor as Miss Annie Creswell, spinster, comfortably off, orthodox Protestant, of Ewenden House, Drearney, and he straightened up, gave his characteristic short laugh, and then said more quietly:

"But I let my mind run away with me. Or—no! Isn't my mind *me?* I expect you think I've got well away from Peter Kharkoff. But, really, Miss Creswell, that man with his great love of truth, his great, mighty truthfulness—it was he who made me see afresh what lies we men live by, or try to live by. (For it can't rightly be called living!) You want me to tell you something about him. He's a Jew, a *poor* Jew who might easily be rich, I imagine. That's something to think about, isn't it?" And he smiled. "As we know he lives at Geneva."

Struck by an idea, which oddly enough (she thought) hadn't come to her before, Miss Creswell asked, "Has he anything to do with the League of Nations?"

"I don't know. But I doubt it. He didn't say anything about it. He's a lonely being, I think. By which I don't mean that he's sad, desolate, derelict. Not a bit of it! But I can't think of him as tied up in a bunch with a lot of men who are always discussing things at Banquets (with a capital letter) and who have to have a government allowance for entertaining. That's not *him*. At Geneva—he lives in a flat—he's got a big library, it seems, thousands of books."

"And yet he's poor, you say?"

"I imagine he is. But he manages books. I suppose rather as I manage scores." Again he smiled.

"What does he do at Geneva?"

"Studies, writes, carves, sculps."

"Is he a sculptor?"

"Yes, in wood."

"Do you mean——"

"He carves statues in wood, he told me. He's done a big one of Christ lately, and by what he said about it I imagine it's as unlike the Christ of convention as anything could possibly be."

"Really! In wood!"

"Is there—you seem specially struck by that?"

"It's only that my niece, Imogen Lowrie, saw what she thought was a very wonderful bust in wood once when she was traveling in Switzerland. It was a bust representing pure thought divorced from emotion, and——"

"By Jove!" The exclamation broke in sharply, piercingly almost, upon Miss Creswell's utterance. "By Jove! That's a perfect summing up of Kharkoff himself! Couldn't be beaten. That's the exact impression he makes on a fellow! And it's the complete apparent absence of emotion in him which makes him so jolly impressive." Mr. Hendry had a habit of introducing schoolboy expressions in the midst of talk which was extremely unlike that of the average schoolboy, and "jolly" was a very favorite word of his.

"But surely emotion is at the back of everything fine, isn't it?" said Miss Creswell. "I know it's the fashion of the day

among our young people rather to jeer at emotion and pretend
to distrust it. But I have always thought that was a pose."

"Sugar they call it, gush and so forth. I know! I know!"

"Do you agree with them?"

He looked very grave.

"You—a musician?" she said, with a sort of pressure.

"I'm afraid we often feel falsely," he said, slowly.

"And this strange man—Peter Kharkoff—do you think he
doesn't feel at all? But, if so, he must be a sort of monster."

Mr. Hendry shook his head, and the upstanding plumes of his
hair moved almost like things vibrating. "I don't know how
to put it exactly," he said. "But it's like this. His thought
seems to come to you with the force of something that's absolutely pure, unmixed with anything else. That's how I felt
it. It reaches you like light. It pierces as light pierces darkness. His mind calls you."

"Yes."

"But I don't know that his heart calls you. Tell the truth,
when he was with me I don't believe I ever thought about
his heart at all."

"What made him come to you?"

"Couldn't say. I didn't ask him and he didn't tell me.
When I opened the window he said, with his heavy foreign
accent, 'Can I come in and have a talk with you?' I looked
at him—of course I'd never set eyes on him before—and I
said, 'Rather! Come in! I'll open the door.' That's how
it was. It seemed to me the most natural thing in the world."

"Isn't it all very extraordinary?"

"I suppose it is. But I don't know that I bother much
about what is extraordinary, or called so, and what isn't. Some
people might call it extraordinary your coming to me about it
this evening."

"So it is, I think. But I couldn't help it." She said the
last words in a low, uncertain voice that struck him as being
full of melancholy.

"What's the matter?" he asked.

"I—I think perhaps—I think that man must be a dangerous man," she said.

"Why?"

"I think he makes people prisoners, prisoners of his mind."

He looked hard at her with a new and profound interest.
"But if it's a fine mind, a wonderful mind? What then?"

"I think it's a terrible thing to be a prisoner," she said. She got up. "Yesterday I knew he had gone. I knew he had left Drearney," she said, standing by the fire opposite to him.

"How did you know?"

"The whole place seemed empty, as if it had been emptied. That was because *he* had gone away."

"That's odd!" he said. "I had the same feeling. I have it now. I've been trying to lose it in work—orchestration. It doesn't do. A man has to stand alone."

"Do you think it would be wise to go to Geneva?"

"D'you mean—Oh, I know! You're alluding to my holiday. But that's far ahead. I don't get away till the summer. We organists only get a month or so. My month will be somewhere about August, I expect."

"Perhaps, by that time you'll have forgotten——"

"Oh no, I shan't."

"And do you think——"

"Oh, I shall go to Geneva sure enough."

"Then he means you to go."

There was a soft rap at the door. Miss Creswell started violently. "Come in!" called Mr. Hendry, in his high, rather sharp voice.

The door opened and the elderly servant appeared. "Canon Barrimore wants to see you, sir, please. I have shown him into the drawin'-room."

"I'll come in a moment, Lucy."

"Yes, sir."

Lucy withdrew, shutting the door discreetly behind her.

"I'll go at once," said Miss Creswell. "I oughtn't to have —I really don't know how to——"

"Please don't! You had to come."

"No—don't say that!" He saw her lips tremble slightly. She pressed them together, held out her hand. "Good-by."

"I'll see you to the door."

They went out into the hall. As he was letting her out she whispered, "Please don't say anything to the canon!"

"Of course not!" He shook her hand in a rather offhand, rough way.

As he shut the hall door he muttered to himself, "Odd! Damned odd!"

CHAPTER VII

"HULLO, Canon! Very glad to see you! Forgive me for keeping you a minute, but I had someone with me."

"I know—Miss Creswell. A very agreeable and intelligent woman with quite a competent knowledge of modern poetry. My wife and I are very fond of her."

"Do come into my room out of this horror, won't you?" And he led his second visitor into the room with the fire and shut the door. Evidently the poor old symphony, which probably no one would ever hear, wasn't destined to be got on with that evening. "That's the best chair!"

The canon at once sat down in it, and Hendry sat down opposite to him on the top of a pile of letters. "Oh, Lord!" he said, jumping up again and removing them. "I've got a bad habit of throwing things down everywhere. May I give you some tea or anything?"

"No, thank you. I am on my way home. But I thought I would just look in on you."

"I'm glad."

The canon seemed preoccupied, Hendry thought, and not so completely, almost complacently, self-possessed as usual. There was something doubtful in his demeanor, something of perturbation in his look. And he had the manner, Hendry fancied, of a man who wanted something, perhaps vaguely, but had come to no conclusion as to the best way of getting, or reaching out after it. After a moment of silence he said, "Don't you find life here all the year round rather unsatisfactory, Hendry? You're an intellectual man, as well as being highly musical. How do you manage among all these dear ignoramuses?"

"Oh, I get on all right. My musical job interests me, keeps me going. Prowse allows me to experiment now and then." He smiled. "If you'll forgive me for putting myself alongside of you, Canon, I think you and I between us manage to keep a few of them immune from the sleeping-sickness."

"Aha!" For an instant the big voice became more sonorous, and a smile began to dawn on the smooth red face. But it died away and was replaced by a queer look of uneasiness. "But I have only three months of it, Hendry, and you have —what is it—eleven in the year."

"Eleven. That's it."

"How do you manage?"

"Well, Canon, I'm one of the fools who are keen on composing. That helps, I suppose."

The canon looked across at him. "Do you feel self-confidence when you're at work?"

"I believe I do, somehow. It may be conceit, but I don't believe I could plow along without it."

"Self-confidence! That's the great thing to have if one is to do anything first rate. But don't you feel doubtful sometimes?"

"About what I do?"

"What you've done—yes."

"Oh, rather! Sometimes I feel I'm the most impotent thing in creation."

"That's a terrible sensation! Weininger says that the greatest geniuses at times feel far more incapable, far less able, than the ordinary man ever feels, and that they even seem to be so."

"The genius can feel and seem a fool no doubt but——"

He was going to say more, but Canon Barrimore interrupted him. "Tell me, Hendry—I have a high opinion of your intelligence—do you think my sermons, if you listen to them——"

"I do!"

"Then, do you think they are as a rule sound?"

"Sound?"

"The clergy too often talk great nonsense in the pulpit. No one can contradict them unfortunately. And so they often exist in a state of great complacency. What about my sermons?"

"They're the best I ever hear in Drearney, barring the dean's. And you're a much more accomplished preacher than he is."

"Yes, that's true. I'm more of an artist. Then my sermons satisfy you?"

"I consider them brilliant."

"Aha!" Again the smile dawned and suddenly faded. "But last Sunday? I felt I didn't do myself justice last Sunday night. How did it strike you?"

"I thought the sermon first rate, absolutely stunning as a piece of work, planned to a T and jolly well delivered. But the coda was thoroughly unexpected. It seemed like a sudden afterthought, as if you'd never meant to have it and just stuck it in anyhow in a hurry, and weren't half sure yourself why you put it in at all. It seemed to me that you finished your sermon and then there jumped up in your mind the thought, 'By Jove, though, perhaps all I've been arguing isn't worth tuppence ha'penny. Perhaps I've got hold of the wrong end of the stick.' I hope you'll forgive me, as you asked my opinion. I can hold my tongue—at times. But if I speak I have to say what I really think."

"You're quite right, quite right! That's just what happened. A sudden attack of mental doubt laid me low for a moment. I have never known anything of the kind before. It was like a seizure. I cannot account for it. It was singularly painful, Hendry, singularly painful. I felt like a man who had carefully planned and built a house and then was moved to try and pull it down with his own hands." The canon looked up again, met the organist's intent eyes, and looked away uneasily, almost guiltily.

"You are wondering why I tell you all this. But I had the feeling I must speak about it to someone. I feel sure that the whole of my congregation last Sunday must have been taken aback by what I did. But no one has spoken of it to me, not even my wife. It seemed as if there was some strong influence adverse to me in the cathedral. But that of course is impossible."

"Why impossible?"

The canon looked up smartly. "Well, I am not, I hope, so conceited as to suppose that everybody in a place like Drearney delights in my sermons or in me. There are other ecclesiastics here, with their wives and daughters. There is our dear, but somewhat difficult, friend the dean. I've no doubt I have plenty of critics, and perhaps some severe ones. But I'm an oldish war-horse, Hendry, and not easily put out by having a few critical minds about me. Indeed, I rather like the feeling of mental resistance. It brings with it the desire to conquer, to convince. One can't debate from the pulpit unfortunately, but mental resistance stings the mind into activity. Of course I always preach from manuscript. Nevertheless, in my study, when preparing my sermon, I always have the thought of the hostile minds I must overcome by my own mental power—if possible, aha—present with me. So—what did you mean by your question?"

Something, perhaps, in the expression of the organist's eyes brought the canon up sharply to the last inquiry.

"Wasn't it possible—or shall I put it like this? Mightn't it be possible that there was a new influence in the cathedral last Sunday when you were preaching, an influence never encountered by you before, and that the force of it was so great as to cause what you described just now as like a seizure?"

"But—but do you know, are you aware of such an influence?"

"I don't say that."

"Was any unusual personality present last Sunday? Any big man? Any famous atheist? But I'm so accustomed to preaching before brilliant men of free-thinking tendencies in London that I can't conceive being thrown out of my stride by an incredulous mind, however forcible."

"But you yourself said that it seemed as if there were some strong influence adverse to you in the cathedral."

"What is it you have in your mind, Hendry?"

"Look here, Canon! Let's have all quite clear between us. What really—exactly—brought you in to me this evening?"

"I felt inclined to look in on you. You interest me, because you are much more interesting than most of the good folk down here."

"That all?"

"What else should there——"

"I don't say there was any other reason. I only ask. Did you feel almost obliged to come my way this evening?"

The canon looked uneasy, surprised, and restlessly uncomfortable. "I should hardly say—well, perhaps I did. Possibly I did!"

"In fact—you did!"

Rather reluctantly, and after hesitation, the canon answered, "Yes."

"Isn't that rather astonishing?"

"I don't quite understand it, I confess." After saying this he looked all round the room as if inquiringly and then back at the organist, who was sitting in the chair opposite to him, leaning forward with his hands between his knees.

"Excuse me for cross-examining you! But have you ever felt obliged to come to see me till this evening?"

"No. Never."

"Something struck me, Canon, when you came it. You

began the conversation by asking me if I didn't find the life here unsatisfactory. Somehow you gave me the impression at that moment that you asked me that because *you* were feeling that the life here was unsatisfactory, dull, empty perhaps. Was it so?"

The canon shifted in his chair, tucked in his chin, as if with an effort after his normal self-confidence and self-satisfaction, then suddenly got up briskly out of his chair, and said in a rather loud voice, as if he had made up his mind to take a strong and definite line, "Yes. It was so. I don't know what is the matter with me today, Hendry, but I don't feel at all my usual self. The occurrence of last Sunday upset me. I have not spoken about it to anyone but you. But I cannot get over it, and I cannot understand it. Apparently you think you do!"

"You will probably think the explanation which I shall suggest entirely ridiculous, Canon.

"What is it? What is it?" exclaimed Canon Barrimore. "I'm quite in the dark as to your meaning. Who was in the cathedral last Sunday? You evidently mean that what happened was caused—though how it can have been, I can't conceive—by the presence of some particular person. Who was this person?"

"I think it must have been a man called Peter Kharkoff, who called upon me here on Saturday after the 3.30 service, and who left Drearney yesterday."

"Peter Kharkoff! I have never heard of him. Is he a friend of yours?"

"I never saw him or heard his name till last Saturday."

"What is he? Where does he come from? How could he possibly affect me?" Canon Barrimore asked these questions quickly and almost irritably, standing by the fire, and staring down at the organist with his very intelligent and rather fiery blue eyes, the eyes of a man with a mind capable of heat and not afraid of emotion.

"I don't say he has affected you. I'll just tell you what I feel about him and leave you to judge for yourself of the possibilities."

"Do! Do by all means! I'm still quite in the dark. I don't understand at all what you intend to convey to me."

"I'll try to make it clear." Hendry paused. During the pause Canon Barrimore again looked about the room, as if inquiringly, and then sat down once more in the chair from which he had got up so bruskly. "This is exactly what happened," said Hendry.

And then he told the canon, but more fully, more eloquently and with greater detail, what he had previously told Miss Creswell.

Canon Barrimore listened with profound attention, without attempting, or apparently wishing to attempt, any interruption. Only when Hendry finished his remarks with the statement, "Kharkoff left Drearney for Switzerland yesterday," did he move in his chair, and open his lips.

"When this man came to you on Saturday did you see him in this room?" he then asked.

"Yes. I was with him in here for a long while. Your invitation to dinner—by the way, many thanks for it—came while he was with me."

The canon was silent. As he did not speak, Hendry at last said, "Do you think my suggestion a very absurd one?"

"That this man was in the cathedral on Sunday night and that because of his being there I was obliged to say what I did at the end of my sermon?"

"Yes."

"It doesn't seem very likely, does it? Besides why should this man, this Russian Jew as you say he is——" He broke off, shifted in his chair, then said, "Do you know if he is a Jew in religion as well as racially?"

"I'm sure that man isn't, could never be, confined within the limits of any religion," said Hendry, bluntly.

"I asked because of course the Jews rejected the Messiah, and therefore any believing Jew wouldn't, couldn't possibly, agree with the main contention of my sermon."

"That's perfectly true. One thing I can tell you. Kharkoff said to me in the course of our talk that probably never before in history had the world seemed so sorely in need of a Savior as now. But that's pretty obvious, isn't it?"

Canon Barrimore ignored the final question. Hendry could see that some new, and perhaps startling, thought had suddenly taken possession of his guest's pliant mind, for his eyes filled with the curious inward look which suggests a man withdrawing from the outer world into the deep and mysterious recesses of himself, and he sat for a moment perfectly still, with his lips pressed tightly together and pushed up towards his nose.

Then he said, "Hendry, I'm convinced that Miss Creswell must have met this man on Saturday after cathedral. Yes, I'm convinced of that!"

"Why?" asked the organist, rather uncomfortably.

"By the way—and *she's* been to see you this evening! Your servant told me."

"Yes, she kindly looked in. She'd been to the service."

"I know. I saw her there. Oddly enough on Saturday in my drawing-room she brought up the subject of a Savior *à propos de bottes.* She was so abrupt that we—Mrs. Sotheby was with us—were astonished. She spoke of a prophecy that anticipated the coming of a Savior from the North. I thought she had been influenced by my mind. I told her so. But——"

He got up out of his chair, as Miss Creswell had done a few minutes before. "But I don't know now. If this man has such enormous mental power as you imply perhaps—but isn't all this rather fantastic, Hendry?"

"I don't feel it to be so, Canon."

"No? Has Miss Creswell met this man? Does she know him?"

"If I were you I should ask her, Canon."

Canon Barrimore looked sharply across at him and evidently came to a conclusion. But he was too much of a gentleman to say anything more on that subject. Subtleties did not easily escape him, and he was very swift at drawing conclusions.

"My visit and hers!" he thought to himself. "Both obligatory—were they?" And a sense of anger came to him, and with it a sense of mental pride which held something of defiance. "I really think," he said, with an attempt at great decisiveness, "that you and I, Hendry, are allowing ourselves to be absurd for once in a way. Don't you think so? I'm afraid I led the way by coming here as I did. We all know in these days what an immense power thought is. I should be the last to deny it. But really I cannot subscribe to your suggestion that this casual traveler, who gives you his name as Peter Kharkoff, is the possessor of the abnormal powers you claim for him. I really——"

"I beg your pardon, Canon," interrupted Hendry, rather dryly at this point. "I am not claiming anything on behalf of Peter Kharkoff. I have merely stated some facts and given you the impressions *I* drew from them. My impressions may be all wrong—but I don't think they are. I am thoroughly

convinced that Kharkoff's no ordinary man. But I don't ask
you to be convinced of the same thing. Why should you?
You have never met him, never seen him. To you he means
nothing——"

"I don't say that! I don't say that!" said the canon.

"But how can he mean anything?"

"I don't know, but—well, from your report of him I should
judge him to be a very exceptional sort of man. Tell me now!
Did he lay claim to any special powers?"

"He laid claim to nothing whatever."

"You told me he has lived in America."

"Yes."

"I suppose you know that a great many charlatans have arisen
in America, religious charlatans who have put forward all
sorts of absurd claims."

"But——"

"There was the Prophet Harris, for instance, who got hold
of even so brilliant a man as Laurence Oliphant. And there
was——"

"I know! I know! And, as far as I'm concerned, you
might cite Mrs. Eddy among them, though the Christian Scientists would probably be ready to think me into some dreadful
illness for saying so."

"Well, don't you think that this man, Kharkoff, may be
something of that kind? We must remember this, that no
charlatan ever can make a great impression on his fellow men,
especially on his well-instructed and clever fellow men, without
possessing powers of some sort, and perhaps remarkable powers.
The worst of it is that they are nearly always mingled with
humbug and with the desire to be important, influential, and
to make money. What are you smiling at?"

"Was I? Do forgive me!"

"Have I said anything you consider absurd?"

"Good heavens, Canon!" Hendry got up. "If you'd only
come across Kharkoff, as I have, you could never put him
among the charlatans. You could never mention him and the
Prophet Harris in the same breath."

"No?"

"No, no, no! The man's so enormously sincere that by
his mere sincerity he throws a terrible white light on our in-
sincerities. He's so simply truthful that by his truth he dis-
covers for us our innumerable lies. We're up to the neck—

up to here"—he put his right hand up to his throat and tightened his fingers—"in lies, Canon, all of us. But he isn't. I'm thankful I met him. I'm thankful he chose to come here and see me. Some day I shall see him again. I shall go to him when I'm free to go. Meanwhile I miss him, and so do you!"

"I miss a man I've never set eyes on?"

"Yes. You miss him just as Miss Creswell——" Suddenly, he stopped, reddened, looked almost guilty.

"Aha!" said the canon. "Then I was——" But he too stopped short, and they looked at each other in silence.

"You miss him!" then said Hendry. "You came to see me today because he came to me on Saturday. He drew you here—not I!"

"I don't believe it!" said the canon. "I don't believe it!" But again he looked about the room as if searching for something invisible. "Tell me one thing," he said, after a pause, in an altered voice. "Did this man strike you as a mystic? Is he a teacher of men? Has he disciples?"

"One thing!" said Hendry.

"Well—well! I confess I am interested, very much interested. Can you answer these questions?"

"I'm not sure that I know exactly what a mystic is."

"Let me give you a definition which I believe to be exact. A mystic is one who consecrates his life to the science or art of the spiritual life."

"I couldn't say that Peter Kharkoff is that. He strikes me as extraordinary not so much because he is what is usually called holy, but because he seems so entirely loosened and free from the chains that seem to bind all other men. It's rather as if he were—what shall I say?—midway between two worlds than as if he belonged definitely to either this world or to some spirit world. He seems to me detached, enormously detached and yet tremendously powerful. He draws you, but not by love so much as by serenity and wisdom. But he's got a mind that searches and that can't, simply can't, be evaded."

"Has he disciples?"

"I don't know. I didn't ask, and he didn't tell me."

"Does he write?"

"I believe he does. But he didn't tell me what."

"Does he write under his own or another name?"

"I don't know."

"One thing more! Although I preached as I did last Sunday, and although I believed every word I said, there's no doubt that numbers of people, great numbers I'm inclined to think, do expect some extraordinary new development in religious experience. You know how ideas get about—one can't say how?"

"Yes."

"There's no doubt that the idea has got about among men that a new Savior may arise in the world in our time. I combated that on Sunday in my sermon. But at the end some doubt seemed to seize me, and I—well, I scarcely know exactly what I did."

"You seemed to me to imply that perhaps after all a new Savior was wanted, and wanted pretty badly."

"Did I? Did I? If, as you seem to think, Peter Kharkoff obliged me by his mental force to do that, the implication is that he believes in, or expects, a new Savior. But what I wanted to ask you is this. Do you think—does it seem to you possible that *he*——"

And there the canon hesitated and broke off. It was evident that he couldn't bring himself to say what he had wanted to say. He seemed greatly disturbed, and his smooth red face expressed intense uneasiness, almost amounting to shame.

"Well, well!" he said at last—for Hendry didn't help him out. "All these speculations are not very fruitful. But the mind—the mind will concern itself with many things. It's voracious—must be eating. And"—he looked up into Hendry's face—"although I'm no pessimist I can see, I can take note, and the turning away from the things which ought to concern and interest the higher part of man is terribly marked in our age. Materialism is ferocious just now. There's something positively savage about it. And you say he has lived in America!"

"Yes."

"Materialism is very marked over there. Not that we have a right to say much, to gird at others! Christ's religion doesn't seem to have very much hold over the mass of men, does it?"

"I can't say I think it does!" said Hendry.

"And he's a Jew too! It's all strange, very strange!"

Again he looked about the room questioningly, anxiously. Then he pulled out of his black silk waistcoat a gold watch.

"I must go. My wife's expecting me. Good-by, Hendry!" And, walking as usual very upright, with his head well up, and his chin held well in, he made for the door. When he was on the door-step, and had buttoned up his black overcoat, he said:

"But what I said in my sermon, all the written part, was right, Hendry. I stick by it every word. The world has had its chance of salvation, and all these new teachers are merely specimens of the second best. And we ought to have no use for the second best. But no doubt that man, Peter Kharkoff, is remarkable. I have your word for that, and your word means a great deal more than the word of most of our Drearney friends. I wonder whether Miss Creswell——"

And then he broke off, and Hendry said nothing, and after a moment of hesitation he went away walking briskly.

At the end of the week Drearney was surprised to learn that Miss Creswell had left Ewenden House for Switzerland, after a brief visit to London. Rumor had it that she had gone to Geneva.

CHAPTER VIII

IMOGEN drove up to the house in Lowndes Square in a taxi-cab with Hugo Dennistone as the December day was closing in. She had been hunting and was in hunting kit, breeches, top-boots, coat, collar, stock and hard hat. From her childhood she had ridden astride. Habits and side-saddles had no place in her young life. Although she had no special wish to be a man she enjoyed getting into breeches, knickerbockers, sports clothes of all kinds. Secretly she thought that she looked her best in them, and perhaps she was right. For her long slim figure was not unlike a youth's, and she had legs that would have done credit to a Gaiety girl.

When the cab stopped in front of Lord Lowrie's magnificent door, red-brown mahogany studded with heavy brass nails, Hugo let go of Imogen's hand, which he had been holding in his all the way from Paddington Station.

"Shall I come up?" he asked, in a very strong, rather gritty voice as he opened the cab door.

"What for?"

"To have a cigar and a whisky and soda."

"You can if you like. But I'm going straight into a bath and I shall stick there with the water up to my chin for a good twenty minutes. What'll you do meanwhile?"

"Browse about among your books to be sure!"

"Hugo, tell me a bit of honest truth for once."

"Right-o!"

"Except schoolbooks, and they don't count, have you ever read a book through?"

"Rather! Of course I have!"

"Which one?"

"That's my secret."

"Oh, well—if you're going to have secrets from me!"

"Of course I am. What sort of a man is it who tells everything to a respectable, nicely brought-up, young, innocent girl? What do you take me for—with the accent on the take?"

"What book was it? It can't hurt my morals to know that."

"Well, if you will have it, it was 'Katerfelto.'"

"Katta—what?"

"Katerfelto."

"Never heard of it."

"Shows your ignorance. It's a damned good book about stag-hunting by a chap called Whyte-Melville."

"Whyte-Melville! I never heard of him."

"Then you don't know your classics."

"What are you sitting there for? Why don't you get out?"

"I thought we were having a literary conversation."

"Get out and ring the bell. I don't want your views on literature. I want a deuced hot bath."

"I won't prevent you." And Hugo unfolded his lengthy limbs, pushed his dark, sleek head and red-brown face out into the fog, stepped down and with a slow stride reached the door and pushed the bell. The door was immediately opened by a very tall footman.

"Hullo, Henry! Here we are! Not broken our necks yet!" said Hugo to the man, in the good-natured, offhand way which made all servants love him.

"I'm sure, sir, I'm very glad," said Henry, in a civil boyish voice. "There's a lady here for Miss Lowrie."

Hugo turned back to the cab. Imogen was just getting out. "Someone waiting for you, Geney."

"Who?"

"A lydy friend."

"I shan't see her. I shan't see anybody. I'm for a hot bath, tea and muffins. Who on earth is it, Henry? Why did you let her in? Where is she?"

"Well, ma'am, it's your aunt, Miss Creswell."

"Towser! Why the devil didn't you say so!"

"Well, ma'am——"

"Don't kill the poor chap! He did say so! Give him a chance to breathe."

"Where is Aunt Towser?"

"In the drawing-room, ma'am, with her ladyship."

"Well then—you're not to say a word about my being home for twenty minutes. Have you got a watch?"

"Yes, ma'am."

"Look at it."

"Yes, ma'am." Henry took out a silver watch and observed it.

"In twenty minutes from now go into the drawing-room and ask Aunt Towser to come up to my room."

"Yes, ma'am."

"Now come on, Hugo! And for the Lord's sake walk softly."

"Aren't I going to be in the way?"

"Not now! I want you to meet Towser. I want to ask her afterwards whether you're any real good or not. She's a virgin, but she's got a shrewd head."

"Then she'll jump to my worth, if she hasn't jumped already."

"Don't tramp—tread! She's only seen you twice."

"Once should be enough with a chap like me."

"Your eyebrows frightened her. I can't think why you don't have them cut when they operate on your hair."

"Make 'em grow ever so much thicker, and then where should we be?"

"In the depths of the jungle without a ray of light, like Stanley when he came across the pigmies. Now go and sit by the fire like a lamb and warm your wool, and I'll come to you presently. Drink, smoke and read if you can. But with all your talk about 'Katta'—what is it?—I don't believe you've ever mastered your letters, not to say *mastered* them."

And she turned into a room opening out of her sitting-room and disappeared, looking like a tall, thin boy, and shutting the door behind her.

Left alone Hugo mechanically felt for a cigar, cut it, lit it and stuck it into his mouth under his short, dense black mustache. Hugo was physically a very male man, almost over-poweringly male. He was very tall, and looked even taller than he was because his strong body was exceptionally lean and wiry, and his legs were very long with thighs that could grip a horse like bands of iron if necessary, though generally he rode with what looked to some people a dangerously loose seat. His head was small and was covered with very thick, black, smooth hair. He had very bright blue eyes under enormous black eyebrows that grew almost like mustaches and had to be carefully brushed early and often. His red-brown, weather-tanned face, with its fine sharp lines, keen jaw, straight nose, and pointed chin, was dark with suppressed hair. He had to shave twice a day, but knew how to finish the job perfectly in under ten minutes, and had a skin which, though it looked fine, was according to him as tough as rhinoceros hide.

He was just twenty-eight, had been through the war with the Irish Guards and come out without a scratch, and was now a young man at large, with just enough money to live on as he wished to live. But, nevertheless, owing to his natural extravagance, natural generosity, and temperamental care-lessness in all money matters, he was perpetually in debt. He enjoyed life amazingly because he was a man of action rather than a man of thought, and because he had a splendidly healthy body which was clever at almost everything active. Vigorous games were no trouble to Hugo. He had far less difficulty in mastering them than the average man has. He played golf, lawn-tennis, polo, squash, and played them well as a matter of course, was a perfect horseman, a first-rate gun and a fine whip. Cards and billiards he was thoroughly at home with. Almost the only sport he had no use for was fishing. Perhaps it required too much calm, too much patience. Anyhow he didn't care for it and left it alone. His life ran by swiftly in a maze of bodily activities. By night he loved to dance. He liked to have a pretty girl in his arms. He liked movement to music. And even after a hard day's hunt-ing he was never too tired to go out, to dance, to make love.

Making love! That had been one of Hugo's chief joys since he had been a remarkably well-grown and forward lad

of fifteen. Instinctively—he breathed. Instinctively—he made
love to a pretty girl. In Ireland he made love to Irish girls,
in England to English girls, in France to French girls, and
so on, being always kind and warm and enterprising with the
"habitable globe of girls" as he had a habit of calling girls
en masse. His successes had been beyond counting, but he
never dreamed of boasting of them. He wasn't what a Christian would have called humble, but he was without conceit.
It didn't occur to him to be conceited. He would have had
to take trouble to be conceited.

His devotion to Imogen Lowrie had not broken him of his
habit of love-making. Nothing probably could have done that.
But he was genuinely devoted to Imogen. Indeed, he was
very much in love with her, and had been so for quite a long
time, and had proposed to her over and over again. If he
married anyone he felt he must marry Imogen. She suited
him. He was "mad keen" on her. She was the girl for him.
He had no doubts about that. Her intellectual and literary
side, her genuine love of art, did not worry him in the least.
She was a "good un" across country, had been down the Cresta
run, didn't know what fear was. Let her read books, and
go to picture shows, and performances of the Stage Society,
and pianoforte recitals, and "all that sort of thing" if she liked
to. The fact remained that she was a wonderful sport and
suited him down to the ground, and that he wouldn't marry
any other girl that had ever been "foaled."

Whether Imogen would ever marry him was another matter.
Hitherto she had amiably refused him. But she didn't seem
in a hurry to marry anyone else, although she flirted outrageously with most of the young men whom she knew. That
didn't worry Hugo very much. Why should it when he was
forever doing much the same thing? He said to her periodically, "You'll come to it, old girl. It's a fence you'll have
to take sooner or later." And he genuinely believed what he
said. She was young. There was no special hurry about it.
St. George's, Hanover Square, wouldn't run away overnight.

Meanwhile Imogen and he were continually together, hunting, dancing, tennis playing, motoring, and generally having a
damned good time. She let him kiss her whenever she was
in the mood for it. She let him hold her hand when he wanted
to. She chaffed him unmercifully and he chaffed her. She
couldn't get on without him. He was her "lead" whenever

she was out with hounds. When she stayed about in country houses he was invariably asked to stay too. Things were
"shaping up" as hard as they could for an eventual wedding.
Sometimes he felt a certain impatience. It would have been
even greater had there been no other distractions in his varied
life. But Imogen didn't demand too much of a man. She
was hopelessly modern in her outlook and knew nearly as
much of life, its necessities—so-called—and its follies as he did.
She wasn't a slave to romance, and had if possible fewer illu-
sions than he had. She would "come to it" before long. Then
they would settle down in a good hunting country, somewhere
in Leicestershire for choice, and life would go on as before—
with a difference. Hugo was not worrying.

Perhaps he was too absolutely well, too absolutely strong
and sound in body to worry much about anything. Although,
as Imogen had told Towser at Drearney, Hugo had broken
nearly every bone in his beautiful body, all the bones had been
properly set and no harm had come of it. You couldn't expect
to keep in the first flight without an occasional spill. And
since Hugo had come out of the war without a scratch he
had a belief in his star which nothing could shake.

Now he puffed at his cigar, straddled his long legs and
stared about the room with his bright blue eyes. Plenty of
evidences here that Geney cared about other things besides
hunting. The long room was full of books, of drawings, etchings, paintings, of china, statuettes, caricatures. Burne-Jones
was represented by a head in red chalk, "Max" by a drawing
which showed a little man with an enormous head, very short
trousers and a stomach the shape of a prize pear, leading another man, much bigger than himself but evidently docile, by
the hand along what might be the Thames Embankment. A
bust by Epstein was startling in its suggestion of cocaine. Near
to it, next to a Beardsley drawing of people being as decadent
as they knew how in a garden, was a fine copy of a Bellini
Christ, one of the treasures of the great gallery in Milan. A
prayer-book with leaves made of jade lay on a table by a signed
copy of poems by Yeats, and George Moore's "Confessions,"
hidden in a loose cover of gazelle skin, dyed green-blue and
gold from the Souks of Tunis. A baby-grand piano, a Bech-
stein, was littered with music. Hugo picked some of it up
and saw names, Cyril Scott, Holst, Poldowski, Vincent D'Indy,
Rimsky Korsakov.

Who were all these fellows? He didn't know them and wasn't sure that he wanted to. But no doubt they were all right in their way. He couldn't remember having heard any of their "tunes" at the Winter Garden. He wondered whether any of them had ever ridden to hounds, under a cloudy sky, with a southerly wind blowing, and a raking Irish hunter between their legs. If not what did they know of the absolute joy of life? Not much more than nothing, in his humble opinion.

He whistled a tune, went over to the fire and stood there warming his back.

It was a first-rate room, this of Geney's, a bit too full of "odds and ends," but cozy and comfortable with its jolly deep blues and its emerald greens, its big chairs that seemed made for a man with long legs, its cute system of lighting which didn't strike you full in the eyeballs, but which gave to everything a "homey" look of its own. First rate being up on the third floor, too, and at the back of the house. And no one ever interrupted you there. Geney prohibited interruptions. Not a soul ever came in unless she rang the bell and sent for them. Geney was a dodger at arranging her life. No mistake about that.

He sat down in one of the enormous armchairs, lay back, and stretched out his legs. His whole body felt full of complete satisfaction after the long day in the open, the hard exercise, the rousing music of hounds. What a good thing life was with its many activities! He looked lazily round Geney's room, for he was beginning to feel a pleasant drowsiness creeping over him. All these books and pictures and music pages, scores or whatever you called them, what a damned lot of sitting about they represented! How could men, real live men with quick blood in their veins, spend their lives in squatting on chairs and swotting over such things.

Geney had told him that some of these writing fellows actually shut out the daylight and turned on the lamps when they got to their work. And what was the good of it all? Who wanted to read all these books? Who wanted to bother over all this music? A good tune—yes! Anyone liked a good rousing tune like, for instance, "The Little Girl Who Played with Me at Ciro's," which they were singing every night at the Golden Theater, but this music that was black with notes and had twice as much accompaniment as tune—

that was a bit too much. Waste of labor, waste of time! A man ought to keep out in the air, move about, see to it that his body was in top-notch condition. Otherwise life was surely not worth a damn.

For a moment an ugly thought came up in Hugo's mind, a thought of the many poor chaps crippled in the war. He knew some of them, fine chaps who hobbled about with wooden legs, armless chaps who couldn't swing a golf-club, or hold a racket, chaps with wrecked bodies who couldn't sit a horse. How did they manage? They kept a brave face of course. That was obligatory. He would have done the same. But how did they manage really? What was it like inside? (By "inside" Hugo meant really in the soul; only he wasn't much given to using the word "soul" even in his private thoughts.) It wasn't much of a life for them. It wasn't a life at all. And he thanked God—a phrase!—that he had come out all right though he had taken so many chances with the rest. For life to him meant incessant physical activity, and he simply couldn't conceive, not really conceive, of a comparatively motionless life. It was all right sitting still for a bit after a day's hunting. But to *have* to sit still, or only hobble about, while the years rolled by! That didn't bear thinking about.

He turned the cigar between his lips and half closed his eyes. A whisky and soda? He knew where to get it without ringing for it. But he thought he'd wait for Geney. She wouldn't be long. When they were married she wouldn't have much time for stuffing over books and picking the tunes out of all that mass of music. He'd keep her busy with other things. They'd live in a first-rate hunting country, and in August they'd be off to the moors, and now and then they'd pack up their traps and make tracks for East Africa after big game, and——

The door into the corridor opened, Hugo heard a voice say, "May I come in?" and Aunt Towser appeared in, though Hugo didn't jump to that, a traveling dress.

"Hullo! Do forgive me. I believe I was dropping off. Been with the hounds all day, don't you know, and then this jolly big fire! Glad to see you. Geney's in the bath, I believe. Good place to be in, too, after a run of an hour and twenty minutes. Afraid I'm rather bespattered. The going was a bit heavy in parts and——"

"Hullo, Towser!" Imogen came in from the mysterious

regions, painted as usual, but looking fresh and lively nevertheless, and wearing, instead of the coat and breeches, a loose
orange-colored gown. "How's Drearney? Have you come up
for long?" She gave her aunt a brief kiss.

"No; I'm only passing through." The reply came in an
oddly brisk and decisive voice, a voice perhaps unnecessarily
decisive.

Imogen looked at her aunt's "get-up." "Where are you
off to?"

A maid came in wheeling a table covered with a sumptuous
tea.

"I'm leaving tomorrow by the morning train for Paris—
and Switzerland."

Imogen drew the sealing-wax lips together as if she were
going to let out a prolonged whistle, but no sound came.

"Winter sports?" said Hugo.

The maid went out.

"Oh no! It's too early for them. Besides they're not
much in my line. No; I am going to spend a little time in
Geneva."

Hugo, who happened to look at Imogen at that moment,
saw a peculiar expression come into her face. It seemed to
him startled and hostile. But it was gone even as he noted
it, and Imogen was busy over the tea table, looking casually
cheery and the least little bit greedy. In answer to a glance
from her, Hugo said, "I believe I will. Muffins don't go with
a whisky and soda somehow, and I feel like muffins."

"You've had tea with the old lady, Towser, of course?"

"Yes, dear. I won't have any more. I'm staying for the
night at the Grosvenor."

"The Grosvenor! You might as well sleep on the platform of Victoria Station!"

"It's extremely comfortable."

"Is it? But why not stay here?"

"It's convenient for an early start." And then she began
to talk to Hugo, briskly, decisively, with a very definite cheerfulness, a very definite ease of manner. Hugo and she knew
each other only slightly. It couldn't be said that they "got
on." They had never really had a chance of either getting on
or not getting on. Hugo was charming to her, as he was
charming to nearly all women. She thought Hugo very attractive considering his brainlessness, but his intense masculinity

caused her at moments an odd sensation of uneasiness, which she didn't fully understand. That evening she was more important with him than she had ever been before. There was, he thought, something even slightly aggressive in her manner. She seemed to be asserting herself, or trying to do so; why he could not imagine. And there was effort about it all. Imogen too—and he could note passing changes in her with the eye of a connoisseur—was not as usual. He was quite sure of that. She sat in her big chair, drinking tea and eating muffins, with a certain cold and detached complacency, preserving the while a slightly satirical expression as if her mind were in lofty regions smiling, but not very happily. She said very little, left conversation to her aunt and her lover. And Hugo felt that she wasn't pleased. Something had put her out. He didn't know what it was.

"What's up?" he thought. And he went on talking about Switzerland, London, horses, health, the Archbishop of Canterbury—how they got to his Grace he could never afterwards remember—the Cresta run, God knows what, till at last he drew in his legs, unfolded and towered up to go. "Where are we shaking a leg tonight, Geney?" he asked. "The Embassy?"

"I'm not sure I shall go."

"As you like it. Give me a call on the telephone at the Marlborough by eleven if you're game for anything."

"I will."

"Good-by, Miss Creswell. I must hop it. Hope you'll have a good time in Geneva."

"Thank you very much."

"If Geney says anything after I'm gone, put in a pally word for me, will you?" His strong lips curled in a lazy smile. For a moment his bright blue eyes twinkled down on her. "Say I'm a jolly good sort—if you can!" And then he was gone.

When the door had shut behind him, Miss Creswell, with a rather hurried and uneasy air, said to Imogen, "What did he mean?"

"Less than nothing, Towser," said Imogen, lighting a cigarette. "Have one?"

"No, thank you. But why should he wish me to put in a good word for him?"

"Cut Hugo, Towser! Cut him right out! We aren't thinking about him?"

"Aren't we?"

"Where's your sincerity?"

"Im, please don't attack me for being insincere merely because I asked you a very natural question about Captain Dennistone."

Imogen said nothing for a moment in reply to this thrust. She leaned back in her chair exposing her smooth white throat, and the loose sleeves of her orange-colored gown fell back from her long white arms, thin but beautifully soft and silky, as she put one of them behind her head, and lifted the other to put back the cigarette she was smoking between her painted lips.

"If you and I are sincere," she said at last, "we shall speak not of poor old Hugo, the hunting man, the dancing man, the man's man and the woman's, the good fellow, captain late of the Irish Guards, member of the Marlborough, and so on and so forth—no! We shall speak of the man who is none of these things, of the man who seems destined to put you and me at loggerheads with each other. We shall speak of the Jew."

Miss Creswell sat more upright, obviously pulled herself together, and said in a voice which she tried to make very firm, but which sounded very self-conscious, "Very well! And why not? We spoke of him at Drearney. Why not here?"

"D'you know, Towser, I admire you tonight," said Imogen, in reply to this brisk defiance, for it sounded like defiance rather than agreement. "I didn't think you had it in you to do what you're going to do. Aren't you afraid though?"

"Afraid! What of?"

"Of such an adventure?" She looked at her aunt with wide-open, scrutinizing eyes. "When you were young—I mean when you were a girl as I am now—I don't believe you ever had an adventure."

"Perhaps I didn't wish for one," interposed Miss Creswell.

"Probably not. But you didn't have one. That's the point. Isn't it rather daring to start in now?"

"I am not starting in, as you call it."

"Aren't you? Just think of it! You are leaving home in the depth of winter and traveling to Geneva (which, by the way, has an awful winter climate) in order to try and make acquaintance with an Israelite who is a total stranger to you and of whose character and antecedents you know practically nothing. As for him he doesn't even know your name. For I didn't tell it to him. You believe him to be a dangerous man."

"Who told you I did?" Miss Creswell interrupted, with startled sharpness.

"Surely you told me so."

"I didn't. I never did."

Imogen looked genuinely surprised. "But I seem to remember——"

"I never said that to you."

"To me! But haven't you said it to someone? Or haven't you at any rate thought it?" Imogen looked at her aunt with searching eyes. "You have!"

She paused, but her aunt said nothing more, and at last she continued, "You are going to pursue this Israelite to Geneva and to force yourself on him, as I forced myself on him that Sunday night. Isn't that an adventure? Suppose I were malicious, which really I am not, and were to tell the Barrimores, or any other of your Drearney friends, what you're up to, what on earth would they think?"

"You don't care what people think! Why should I?"

"I don't know why you should. But don't you?"

"No!" said Miss Creswell, with a smart attempt at defiance which didn't quite come off. "My dear Imogen," she added. "You were good enough to show me the easiest way to unconventionality, so you should be the last to blame me for taking it, or"—she made a little significant pause before continuing—"or to try to dissuade me from taking it, however subtly."

"Towser, I didn't think you had it in you to be so catty!"

"Why don't you wish me to go to Geneva?" retorted Miss Creswell.

"Did I say——" Imogen stopped short and smiled contemptuously, but evidently at herself not at Miss Creswell. Then she looked down for a moment as if considering. During that moment—perhaps it was the paint's fault—she resembled in some degree a strangely improper Sphinx. The profundity of thought—Imogen could think—under the paint made her look hard and mysterious. She finished her thought-process with apparent deliberation, then looked up and said:

"You're right. Why should I grovel down to a lie—that wouldn't even fulfil its destiny by deceiving? As you hated

my going away from you that Sunday night I hate your going
off to Geneva. Isn't it preposterous? That you and I should
be quarreling over a man?" And she laughed. "But at any
rate," she added, with characteristic coarseness, "it's his mind
we are quarreling about, not his body. At least, I suppose I
may acquit you of any body-snatching intention, mayn't I?"

To Imogen's genuine surprise Miss Creswell blushed, and
the blush became violent, painful.

"What's the matter, Towser?"

"Nothing, nothing! I have no idea why I'm being so absurd
—at my age."

"But *is* it his——"

"No; of course not!"

"But then why——"

"I don't know!" Miss Creswell was quite evidently confused, painfully, pitiably confused. "I don't know, I don't
know!" she repeated.

"But you surely don't mean that——"

"Don't let us discuss it."

"Discuss what?"

"Don't let us talk about it any more. I have made up my
mind and I—I——"

"I begin to think," said Imogen, interrupting, "that Peter
Kharkoff is a dangerous man for you to have anything to do
with. Aren't you at all afraid of doing what you are going
to do?"

"What nonsense! Afraid! What is there to be afraid of?"
Miss Creswell looked at her niece with the anxious eyes
of one longing to be reassured.

And suddenly Imogen, proud in the self-possession of her
youth, felt a sense of pity for this middle age which seemed
to her so much less capable, so much more nervous, than she
was or could ever be. "That's what we don't know," she
said. "If we knew, what cause for fear could there be to
us here, in London? It's the incalculable that brings fear
with it, I suppose. And *he's* incalculable."

The flush had died away from Miss Creswell's face, which
now looked unusually pale.

"The Unearthly!" added Imogen, in a slow, lingering voice.

"I wish you wouldn't call him that, and I can't think why
you do!" said Miss Creswell, with a sort of startled irritation.

"I feel him as that. Look here, Aunt Annie——"

"Yes? What is it, Im? Why don't you go on?"

"I'm sure you'll take it in the wrong way, but here goes! Shall I come with you to Geneva?"

Miss Creswell's face became rigid. "Yes, certainly, if you like," she said in a voice that sounded like the counterpart of her face. "But surely you must have lots of engagements. And then your hunting and—and Captain Dennistone! How would you manage? I'm leaving early tomorrow, you know. I've taken my seat and I can't put off, because if I do——"

"It's all right, Aunt Annie; I can't easily get away. Besides I should hate that beastly cold climate. London's bad enough, but to be close to rushing water and blown upon by winds from Mont Blanc! My Lord! Not for this child! In St. Moritz you get the sun, and the sun's worth all the men, Jews and Gentiles both, in the world, though *you* mayn't think so. I shall stick here, I expect, till the old lady starts for Sainte Maxime and the villa, end of January, I suppose."

"Are you going with her?"

"I may, and enter for some of the tournaments at Cannes. I can cover the distance from the villa to Cannes easily in an hour and twenty minutes with my Sunbeam two-seater. And heaps of people would be glad to put me up at Cannes if I want to be there."

"Oh, I know! You're so popular with everybody." She got up to go. "Well, good-by, Im! By the way, to return to Captain Dennistone——"

"Old Hugo—yes? What about him?"

"He's certainly not intellectual, but I think he's a very nice fellow. And I'm sure he'd be a very kind and good-natured husband."

"A thousand thanks for the information, Towser."

"Well, he asked me to say a good word——"

"And, like a Christian lady, you've said it. I'll let Hugo know, when next I meet him. Here comes the lift! Good-by, Towser!"

"Good-by, dear."

The lift sank with Miss Creswell in it. Imogen stood by the well, staring down through the iron-work gate, till she heard a slight click in the distance below, and a murmur of voices which almost immediately died away. Then she went back into her room and shut the door.

Although she was so cool and self-possessed she felt that

she had had a shock. She felt like one who has received a blow from fate, something unexpected and unpleasant which had quite changed her outlook for the moment. In addition to that she felt that she had been heavily "scored off," and by the last person who could have been expected to score off her. Towser's plan about Geneva was surely a revenge upon her, Imogen, for what she had done at Drearney, and really it was quite a neat revenge. She couldn't deny that.

She regretted her suggestion about accompanying her aunt to Geneva. She oughtn't to have made it. In making it she had given herself away, and though she had immediately withdrawn it, when her aunt had begun to suggest difficulties, Towser had scored again. Not that that mattered! She was really attached to Towser, but she didn't relish not having her own way. Decidedly she was not having her own way just now.

She sat down in a chair by the fire and brooded with lowered eyebrows. One thing stood out in her memory of the interview which had just come to an end: Towser's violent blush when she had spoken about the mind and body of the Jew. What had that meant exactly? Imogen recollected clearly that when, at Drearney, she had suggested that her aunt had fallen in love with the stranger whom she had met in front of the photograph shops, her aunt had looked and had evidently felt satirical. That meant complete detachment from any smallest feeling of merely physical attraction towards the unknown man. But now surely that detachment no longer existed. Towser was painfully self-conscious about Peter Kharkoff. Yet she had not seen him again. Possibly it was the event of the Sunday evening which had changed her. She had been very angry. She had said that she had been angry because she had felt mentally jealous, and only because of that. But was it really possible for a woman to be jealous only with her mind? Imogen now began to doubt whether it was possible, and she doubted partly because of her own feelings.

As she sat there alone by the fire she felt strangely depressed, strangely irritated, strangely frustrated. She thought of Towser's situation and her own. Towser was now on her way to the Grosvenor Hotel. Imogen had said that to sleep at the Grosvenor Hotel was much the same as sleeping on the platform of Victoria Station. That was her way of saying that in the bedrooms of the hotel you could hear the trains coming into, and going out of, the great station below. Towser would sleep in such a bedroom. She would lie in one of the enormous beds specially selected for the appropriate greeting and solace of tired travelers from over the sea. She would lie there and listen to the trains and think to herself, "Tomorrow I shall be in one of you, and you will speed me away through the Kentish landscape till the sea comes in sight. And then —Good-by to England!" And thinking this she would enjoy the ugly noises coming up from below in the darkness. They would suggest to her what she wanted, what she would be longing for.

Imogen now felt acutely that she was longing for the same thing, and she realized, as she had not realized before, what her aunt's feelings must have been on the Sunday night in Drearney when waiting for the sound of the hall door-bell.

It would be far worse waiting for news from Geneva.

Ever since her departure from Drearney Imogen had been feeling unusually restless, unusually dissatisfied with her life. She had filled up almost every moment of her time. She had hunted, danced, played bridge, gone to plays, to suppers. She had been specially amorous with Hugo, letting him go very far. But all the time she had felt horribly dissatisfied. And now she felt surprised, angry, injured. Surprised—for she had never thought her aunt capable of stealing such a march on her as this, or showing such almost wild decision. Angry— because she had not done what her aunt was going to do now. Injured—because—but that was an intensely intimate feeling, and jealousy was coiled all round it like a serpent coiled round a rod. And she knew that her kind of jealousy was not purely mental. The body was taking part in it.

The ting of the telephone bell startled her. She went to answer it, feeling sure it was Hugo who had rung her up. And it was Hugo asking her whether she was going to meet him that night. "Yes," she said. "I will meet you, and I'm going to dance till five in the morning!"

She was as good as her word. But all the time she was dancing, laughing, and flirting, and driving Hugo to the end of his not very long tether, she was wishing she was stretched out in one of the enormous beds of the Grosvenor Hotel, and hearing the sound of the trains, with the knowledge in her mind that on the morrow one of them would take her away from this London, and bear her to the sea—and escape.

Book Two—In Geneva

CHAPTER I

WHEN Miss Creswell was actually in the train with the Times and the Spectator en route to Dover she began to be amazed at her own temerity. She had never done anything like this before. Though she was quite an independent sort of woman, and had often traveled alone, and was thoroughly accustomed to managing for herself without a maid or a companion, this was a new departure. Her object this time in traveling was not a country but a man, a man whom she didn't know and whom she had thought of and spoken of as dangerous. She was fifty-five and she was now for the first time in her life running after a man.

She was conscious of a loss of dignity, even of an occasional under-sense of humiliation. Nevertheless, not for a moment did she wish herself back in Ewenden House among the good people of Drearney. She had come away from Drearney without telling anyone there, except of necessity her servants, where she was going, or even that she was going. And she had condescended to asking the servants not to speak of her approaching departure till she had gone. She had invented plausible reasons for her desire for secrecy. She forgot now what they were. But of course by this time "everyone" knew.

Before she had left she had met the Barrimores two or three times, and had had some conversation with the canon. Neither of them had been at ease, and she had felt certain that he was refraining when with her from doing something which he longed to do, from asking some vital question, from making some unusual statement. She had felt an undercurrent of secret communication between them, which neither had chosen, or perhaps had been able, to avow. And in that undercurrent she had felt the influence of the Jew. That the canon had gathered from Mr. Hendry by chance knowledge, or at any rate suspicion which practically amounted to knowledge, of her meeting with Peter Kharkoff she of course didn't know. She didn't even know for certain that the organist had spoken about his unusual visitor to the canon. But she guessed that he had. Canon Barrimore must surely have been lured to Mr. Hendry's house by the same strong influence which had lured her there. And she felt nearly sure that he had not left the house without learning something about Peter Kharkoff. If so, their mutual knowlege, not spoken of, hidden, was surely the cause of the uneasiness which had prevailed between them. Each of them had wanted to speak about the Jew, and neither of them had chosen to.

Miss Creswell could see before her as she sat in the train the canon's self-conscious blue eyes. And what had her eyes been like? She had not spoken to Mr. Hendry again before she went away. She wondered what his feelings would be when he learnt that she had gone to Geneva. She knew very well, or believed she knew what Imogen's feelings were.

She remembered how she had blushed when Imogen had spoken of body-snatching. And she remembered the rigid sensation of intense protest—as if the whole of her, soul and body too, had been protesting—when Imogen had suggested coming with her to Geneva. The suggestion had come upon her like an outrage. She had wanted to fight it off. And of course Imogen had seen that. There was a new and dreadful comprehension between her and Imogen since the appearance of the Jew in Drearney. They understood each other as women do who hate.

And yet she knew that she really loved Imogen. And she believed that Imogen was really very fond of her. The fact was that her jealousy was met by an answering jealousy in Imogen. And could such jealousy be purely of the mind?

She pondered over that as the train rushed on through a landscape drowned in the mists and dews of December. There was no frost, no snow. But humidity saturated the land, and no pale sun showed his wintry face to the leafless woods, the soft plowland, the meadows silvered with moisture. She pondered over that but didn't come to any quite definite conclusion. For she was rather ignorant about the very intimate bodily things which generally lie at the root of any acute jealousy. It was a fact that she had never loved a man. She always felt that she was a quite normal woman. Yet she had never come across a man whom she had longed to live with as his wife, and whom she had longed to have as the father of her children. Often, in long-ago days, she had thought of marriage and motherhood with desire. But she had never met *the* man, and so she had never married. For she had felt an almost fierce repugnance at the thought of entering into the marriage relation with any man merely because he was a male and could make her a mother. She was, perhaps, for all her healthy common sense (now, she supposed, in abeyance) a rank idealist, and had made of her unborn children a sacrifice to her ideal.

And yet now, in her middle age, she knew jealousy.

At Dover it was bitterly cold, with what land-lubbers call "a heavy sea," and what sailors call "a cap full of wind," but Miss Creswell stayed on deck. She hadn't engaged a cabin, and she disliked the idea of going below among the sea-sick, of whom, fortunately, she was never one. While she was sitting well wrapped up on deck, with her feet buried in a thick rug, she saw someone whom she knew, a certain Elwyn Barnett. He was a man of about thirty-five, whose people had a place called Thorbury Manor some six miles from Drearney. He was in the Foreign Office, and when she saw him she remembered having heard that he had been several times to Geneva on business connected with the League of Nations. At once it occurred to her that he might know something about Peter Kharkoff, if Kharkoff had lived in Geneva for any long time. It seemed to her quite impossible that such a man could live hidden and unknown in a town as comparatively small as Geneva. Presently Mr. Barnett, who was walking up and down, saw her and came up to her. He was a red-brown man, with red-brown eyes and a pleasant, though rather too convinced manner, very sure of himself, very sure that what he thought was "it," that what he said was undoubtedly "just so." He was one of those fortunate men who, knowing some-thing—it may be two or three foreign languages—go through life happily unaware of their profound and abysmal ignorance of the greater part of the realm of knowledge.

Seeing Miss Creswell, a county neighbor, and a "very decent sort of woman" into the bargain, Mr. Barnett came up to her, got hold of a deck-chair and sat down beside her.

"Going to Paris?" he asked, in a brisk dry voice which seemed located in the upper part of his throat.

"Yes. And you?"

"I'm on my way to Geneva. I go there from time to time on business connected with the League."

"Then you can tell me something, if you will. I am only staying one night in Paris. Then I am going on to Geneva too. I've been there, but I've rather forgotten it. Can you recommend an hotel?"

"If I were you I should go to the Bergues."

"The Bergues?"

"The Hotel les Bergues. It's the most up to date. Good bathrooms. Good food. I like it."

"I seem to have heard—isn't there a rue les Bergues?"

"I dare say there is somewhere."

"Oh, then the hotel you speak of isn't in that street?"

"No. It's right on the Rhone. The front that is. Some of it looks on to the rue de Mont Blanc."

"I'll go there."

"Then I shall see you. I shall be there for a few days."

"I suppose you know lots of people in Geneva."

"Oh, I know a good few of the League crowd, of course, and some of the old Swiss families."

"There are a good many Russians at Geneva, aren't there?"

"There used to be heaps before the Revolution. Not so many now, I fancy. Or, if there are, one doesn't see much of them. But of course all over Switzerland there are Russian refugees."

"That's what I thought."

She was silent, turning over in her mind how to introduce the name of the Jew. Meanwhile Mr. Barnett, who was evidently, like Miss Creswell, a capital sailor, talked briskly of the League and Geneva.

Presently, finding subtlety beyond her—perhaps the strong north wind had blown it away—she said, "Have you ever heard of a man called Peter Kharkoff? Someone spoke about him to me somewhere once as a remarkable man. I think I heard that he lives at Geneva."

Mr. Barnett got partial hold of his red-brown mustache with his flexible under-lip, and his red-brown eyebrows came down above his large, self-possessed eyes of the same color. "I've certainly heard the name," he said. "Stop a bit!"

Miss Creswell stopped a bit, almost holding her breath in an ecstasy of eagerness to hear more.

"I know!" at length said Mr. Barnett. "I know! Miss Baynes—Edie Baynes—she's a clever girl, woman rather, in the League—told me about him. He's an American Jew, isn't he?"

"I fancy I was told he was a Russian Jew."

"Probably! But been in America a long while."

"I dare say he has."

"That's the man! Kharkoff—yes! She told me about him."

"Has he anything to do with the League?"

"Oh no, not he! I think she said he lived a very retired sort of life. He's got a big library, I believe, thousands of books. I imagine he's a savant, a recluse. I think she said he wrote but not under his own name, and that she hadn't been able to find out what the name he wrote under was. She seemed very interested in him, very curious about him, I remember now. She's a woman who's very keen on the intellectual side, a regular ferret after food for the mind."

"She must be interesting. I wish I knew her," said Miss Creswell.

"If you come to Geneva while I'm there I shall be delighted to introduce her to you," said Mr. Barnett politely.

And then they talked of other things, and soon Calais, looking cold and drearily hard in the wind, came in sight, and in the bustle of preparations for departure they lost sight of each other.

Miss Creswell spent one night in Paris at the Hotel Lotti in the rue de Castiglione. On the following morning she took a day train, which was due to arrive in Geneva at ten minutes before midnight. Before starting she had taken the precaution of telegraphing to ask for a bedroom and bathroom at the Hotel les Bergues.

The journey seemed to her very long, especially when the daylight failed and darkness settled over the flying landscape. The lamp in the carriage was so placed that it was impossible to see print easily. She had to give up the attempt to go on reading. This was after tea, at about five o'clock. There were still nearly seven hours to be got through somehow. Dinner in the restaurant car would account for one. The rest must be endured with patience, and must be passed in sleep, or in thought. She knew she couldn't sleep, but she sat back in her corner facing the window and shut her eyes.

There were two other people in her carriage, a man, who looked like a South American, elderly, yellow and weary, and a woman, evidently English, perhaps thirty-two, or anything up to thirty-five. This woman was deep in a book, and though the light had faded, and the lamplight was faint, she sat well forward in the middle seat on the side opposite to Miss Creswell, and holding the book as near to the light as possible she continued always reading, although obviously with difficulty. Before she shut her eyes Miss Creswell had tried to see the name of the book and had failed. The woman was well dressed in a coat and skirt, with a collar and tie, and a small, but smart, round black hat. Her hair was thick and fair, her eyes were large and very light brown. She looked capable, intelligent and somehow ardent. But she looked also as if she had lived in the body as well as in the mind, as if she had made an almost gluttonous meal on the fruit of the tree of knowledge.

Miss Creswell wondered who she was. Perhaps she would have spoken to the stranger in the course of the journey but for the book. But the book was so engrossing that it evidently blotted out companionable humanity from the consciousness of the reader. And the journey at last came to an end without a word being exchanged between the two women. As for the elderly South American, muffled up in a sable-lined coat, which he kept on in spite of the artificial heat in the carriage, he smoked cigar after cigar and never uttered a word.

At five minutes past midnight the train glided into the station of Geneva. Directly Miss Creswell reached the door of the long carriage and began handing out her small luggage to a waiting porter below her she was aware of the cold and mysterious breath of snow, suggestive of stillness, pallor, hidden things. The midnight city was wrapped in a garment of snow. Its lights shone upon snow. Its river rushed eddying between snow-covered banks.

The hotel omnibus was waiting. Miss Creswell followed her porter out of the station to it, feeling tired, almost dazed, and strange in the keen night air. As she stood for a moment, waiting to see her luggage put on the roof and inside, and to pay the porter, she felt that this was indeed, to quote Imogen's expression, an adventure. With the exception of Mr. Barnett, who was no doubt only there for a very few days, she had no acquaintance in Geneva. An unknown Jew was her only reason for being there in this dead season of the year when travelers were few. And yet she had had to come, and she didn't regret having come. The thought of Imogen in the garden of the Dane by night was with her. Imogen was not there. In her heart she thanked God that Imogen was far away in England, that those painted eyes would not look on her here, that those painted lips would not comment on her doings, or call her "Towser." She rejoiced in her solitude, because it seemed to mean freedom.

The porter, having put up and in the luggage, came and stood by her. She paid him. But the man in uniform from the hotel was still away, looking to see if there were any more travelers for him, and Miss Creswell didn't at once get into the brightly lit omnibus. In spite of the really intense cold she remained out in the air, looking towards the vague lights of the city below, near to the entrance to the rue de Mont Blanc. She was trying to recall her sensation in Drearney on the day of the Jew's departure. She was trying to draw in from the almost entirely hidden city another sensation. In the darkness, broken by hints of light here and there near by, and by a faint gleam of gold in the distance, she was saying to herself, "Do I feel that he is here?" But it seemed to her that she was too vague and too tired to know. Suddenly in the midst of the snow a great fatigue came over her. The hotel man came up. There were no more travelers. She got into the omnibus. The door was shut. The motor purred. They glided away down the hill towards the lake and the river.

At the bottom of the rue de Mont Blanc the omnibus turned sharply to the right and drew up at the door of the hotel facing the Rhone. The night porter came from his bureau on the left of the hall. Yes, a bedroom and a bathroom were reserved for Mademoiselle Creswell on the second floor. He led the way towards the lift.

The hotel was very silent. In its corridors one felt the lateness of the hour. Miss Creswell had an odd feeling that almost everyone was asleep. She liked her room and the shining white bathroom.

"The luggage will come up directly, madame," said the porter in French.

"Thank you. You sit up all night?"

"Yes, madame. It is a habit. I have done it for fifteen years."

He was a short, oldish man with exhausted eyes. As he went out she wondered how he passed the night hours. The luggage was not brought up immediately, and she went over to the window in front of which yellow curtains, with borders of pale blue and white, were drawn. The window was the size of a door, and surely opened on to a species of balcony. She unfastened it. Behind were another window and a heavy wooden blind. She found the cord and pulled the blind up. Then she opened the second window and looked out into the snow-bound night. The Rhone ran just beneath her. She could hear the noise of the water hurrying past to a weir a little way lower down. Across the water, beyond the famous islet, she saw some brilliant lights shining. People were still up in the cafés over there. She wondered where the rue les Bergues was, how near or far off. She wondered whether the Jew was there. Suddenly it occurred to her that he might be away from Geneva. He might be traveling. If he were, what a useless journey she had undertaken. Geneva in the winter, in the snow, and with him away! She wouldn't stay—she would leave at once. But she couldn't go back to Drearney. Something in her revolted from the thought of doing that.

There was a tap at the door.

"Entrez!"

The hall porter came in with her luggage and looked astonished at seeing the wide-open windows.

"I wanted to see what the view was," she explained. And she began to let the shutter down after closing the outer window.

He came over to help her. "It's very cold, madame," he said. "One of the coldest winters we have had. That's how it is here, cold in winter and hot in summer."

He undid the straps of her luggage and went out. She took a hot bath and got into bed. The room was splendidly warm from the heating apparatus. The bed was soft, but not too soft. The pillows were the right size. But though very tired she did not feel sleepy, and knew that she couldn't sleep for some time.

Her mind saw many things; the photographs in the bow-windows of the dignified little shops, Canon Barrimore tucking in his chin as he wondered why clever men came to hear his sermons, Mr. Swarpes floating forward with imperial dignity to show important nobodies to their stalls, Imogen's heavily painted face and tall slim body, Mr. Hendry with his up-leaping hair, the veiled heavy eyes of the Jew, and then the same eyes large, widely opened, profound with depths upon depths of thought.

"My life!" she thought. "Those figures, and many others, they make my life." But then a voice within her said, "No. That is not so. Your real life is within you, a burden you carry always unaided. In your thoughts, in your emotions you live, not because of those figures who come to you, and go from you, and from whom you are destined to be separated. They are in your life, as shadows may be in a room. But your life is independent of them, and theirs is independent of you. You are really alone with God."

She lay awake for a long time in the dark with the crowding companions whom the mind is never weary of bringing to the birth. And herself was all that company. Never before had she been so conscious of her own ego, and of its separation from all other individualities. It was as if the message were sent to her, "You have traveled out here moved by the desire to try to sink yourself in another. What is the use of that?"

And she felt as if the Jew didn't want her, as if she were an intruder in this city where he dwelt. But it was too late now. She had come, and she knew that she could not go back without making at least the attempt to draw nearer to him.

On the morrow it was snowing, though not heavily, and Miss Creswell unpacked slowly, arranged her things and "pottered about." She enjoyed her breakfast and lingered over it. She read the Journal de Genève. At half past twelve she went down to the restaurant on the first floor to lunch. As she was passing by the entrance to the big central hall, where people gather for conversation, where teas and dances are given, she saw Mr. Barnett there in conversation with Mrs. Sotheby. They saw her. Mr. Barnett got up, and she went to speak to them. She was surprised at seeing Mrs. Sotheby, but that energetic and strenuous-minded woman seemed even more surprised at seeing her.

"The Barrimores' drawing-room—and here!" she exclaimed. "How astonishing! I didn't know you had anything to do with the League."

"I haven't," said Miss Creswell.

"Well I have, or I shouldn't be here in the snow." She

paused and looked at Miss Creswell with her small bright eyes, evidently expecting some explanation from the latter of her presence there. But none came, and after an instant she said, "Didn't the canon give us a surprise on that Sunday evening?"

"Yes, he did."

Mr. Barnett inquired what the allusion meant and Mrs. Sotheby explained. She had a marvelously lucid mind, and a great command of language. Now she drew a perfect word-picture of the wrecked sermon and of Canon Barrimore with it on the rocks, derelict, amazed.

"How very extraordinary!" said Mr. Barnett. "Barrimore must have lost his senses to do such a thing. What's the explanation?"

"Nobody knows," said Mrs. Sotheby. "We didn't dare to allude to the matter, Mrs. Barrimore and I—that is before the canon. But we did speak of it to each other. She was quite alarmed about it, and told me she wished she could call in a doctor. She attributed it to something seriously wrong with his health."

"It wasn't that," Miss Creswell couldn't help saying.

"No?" said Mrs. Sotheby.

"Well, I must go into lunch. I hope I shall see you again."

"I'm out nearly all day. I have to be. But I shall be here for tea today at half past five. We might meet then."

"Do let us." And then Miss Creswell went in to lunch.

"She's a nice woman," said Mrs. Sotheby to Mr. Barnett. "What has brought her here?"

"I don't know, and evidently she doesn't want me to know."

"Really? What makes you think so?"

"I feel it."

"But a dear woman like that can't be up to anything that needs hiding."

"It may not need hiding," said Mr. Barnett, with decision. "But she certainly wants to hide it. Now what do you think of that view of Monsieur Thomas with regard to——"

And then they talked "League" while they waited for a Frenchman and a Japanese who were going to join them at lunch. But before these two personages arrived Mrs. Sotheby referred again to Miss Creswell. "She looks typical," she said. "Doesn't she?"

"Yes, the typical well-off, reasonably well-educated, thoroughly healthy and healthy-minded British spinster lady."

"Just that! But she's rather surprising. I noticed that in Drearney, and I notice it again here. Now how could she possibly know that Canon Barrimore's catastrophe—for it really was that—was not due to any failure of health, when his own wife didn't know?"

"I wondered about that too. But what happened in Drearney to surprise you?"

"It was only a trifle, but it certainly took her quite out of the typical." And then she told him of Miss Creswell's very abrupt allusion to a Savior from the North. Before he could comment on this rather curious bit of news his two guests arrived simultaneously, and they went in to lunch. But during that meal he found time to glance more than once at Miss Creswell sitting alone at a small table in a quiet corner of the room, and he began really to wonder what she was up to in Geneva.

CHAPTER II

ABOUT three o'clock that afternoon, wearing a thick coat of musquash, and a pair of "Jemimas" over her shoes, which made her feet look very large, but which she hoped would keep them warm and dry, and carrying a stout walking-stick, Miss Creswell came down into the hall of the hotel, and went up to the bureau. From the little room behind it a smiling man came forward, in whom she recognized with pleasure an old friend of Italian days.

"Oh, Mr. Klein!" she said. "You here!"

"Yes, madam. Since the war I have given up going to Egypt and Italy, and settled down in my own country. I stay here summer and winter. Very glad indeed to see you here. What can I do for you?"

"Well, I want to know whether the rue les Bergues is near to this hotel."

"The rue les Bergues? This is the Hotel les Bergues, but I don't seem to know—one moment, madam!"

He went into the little room and came back with a directory.

"This will tell us! Rue—les—Bergues." He turned over the leaves with amazing rapidity. "Ah!—here it is! Rue les Bergues!" He murmured something to himself, then looked up. "It is on the other side of the river, madam. You can take the tram from——" He gave her minute directions.

"How far do you think it is on foot?"

"In this snow—perhaps a quarter of an hour, madam."

"Thank you. I think I'll walk. I like exercise and I'm not afraid of air."

Mr. Klein smiled. "You are English, madam."

"Is it such a wonderful feat?" She smiled too and went out by the revolving door.

There was a bitter breeze outside coming over the snow and over the water. She looked down at the swans and wondered how they could be happy in their winter lives. Crossing the road she kept along the path, with the river on her right, passed the newspaper kiosk, in which she saw peering at her a crouching woman muffled in a shawl, and turned on to the bridge following the tram lines. Vaguely she remembered from a former visit that on the other side of the lake, beyond the last houses of the town, there was a pretty pleasure-ground for the citizens called the Parc des Eaux Vives, with a restaurant and near-by the Geneva tennis club. Somewhere in that direction, but up on the hill, if her friend of the bureau was right, lay the rue les Bergues and the house she was seeking.

Going was difficult, and she walked slowly in her rather too loose Jemimas, using her stick. The breeze blew the snow flakes against her face. She felt them melting on her cheeks, and tears ran out of her eyes. And again, as on the previous night, she thought, "Imogen was right. This is an adventure."

The first, really the very first, she had ever had! And she was fifty-five. What would come of it? How would it end?

Even now she didn't know what she was going to do when she reached the rue les Bergues, and stood before number seven. But she longed to see the place where he lived, the place from which that great force of thought came out into the world, and surely affected those who dwelt in this place; such of them at least as were sensitive, as evidently she, Canon Barrimore and Mr. Hendry were sensitive. And Imogen? But she didn't want to think of Imogen today.

Having crossed the bridge she went on into that part of the city which lay on the farther side, and, following carefully the directions she had received, presently turned to the left and made her way towards the outskirts of Geneva. Things began to look suburban. She could not be very far off now.

There was no cheery bustle of city life here. There were no big, bright shops, no cafés, no cinema houses. An air of dull and respectable stagnation prevailed. Perhaps because of the bitterly cold weather, the nipping breeze and the snow, which fell always steadily though lightly, scarcely anyone was about. Such shops as there were looked unattractive, almost furtive. Here and there a detached, naked house appeared, standing in a bit of snow-covered ground which in a different season might perhaps look like a garden. The city seemed to Miss Creswell to be fraying away. She felt that she was now almost, if not quite, in its tatters, that very soon the fabric of it would have entirely disappeared. At a corner she stopped and stood still, wondering whether she had not missed her way, or been perhaps wrongly directed. Beyond her, in the direction as she believed of the French frontier, stretched an unmeaning road flanked by nondescript houses, houses in which she could not imagine anyone living, although they looked quite respectable as most things do in Switzerland. To her left stretched another thoroughly suburban road, in which there were several fair-sized, but neglected-looking houses, some of which showed a certain dull fantasy in their construction and ornamentation. On the façade of one there was a painting of a balcony, with a painted figure of a woman leaning over it, such as may sometimes be seen in Italy. Down this road in the middle of the snow a small tabby cat, with ears laid well back, was stealing with an air of purpose. Miss Creswell looked at this cat, the only living thing in sight. Its creeping movement oddly enticed her. (She didn't know why.) She followed it and in a moment saw painted on a plaque the words: "Rue les Bergues."

So this was where he lived!

She stood still again. Suddenly she felt full of hesitation, almost of fear, and she remembered how, in Drearney, on the Sunday night when Imogen and she, very late, had got up to go to bed after the long talk about the Jew, Imogen had shivered as she said, "A Savior from the North! How cold it sounds!" And now here she was all alone, and it was bitterly cold, and the snow was falling upon her and about her.

Now the cat had disappeared. It must have slipped between some railings into a bit of garden ground and vanished in the snow, always moved inexorably by purpose. Miss Creswell, ridiculously, felt lonelier without it, and indecision came upon her. The strong, even violent, impulse which had driven her

away from Drearney and across the sea to Switzerland seemed
to grow faint within her, like a thing losing its strength in
the snow. The cold lay upon her like a spell which was affecting her mind. She felt inclined to turn back, to hurry away
to frequented streets, to the sound of trams and of passing feet.
She thought of her comfortable hotel as one thinks of a haven.
She even turned to go back. But her feet were held fast.
She couldn't do that now. She must at least go as far as the
house where he lived and just look at it. Then she would
return whence she had come. And she walked on very slowly—
the snow lay thick in the rue les Bergues—looking for the
numbers of the houses. She saw number one. It was on the
other side of the deserted road. She went on a few steps, and
saw number two on the same side. The houses were numbered
consecutively. Then she crossed over and walked on rather
more quickly. Number six—number seven.

She stood still. Number seven was a large, evidently old
detached house, with a ground floor and two stories, standing
in a snow-covered plot of ground in which were three or four
plane trees. A railing divided it from the road, and on either
side, to right and left, the railing ended in a low stone wall
which served as a protection to the garden. The house resembled one of those typical dwellings of the Swiss upper class
which may be seen in Bâle. It looked cold, solid, uninteresting and reserved. Obviously it must contain some good rooms.
Also obviously, however, it could not belong to an owner-
inhabitant who was rich and careful of his dwelling. It had a
neglected, gone-to-seed appearance. Yellowish white, it evidently needed a new coat of paint. The iron-work of the railing was rusty and tarnished. Much of the paint had been
knocked off the buff-brown front door. The coping of the
stone wall was uneven. A stone had come away here and
there and had not been replaced. The house was not actually
repellent. Hundreds of houses in Paris are, but very few in
Geneva, or in other towns of Switzerland. It did not look
dangerous. But it looked in that weather dreary with a bleak
dreariness, Calvinistic perhaps, almost sour if a building can
look sour. It was difficult to believe that anyone had ever
laughed within it, or even smiled, that life had ever pulsated
behind those walls and those large, grim windows, that hearts
could beat strongly in such a house, or minds think eagerly
and hopefully. In the falling snow its aspect was freezing.

There was no sign of life about it, but all the blinds of the windows were up.

In the garden, to the right of the house as she stood now facing it, Miss Creswell noticed an outbuilding made of wood, rather large, with a very large window on the side facing the road, a tall studio window, covered with some drapery. This outbuilding made her think of the Christ carved in wood which Mr. Hendry had spoken of as the work of "the Unearthly." Had it been carved in that wooden building?

After a long pause of hesitation, which followed upon the pause of observation, she conquered a painful reluctance with one of those fierce moral efforts which cost the human being so much more than almost any physical effort, opened the iron gate, walked up the snow-covered path, mounted three steps to the porch and pushed the front door. This push was quite instinctive. She didn't look for a bell. The door yielded and she found herself in a bare lobby, with a bare, stained staircase rising in front of her, and doors on either side, leading, she supposed, to apartments. On the wall she saw fastened a wooden plaque in which cards could be introduced. She went up to it and read: *Rez-de-Chaussée,* M. P. Heinz. Otto Braun. *Etage I.* Pierre Lecave. Serge Kropinsky. *Etage II.* P. Kharkoff. So—he was here. This was his home.

There was dead silence in the cold, bare lobby. A deadly silence seemed to brood in the house. Miss Creswell looked at the uncarpeted staircase, made another moral effort, and went up it. She passed the first floor, where, again, she saw doors to right and left, doors doubtless leading to the apartments of Pierre Lecave and Serge Kropinsky. She reached the top landing and stood before a door with a letter-box. Immediately above the letter-box was nailed a card on which was written in a large, thick handwriting: "P. Kharkoff." To the right of the door was a bell. Miss Creswell pressed it, and waited.

No one came. She heard not a sound behind the big, solid door. She waited for what seemed to her a long time. She pressed the bell once more. Again she waited but there was no response. She had a ridiculous feeling that she was being repelled, rejected, deliberately repelled and rejected. A sensation of blank humiliation came to her. Nevertheless she pushed the bell again and again. There was no reply. There was no sound within. If "P. Kharkoff" were indeed there he did not choose to see anyone. But perhaps he was not there.

She descended the stairs and went out into the snow. Once there, with the cold breeze on her face, the snowflakes melting on her cheeks, she hurried away towards the center of the town, towards the shops, and the trams, and the cinemas, and the bustle of human life. Before long she was in the chief street of Geneva, and found herself before the large book-shop of Coiret. The windows were temptingly full of well-arranged books. She stopped. She decided to go in and buy something to read. She entered. A middle-aged woman came forward. She had a rather aristocratic and intellectual face, looked austere and high-minded.

"I want something interesting to read, please," Miss Creswell said in French. "Can you recommend anything?"

"A novel, madame, memoirs, philosophy?"

Miss Creswell looked at the woman. "Won't you suggest something you have read and like?"

The woman smiled, went away and came back with two books. One was "The Way of Initiation," by Rudolph Steiner; the other had the title "Sérénité" and no author's name. Miss Creswell bought them both on the woman's recommendation.

"I know about Steiner, of course," she said. "But whom is this book by?"

"I don't know for certain, madame. But it is interesting."

Miss Creswell took the books and went back to the hotel.

At just before half past five, remembering her engagement with Mrs. Sotheby, she went down into the great room near the restaurant. A few people were there, reading papers, talking, drinking coffee and tea. In the distance a little band was playing, but not for dancers. There were no dancers that day. Miss Creswell sat down in an armchair opposite to the main entrance and waited.

In about five minutes she saw Mrs. Sotheby coming in with the fair-haired woman whom she had traveled with in the train, the woman who had read with such intensity in the difficult light. Mrs. Sotheby came up, apologized for being a little late, and then introduced to Miss Creswell, "My friend Miss Baynes, who works here in the Library of the League."

So—this was the clever girl, woman rather, Edie Baynes, who knew Mr. Barnett and had talked to him of the Jew. Miss Creswell greeted her with an eagerness which she tried to disguise.

"We traveled in the train together yesterday," she said.

"To be sure!" said Miss Baynes in a low, agreeable voice, a voice with distinct charm. "I have been in Paris for two days."

"And you were deep in a book. I wondered how you could see to read."

"What was it?" said Mrs. Sotheby, who had been ordering tea. "Anything specially interesting?"

"I found it so," said Miss Baynes. "It was a book called 'Sérénité.'"

"By whom?"

"I don't know. No author's name was given."

When she said that Miss Creswell had the feeling that she was concealing something. She didn't know why this feeling came to her. Nor could she find any basis for it. It just seemed to her that Miss Baynes was not being quite truthful.

"Let's go over there to that quiet corner!" said Mrs. Sotheby. She turned and indicated where they would be to the waiter. The band was playing the tune everlasting, "Mon coeur s'ouvre à ta voix," from "Samson et Dalila." Miss Creswell remembered that Mr. Hendry hated it. She had heard him call it "sugar and spice and all that's—nasty."

They sat down. Tea was brought. Mrs. Sotheby inveigled them briskly into a fairly ardent conversation. Her mind seemed to be always in a pleasant state of heat, and always reaching out after fresh food. Its activity was remarkable and it never showed fatigue. When she was not busy with some work or other she was talking with interesting people and tasting their minds. Or she was ardently playing some game. For she had a strong love of physical, as well as of mental, exercise and brought to a game as much intensity, and desire to succeed by mastering the science of it, as she brought to knotty problems for the mind. By day she was always putting forth energy. At night in bed, with a lamp behind her, she read voraciously.

And Mr. Sotheby? He was a quiet man whom she loved and who loved her.

Miss Edie Baynes had a mind of a different caliber, Miss Creswell believed. But she couldn't quite "make" Miss Baynes "out." As was fitting in a librarian she evidently had a great love of books. But Miss Creswell felt perhaps rather than actually thought that she had another side which was far from

being purely intellectual. Once or twice, while the little band
was playing the voluptuous music of Saint-Saëns, Miss Creswell detected on Miss Baynes's pale face—she had a clear white
complexion—a curious expression which, to her, suggested
greed, and which obscurely troubled her. And she wondered
about Miss Baynes's life.

"I am unmarried, and so is she," thought Miss Creswell.
"But surely she has had many experiences which I have always
considered as not possible for a"—and then her mind had
paused for a word, and could find none except the out-of-date
word "respectable"—"for a respectable woman." And then
again, as in Drearney with Imogen, she felt a sense of rebellion against her own pure past such as she had never felt till
within the last few days. And in the sense of rebellion was
surely the Jew.

Towards the end of tea she said with abruptness, "I didn't
see the title of the book you were reading in the train yesterday,
Miss Baynes, but oddly enough I went into a book-shop just
now, and the woman there recommended 'Sérénité' to me as
interesting, and I bought it."

"Did you?" said Miss Baynes, lighting a cigarette and
putting it into a holder; Miss Creswell noticed that she had
beautiful hands. "Everybody here seems to be reading it."

"I shall get it," said Mrs. Sotheby. "Does it teach one
to be serene?"

Serenity was certainly not Mrs. Sotheby's "note," though
she often looked, and probably often was, a happy woman.
But she was obviously traveling too fast to be entirely serene.
She had more in common with a motor bicycle than with a
pool of still water, reflecting, because of its quietude, the dream
of tranquil nature.

"It should," said Miss Baynes. "But how many people are
teachable? I think the average human being reads and forgets.
I think it is very rarely that a book, however remarkable,
makes a mark which lasts on any human mind. One often
hears of books 'forming' the mind. I wonder if they do. It
sometimes seems to me that our minds really assimilate only our
personal experiences, and if they are 'formed' at all, are formed
by what we do and suffer, not by what we read."

This was a topic of conversation after Mrs. Sotheby's heart,
and she flung herself upon it with a joyous energy almost
brutal. Miss Creswell, who felt herself to be intellectually

inferior to her two companions, but who was too sensible to suffer in her pride because of that feeling, sat listening while they talked. Miss Baynes interested her very much, but not only because she was obviously a clever woman, and not only because of what Mr. Barnett had said about her. All the time that she was with her Miss Creswell felt increasingly that she was with one who was secretly sad because of knowledge. Imogen too had a good deal of knowledge in spite of her youth, Miss Creswell supposed. But this "Miss Baynes" had surely felt much more acutely than Imogen had ever felt.

When Miss Baynes got up to go she looked at Miss Creswell and said, "I suppose you aren't staying long here?"

"I don't know. I don't know at all. Possibly I may."

Mrs. Sotheby looked interested, even curious, but obviously tried to hide that. Miss Baynes too, Miss Creswell thought, showed in her expression a stirring of something like wonder.

"I'm a free agent," added Miss Creswell, with an attempt at cheery lightness. "If I like a place, a hotel, there's no reason——"

"Then perhaps we shall meet again," said Miss Baynes, cordially enough, but without any special pressure which indicated desire.

"Might I come and see you sometime?" said Miss Creswell quickly.

"Certainly. But I'm afraid I'm out all day. Perhaps you'd come one evening after dinner. I live in a flat not far from the casino. This is it." She gave Miss Creswell a card. "Perhaps you'll telephone? Sometimes I'm out—dancing."

"I believe you all dance in the League!" said Mrs. Sotheby.

"Most of us do. Good-by."

She was about to go when Mrs. Sotheby laid a hand on her arm. "I wanted to speak to you just for a moment about the last speech of Lord Robert Cecil. I can't understand why France——"

"I must go. I've got letters to write."

It was the usual excuse, but Miss Creswell made it in all good faith. A moment later she was up in her bedroom. She went to the writing table, sat down and took up a pen. Then she turned round. The two books she had bought that day were lying, wrapped in paper, on the mantelpiece. She looked towards them, got up, untied the parcel, took up "Sérénité" and opened it at haphazard.

Five minutes later she was sitting in the one armchair her room contained buried deep in the book.

CHAPTER III

On the following day she telephoned to Miss Baynes and asked if she might call on her that evening. Miss Baynes was very sorry, but she was dining at the restaurant in the Parc des Eaux Vives with some friends. There would be dancing afterwards. Otherwise she would have been delighted to see Miss Creswell. Perhaps Miss Creswell could call about nine on the evening of the morrow. Miss Creswell eagerly said that she would do so. But when she came away from the telephone, she felt that it would be very irksome to have to wait till then for the information she wanted.

Although she had been studying "Sérénité," although it had interested her profoundly, she was certainly not serene. On the contrary she tingled with impatience to take a decisive step forward. She found herself being utterly unreasonable. She found herself condemning Miss Baynes and her friends, probably all of them people "in the League," for dancing in a public restaurant at night after the labors of the day were over. It was not "suitable," Miss Creswell said to herself, like a modern Pharisee, to mix up work for the peace of the world with the fox-trot, the hesitation-waltz and the tango. It seemed to her that everyone was feasting and dancing except herself. Miss Baynes might surely have stayed at home that one evening. But no! She must be dining and dancing and "having a wonderful time." And yet she professed, according to Mr. Barnett, to care for the things of the intellect. Probably that was only a pose. And then Miss Creswell remembered a woman reading for hours in a railway carriage with a book held up towards a lamp. No, it wasn't a pose. But Miss Baynes's intellectual side was certainly balanced, or perhaps overbalanced, by traits which were far from intellectual.

During the day, which wore away slowly enough, Miss Creswell had ample time to face her situation in Geneva. She had nothing, absolutely nothing to do there in this winter weather, unless she could make an advance on the path she had come there if possible to tread, the path which led towards the Jew.

The day was wasted, utterly wasted, unless she made a step forward. She felt in a desperate hurry, and partly because she could not help being painfully self-conscious about her solitude in this foreign hotel. Unless she did something definite, had something definite to do and was occupied in doing it, everyone would wonder why she was there. They were wondering already. She knew that. She had not missed the inquiry in the eyes of Mrs. Sotheby and of Mr. Barnett. They couldn't conceive what had brought her there. Miss Edie Baynes too must be curious. It seemed to Miss Creswell that even the hotel people were asking themselves why she was there all alone. She felt self-conscious even about the waiters, the director, the young gentlemen in the office, and her friend the hall porter.

At lunch that day she saw neither Mrs. Sotheby nor Mr. Barnett. They must be out lunching with "the League," that mysterious phenomenon which means so much in Geneva, and which men of good intent hope may come to mean so much to humanity. Miss Creswell found herself wishing almost furiously that she had something to do with the League, that she was a League librarian, like Miss Baynes, or a secretary, or a member of some committee—she was dreadfully vague about the League—or even a typist connected with it. Anything to have a reason which she could publicly proclaim for being in Geneva!

After lunch, and sitting about in the big hall till she was ashamed to be seen there alone any longer, she went upstairs, put on her outdoor things and went in desperation to a cinema house. There she saw "Charlot" going through manifold tribulations in a Turkish bath, and Miss Pearl White in a tremendous drama of passion and wild adventure, accompanied by a violent piano performance. Few people were there, and it seemed to Miss Creswell that the few who were present regarded her with curiosity and satirical suspicion. She was the only solitary person in the small audience. Every other woman had a companion.

At five she issued forth into the snow and went to a tea shop. At a quarter to six she was back in the hotel and went up at once to her room.

When she was there, with the door shut, she felt driven. Outside by the rushing river she heard a sound of traffic oddly muffled by the snow. The night was closing in, a night which held nothing for her. How was it that in Drearney she had not minded her solitary evenings? Her whole life was upset. She saw it in disorder. She could not understand how for so long she had lived contentedly with so little. And she was alarmed and chilled by the prospect of having to continue living as she had lived for many years.

"I can't go on like that!" she thought dismally.

But what else was there for her to do?"

And tonight? Was she to spend a lonely evening in the dining-room and hall of the hotel, or perhaps in this bedroom? She felt it would be intolerable to do that. And she thought of Miss Edie Baynes and the restaurant in the Parc des Eaux Vives. Should she go there? Should she venture there alone? Why shouldn't she dine there? It would be something to do. She wanted to see Miss Baynes as soon as possible. She felt that she couldn't wait till the evening of the morrow. She must do something tonight. Certainly it wasn't pleasant to go all alone to a perhaps crowded restaurant where there was dancing. She would see people staring at her. It was quite certain that everybody would be astonished at seeing a middle-aged English woman dining alone in such a place. Nevertheless why shouldn't she go? Imogen did what she liked, went wherever the fancy took her. Miss Creswell resolved—and really in her case it was almost a frantic resolve—that she would do the same. And presently she put on an evening dress and a hat, had a taxicab called, and at a quarter past eight started off for the Parc des Eaux Vives.

Mr. Barnett, who was sitting at a long table in the restaurant of the Parc des Eaux Vives, between Mrs. Sotheby and Miss Edie Baynes, bent over to the former at about half past eight, and said in a low voice, "The mystery deepens!"

"What mystery?" asked Mrs. Sotheby, detaching herself from an eager conversation with a tall young Frenchman.

"Our mystery! The enigma from Drearney has just walked in and is actually going to dine here all by herself. What can it mean?"

"The enigma—Miss Creswell? Where is she?"

"Over there, close to the table where two women of the town are dining merrily with the Spaniard who looks like a Moor, and his South American friend, Dousmanos. Be careful! She's very self-conscious and on the alert."

"I see her," said Mrs. Sotheby. "Poor dear! She looks horribly lonely."

"What can it mean? D'you think she's one of the middle aged who has been bitten by the modern tarantula? Shall we see her spring up presently and swoon through the tango in the arms of the velvet-eyed professional who, I'm told, calls himself Juan de Lara? She must have some great reason for coming to dine at a place like this all alone."

"I'm quite sure she hasn't come to dance," said Mrs. Sotheby. She leaned over to Miss Baynes. "Edie!" she said.

"Yes? What is it?"

"There's poor Miss Creswell dining all alone."

Miss Baynes looked and said, "She telephoned asking if she might call on me tonight. I said I should be here."

"Has she followed you?"

"The fascination of the serpent," said Mr. Barnett.

"Of course she can't have come for me," said Miss Baynes. But she said it rather doubtfully, and looked again towards Miss Creswell. Just then Miss Creswell looked at her eagerly, blushed slightly and bowed. "I believe she has come for me," said Miss Baynes. "But why?"

"I spoke about you on the boat on the way here," said Mr. Barnett. "I told her you were clever. She seemed interested and I promised to introduce you to each other if possible."

"But why should she be interested?" asked Miss Baynes.

"Ha!" said Mr. Barnett, looking like a man who had found something. He had remembered the conversation about the Jew. Mrs. Sotheby's Frenchman spoke to her again, and Mr. Barnett began to explain things to Miss Baynes.

From her table in the distance Miss Creswell saw them in deep conversation, presently saw Miss Baynes lift up her head and send a long and intent look at herself. "They are talking about me!" she thought. And she felt more self-conscious in her solitude.

The restaurant was crowded that night. At the table next to Miss Creswell's, two cocottes, one French, one anything you like—spurious even in mystery—were slowly eating an elaborate dinner with a short bronze-brown Spaniard, who looked as if his parents must have hailed from Morocco, and a tall, lithe South American with sleepy, lascivious eyes. From time to time these four persons, as Miss Creswell did not fail to notice, examined her with a sort of satirical interest, as panthers might examine a quiet tabby cat whose only jungle was the shrubbery in an English garden. Now and then she was sure they spoke about her. And the two women showed a sort of amused interest in her small and plain black hat, which had an aigrette on the right side. There was something wrong about that aigrette. Suddenly Miss Creswell felt certain of that, and certain that those two improper marvels had spotted it. And now "the League" was talking about her.

She felt as if she were blushing inside, as if all her organs were blushing. And she tried to look at no one, to concentrate on her dinner, on her glass of Graves. (She had ordered a half-bottle of Graves and a half-bottle of Montreux water.) But now and then she had to look up. And it seemed to her that each time she did so she immediately caught the eye of Miss Baynes, Mr. Barnett or Mrs. Sotheby. She had nodded to them all by now, and had tried to make each nod careless and natural. But a sense of guilt had seemed to her to be manifest in each of those movements of her head. She felt guilty—because of the Jew. She felt like a pursuer who had been found out. A glass-like sensation made her mind secretly wriggle. All her usually hidden wishes and thoughts seemed to lie in her fully exposed, like things exposed behind glass.

Nevertheless she did not wish that she hadn't come. The dulness of her bedroom tonight would not have been bearable. Here she was miserable and lonely and very uncomfortable, but she saw life, she felt life, and expectation was alive in her.

Near to her were some musicians. And they played really well. The pianist looked to her like a smiling madman. He was young, dark, flat-faced and clean shaven. His eyes glittered with a light that suggested mania. He smiled perpetually, a sly and improper smile, glancing round from one diner to another, threw his head back, wagged it gently and played brilliantly without looking at any music or at his hands. The violinist, probably a Hungarian, played sensuously, caressing his violin, and often walking about among the tables. Once he came close to Miss Creswell, and standing a little behind her poured forth a stream of passionate music, while the surely mad, but very efficient, pianist played looking at her with his smiling eyes half closed, and wagging his head at her gently.

And then it seemed to her as if all the people in the restaurant were laughing at her, were whispering to her with their minds, "Why are *you* here? What do *you* know about it all?"

She was thankful when presently a two-step was played, and people began to move, to get up, to go into a lighted room just beyond the restaurant, and to dance.

Miss Edie Baynes went away with a handsome young man, fair with a white skin and blue eyes. He was a Swede and looked powerfully athletic. Through the large opening just by the band Miss Creswell saw him take Edie Baynes gently in his arms, and lift her—so it seemed—into the dance. And Edie Baynes's curious face, which seemed full of knowledge, and ardor and sadness, was like a face dreaming as she slipped away among the moving figures in the room.

The pianist thundered as he smiled. His left hand made the bass sound like the rumble of drums in some forest depth. And Miss Creswell felt the black world, the nigger world, in the music. And so this was civilization, the civilization that was planning, or was supposed to be planning, for the peace of the world, taking its pleasure!

Mrs. Sotheby was dancing with Mr. Barnett. In spite of her keen intellect she despised no pleasures which she deemed healthy for the body. Others from the League table were also dancing, among them a very tall woman of middle age, with jet black hair and a white face, and a little girl with frightened gray eyes that were very attractive. She was dancing with a Swiss boy, who looked full of animal spirits, and who often put out his tongue as he danced.

Presently the music stopped. Everyone stood still, as if surprised, looked vague for an instant, and then began softly and feebly to clap hands. Thereupon the pianist threw back his head, as if entranced or under the spell of a drug, flung his long hands on the piano, and back came the nigger world and the dance began again.

Miss Creswell was now alone with a cup of black coffee and a glass of brilliant green crème de menthe. She must prolong her meal, must have something to do. Otherwise she would have to get up and go. She could not just sit there, being stared at and staring.

In a short time the dance ended and people flowed back into the restaurant, looking grave and preoccupied. There was little joy in the dancing. There was even, Miss Creswell thought, something stern, almost ritual, about it. And yet, she also thought, there was something improper, something negroid, about it too. She couldn't conceive how any middle-aged per-

son could take part in it. But she had seen gray-haired fat
men, and women obviously as old as herself, dancing with
great self-possession.

"Hullo, Miss Creswell! Are you a dancer?" Mr. Barnett
had come up with Mrs. Sotheby and was bending down to her.

"No," she said.

"Won't you come and sit at our table?" said Mrs. Sotheby.
"We are pooling our dinner. There's no hostess. Do come."

"Thank you. I will with pleasure."

Confusedly she drank her liqueur, as if it had been water
and she was thirsty, got up and followed them to the table of
the League. There she was introduced to several people,
English and not English, and presently found herself speaking
to Miss Baynes, who said something about regretting her enforced refusal of Miss Creswell's proposed visit. While she
was replying the music began again, and immediately the
Swedish athlete looked at Miss Baynes, and she went off with
him into the dance-room, obeying his glance like one hypnotized,
Miss Creswell thought. And she wondered about Miss
Baynes as she talked to a civil Swiss colonel who had just been
introduced to her. And through his polite conversation, as
through holes in a grating, a tango streamed over her like
colored and perfumed water.

It was getting late, and she had begun to think that she
ought to go home, when at last Miss Baynes missed a dance
with the Swede. He had asked Mrs. Sotheby. Miss Baynes
with her large bright eyes, which in spite of their brightness
looked tired, watched him going with intentness. That was
her "note," a curious sad intentness. Then she looked round
and her eyes fell on Miss Creswell. She detached her nature
from the Swede, traveled out of his empire, moved and sat
down by Miss Creswell.

"Does all this amuse you?" she asked. And again Miss
Creswell admired the sound of her voice.

"Yes, for once in a way."

"I often come here with my pals of the League. It's an
escape from serious things. Besides dancing is the passion of
this Europe, and of America, too, I suppose, and keeping out
of it would mean too much loneliness. Bridge helps, but you
can't let everything go in bridge."

"No. But can you in dancing? I had just been thinking
how stern it was."

"Stern?"

"Well—to look at."

"I dare say. Yes." She seemed to consider. "There's a new sort of gravity in Europe's pleasures, I suppose," she then said. *"Lo joie de vivre* has been affected by that past exhibition of the voluptuous—*la joie de mourir."*

Miss Creswell felt disagreeably moved by that remark and the lingering tone, almost like a sigh, in which it was made.

"And yet it is all done to nigger music!" she said.

"Quite right! What are we but niggers, white niggers?" said Miss Baynes, with a slow pressure of deep-seated contempt. Miss Creswell felt disgusted, but she felt deeply interested too. "May I drive you home presently?" she said. "Unless you are staying very late."

"Thank you. But I shall stay very late. And Baron Nordstrom is driving me back. You're coming tomorrow night, aren't you?"

"Yes, if you are quite sure that——"

"Of course! I know why you want to know me, why you are interested in me." Miss Creswell flushed deeply. "Mr. Barnett put me on the track. We can't talk about it here."

And then almost directly Miss Creswell decided that she must go home. A non-dancer must not linger unwanted in this atmosphere of ritual.

As she went out alone—she chose a moment when people were seriously at work in the fox-trot—the pianist turned on her and enveloped her in his madman's smile. Then she was out in the snow and getting into her cab. The lights and the music faded as the motor slipped away among the trees.

As it turned out of the park into the roadway by the lake, and she saw the jeweled lights of Geneva shining across the water, Miss Creswell put her head out of the cab and called to the chauffeur. "Chauffeur! Do you know the rue les Bergues?"

"Madame?"

The man pulled up. Miss Creswell repeated her question.

"Oui, madame."

"Please go back by the rue les Bergues, and when you get there drive very slowly."

"Bien, madame."

He drove on for some time, and presently slowed down suddenly.

Miss Creswell looked eagerly out. The lake had vanished. They were in a deserted thoroughfare with detached houses on either side. Before she had time to find out in which part of the street, *his* street, they were, she saw high up in a house they were passing a solitary light.

"Please stop!" she called out. The man stopped the car. "I want just to see—one moment!"

She looked out, then opened the door and got out. The snow was deep, and she had on smart shoes and silk stockings. But she walked across the path. Yes, it was number seven! She saw the outbuilding, like a studio, standing black in the snow-covered garden. She looked up. The light shone out from the top floor of the house. For a long time she stared up at it, standing in the snow.

He was there. The light shone in one of his windows. All the rest of the house was dark. What was he doing up there? Would he answer if she went up and again rang his bell? She longed to go up the stained, uncarpeted stairs, to stand outside his door, to summon him. But she dared not do that. As she looked at the light she was terribly enticed. But something in her was afraid. And after a moment she got into the cab and told the man to drive to the hotel.

On the following evening, after another desultory day, helped a little in its passing by an afternoon concert, Miss Creswell set forth after dinner to call on Miss Edie Baynes. She wore a day dress, her fur coat, and the Jemimas. She had decided that she would walk as Miss Baynes lived so near, not far from the Hotel Beau Rivage, but in a street withdrawn from the lake.

She trod slowly through the crumbling snow, using her stick. Crossing the end of the rue de Mont Blanc she passed the Hotel de Russie, and went on, having the lake on her right, till she reached the Hotel Beau Rivage. Here she turned to the left, and after a walk of a few minutes, and one or two halts to inquire the way of respectable-looking pedestrians, she came to the building in which Miss Baynes had a flat. It was a modern house but there was no lift, and Miss Creswell, in her loose Jemimas, ascended slowly to the third floor, and rang a bell by a door on which a card was pinned with Miss Baynes's name printed on it. Miss Baynes opened the door and greeted her, not warmly but with quiet politeness.

"I live here all alone," she said, shutting the door. "I have

a woman who comes in by the day and 'does' for me. I go
out to dine, to a little hotel near by where the food is quite
good, unless I'm dining with friends. Do put your stick here.
Oh—your overshoes. Here's a chair. Shall I help you?"

"No, no. They're quite easy to take off. Have you been
out to dine tonight in the snow?"

"Yes. I'm just in. But I think I shall go out again
presently. Do come in." And she led the way into a small,
well-furnished sitting-room, containing a good many books,
which opened into a farther room, her bedroom as Miss Creswell found out later.

"You're going out again!"

"If I can persuade you to come with me after we've had a
talk. I thought of dropping in at the casino. I often do that
and take a turn or two—the band isn't bad—before I go to
bed. You think me restless!"

"But why should——"

"I can see you do. And so I am. So I am! We are all
restless here, I think, we of the League. Perhaps it's because
we are all living away from our own countries and our own
people. I don't know. Perhaps it's the malady of our age.
This incessant dancing, even by the elderly and the old—it's
surely a sign, don't you think?"

"I don't know. I never dance."

"Perhaps you will!" said Miss Baynes. And her large
bright eyes rested intently on her visitor's face. "I shouldn't
wonder," she added, in a slow, meditative voice.

"Never!" said Miss Creswell decisively. "My folly will
never run in that direction."

"Will it *run* in any direction?" asked Miss Baynes, holding
out a box of cigarettes which Miss Creswell refused. "I
smoke all the time," she added. "Smoke and inhale though
I know it's bad for me." And she lit a cigarette. "Do you
know Peter Kharkoff?" she then said, bluntly.

"No," said Miss Creswell.

"I thought that was why you cared to know me."

"But you interest me," said Miss Creswell quickly. And
that was quite true. "In the train you interested me. But
—of course Mr. Barnett told you. I saw him telling you at
dinner yesterday."

"Yes. Your conversation on the boat. That made me
suppose——"

"No. But I'll tell you. I'll explain. I want to explain."

A sudden great desire to be perfectly frank had come to Miss Creswell, after these days of loneliness and uneasy waiting; and the fact that Miss Baynes was a stranger, and didn't live in England, made frankness not difficult to her at this moment. Perhaps also there was something in Miss Baynes, some faculty of comprehension, some boldness of outlook, not impudent but rather intellectual, which drew Miss Creswell on without her being consciously aware of it. Anyhow she told Miss Baynes with eagerness her story of Peter Kharkoff's appearance in Drearney, and told it in detail, only leaving out names. And Miss Baynes listened, making no interruptions, with her bright, tired eyes watching the speaker.

"And so when I heard that you knew Peter Kharkoff I was very anxious to meet you," Miss Creswell said, when all had been told.

"But I don't know him," said Miss Baynes.

"You don't!" said Miss Creswell with a sense of lamentable disappointment. "But I understood from Mr. Barnett——"

"He cannot have said I knew this man, Peter Kharkoff."

After a pause Miss Creswell said, "No; I remember now that he didn't say so actually. But from what he did say I implied——"

"What wasn't the fact. We often do that. No. I wish to know Mr. Kharkoff, but he knows nobody in the League, and apparently wishes to know nobody."

"Then he has nothing to do with the League?"

"Nothing whatever, so far as anyone knows."

"But—yes? How do you mean? You think he has some secret connection with the League?" A horrible idea suddenly started up in her mind. "Surely you don't mean that Mr. Kharkoff is a secret agent, or—or—a spy—anything of that kind?"

"In the pay of one of the nations not yet admitted to the League? Oh no—no!" She was smiling.

"Then what is your exact meaning?"

"It's such a strange meaning that I hardly know how to put it into words."

"But please do try to."

"I don't believe that Mr. Kharkoff's choice of Geneva to live in is fortuitous. I do believe he is living here because the League is functioning here."

It seemed to Miss Creswell that there was something mysterious in Miss Baynes's tone and even in her look as she said that.

"Indeed!" she said, rather at a loss. "But if he has nothing to do with the League and knows no one connected with it!"

Miss Baynes said nothing. She was now staring straight before her. She went on smoking.

"I'm afraid I don't understand," Miss Creswell said after a moment.

"And perhaps I don't either," said Miss Baynes. "The fact remains—I've taken the trouble to ascertain it—that Mr. Kharkoff was never seen or heard of here until the League was set up here. It may be said that he came here when the League was established here."

"And that wasn't chance?"

"*I* don't think it was."

"Have you known about him long?"

"Yes. At least it seems to me a long time. When I first came out here I came with great enthusiasm. I won't bother you with all that. But I had what I thought of as high ideals. I lost a man in the war. He wasn't a husband, but that didn't matter. I lost him . . . and somebody else as well."

"Somebody else?"

"We won't talk about that." Miss Baynes frowned and her eyes nearly closed.

Miss Creswell had a momentary strange feeling that there was a third presence in the room, a tiny presence, a very young even infantile presence. And as she gazed at Miss Baynes the thought was with her, "She was one of those who gave herself too soon, because of the war."

"When I got a post out here in connection with the League I resolved to put my sorrow behind me. We were going to work for peace. That was worth doing. I thought then the only thing worth doing. I imagined coming out here to live in the midst of people with noble ideals, people on fire with enthusiasm for a great cause. Well, I've been out here for a good while, and it isn't quite like that. No. We're not so bad. We're no worse than others. But then what are the others? I passed through a period of acute disillusion before I—what shall I call it?—before I got down on the level again. But the getting there cost me a lot. And I

lost most of my faith, if I really had it, in human nature. And
then I read a book. There was no author's name on it. It
was anonymous, short, unpretending. But it made a great
impression on me. The subject was the supreme value of
thinking always rightly. The book was called 'Your Companion.' "

"What was the companion? The——"

"That's it! The mind. I wanted very much to find out
who had written that book. At first I couldn't. Finally I
inquired at a certain book-shop which is run by a Swiss woman,
very intelligent, peculiar, a woman with ideals—the sort of
person who would be called a crank by nearly all English
people."

"I know."

"She told me she wasn't sure, but she believed it was written
by a Russian Jew called Peter Kharkoff. She told me a lot
about him: that he had arrived in Geneva just when the League
was being established here, that he sometimes came to her shop
to inquire about or buy books, that he was a recluse, but that
there was nothing extraordinary about him, no pose, no affectation, no desire to impress or to attract attention by oddity. I
must tell you that she is a bit of a Steinerite."

"A follower of Doctor Steiner?"

"Not exactly that! But she thinks Steiner a genius, and
has often been over to Bâle to visit the Academy for the study
of occult sciences at Dornach."

"Does she know Peter Kharkoff?"

"Yes."

"Oh, of course, you said that he came to her shop!"

"Yes; but she knows him outside the shop. All she said
made a great impression on me. She thinks him phenomenal
—Peter Kharkoff."

"How phenomenal?"

"She thinks him entirely free from all animal passions.
What's more she believes he has always been like that. It
seems impossible, doesn't it?" She lit another cigarette. She
had already smoked two. "Most of us are niggers, I think,
white niggers, as I said at the Eaux Vives last night. I've no
more real belief in white civilization, in the white man's mission, and all the rest of the jargon. The black troops from
Africa have seen what we are, and *we* have seen. But he's
not as we are, it seems. It was she who made me feel what

that man must be. He does a great deal of work. He writes
and he carves. He's got an atelier."

"I know."

"You know?"

"Yes, I've seen it from outside." And then Miss Creswell
told Miss Baynes of her visit to the rue les Bergues and her
vain attempt to have speech of Peter Kharkoff.

"I never ventured to do that," said Miss Baynes when
Miss Creswell had finished. "I only tried to get to know him
through Madame Coiret. But when he knew I was of the
League he avoided meeting me."

"Why, I wonder."

"Madame Coiret has a theory about him."

"Yes?"

"She believes he is here because of the League, and that
he is trying to influence the League by the power of his
thought, and that he doesn't wish to know anyone belonging to
the League—as I may be said to belong for instance—because
he wants to keep his thought-power perfectly pure, quite untarnished. She is convinced absolutely that he is here in
Geneva because he is trying to act upon the League through
thought-power. And she thinks that his thought-power is
unique; in fact that he isn't as other men. With regard to her
belief that he isn't as other men—I'm bound to say I agree
with her."

"So do I! So do I! But have you seen him?"

"Yes, several times in the street, and once at a concert given
by the Rosé Quartet—strings, you know. But I agreed with
her even before I saw him."

"That's strange."

"Yes, so I thought. But it was so."

"But why? I mean how could you agree without—I mean
merely by another's report of him? Had you such absolute
confidence in Madame Coiret?"

"No; it wasn't that. All I can say is that I just did."

Miss Creswell remembered that Imogen had seemed to receive exact truth concerning the Jew, and to know that it was
exact, through her. And now here in Geneva a precisely similar occurrence had taken place. Only Madame Coiret had
been in her—Miss Creswell's—place and Miss Baynes had
been in Imogen's.

They sat for some time in the little sitting-room talking

always about the one subject that engrossed them. And Miss
Creswell presently received the impression that the sad recklessness which she believed she detected in her companion had
been accentuated by Peter Kharkoff's refusal to have anything
personal to do with Miss Baynes. From various things Miss
Baynes either said, or allowed to be known through hints,
Miss Creswell gathered that here was a woman who, floating
more or less derelict on the ocean of life, had seen something
which she felt could bring her into safety and stability, perhaps even into happiness, if she might reach it, stretch out and
get hold of it. But—there was the embargo. And so the
great sea in which she was drifting seemed more terrible to
her than it had before, and in it she felt more lost, more near
to drowning. Perhaps the impression was wrong. But Miss
Creswell had it and it came to her in clearness, with sharp
outlines.

She felt certain that the austere-looking woman who had
recommended her to buy "The Way of Initiation" and
"Sérénité" was no other than Madame Coiret herself, and she
learnt from Miss Baynes that in all probability the latter book
was one of the anonymous works put forth by the Jew.

"Ah, that was why you——" she said, and stopped.

"What is it?" asked Miss Baynes.

"I noticed in the hotel, when we were speaking about that
book, and you said you didn't know who had written it, that
you were not being quite sincere," said Miss Creswell with
unusual bluntness.

"Did you? You are right. I feel sure it is by him. It's
all I can do—taste him through what I believe to be his writ-
ings. I'm of the League and he doesn't choose to know me."
She sighed, and threw away another cigarette end.

Miss Creswell felt her uneasy restlessness. "Really," she
said. "I must go. I know you want——"

"Come with me! Won't you?"

"To the casino? What is it like?"

"Come and see."

"But it must be getting late."

"Nothing happens there till late."

Miss Creswell felt both reluctant and desirous. She wanted
to go, but she felt half afraid of going. She remembered her
age, her looks. Her looks especially troubled her at that
moment. For the first time she absolutely realized her un-

questionable respectability, self-consciously realized it. Even
the way she did her hair and put on her hats was respectable.
What would such respectability look like in the casino at eleven
o'clock at night?

"You will come?" said Miss Baynes, looking at her with
the curiously bright and curiously tragic eyes.

And Miss Creswell said, "Yes."

CHAPTER IV

AFTER Towser's departure for Switzerland Imogen saw to
it that her life was if possible even more complicated than
usual. She had always had within her the restless urge to be
"in" everything that was going on, to touch, or to grasp life
at as many points as possible. Rest, quiet, calm, the tranquillity of a serene existence had never had any attraction for
her. But now the thought even of such an existence had become hateful to her. Even Hugo, who was accustomed to
her in all her changing moods, in all her vagaries, was mildly
surprised by the fury of life which followed on that hunting
day when he had revealed the great secret of his concentration
on literature. For Hugo's activities, though incessant, were
never feverish. In his case strength of body seemed to drive
him along, and in a way that was healthy enough. But with
Imogen it was different. Her mind, her very nature, seemed
at this period goaded, as if the very devil were after her. So
Hugo thought and didn't scruple to say. But she didn't bother
much about what Hugo thought or said. The slave's mental
processes, the slave's remarks, are seldom considered important.
And Imogen always thought of Hugo as really her slave, despite
his intense masculinity, his independence and self-possession,
even his daring and audacity.

"He's mine!" she thought. "And whenever I choose it he'll
be more mine than he is now."

For she didn't intend to let Hugo run wild in a certain
way, as she knew he ran wild now, if she married him. And
secretly she expected some day to have him as a husband. Then
he must belong to her entirely. Her young pride would demand that. She didn't intend that her set should have the
chance of saying that she wasn't enough to satisfy Hugo. And

she felt that she could thoroughly satisfy him, though he could certainly never fully satisfy all of her. For she had the restless and clever brain which he lacked, a thousand desires, esthetic, subtle, delicately sensuous even, which he could never even understand.

"I'm one better than poor old Hugo!" she often thought, and had no doubt that he and all her friends thought so too. For she had a high opinion of herself and every assurance that it was shared by those about her.

She was one of those audacious young women who can always command plenty of flatterers. She expected flattery, and the expectation, being marked and very strong, caused it. In Imogen's set it was an understood thing that she was remarkable. People didn't question the fact that she was a brilliant creature and had a right to do whatever she chose. A mere insolence from her was hailed as a marvel. If she said a smart thing it was repeated through her circle with almost as much respect as if it had issued from the Burning Bush. Her good looks were asserted to be beauty, and her intellectual attainments, excellent but not extraordinary, were lauded as if she were a genius combined with a wit. When she uttered a criticism it was pronounced to be the final verdict. Imogen had said it. That was sufficient. It was, it must be, so. Her sayings and her doings were talked of through the town. The cleverest men were in her pocket or at her feet.

And what was she after all? Merely a clever and pretty painted girl of twenty-one, with immense hardihood, unbounded assurance, high courage and even higher "cheek," but without creative power, without genius, without simplicity and without modesty. She could not bring to the birth, but she could make a brilliant and caustic comment upon the children of another. Because of her fearlessness she was feared, because of her vanity she was admired, because of her open, and subtle —for she could mingle the blatant with the delicate—demand for everything life has to offer she was even loved. Clever men found her clever. Subtle men thought her remarkable. There were even latter-day saints who believed she had a beautiful nature and had, in spite of her worldly triumphs, kept it untarnished from the world.

So easily, so quickly, can a legend be created in silly London. So ready are even the important and the genuinely valuable to be foolish when a pretty and cheeky girl is concerned.

Sometimes, in the secret chamber of her soul, Imogen wondered at her own triumphant success. Oftener she just took it as her due, and as the logical working out of the law of demand and supply. She demanded all this and so her world hastened obsequiously to supply it.

It continued to supply it now but Imogen was not satisfied. Since she had seen Peter Kharkoff at Drearney, and since her aunt had departed for Geneva in quest, as she knew, of him, nothing that she did satisfied her. And it was this perpetual sense of acute dissatisfaction which led her to complicate her life even more than it was complicated already, piling distractions, physical, mental, affectional, one on the top of the other.

Always she was haunted by the memory of the Jew and by an intense desire to be with him again. She was haunted too by a creeping jealousy, so unwarranted, so absurd, so humiliating, that she could scarcely acknowledge it even to herself, jealousy of the woman who had gone to Geneva. The woman —yes! For in that jealousy her aunt became just that, another woman who was where Imogen wished to be because of a man.

As the days went by and Miss Creswell sent no communication to her family, Imogen's unrest increased. Christmas was now quite close. Towser would have to write for Christmas, unless she came back to pass the festival in England. Her sister, Lady Lowrie, Imogen's mother, wondered about that and expressed her wonder. Knowing nothing about Peter Kharkoff, Lady Lowrie had no idea why her sister was staying in Geneva in the depth of the winter.

"If she wanted a change why Geneva?" she said. "I would have lent her the villa but she wouldn't hear of it. Whatever can she be doing all alone in Geneva?"

"Preaching peace to the League of Nations perhaps," said Imogen flippantly.

"And not a word from her!" continued Lady Lowrie. "Evidently she's staying on. When I know her address I shall ask her to come back by the Riviera in February, if she remains out there over Christmas. D'you think she will?"

"Who knows? Towser's capable of anything."

"Is she? In the family we have always looked on her as the quiet one."

"The devil you have! Well, as Hugo says, the quiet ones are always the worst!"

"What *do* you mean, Imogen?" asked Lady Lowrie, who

was always delightfully slow in the uptake, and who had none
of her daughter's sharp cleverness. "Annie has never done
anything to cause us anxiety."

Just then a vision of her aunt rose up before Imogen's mental
eyes, and she broke into a fit of laughter. "Perhaps she's
reached the dangerous age, old lady," she said.

"Is there a dangerous age?" asked Lady Lowrie, with the
elegant vagueness characteristic of her.

"There is indeed. Every woman surely must pass through
at least one perilous moment in the course of her life. Perhaps Aunt Towser's perilous moment has come at last."

And then she went out of the room leaving her mother, as
usual, wondering what it all meant. That was Lady Lowrie's
usual state of mind in connection with the only child she had
managed to give birth to. With Imogen she was forever wondering what it all meant, and Imogen never told her. It would
have been too much bother.

Just before Christmas Miss Creswell did condescend to communicate with her relatives, wishing them the usual stereo-
typed Christmas happiness—"Christmas Cheer" Imogen called
it sarcastically—and informing them that she was "so comfortable in Geneva," and had made "such good friends" there,
that she had given up the idea of spending Christmas at home.
There was no mention of the Jew in her letters. She sent
Imogen a pretty little Geneva watch, slung on a chain of
platinum and gold, as a present.

Imogen read her aunt's letter—Miss Creswell had written
to her as well as to Lady Lowrie—again and again. She even
"pored" over it, shut up in her long third-floor sitting-room.
And she was indignant at its cruel reticence. When she had
gone out into the night in search of the Jew, at least she had
been thoroughly frank afterwards. She had soothed Towser's
angry feelings, she had told her everything, had kept nothing
back. And in return she was met by this coldly deliberate reserve. Towser wasn't playing the game. Imogen looked at
the little watch and detested it. But of course she sat down
and wrote a charming note of thanks and good wishes to
Towser, and of course she made no allusion to the subject which
united and divided them. Nevertheless she realized, when she
had signed "Im" to the note, that she couldn't close it up in
an envelop without inserting a cause for uneasiness. And
she added the following postscript:

By the way I shall probably run out to St. Moritz for January to indulge in winter sports. ski-ing, the Cresta, and so on, before going to the villa. So if I turn up at Geneva on the way don't let your hair tumble off with surprise.

Of course she knew that Geneva wasn't on the way to St. Moritz. But that didn't matter. She had only at that moment thought of going to St. Moritz. But by the time she had addressed the letter she had made up her mind that she would go. And she told her mother she was going in her usual casual way.

"I shall be off to St. Moritz early in January, old lady. I've had enough of this." "This," it seemed, was London in soft and foggy weather.

Lady Lowrie was not surprised. Imogen was forever darting about from place to place. Since she had been seventeen she had never been a fixture anywhere. So Lady Lowrie merely said:

"Whom are you going with, dear?"

"That's to be seen. I'll probably turn up at the villa some time in February."

"You've had enough hunting?"

"One never has enough hunting if one cares for hunting at all. But I think I'm for a change." She paused. Then she added gravely, "Besides, old lady, I'm getting the least bit anxious about our Towser."

"But Annie is quite accustomed to traveling alone. Why she's been to Greece and Corfu, and——"

"Traveling—yes. But I think this passionate squatting in Geneva's damned odd, old lady."

"Passionate squatting—dear!" said Lady Lowrie, with the densely serious face which indicated severe mental processes obtaining within her organism. "What do you mean? Surely, Annie——"

"Don't probe, my sweet! I think this matter of Towser's continuing existence in the Hotel les Bergues wants looking into. That's all. I may take her on the way to St. Moritz."

"But you go to St. Moritz by Zurich surely, dear."

"Cook's tourists do. But Cook isn't a law for me."

"Of course not. I know that."

Imogen went out of the room. She was feeling hard and oddly humiliated. What she had spoken of doing, what she now knew she would do, had caused in her this sense of humilia-

tion which was disagreeably novel. To follow Towser un-
asked, unwanted, to arrive in Towser's hotel and to have her
arrival hated—not very glorious, was it? Towser hadn't followed her on that Sunday night in Drearney.

But the Hotel les Bergues! Imogen believed it was that
name on Towser's letter paper which had "put the lid on."
For she still had a visiting card hidden away in a despatch box.
And on it was printed "7, Rue les Bergues, Genève." If
Towser had been staying in the Hotel de Russie, or the Hotel
Beau Rivage, perhaps Imogen wouldn't have had to do what
she was going to do. She wasn't sure about that. But she
was now quite sure that she would go out to Switzerland.
The force of the urge within her was too great to be resisted.
Besides she had always followed her whim. (She now called
what she was going to do a whim, strove to think of it as a
caprice. But she knew quite well it was neither.)

Immediately after Christmas she told Hugo what she was
going to do. The weather was still soft and excellent for
hunting and in consequence he was surprised. For he knew
that Imogen's love of hunting was a genuine passion.

"After the Cresta again!" he said rather blankly. "Determined to break your neck, are you?" And he fixed his bright
blue eyes on her beautiful throat. "Why not break it over a
good, sound bullfinch," he added, "with hounds running on a
hot scent, and die to music, the best music I know?"

"I've no intention of breaking my neck and dying to any
music," said Imogen. "Besides frost may come any day.
January's always the worst month in England."

"Want me to come with you?"

"No," she said. And only when she said it did she know
how definitely she didn't want old Hugo to come with her to
Switzerland. "We can do a good deal," she added. "But we
can't go to St. Moritz together."

"Then rout out a chaperon."

"Put an advertisement for one in the Times if you like, and
see what happens."

"Better marry me, old girl, and we'll go bobbing for a
honeymoon." They were up in her sitting-room, and he caught
hold of her hand. "Come on! Take the fence, Geney. Why
not? You're not one to hang back from an obstacle. You
know perfectly well you mean to land on the other side one
day, so why not——"

"I don't know anything of the kind!" she interrupted, with sudden fierceness.

A tremendously masculine intentness showed in his eyes, and he gripped her hand more closely. "Come, Geney! We've gone pretty far together. We shall have to go to the end of the road. You can't hold me off forever, you know."

As she looked at him with a very complete comprehension, she thought of the Jew's strange lack of all sensuality, and she wondered, knowing herself pretty thoroughly in one way, how such a man could draw her away from a very complete man like Hugo. A voice within her said at that moment, "He'd never want you as Hugo wants you." And it was a voice which seemed to rise up out of the depths of knowledge. Nevertheless, and even at that moment, she passionately wanted to go to Geneva. And she was jealous of Towser as she had never been jealous of the women whom she knew to be, casually but intimately, in Hugo's life.

How could that be? What did it mean?

She pulled away her hand with very definite force. "I'm not in the mood for all that now," she said. "Do stop it, Hugo."

"I don't know why I stand what I do," he said, in a surly voice. "Upon my soul, Geney, you want a damned good bringing to heel."

"You're not the man who could bring me to heel."

"I don't say I am. Fact is I've never seen the fellow that could." As he spoke the last words he was looking straight at her, with hard, disappointed eyes. And when he had spoken he still kept his eyes on her in silence for an instant. Then he said, "Have you?"

"You know me pretty well. Is it likely?"

"By Jove—you have!" he said.

Imogen felt that a phenomenon had occurred, two phenomena even. Number one: Hugo had actually been subtle. Number two: she was actually blushing under cover of her beautifully complete make-up.

"What's the matter?" he added suspiciously. "Who's the fellow? Anyone I know?"

She looked at him and knew that an evasion would "cut no ice" with him in his present mood, and with his present, strangely ascertained certainty. So she attempted none, and merely said, "That may be true—what you've chosen to assert

—or not. I don't affirm or deny. I simply decline to be cross-examined."

"Geney," he said, coming nearer to her. "That fellow has something to do with your going to St. Moritz."

"Since when have you become jealous?" she asked. "You and I have never troubled to be jealous of each other. I know quite well you have to do with other girls. Do I ever try to stop you? Do I ever ask you to be a plaster saint?"

"All that's nothing."

"Why is it nothing?"

"Because it's a necessity and it doesn't touch *you*," he said, with a sort of soft brutality. "If you'd marry me I should drop it all from the wedding day."

"Very good of you to say that!"

"Geney, what's up with you? Who've you run up against? What's he up to in Switzerland?"

She shook her head, and made answer, "Nothing doing, Hugo!"

He looked savage, but he said nothing more on that subject until he was on the point of going away. Then he just shook her hand coldly and said, "I may not be the man to bring you to heel, but neither are you the girl that can keep me on a string forever. I've had about enough of it, Geney. Go to St. Moritz. Go anywhere you damned well like. I'll ask no more questions. But when you come back you'll either marry me or we'll cry quits and I'll be off to other pastures. You've kept me hanging about long enough. Better keep clear of the Cresta or you may break your neck."

"And much you'd care if I did!" she said. But she turned up the tail of the sentence and made it sound like a semi-question. Perhaps Hugo didn't notice that. Anyhow he didn't make any rejoinder. He went striding out of the room without another word, leaving her secretly amazed.

She felt the power of the Jew in his outburst of jealousy; she felt the influence of the Jew in his unexpected subtlety; and in his knowledge of the unrevealed—for what revelation had she been guilty of?—she felt the lure of the Jew.

Never before had she had such a scene with Hugo. She had flirted outrageously with many men and he had known of it, had even been witness of it. But not one of these men had he feared. Yet he feared the Jew, of whom she had never spoken to him, of whom he had, she was certain, never heard.

He felt the Jew then in her. She carried report of the Jew's power within her and made it felt without intention, even indeed against her desire and will. She had longed, as she had said to Towser, to creep into the Jew's mind, and to lie there in hiding. But what had happened was this: he had crept into her mind, he lay there in hiding, and began to make his presence there felt.

That day Hugo had ignorantly revealed to her something about herself of which she had not been fully conscious. And because Hugo feared she began to fear the Jew. She remembered how she had shivered at Drearney when she had murmured, "A Savior from the North." Now, left alone in her warm familiar room, she shivered again, and a warning seemed to be upon her, to lie upon her like a weight, making her feel as if in the whole of her—nothing of her left out—that she had better not go to Switzerland, that she had better pull up now on the edge of the course, not throw the reins on the horse's neck, and let it gallop with her into the unknown.

So strong was her sense of that weight of warning that perhaps she would have heeded it, in spite of the hatred she felt at the idea of yielding to a feeling of fear, she who had always prided herself upon being a girl of high courage both mental and physical. But exactly in the moment of hesitation her telephone sounded. Henry was asking whether he might bring up a telegram for her which had just come. He brought it. It was from Towser, and was as follows:

Dead season here weather very bad fear you would find it dull could join you instead at St. Moritz meeting you at Zurich fix date love: Towser.

"Any answer, ma'am?" asked Henry.

Imogen glanced up at him from the telegram, and he was surprised at the expression in her eyes though he didn't show it. Afterwards he said about her eyes below stairs, "Miss Imogen looked as if she wanted to do something crool, downright crool!"

"What did you say?" she asked.

"Beg pardon, ma'am. I only asked whether there was any answer?"

"Oh! Yes, there is an answer—of course. Just wait, will you?" And she walked slowly to her writing table, sat down, took a pen and, after a moment of consideration, wrote in her large, decisive hand:

Delighted you will come to St. Moritz with me but not Zurich will pick you up at Geneva expect me on——

She paused and thought for an instant. "What day is it, Henry?"

"What day, ma'am?"

"Yes. What's the date?"

"The twenty-ninth, ma'am, of December."

"I didn't suppose it was August. Thank you."

She added to her telegram the words:

January fourth please take room love: Im.

"Here you are, Henry. Get it off at once."

"Yes, ma'am."

When he had left the room Imogen smiled. But it wasn't a very pleasant smile. "So much for little Towser!" she said to herself.

She went downstairs to the first floor. Lady Lowrie was in the drawing-room reading "The Rosary" for the fourth time, with an uncut volume of Proust on a table beside her. Imogen came up to her.

"Merciful powers, old lady! 'The Rosary' again!"

Lady Lowrie's handsome Du Maurier face became faintly pink.

"I took it up by chance. I'm going to read the one you recommended afterwards, but it isn't cut and——"

"Quite right to leave it alone. It's a good rule never to read an author whose books are uncut. I've come to tell you that Aunt Towser's telegraphed offering to go with me to St. Moritz. Isn't she an old dear?"

"That's capital. Your father will be pleased."

"Why?"

"Well, dear, though he never says anything I think he really prefers it if you have a competent chaperon."

"Is Towser competent? We'll see. Anyhow, I'm going to Geneva to pick her up and carry her off to the snows. I shall start on the second and spend a couple of nights in Paris. They'll put me up at the Embassy, I know. I'm glad 'The Rosary's' cut."

"You'll come to the villa from St. Moritz?"

"Shouldn't wonder if I do."

"And of course we shall have room for Captain Dennistone."

"Hugo? I'm not sure I shall want him there. We've just been having a scrap."

"A scrap, dear? What of?"

"A scrap! A row! Bad language and blows!"

Lady Lowrie looked deprecating and pathetic. She was still very good-looking, though some of her friends said that she had *"une tête de chameau,"* perhaps because her neck was unusually long and her head was distinctly small.

"I'm sorry for that," she said. "Who started it?"

"Hugo, of course. No, I believe I did."

"I'm sure it will blow over."

"With the accent on the blow. Well, I'm off to Reville's and Molyneux."

When Miss Creswell received Imogen's telegram—it came on the morning of December 30th—she felt like one who, having trodden a difficult path with, as she supposed, great wariness, found herself unexpectedly caught fast in a trap. She had made a sacrifice, and that very sacrifice had been adroitly turned to her disadvantage. Horrified at the thought of Imogen's advent in Geneva, she had resolved to leave Geneva, where she wanted even terribly to remain, and to travel up into the region of ice. Anything to keep Imogen away from Geneva. And now Imogen was coming there and was going to take her aunt away. So that nothing was gained. Indeed it might be said that nothing but loss had resulted from Miss Creswell's carefully thought-out telegram. She felt very angry and distressed in her trap.

She had now been in Geneva for over three weeks, and she had not yet made acquaintance with Peter Kharkoff. Nor had she seen him in the street or in any public place. Nevertheless, till Imogen's letter had come she had been neither dissatisfied nor unhappy. She had not even been restless after the first two or three days of uneasiness and self-conscious misery. Having made up her mind definitely to stay on, and having got to know Miss Edie Baynes, a curious contentment, a curious peace, had come to her. She was free, her own mistress, and could wait. He was near. She would know him presently. She had only to wait for a little while. She had an inward

assurance that very soon she would know him. But it now
seemed that their meeting must come in his own good time.

Through Miss Baynes she had got to know, really to know
outside of the book-shop, Madame Coiret.

Madame Coiret was an interesting woman with a touch
of gentle distinction and an evidently fine nature, a nature
that aspired. But she did seem to Miss Creswell, as Edie
Baynes had hinted she might, to be a bit of a crank. Left a
widow and childless many years ago she had turned her love
of books to practical account. She had set up a book-shop in a
very small way, had gradually drawn customers to her, had
begun to prosper, had enlarged her business, had moved to the
center of the town, and now was mistress of probably the best-
paying, and most-considered book-shop in Geneva. She was
a businesslike woman, though not grasping. She knew how
to make and to keep money. But she had another side to her
character, a curious other-worldly side, which seemed to have
its way out of business hours. Miss Baynes had once said to
Miss Creswell that Madame Coiret was a business woman for
eight hours of the working day, a visionary during the rest of
the time. And there seemed to Miss Creswell to be some truth
in this.

She was one of those curious people who, rejecting the tenets
and teachings of established religions, nevertheless are incessantly preoccupied about what may be called spiritual matters,
and about the guidance and advancement of the soul. And
what she was able to believe was often even more extraordinary
than what she was unable to believe. But she was so earnest
in her beliefs, and so obviously sincere in character and free
from ordinary selfishness, that even those who smiled at her
esteemed her.

Miss Baynes, for instance, was even fond of her, though
their two characters might be said to be almost in opposition,
Madame Coiret being austere and Miss Baynes the reverse of
austere. And Miss Creswell "took" to her at once, although
she was anything rather than orthodox. But Miss Creswell
had a special reason for being drawn towards her.

She was a friend, or if not absolutely that, a fairly intimate
acquaintance of the Jew. And she allowed Miss Creswell
to talk about him to her. For Miss Creswell had from the
first thrown off reserve with Madame Coiret, as she had soon,
though not immediately, thrown it off with Edie Baynes.

She allowed Miss Creswell to talk about Peter Kharkoff to her but she did not say very much about him herself in return. It seemed to Miss Creswell that Madame Coiret could not bring herself to talk about him in any casual or gossiping way as women are apt to talk about those they know to other women. About Doctor Steiner, whose adherents surrounded him at Dornach near Bâle, she spoke freely and with admiration, as one may discuss a famous author, or painter, or profoundly learned teacher and guide of men. But evidently she could not talk like that about Peter Kharkoff. The mystery in him seemed to fall upon her when his name was mentioned. Miss Creswell noticed that a peculiar look came into her eyes, rather small, dark gray, and sunken, when her mind was on him, a withdrawn, mysterious and deeply reverent look.

Miss Creswell, in her frankness, had even told Madame Coiret of her visit to number seven rue les Bergues and of her vain attempt to see Peter Kharkoff there. She had not forgotten the delicate rebuke in Madame Coiret's sunken eyes, or the sound in the voice which had said, "Monsieur Kharkoff was probably in and didn't reply. He sees very few people."

Miss Creswell, feeling rebuked, had told Madame Coiret of Mr. Kharkoff's unconventional visit to Mr. Hendry uninvited, unexpected. But Madame Coiret had only said, "What he may do, it is not for everybody to do." But immediately afterwards, as if to soften any possible resentment or depression which might have been caused by her words, she added gently, "I know how much you wish to know Monsieur Kharkoff. I hope an opportunity for a meeting will come about presently. Just now I believe he is seeing no one though he is here in Geneva."

Miss Creswell received the impression—it might be a wrong one; she did not believe so—that Madame Coiret was quietly testing her, in order to find out whether her desire to know the Unearthly was genuine, lasting and intense, or whether it was merely the foolish, perhaps hysterical caprice of a middle-aged spinster lady. She was resolved to prove to Madame Coiret that she was not wholly unworthy, that her desire was deep and irresistible, a governing desire for which she would make sacrifices willingly.

And then had come Imogen's startling letter. Instantly Miss Creswell had resolved that Imogen must be prevented from coming to Geneva. Her telegram had been carefully

thought out and had caused her great searchings of the heart
before she sent it. She hated the idea of leaving Geneva even
for a few weeks for the uproar and turmoil of St. Moritz
in the winter sports season. Yet she would do even that.
Anything to stop the pursuit of Imogen. And then had come
the answering telegram, and Miss Creswell had realized
Imogen's delicate malice, and her own impotence when pitted
against the hardihood of modern girlhood.

She wanted to do something, to make another attempt to
stop Imogen from coming. But she knew Imogen very well,
and she could think of no plan capable of causing a change
in that horribly determined mind. Certainly she might go
away in a hurry, and telegraph to Imogen that she was going.
But to do that would be to leave the field open to her rival.
(She had come to think of Imogen quite definitely as that.)
Imogen, she was sure, would come to Geneva whether she
were there or not. She was an excuse. But girls like Imogen
do what they want without troubling to search for excuses.
After much heart searching and agitated mental debate Miss
Creswell did just nothing. She sent no more telegrams. She
did not take a room for her niece. She couldn't bring herself
to do that. In great perturbation and distress she waited, telling no one that a relative was going to join her.

She waited till January the third.

On that day—that last day, for Imogen was due to arrive
on the morrow, though no further communication had come
from her—Miss Creswell was seized by a desperate conviction
that she couldn't remain inactive any longer. There was something she must do before Imogen arrived, and yet it was
something that she was now ashamed to do, indeed scarcely
dared to do. But suddenly she felt that she had to do it, that
she couldn't face Imogen until she had done it, that if she
didn't do it before Imogen came she would be delivered utterly,
like a naked defenseless fool, into that audacious young woman's
hands. She must know Peter Kharkoff before Imogen came.
She must be able to say that she knew him. Otherwise
Imogen's contempt for her would be limitless, and to it would
be joined her own self-contempt. For now that her niece's
arrival was close upon her she realized the absurdity of the
situation. Imogen had followed Peter Kharkoff the only time
she had seen him, had made his acquaintance and had a long
interview with him. She, Annie Creswell, had pursued him

to a foreign land, and, now that she was there, had been there
for over three weeks, hadn't definitely advanced one step
towards him.

If she found that out how inextinguishable would be
Imogen's young laughter. She mustn't find it out because it
mustn't be so when she arrived.

And Miss Creswell got up in a small fever of agitation, put
on her "things," and, deliberately denying herself any time
for quiet consideration, hurried over the bridge to the book-
shop of Madame Coiret.

CHAPTER V

MADAME COIRET occupied a flat above her shop, with a
faithful Swiss maid who looked after her devotedly, but in
business hours she was always to be found either in the shop
itself, or in one of the smaller book-rooms opening out of it
at the back towards the river. On this particular afternoon,
when Miss Creswell hurried in from the street driven by a
purpose of which she was more than half ashamed, but which
nevertheless she was determined to carry out, Madame Coiret
was not to be seen, and the three young Swiss women who
helped her in the business were all busy with customers. For
it was four o'clock, a favorite time for shopping with the people of Geneva, and two American travelers had looked in,
attracted by books they had seen displayed in the window.

Miss Creswell stood waiting till she could be attended to,
and meanwhile began to look at the books lying about in carefully ordered confusion.

Just at first she was not aware of anything unusual in the
shop. She saw two or three Swiss being shown various books,
heard them asking quiet questions in French. One of the
Americans—the two had not come in together, were in no
relation with each other—was inquiring about a work by
Romain Rolland, "Au dessus de la mêlée." The other, an excessively lean elderly man, with a clean-shaven wrinkled face,
thin gray hair, large spectacles with remarkably bright eyes
behind them, and wearing a sort of gray shawl laid on his
narrow shoulders and enfolding his long, small neck, was asking for a book in a wiry voice. Miss Creswell heard the

words: "By Steiner—Rudolf Steiner, the head of the Academy near Bâle, young woman," spoken in English. The "young woman," also speaking English, said she wasn't sure whether they had the book in stock but she would go and look. As she went she passed by Miss Creswell, smiled a civil greeting, and said in French, "I'll attend to you in a moment, madame."

"I've only come to have a word with Madame Coiret if she's in."

The young woman glanced at Miss Creswell with very light, steady eyes, that looked newly washed—as Swiss eyes often do —and answered, "She's in one of the back rooms with a customer."

"By Steiner—Doctor Rudolf Steiner!" said the elderly American. "I see other books of his in your window."

"Yes, sir. I'll see at once." And the young woman went away towards a book-shelf at a distance.

Miss Creswell looked towards the farther part of the shop, beyond which the small rooms filled with books were. And she saw that the elderly American was also looking in that direction. And something—at least so it seemed to her—in his pose, the turn of his head, the curious steadiness of his gaze, made her think, "Why does he look like that?" Immediately afterwards she remembered that she, too, had been gazing towards the book-rooms and perhaps with a scrutiny like his. But then she knew Madame Coiret was there with somebody. She watched the American, she couldn't help watching him, and then she knew something else. She knew that the "customer" with Madame Coiret was Peter Kharkoff. And she seemed to have gained that knowledge somehow, in some queer, inexplicable way, through the American. He was much nearer to the book-rooms than she was. Could he see—hear?

At that moment the assistant came back from the book-shelves, and went to the American. "I'm very sorry, sir, but we haven't that book in stock. Can I order it for you?"

"Can I order the book for you, sir? I think we could get it in two or three days."

The American, who had not answered the first question or looked at the girl when she put it, turned round. "Never mind the book, my girl. I can get it in Bâle when I go there. Who's in there?" And he pointed with a long, thin fore-finger to the back of the shop. "Who's that I hear talking?"

"It's a customer, sir, with our employer, Madame Coiret."

"Is it a Mr. Kharkoff?"

The girl looked astonished. "Yes, sir."

"Ah!" said the American. "So he's in Switzerland, is he?"

"Yes, sir."

"Staying here?"

"I suppose so, sir," said the girl, who was now beginning to show signs of defensive surprise.

"Ah!" said the American again. He stood silent and still as if listening. Then he said, "His voice is unmistakable. That's sure!" He hesitated a moment, as if in doubt about something, then nodded and walked out of the shop, drawing the shawl more closely round his neck and shoulders.

The assistant came over to Miss Creswell. "I think madame will be able to speak to you in a moment, madame."

"Thank you," said Miss Creswell, speaking with unnatural calmness and dignity. "What a curious man that was."

"He comes in now and then when he's in Switzerland. He's a great admirer of Doctor Steiner and is on his way to Bâle, probably for lectures, or perhaps to see a performance at the Dornach Academy."

"Is the Academy very——" Her voice petered out.

From the shadowy background of the shop, where the smaller rooms lay near the river, Peter Kharkoff emerged, walking slowly with a large book held in his left hand and lying close in the crook of his left arm. Behind him came Madame Coiret in her black dress, white collar and cuffs. Their conversation was evidently over, and probably good-bys had been said, for Peter Kharkoff walked forward like a man who felt himself to be quite alone, free from all social obligations, serenely away in his own world.

When Miss Creswell had learned that he was in the shop she had made up her mind to take this unexpected opportunity, and either to speak to him—she didn't know under what pretext—or to ask Madame Coiret quickly and secretly to introduce her to him. But now she did neither of these things. Although he came up to her and passed by her she could not do either of them. Indeed, she was not as Imogen. And with this man she had no audacity. It seemed to her that perhaps with a lesser man she might have found some— but not with him.

She gazed at him as he passed and the enormous impression

she had instantly received when she had looked into his face
at Drearney was with her again, and even intensified. She
had felt a sort of occult fear of this man. She had said that
perhaps he was "dangerous." She had doubtless felt that perhaps it was so. But she now knew that any danger which
might lie in him, for her or for others, came not from any
evil, any least drop of malignity in him, but from the fierce
attraction of his power. That it was which drew her, as a
very small thing may be drawn to a thing that is great. That
it was which created in her the intense, almost overmastering
desire to sink her personality in his. She felt herself as a
drop just then. And the ocean was near. And she remembered Imogen's words about "a great view of the sea."

She saw a man, tall, broad, with the curious blunt features
which had made her think of a lion, the large, veiled eyes, the
unmistakable impress of Israel. He wore a heavy dark overcoat, one of those large black hats worn by many of the Swiss.
She glanced at his hands. (He wasn't wearing gloves.) They
were large, neither fat hands nor yet very thin. They had
none of the sinuous grace, none of the agile cunning, of the
delicately subtle and adroit artist. They seemed to her quiet,
powerful, and amazingly unselfconscious hands. He went on.
He was gone.

And Madame Coiret was speaking to her. What Miss Creswell said in reply she didn't know. But, in a moment, she
found herself in one of the small book-rooms with Madame
Coiret, and she was saying to her, "I didn't come for books.
I came to see you."

"Yes?" said Madame Coiret, in her quiet, self-contained but
earnest voice.

"I came to ask you, to beg you to introduce me to him."
"Mr. Kharkoff."

"But when I saw him again I felt I had no right whatever
to intrude upon him. And yet others don't feel like that."

And then, sitting in the little room, surrounded by the walls
of books, she told Madame Coiret all about Imogen, and that
Imogen was coming, and that she knew why Imogen was
coming, and her feeling about this intrusion upon her freedom.
She even told Madame Coiret exactly what it was which had
driven her to the shop that day, the ugly, but overwhelming,
feeling that she must be in advance of Imogen, must escape
from the thrust of the inextinguishable laughter.

"But when I saw him—I couldn't. All those little wretched things shriveled up in me. But already I begin to feel them again. And I hate her coming. I know exactly what she will do. When she finds out that I have been here all this time and haven't got to know him she will laugh at me. And then she will go—she has no fear of anybody, no reverence for anybody—she'll go and call upon him. And he will answer. I know that. I can feel it. When she is there and rings his bell he will be at home, and he will answer."

Without being actively aware of it she said the last sentence with the vital energy which jealousy can always prompt, even in the sluggish. When she had finished she looked at Madame Coiret, perhaps instinctively seeking for assent to her fierce mental protest, for sympathy with her bitterness. But Madame Coiret only looked at her with a sort of reticent gravity and said:

"You ought not to give him that part of humanity as your tribute. He deserves something better than that."

It was a severe rebuke, but it was given so quietly, so simply, and with such exceptional sincerity, that Miss Creswell did not resent it. Indeed it struck her as so deeply true that she accepted it as if with her whole nature, completely. Before she could say anything in reply one of the assistants came into the room.

"Pardon, madame, mais——"

"I'll come, Rosalie."

The assistant went out, and Miss Creswell hastened to say good-by. Although she had failed in her purpose, although she was going away with apparently no greater prospect of knowing Peter Kharkoff than she had had when she had left the hotel, she was ready to go. She even wanted to go away and to be alone. Something had happened. She thought of it just then as something outside her. It was really something within her. The happening was not Madame Coiret's rebuke, but what it had brought about in the woman rebuked.

As she walked home to the hotel she felt a sense of relief, as if an ugly burden, which she had been forced to carry, no longer weighed her down and irked her. She thought of her telegram to Imogen, and of Imogen's reply; rapier play—wasn't it?—between two hostile women, or rather between a woman and a girl. Each had thrust at the other. She had come off second best in the encounter. But what did that matter now?

Madame Coiret had gently rebuked her and suddenly she had
seen a ray of clear light. She felt that she would be able to
meet Imogen on the morrow without dread. Certainly she
could not exactly even now welcome the coming of Imogen.
But her dread of the girl was gone. For the moment? She
hoped not. She even ventured to believe not. For something
had happened, and it seemed to her big.

"You ought not to give him that part of humanity as your
tribute. He deserves something better than that."

Till now Madame Coiret was the only human being Miss
Creswell had met who could be said really to know Peter
Kharkoff. Imogen and Mr. Hendry had met him and talked
with him, but each of them only once. That was not knowledge. Madame Coiret, however, knew him. She had always
been very reticent with Miss Creswell about him, but her
very reticence had, Miss Creswell now believed, conveyed a
great deal. There are things and people one cannot chatter
about, and they are not the small things and the small people.
Madame Coiret knew him, and today, in a couple of pregnant
sentences, she had surely expressed her view of him and also
him.

Miss Creswell believed that she would not be able to wrangle
about him any more, either with Imogen or with anyone else.
Imogen, when she came, might laugh at her, would no doubt
laugh at her. But now she would be able to bear it without
difficulty or trouble of the soul.

Her tribute to him mustn't be feverish jealousy, quarreling,
envy, malice. She looked back and saw herself as horribly
unworthy. She looked forward and hoped to compass a conduct the reverse of what hers had been. She felt the Jew
through Madame Coiret, as well as through his own personality. It was somehow as if Madame Coiret had explained
to her with concentrated lucidity something which she had
obscurely felt, but only with a confused sense of its meaning.

That evening when she came down to dinner she found the
elderly American whom she had seen in the book-shop dining
at the next table to hers, a book by his side, the gray shawl
still round his shoulders. He glanced at her through his large
glasses, and she noticed an odd glitter in his eyes. Then he
returned to his book. He ate slowly, fish and vegetables only,
and seemed to be absorbed by what he read. Sometimes he
let the food lie on his plate, and turned page after page with

out putting a morsel into his mouth. He drank only water.
Miss Creswell resolved if possible to speak to him after dinner,
though he did not look like a man who would welcome casual
conversation from a stranger. Although his eyes were obviously observant there was something remote and fanatical in
them. He did not look like a lover of his kind.

She finished her dinner while he was still reading, and occasionally eating a small portion from a mess of potatoes and
beetroot, which, by his orders, had been brought to him in a
salad bowl. She got up and went into the hall, sat down by a
table near the entrance and ordered a cup of coffee. Then she
waited and looked at the New York Herald. In about a
quarter of an hour the American came in on thin, bending legs,
drawing the shawl about his neck with his right hand and
carrying his book in his left. He stood still and glanced about
the hall with rather a sour expression, then sat down not far
from Miss Creswell, and took out, clipped and lighted a tiny,
pale-brown cigar. He put his book down on a table. Evidently he had read enough for the moment.

She glanced at him, hesitated, returned to her paper.
"Mrs. Van Prunt was beautifully dressed in gray marocain."
Was she indeed? How interesting! "Miss Emily Bibber
wore the latest creation from Paris." Heaven be praised for
that! She put the paper down, sought in herself for hardihood like Imogen's, got up and crossed over to the American.

"May I venture to speak to you for a moment?"

"Heh?" He sat looking up at her with repellent surprise.
She had a dreadful and ridiculous memory of a lesson Canon
Barrimore had read in the cathedral at Drearney, the story
of Joseph and Potiphar's wife. What was the old man thinking? In the midst of her confusion she nearly laughed, but
she managed to say, with earnest gravity.

"I was in Madame Coiret's book-shop today when you were,
and I heard you speaking about Dr. Steiner and the Academy
for the study of occult sciences at Dornach."

The expression in his eyes changed. "Are you one of
Rudolph Steiner's adherents, ma'am?"

"No, I couldn't say that. But I am interested in his writ-
ings, and I thought perhaps I might venture to ask you a
little about him and Dornach.

"Sit down, ma'am, sit down. I'm quite at your service."

Miss Creswell sat down, feeling terribly insincere. But

when about eleven she got up to go to bed she had been rewarded for what she thought of as her "venturesomeness."
For she had learned something more about the Jew.

The American—Martin Heylen was the name he had given
—was, as she had supposed, a crank and evidently a very rich
crank. His main interest in life was what he called "religious
and occult experience." And, as cranks will, he had obviously
taken pains to "get into touch" with as many other cranks as
possible, both in the States and in Europe. A pilgrim through
various religions—he had assured Miss Creswell that at one
time he had even been a Moslem—he had sought out the
leaders of many cults, and had probably spent his money freely
among them. He was just now particularly interested in the
teachings and the art manifestations of Dr. Steiner, and was
on his way to Bâle, from which place he was in hopes of going
out to some performances at the great wooden building which
he called "The Goetheanum."

It was she who had brought into the conversation the name
of Peter Kharkoff, and immediately she had noticed that Mr.
Heylen felt both hostility to, and admiration for, the man whose
remarkable voice he had recognized immediately in the book-
shop. She gathered that his hostility had its source in the fact
of "Mr. Kharkoff's" solitude of spirit and apparent indifference to money. His admiration had, perhaps, a better foundation.

Always busily in search of remarkable men who were concerned about other than material things, Mr. Heylen had
come to hear of Mr. Kharkoff in New York as a solitary Jew
who possessed immense mental power, and who lived, apparently, in the mind and for the cultivation of the mind, "lived
for thought instead of for life," as Mr. Heylen had put it.
He had sought Mr. Kharkoff out and—but evidently only with
great difficulty—had at last "got into touch" with him. He
was a man without followers, without "adherents." He was
not a teacher, had no disciples, made no claim to be remarkable,
or greater than other men. But on the few who came into
contact with him he evidently made a prodigious impression.

Miss Creswell had gathered from Mr. Heylen that the
impression made on him had been prodigious, and that he
had endeavored to force Peter Kharkoff into the position of a
teacher and the leader of a cult, but had been quietly, even
gently, evaded and finally escaped from. Hence the hostility.

The rich crank had not liked to see such a prize beyond the reach not only of his influence but of his money. The would-be worshiper had been sorely injured by finding his worship quietly put aside. But his sense of injury had not prevented Miss Creswell from realizing that he thought Peter Kharkoff phenomenal, and was still deeply, almost angrily, interested in him. It was indeed evident to her that Mr. Heylen had been greatly excited and intrigued by the discovery that Peter Kharkoff was living in Geneva, and more than half regretted not having taken the opportunity which had presented itself so unexpectedly of speaking with him. Mr. Heylen had spoken with enthusiasm about Dr. Steiner and his very remarkable activities, but Miss Creswell had noticed that his way of speaking about Peter Kharkoff—and she thought perhaps in despite of himself—had been tinged with something like awe.

One statement of his about Kharkoff had specially struck her. He had said, "The man is absolutely exceptional, so far as I know, in one way. It's this, ma'am. He doesn't seem to care to act upon individuals. Of course he does act upon them. Such mental power can't help itself. He acted upon *me,* though I don't think he was trying to. What he aims at, I believe, is to act upon mankind in the mass. Of course the mass is made up of individuals. That's sure. We can't get away from that. But Kharkoff likes to deal with individuals not separately but en masse. Wonder why he's here in Geneva. I shouldn't wonder, mind you"—and at this point his eyes had glittered fiercely behind his glasses—"if he's trying to act upon the League by thought-power. Some would laugh at such an idea";—here he had scrutinized her closely—"you don't, I see. No more do I. I know too much. Men and women, aye, scientists and priests and politicians, they laugh at most of the greatest truths. Poor things! I laugh at them, ma'am. And I say I shouldn't wonder if Peter Kharkoff's here doing just one thing. And what's that—you say? I'll tell you, ma'am." (And here he had made a long pause, and his lips had worked, and his eyes of a fanatic had seemed to bulge at her for a moment.) "What's that?" he had resumed, lifting his wiry voice into sudden sharpness. *"Thinking* peace, ma'am. Aye—just that! *Thinking* peace! And what that man thinks is like a great white light that goes to the darkest places."

It was soon after this that a clock had chimed somewhere, recalling Miss Creswell to remembrance of time, and that she had got up to go. But before going she had ventured on one or two questions. Mr. Heylen knew nothing of Peter Kharkoff's past life before he had met him in New York. Nor did he know anyone who knew any more than he did. The man was there, a Portent. Mr. Heylen had not sought to dive into his past. One day he was gone. Now he was here in Geneva, a mystery, a Power.

Mr. Heylen's eyes had positively blazed in those last few moments of talk. But he was a crank, a fanatic. That was obvious. "Switzerland!" he had said. "These men come to Switzerland, to one of the smallest of all countries. Why's that? There's quiet here. The mountains keep out something, ma'am, something that these men don't want. Thought-power! Perhaps it's at its height here. Steiner's here! Romain Rolland's here—they tell me. And Kharkoff is here. What's the greatest power we know, ma'am? Thought! The power of thought! I look upon Kharkoff as the embodiment of that power. But he didn't want me! He didn't want me!"

And suddenly his voice had become dry and peevish, and the light had gone out of his eyes, and he had pulled at his shawl with a yellowish hand, and she had left him calling to a waiter for a glass of water with a squeeze of lemon in it.

He was a crank. He was what is usually called "an impossible sort of man." Miss Creswell realized that thoroughly. But she realized, too, that he was a conscious searcher after something that was surely worth having. And she could not help putting him in her mind with Mr. Hendry, the organist at Drearney. Only Mr. Hendry was free from even the least touch of mania, she thought, and Mr. Martin Heylen certainly had "a screw loose." Perhaps that was why Peter Kharkoff had sought out Hendry and had gently evaded Heylen. Discrimination must be a powerful factor in that extraordinary mind.

When she was in bed Miss Creswell lay very still thinking of the American's strange suggestion that Peter Kharkoff's reason, sole reason probably, for being in Geneva was to "think peace." The suggestion of a crank? The suggestion of one on the borderland between sanity and insanity? Most men of sense would merely laugh at such an idea and forget it immediately. But Miss Creswell (not a man of sense) could not do that. And she remembered her first evening with Miss Edie Baynes, and all that Miss Baynes had told her about

Madame Coiret and the Jew. Madame Coiret had not been quite so outspoken with her. But she believed what this Mr. Heylen believed.

Could it be true? And if it were true, was not Peter Kharkoff not merely a crank but a king of cranks? And yet Edie Baynes had evidently been ready to believe what Madame Coiret and Martin Heylen believed. And Miss Baynes—Miss Creswell knew her much better now—had a competent, even a rather hard intellect, combined perhaps with an often unsatisfied body. Like Imogen apparently, before the Sunday evening interview in the Dane, Edie Baynes, not having seen, or rather not having known, was ready to believe.

If, as Mr. Heylen had suggested, Peter Kharkoff did not concern himself with individuals but devoted his power to action upon mankind in the mass, nevertheless he was not able to escape from the necessities attaching to his own abnormal faculties. Miss Creswell was quite certain that she had never before met anyone who made vehicles of people as he did, vehicles for the reception and dissemination of himself.

And in the night a group of people rose up before her silently, like phantoms full of meaning. In this group were Canon Barrimore, the organist, Imogen, Edie Baynes, Madame Coiret, Martin Heylen. And there was one other, a middle-aged woman with smooth hair and a fresh complexion—herself.

It seemed to Miss Creswell that she lay there quietly in the darkness and looked at this group of human beings, and knew that they were messengers, people who carry news. Presently they began to fade away. That was how she felt it. But then a strange thing happened. As they faded another figure dawned out of the darkness and presently remained alone. And it was the figure of Hugo Dennistone.

But Hugo Dennistone did not know the Jew.

CHAPTER VI

On the following day no telegram or letter came from Imogen. It was her way to be casual. Miss Creswell was certain she would come. The daylight hours passed by. Evening fell. The traveler had not appeared. Miss Creswell was now convinced that Imogen had taken the midday express from Paris and would not be in Geneva till midnight, and, having since the interview with Madame Coiret in the bookshop overcome what had seemed to be an invincible reluctance, she went to the office and engaged a room and a bathroom for her niece.

While she was dining she received a telephone message from Edie Baynes, "Can you pick me up and come with me to the casino tonight?" After a moment's hesitation she decided that she would go. Martin Heylen was not in the dining-room that evening. He had probably started for Bâle. She had nothing to do and she meant to sit up for Imogen. A visit to the casino would fill up the time.

Already she had been with Miss Baynes to the casino on two or three occasions. She did not know exactly why Miss Baynes asked her to go. She didn't dance and Miss Baynes went there to dance. She was—she knew that—totally out of place in the casino at night. Her mere appearance told everyone that. Yet Miss Baynes asked her to go, and she had been, and now she was going again. The place had a queer, ugly fascination for her. In it she was able to take a peep at a life which seemed very strange, very foreign to her, a life that repelled her and that also roused in her curiosity and something else, indefinable by her.

That evening, when she and Miss Baynes were walking to the casino, she said, "Why do you care to have me with you?"

"For company."

"I'm really very much out of place in the casino. I'm sure you can see that."

"Why do you come?"

"I don't quite know."

"And perhaps I don't quite know why I ask you to come." After a silence she added, "What a lot of little things we do without defining our reasons for doing them. And yet I suppose the reasons must always exist. I often feel that my life's like a spider's web, full of tiny, criss-cross threads. There is surely a reason for every one of those threads, and probably something in me secretly knows it. But that knowledge doesn't always rise into my ordinary consciousness. I believe we often feel more ignorant than we really are, though I dare say, if they were asked, most people would declare that we are much more ignorant than we feel ourselves to be. Here we are!" The lights from the casino shone out upon them and the snow.

People were dancing that night in a downstairs room. There were not many dancers. There were seldom many dancers at night in the casino except on special occasions. Miss Creswell and Miss Baynes sat down at a little table and ordered coffee, and then almost immediately, the Swede, Baron Nordstrom, appeared, spoke to them both—Miss Baynes had introduced him to Miss Creswell—and asked Miss Baynes to dance.

He was younger than Miss Baynes, and very good-looking. Miss Creswell wondered whether he cared for her, or whether he danced with her because she danced very well. Although Miss Baynes was not pretty, not fresh, and not very young, she had some seduction. There was something strongly sexual in her, and it was apparent when she danced. Her whole body showed it, her face, the pose of her head, her hands.

Miss Creswell thought Edie Baynes had perhaps even more seduction than Imogen had, though she was sad and had none of Imogen's conquering impertinence.

Close to her were some of the girls of the casino, cocottes who were paid a small weekly wage, in return for which they had to attend at certain fixed hours and to dance with anyone who came up and asked them. They were a strange crew.

One girl was a German, fair, pretty, with stolid blue eyes, and hair such as opera singers wear when they play the part of Marguerite in "Faust." She was sitting, in a gray dress trimmed with white fur, by an amazing creature who looked like a live coal, black and red, with a large round head covered with smooth, oily black hair, in which were stuck several enormous pins like weapons, a copious bust, brown arms, an incipient mustache, several provocative moles, and a voice and laugh like a man's. From time to time she sprang up and danced with one of her paid companions, shaking her broad uncovered back, waggling her nude shoulders, advancing and drawing back her hips. Huge black earrings hung from her large brown ears. She laughed with coarse impropriety. Miss Creswell wondered what such a creature was really like, was like "inside."

There were other girls of various countries, most of them aiming at the improperly fantastic in make-up, manner, dress. All were heavily painted. Most of them wore their hair in tortured confusion. But two of them had heads as smooth as billiard balls, which shone under the lights as they danced. Two professional male dancers roused Miss Creswell's half-pitiful curiosity.

They were both young, between twenty and twenty-eight, both excessively thin, both effeminate-looking, both graceful in a sort of contemptible way. Both too had a manicured look, a smooth, polished, meaningless, scented look. One of them had the face and eyes of a being on the way to consumption, an intensely conscious expression which seemed most marked in the region of the cheekbones: The other, who was taller, with a very definite waist, had surely better health. But he was terribly epicene. A gold bangle caught the light on his left wrist. He was dancing with a fat old lady, crowned with ostrich feathers, and miraculously compressed into a tight-fitting green satin gown. He smiled down on her. Her powdered cheek touched his shoulder. Her large ankles, clothed in flesh-colored silk stockings, wriggled heavily in the fox-trot. She paid him to dance with her.

"What a way for a young man to make money!" thought Miss Creswell, as she listened to the thud of the tamborine, the monotonous banging of the piano, the more poignant music of the strings.

From time to time Edie Baynes came back to her, and sat with her, while Baron Nordstrom went off to another table, where a friend of his was sitting, a stern-looking Danish athlete from Copenhagen. And once the baron danced with the fair-haired German girl, while Edie Baynes watched them intently with her curiously sad eyes. The room was very hot and brilliantly lighted, but when a tango was played the ordinary lights were turned off, and colored lights, deep blue followed by rose-color, bathed the dancers.

When the tango was over Miss Creswell said that she must go back to the hotel as she was expecting her niece, and didn't want to be out when she arrived. Edie Baynes said she would come too. She told the baron that she was going. He was sorry and bade her good night, speaking accurate English in the heavy, accented fashion of the Swedes.

As Miss Creswell and Edie Baynes went out, the latter said, "He's staying because of that little German girl."

Miss Creswell felt rather embarrassed. She didn't know what to say, and murmured something about pitying "those poor girls."

"I don't pity them," said Miss Baynes. "I think they probably enjoy life far more than lots of respectable women do. Those girls have an extraordinary fascination for men, and even for splendid men. Oh, how rotten life is!" There was a desperate sound in her voice. She added, "You asked me why I invite you to go with me to the casino sometimes. I believe it is because you aren't a white nigger."

"A white nigger!"

"Don't you remember? I said once that we were all white niggers. Well, you aren't. D'you know that I'm thirty-five?"

"Are you? I'm between fifty and sixty."

"Yes! But to you I don't believe it matters. But to me——" She broke off. After a moment she went on, "I can't tell you how I dread middle age—I can't tell you. The thought of it haunts me day and night. I'm fading so fast, and there is no stopping it. If only I could have got to know that man, Peter Kharkoff, I think he would have helped me. But what do I matter to him? They say the Sphinx—I've never seen it—looks beyond everything into eternity. I think he's like that. I know he can't see me. Here's my corner. Good night. You aren't afraid to go the rest of the way alone? Then good night again, and forgive me!" She just touched Miss Creswell's hand, and walked away through the snow towards her little flat in a side street.

Miss Creswell stood still for a moment looking after her. A clock began to strike melodiously. The sound came to Miss Creswell from the other side of the river clearly in the still winter night. Stars were shining. There was not a cloud in the sky. The air was intensely cold, almost like the air on high plateaus among the Alps. The clock went on striking. Was it twelve o'clock? Miss Creswell had not realized that they had stayed so late in the casino. Now she hastened on, hoping that she would get to the hotel before Imogen arrived. But just as she reached the end of the rue de Mont Blanc and, before crossing it, glanced up the broad street to make sure that no traffic was approaching, she saw the bright lights of a motor-car coming swiftly towards her. It was the omnibus of the Hotel les Bergues. She stood still. As it passed her she saw Imogen wrapped up in furs sitting in it facing her. Imogen's maid was opposite. It seemed to her that Imogen looked out of the omnibus straight at her. But she was not sure about that. The omnibus swung round to the right. She followed, she had to follow, and saw it draw up in the snow before the hotel. Imogen was just getting out.

"Hullo, Towser!" she called in her nonchalant voice. "Here I am! I say it's damned cold though. What have you been up to at this time of night? I spotted you at the crossing."

"I've been to visit a friend."

"A friend?" The voice was less nonchalant.

"A Miss Baynes who works in the League, and whom I've got to know here. How are you, dear?" They kissed. "Good evening, Harriet."

"Good evening, ma'am."

"How's the hotel?" asked Imogen.

"Very comfortable indeed."

"Got me a room?"

"Of course."

"Not many people here, I suppose, at this time of the year?"

"No; not very many."

"I hope you don't hate my coming like this to pick you up?"

"Why shouldn't you come?" said Miss Creswell gently. She was thinking of Madame Coiret, was pinning her mind on Madame Coiret. "I'm very glad to see you," she added with quiet definiteness. "Now I'll show you your room."

When they were in it and the luggage was brought up Imogen asked the porter with the exhausted eyes whether it was too late to have a drink. He said no, and she ordered whisky, hot water—"boiling, mind"—and sugar. The man went to get these, and Imogen told Harriet just to put out her things for the night and not to unpack.

"Where's your room, Aunt Annie?" she then said. "Is it on this floor?"

"Yes, only three doors off." (She gave the number.)

"I'll come there with you, if I may, while Harriet's messing about. Harriet, come and tell me when my drink arrives, will you?"

"Yes, ma'am."

"Which way? Right or left?"

"This way, dear. They're very nice rooms, aren't they?"

"Rather!" And then Imogen did what Miss Creswell had done when she had arrived in the hotel. She went over to the window, put up her hand, hesitated, then said, "D'you mind if I just have a little squint out into the night?"

"Do, if you like. But they're double windows. The cord's on the right."

"Don't you bother. I'll manage."

When the shutter was up, and she had unlatched both the windows, Imogen stood quite still looking out. Standing behind her Miss Creswell could hear the rushing sound of the Rhone. What was Imogen doing? Miss Creswell believed that she knew. The girl looked very tall, very young, as she stood there. She moved, put up her hands to her head and took off her hat. Then Miss Creswell heard her murmur something as if to herself.

"What did you say, Im?" she asked.

"It's good to be here!" The girl turned round. "I was so sick of London, and Paris seemed worse, though they put me up at the Embassy. Well, I must shut the window, or you'll be frozen."

"You too."

"I like it. The cold gives me a Northern feeling."

"And you like such a feeling?"

"Yes—tonight. There ought to be purity up in the North." Purity! Miss Creswell was astonished. That wasn't a word that came very readily on Imogen's lips as a rule. "Like there is in Hans Andersen's fairy-tales, and in Grieg's song—I forget the name. But it's about being far up in the North, where even the fir trees die away—at least I think so. Ah! There is magic in the North, white magic!"

She drew a deep breath, then slowly closed the windows and let down the shutter. When she turned round Miss Creswell saw that there were tears in her eyes. "And so you don't hate me for coming?" she said.

"No."

"I wonder why. I thought you would."

"I thought so too, but I don't."

"That's good! Come in!" A tap had come on the door.

"Forgive me! It's your door. But it must be Harriet."

It was Harriet, to say that the drink had been brought. "Coming!" said Imogen. Harriet went away. "Well, I must go. Are you tired?"

"No."

"Shall we get into something loose and have a talk?"

"Yes, if you like."

"There are so many things—and as you don't hate me——"

"I'll come to you," said Miss Creswell.

When Imogen had gone Miss Creswell got out of her

dress quickly. She wanted to be quick, lest the kind feeling in
her should change, lest the ugly things should show their heads
before she had time to take some more steps on this new path
she was treading. If she could only get a good way along the
path it would be less easy to pull up. The movement onwards
would surely give an impetus to her nature. The help of
custom would come. She wanted, even ardently, to behave
"like a gentleman" tonight.

When presently she returned to Imogen's room she found her
lying on a small sofa, clad in a remarkable wrapper embroidered with dragon-flies, smoking a cigarette, and sipping her
hot drink. Harriet drew up an armchair for Miss Creswell,
said good night, and went away at once to her room. Evidently
she had been told to make herself scarce.

"Do sit down, Aunt Annie."

Miss Creswell sat down in the armchair, rather wondering
why Imogen had dropped calling her by the familiar name.

"When are we going to St. Moritz?" said Imogen.

"Whenever you like," said Miss Creswell.

"You will really come?"

"Yes," answered Miss Creswell, trying to keep reluctance
out of her voice, "I said I would and of course I will."

"Yes. But your proposition was contingent on my traveling
to St. Moritz via Zurich, wasn't it?"

"You didn't take it like that, did you?"

"No. Because I was malicious. I knew you wanted to
shunt me, and I didn't want to be shunted."

Miss Creswell was silent. She didn't know what to say.

"Do you suppose I really want to go to St. Moritz?" said
Imogen.

"Why not? You've been there before. I thought you
loved the Suvretta House."

"So I did. But the mob! And the Jews! Since the war
St. Moritz is as bad as Brighton."

"Do you still keep up your old hatred for Israel?" said
Miss Creswell.

"I'm afraid of Israel, I'm afraid." She spoke with a peculiar significance. Her eyes were fixed on the aunt.

"I don't think you have it in you to feel fear of anything,"
said Miss Creswell.

"You're wrong. I could feel the peculiar type of fear
which is housed in the imagination."

"What has Israel to do with that?"

"There's power in Israel, terrible power. It's spreading all over the world. It has touched us—you, Aunt Annie, and me. While I have been traveling here I have realized that, the Jewishness of the power that has drawn me here, and you before me."

"Do you realize the Jewishness of another power which once tried to save the world?" said Miss Creswell.

Imogen pulled herself up sharply. She had stretched out her hand towards the tumbler of steaming liquid which stood on a table beside her. Now she drew it back. "Do you mean —surely you don't connect the two powers?" she said.

"I didn't say so."

"But do you?"

"Do I?" said Miss Creswell, speaking as if to herself, solemnly, thoughtfully. "I don't know—yet." She sat very still.

Imogen lay staring at her with concentrated attention. At last, as Miss Creswell said no more, Imogen spoke again, "You have seen him?"

"Yes, once."

"Only once! You spoke to him, of course?"

"No, I didn't." And she said it quietly, without any shame, without any fear of that inextinguishable laughter of which she had thought with a creeping of dread. "No, I didn't. Shall I tell you why?"

"Yes—please do."

And then Miss Creswell unburdened herself to Imogen. She was tremendously frank, not entirely because she wanted to be frank, but partly because she felt that for her just then there was moral salvation in frankness. Imogen listened with deep attention.

When at last Miss Creswell had finished, Imogen said, "You are an old dear!" But she said it quite without flippancy, quite without any of that condescension which youth sometimes shows to age. "I always felt you were," she added, "and tonight you've proved me right. You might so easily have hated me for what I've done, for following you out like this. I'll tell you what I ought to do now."

"What?"

"Take the morning train back to Paris and London!"

Miss Creswell smiled.

"And Hugo?" she said.

"Hugo? What's he to do with it?"

"Don't you ever miss him when you're away from him?"

"Miss old Hugo! But he's practically always there now."

"But when he isn't?"

"Aunt Annie——"

"Why do you call me that?"

"Somehow tonight you don't seem to answer to Towser. Aunt Annie, you've been awfully frank with me. I'll return the insult. Since I've seen Peter Kharkoff Hugo doesn't mean half so much to me as he did, or as I thought he did."

In spite of her warm feeling of Christian charity, which had grown since resolutely she had exercised it, Miss Creswell felt a coldness creep through her when Imogen said that. "I don't quite understand," she said.

"Nor do I. I wish I did. I should feel safer then."

"Safer!" said Miss Creswell. And the cold increased in her.

"Yes. Hugo's in London. When I'm there I know it, and it doesn't much matter. *He's* here. I know it. And it matters tremendously."

"But you surely——" She broke off, then forced herself to go on. "But, Im dear, I can't believe that you—I mean that it's impossible that you——" Again she broke off.

"The question is," said Imogen, in a very clear and definite voice, "whether anything is impossible when it comes to a woman and a man."

"What do you mean by that?"

"Don't ask me. I couldn't explain tonight. I've been traveling all day and I suppose I'm tired. It's one o'clock, you know. Shall we start for St. Moritz tomorrow?"

"So soon?"

"Yes, you and I—both of us, and never come back here? Shall we?" Their eyes met. Imogen said, "We shan't."

Miss Creswell was an excellent sleeper as a rule, but that night she lay awake. Directly after Imogen had made that very definite statement about not going to St. Moritz on the morrow she had shown signs of weariness. Miss Creswell had suspected a little bit of acting on the part of the not unsubtle girl. But she had decided to go at once. The conversation had taken a dangerous turn. It was better to break it off. And she had said good night and gone. She had returned to her room, finished undressing and got into bed.

And then the gallop of thought began.

Two extraordinary things had come up from the depths in the course of that conversation just finished, one out of her depth and one out of Imogen's. Of her revelation—for hadn't it been that?—a revelation to herself and a revelation to Imogen!—she made up her mind that she dared not think. And so she concentrated on Imogen's.

The girl must have meant that the Jew enticed her not merely as a mind but in another, a wholly different way. If she had not meant that, she could not have spoken as she had spoken, could not have forged that link between Hugo and the Jew. Miss Creswell was accustomed to think that some day, in her own good time, Imogen would marry Hugo Dennistone. She had supposed that Imogen loved Hugo "in her own sort of way," not a very romantic way, perhaps, but then the modern way is often not very romantic. She had probably supposed that it was not "in" Imogen to love romantically, passionately, perhaps desperately. Imogen's look, manner, language—full of slang and absurd expressions—had never suggested anything of that kind. Even her intellectual as opposed to her frivolous and sporting side had always seemed to Miss Creswell the least bit hard. There had seemed to be very little softness in Imogen.

But tonight Miss Creswell saw possibilities in her niece which she had not suspected. And they frightened her, as things frighten people who lie wide awake at night, in a sort of morbid nightmarish way. She imagined terrible complications in the future, complications which even at last became blasphemous in her imagination, which made her shudder as she lay in the soft, comfortable bed. What was coming? What was Imogen going to do? What—and that was far more important—was Imogen going to become?

Pure thought—and physical love, the love that cannot help lusting after complete satisfaction! What might not come from the thrust of one towards the other, from the other's reception or rejection of that thrust? But could any man born of woman be utterly free from those moments when thought is submerged in the stream of desire?

"How can I be thinking like this?" said Miss Creswell to herself at this point. She was startled by the thought capacity which seemed violently developing within her. "I must sleep! I *will* sleep!"

But the gallop went on. Was it a gallop to the abyss?

White magic! The tears, the unwonted tears in Imogen's eyes! And that strange reference to the beauty and the fascination of the North, "where even the fir trees die away." How unlike Imogen—at least unlike the Imogen Miss Creswell had thought she knew—that reference had been. Something had surely come to the girl across the cold river under the stars, had come to the girl in the night!

"And my thought, the thought that startled Imogen and startled me?" From whence had that visitant come?

It was past four when at last Miss Creswell fell asleep.

CHAPTER VII

Miss Creswell woke about eight o'clock the next morning. She got up, had her bath and rang for her breakfast. It was brought, and the Journal de Genève with it. She ate and drank slowly, reading the paper. When she had finished, her watch pointed to half past nine.

After a while she rang for the housemaid and asked her to go to the bedroom of Harriet and ask the maid to come to her for a moment. Harriet came, and in answer to a question said that her mistress was still fast asleep.

"Just let me know when she wakes, will you, please, Harriet?"

"Yes, ma'am."

"Perhaps I'll come to sit with her while she has her breakfast."

"Yes, ma'am."

Harriet went out, and Miss Creswell "pottered about," then wrote a couple of letters and did a little more reading. It was nearly a quarter to eleven when there came a light tap on the door.

"She's awake at last," thought Miss Creswell as she answered, "Come in!"

The door opened and a small page boy appeared. *"Une dépêche, madame,"* he said, smiling.

"For me? Thank you." She took the telegram, without looking at the name on it, and as the small boy went out she tore it and began to unfold the paper. While her fingers

were doing this, they felt—that was exactly how it seemed to
Miss Creswell—that what they were doing was dreadful.
Miss Creswell felt that they were trembling, or at any rate
she imagined she did. And then her mind said:

"In this telegram there's some horrible news!"

She stopped, hesitated. It seemed to her imperative that
she should have at least one more moment devoid of the knowledge which that piece of paper was surely going to give her.
Something abominable had happened. The statement of it was
there on that paper. She wanted, needed, one more moment
of ignorance.

But the inevitable can't be avoided, and at last she looked
down on the paper.

> Poor Hugo had frightful accident hunting field neck perhaps
> broken but is alive wants you love: Mother.

"Wants *me!* Hugo wants *me*!"

That was Miss Creswell's first idiotic thought as she looked
at the words. Poor Hugo Dennistone, that splendid man,
had broken his neck. And that was awful. "But why does he
want *me?*" In an instant, however, that folly of the mind
passed away and Miss Creswell was able to see the word
"Mother" with understanding, and to realize that she had
inadvertently opened a telegram from her sister intended for
Imogen.

"Why was it brought to me?" That was the next useless,
unmeaning thought. Then she looked at the paper and saw
the words, "Honble. Imogen Lowrie, c/o Miss Creswell," etc.
A very natural mistake in the bureau. Yes. But it meant
that now she had to go and tell Imogen.

And then Miss Creswell's mind cleared, and she seemed able
to grasp the whole matter of Hugo's tragedy. If really his
neck had been broken he was probably, almost certainly, dead
by now. Hugo Dennistone—dead. She was ashamed of herself for what happened now, but it happened inevitably and
she couldn't help it. The thought of Hugo removed brought
another thought with it. His death, coming at this moment,
seemed to clear a road for Imogen, the road that led towards
the Jew. For Hugo, after all, had meant something to Imogen,
perhaps even much. But how much? Probably Miss Creswell
would soon know about that.

She took up the telegram and went slowly out of her room. In the corridor she saw Harriet. "Harriet!" she called softly.

Harriet turned round. "Yes, ma'am?"

"Is Miss Imogen awake?"

"Yes, ma'am. She has just rung. I am ordering her breakfast. I was just coming to tell you."

"I'll go in and see her."

"Yes, ma'am."

Miss Creswell went to Imogen's door, knocked, and without waiting for an answer went in.

"Hallo, Towser! I slept awfully late. What's the matter? What's that in your hand?"

The girl's face had changed from careless insouciance to fixed intentness.

"Im—there's bad news."

Imogen sat straight up. "The old lady isn't ill?"

"No."

"My father——"

"No."

"Stop! I know! It's Hugo! Hugo's had an accident!" She stretched out her hand.

"Yes."

She took the telegram and read it. "Neck perhaps broken——" she said aloud. She shook her hand. "No, no, no! That's mother—that isn't—no, Hugo hasn't broken his neck. It's just another accident—just another accident!" But she went on staring at the telegram, and her eyes were very wide open. They looked unnaturally large. "It's just another accident, I know that."

"But——"

"I just know it. It may be worse than any of the others. That's possible."

She sat still in the bed for a moment. Then she said, "There's only one thing to do. I shall telegraph to Marfield, Hugo's man, and get the truth from him."

"And if it's what Minnie says?"

"I shall go back to England at once."

Harriet came in just then with Imogen's breakfast.

"I want a telegram form, Harriet, at once."

"Yes, ma'am." Harriet put the breakfast down on a table.

"I expect there's one in the writing table over there. Look in the drawer."

"Yes, ma'am."

"Is there one?"

"Yes, ma'am."

"Just give me the blotting pad, and dip a pen in that ink. I'll write it here."

Harriet came to the bed with the form, the pen and the blotting pad. And Imogen began to write. Meanwhile Miss Creswell stood by the bed marveling at the bizarre unexpectedness of life, but in a dull sort of way. For now she began to feel the force of the shock which had come with the morning. And she saw Hugo in his masculine strength, his tremendously male strength full of almost embarrassing forcefulness. And something in her began to cry out in pity for him as he surely was now.

"That's it," she heard Imogen's voice saying. "Aunt Annie!"

"Yes?"

"This is what I'm sending to Marfield: 'Telegraph to me here exact nature of Captain Dennistone's accident and where he is without delay, will come at once if serious,' and the address and so on. Here, Harriet! Oh—Captain Dennistone's had another accident in the hunting-field."

"I'm very sorry, ma'am."

"Yes . . . it's bad. Have that sent off at once, will you, and pay a reply."

"Yes, ma'am." Harriet went out, looking alarmed.

"A pity Harriet has unpacked," said Imogen, directly the maid had gone out. "I'm sure I shall have to go. I can't let poor old Hugo down if it's really bad. But you know the old lady! She always gets the wrong end of the stick if it's possible. Till the answer from Marfield comes I'm not going to believe it's worse than it's been half a dozen times before." She said the last words with obstinacy. "Now I'm going to eat my breakfast," she added. "Sit down, Aunt Annie, if you're going to stay."

"But perhaps you'd rather I——"

"No, no. Do sit down. We aren't two fools. I'm not going to make a fuss. We must go on as usual till I know."

"How strange if you do have to go!" Miss Creswell could not help saying.

"Won't you be glad? Is that what you mean?"

"How could I be glad of such an awful thing?"

"You might, without wishing to be. You might, even

hating to be. It's no use our thinking, and pretending, that
all our feelings are what people expect them to be. They
aren't. They're often exactly the reverse. Only we don't
care to say so."

"I don't want—I never could want Hugo Dennistone to
suffer and to die. He's a splendid young man. I have always
liked him. I hoped you would marry him. I hope so still."

"Don't get upset, Aunt Annie. I wasn't accusing you——"

"No, of course not. How—what shall we do till the answer
comes?"

"Go on as usual. But I shall make Harriet pack up." And
then she began to talk of other things, deliberately, but with
unusual gravity. Miss Creswell didn't know exactly what,
or how much, she was feeling.

The day passed somehow. There was a constraint between
the two women. In spite of themselves they seemed to be on
terms that were almost formal. They went out for a walk
after lunch, through the town, by the lake. Not a word was
said about Peter Kharkoff. Very little was said about Hugo.
In their suspense they were silent about the important things.
Evening had fallen when a telegram came for Imogen. Miss
Creswell was with her in the hall when a page brought it in.
Without a word Imogen took it and opened it. Miss Creswell
looked away from her while she was reading it.

"It is from Marfield," the girl said. "Here!" And she
gave it to Miss Creswell.

Miss Creswell looked down and read:

> Mr. Hugo's back badly injured is in nursing-home Bentinck
> Street no immediate danger but doctors think crippled for life
> sends his love: David Marfield.

After reading these words Miss Creswell went on looking
down at the telegram. But she no longer saw any words, or
even the paper. Tears prevented her from seeing.

"Poor fellow!" she thought. "Poor fellow! And—sends
his love."

"I'm sorry," she said, when she could speak. "I'm sorry!"

"Of course mother was wrong," said Imogen.

"Wrong?"

"Yes. But it's pretty bad. I can't see Hugo living a cripple's life. I can't see that. And the last time I saw him he
told me not to break my neck on the Cresta."

"Did he?"

"Yes. He said, 'Better keep clear of the Cresta or you may break your neck.' And I said, 'Much you'd care if I did!'"

"Oh—Im!"

"Yes. And now see how it is! We don't know much, do we?"

"No. We know nothing."

Miss Creswell looked at Imogen now for the first time since she had read the telegram. There were no tears in Imogen's eyes. She looked, Miss Creswell thought, much as usual, grave, rather hard even, perhaps—yes, surely rather hard. When she looked the girl got up.

"I shall leave for England tomorrow," she said.

"Not—not tonight?" ventured Miss Creswell. "I would come with you."

"Oh no, Towser. I won't drag you away. I've got Harriet. I shall start by the earliest train in the morning. I'm going to send some telegrams. I will be back in a moment. Shall I find you here?"

"Yes. I'll stay here."

Imogen went away.

"Why doesn't she go tonight?" was Miss Creswell's thought. "If—if a man had sent his love to me *like that* I should have gone. But perhaps there isn't a train. Perhaps she knows there isn't a train. I do hope it's that."

And when Imogen presently came back her aunt couldn't help saying, "Perhaps there isn't a night train."

"A night train?"

"Yes, to Paris. I dare say there isn't."

"I don't know. I haven't asked. I'm going by the first train tomorrow." Miss Creswell said nothing and Imogen added, "Marfield put that there's no immediate danger."

"Yes. I'm thankful for that. But still——"

"It's a question of a few hours only."

"Yes, I know." Miss Creswell was thinking of a crippled man lying on a bed in a nursing-home in London, and wondering whether someone would come, someone to whom he had sent his love.

"I've telegraphed to Marfield to say I'm starting tomorrow. I've telegraphed to Hugo too."

"I'm glad; I'm sure he'll value that, poor fellow."

"I know of course exactly what you're thinking, Aunt Annie."

"But I'm not——"

"Yes. You're thinking that I'm a heartless brute not to start off at once, now, if there's a train. But there's something I mean to do before I start. And it may take a little while."

"What is it?"

"You can't guess?"

"No. It's seven now. The shops will be shut."

"It isn't the shops. No. Directly after dinner, and I want to dine now, I'm going to the rue les Bergues to try to see Peter Kharkoff." As she spoke she got up. Miss Creswell got up too. "Let's keep out of the dining-room. There's a grill-room downstairs. Let's go there and eat something quickly and be off."

"You mean—you want me to come with you!"

"Yes. This isn't a question of trying to cut you out with a man. This is something bigger, more serious than that. I think perhaps I was led here just now, was meant to be here when this awful thing happened."

"But why? What can your being here have to do with poor Hugo Dennistone's accident?"

"Difficult to explain. But I have an intuition that if I see Peter Kharkoff before I leave tomorrow it may somehow help Hugo."

When Imogen said that, Miss Creswell remembered the waking vision she had had on the night before Imogen came, a vision of the carriers of news, of the messengers who had come into contact with the Jew and mysteriously bore witness to him. Of them Hugo Dennistone had been one. She had seen him in the night and had wondered.

Now she felt that perhaps she had had a premonition of that which was to come, which was on the way.

"Will you come with me?" said Imogen.

"I don't know. I must think. I can't tell in a moment."

"Anyhow let us go down and get dinner over. We must eat, I suppose."

They went past the bar, where two Americans were seated before the counter on high stools drinking cocktails, descended a narrow flight of stairs, which was abruptly lit up by a boy at the bottom as they descended, and came into the small, cozy grill-room of the hotel. It was empty.

"Thank God! Nobody here!" said Imogen.

Hearing them, a waiter came in from a room at the back. They went to a table in a corner and ordered the dinner *à prix fixe* which was ready. The waiter brought the soup very soon, and they began to drink it in silence.

Miss Creswell hadn't made up her mind yet whether she would do what Imogen wished, or at any rate had asked, her to do. She had been greatly startled by the proposition. Remembering Madame Coiret's evident reluctance to disturb Peter Kharkoff's life by trying to bring anybody into it, remembering Edie Baynes's desire which had remained ungratified, remembering her own intention in Madame Coiret's book-shop, and her incapacity to carry it out in action when the moment to do so arrived, Miss Creswell was almost frightened at what Imogen meant to do, and didn't know whether she would dare to join in it. Yet she could scarcely bear the thought of letting Imogen see the Jew alone for the second time, while she, deliberately, remained away, in solitude—agonizing because of her own impotence to dare.

"Are you coming, Aunt Annie?" said Imogen at last.

"Do you think we ought to go?" said Miss Creswell. And then she brought forward her doubts. She spoke of Edie Baynes, of Madame Coiret. Finally—she kept this to the last, perhaps from a sense of shame—she told Imogen of her own useless visit to number seven.

"You actually did that!" said Imogen, apparently with surprise.

"Yes; but he didn't answer."

"I shall go tonight. I must go. But if you like we'll visit this Madame Coiret first, and ask her to help us, if she can, to get to him."

"If you do that I will come with you. But if Madame Coiret doesn't wish us to take any further steps I can't do more. And I hope you won't, Im. There are lives it is impious to intrude upon."

"Impious!" Imogen looked across the small table at her aunt, and opened her lips to say more, but remained silent.

When dinner was over she said, "Aunt Annie, you must wait a little while. I have something to do, and I shall want perhaps half an hour to do it in. I'll join you in half an hour, in your room or in the hall, whichever you like."

"I'll be in my room."

"I'll be as quick as I can."

Miss Creswell wondered what Imogen was going to do. It was evidently something that the girl thought important. When presently Imogen came to her aunt's room Miss Creswell saw at once what it had been. All the make-up had been removed from Imogen's face and neck. The blue shadows were gone from beneath her eyes. Her lips were quite pale.

Miss Creswell said nothing about this startling transformation. Nor did Imogen. They went down and set out on foot for the book-shop on the other side of the river.

Miss Creswell knew that Madame Coiret seldom went out in the evening. She was not of those who go to "the pictures," or who love to see French plays on the everlasting subject of adultery. Only a lecture, or a good concert of the Suisse Romande Orchestra conducted by Ansermet, or a pianoforte recital, or a performance of string quartets, could draw her away from her flat after business hours. Miss Creswell had little doubt that they would find her at home. And they did. In answer to a ring the elderly Swiss maid came down the passage of the flat, opened the door and said that Madame Coiret was in. As they stepped in Miss Creswell felt very glad that Imogen had removed all the make-up. Madame Coiret always looked austere. Imogen's usual face would have surely disgusted her. And it would have seemed horribly inappropriate in connection with such an errand as theirs.

They found Madame Coiret alone in a small, simply furnished sitting-room, free of armchairs and sofas, but with a good many books in it, neatly arranged, and a cottage piano, a Bluthner, standing against the wall. Miss Creswell introduced her niece, and Madame Coiret welcomed them civilly and without showing any surprise at their visit.

"I must explain to you why we have come, disturbing you like this," began Miss Creswell, feeling the obligations of English conventionality strong upon her. "My niece knows Mr. Peter Kharkoff."

"Indeed!" said Madame Coiret. She looked with a new intentness at Imogen. "Now I remember that you told me something about this young lady," she added.

"Did she?" interposed Imogen, with her usual complete self-possession. "I followed Mr. Kharkoff at night, when he was in England, caught him up and had a long talk with him. I asked him for his address and he gave it to me—number seven, rue les Bergues. I'm leaving for England tomorrow and I want tremendously to see him tonight."

"Then why do you not go to see him?" asked Madame Coiret in her gently direct way.

"My aunt thought we ought to come and speak to you about it first, and see whether you—I believe you're a friend of Mr. Kharkoff's, aren't you, madame?"

"I know Monsieur Kharkoff," said Madame Coiret. "I don't say he would call me his friend."

"Can you help us to get to him? The fact is I've had terrible news from London. A dear friend of mine, a splendid chap who wanted to marry me, a real man, has had an awful accident."

"I'm very sorry."

"I want to speak to Mr. Kharkoff about it."

"What could he do?" The question came softly. There seemed no sarcasm in it. To Miss Creswell it sounded like a test question.

"I think that man could do more than other men if he would," said Imogen.

"You want him to do something for an individual?" said Madame Coiret. All this conversation was spoken in French. She laid a stress on the word *individu*.

"Won't he? What do you mean, madame?"

Madame Coiret glanced at Miss Creswell. Miss Creswell said nothing. "I cannot tell what Monsieur Kharkoff might choose to do. What he *can* do is a different matter."

"Will you help us?" asked Imogen. And she spoke with unusual earnestness.

"I have no telephone to Monsieur Kharkoff's apartment. He does not use the telephone here. That is, he does not have one in his rooms." She paused, and seemed to be thinking. Then she looked steadily at Imogen again. "You had better go to number seven, rue les Bergues, and ring at Monsieur Kharkoff's door," she then said.

"But my aunt did that once and there was no answer."

"If there is no answer that is final," said Madame Coiret.

"Do you think he will be in?"

"Probably."

"Then if there is no answer that means he won't receive us."

"He has the right to answer or not to answer."

"Yes. I suppose so."

"That is all you can do," said Madame Coiret quietly. "Do not ring more than once."

"Why not?"

"If he is in he will probably hear the first ring. If he is in, and does not hear it—that is possible—please do not ring again. I beg you not to."

Imogen looked at Madame Coiret, and then said, "I promise you, madame, that I won't."

"Thank you."

And then they got up to go. Madame Coiret bade them good-by with a sort of reticent cordiality.

When they were once more outside, Imogen said, "Is she typically Swiss?"

"I don't know. But I shouldn't think she was typically anything."

"No. Nor I. I like her, but I could hardly say why. She's severe. But she's somebody. Very much somebody. And she's strange too, but in a sort of well-ordered way. I believe I can understand why she knows *him.*"

"Yes."

When they were below in the street Miss Creswell looked about for a cab. She could not see one. But in a moment a tram stopped close to them.

"Let's see if we can get near there by tram," said Imogen. She inquired of the conductor. "Yes, we can. We shall have to change once. He'll tell us where. And we can easily walk the rest of the way."

They got in.

Presently they changed, and after a few minutes in the second tram were told by the conductor to get down, follow a street on the left and then turn to the right.

"Et alors vous serez dans la rue les Bergues, madame."

"Merci, monsieur."

They got out. The bell sounded. The pale-blue car, brightly lit up and clean, glided away into the night.

"We go to the left and then turn to the right," said Miss Creswell.

"Yes," said Imogen in a low voice.

As they walked down the deserted road—it was rather a road than a street—Miss Creswell said:

"Im!"

"Yes?"

"I wish you would tell me what it is you think Mr. Kharkoff could do for poor Captain Dennistone. You surely don't suppose that he has some unusual medical knowledge, or that——"

"Medical knowledge! I'm not thinking about Hugo's *body!*"

"Then——"

"Aunt Annie, you know Hugo, though not very well. Tell me this—have you ever seen a more bodily man than Hugo? Have you ever met a man who lived more in the body, and through the body, than he did?"

"I dare say he did. I suppose he did." She remembered having felt a certain strange uneasiness at the maleness of Hugo, at his almost overwhelming masculinity. "Yes, I think you are right," she added.

"Imagine such a man deprived—for I suppose it comes to that when a man is completely crippled by an accident to the spine, and I feel no doubt now that Hugo has injured his spine irreparably—imagine such a man deprived of the life of the body! You know what I mean, the real life of the body. Imagine that! What's he going to fall back upon? How's he going to get along? A man who never opens a book, whose whole instinct it was to be in movement, and out of doors whenever possible! Imagine——" She broke off, was silent for a moment, and then said, in a different voice, "Peter Kharkoff might help Hugo in the new way of life I suppose he'll have to walk in. God, Towser, what a lot of help he'll need! Here we go to the right."

"Yes, dear."

They turned into the rue les Bergues and walked on without speaking till they got to number seven. Here they both stopped on the path in front of the small iron gate.

"This is it."

"Which floor does he live on?"

"The top floor."

"There's a light—look!"

"Yes; he must be in."

But still for a moment longer they stood where they were, and Imogen said in a low voice, "What do you think Madame Coiret meant by telling us not to ring more than once?"

"I don't feel sure."

"She said that probably he would hear the first ring, but that if he didn't hear it we must not ring again. Don't you remember? She even said, 'I beg you not to.'"

"Yes. And we must not do it."

"Perhaps she thinks—perhaps he——" She stopped and looked up at the light. As she looked it moved upwards, sideways, and then disappeared. "It's a lamp, and someone has lifted it and carried it out of the room it was in," said Imogen.

"Come, dear—let us go up—if you are going."

"We are going." Imogen opened the iron gate and they walked up the garden path.

"Just push the door!" said Miss Creswell.

Imogen obeyed. The door yielded, and they found themselves in the bare lobby, which was lit by a small electric lamp. The staircase was also faintly lit with a sparing use of electricity. They began to go up it. When they reached the first floor, Imogen said:

"I can't help my promise, Aunt Annie. If he doesn't answer at the first ring, I shall have to ring again. Now I know he's in I can't go away without seeing him."

"But it may not be he who moved the lamp. It might be someone else, a friend, or a servant."

"I'm positive it was he."

"In any case I don't think we ought to——" Her voice died away. They had reached a turn of the stairs, and could see part of the top landing of the house by looking upwards. The light was brighter there than on the staircase, and Miss Creswell had the feeling that to the habitual illumination of the landing at night some light had been added. She was right. When they mounted to the landing Peter Kharkoff's door was wide open, and he was standing just outside it holding a strongly glowing lamp in his hand, and looking towards them.

CHAPTER VIII

IMOGEN went straight up to him and held out her hand. "Were you expecting us then?" she said.

He took her hand. "You are the girl who walked with me in Drearney—changed a little." His eyes were fixed on her.

Imogen flushed.

"Yes, slightly. This is my aunt, Annie Creswell." Somehow she couldn't put the prefix "Miss" before the name.

The Jew turned his large veiled eyes to Miss Creswell. "I saw you in Drearney too. I was standing beside you. But we didn't speak in words, didn't say any words to each other."

"No."

He took her hand, too, slowly, with an air almost of being unconscious that he did so. He was holding the lamp all the time in his left hand. Miss Creswell noticed that he was dressed in a loose suit, evidently old but scrupulously clean, of dark-brown cloth. His very thick hair, which rose up in front above his low broad forehead to an unusual height, was parted at the left side. He had on a soft shirt with a soft, low, white collar, and a small spotted blue and white bow tie. He was wearing dark slippers. Everything about him was neat and simple. There was no dirt, no slovenliness, no disorder. But there was nothing, not a touch, that suggested fashion.

Although he had spoken to them with great kindness, and was now looking at them, Miss Creswell had very strongly the feeling that they, and their coming unexpectedly in the night, had caused in him absolutely no emotion. Although she felt, or believed she felt, a tremendous influence pouring out of him like a great invisible, inaudible stream, she had a sensation that he was far away from her, remote from her, working in the distance. And the distance was vast.

"May we come in?" asked Imogen.

"Yes, please," he answered.

And again Miss Creswell had the conviction that all this caused in him no emotion. There was, of course, no reason why it should cause in him strong emotion. But she seemed aware that he was quite without the little, and surely natural, emotions of surprise, wonder, and instinctive demand, which such a visit as theirs, at such a time, and with no reason given, would be likely to call up in any ordinary man.

He held the lamp a little higher, and moved to one side to let them go in. Miss Creswell went in first. Imogen followed her.

As Miss Creswell stood in a long broad passage, or corridor, lit only by the Jew's lamp from behind, she heard the door shut. And she thought, "Actually I am in his home, where he lives, where he works and thinks." And it was to her a tremendous thought, and the greatest part of it was the last.

There was no carpet in the corridor. She stood on scrubbed bare boards. The whole of the wall on her left was covered with plain book-shelves of wood that looked like unpainted deal, and these book-shelves were all filled with books, either poorly bound, or in paper covers. She saw at once that there were no handsome bindings. A small thin ladder stood against the book-shelves so that the top books could be got at.

She stood still, with Imogen by her, and Peter Kharkoff, always carrying the lamp, passed them slowly (he had a slow walk, that looked heavy but that was very quiet) and opened a door just beyond them on the right. "Please come in here."

They obeyed, and came into a small room, lined, like the wall of the corridor, with books on plain shelves of unpainted wood, and opening on both sides into other rooms full of books. In the room, in the middle of the floor, there was a large, plain table, like a writing table. But there was absolutely nothing on it except an hour-glass with its moving sand. Before it stood a large chair with a worn leather cushion. Against the book-shelves, just not touching them, stood formally three cheap straight chairs. There was no carpet on the floor which was of clean yellowish-white boards. There were no window curtains. But there was a thin white blind drawn over the window. There were no ornaments, there were no superfluities of any kind in this room. It was well warmed, and the silence in it seemed to Miss Creswell to be unusually intense, like silence living, not silence dead. She told herself, however, that her imagination made her feel the silence like that, and that of course it was merely the perfectly ordinary stillness prevailing in a solidly built Swiss house, standing detached in a suburban road unfrequented by traffic in the night.

"It's very quiet here!" Imogen had spoken, in a withdrawn voice.

The Jew set down the lamp on the table, and went to fetch out from the wall two of the small chairs. "Won't you please sit there?" he said, to Miss Creswell, pointing with his large, oddly natural-looking hand to the big chair.

"Oh—but it's yours. I'm sure you use it."

"I hope you will take it."

She sat down in it at once with the big table between her and her two companions, who sat down on the two small chairs.

And then something extraordinary happened, something very simple, and yet so unusual as to be extraordinary. There was a prolonged silence, and it seemed perfectly natural and inevitable. Miss Creswell felt absolutely no awkwardness in it, no sense that she, or that somebody, ought to be talking, as invariably happens if a silence falls on a social occasion between people who are together for the purpose obviously of speaking, of exchanging words which are supposed to convey thoughts of some kind. Miss Creswell found herself sitting quite still, with no desire to speak or to move, yet with no uneasy sensation such as sometimes overcomes a person who is being hypnotized, or who is endeavoring self-consciously to make the mind blank and to relax all the muscles of the body.

Looking across the broad table, past the shining hour-glass (Peter Kharkoff had set down the lamp on the table beside it.) she saw her niece in an attitude of peaceful repose, looking down. What Miss Creswell thought of as "the modern look" had gone from Imogen's face, which looked strangely simple, young, even almost childlike. And though very grave it was not sad. The absence of paint, cream, powder, naturally altered the face. But the greatest alteration was in the expression. And Miss Creswell remembered the girl's remarks about jazz when they were walking to the cathedral in Drearney, and that terrible description of hers, "We products of catastrophe." And then she had said, "We want jazz. Jazz stamps on the under things. 'Down, down, you devils—down!' That's what jazz says." Where was the Imogen who had said that now? Where was the Imogen of even half an hour ago? Gone surely! And then Miss Creswell looked away from Imogen to the Jew.

A big man sitting on a small straight chair usually looks awkward or uncomfortable. Peter Kharkoff looked neither. He was sitting upright with his hands resting on his legs just above the knees. And when Miss Creswell glanced at him she met his large eyes. They were not widely opened, not staring. Like his hands they looked wonderfully natural. Quietly they looked at her eyes, not into her eyes. And she felt, "Imogen was right to come. We shall not go away from here empty handed. Something will be given to us, or we shall get something here that we shall surely be thankful for."

Indeed were not they getting it already? She felt strangely, marvelously serene, as if the mind, perhaps even the soul, like the body, were resting quietly and completely. And the strangeness of the feeling made her understand how restless, how tormented, the mind and soul often are. This mind and soul repose was to her like a new experience.

Imogen had said that jazz stamps on the under things, driving the devils down to the lowest place of their habitation. And when she had said that, she had implied that the under things were of necessity ugly, even horrible, in some sad and lamentable way. But Miss Creswell seemed now to be aware that in human beings, certainly in herself and, judging by Imogen's face, in Imogen also, there were under things which were not ugly and horrible, under things perhaps even beautiful and holy, but which lay usually neglected in the dark. And it seemed to her that Peter Kharkoff had the power to release these beautiful and holy under things, and that he was using that power now. With him certainly she felt small, because she recognized in him powers which she could not even comprehend, and certainly could never aspire to, but she also felt that she was greater than she had suspected.

How long the silence in that little room lasted she did not know. It was broken at last by the Jew. He moved, raised his hand a little and then said, in the voice that was deeper and more powerful even than Canon Barrimore's:

"Tell me—won't you?" As he spoke he looked at Imogen.

Then she moved. She looked across the table at her aunt, seemed to hesitate, and then said, "There's a man in England. He loves me. He's a very physical man——" She stopped, and looked at the walls covered to the ceiling with books. "Perhaps you can hardly believe that there are men, so-called educated men—well"—the voice sounded suddenly apologetic—"gentlemen—that's our name for them in England, or it used to be—who care nothing for books, never open a book, much less read a book through. But there are. Lots of men are like that. He is—this man who's very fond of me. He's a man who has always lived for the body, I think. I think—of course I can't be absolutely sure, but I think he has always felt himself more as a body than as anything else, than as a mind or a soul."

The word "soul," used by herself in connection with Hugo, brought a very faint smile on her lips.

"Of course we can't help thinking, whether we want to think or not, but I believe, if it's possible"—she seemed asking a question just then—"that Hugo, the man I'm speaking about that is, that he has always felt much more keenly than he has thought. The body's been his god and not the mind."

Again she looked round at the books and then back to the Jew.

"But now suddenly he's left alone—that's how it seems to me —with his mind and—and soul, I suppose. And, as far as I know, he's got to be practically alone with them for as long as he lives. He's had a terrible accident out hunting—riding after hounds and a fox—and they say he'll be a cripple for life, have a body that's useless, in his sense of the word, for the rest of his life. What's he going to do?"

She stopped for an instant, then went on.

"I can't see him living as a cripple. And yet he may have to live. I can't see him always lying down—being—being forced to be still. Some men—yes! But not him! He's really always seemed to me the most physical man I've ever known, tremendously physical. One has felt him always, at every moment, as a wonderful body living gloriously. And now it's all over. It's suddenly all come to an end forever—I believe. And I can't see how he's to face it, to endure it. Can you?"

She said the last words as simply as a child, Miss Creswell thought. But then she added, "But of course you have never seen him."

"I have seen others like him," said Peter Kharkoff, "so far as one human being can be like another."

"Then—what can such a man do when all he cares for comes suddenly to an end, when everything's at an end for him?"

"You talk of the end. But I can see it as the beginning."

"I know what you mean. I'm pretty physical myself, but I care for the things of the mind too. I care for beauty. I care for art. I almost worship brains secretly." She glanced at her aunt, and went on. "But he's never cared about things of that kind. I can just imagine—barely—that such a horror might be a sort of beginning for me. But not for him!"

"For him just as much as for you or for anyone," said Peter Kharkoff.

"I don't see how."

"Perhaps you will come to see. What are you going to do?"

"About him?"

"What are you going to do?"

"Well, just for the time I can't see far ahead. Perhaps you can. I am sure you can. But I can't. I am going back to London early tomorrow. He's in London in a nursing-home. I'm going to him. Of course I shall try to help him. Not that I can—really. But I'll do my best. I can't do less than that. He's been very fond of me. He's not been a faithful man in the body, but he's been very fond of me."

Peter Kharkoff stretched out his hand slowly towards the table and turned the hour-glass. When he did that Miss Creswell felt the irresistible onward movement of life as she had never felt it before.

"You are going to him," he then said, with his heavy, curious accent, not at all pretty but somehow powerful. "Are you going to stay with him?"

"Stay with him?"

Imogen looked startled.

"I don't know what's going to happen. I can't know yet."

"Can't you?"

Peter Kharkoff was looking at her steadily.

"I don't know. I don't—honestly!" she said.

And there was a sort of heat, a sort of anger even, of the anger that comes from rebellion, in the reiteration.

"I must have time to know."

"Time!"

He looked towards the hour-glass, and then it seemed to Miss Creswell that this man who measured time really took very little heed of it.

"But such knowledge is in there." He touched himself. "Folded up in us, part of us. We know ourselves as nobody knows or can know us. When a man says of another, 'I know him better than he knows himself,' it is never true. It cannot be true."

"I'm not sure that I agree with you," said Imogen.

And when she heard the girl say that, Miss Creswell felt for a moment indignant, as if an outrage had been committed upon the Jew. Was Imogen going to dare to pit her opinion against his knowledge? Could such a thing be possible?

"I'm not sure," Imogen added, "that you don't know me much better than I know myself. But I've never met anyone else that I could think that of. You must have trained your mind as surely no other man has trained his."

Peter Kharkoff said nothing. After a moment Imogen said:

"I shall go back tomorrow, and try to be of some use, of some help. But I know that"—she stopped, hesitated, then went on steadily, almost with hardness—"I know that I could never sacrifice my life, all my life, for another. I couldn't offer up my life as a sacrifice to another. If that's what you meant just now? And I think perhaps it was. I'm too fond of life for that. I'm young. I must live. I mean to live. But all the same I want to help Hugo, and I shall try to. It won't be much use, but it will be a little use. I know that."

All the calm and all the look of a child had gone out of her face. And her manner had changed too, though not so markedly. It was more like the manner of the usual Imogen than it had been. There was a touch of self-assertion in it, a touch of strong, though girlish, pride, even of petulance. She looked at Peter Kharkoff, and Miss Creswell thought there was some hostility in her eyes.

"I don't believe in complete self-sacrifice," she went on. "I think—I think there's something abject in it even."

"Do you?"

"Yes."

"Possibly you will not always think so."

"I'm quite sure I shall. One is put here to live, not to give up everything that means life."

"Tremendous changes are possible in the mind, in the soul. Who knows when they will come, where they will lead to? When people talk of change they mean moving from one place to another, as you have come from London to Geneva, as I have come to Geneva from America. But is that change of any importance? Do you think *you* are fixed, that *you* are not going to change? I don't."

"I might change, of course. But not so much as that."

"You are afraid of changing so much as that."

And when he said that Imogen knew that it was true. The idea that possibly, at some future time, through the operation of some obscure influence within her, she might become utterly unselfish, filled her with dread.

"Why are you afraid?" asked Peter Kharkoff.

"But I'm not. I'm not afraid of anything," said Imogen defiantly. "You don't understand me. But why should you? You don't really know me."

Peter Kharkoff attempted no denial of this assertion. Miss Creswell realized that he had none of the pride of intellect which is almost always to be found in exceptional men. Indeed she believed that he had no pride at all. He seemed to be outside, entirely outside, of all the ordinary pettinesses which afflict humanity. She had been angry—for him. But now she felt almost sure that he was incapable of anger as, perhaps— she did not know—he was incapable of love. And of suffering? She looked across the big table at him steadily and wondered about that. His face was very grave, even profoundly grave, but his gravity seemed to her to be the gravity of wisdom rather than of melancholy or active sadness. And again she felt his remoteness. Where was his mind at this moment? Part of it was with them, perhaps, with Imogen and herself, but only a very small part. And where was the rest? Again she was attacked by an intense desire to be in his mind, to be part of it so that she might be able fully to understand it. As she looked at him he said:

"If you cannot know fear you are beyond all other human creatures."

When he said that Imogen's face was flooded with red.

"I can only say that up till now I don't think I've ever been really frightened of anything," she said in a voice that had lost its assurance.

"You are not afraid of going back tomorrow to London to see that friend of yours?" asked Peter Kharkoff. "You have not even the fear of deep pity?"

Imogen stared at him as he said that, continued staring at him after he had said it.

"You are not afraid of confronting his mind and soul in the dust and the ruins of all he thought of as life?"

Again Peter Kharkoff was silent, and Imogen did not speak, but only sat very still looking at him.

"Have you ever seen despair, what is called despair, in a human being who cares for you? Have you no fear of seeing that?"

"I don't know. I haven't had time to think into all that yet."

"You say you are completely fearless. But you are only beginning life. How can you know such a thing? Do you believe that you really know what life is?"

"I think I know it as well as any girl of my age can know it, and far better than most girls of my age do."

Again Miss Creswell noted the defiance in Imogen. There

was surely hostility in her against the Jew. He had no sort of hostility to her. Probably he was incapable of hostility. Miss Creswell believed so. But Imogen's strongly assertive nature, which had seemed just at first utterly subdued by the personality of this strange man, was now evidently rising, or trying to rise, in revolt against him, was trying to fight his influence. And how useless that was! Miss Creswell longed to tell Imogen of the uselessness of her revolt, but she was held in silence.

"There are so many different sides of life," Imogen said. "I dare say I know some that you don't know. My aunt"—she glanced at Miss Creswell—"has lived much longer than I have, but about certain sides of life I think I know much more than she does. Don't I, Aunt Annie?"

Miss Creswell started. She had not expected to be addressed. All this time, quite naturally, she had been left out of this strange conversation. Now she was appealed to.

"Perhaps there is a way of seeing life as a whole," she said seriously. "Not in little bits."

She looked at the Jew. She felt that he was able to see life as a whole. And Imogen's rebellion and attempted explanation of that rebellion seemed to her futile and ridiculous.

"How can any mere human being see life as a whole?" said Imogen petulantly. "Even the greatest philosophers haven't been able to do that. In all the history of the world I can only think of one whose recorded sayings give me the impression that he saw life whole, in the round as it were, and understood it completely."

"Who was that?" asked the Jew in his deep, heavy voice, that could be soft, and could surely never be harsh.

Imogen looked at him, but she did not answer him. Suddenly restlessness came to her. She moved, looked across at Miss Creswell. And Miss Creswell saw in her eyes, which looked strange, scarcely like Imogen's eyes without the painted shadows beneath them, an appeal, a definite appeal.

"I think we ought to go," Miss Creswell said, suddenly recalled to formality, to a sense of the conventionalities, which they had broken through completely by coming to this man uninvited. "We mustn't take up too much of your time."

She looked at the sand slipping downward in the hour-glass.

"You have been very kind to receive us, very kind indeed. But we mustn't presume upon——"

"Don't, Aunt Annie!" interrupted Imogen almost savagely at this point. "It wasn't that I meant!"

"Im, please! I don't know what——"

But Imogen turned away from her to the Jew. She had pulled her little chair close to the table. Now she leaned an arm on it. Her body was turned sideways. Miss Creswell saw her in profile, bathed in the strong light from the well-trimmed lamp, light softer, more mellow, even in its brightness, than that given by electricity.

"We've never explained why we've come here tonight, and you've never asked us," she said. "It's because of something in you, something extraordinary. We both felt it at Drearney, and so did others. But I don't want to speak of them. We did. It drew me to you that night after the service. It brought my aunt across the sea here. You didn't want us. But something in us, or we, perhaps the whole of us, wanted you. I don't know why. I followed my aunt. I felt that I had to. Now, tomorrow, I've got to go away. I ought to have gone tonight. That man wants me. But I felt I couldn't go away without seeing you. And I pretended to myself that I wanted to see you tonight because of him—the man who is fond of me. It may have been partly that. I think it certainly was. I had a feeling that he'll need some peculiar help in the future, help quite out of, quite beyond the ordinary, and that only you could give it. I feel that still—much more now—here. But I dare say I was selfish in staying on tonight, in coming here. I expect I was. However, we'll drop that—I mean my selfishness, if it was there. And I'll just ask you one thing, and then we'll go. If the man I am going to is doomed to lie a cripple for the rest of his existence, and if he goes to pieces under his doom, can't face what he's got to face —oh, I know that's a contradiction, but it's just what I mean, and I must put it like that!—will you help him if I ask you to? Will you come to his rescue?"

She stretched out a hand as if she were going to touch Peter Kharkoff, but she didn't touch him. She paused, then drew her hand back. He sat still, as if considering. Miss Creswell thought he was, perhaps, going to refuse Imogen's request. Again she felt that the silence in this small room lined with books was an unusual silence, a silence full of something, not emptied. At last he said:

"If *you* help him I will help him."

"If I—" said Imogen.

"If *you* help him you can come to me for any help I can give. But you must prepare the way for me."

And then they were all three on their feet. Miss Creswell did not know who had given the signal for that simultaneous rising up. The last words of the Jew had had an absolutely final sound as he spoke them. There was no more for the two women to do in that room now, and they must go, must leave the Jew to his life in the night. That she felt, that she knew. And perhaps Imogen had the same knowledge and it had brought her to her feet. Or perhaps—but there were things Miss Creswell, not being mentally audacious, dared not contain in her mind. Peter Kharkoff lifted up the lamp. They all passed out into the book-lined corridor.

"What are all those books?" thought Miss Creswell. "Is 'Sérénité' among them?"

The outer door stood open. The landing, faintly lit, was before them, the dingy staircase—the outer world. Good-bys were said—she supposed. But there were no hand-clasps this time. She began to descend the staircase. Imogen was behind her. She heard the girl's high-heeled shoes on the stone steps. She looked back to see the last of the Jew.

But the lamp was gone, and the door was shut.

She went on slowly down the stairs, always hearing behind her the tap, tap of Imogen's high heels. And they suggested to her, by the light sound they made, a return towards the frivolities and the artificialities of life.

At the bottom of the staircase she stopped. Imogen came up with her, and they went together to the big front door of the building. Imogen pulled at it. But the door had evidently been shut for the night. It did not yield to her touch, and when they examined it they found that the latch had been let down. Imogen pulled the latch back. The door opened and they passed out into the cold winter night, and shut the door behind them.

As they walked down the path to the iron gate Miss Creswell said, "D'you see that wooden building with the plane trees by it? That must be the place where he works, I think."

Without being aware of it, quite naturally, she said the words in a low, unusual voice, rather like the voice of a reverent worshiper. To her great surprise Imogen answered with intense exasperation:

"And it's very ugly! All this is ugly: the road, the house, the garden, if you can call it a garden! It's all ugly, un-esthetic, repellent! No one who cared for beauty could possibly live here for five minutes."

They had passed beyond the iron gate now, and were out on the narrow path which flanked the road. A thaw was just setting in. The air was still very cold, but with the peculiar raw coldness which is characteristic not of frost, but of thaw. The snow was degenerating. Dark patches showed in it. In the gutters there was already water, and water dripped surreptitiously from the trees. Mist hung in the air, and showed round the lit lamps here and there, like a frail garment drooping from some invisible support. In the stillness the only sound they could hear was the faint drip, drip from the trees.

"Could anything be more beastly, more beastly in an absolutely ordinary, dull, suburban way than this?" continued Imogen, standing still. "I ask myself, how can anyone live in such a road as this? Such an existence must be the negation of what I call life."

She looked up at the house they had just left, and so did Miss Creswell.

"And as to that house——"

She stopped. While they looked, they both saw on the top story a light move sideways, descend, remain stationary.

"It's his lamp!" said Miss Creswell, still in the hushed voice. Imogen shot an almost vicious glance at her.

"Oh, Aunt Annie!" she exclaimed, "for God's sake don't let us be a couple of abject fools! If there's one thing I hate more than another it's the worshiping woman. Every callow curate has his fatuous worshipers, every vicar, every bishop, every known man, be he writer, painter, pianist, politician, or merely one of the Rudins of the world, a talking windbag. And such women degrade themselves and degrade the men they worship. No man, I don't care who he is, is worthy of being worshiped. I know them all too well."

"He isn't like them," said Miss Creswell, with a totally unusual fierceness.

"All men are like them—all, all, all! Come along! I shall catch cold if I stand here any longer."

She started off down the road, turning away from the house where the Jew lived with a sort of angry resolution. Miss Creswell kept beside her.

"Im dear, I can't think why you——"

"No, of course not! Does anyone ever know why? That's the curse of life."

"But what has happened to make you so angry?"

"I'm not angry. But why should I be ordered by a stranger to play the part of a modern St. John the Baptist? Can you tell me that, Towser?"

"St. John the Baptist? What d'you mean? Please don't be blasphemous."

"Blasphemous! What is blasphemy? I'm certain you can't define it. Why is it blasphemy to allude to a well-known historical character?"

"But the way you said it! Besides I don't understand what you mean."

"Didn't I ask him to help Hugo, and didn't he make it a condition that I was to prepare the way for his coming to help Hugo? Now do you understand my allusion?"

"I think it's a very far-fetched comparison. Besides if you pretend that what Mr. Kharkoff suggested——"

"Suggested! He made it a condition."

"Well then—laid down, if you prefer it so, puts you into a position—a situation akin to that of—but I can't talk about it. It's too—it isn't right to talk in such a way."

"But I want to know what you mean. Please go on! I must know."

"I was only going to say that, as we all know, St. John the Baptist was sent to prepare the way of the Lord."

"Well? What then?"

"What then? Why, Im, you must see what the implication is!"

"Tell me what it is!"

"No. I can't. I don't wish to talk about it. But I don't think—we turn here. I wonder whether we shall soon find a tram."

"Let's walk all the way back. I detest trams: blue, shining monstrosities full of Swiss humbugs."

"I can't think what has come to you, Im. I've never seen you like this before."

"Do you mind walking?"

"No. What is the matter?"

Imogen walked on for two or three minutes without making any reply. Then she said:

"Towser, I'm sure it is a mistake in life ever to go to anyone begging for favors. To do that puts you at once in an inferior position. And it gives the person you go to a feeling of tyranny. The consequence of that is that you are bound to suffer in your pride even if you are accorded the favor you go to ask for. Human beings aren't, can't be, whole-heartedly generous. There's always some condition attached to the granting of a favor, either tacitly or blatantly. That's what has happened tonight. I hate myself for what I have done tonight. I ought never to have done it. I don't really know what drove me to do it. That I should go to a Jew to ask a favor, and on Hugo's behalf too! That makes the thing so ironic. Hugo hates Jews. Even in London, where they swarm as the sands of the sea, he has nothing to do with them. And then I go to a Jew about Hugo! And the Jew makes conditions. It's revolting!"

"I don't agree with you. I see nothing revolting in it."

"No. But you didn't ask any favor. You just sat there in absolute silence. You were simply a spectator while I was the fool. Is this the way?"

"Yes, I think so."

"They say lookers-on see most of the game. Do you mean to tell me that you didn't grasp what was happening?"

"Of course I did. And I thought it was very beautiful."

"Beautiful! Why?"

But Miss Creswell couldn't answer that impatient question with swiftness. She was unable to express concisely the feeling she had had during the long preliminary silence which had been the preface to the conversation between Imogen and the Jew. It seemed to her that she knew why there had been beauty in what had happened in the little bare room, but that it was impossible to state her knowledge. And at last she was only able to say:

"I can't exactly say why. But I felt that he had the power to—to—to bring out——"

"Bring out what?"

"It's very difficult to explain, especially as you are in this rebellious mood, dear."

"Rebellious! And why shouldn't I rebel against attempted tyranny?"

"Tyranny! I can't see tyranny. I can't see it as you do."

"Then you can't see it as it was. What happened was this.

Peter Kharkoff was trying all the time to wring a promise out of me."

"What promise?"

"A promise that I would dedicate my life to poor Hugo, that if his life—Hugo's—is destined to be a martyrdom I would link my life to that martyrdom, share it, sink myself into it, give up my life voluntarily because poor Hugo has been forced by this awful accident to resign his life, all the life that was real to him. I know it sounds dreadful, cruel perhaps, to talk as I am talking. I dare say you think I'm a heartless beast. I'm not. But I do resent this extraordinary attempt on the part of a stranger to—to drive me forcibly into sacrifice, without knowing even whether I have in me the great reason for sacrifice, the woman's sufficient, all sufficient reason."

"You mean——"

"Of course I do! Of course I do!"

She walked on swiftly. They were now coming into the more frequented part of the city, were out of the dreary silence, which had been broken only by the sound of water dripping to the sodden ground from the leafless trees now losing their covering of snow. Tram bells sounded occasionally. Now and then strangers passed by. There were lighted houses about them. But Imogen seemed quite unaffected by changing conditions. It was obvious that she was not living through the eyes, but was led captive by the ruling mind within her.

"Towser, I know you're condemning me all this time," she went on. "But I can't help it. I'm in the mood to be brutally frank tonight. I'm fond, very fond of Hugo. I'm horrified at what has happened to him. I feel sick inside when I think of it. I told—I said tonight that I wasn't afraid of anything. It wasn't true. I am. I'm afraid of seeing Hugo as I shall see him in not many hours. I dread that unspeakably. I long to help him, to comfort him somehow. And I told you—or I told him, Peter Kharkoff, was it? I'm getting confused by all this! I said I knew I could be of some help to Hugo. But now I don't believe I can. For I don't love Hugo, not really. It's no use pretending. I don't, I don't. I want to even, because I pity him so. But it's no use. I don't love him. And the awful thing is that I might perhaps have loved him eventually—in a way, if there are different ways of love—if this hadn't happened, if his splendid body, and all it meant of activity, and strength, and glory hadn't been

wrecked, as it must have been wrecked. But I couldn't love
Hugo wrecked, shattered, helpless. I couldn't, because his
mind never meant much to me. I've always cared for Hugo
as a body, a conquering body. And that's all gone forever."

"But perhaps it hasn't. Perhaps——"

"I know it has, and *he* knows it has."

"How can he know such a thing?"

"Anyhow it is so, it is so. I feel it in every fiber of my
being. Besides the telegram was explicit enough—'think
crippled for life.' The doctors would never have said that if
there were the slightest chance for Hugo. No. I feel there
is no hope of anything like recovery."

"Well, dear, all you can do is to help Hugo as much as you
can. No one will expect you to——"

"I don't care what people expect. I don't bother about
people's opinions. I never have. That's why they bother
about mine."

"Then," Miss Creswell could not help saying, "why are
you so upset by what has happened tonight?"

"Because I feel I have put myself in a false position. Because I humbled myself to a Jew. And—and you see how
he took advantage of it."

"I don't agree with you at all," said Miss Creswell with
sudden heat.

"And the worst of it was he didn't care. In spite of his
apparent gentleness and kindness there's something absolutely
inhuman about that man. Didn't you feel it?"

"Inhuman? In what way?"

"Perhaps in every way. Didn't you feel it?"

"He's absolutely unusual of course."

"Yes. And why is he unusual? What is it makes him
unusual?"

"I suppose his great mental power."

"It isn't only that. I know lots of brilliantly clever and
deeply learned men. But not one of them has the peculiar
effect on me he has. And tonight I think I know why that is."

"Why?"

"Because of his enormous indifference, Towser."

When Imogen said that, her voice changed. It had been
quivering with excitement and passion. Now it sounded grim
and hopeless. Miss Creswell said nothing.

"Didn't you notice it? Didn't you feel it?"

"I think I know what you mean."

"It's almost like the indifference of nature. I've never felt anything like it before in either man or woman. Oh, how I resent it—and yet——"

"Yes? What?"

"And yet it draws me. There's a sort of horrible fascination in it."

When Imogen said that, Miss Creswell thoroughly understood something. She had thought of it, she had suspected it before. Now she just simply knew it. And she was invaded by a dreadful uneasiness. There was no jealousy in it. She had passed beyond that ugly condition. She could now look back on her feelings in Drearney with a sense of wonder. But then she had never spoken to the Jew, had never sat with him, had never fully felt his atmosphere. His force she had felt, but not the exact quality of it, the quality she had been conscious of tonight. Tonight she had felt that quality, and it had banished from her the ugly sensation of acute jealousy which had caused her so much pain on that night in Drearney, so much pain ever since that night. What had just happened in Peter Kharkoff's flat proved that to her absolutely. For she had been able to sit unnoticed in the shade while Imogen and he had talked together with as much freedom and indifference apparently as if she had not been there. (Until Imogen had needed something from her!) Yes, she had sat there absorbed in attention, without one pang of jealousy. And the reason of that lack in her had not been something in Imogen but something in Peter Kharkoff.

"He doesn't care!" she heard Imogen saying, as if to herself. "He doesn't care!"

And they walked in silence till they drew near to the bridge, and could see the starry lights of the hotels on the other side of the river and the lake. As they were coming on to the bridge Imogen said, in a voice from which all the excitement, the heat, the passion had died away.

"What are you going to do, Aunt Annie? There's no St. Moritz to plague you now. You must be thankful for that."

"I only wish that this awful thing hadn't happened, and that we were going to St. Moritz."

"But it has happened. Nothing can ever change that. I must go home and face it, see it. And what are you going to do?"

"Let me come with you. Shall I?"

Imogen seemed to hesitate for a moment. Then she said,
"No. That wouldn't be fair. And besides, you could do
nothing."

"I know that. But I could keep you company on the
journey."

"You're a dear to suggest it. But I believe I'd better travel
alone. I've got such a lot to prepare for."

"Very well," said Miss Creswell.

And it was impossible to tell from the sound of her voice
whether she was sorry or glad.

As they reached the end of the bridge and saw the lights of
the rue de Mont Blanc stretching away in front of them to
the hill near the station, Imogen looked at her aunt and said
in a hard decisive voice:

"One thing I've made up my mind about, absolutely made
up my mind. Whatever happens, in whatever state I find poor
Hugo, I shall never, never ask Peter Kharkoff to try to help
him."

Miss Creswell said nothing, and after a moment Imogen
added:

"How could a Jew help a man like Hugo? The idea is
ridiculous. But, even if he could, after tonight I should never
ask him. I hate people who make conditions. Generosity,
true generosity, never does that. But who could expect
generosity from a Jew?"

"Oh, Im!" said Miss Creswell.

And then—she couldn't help it; she had to do it—she repeated the words Madame Coiret had said to her in the book-
shop to Imogen:

"You oughtn't to give him that part of humanity as your
tribute. He deserves something better than that."

"Who said that?" asked Imogen sharply, as if startled.

"I say it."

Miss Creswell saw her niece's eyes examining her closely,
and they looked like the eyes of a stranger now that the
painted shadows were away.

"Those are your words?"

"I say them to you. They are true."

"I give what I choose to give. And what I choose to withhold I withhold."

"Perhaps we can't always choose," said Miss Creswell gently.

"There may come a time when the choice is not of our making."

And then they reached the hotel.

Next morning by an early train Imogen started on her journey to London.

Book Three—At Sainte Maxime

CHAPTER I

LORD LOWRIE, Imogen's father, had a property in the Var, on the shore of the Gulf of Saint Tropez, near the little sea town, or village, of Sainte Maxime. It was called the Villa Sainte Maxime. When almost a young man Lord Lowrie had bought the ground on which the house now stood among pine and mimosa trees, and with the help of a friend who was an architect had planned and built himself the house.

Although on the Riviera within easy distance of Saint Raphael and Valescure, and only an hour and a half from Cannes in a fast motor, this retreat was still more or less "in the wilds." From its many windows only the wash of the sea was audible in the still nights of spring. Even during the daytime there was scarcely any sound of traffic, although the house, standing close to the sea, was of necessity not far from the highroad which hugs the coast all along the Riviera. Now and then the characteristic note of civilization, the hoot of a motor-horn, could be heard in the distance as a car spun by on its way to Cannes, or to Hyères, Toulon, Marseilles. But usually the silence about the butter-colored house with its pale-blue shutters was profound, and was broken only by the whisper of the breeze among the pine, mimosa and cork trees, by the tinkle of the little stream which ran surreptitiously through the scrub, and by the melodious voice of a bell from Saint Tropez on the shore of the opposite side of the gulf, calling across this sheltered arm of the radiantly blue and deep-purple sea.

About the villa Lord Lowrie had laid out pretty and well-kept, though not very large, gardens. An avenue planted with mimosas led up to the house, to the right and left of which were some splendid palms. Beyond the gardens on all sides stretched scrub intermingled with groves of cork, pine and olive trees. In front of the house there was a view of the gulf, of the town of Saint Tropez, massed closely along the sea edge on the southern shore, of low hills, of the Bay of Canebiers and of the Pointe Capon.

Many of the Lowries' innumerable friends and acquaintances, frequenters of Cannes, Nice, Monte Carlo, Menton, tennis players, golf players, players of baccarat, roulette, lovers of the crazy life of enormous casinos, openly pitied Lady Lowrie because her husband had wasted his money in building a house and laying out a property in such an out-of-the-way place. When busy paradises were so near, just round the corner as it were, on the Californie hill, at Cap d'Ail, Cap Ferrat, Cap Martin just below Monte Carlo, why Sainte Maxime?

The answer to that question lay in Lord Lowrie's character. Though not a brilliant he was an unusual man. He was queer enough really to like peace and quiet. He cared nothing for public life, had absolutely no ambition and was perfectly contented without society. Mobs of people simply bored him. The clatter of a myriad tongues pouring forth unadulterated nonsense didn't cheer him at all. He was far livelier with two or three people than he was in the midst of a crowd. And he had a passion for reading, though he read entirely without plan. One day he would be immersed in a French novel. On the next he would be deep in William James, or Papini, or Oliver Lodge, or Knut Hamsen.

He had been a great lover of games, had played in lawn-tennis tournaments, and had worked literally "like a nigger" to get down his handicap at golf. Three years after starting golf his handicap had been four. At four it had remained. He could not get down to scratch. And one day he had locked away his golf-clubs, taken his tennis-racket out of its press, and said to himself, "No more games for me! They worry a man."

From that day—he had been about forty then—to now, when he was just fifty-six, he had never gone on a tennis-court or walked round a golf-course again. Yet his health was excellent, and he looked younger than his age. He was rather short, with a clear complexion, gray eyes, a tiny gray mustache, and a well-shaped bald head with some gray hair, cut very short, round the sides and back. Cheerful, totally without ostentation, quietly pleased and satisfied with a simple, comfortable life, he nevertheless spent much of his time—so his friends said—in the clouds. Although he seldom talked about it he was deeply interested in spiritualism and in all matters "appertaining" (his word) to another world. He dressed neatly and quietly and detested what he called "show." People thought he was a queer sort of father for Imogen to have.

Every year, soon after January came in, Lord and Lady Lowrie left London for the villa, and in the villa they invariably remained till the end of April or the middle of May. They often had two or three guests with them. Imogen popped in and popped out and away as the fancy took her. People motored over from Hyères, Valescure, Cannes, lunched, had tea, played tennis, sometimes dined and drove home by moonlight. But on the whole it was a very quiet life at the villa, and both Lord and Lady Lowrie enjoyed it very much in their different ways; she because she was deliciously stupid and loved ease and "no trouble," he because he was fond of the house he had built and the garden he had made, had plenty of time for reading, and could take endless walks in the woods, over the hills and by the sea, without being pestered by people.

Grimaud knew him, Beauvallon knew him, Saint Tropez by the water, Ramatuelle perched on its hill, La Garde-Freinet, La Croix, Cavaliere, Lavandou. When the fancy took him he would go out to sea with the fishermen, or on a Sunday commit the outrage of shooting foxes with the peasants of his neighborhood. He had been known to stand for an hour on a dusty road watching brown men in their shirt-sleeves playing their peculiar game of bowls with wooden balls astonishingly small in size. And always, whatever he was doing, he seemed to be quietly enjoying himself.

He was "an odd fish," and apparently also a happy man.

It was nearly the end of March, more than ten weeks since Imogen's brief, tormented visit to Geneva, when a train with an "invalid carriage" attached to it drew into the station of Sainte Maxime and stopped by the platform edge. Lord Lowrie and Imogen were waiting on the platform. Outside stood two motors, one a sort of ambulance-motor, and a luggage cart, surrounded by a small group of curious citizens and a number of eager children. The invalid carriage was presently detached from the small train, which then puffed stertorously away in the direction of Beauvallon, and Imogen and her father went up to it, accompanied by a couple of man servants.

Imogen was looking oddly nervous and excited. Her painted lips were compressed. Her usually smooth forehead was drawn down and showed two short lines between the eyebrows. She kept on opening and shutting her right hand as she waited for the carriage door to be unfastened.

"Why don't they——" she began.

The door was opened, and a young man bearing a rather strong resemblance to Douglas Fairbanks quickly got out.

"Who are you, please?" said Imogen.

The young man took off his bowler hat.

"I'm Arthur Milligan, ma'am, Captain Dennistone's male nurse."

Imogen's lips twisted sideways.

"Good morning, Milligan."

"Good morning, ma'am."

"This is my father."

"Good morning."

"Good morning, my lord."

"Tell us," said Imogen, "how did he get through the journey?"

"Not at all badly, ma'am, considering. We'll get him out in a moment."

"These men will help you," said Lord Lowrie.

"Thank you, my lord."

"Oh, God!" said Imogen, under her breath. "I can't stand this. Father!"

"What is it?"

"I'm going to see if it's all right outside."

And she turned away and went out into the road. When she got there she was immediately confronted by the eager little crowd, some of whom politely saluted her.

"*Bon jour! Bon jour! Mais qu'est ce que vous faites ici? Il n'y a rien à voir ici, mes amis. Je vous en prie! Je vous en prie!*"

She turned to the children and forced a smile.

"*Allez! Allez vous en, mes enfants!*"

She waved her hands. The people, looking grave and more curious, retreated to a little distance, hesitated, paused. The children ran off, stopped short, stood whispering and craning their necks in the dust. Imogen turned sharply away from them. Unexpected, unwanted, but irresistible tears had come into her eyes. She walked on, going away from the motors. And the tears actually ran down her cheeks. She took out her handkerchief and used it almost viciously.

"Damned fool!" she muttered.

But for Hugo to arrive anywhere like this! For people to be waiting in the sunshine and the white dust to have a good look at the unusual phenomenon of Hugo! How awful and how ironical! And, when she had dried her tears, she saw life, like a goblin, a huge, hideous, perching goblin, shrieking with laughter at human beings engulfed in their ignorance, standing up to their necks in the shifting quagmires of uncertainty.

She turned round; she had to turn round and go back. And when she had turned she saw at once that the people were back in their former place of waiting, and that the children were once more crowding round the motors. And in their midst was something being carried out of the station lying flat, or nearly flat, on a sort of stretcher. Hugo! So, now he came to the azure coast of the Riviera.

Imogen made a fierce effort, banished memories, drove them out, tightened her lips, and walked quickly up to the thing lying flat, or nearly flat. She came up just as it was going to be placed in the ambulance-motor under the careful supervision of the young man with the resemblance to Douglas Fairbanks.

"Hullo, Hugo!"

"Hullo, Geney!"

She bent down over the long, stretched-out figure, and looked into the carefully shaven face. (Hugo must have been shaved in the train.)

"Glad to see you! Are you awfully tired with the journey? I always get played out coming down here from Calais."

"I'm all right."

She took and held a hand that was lying by the side of his body. "Well, we'll meet in five minutes at the house."

"Yes."

She gave the hand a squeeze which was gently returned.

Then they lifted him into the ambulance.

As she turned away she saw Marfield, Hugo's man, a short, very upright, dark fellow of about thirty-eight, who had obviously once been a "regular," helping to put some bags, etc., into the luggage cart. He looked painfully grim, but managed a smile when she greeted him.

"It's pretty bad, isn't it, Marfield?"

"It is, ma'am. And Mr. Hugo came through the war without a scratch to end up like this."

"Desperate, isn't it? But we must do the best we can."

"Yes, ma'am. At any rate there's a good bit of sun here to shine on him."

"Imogen!"

"Coming, father!"

"We'd better be off. Then we shall be at the house to receive him. It's wonderful how well he looks."

"Isn't it? The face is the old Hugo. But the body—that's the new Hugo."

"Poor chap! Poor chap! And the voice is so strong. The same strong, gritty voice."

"If I shut my eyes when he's speaking I could almost swear he's upright. But he'll never be able to sit straight up again. Sir Mervyn Jones told me so. Never! Never!"

She was silent. So was Lord Lowrie. She glanced at him wondering what he was thinking, feeling. In his cheerful reticence, his curiously withdrawn contentment, her father was often an enigma to her.

"What's he going to do?" she said. "How's he going to get through the time?"

"This life is only a very passing business," said Lord Lowrie. "Don't you feel it so?"

"No; I can't say I do."

"Nor did I when I was young. To be scratch at golf— the want of that—took up a lot of my mind then. When at forty or so I found I should never be scratch I began to realize that there is plenty of interest ahead of us."

"Ahead of us?"

"On the other side of the Rubicon."

"I think it would have been better for old Hugo if he had taken that brook in his stride. But he hasn't, and he's young yet. I can't imagine what's going to happen. It lies on me like an enormous weight."

"Well, my dear, he hangs on to you. One can see that. His eyes when you came up to the stretcher gave it all away."

Something in Imogen shuddered when her father said that.

The motor turned in at the gateway. The lines of yellow mimosas flitted past on either side, or seemed to, deceptively. As the car stopped Imogen laid a hand on her father's arm, and said in a low, fierce voice:

"Father, do you wish me to dedicate my life—you know what I'm like, or what I am, better say that!—to a helpless man? Wouldn't that turn out hell for both of us?"

"My dear, I wish you to do what your heart consents to."

Then a servant opened the door of the car, and the tall figure, and swanlike, or camel-like, neck of Lady Lowrie became visible in the hall.

What had been happening in Hugo's brain and soul since the accident which had in a moment, and permanently, transformed his life, nobody knew but himself. He had not tried to tell it to anyone. Marfield knew something, having seen him at the beginning in moments of fierce physical pain. Doctors, nurses knew something. Imogen knew something. But the secret was really kept, the secret of the whole.

And Imogen kept her secret. Only now and then, as in the motor to her father, did she let out a hint of the turmoil she had lived in ever since she had known of the accident.

Before it had happened she had often thought that some day she would probably marry Hugo. But when it had happened, even in the midst of her horror and pity, she had known that she did not love him, as she put it, "really." If she had really loved him the whole of her would not have rebelled against the idea of self-sacrifice as it did rebel now, would not have rebelled too against the unspoken expectation of many who had watched her association with Hugo.

Since Hugo's tragedy Imogen had become aware of a fact which, with all her sharpness of observation, she had not detected before, the fact that the world, under all its egotism and selfishness and hardness, maintains an almost childlike belief in the readiness of women for self-sacrifice where men are in question. And this childlike belief issues forth to the world in the guise of expectation—an expectation quite as firmly rooted in women as it is in men.

Imogen was fully and angrily aware that "they," by which word she meant all the human beings who were in more or less close contact with her young life, were now looking confidently to her for self-sacrifice. And though she had hitherto been extraordinarily independent of opinion she was now intimately affected by the stare of these eyes turned towards her. She could almost hear the remarks being made in her set: "She'll stick by him now he's down and out, poor chap!" "She kept him on a string when all the other women were after him, but now she'll show him what she's made of." "Under all her frivolity Imogen's a fine creature and she's going to prove it now——" And so on, and on, and on!

Yes, her little world, which seemed to her quite large, and which was really, as little worlds go, quite important, believed in her moral beauty implicitly.

And the Jew? But she tried not to think of him at this time. For he represented to her all those realms of the mind into which Hugo had never penetrated, about which he had never shown the least scintilla of curiosity. And they enticed her, all that part of her which had never had anything to do with Hugo, which had never been attracted by him.

Sometimes she thought that with her body she had almost, or quite, loved Hugo, but that she had never loved him with her mind, her brain, her intelligence. His wonderful body had drawn her, his competent, even brilliant, masculinity, the careless charm, charm of a conqueror, that had always gone with it. But now all that was suddenly withdrawn. His body was impotent to prove his daring. It was less than the bodies of all ordinary men. And his mind had never fascinated her.

She imagined the Jew stricken down as Hugo was stricken—for she had to think of him sometimes, in spite of her effort not to do that—and she felt that the sum of him would hardly have been diminished by such a happening. And yet he was tall, and big, and probably strong. There was power in his body. His physique was even striking. Yes; but the power within outweighed it completely. And that power would have existed, perhaps have been even intensified, in a powerless body. It was not an emanation of the body as Hugo's "atmosphere" had always, queerly, seemed to be. There was a terrific independence in the mentality of the Jew.

Imogen at this time wanted to love because of pity. She found that she couldn't do that. Nevertheless she had tried, was trying now with all her might, "to play the game." She had done her very best to help Hugo in London when he lay in the nursing-home, and as soon as the doctors had said that it was possible for him to travel by easy stages into a warm and sunny climate she had urged his coming out to spend a long time at the villa. Pity, even a great tenderness of pity, made her long to do everything possible for Hugo in catastrophe. But she knew that there were things which it would not be possible for her to do. And sometimes she was secretly afraid that all she was doing manufactured deception, increased the expectation of her little world, the expectation which irritated her intensely.

What Hugo expected, whether indeed he expected anything of her now, she did not know. There was so much now that she did not know about Hugo. And yet, perhaps oddly, that not knowing didn't really interest her, as it interested her profoundly in connection with the Jew.

Sometimes she thought of that saying of the Jew's about preparing the way for him. Would he call what she had been doing, what she was doing now, a preparation of the way? That didn't matter, since she was never going to ask him for help. On that night when she had spoken with such violent frankness to Towser she had made up her mind. And she was not going to change it. But she sometimes wondered—just as a sort of mental exercise—whether the Jew would call what she was doing a preparation of the way.

Before they had brought Hugo out she had gone to stay with some friends at Cannes. It had been the height of the season there, and Imogen had thrown herself, almost with fury, into everything that had been going on. She had played in two tennis tournaments, the Nice international tournament for the South of France Championships, and the following big tournament at Cannes.

She had tried, as it were, to drown herself in bodily activity and she had been surrounded by incessant activity of the body. Wherever she had looked she had seen men and women, vital to their finger-tips, running, leaping, turning, stretching upwards, bending swiftly, throwing up the little white ball, driving it through the bright sunshine. How beautiful, how wonderful the body was! Only now she realized that, now that she had sat by that bed in Bentinck Street, and known the body inert. And she had seen a great polo match, men showing the prowess of the body on animals more active than themselves, animals with whom they had seemed one, as Hugo had always seemed one with his hunters, with any horse he rode. And at night she had danced, and seen bodies, masses of happy bodies, moving lightly to music. And through it all the tragedy, and the repulsion, of Hugo had been with her.

For, and that was horrible to her, she felt repulsion at the powerlessness of Hugo's body. It almost frightened her at moments. The sudden silence of the machinery that had whirred as if endowed with a motion-life which must last forever was awful to her. Hugo's face was unaltered. Now that many weeks had elapsed since his accident, indeed nearly three months, the ghastly look he had had when she first saw him in the London nursing-home had disappeared. There was no unnatural pallor. It could not be said that he looked like a very ill man. But the incessant stillness of him was awful to Imogen. Each day he was dressed by Marfield—how Imogen did not know. Shaved, brushed, still retaining the smart, well-groomed look which had always been characteristic of him, he lay on his back on a specially constructed couch with small wheels, which could be swiftly moved about without noise.

He lay there—ready for what? Ready for the day, for the many days, for the weeks, for the months—for life. Sometimes, often, she looked at the long, well-made, well-dressed body lying at full length on the couch, and had a fantastic impression of a lazy Hugo, of a lounging, useless, effeminate man, of a fainéant, the type of man she "couldn't do with at any price." And this impression was fostered by the fact that Hugo could use his hands and his arms, though he could not raise himself up from a recumbent position, was absolutely powerless to do that. Very often he just looked like a tall, strikingly good-looking young man who, being abominably lazy, chose to lie at full length on a couch instead of sitting in a chair, standing, or walking about like other men. And even though she knew what he had been, and why he had to lie still, she could not banish the occasional and horribly unreasonable feeling that he was less than other men who had the power of movement. She knew that he was not less really, that he would only have been less if his perpetual attitude were caused by his own will and inclination instead of by *force majeure*. Yet the fantastic impression haunted her although she hated it. And she became weary, in a sort of mentally exhausted way, of seeing Hugo always lying stretched at full length.

Her natural restlessness too was increased by his immobility. Ever since she had been a very young girl Imogen had suffered acutely from the mania which is the curse of so many modern women, the mania of restlessness. Movement with her was almost a necessity. She had excellent physical health and scarcely knew what it was to feel tired out. Her mind was alert, voracious, greedy. She had a passion for pleasure, for change, for excitement. Life to her meant incessant activity, doing things, being perpetually "on the go." Certainly she read, but she read quickly, tore the heart out of a book between one active pleasure and the next. Certainly she talked to

clever men, but then her mind was at the gallop, and her love
of flattery was being fed. Now and then she even sat in a low
armchair, or lay on a sofa in her room in Lowndes Square,
smoked cigarettes and thought. But when she did that she was
planning for fresh pleasures, excitements, exertions; she was
not sunk happily in calm, was never dreaming or deep in mental
contemplation.

No girl, therefore, was less suited by nature than was Imogen
to sit by the couch of a motionless man and try to cheer him
with conversation.

Lord Lowrie was thoroughly at home with quiet, was indeed
quite at his best in a quiet atmosphere. Lady Lowrie loved
sitting about and was lethargic both in body and mind. Imogen
hated quiet, starved in quiet, could, it seemed, only be nourished
on perpetual excitement.

Her present effort for Hugo, therefore, was in the nature of
a genuine sacrifice. And, unfortunately, she felt it to be so.

She had never hated herself as she hated herself at this time.
For she wanted her whole nature to be in accord, in perfect
harmony, with the pitiful part of her. But it was not. Much
of her was always struggling to be away, was longing to be
out in the great life which had been hers and Hugo's together,
but which could never be Hugo's again. It was she who had
incited the doctors to consent to Hugo's difficult journey out.
It was she who had suggested the plan to her father and
mother. No one was responsible for Hugo's presence in the
villa but herself. And all her set knew that, and were full of
praises for her (expected) conduct, full of expectation of further developments towards even more romantic nobility.

They did not know, were far too careless even to guess at,
the difficulties of this new situation. Imogen was "turning up
trumps," was showing herself to be a right down good sort,
was proving that the typical modern girl is just as good as,
and probably a great deal better than, her mother and grand-
mother were when "it comes to the pinch." What could be
more satisfactory? Her world saw itself pleasantly reflected in
the moral beauty of Imogen. Her numerous girl friends
thought to themselves, "If I had the opportunity I should do
exactly the same as Imogen," and subsequently reveled in the
pleasant conviction that such an opportunity would never
present itself to them. In fact Imogen's set warmed its hands
at the fire of Imogen's burnt sacrifice.

Meanwhile Imogen was at terrible odds with life, at terrible odds with herself.

Many things secretly tormented her at this time. One was this. She, who had never known the meaning of shyness, often felt shy with the new Hugo. Often she did not know what sort of manner to assume when she was with him. And the fact that she had to think of assuming a manner proved to her that she was not able to be natural. She felt herself forced to try to accommodate her strength to his weakness, to try to beat down the natural *joie de vivre* which couldn't be killed within her by his accident, lest it should make the contrast between them present itself to him as too horrible, too insufferable.

Another thing which tormented her was this. She no longer knew what to talk about with him.

Formerly she had never been at a loss for conversation. Hugo had never been what she thought of as an interesting talker, as many of the men she knew intimately were. But that fact hadn't seemed to matter when they were linked together by the bodily activities, and by the many light pleasures of life, which they had shared with such comradely gusto. Talk, natural talk, lively, cheery, haphazard talk had sprung up out of them to their lips without effort, because of life. Life had given them talk. They had never had to burrow self-consciously to seek for it. Games, hunting, dancing, theaters, suppers, the absurdities inherent in the great panorama, had provided them with innumerable topics for conversation, for jokes, for chat. It had seemed as if their bodies had talked of their own accord.

All that was over now.

One day—Hugo had been at the villa for a little over a week—Imogen had a conversation with the nurse, Milligan, about him. By this time of course she had often met Milligan, had formed a definite opinion about his character, was growing accustomed to his presence in the house. But she had never had any intimate talk with him. Marfield was jealous of him, but even Marfield acknowledged that he was "a capable young fellow, and seemed to know his job." Everyone else in the house liked him.

It was night when she talked to Milligan. She had been upstairs after dinner sitting with Hugo. When she came down feeling dreadfully restless she had gone out alone into the garden. The night was reasonably warm and perfectly still.

The scent of mimosa was strong in the air. On the far side of the Gulf of Saint Tropez the lights of the town were strung, like glittering beads on an invisible thread, across the breast of the velvety darkness. A lighthouse winked far off in Calvaire. The murmur of a small stream was just audible running down through the wood beyond the garden on the right of the house. In the sheltered gulf the sea lay very silent.

Imogen had put a fur round her, but her head was uncovered. As usual she had a cigarette between her bright-red lips.

She walked about the garden restlessly for some time. The calm of the night was wonderfully expressive; she realized it but could take no part in it, could not receive it into herself. She was feeling desperately depressed. She could not remember that she had ever felt so depressed before. When she had been in London just after the accident she had been "keyed up" by excitement; by painful excitement certainly, but still it had buoyed her up. And she had been in London surrounded by friends and acquaintances. It seemed to her that she hadn't had time to think much. Now she had far too much time.

Life lay before her, her life, and she could no longer look ahead into it, as she had at any rate seemed able to do before Hugo's catastrophe. She saw no prospect. It was as if a wall was before her. She had come up to it and was standing impotent before it. The dulness of such a situation was awful. She longed to do something strong and definite, to break out into something. And, longing thus, she thought of Hugo's situation, lying up there in that room looking out over the sea, condemned to lie on his back probably for many years.

"How can he stand it?" she thought.

And then she realized how little real communication there was between her and Hugo. He could know nothing of her endless debatings, of her fear of the future, of her desperate uncertainties. And what did she know of him?

In the distance of the garden, lower down than where she was walking, she saw a small glow. She guessed that behind it might be Milligan, getting some air before going to bed. She knew he was an open-air sort of man. Indeed, he had a love of fresh air that was almost a mania. She walked downwards towards the little glow, and when she was near it called out:

"Who's that? Is it you, Milligan?"

"Yes, ma'am," replied a light baritone voice. "I was taking

a little walk before turning in. I hope you don't mind my——"

"Of course not. I know the smell of that cigar. It's one of Captain Dennistone's."

"Yes, ma'am. He kindly gave it to me."

Milligan was beside her on the path now, hatless. His head was small and covered with smooth, straight, light-brown hair. His face was clean shaven and rather pale. His eyes were hazel and had an extraordinarily kind, honest and ready look in them. He had broad shoulders and held himself like an athletic man. His manner was gentle yet not without firmness. Altogether he looked straight and self-respecting. He was about twenty-seven.

"I'll take a little walk with you, Milligan," said Imogen. "I want to have a talk with you about Captain Dennistone."

"Yes, ma'am, certainly. Shall I put away the cigar?"

"What? For another time? Would you insult a cigar of that brand? No. Go on smoking. I'll smoke too." And she lit yet another cigarette. "We'll walk up and down here among the palms."

"Yes, ma'am. They are fine and no mistake."

"Oh, yes, they're all right. There's nothing much the matter with this place if you can stand the quiet."

"I like it, ma'am, after London. But I always was one for the country."

"And yet you've become a nurse and live in London, don't you?"

"Yes, ma'am. But I get down to my home a good bit."

"Are you married?"

"No, ma'am. But I have my home not very far from Uxbridge, and I get down when I can. I am very keen on football and cricket. I wanted to be a cricket professional, but my dad said if I did he'd never let me in his house again."

"Why on earth?"

"Dad hates games, ma'am—thinks they're waste of time. Horses is his job. As I couldn't be a pro I started studying for a male nurse, massage, x-rays and all that sort of thing. But I play football and cricket whenever I get the chance. Our football team didn't have a defeat this last winter, ma'am. And we played some jolly good clubs too; in a small way, of course."

"You were in the war, weren't you?"

"Oh yes, ma'am. A lot of my time I was in Serbia. The Serbs are very good fellows. Some of them write to me now."

"And of course Captain Dennistone was in the war too."

"So I heard, ma'am. In the Irish Guards."

"Yes. He came through without a scratch, and now look at him!"

"I'm very, very sorry for Captain Dennistone, ma'am."

"It's for life of course. I know that."

"Yes, ma'am, it is. When the back——"

"Yes, yes. I know! I know! The doctors told me. And he knows too."

"He does, ma'am, of course."

"Does he ever talk about it to you?"

"He has, ma'am. We get on very well, him and me."

"What does he say?"

"Well, he said to me once, 'Milligan, old chap, I've got to put up with it somehow, but it's a bad job!' And another time I remember he said, 'It would have been better to go out under fire doing something for one's country than to wear out people's patience lying here like a china doll.' He does use some strange expressions, ma'am, at times. But of course I knew what he meant."

"Of course! What's he going to do, d'you think?"

"Do, ma'am?"

"For the moment he's here, of course. And if he likes it we shall keep the house open until the end of May. But I was thinking of the future."

"I don't know, I'm sure, ma'am. Captain Dennistone's never spoken about that to me. Of course, ma'am, if I may say so, he holds very much by you, very much indeed."

"We're old friends. We used to hunt together."

"He hangs on to the memory of that, ma'am, no doubt. You'd hardly believe——" And then Milligan diverged into souvenirs of other patients of his, and told Imogen a good deal about the psychology of male invalids.

"You seem to get very fond of your patients," she said presently.

"I do, ma'am, of some of them. If I don't like anyone I don't stay with him, not for long. It's no good."

"And you like Captain Dennistone?"

"I do, ma'am! I admire him too. He's a man and deserves the best."

"Ah! And he's got the worst."

"Don't say that, ma'am."

"Why? What else can I say?"

"There's worse fates than Captain Dennistone's, ma'am. He's got something many men in his condition might have to do without, have had to do without, I might say. I'm sorry to have to say it, but a good many girls in the war went back on chaps that were badly wounded, disfigured, you know, and —and sometimes worse than that, things one doesn't care to talk about except among nurses, you know. I could tell you some very sad stories. But Captain Dennistone's one of the lucky ones in respect of that. And after all, ma'am, say what they may, we don't live altogether by the body, do we? I'm sure no man's fonder of cricket and football—especially football—than what I am, but still——"

He paused, and looked at her with his kind hazel eyes as if seeking assent from her. But she didn't say anything. He wondered why. How fast she smoked! That struck him just then. But he had noticed that women usually smoked much faster than men.

"Captain Dennistone seems to like hearing me talk to him about cricket and football and boxing. I do a good bit of boxing, or rather I did, ma'am, before I had dysentery and malaria. —But there's other and better things than them, ma'am, isn't there? Though I'm all for young fellows keeping their bodies fit. But what I mean is that a man wants more than that to make him happy. So that even if he has the bad luck to get it in the neck as Captain Dennistone has, he can still say he has something to look to."

"Well, good night, Milligan."

"Good night, ma'am. I hope I haven't——"

"No. But I must go in, or the old—or my mother will be wanting to drag the gulf to see if my body's there. Do all you can for Captain Dennistone."

"I will, ma'am, indeed. There isn't much I wouldn't do for such a man as he is; a gentleman too, ma'am, of course, but you——"

"I prefer *man*. Good night."

And she went towards the house leaving Milligan rather perplexed. He was sensitive enough to feel that he had said something which had distressed her. "Upset" was his word for it. But he couldn't think what it was.

When she had left him Imogen went straight into the house. They had no guests except Hugo with them at the moment, but Towser was expected on the morrow from Drearney.

It was past ten o'clock when Imogen came in. Lord Lowrie was already established in his library with a pipe and plenty of books, and Lady Lowrie had just got up from her sofa in the drawing-room to go to bed. She was a woman who required great quantities of sleep.

"Going to bed, old lady?" said Imogen.

"Yes, dear. The soft air today has made me unusually sleepy. And, besides, I want to feel brisk when Annie arrives. Have you been in the garden?"

"Yes, with Milligan."

"With Milligan?" said Lady Lowrie, looking mildly surprised and slightly craning her beautiful neck.

"Yes. I wanted to talk to him about Hugo."

"He seems a very nice young man. He's always very polite to me. Did he say anything about poor Hugo?"

"Yes, he did. He said very much what father said."

"Your father? What was that?"

"Father said that Hugo hung on to me. And Milligan said that he held very much to me, very much indeed."

"Well, dear, he does, poor fellow. Anyone can see that. And I don't wonder at it. You've devoted yourself so entirely to him ever since his dreadful accident."

"Naturally I've tried to do my best. Who wouldn't? But Milligan seemed to think—you know how natural and simple in a way he is!—he seemed to take it for granted that I shall always—that I practically belonged in Hugo's life and should always belong in it. He spoke of Hugo *always* having something to look to. That something was myself."

"Really! Did he?"

"Yes."

"Well, isn't it true? You and Hugo have always——"

"Old lady, I don't mean to marry Hugo, and I think it is time people realized that."

"Marry, dear? But who thinks of poor Hugo marrying now?"

"I don't know. But my not marrying Hugo would mean eventually my marrying someone else."

"Of course, dear. Naturally you will marry."

"Well, what about Hugo then?"

"When, dear?"

"When I marry of course!"

Lady Lowrie drew down her brows in her perplexed look.

"Oh, then! Well, I scarcely know. But there's time enough."

"Is there? Are you sure?"

"Are you fond of somebody? Do you wish to marry someone?"

"No. But sometimes kindness turns out to be cruelty."

"Kindness! How can it? Cruelty is surely the opposite of kindness."

"Quite right! When you've got Aunt Annie to keep you company I may be off to Cannes again. Tiny wants me to go to the château."

"But then what will poor Hugo do, dear? Can you leave him all alone here?"

"You're sleepy, old lady. Better go to bed."

"Yes, I want to feel brisk tomorrow for Annie."

That night Imogen felt, unreasonably enough, perhaps, like one confronted by a conspiracy. And she thought of it as started by the Jew. He had been the first, she thought, to imply an obligation on her part towards Hugo, a serious, binding obligation. He had not actually stated it in words. But his whole manner, his look, had implied that he was conscious of it. Perhaps, though, that was her fault, because she had made her feeling for Hugo the excuse for coming by night to the rue les Bergues. But now in this conspiracy to trammel her freedom of action were others; her father, her mother, Milligan, and, in the background, the whole crowd of her set.

She revolted against this silent conspiracy. She felt anger against the conspirators. What right have people to expect from others abnegations not called for from themselves? And she felt the pressure of this multiplied expectation as she had never felt the pressure of opinion before. And the Jew seemed to her to be leading it, guiding it, directing it with intention to her. It was as if she felt him at work in connection with her. And she remembered expressing to Towser her fear of Israel. The remark had been made half in whimsical fun. Hadn't it? She fancied so. But now it seemed to her a saying wrung out of premonition. For the power of Israel seemed to be upon her.

"I'm going to break out of this!" she said to herself viciously.

"I've never been governed yet, and I'm not going to be governed now. Tomorrow I'm off to the château!"

CHAPTER II

HUGO never complained. That no doubt was his idea of "putting a good face" on his terrible misfortune. He did not complain, but he was without the power to act a difficult part cleverly. By nature he was a straightforward kind of fellow, not much given to concealing his likes and dislikes, his desires and his rejections. In the fulness of his health and strength he had often shown his joy of life plainly, even boisterously. When he had felt cross or "put out" he hadn't scrupled to show that too. In his love-affairs he had sometimes displayed a certain subtlety which had belonged to the charm he had had for most women. But the charm and the amount of subtlety which went with it had been wholly unconsidered. Great lovers are seldom without that form of subtlety though they may lack all the other forms. And Hugo had been a great lover with a strange background of unexpected faithfulness in his lasting affection for Imogen. Now all the women had dropped away out of his life, like shadows falling into a gulf, and into his helplessness had been born a great concentration.

And he didn't know how to hide it. For the inertia of his body seemed to cause violence in the motion of his feelings. Since he had become a cripple he had felt much more intensely than ever before, and in a quite different way. Although he did not put it so to himself his feelings seemed to have gained in poignancy by being disconnected from bodily things. Formerly the glorious pleasures and satisfactions of the body had seemed always to prompt his feelings. Now his feelings came like lonely things unprompted, naked, fierce in their nakedness. And he hadn't learned yet—if he could ever learn—how to hide the fierceness, the nakedness of them.

And so, when the next morning Imogen came into the upstairs room which Lady Lowrie had given to Hugo as a sitting-room, and in her most casual manner, but looking aside, told him that she was off that day to Lady Vesie's château in the hills above Cannes for a visit, he showed his startled surprise, and taught her the lesson of his now terrible sensitiveness. He didn't show it in words. What he said was:

"Going to Tiny, are you? Then you're sure to have a good time. Give her a friendly word from me, will you?"

He didn't ask how long the visit was going to last, whether there was any special lure which took her suddenly to the château. He didn't ask anything. But the look on his face was an undressed look, told her more than his words could have told her. She hadn't missed it because, when he spoke, she had felt obliged to look at him to see how he was taking the news of her departure. A dreadful curiosity had possessed her just then. And there was vanity in it. But when she had seen the expression of fright in his bright blue eyes, the startled movement of his lips when he had finished speaking, and then, immediately, the swiftly produced smile which had tried to bid her go to her pleasures without being hindered in her enjoyment by any thought of him as a cripple, something within her had suffered acutely, something had seemed to be weeping. And she had nearly changed her mind, given up the visit, stayed with him.

That look had given her a shock, had almost terrified her. For in it had been visible the menace of an exclusive affection, strong, permanent, concentrated, such an affection as cannot be easily or lightly put aside, ignored, even by one who has the definite intention to be selfish in life, the definite will to live according to the dictates of a tyrannical nature bent upon pleasure and freedom. But she had gone. For she had remembered the word of the Jew and her fear of unselfishness in Geneva. That fear was deepening now. But she was not going to be numbered among the abject. Youth has a right to live fully, to enjoy. The dedication of youth to pain is an outrage, and must surely be against the intention of the power which imagined youth and then created it. So Imogen argued. But the very fact that she argued and mentally debated such a point proved that a strange influence had affected her, was even, perhaps, stealing over her.

At the château she found a large party of people, all bent on pleasure, fun, activities. The last big tennis tournament of the season on the Riviera was being played at Cannes. Several of the players in it were staying with Lady Vesie. All day long Imogen was out of doors at the Cannes Tennis Club. In the evening there were dinners, visits to the opera and to the casino, baccarat and, of course, dancing. In the early mornings she went to bed—tired. And she felt that the reason why she was unexpectedly tired lay in the mind. She was no longer wholehearted in gaiety. Her *joie de vivre* was not what it had been. A shadow lay over it.

All the people staying in the château, with the exception of three Americans, knew Hugo. All liked him. All had expressed their grief to Imogen at the ruin of his physical life and had asked with apparent eagerness about his condition. But even while she had been answering their inquiries she had known, "They don't really care. They haven't time really to care." And for the first time the deep-seated and perhaps designed carelessness of the world about the troubles and miseries of "others" was driven home to her.

In thinking about that Imogen had said to herself at first, "Perhaps it is that they dare not care." But almost immediately afterwards had come the conviction: "No, it isn't that. The truth is that they cannot care." And, realizing that, she had realized two lonelinesses, Hugo's loneliness and her own. And a chill which had seemed to come, like a breath of wind over fields of ice, from out of the future, had fallen upon her.

What Hugo had suffered would certainly never be her lot. She was convinced of that. The chances of life are extraordinary, but not so extraordinary as that. But what might she not have to face some day? And when she had to face it, which of all her many friends and adorers would take the trouble to stand by her and to continue standing by her? And then she imagined a reversal of fortune. She imagined the accident to Hugo as her accident. She saw herself lying crippled on his couch instead of him. What would Hugo have done? How would he have been to her? If all the glory of her young vitality, if all the lure of her youthful powers, had been knocked away from her by a hammer-blow, such as had fallen upon him, would he have cared for her less, or more, or not at all?

One night she lay awake for hours thinking about that.

She was exasperated by an assumption that evidently prevailed among Lady Vesie's guests. The word had certainly gone about that Imogen Lowrie had a large fund of unselfishness at her disposal and was now beginning to spend it lavishly for the benefit of Hugo Dennistone. Whatever surprise there might have been at first among Imogen's "pals" at the discovery of this fund had already begun to die down. They were already beginning to feel disastrously at home with this supposed virtue. Imogen had too many evidences of that fact to be able to doubt it.

Her visit to the château was assumed to be a little holiday which would of course soon come to an end. Formerly the assumption had been that the wonderful Imogen's life was a lasting holiday. One woman spoke of "the dear duties you've so nobly undertaken" as if they were to last for eternity. Another, supposed to be a great pal of Imogen's, Lois Tremayne, alluded earnestly to the "wonderful reward" which must be the guerdon of those who tread the path of self-sacrifice, and even had the "cheek" to add a pious hope that some day a chance akin to Imogen's might be offered to her.

Meanwhile of course there was "nothing for it" but to go on enjoying herself.

There seemed to be a general agreement among the whole company of women that there wouldn't be much seen of Imogen during the London season which was now close at hand. "She won't have time for all the rubbish of so-called pleasure which we put up with!" said one pretty girl, in a plaintive voice designed to match the curve nature had by chance given to her lips. "She has better things to do. Imogen's at grips now with the real humanities."

The men of course took quite a different line. But it was equally exasperating to Imogen. They evidently admired her genuinely for "sticking by poor old Dennistone," and showed their admiration in manner more than by words, as is the way of Englishmen. But they also now evidently took it for granted that she was mad keen on the poor chap. And, showing a solidarity of sex not uncommon among men, they tacitly indicated their view of the situation by avoiding all attempts at flirtation with Imogen.

As she was accustomed to being laid siege to, this marked departure from the normal on their part proved the sincerity of their belief in her devotion to Hugo. He had lost practically everything that makes life worth living to a man. But he had one piece of property left—Imogen Lowrie. Their code made it the right thing to abstain from all interference with that. There wasn't a man among them who would try to use the powers which Dennistone had been deprived of to take away his girl. Later on in the course of this life anything might happen. Men aren't made of plaster, and girls, even self-sacrificing girls, aren't free from nature's promptings. The way of the flesh not infrequently runs parallel with the way of the spirit, and there are many little side-paths uniting them. But for the moment Dennistone's tragedy was a fresh tragedy. When it grew stale, as every tragedy must, human nature might once more make its little mistakes. Meanwhile there was a code to be observed. And they meant to observe it.

Again, in the château, Imogen felt herself to be face to face with a conspiracy, a soft, subtle, but perfectly definite conspiracy. Things were not as usual. Everything about her and in connection with her was changed because of this mental attitude of people towards her. And she was conscious of the power of thought as she had never been conscious of it before, in a widespread way. In the Jew she had been conscious of it of course, conscious of it in the confined, individual way, as the exceptional attribute of one man. But this was thought spread about through many differing minds, thought percolating as water percolates through porous soil. And she hated it, and she began to be obscurely afraid of it.

"What do they all expect of me?" she asked herself.

It wasn't difficult to answer that question. She was certain that they expected her presently to marry Hugo, as she would perhaps have married him if the accident had never happened. Had they troubled, had anyone of them all troubled, to think down into the matter of such a marriage, to think what it would mean to her? They were—she was convinced of it—thinking of Hugo rather than of her. They were thinking of the man. And doesn't the world always think of the man first in any great question in which a woman and a man are concerned? Hadn't Peter Kharkoff thought of the man when she had put Hugo's case partially before him, rather than of her, although he only knew of Hugo, while he knew her, was actually with her when his thought was on the man? Perhaps, in this particular case, her little world's outlook was affected by ordinary human pity, which unconsciously demanded that such consolation as was possible should be given to Hugo for all that had been taken away from him.

"But—I—I—I!" she thought in a burst of excited egotism. Am I to pay the price which ought to be paid by fate?"

She hated her own thoughts at this time. She knew that most people if they knew of them would call them unnatural. As if all women thought on a pattern! As if all women had the lust for self-sacrifice!

Yet she felt horribly unhappy when she thought of making Hugo unhappy. When she remembered the look of fright in his eyes something in her yearned over him. In that look she had seen surely a stricken soul. The sight of that was far more intimately poignant than the sight of a stricken body. Somehow—it was very absurd really!—she had seemed to see Hugo for the first time in that look of fright, that scared look.

She could not get his eyes, as she had seen them just then, out of her memory. And there had been an odd, flattened look about his cheeks too. How could that have been? His cheeks had seemed to shrink, to be suddenly flattened like something soft altered in shape by a blow.

If Hugo had looked like that because she had told him without preparation that she was going away for a week, what would his eyes be like if one day she had to tell him that she was going to marry another man, a man strong, active, ready for anything, what people call "a real man"?

And with that thought there came again the thought of the Jew.

Hugo hated Jews. He had never made friends with a Jew. About Jews he had always been absolutely unreasonable. And yet she had been to a Jew about Hugo, and had even asked a Jew to help Hugo. She remembered the last interview she had had with Hugo in health. In that interview they had quarreled—because of a Jew. Hugo had suspected something, had even strangely guessed that her journey to Switzerland was caused by a man who was in Switzerland. Now suddenly, in the château, Imogen realized that the journey had ended in her asking this man of whom Hugo had shown jealousy to help Hugo, and she had a feeling that, though she had undertaken the journey as she had thought of her own free will, really perhaps she had been deliberately led to Geneva on Hugo's account.

But she had made up her mind—hadn't she?—to have nothing more to do with Peter Kharkoff.

Now, faced by this silent conspiracy, and remembering the scared look in Hugo's eyes, she began to long for moral help, she began to long for someone to whom she could unburden herself. She realized her loneliness of spirit. Her normal self-confidence was abated. And the thought of the Jew began to be continually with her. Although she now had definite fear of him, a fear which seemed growing, his attraction for her was greater than ever. It was as if she wanted to reject him, and couldn't. She knew that no man whom she had encountered in her life had made an impression upon her such as he had made. His great indifference had won upon her far more than the concentrated assiduity of other men.

If he had suffered as Hugo suffered, had wanted her in his suffering as Hugo wanted her, how would it have been?

She tried not to think about that. But now she found that her thoughts were continually leading her to the feet of the Jew.

She stayed for ten days at the château, and all the time she was there she tried to drown thought in gaiety. There was a fever in her blood, but it was not a fever of joyous youth carried away by heady excitement. In it or beneath it there was a deep uneasiness, a deep melancholy. She was apprehensive of the future.

In the good-bys at the château she was conscious again of the conspiracy. She was being dismissed to her path of duty which, it was assumed, was lit up, made easy, by love.

But whenever she thought of the Jew she knew she didn't love Hugo. The Jew made her know that even her deep pity for Hugo was not akin to love. She longed for it to be akin now, since she had seen the real Hugo in his scared eyes and lips that couldn't keep still, but it wasn't.

She had to make an ugly confession to herself at this time. It was this: that the sensuality in her rejected the crippled man.

She motored back to Sainte Maxime wondering what was going to happen. Since she had been at the château exasperation and fear had increased in her. She didn't believe that she would be able to let things drift on much longer. If Hugo became accustomed to her continued presence, if she gave herself up too much to him, surely she might presently feel that she was caught fast in a net. She might not have the hardihood or the brutality to break out. The situation would become too difficult. She wouldn't be able to handle it. There was still time for caution or even for cruelty. But she must not let things drift.

As the motor drew near to the villa she was struck by the tranquillity of the atmosphere which seemed to be embracing

this arm of the sea. The water of the gulf was fiercely blue
dashed with long streaks of purple. But the strength of color
did not quarrel with the peace of the atmosphere for the sea
lay perfectly still. Even along the shore there wasn't a ripple
perceptible to Imogen. Every afternoon a wind, sometimes
small, sometimes showing strength, springs up in the gulf.
Now towards evening that wind had completely died away.
Across the water the massed houses of Saint Tropez along the
harbor looked like an oil painting, bold dashes of yellowish
white on a stretched canvas. All around, the hills were folded
in a dream. After Cannes this country seemed remote, a tract
of nature in exile from gaiety. The hush of it frightened
Imogen. For at its core she felt a crippled man concentrated
on her with all that was left of him. And Hugo assumed
suddenly an awful importance in her life. She saw him as a
dark shadow growing abruptly in height on a wall, towering
till its head was lost in the invisible.

He did not know that she was due to arrive that evening.
She had not let anyone know when she was coming back. Her
room was always ready. And she had a wish that was also a
dread in her, the wish to surprise Hugo. She had seen him
startled by her going. She must see him startled by her coming.
She felt that she had to see that.

The motor turned through the gateway into the avenue
of mimosas. It flashed past somebody who had stood quickly
aside under the trees, a woman holding something. Imogen
leaned out of the window. She caught a glimpse of Towser
laden with apparatus for her business of painting in water-
colors. She waved. When the motor stopped she went back
down the drive.

Miss Creswell and Imogen had not met since they had been
together in Geneva. Miss Creswell had stayed on for a time
after her niece had left her. When she had passed through
London on her return to England Imogen had managed to
avoid seeing her without giving offense. She had felt a curious
instinctive desire not to see Towser just then in the midst of the
trouble about Hugo. The memory of her passionate outburst
of frankness, after the visit to the Jew, had made her reluctant
to meet her aunt's eyes. Towser knew too much about her.
But now the inevitable must be encountered with hardihood.
And she welcomed her aunt in the drive with her usual apparently light-hearted greeting.

Miss Creswell had been out since lunch sketching. When she visited her sister she was perpetually out sketching. Sometimes, when she was at home, for months she did not take a brush in her hand. But usually, as soon as she was abroad, removed from the duties and pleasures connected with her home and her Drearney friends, the passion for painting seized her and she gave herself up to it with greediness. She had studied hard as a girl, had great facility in water-color, and had also a considerable knowledge of drawing. Her work was sound, without being actually brilliant, and had none of the feebleness and pretty-prettiness of the average amateur.

In answer to her niece she said that she had crossed the gulf to Saint Tropez in the motorboat belonging to Beauvallon and had been painting in the harbor there.

"My first day out!" she added, as they walked into the house.

"Your first!" said Imogen incredulously.

"Yes. I've been spending a great deal of my time with Captain Dennistone."

Imogen sent her a keen, questioning glance.

"Hugo! That's good of you, Towser."

"I don't think so. I should be only too thankful to be of any use or comfort to him if I could. But I can't. Oh, Im,"—she put a hand on her niece's arm—"how thankful he'll be to see you back. He doesn't know—we none of us knew that you were coming back today."

"I wasn't sure myself till this morning. How d'you find him?"

It was a horribly stupid question, and she didn't know why she asked it. Directly she had asked it she repented of it.

"Do you want me to say what I really think?"

"Of course. Why not?"

"Well, he makes me think of Lazarus."

"What do you mean, Aunt Annie?"

"There's something—it's as if some part of him were dead, but in such a way that the right voice could bring him to life."

"Some part! Of course his poor body——"

"No. I mean something else."

"The voice which brought Lazarus to life, according to the Scriptures, hasn't been heard on earth for nearly two thousand years."

"*I* was no good."

"And evidently you think *I* can't be of any good. Or—or did you mean me just now?"

"No, no; I didn't."

"Then you think I'm of no use to him?"

"Im, he clings to you. If you abandoned him I think it would take the last ray of light from him. But I don't think even you can accomplish certain things in connection with him, partly because you haven't certain faculties, and partly—don't be angry with me—because I don't think you are whole-hearted."

Imogen was silent.

"Are you angry?"

"No. I know what you are driving at, Aunt Annie. I know quite well."

And then Lady Lowrie swam lethargically, like a weary swan, out of the drawing-room and almost immediately Imogen went upstairs to see Hugo.

"Whole-hearted!" she thought. "And father said, 'Do what your heart consents to.'"

As she came near to the door of Hugo's sitting-room she walked softly, and when she got to the door she stood still for a moment beside it.

Within she heard the sound of a voice, and almost immediately was able to distinguish some words.

"You see, sir, I never seemed to have any difficulty bowling overhand. Even as a boy I had what they call a natural break, and could get a lot of work on the ball. Lobs somehow I was never any good at. The funny thing about lobs is that fellows who aren't bowlers at all so to say, not what you'd *call* bowlers, are often nailers when it comes to pitching up lobs. If you remember, E. M. Grace, who was such a wonderful point, could often get a man out by——"

And then Imogen opened the door.

Opposite to the door was a large window down to the floor which gave access to a balcony. Hugo's couch was placed exactly in front of this window, not sideways but facing it, so that the back of his head, as he lay, was turned towards Imogen coming in. Arthur Milligan was sitting beside him eagerly talking. But when he saw Imogen he stopped at once and got up.

"Oh—good evening, ma'am," he said.

"Good evening, Milligan!"

She came up to the couch and quickly sat down in Milligan's chair.

"Hugo!"

Hugo's face was scarlet, and his blue eyes looked startled and full of a sort of pain of joy, as if sudden joy had given him such a shock that pain had to mingle with it.

"Geney! Are you back? What? Back, are you? But we didn't expect you today. We weren't expecting you. We—were we, Milligan?"

"No, indeed, sir."

"Well, anyhow here I am."

"To be sure!"

She had taken his hand, and now tried to let it go, but his fingers held on to her, not hard, very softly.

"Did you have a good time at Tiny's?"

"Did I?"

She saw the flush gradually die down on his face.

"Well, I suppose I had what's called a good time, what you and I used to call a good time."

"Yes?"

Milligan moved towards the door, but Imogen called him.

"Don't go, Milligan. I shall be off in a moment."

"Yes, ma'am."

"I hear Aunt Towser's been with you a good deal."

"Yes; she's been very kind."

"We've been going to Sainte Maxime, ma'am, just for a little outing, Captain Dennistone's been taking tea at the—what's it called again, sir?"

"Ermitage de Provence."

"That's it, ma'am, the Hermitage dee Provongse. You look right on the harbor from there and can see the life."

"That's it," said Hugo with a faint smile. "Men loading wood on a black barge that'd do to take you over the Styx, and unloading green barrels. And there are a couple of old sailing vessels lying at anchor. A gramophone plays ragtime at the back of you, and there you are! I'm glad to see you back, Geney. You must tell me about it all presently."

"Yes, after dinner."

"Anyone there I know?"

"Oh yes." (She ran through some names.)

"All the old crowd!" he said. "And carrying on as usual, of course?"

"Yes. They've only got one way of living."

"It wasn't a bad way either," he said.

And he let her hand go.

"Now I'll go and take off my hat. Back again presently."

"Right!"

As she turned away she heard him sigh faintly. Before going out of the room she happened to look down on a small table which was close to his couch. On it, by a vase of mimosa, she saw two books and the Times. She bent and picked up the books. "Sérénité." "Votre Compagnon."

"What are these?"

"Your aunt kindly dumped them here. I haven't looked at them yet. I'm not a great hand at reading, as you know. And they're French. I can manage the French all right though. I mean to have a shy at them presently. Something to do, and she swears by them."

"There's no name in them," said Imogen.

She had opened the books one by one and looked at the title-pages.

"No," said Hugo. "But they're not by Whyte Melville so perhaps I shan't be able to plow through them."

"Oh, Hugo!" she said.

Milligan moved and slipped quietly out of the room, after a side glance at her. Although she was a girl very conscious of those about her she did not notice his going. Suddenly a winter evening came back to her, a conversation in a cab after a day's hunting, a tea up in her guarded room, Hugo luxuriously resting the body which had been gloriously active all day. And the music of hounds! Once Hugo had spoken of dying—or "going out"; wasn't that the expression?—to that music. How much better if he had gone out, with hounds running on a hot scent and green England all about him. Pity overwhelmed her and an extraordinary impulse rose clamoring in her—like an enemy! Should she throw away her future, the life which she surely needed? Should she go to Hugo, bend down to him, say to him, "Marry me. I'm yours! Take me into your wrecked and powerless life." If she did that she could never "go back on it." She wasn't the girl who could ever jilt a man in Hugo's condition. The words once said, the deed would follow. The thing would go through. Should she do it? At that moment she was conscious of fear, almost of dread, and also of a sort of tremendous pressure, as if

something, some force, were urging her to an irrevocable act,
to an act which she had absolutely resolved never to commit.
She felt impelled.   Yet she also felt that something in her
was crying out in protest, was struggling against the invisible
force which seemed taking hold on her life.

"What's it, Geney?" said Hugo.

The books were still in her hand, but she didn't know that.
She had forgotten they were there.   Now she tightened her
fingers round them.   Hugo was looking up at her, and she
saw a flame of hope in his eyes.   She knew he was longing, was
even trying—in vain—to raise himself a little towards her.
He couldn't do that.   He would never be able to do that
again.   But he slightly lifted his arms, and she saw that they
were trembling.

"Yes?" he said.

And then she couldn't resist.   She quickly knelt down by his
couch, leaned over him and said, "Hugo, will you marry me?"

"But I'm a hulk now!" he said.   "I'm no good.   Could you
stand me, Geney?   Could you put up with me?"

"Yes, yes, yes!" she said—scarcely knowing what she said—
"*You* aren't changed.   What's the body?"

As she spoke she looked into his eyes, and for a moment she
was rewarded.   She was rewarded—and she was terrified.   For
she knew that after seeing the look Hugo's eyes held at that
moment she could never try to release herself from the word she
was giving.   Perhaps he wouldn't hold her to it.   That didn't
matter.   What she had seen would hold her to it forever.

As she kissed him she knew that she was the prisoner of the
future she had abruptly made inevitable.

CHAPTER III

A few minutes later Imogen was up in her room, and Harriet was unpacking the trunks that had been to Cannes.   She
looked at Harriet, said something—she didn't know what—
and went into her sitting-room.   She shut the door between
the two rooms, went to the open window and looked out to
sea.

"What have I done?" she thought.

She had come back from Cannes to do this!   And she had

not known, she had not had the least suspicion that she was going to do it while she was driving towards the villa. Indeed she had absolutely made up her mind that the thing expected of her by those whom she had thought of as conspirators was the thing that she would never do.

Perhaps for the first time she felt that her life didn't belong to her, that she wasn't captain of it, that it was the prey of some power outside her, and that she had no control at all over it. Hitherto, like most of those who are young and audacious, she had been companioned by the feeling that she could do pretty much what she liked with her own. And she had thought of her life as her own, her possession, something precious which she could deal with as she chose.

And now, without meaning to, she had made it over to Hugo, to the man lying helpless on the couch in the room below hers!

Without meaning to!

She looked away from the sea and down at her right hand. It still held a book, one of the two she had taken up and spoken about to Hugo.

"Votre Compagnon."

She opened it, glanced at it, then hastily laid it down. She felt sure that it was one of the anonymous works put out by Peter Kharkoff to influence the thoughts of men. And now abruptly her thoughts swung from Hugo to him, and she remembered the condition he had laid down when she had spoken to him about Hugo.

"And so I've done it, I've prepared the way!" she thought.

The thought struck her like a bolt. She came away from the window and threw herself at full length on a sofa. And she remembered her fear of unselfishness and the Jew's comment on it. He had divined it and he had stated it. He had said to her, when she had said that she couldn't change into a completely self-sacrificing woman, "You are afraid of changing as much as that."

And now what had she done? In a moment of unaccountable impulse she had offered her life to a cripple. But the horrible thing was this. Although she had had the impulse to do what she had just done, she knew that her heart had not really consented to it. Deep pity had swept over her, but it was not a pity so deep as to drown all thoughts of self, all selfish desires. Already she regretted what she had done, was afraid of it, felt desperate about it. And the desperation grew till it was like a disease within her, till she seemed to be feeling it physically. It sent all through her a tingling heat like the dry heat of fever. She saw, as if with the eyes of the body, a dedicated life, a life lived for another, days, weeks, years, spent in living unnaturally because of another, a life bent down over a couch, a life almost immobile passed in the company of a motionless man. Could she bring happiness by being unhappy? Could she help Hugo by torturing herself?

She tried to get rid of her desperation by thinking of his new-born joy. For she knew that, in spite of his condition, for the moment he was very happy. She had seen that, felt it. But could that happiness continue? She didn't know. She didn't believe that it could, unless the power was given her to act with consummate art.

The fear she had felt in the Jew's flat, the fear he had commented upon, had been well founded. She knew that now. A virtue may be terrible as well as a vice. And she saw herself punished, almost murdered by virtue. The virtue of Christ nailed him to a Cross. But she did not wish nails to be driven into her; she did not wish to be stretched upon a cross of her own contriving. And the passion for life boiled angrily up in her.

She sprang up from the sofa and went again to the window. Standing there she could hear the sound of voices coming up from below her. Milligan and Hugo were talking. When he knew, how Milligan would admire her. He had condemned those girls who had thrown over their lovers injured, disfigured, mutilated in the war. But she understood those girls. They had wanted life. They had needed the joy of life. Their youth had instinctively stretched out hands to the happiness of life, had turned away shuddering from life's horrors. And people had called them selfish, unwomanly, cruel.

At any rate they would not be able to call her cruel. She would not have been cruel to Hugo.

Listening to the murmur of those voices from below she began to wonder whether it was in her to find some comfort in the good opinion of those who still valued the so-called virtues, who gave to them more than lip service.

She had always believed that she defied opinion, that she really didn't care what people thought about her. But then she had been always surrounded by admirers. Her set had seemed to delight in her egotism. Her vanity had earned the reward of incense. Her insolence had been discreetly named character.

As she stood by the window the values seemed changed. For the moment at any rate all defiance had gone out of her. She wanted the guerdon of praise for the strange sacrifice she had suddenly decided to make. She wanted sympathy, understanding, mental upholding. And she would never be able to ask for them, for she would never be able to acknowledge that a sudden storm of pity had swept her away, and that she regretted that, but was a girl who held to her word. She would have to pretend, to Hugo, to her father and mother, to her aunt, to Milligan. Not to pretend would be treachery to Hugo. She couldn't be treacherous to a man in his condition who loved her as he did. She saw herself horribly alone, and she saw life like a thing receding from her into the distance.

The sound of the voices beneath her windows had ceased. Evening was coming, and the hush of nature grew more profound. She knew it must be nearly or quite time to dress for dinner, but she remained at the window. Beyond it was a small balcony. She stepped out on it, drew a chair up to the rail and sat down.

"Why have I done it? What made me do it?"

These questions persisted in her. The change that had come into her was so abrupt, had been so unforeseen, that she was still almost incredulous about it in spite of her feeling of desperation. She had not supposed that she could yield like that to a sudden impulse, that her brains could "let her down" in such a startling way as they had. She hadn't known that she was so incalculable.

She looked again out to sea, and across the gulf to the low hills and the sea town opposite. The town was fading, was becoming one with the landscape, almost one with the still sea that lay at its foot. A grayness was creeping into the sky. The stillness of the evening seemed to her gray, not blue. And she saw life as gray. It seemed to her that what she had just done, in which a certain future was implicit, had made her one with calamity. Fate had stricken Hugo, but she, unstricken by Fate, had chosen calamity when she had said she would marry Hugo. Using her hard young intellect she said to herself, "I've done the typical womanly thing, the sort of thing the heroine would be certain to do in one of the books the old

lady reads. I've behaved exactly as a Florence Barclay girl
would have behaved in similar circumstances. And I'm not
like that. I'm just the contrary of that."

And she saw herself as a ferocious egotist gone astray in
the gardens of self-sacrifice.

"My God!" she couldn't help thinking horribly. "How
dépaysée I shall be in them!"

She heard a tap on the door, and Harriet came in.

"It's twenty past eight, ma'am."

"I'm coming!"

Harriet disappeared. And again Imogen looked out to sea.
And then she saw the way. And it was prepared. For she
had done the unimaginable thing, the thing that, ridiculously,
she still felt herself incapable of doing though she had
done it. "If I told *him* he would be bound to do his part!"
she thought. "I have his promise."

But she had resolved to have nothing more to do with the
Jew. And suddenly she was deeply afraid of him; suddenly
she felt that she had promised herself to Hugo because the
Jew's influence had been upon her. It must have been that.
When he had spoken of a preparation of the way, that must
have been in his mind—her act of definite self-sacrifice. And
now his will in her had been accomplished. Secretly he had
required something of her. And now she had given it to him.

Hadn't she really just given him her life?

As she looked out to sea she felt that he must know what
she had done. She imagined him sitting in his little room by the
hour-glass, knowing. The night was coming on. Soon his
lamp would be lit. She saw the faint and fleeting gleam of
the lighthouse beyond the soft outline of the hills behind
Saint Tropez. She imagined it to be the gleam of his lamp.
And again she was preoccupied by the thought of opinion.
Would he praise her for what she had done, for what she was
going to do? If he did would that help her?

Below in the house she heard the sound of a gong. She got
up and went into her bedroom. She dressed for dinner
quickly and went down without looking in again on Hugo.
He always dined upstairs. He preferred to do that. And Milligan dined with him.

When she went down she hadn't decided whether or not she
was going to say anything to her people that night about what
had just happened. She and Hugo hadn't spoken about that,

hadn't discussed anything. And she knew that Hugo would
say nothing till she did. If she had the heart to be an utter
brute she could still get out of it, and no one would know
except Hugo and herself. No one? And then she saw the
Jew sitting under the lamp by the hour-glass.

Wouldn't he know?

At dinner she made a great effort and probably seemed to
be just as usual. Soon after it was over she said she would go
upstairs and see how Hugo was getting on. She found his
couch drawn up near an electric light which shone over a book
he was apparently reading on a movable book-rest. Milligan
was not in the room.

As she came in she thought, "I'm coming into my new
life, to what is going to be my life in the future. How am I
going to bear it?"

She went up to the couch and said, "Reading, Hugo? Isn't
that rather wonderful?"

"Everything seems wonderful tonight," he replied.

She drew a low chair near to his couch and lit a cigarette.

His blue eyes were fixed upon her. She knew that, but
she felt just then unable to meet them. She was afraid he
would be able to read in them something of the desperate
turmoil in her mind.

"Almost too wonderful!" he added.

"Why—too wonderful?"

"I don't know. But I can hardly believe it's going to last.
Did you mean it, Geney?"

She wanted to hesitate, but she answered at once, "Of course
I did."

Something within her said violently, "You can't go back.
You're not a brute. You're not a cad. You can't go back."

"I don't believe I ought to hold you to it, Geney. You're
such a wonderful live wire, and I'm such a dull dog now."

"Rubbish!"

"Oh, I know I used to be all right. I was never anywhere
near up to you in brains. But I didn't mind that when I
could do everything a man needs to do. I felt it was all right
then. You could think for two, and I felt sometimes as if
I'd the go in me to act for a regiment. But I shall never
be an interesting chap. Some of your friends might be all
right even lying as I do like a log. But everything that was
worth anything in me has been knocked away."

"It hasn't. You've got a heart and that's worth more than any brains."

After a pause he said, "I wasn't sure till this evening that you really cared tuppence about me. I thought perhaps it was all pity. And—and I didn't want that."

She looked up then and saw a painfully searching expression in his eyes. Quite evidently he was in doubt about her whole-heartedness. She smiled and laid a hand upon his.

"In the old days I played about a good deal. And so did you. But I think I always meant to marry you some day. I believe I always knew we should be married in the end."

"Ah—but not like this!"

"No, not like this. But it might have happened in the war. I mean you might have been disabled in the war like scores of splendid fellows. If that had happened would you have expected me to let you down?"

"No. You're too thoroughgoing English for that. But hunting's different. I was out for pleasure. I wasn't out for my country."

"It's all the same to me."

"Don't be angry, Geney!"

"Angry! What about?"

"At what I'm going to say. Somehow I scarcely thought you had it in you to do such a thing for any man. I mean apart from the war. When a fellow's knocked out for his country it's a different thing. Love of country comes in there, and helps. But I scarcely thought you could care for anyone enough to make such a sacrifice."

"I know. Because I cared so much for myself. Hugo, you mustn't expect too much from me. I shall often be horribly trying. I shall be restless. I shall—I shall run away after all sorts of pleasures. The will-o'-the-wisps will call me and I shall follow the light of their torches. But I'll try to be stanch to you."

"It's awful, Geney. I feel I ought to refuse to let you do it. I feel that everyone, all your pals, will think me a damned scoundrel for letting you do it. They'll say I ought to stick it out alone, that I've no right to let a woman tie her-self up to my infirmity."

"Who cares what they say?"

"But have you thought it all out?"

"Yes, yes, yes!"

He didn't say anything more for a minute, but lay with his eyes fixed upon her. In the silence she wondered whether he was trying to read her, whether he was able to read anything of what was going on in her mind. He was giving her her chance. He was being generous to her, was holding open the door to facilitate her escape. There was still time for her to rush out into liberty. She knew that. She realized it thoroughly. As she sat there she seemed to see the open door and Hugo holding it open. But she couldn't go back on her word, couldn't give Hugo another blow, dedicate him to a life of motionless loneliness.

She felt that she was prevented from doing that by something within herself which was governed by something that penetrated to her from outside. She had started impulsively on a path, and she must go forward along it. There was nothing else to be done. She had to be unselfish in spite of her fear, her horror almost, of her own unselfishness. She had to practice a virtue reluctantly. But she had the grace when she looked at Hugo to hate her own reluctance.

"What will your people say?" Hugo said at last.

"They are fond of you. They'll always be fond of you."

He sighed. It was evident to her that he wasn't quite at ease with his new happiness. Perhaps he was thinking how different he had expected it to be. She wondered whether since the accident he had ever dared to think of marriage with her as a possibility, or whether the conception he had formed of her character had prevented that. And with that wonder came a great curiosity.

"What were you expecting in the future?" she asked him.

"When?"

"Let us say yesterday?"

"I tried not to think about it. I tried to shut it out of my mind."

"Do you feel I can give you any happiness?"

"Yes—if you are happy in what you're doing."

She trembled at the thought of his possible insight as she had never trembled in the presence of danger, and under the pressure of this thought sought the safety of semi-frankness.

"Happy!" she said. "I think I should have to be pretty heartless if I could be perfectly happy with you now. What's the good of pretending, Hugo? A tragedy's happened, and nothing either of us can do can ever do away with it. You and I had thought of a very different life from the one we shall have to lead."

"You can lead it still," he interrupted quickly. "I won't have you tie yourself——"

"Yes, yes, I know! But we should have led it together. That will be the difference. We can't ever be happy as we hoped to be. But——"

She looked at him and paused. Perhaps unconsciously she happened to fix her eyes on his left cheek. (She was sitting on the left of his couch.) He began to look uncomfortable, shy almost, and put up a hand to his cheek.

"What's the matter?" she asked. "Why do you do that?"

"I thought—weren't you noticing——"

"What?" she asked.

"I have to let Marfield shave me now, and I can't have him do it twice a day. It hurts too much. When I——"

Then something unsuspected, almost desperately womanish, overwhelmed her for a moment, and she bent over Hugo, took both his hands in hers, held them fast, squeezed them.

"My poor old boy! As if I were looking at that! As if I cared about such a thing as that!"

That helplessness of his went straight to her heart, and at that instant no regret for what she had done or was going to do was left in her. Instead, a half-savage desire to rush on along this strange path came to her and she said:

"Now I'm going down. I'm going to tell them."

Before he could say another word, she had sprung up impetuously and gone out of the room.

She found her mother in the drawing-room confusedly engaged in a struggle with a patience, while Towser sat reading a book. Lord Lowrie was not in the room. As she came in Towser looked up. She looked. She stared.

"Where's old papa?" asked Imogen, returning her aunt's gaze with hardihood.

"What, dear? Will that ace never come out?"

"He's in the garden, I think," said Miss Creswell. "I smelled the smoke of his cigar a minute ago through the open window."

"Thanks, Towser. I'll go and find him."

She went out of the room and into the garden, where she found her father cheerfully contemplating the night on one of the lower terraces. She went up to him and put her arm

through the crook of his as he stood with one hand in the
pocket of his smoking coat.

"I've come to tell you a piece of news. I'm going to marry
old Hugo."

Lord Lowrie turned a little and looked at her.

"Are you surprised, old papa?"

"Yes," said Lord Lowrie.

"You thought me too selfish to do such a thing?"

"I thought in time you might possibly come to it, but not
yet. What has speeded up the pace of your resolve on self-
sacrifice?"

"Don't call it that!"

"But isn't it that?"

"Hugo deserves everything I can give him. He's worth
more than I am."

"And your heart consents to what you are going to do?"

"I remember your saying that. But when you said it I didn't
think I should ever do what I am going to do."

"Then your heart has changed."

"I don't know. I don't know what has changed, what's
happened exactly in me. But I'm going to marry Hugo."

"Have you told him so?"

"Yes. I told him today when I came back."

"Then you decided while you were at Cannes?"

"No. At Cannes I had made up my mind never to marry
him."

"The impulse was sudden!"

"Yes, absolutely! But I shan't change. If there were the
slightest chance of my changing my mind, I shouldn't have
told Hugo."

"No. That wouldn't have been fair. The poor chap's had
enough trouble without that being added to it."

"What d'you think about it, old papa?"

"My dear, I don't quite know. And it doesn't much matter.
It's a long while since I came to the conclusion that what I
think isn't of any great consequence."

"I know someone who wouldn't agree with that. At least I
don't think he would."

"Who is the gentleman?"

"It's a—Jew man."

"A Jew! I had an idea you didn't make friends with Jews
easily."

"This is a very exceptional Jew."

Lord Lowrie seemed to be struck by his daughter's manner and voice. He looked at her with an almost sharp curiosity.

"Exceptional, is he? Well, there are plenty of very interesting, cultivated Jews. I have no dislike of Jews. Cut all the Jews out of the world, and the arts would be stricken. As executants and patrons of art the Jews are of immense value to the community. Only fools can doubt that. And their value to science is known to all of us."

"My Jew doesn't belong to any recognized type, but he'd interest you most tremendously, old papa."

"Tell me something about him."

She opened out to her father and gave him a sharply drawn outline of Peter Kharkoff. Lord Lowrie was deeply interested.

"Just the sort of man I should like to meet! Just the sort of man! But why did you say that he wouldn't agree with me about the impotence of the average man's—and I'm average —thoughts?"

"Because I am sure he uses thought as a weapon, and doesn't consider thoughts as negligible things. I scarcely know him, but he's made me feel about thought as I never felt before I met him."

She turned round and saw a light shining in Hugo's window.

"Go up to Hugo, will you, old papa, and say a kind word about—about our engagement. I know he thinks he ought to have refused my offer."

"Then it was you who——"

"Oh yes, it was I! Or some influence working in me. Aren't we the homes of influences?"

"I thought you always prided yourself on being absolutely independent and ungovernable."

"I did! But remember my age, old papa! Even a fool may surely be forgiven at twenty-one! And now I'm going to tell the old lady and Towser."

CHAPTER IV

BECAUSE of Hugo the Lowries were not having guests in the villa that spring, except Miss Creswell who was of course one of the family. Lord Lowrie had thought that it was "early days" for Hugo in his affliction to be surrounded by lively people whose gay activities must bring into greater relief his inability to live like others. Lady Lowrie agreed with her husband. Secretly, perhaps, they were both not indisposed to enjoy the peace which resulted from their apparent self-sacrifice. Now and then a visitor dropped in by motor, and after a short stay of an hour or two was taken by the Riviera. But April had come with its warmer days, its balmier nights and its flowers. Already the tide of the gay world was setting northwards.

As Beauty drew nearer to that lovely coast, beauties had their trunks packed and prepared for flight. Paris was calling. London was calling. Why linger when there would soon be no attraction except the loveliness of nature and the golden sunshine to drape it? The annual chapter of Exodus was being busily written, and life at the Villa Sainte Maxime would soon be in no danger of even casual disturbance by visitors.

Imogen's "set" had been duly informed of her engagement to Hugo, and had taken it in quite the right spirit, as the appropriate conclusion to a love-affair not without elements of romance in an unromantic age. Public praises of her moral beauty were loud and numerous. Private remarks were not always on the same elevated level. There were those who wondered how she would "stick it" when it came to the pinch of matrimony, those who argued that of course Hugo wouldn't —couldn't—try to hold her too tight, considering that really now he wasn't much more than a quarter of a man. Imogen would of course find compensations in the future, and no one would blame her if she did. In any case, she had risen up to the heroic and shown the world what the maligned modern girl was capable of. And that was very satisfactory. Her numerous girl friends went about with an added complacency, pluming themselves on her noble self-sacrifice, which helped to show them all up in the proper light.

The old lady had received the great news without surprise. She had indeed "always expected it." She was very fond of "poor Hugo" and glad that he should have something to compensate him for his terrible misfortune. But she wondered a little about her daughter. She hoped Imogen realized what she was doing. Imogen assured Lady Lowrie that she did, whereupon Lady Lowrie hastened to throw away any doubts

and anxieties which were beginning to beset her, and was sure
it was all for the best.

Lord Lowrie's acceptance of his daughter's decision might,
perhaps, seem surprisingly prompt and easy. Imogen could
not help thinking about that. But she had become accustomed
to her father's peculiar casualness about the matters of life on
this plane. Having everything he wanted, and an excellent
digestion into the bargain, he could afford to be charmingly
unworldly. Apparently he had trained himself to look upon
this life as a quickly passing show peopled by shadows on the
way to other lives in which they would learn gradually to
become less absurd and more definite. He could not, therefore,
like more ordinary fathers, attach enormous importance to his
daughter's matrimonial intentions and plans. And in fact
he was secretly pleased to find in her a capacity for self-sacrifice.
He had hitherto thought her to be enormously worldly. Now
he was able to suppose that she had inherited certain moral
qualities from him. Imogen didn't hold to "all the rubbish"
as tenaciously as one had been inclined to believe she did. He
had never attempted to influence her. That wasn't his way.
But it seemed that she had drawn something from him nevertheless, and he thought it was something worth having.

Miss Creswell's behavior had slightly puzzled Imogen.
When she had first heard the news she had seemed genuinely
surprised, even startled. She had said very little, indeed nothing thoroughly unreserved; nevertheless Imogen had noted her
astonishment. But almost immediately that astonishment had
seemed to die out of her and to be replaced by a great contentment. She moved in a smiling serenity which presently
began to irritate her niece. For Imogen at this time knew nothing of serenity.

Miss Creswell had stayed on for a time at Geneva after
Imogen's departure. She had formed a strong friendship with
Madame Coiret, and she had become intimate with Edie
Baynes. But she had not met Peter Kharkoff again. And she
had not tried to meet him. Since that one visit to him she
had been satisfied, strangely satisfied, to "let things be." Her
former mental agitation and mental jealousy had subsided. She
even was able to look back on them with wonder. Upon her
the Jew had produced an effect exactly contrary to the effect
he had produced upon Imogen. In Imogen he had awakened
passion and rebellion, to Miss Creswell he had brought a

curious calm, a stability of peace. And this calm, this peace of the mind and the nature, seemed now to have been increased by what Imogen had told.

One day Imogen could not contain her irritation at her aunt's happy serenity, and she said:

"What on earth is there to be so damned happy about, Towser?"

"Happy!" said Miss Creswell, startled by this sudden onslaught.

"Yes. Is it the sketching, or what? If it is I think I'd better have some lessons at the Slade or somewhere. They say fishermen are the happiest sportsmen. Evidently painters in water-color are the happiest of all God's creatures, fishermen included."

"I hope I don't seem unkindly happy," said Miss Creswell. She seemed to consider for a moment, then added, "But it's true, I suppose. I'm much happier since I've been to Geneva."

"Well, I'm damned well not, since I've been!" said Imogen almost ferociously.

"Are you unhappy now?" asked Miss Creswell. "Do you regret what you've done?"

Imogen didn't answer at once. At that moment she longed to indulge in a frank outburst, to liberate her soul. But she didn't want to be a cad. And she felt that she had a great duty to Hugo.

"No," she said at last. "I don't regret it. If it hadn't happened I would do it now. But it's useless my pretending that life in the future will be an easy life. You remember what you said about Hugo reminding you of Lazarus in a way?"

"Yes."

"Well, you're right. I can do a great deal for Hugo. But mine isn't the voice that can call the whole of him to life. There's something which escapes me, do what I will. And I'm trying to do my best."

"Go on trying. Surely a reward will come."

"Oh, I'm not out for any reward."

"All the better."

"I'm just doing what I can."

Miss Creswell couldn't help being undiplomatic, couldn't help saying, "It's all very strange. But I think you had to do it."

"Had to?" said Imogen sharply. "Have you become a fatalist? Is that the latest development?"

"I don't know how you define fatalist, Im. But I believe a great reason is at the base of everything important we do."

"Dear me, Towser! How you and I differ! Now I feel more and more the dreadful littleness of things and you seem impressed by the enormous magnitude of everything. I see humanity, myself in the crowd, like worms crawling under the vastness of an unheeding sky. How are we important? Why even our own kind don't bother about our greatest sorrows, our greatest misfortunes, and yet we might surely be sorry for each other. But not a bit of it! 'Fall out of the ranks! Rot in your corner, and on with the dance!' "

"You haven't said that to Hugo Dennistone. You haven't left him to rot in his corner."

"No, that's true. But isn't what I say true of the world in general?"

"If it is what has made you an exception?"

"What are you driving at, Towser?" asked Imogen.

"Don't you remember that you were to prepare the way?"

"Well?"

"Haven't you prepared it?"

Imogen was silent.

"I think you have," said Miss Creswell.

At this moment Arthur Milligan knocked at the door of Imogen's sitting-room in which this conversation had taken place.

"If you please, ma'am," he said. "I thought you might like to know that I'm taking Captain Dennistone out now. We mean to go to the Hermitage dee Provongse."

"Thank you, Milligan. It's a lovely day. Captain Dennistone ought to be out."

"Yes, ma'am. We shall go on the terrace."

"What terrace?"

"At the Hermitage dee Provongse, ma'am."

"Oh—yes! And look at the life in the harbor, barges having wood loaded on them, green barrels being unloaded and so on. I know! Captain Dennistone told me."

"There isn't very much going on, ma'am, to be sure. Still it's something for Captain Dennistone to see."

"Tell him I'll come too. We'll have tea on the terrace and listen to the gramophone. There is one, isn't there?"

"Yes, ma'am. It plays chiefly dances."

"That's it. I'll join you."

"I'll tell Captain Dennistone, ma'am."

Milligan went out. When he had gone Imogen turned to her aunt.

"God, Towser! That one's future husband should have come to this! Sometimes I feel desperate. Sometimes I think I shall have to——" She pulled herself up short. "I must go and get my hat."

It was a brilliant April day, intensely blue, with a sun that gave out real heat, and a warm breeze, almost a wind, which had sprung up in the afternoon, and made waves tipped with foam crests in the Gulf of Saint Tropez. Nature had a joyous, even a lusty look, full of buoyancy, energy, enterprise. When the evening fell a romantic calm would fall with it over the hills, the woods, the sea. The buoyancy would be subdued to a mystic stillness. But now, under the golden sun, the waves were dancing, the pine trees were murmuring, the mimosas were shaking their tresses, and every flower in the garden was enticed into movement.

When Imogen came downstairs she found Hugo already outside before the hall door, lying covered with a thin rug on the high couch with large wheels to which he was lifted by Marfield and Milligan when he was taken out for what Milligan called "a nice airing." He gave her a smile in which eagerness and wistfulness seemed to be mingled.

"Very good of you to come with me, Geney! But it's an expedition."

"I know. You're bound for Sainte Maxime."

"Yes. D'you think you want to come?"

"Of course I do. We're going to have tea on the terrace of the Ermitage de Provence. Off we go, Milligan!"

She tried hard to speak cheerily, to banish the depression almost amounting to despair which she was feeling from her voice. But she was almost sure Hugo saw through the pretense. Ah, how different this was from the many departures she and Hugo had joined in in former days: departures on mettlesome horses in the dawn cub hunting, or later when the pale sun was up, to meet with the Quorn, the Whaddon Chase, the Pytchley, the Badminton. Or they had slipped into Hugo's racing-motor and away. The country had reeled by them as Hugo let the motor have "the run of its teeth"—an absurd

phrase of his to indicate full speed ahead. Or she had nipped
up to the box seat of the coach when Hugo was driving four-
in-hand, and had heard the wind sing in her ears as he gave the
horses their heads, and they were off to the music of ringing
hoofs on the great Bath Road, or on one of the other fine
coach roads of England. For despite his modernity Hugo had
a love of the past in his blood and had often said in Imogen's
hearing that it was the old sportsmen moldering in many a
rustic churchyard with the daisies over them who had made
England a country no sportsman could help loving.

And now she was walking by his invalid's couch pushed by
Milligan, and they were going to look at the "life" in the port
of Sainte Maxime on the Gulf of Saint Tropez.

Although Lord Lowrie had given the name of Sainte Maxime
to his property it lay between the little town and Beauvallon,
and was, perhaps, some twenty minutes' distance on foot from
the former. The road wound along the edge of the gulf and
was not much frequented. Now and then a peasant appeared
on it, a wood-cutter or a worker on the land; now and then
the chasseur from the Golf Hotel at Beauvallon spun by on
his bicycle, or some visitors at the hotel stirred up the dust
on their way to probe into the picturesque mysteries of the
town. Sometimes the doctor drove by in a hired victoria.
And from time to time a motor flashed along by the sea,
giving out a cry at the sharp corners of the road.

Milligan was very careful about motorcars, and kept Hugo's
wheeled couch well to the right of the highway as the three
of them went on slowly towards their bourne, the Ermitage de
Provence. He had grasped the rule of the road before coming
to the villa. Among many other things the Great War had
taught him that.

"Though why the French should make the traffic meet on
the right and pass on the left I don't quite see, ma'am," he
observed to Imogen.

"I imagine it's got something to do with keeping up the
Entente Cordiale," she replied.

He smiled. He was always ready to smile at Imogen's
jokes. Although he greatly disliked the smother of paint
which covered her face he considered her a thorough good
"sport" and admired her whole-heartedly for sticking to the
man in distress who was for the time his employer. Although
he had seen many horrors and much suffering both physical and

mental, he had remained in possession of a very soft heart. And now that he knew Miss Lowrie was going to marry Captain Dennistone she had taken her place among his heroines and become in his estimation not only a sport but also a "damned fine kid." Imogen didn't know that Milligan mentally called her a kid, but she knew that he set her very high among women.

During the slow progress by the edge of the dancing sea there was little conversation. Milligan was busy pushing the couch. Imogen walked beside it, or near it, but said scarcely anything to Hugo, who lay on his back turning his blue eyes from side to side, looking at the trees, the scrub, the water, with the deep gravity which was now characteristic of him, and which he had not lost since his great understanding with "Geney." Once a carriage went by containing two English ladies wearing mushroom hats and huge floating veils, who turned their old heads cautiously to stare down at the crippled man. And Imogen saw Hugo stare back at them with a sort of defiance in his face. Then he looked again towards the sea.

When the houses of the town came in sight and the row of striped blue and white bathing-huts Imogen said to Milligan in a low voice:

"When you've wheeled him on to the terrace you might leave us for a little while; I'm sure you'd like to look round by yourself. We shall be all right for half an hour or so. There are boats. Wouldn't you like to go for a row?"

"Thank you, ma'am. I believe I should. I've seen some quite decent boats. And I believe very much in rowing, specially for the chest and arms."

"Do go then, and have a good time."

And when the couch had been wheeled on to the terrace in front of the little restaurant, and pushed up quite close to the iron railing, she said, "Milligan's going out for a row while we have tea here."

"Do go, Milligan. The sea's not too rough, eh?"

"Oh no, sir. I've often been out in weather much rougher than this. There's no sea on at all really. Look at it!"

"Be off then. You scarcely get any exercise here. And I know how keen you are on it. Put me so that I can see you start."

"Right, sir!" He turned the couch. "That's it, I think."

"And now let's have tea, Geney, shall we?"

Imogen heard a strong effort after cheeriness in his voice.
"Yes. Good-by, Milligan."

"Good-by, ma'am."

Milligan went away, and Imogen ordered tea from a woman
who came out from the café behind them.

"Shall we have the gramophone, Hugo?"

"Oh no—for God's sake!" After an instant he added,
"Milligan thinks it cheers me up. But I hate to hear ragtime."

She sat down beside him. Beyond the railing and the road
lay the so-called "harbor" of Sainte Maxime, a bit of water
protected by a mole and breakwater of stone. On this bit of
water lay two or three barges laden with logs of wood, a couple
of sailing-boats at anchor, and one battered and storm-bitten
sailing-ship. On the wharf stood a row of barrels recently
unloaded, perhaps from this ship. On the stone-paved jetty,
behind which rose a high wall, a few men were at work loading more logs on the barges. Three men lounged vaguely at
the edge of the sea, smoking pipes, now and then exchanging
a few words, spitting and staring at the barges. Against the
wall leaned with one shoulder a young man with a blue jacket
tied round his throat by the sleeves and wearing on his black
curls a peaked cap. His shirt sleeves were rolled up, and his
muscular bare arms were folded across his broad chest. Alone
and not smoking he just stood there taking his ease in the sunshine apparently quite contented. His weather-beaten red
face and his small black eyes looked perfectly calm. No one
spoke to him or took any notice of him. A few people walked
by now and then and presently a perambulator, containing a
very fat and placid child of perhaps a year old, paused in front
of Imogen and Hugo, and the young woman who was pushing
it entered into conversation with a bulging elderly woman in
mourning and a little man in baggy trousers and a dark jacket,
who had wispy gray hair and a very red nose. The child lay
vaguely agitating its fat hands and occasionally emitting a bub-
ble of saliva.

From the distance came a faint sound of military drums.
Milligan had walked away to the right, where a long wooden
jetty ran out into the sea between the Ermitage de Provence
and the bathing-huts. Presently Imogen saw him speaking to
a boatman. Then he took off his jacket, waistcoat and hat,
rolled up his shirt sleeves, stepped into a white boat with a
green line of paint, took a pair of oars and pushed off.

"There goes Milligan!" said Imogen. "Can you see, Hugo?"

"No, not yet."

"You will in a minute. He's coming this way. There he is."

"Now I can."

He stared. She felt that he was longing to raise himself up.

"Milligan's a good fellow."

"Yes."

She made a gesture. Milligan let an oar go for an instant and touched a hand to his forehead, then started rowing vigorously. The woman of the restaurant came out with their tea. Imogen poured it out. She was giving Hugo his cup when suddenly a wheezy shriek came from the house behind them and they were bathed in a husky torrent of jazz.

"My God!" said Hugo. "She thinks—Geney, do stop it!"

Imogen sprang up and her nerves seemed to jump within her.

"We want jazz!"

Had she really ever said that? She hurried into the café.

"Please stop that!" she said in French.

"Mais, madame, le pauvre monsieur——"

"Not today, please! He doesn't want the gramophone today."

"Pardon, madame! Mais j'ai pensé que le pauvre monsieur——"

"It's very kind of you. Another day, perhaps, but not now."

"Bien, madame!"

And the woman, looking rather sulky, went across to the wheezing monster and brought its hideous activities to an end.

"Thank you, Geney," said Hugo, when she came back to the tea table.

And he said nothing more. She sat down beside him and poured out some tea for herself. There was a plate of odd-looking gray biscuits on a tray. She offered it to him.

"They look rather venerable, don't they? Have one?"

"Thanks."

He took one. Imogen struck a match and lit a cigarette. Silence reigned between them and she didn't know how to break it. She stared across the railing at the stagnant harbor, kissed by the glorious sunshine, but stagnant nevertheless to her thinking. The three people were still talking round the perambulator in which the fat baby was still blowing bubbles.

The man with the tied sleeves still leaned his shoulder against
the stone wall. The men went on loading logs of wood on the
barges. The few loungers spat meditatively into the water.
Milligan and his boat had disappeared.

Hugo made a slight movement with his right arm.

"Oh, you've finished. Have another cup?"

"No, thank you."

"Another biscuit?"

"No, thanks."

"Have a cigarette?"

"Yes, I think I will."

She gave him one, struck a match and leaned down to him.
As she put the match to his cigarette, she saw the expression in
his eyes. She threw the burnt match away, then said abruptly,
"Hugo!"

"Well, Geney?"

"You like being out here in the villa, don't you?"

"Yes. You know I do."

"As well as anywhere else?"

"Better."

"I'm sure father would keep the house open all through May
and on into June if you like."

"He mustn't keep it open for me."

"Oh, he loves being here and so does the old lady. But
now I want to ask you something. I know someone, a man
who's living in Switzerland at present."

"Switzerland!"

A shadow seemed to pass across Hugo's face, and an anxious
expression came into his eyes. He looked scared, almost as he
had looked when Imogen had told him that she was going to
Lady Vesie's château near Cannes.

"Yes?" he added quickly. "What about him?"

"I think he might be able to do something for you."

"For me? Is he one of those Swiss doctor fellows then?
But it's no use. Absolutely not. There's nothing to be done."

"But—wait! He isn't a doctor."

"Then how could he do anything for me?"

"I don't know," said Imogen.

She suddenly realized how difficult, how almost preposterous,
was the adventure on which—again driven abruptly by impulse
—she was perhaps embarking, how difficult it would be to
explain matters to Hugo in such a way as to bring him any

conviction of the strange powers which she had felt in the Jew. Painful hesitation seized her. The two short lines appeared between her eyebrows. She saw a faintly suspicious look on Hugo's face. His eyes were fixed upon her sideways.

"I don't understand," he said.

Something in his look and in his tone made her feel angry.

"What's the matter?" she said sharply. "Why do you look at me like that? Are you suspicious of me? Don't you trust me?"

While she was speaking her anger increased and with it came a sense of being wronged.

"If you can't trust me now what sort of a future shall we have?" she exclaimed. And she spoke with a bitterness which startled herself.

"But I do trust you," he said, again looking scared and for a moment oddly boyish. "It's only that—Geney, I can't help it, I'm haunted by the feeling that if I marry you I shall do you a dreadful wrong, and that if you don't see that now you will come to see it some day. But I want you so awfully that I don't know how to give up my one chance of happiness. You mustn't be angry if I'm sensitive, if I—whenever I think of other fellows it has to hurt."

"Forgive me!" she said, putting a hand on his. "I only want to help you." She remembered her aunt's words, and added, "I feel I can do something for you, my dear, but there's a lot I can't do. And I have a strange feeling—it's a conviction, I think—that this man, only this man, could do what I can't do."

"But what is that?"

"Don't ask me. I don't know. But just let me tell you something about him."

And then she began to tell him about Peter Kharkoff. There was much that she felt she couldn't tell. For instance she didn't say that Peter Kharkoff was a Jew; she didn't say that she had spoken to him of Hugo; she didn't say how she had met him; she didn't mention her aunt's meeting with him, or any of the happenings at Drearney. She simply tried to give Hugo an impression of the impression Peter Kharkoff had made upon her, an impression of his intellect, his power, his unworldliness, his unlikeness to all other men, his large simplicity and his curious and totally unselfconscious authority. When she stopped speaking he said only:

"You went out to Switzerland to see him again, didn't you?"

"I was going to St. Moritz and went to Geneva to pick up Aunt Towser; but I knew he was there."

"You saw him of course."

"Yes, once."

"Why do you tell me about this fellow? You know clever chaps were never in my line."

"He isn't a clever chap."

"But, Geney, what on earth could a man like that—granted he's all you take him for—do for me? I'm done, absolutely done. I had it all out with the doctors. And I'm done."

"Doctors are for the body. But there's something else besides the body."

He didn't speak for a moment. Then he said:

"Of course there is. I know that, and perhaps better than most fellows now."

"Peter Kharkoff could help that something else, Hugo. I'm convinced of that."

"Why not send for a parson and have done with it?"

"You've never seen him, so you can't understand. That's not your fault."

"I may as well tell you, Geney, that there's very little can be done for me now. But all there is could only be done by you."

"No, no, no!" she exclaimed. "Compared with him I'm nothing, less than nothing."

"You're all I want," he said.

"That isn't true. I'm only a little bit of all you want and need."

He didn't contradict her but lay silent, looking out at the harbor, staring out, at the barrels, the logs of wood, the barges, the battered old sailing-ship, which had surely knocked about for many years in the obscure ports of the Mediterranean.

The perambulator with the child in it had disappeared.

"It's good of you all the same," he said, after a long pause.

She sat very still. She gazed at the sea, at the hills. The open sea was shut out from her view by a large square house, which stood on the left beyond some palms in the garden, or yard of the café. She saw only the water that seemed confined among the hills. And she saw her life, confined, shut in among narrowing circumstances. A great obstinacy woke in her. She resolved that she would carry through this adventure, for her own sake as well as for Hugo's. Selfishness was at work in her, hand in hand with unselfishness.

"Hugo," she said, "it's impossible that you can understand without knowing this man, absolutely impossible. I want you to trust me. I want you to take it from me. I feel that you must know this man, that it's meant you should know him."

"But he isn't here!"

"If he came here would you allow him to help you if he could?"

She said it because she had to say something. But there was irony just then in her outlook on herself and on Hugo. The thought of Hugo trying to allow or not to allow anything in connection with Peter Kharkoff filled her whole mind with a sarcasm that was pitiful. But she had to say something, and Hugo wouldn't know.

"He couldn't help me, but of course I should behave myself to any visitor in your father's house."

There were hostility and pride in his voice. She felt that he was stiffening with reserve.

She said nothing more, and soon Milligan rowed in from the gulf, and not long afterwards they went home along the sea.

The breeze was dropping now. Quiet was stealing over this hidden corner of the world. A boat with two sails, one white, one orange-colored, was tacking in the distance of the sea, making for the harbor of Saint Tropez. The deep voice of the bell of the church there came to them over the water. The chasseur from Beauvallon spun by on his bicycle carrying the post from the Golf Hotel to Sainte Maxime. No one else passed them. Evening was coming. The sea was dropping into sleep. Imogen walked beside Hugo's wheeled chair in silence. Milligan glanced at her from time to time but said nothing. Her painted face looked severe, almost old. And Captain Dennistone's face, he thought, looked unusually tense and grim.

"I hope they haven't been having a scrap!" thought Milligan anxiously.

He was beginning to identify himself with his employer. And he wouldn't for anything see matters go wrong between the crippled man and the damned fine kid.

CHAPTER V

THAT evening, after dinner, Imogen spoke again to her
father about Peter Kharkoff and said she wanted to write to
him and ask him to stay at the villa. Lord Lowrie assented
almost eagerly.

"Of course ask him. Get him here by all means if you can.
I wonder though whether he'll come."

"So do I. If he does come you mustn't expect him to dress
for dinner."

"Dress for dinner! Who cares about dressing for dinner?
I never heard that Socrates dressed for dinner or Pythagoras,
either."

"And you mustn't monopolize him, old papa. It's for Hugo
I want him."

When she said that, Imogen felt a little less than sincere.
And yet she hadn't told her father a lie. Only she had suppressed a part of the truth.

"Ask him by all means," rejoined Lord Lowrie, taking no
notice of her injunction. "A remarkable man is always an
asset. I flee the herd as the wicked flee when no man pur-
sueth, but I love a man of value as I love a lodge in a garden
of cucumbers. Invite him. I only hope he comes."

And then Imogen got up, and Lord Lowrie refilled his pipe
and cast a glance that was lustful at the third volume of
Gibbon's "Decline and Fall."

"Great times, those old Roman times, Imogen! Just think
of it! Elephants going into battle! And now we've come
down to tanks!"

"And risen up to airplanes, old papa. Don't forget that."

"Waspish atrocities! Give me an elephant covered with
trappings of crimson and gold. Good night, my dear."

He puffed out a great cloud of fragrant tobacco smoke and
returned to the Roman Empire.

As she went to her sitting-room Imogen pondered on egotism.
Not very long ago swimming in egotism herself, she hadn't
bothered very much about it in others. Now she was beginning to find it everywhere. Even her father had immediately
begun to think of himself in connection with the unknown Jew.

"And I?" she had grace enough to think.

When she reached her room she went at once to the writing

table and sat down at it. She meant to write to Peter Kharkoff immediately.

Soon after eleven there came a tap on the door. She started violently. Her nerves felt all on edge.

"Come in!" she called.

The door opened, and Miss Creswell appeared.

"I've only come to say good night."

"Oh—good night, Towser. Where's the old lady?"

"She fell asleep over a patience. It wouldn't come out."

"It never does. But where is she now?"

"Gone to her room. She was so sleepy that I suppose she forgot about you."

Imogen saw her aunt's eyes looking at her intently.

"I'm writing to *him*," she said. "Father said I might. I've asked him to come here."

Miss Creswell said nothing, but she did not look surprised. The window was open. In the silence they heard the faint wash of the sea.

"Isn't it strange?" Imogen added. "While I was writing I seemed to see an hour-glass on the table. And the sands were running out very fast. What did that mean?"

"You were thinking of the hour-glass on his table."

"I don't know." She shivered.

"Are you cold, Im?" said Miss Creswell. "Perhaps you ought to shut the window."

"No; it isn't that. But—I wonder if the sands are running out for someone I know. I wonder if someone I know very well is going to die."

"Whom are you thinking of? You don't mean——"

"Hush! Don't say a name—don't!"

She held up her hand, and shivered again.

"I don't understand, Im."

"Nor do I. Good night, Aunt Annie."

CHAPTER VI

IMOGEN went to bed very late that night. She had taken a long time over the writing of her letter and the letter was a long one. It was strange, but as soon as she had resolved to communicate with Peter Kharkoff and had begun to write to him, she felt an astonishing sense of relief, as if she were casting off a burden on to shoulders that would be able to bear it, not merely without difficulty but with triumphant ease. And this sense of relief drove her pen forward.

Never before had she written such a letter as she wrote to Peter Kharkoff. In it she was tremendously frank. Indeed it was a confession, a complete unburdening of her mind and heart. Having begun to be frank she could not stop. The new joy of complete sincerity carried her away and she realized that such joy must be a very rare experience in the soul of any human being. Hitherto, she had supposed herself to be very sincere in her daring, in her carelessness of the opinions of others. Now she had to grasp the fact that even she, the audacious Imogen, passed a great deal of her time on the defensive behind barriers of mental reserve.

When she had finished her letter she put it into the drawer of her writing table, enclosed in an unfastened envelop. She meant to reread it in daylight. But when the morning came she didn't dare to do that. She was afraid that if she read it again she wouldn't send it. And she felt that it ought to go. So, keeping her eyes away from the fragment of writing that was visible above the envelope's edge, she quickly thrust the letter lower down and stuck down the flap above it. Then she wrote the name and address and gave the letter to be posted.

When it had gone she suddenly felt as if she received a soft blow from the irrevocable, and was conscious of a tremor of doubt.

"What will he think when he reads my letter?"

That was her first thought. And it was followed immediately by another thought.

"What will his answer be?"

She had asked him to come to Sainte Maxime if only for a few hours. Now she was wondering whether he would come.

Presently to this wonder was added an anxiety that became painfully intense. Several days went by, and no answer came to her letter. Was silence going to be the only answer she was to receive? When Imogen asked herself that question she knew how complete had been her dependence on the Jew, and what a terrible reaction must follow upon his tacit rejection of her appeal. (For of course his abstention from reply must mean that her appeal was rejected.) Yes; although she had been so angry with Peter Kharkoff, although she had rebelled against him, her dependence upon him had nevertheless been complete.

That knowledge which was now with her humiliated her. Yet she was not angry as she had been in Geneva. Her anxiety was too great to be mingled with such a common feeling as anger. Her condition was not unlike that of a child waiting for a communication from a parent or guardian, who, in the child's opinion, has the power to order its fate. She had never known anything like this before.

But something more strange succeeded this feeling in her presently. Her anxiety faded into a marvelous patience. Although the chain of days was lengthening and she had received no reply from Peter Kharkoff, she passed on from that reaction of fear into a marvelous calm. And she had the intimate sensation that this calm was sent to her by him, that he was giving it to her deliberately.

It was quite irresistible. It seemed to flow over her and to take possession of her. She was wrapped in it. She felt it folded about her almost like a garment of the softest silk about a nude body. But how much more soft and intimate was such a wrapping to the soul than could any wrapping be to the body.

"Did you send that letter, Im?" Miss Creswell asked her one day.

"Yes," she said.

"Haven't you had any answer?"

"No."

Miss Creswell looked surprised. But her surprise was caused rather by Imogen's quiet manner in making the announcement than by the fact stated.

"Hugo Dennistone was asking me about it," she said, after a moment.

"Hugo!" Imogen said with quite a different voice. "But what, Towser?"

"Well, it seems you spoke about Peter Kharkoff to him."

"Yes—before writing my letter."

"He hasn't forgotten that. Yesterday in the garden he asked me whether anyone was expected at the villa. I said that people were leaving the Riviera now and going North, and that Minnie hadn't said anything to me about any guests."

"What did he say?"

"He said that he understood from you that possibly a friend of yours called Peter Kharkoff was coming."

"Was that all?"

"Yes. But I gathered the impression that his mind was dwelling persistently on the subject."

"Dwelling? Painfully, do you mean?"

"I don't quite know about that. Hugo Dennistone is very reserved and uncommunicative with me, poor fellow. But I am certain he has been thinking a great deal about whether this visit is going to take place or not."

"He has never mentioned the subject to me. Since that one conversation we had he has never alluded to Peter Kharkoff."

"Well, Im, I may be wrong. But I think—I have a feeling that Hugo Dennistone wants Mr. Kharkoff to come here."

"Then he has quite changed."

"But so have you."

"I!" Imogen said, rather sharply.

"Yes. You're generally so impatient. When you want anything you're in such a hurry to have it. And now you're so calm, so patient. I hardly know you."

The patience, the calm which her aunt had noticed still prevailed in Imogen. She thought of them now as necessary preliminaries to something vital which was on the way. She compared this period of waiting with that strange silence which had opened the interview in the rue les Bergues.

Her aunt's words about Hugo had roused her curiosity. She longed to ask him whether, in spite of his obvious hostility when she had spoken to him about Peter Kharkoff, her words had eventually bred in him the thought that perhaps this man might be able to do something for him which a parson could not do. But she didn't ask him this. Something held her back from that question. But though she said nothing to Hugo she could not resist at last speaking to Milligan.

"What do you think about Captain Dennistone?" she asked him, trying to speak casually.

"How d'you mean, ma'am?" said Milligan. "I'm afraid he'll never be any different from what he is now."

"I know. But how is he in himself? D'you notice any change in him? You're so much with him, and I think you're very observant. Is he—is he getting at all accustomed to his condition?"

"Oh no, ma'am! But how could we expect it? It's early days yet."

"I know! I know! I didn't mean to put it like that. It's

only that I'm so anxious that his sufferings shouldn't get worse and so afraid that they may."

"Of course you help him very much, ma'am. I don't really know what he'd do without you. But even with that—you see, ma'am, he feels his difference from other men, specially now you've said you will stick to him. It may seem foolish but how can he help it? He feels you are fit for the very best, and that—I'm afraid Captain Dennistone's passing through a very bad patch, ma'am. As you ask me I have to say the truth. He never complains. Sometimes I wish he would. The worst of it is he isn't one who cares much for reading, or anything like that. Miss Creswell kindly lent him two books. He's had a try at them both but he couldn't get on with them. He said, 'Books are no good to me, Arthur.' (He's taken to calling me Arthur sometimes, ma'am.) 'I never was much of a hand at books. Horses were more in my line. That's a pity now.' And what could I say? Tell the truth, ma'am, if you'll excuse me for saying so, I'm afraid Captain Dennistone's going through hell."

As he said the last words he looked at her with sudden intentness, and she had a feeling that he knew something which she didn't know, and was perhaps wondering whether she knew it. She was silent and at last he added:

"It's difficult to know what to do for the best."

"Yes. If what you say is true it seems that I'm not of much use to him."

"Oh, ma'am, indeed you are! He puts you far before everyone, but——"

"That's all right, Milligan. I'm not the whole world, and don't want to be the whole world to anyone. I wish Captain Dennistone hadn't become so reserved. Often I——"

"It's keeping things in, ma'am, for fear of breaking loose, and then everything might get out of control. I've seen lots of men like that in the war. We used to call it putting up the shutters."

"Ah!" she said.

She stared at him for a minute, but as if she didn't see him. Then she went quickly out of the room.

Within an hour she had sent a telegram to Peter Kharkoff.

"Please come if you can—Imogen Lowrie," and the address.

On the following day there was no answering telegram from the Jew. In the afternoon something happened. Towser

abruptly announced that she must leave for Drearney on the
morrow. She had already lingered on much later than usual.
For she was one of those who like to see "the primroses come
up" when spring bedews England with her copious and no
doubt useful showers. Imogen guessed that Towser had de-
layed in the hope of perhaps seeing Peter Kharkoff at Sainte
Maxime. But now something had gone very wrong in the
garden at Ewenden House, and her gardener's soul was aflame
with anxiety. She must pack up and go. And pack up she
did with practical celerity.

Just before she started for the station she asked Imogen to
come into the garden. When they were there she said:

"So you've had no word from him?"

"None."

"That's strange."

"Is it?"

"Don't you think so?"

"I don't know. That man lives in his own way, acts in his
own way. As father says, most men open their mouths to say
'Baa.' But he doesn't. Even if he doesn't come, somehow I
feel he is here. A paradox, Towser, and a truth. But I still
think his body will come here. I don't know why. I write.
I telegraph."

"Have you telegraphed?"

"Yes, the day before yesterday. No reply."

"Well then——"

"Have you forgotten the silence in his room in the rue les
Bergues?"

"I shall never forget it."

"I feel as if this waiting were like that silence—a prelude."

"But time's drawing on."

"Yes. The sands are dropping in the glass. But I can
wait."

"The change I feel in you is marvelous, Im."

"Not so marvelous! Underneath I'm what I was. Don't
you remember my outburst after we had left his little room?"

"Indeed I do."

"There may be others. But now I feel very still, very
calm."

"Hugo Dennistone doesn't. I've just been up to say good-by
to him. He seemed horribly restless, I thought, and his eyes
looked quite feverish."

"Towser," said Imogen, stopping in the path. "I know what it is. Already he feels the Jew."

"Does he know Mr. Kharkoff is a Jew? Did you tell him?"

"No. If he ever sees Peter Kharkoff he will know at once. But then it will be too late."

"Too late for what?"

"For Hugo to be able to hate Peter Kharkoff."

At this moment a faint contralto voice uprose within the precincts of the house.

"An-nie! An-nie!—Motor—car—late—station!"

"The old lady's getting into a panic."

"Im! As if dear Minnie ever got into anything so vital as that! Well, good-by, dear."

"Good-by, old Towser. Go back to your tulips, and leave us to our roses and arums and bougainvillea."

"And to what else?"

Miss Creswell took hold of Imogen by the shoulders and looked into her eyes.

"To what else?" she repeated.

"An-*nie!* An-*nie!*—don't take—miss the——"

And then Miss Creswell hurried away and got to the station in time.

When she had gone Imogen was conscious of a strong sense of relief. This puzzled her, for she had not known that she had any desire to get rid of her aunt. Yet now that Towser had gone back to the tulips a new liberty seemed to dwell in the house. It was as if a sweeping and garnishing had taken place, as if now things were ready and had not been ready before. A conviction came to her that her summons to Peter Kharkoff would not much longer remain answered.

It was now the beginning of May. The season on the Riviera was over. At Cannes the Carlton and all the other big hotels were shut. A few people of course lingered on in the villas. And many a pension still held its population of elderly ladies with nothing to do and small steady incomes. The real people of the Riviera, the people who belonged there, who drew their looks and not a few of their emotions out of its sun-warmed soil, began to show their dark heads and nut-brown faces. But the painted women and the gambling men, the adventurers and adventuresses, and most of the wolves that come out of the Northern cities in droves to carry off the prey that is dangled before the eyes of the greedy along the glittering sea, as if in sheer invitation to teeth and claws—all these were going, or had already gone, except from Monte Carlo. And Monte Carlo is quite a long way from Sainte Maxime.

Usually at such a time Imogen would have been horribly restless for Paris and London if she had been forced by circumstances to stay on in the villa. For although the villa was in a place comparatively remote, nevertheless even there one felt in some mysterious way when the season was over. The dusty roads were deserted or almost deserted of motors. Few yachts glided into the gulf. The motorboat of Beauvallon crossed the sea but seldom to Saint Tropez, and when it crossed held only two or three passengers. Brown men from hidden places appeared from time to time upon lonely bits of coast, rushed shouting into the shining sea, and afterwards lay warming their lusty bodies in the ever strengthening rays of the sun. In vine-clad arbors dark peasants and seamen sat to drink. And they seemed at ease with nature, held close by the sun-kissed earth as fashionable crowds never are nor can be. The life of this region became Mediterranean, and, so it seemed, suddenly. The cosmopolitanism died out of it. Fashion had gone. Nature remained, and seemed freer, finer, more beautiful, more wonderful, left to its own people, to those who really loved it, though often, perhaps, unconscious of their love.

Towser gone, the gay world gone—Imogen waited.

Naturally, she spent much of her time with Hugo and sometimes she noticed the look of feverish restlessness in his eyes which her aunt had remarked upon. It was only there now and then. Often his eyes looked weary with a sorrow—sometimes Imogen thought of it as a despair—which he never expressed. He talked very little. Sometimes when she was with him for long periods he said nothing. Then he would make an obvious effort, would rouse himself to a pitiful attempt at cheery conversation. She knew that in his tragic condition of body he had become aware of his mental limitations. These had not troubled him when his body was strong and his health was superb. Then he had been contented, more than contented, often riotously satisfied, with his bodily powers. But now they were withdrawn the comparative impotence of his mind appeared to him, like a thing unclothed and showing the unattractiveness of its nudity. And for the first time he bitterly regretted not being what he called "clever." And Imogen divined or sometimes perceived this regret. Now and then he even hinted at it.

"An invalid ought to be brainy," he said to her once. "An athlete or a sportsman needn't be. He's all very well without brains. But, by Jove, a cripple needs 'em."

And another time he said:

"If you've got to keep lying down you want a bright mind for company. I see now there's a lot more to the mind than I used to give it credit for. It's no use laughing at the fellows who swot over books and things. They fill up their minds, and I expect the chap was not far wrong who said that a full mind's better than an empty one."

"Then why not begin to fill up your mind now, Hugo?" she asked him.

But he answered gloomily, "I'm not that kind. One has to begin early with that sort of thing. Once you get the love of the open into your blood it's too late. There's no driving it out."

"Jack London loved the open but he loved books as well," she answered gently.

But he only said, "I expect he was a bit of a freak," and dropped the subject.

Sometimes she felt that he was on the edge of speaking to her about Peter Kharkoff. Then she saw the feverish look in his eyes and knew that despite the motionlessness of his body his nature must be in torment. More than once she surprised him looking at her with sharp intentness, as if trying surreptitiously to read what was in her mind. And she was certain that in those moments he was thinking about the Jew. But whether with hostility, or with a more strange and mysterious desire, she couldn't divine. It seemed to her almost incredible that Hugo could wish for the coming of the Jew. Nevertheless she wasn't at all convinced that Towser's conjecture was ill-founded. The power of the Jew might be upon Hugo although he was unconscious of it. Her power was surely not upon this man to whom she had so abruptly offered her life.

She sometimes felt painfully that she could not make him happy. He loved her. He clung to her, even desperately. But she did not make him happy. Perhaps nothing could give him happiness now. And yet he had told her that he could be happy with her if she were happy in giving herself to him. Perhaps, then, in spite of all her care in playing a part, he had divined the lack in her of which she was always aware, the lack of the passionate abnegation which is so easy to passionate love. Perhaps not even her mysterious and absolutely genuine calm had been able to blind him to the truth, that she had acted as she had rather because of a prompting from outside than because of an inner impulse that was part of her very spirit.

In the second week of May the weather suddenly became very hot. Milligan had taken to bathing in the sea, and every morning swam far out into the blue water of the gulf, while Hugo from his couch on the shore watched the activity which he longed to share. Lady Lowrie was already beginning to talk about the return to London. And still no message came from the Jew.

One day Imogen's unusual and long-continued patience suddenly came to an end. The evening before, restlessness had seized her. She slept very badly and got up in the morning a prey to depression. When the post arrived and there was no letter from Peter Kharkoff she said to herself with finality:

"That's an end of it! I've been a fool. I did what he wished me to do. I prepared the way and now he's let me down. He's done with me. I've humiliated myself in vain."

Many mornings had come and gone without the message she desired and yet her feeling of calm had remained with her. Now, for some reason she didn't understand, it deserted her, leaving her face to face with hopelessness.

"He's let me down! He's let me down!" she repeated to herself. "There's nothing to look for. I must make the future for myself as best I can."

But how to make it? She felt helpless. She had offered her life to Hugo. What more could she do? The gift had not made him happy, and the making of it had not brought happiness to her. And she knew how false are many of the clichés dinned into the ears of mankind. In the average love story devoured by a greedy public such a situation as she and Hugo were in would certainly have brought an abundant harvest of sentimental joy. She, the woman, would have gloried in self-sacrifice; he, the man, would have been rendered perfectly happy by her presence, her care, her affection. She would have been the ministering angel, he the thankful recipient of her attentions, glad almost to have been stricken helpless that he might have the opportunity of proving her love.

And the stark truth of the situation was that she felt desperate, and that he—but she could not tell exactly what he felt. Only she knew that what she had done had not made him happy.

It was afternoon. Heat brooded over the silent house. Lady Lowrie was secluded in her bedroom, perhaps asleep. Lord Lowrie had vanished. Probably he had gone for one of his long strolls in the surrounding country. Often he disappeared for hours without a word as to where he was going. Imogen had been walking aimlessly in the garden. Presently, as she approached the house, she saw Milligan on the balcony of Hugo's sitting-room. She beckoned to him to come down to her, and in a moment he joined her on the terrace in front of the drawing-room windows.

"What's Captain Dennistone doing?"

"Having a look at the Morning Post, ma'am."

"Isn't this place a desert now?"

"But——"

"I mean the Riviera! Can't you feel it? Can't you feel that everyone's gone? There isn't a soul left, not a soul!"

Abruptly, while she spoke, an impatience which seemed injured surged up in her.

"Has Captain Dennistone said anything to you about the future in England?" she added without waiting for any rejoinder from Milligan.

"No, ma'am. But it seems to me he's waiting for something."

"Waiting! What for?"

"I don't know at all, ma'am. I couldn't say. Perhaps he's got some idea in his head. I think he must have, but he hasn't said anything about it."

"What can there be for him to wait for?"

"Well, ma'am, it's difficult to say."

"*I* don't know. *I* see nothing. *I* can think of nothing!" Milligan was silent.

"What's the time?" said Imogen with almost savage abruptness.

Milligan hastily took out his watch.

"Not far off five o'clock, ma'am."

"Let's do something. Let's get away from here if only for half an hour."

"What can we do, ma'am?"

"Let's go to Sainte Maxime again, and look at the green barrels and the logs."

She swung round till she was facing the house, looked up at Hugo's open window and called, "Hugo!"

"Yes, Geney!" came his voice from within.

"I'm going to take you to tea again at Sainte Maxime! And this time we'll have the gramophone."

"Jazz! We products of catastrophe we want jazz!" She had said it lightly. She felt it now with a sort of desperation. Down with the under things! "Down, down, you devils—down!" And when presently they were once more on the terrace of the Ermitage de Provence, under the shade of the awning and of the small plane tree which stands there apart from the palm trees, she said to the woman who came to bring them tea, "Turn on the gramophone this time, will you? We want to hear it today. Turn it on and keep it going, one dance tune after the other!"

The woman—she was fat and looked very soft—smiled.

"Certainly, madame. It's a very good gramophone. We got it from Marseille."

"Let's have it. I'm longing to hear it."

The woman went away to the saloon just behind them, and in a moment the wheezy shriek of the abomination was loud in their ears.

"That's fine, isn't it, Milligan?"

"Very nice, indeed, ma'am."

"Are you a dancer?"

"Well, ma'am, I have danced, but I'm very awkward on my feet. Round my home they call me the dancing bear."

He smiled, and looked at Captain Dennistone for an answering smile. But none came. Hugo was staring at his knees, and his face looked grim and set. The heat under the plane tree was great although the afternoon was beginning to wane. The noise of the gramophone seemed to increase it. It called up to Imogen a vision of sweating niggers beating palms, horribly not black, together and trampling dust with jigging bare feet. She felt brutal as she listened, and that she must show her brutality, display it naked. Whence did such a horrible feeling come? She didn't know. Out of the depths of her, she supposed, where the good and the evil of her lay intertwined like snakes. And sometimes one must let loose the evil, give it its fling, see its face in the daylight.

"The dancing bear! I don't believe that. Why, you're so athletic: a cricketer, a footballer, a boxer too! And a boxer must be light on his feet. I know several boxers. I know Carpentier. Boxers have to be springy. Don't they, Hugo?"

"What, Geney?"

"I say that boxers have to be light on their feet. Carpentier's like a man on springs. Isn't he? And here's Milligan saying that he dances like a bear although he's a boxer."

"Oh!"

"Aren't you listening?"

"I'm trying to, Geney, but that ragtime——"

"But since the war our lives are set to ragtime. You don't mean to tell me that ragtime bothers you."

"Well, in all this heat and with such a deuced bad gramophone——"

"Bad? Why it's come all the way from Marseille. They bought it at Marseille. The woman in there told me so. And then you run it down! That's too bad; isn't it, Milligan?"

"I must say, ma'am, I've heard better ones in London."

"In London! Of course! But who'd compare Sainte Maxime with London?"

And then, as she reiterated the well-known word, there rose up before Imogen's mind all she was missing, had missed in the last four months, and with it an ugly consciousness of the shortness of youth for a woman. How could she give up life? By life she meant the restless, full, brilliant, varied, continually changeful life she was accustomed to. This year she had lost nearly four months, nearly a third of a year of it. She longed to go back to it. It called to her with a voice as penetrating as, but far sweeter than, the voice of the gramophone which had been bought at Marseille. Hugo was down and out. That was terrible, but it wasn't her fault. She couldn't help it. It was the doing of Fate. Her fate was separate from his. Whatever she did it must remain separate, even as their bodies, their souls, their minds were separate. They, she and he, might try to share life, but she must go on her way and he must lie still. What would the future, as they had settled it was to be, the married future, be like? She felt frightened of it today. When she contemplated or tried to contemplate it a dull despair crept over her. She felt herself to be so dreadfully unsuited to long-continued self-sacrifice.

She looked out now over the tarnished iron railing of the

terrace, and she was weary of the empty blue sea in the gulf
and of the little town opposite massed along the edge of the
water like a painting with sunshine falling over it. And she
was weary of the tiny harbor, with its anchored sailing-boats
and its two or three filthy barges and its three or four nondescript loungers. Behind her the gramophone beat out ragtime
relentlessly. And she saw the thick lips of the niggers, their
bare, scaly feet dancing in the dust, their bulging eyes, their
quivering, sweating bodies. And her body tingled with an
almost crazy desire for movement and change and people.
Suddenly the last shred of her patience and calm was stripped
from her, and her soul seemed revealed to her bereft of the
wrappings in which it had been swathed. And it was a wild
thing that wanted wildness.

"It's true, ma'am, there's plenty of difference between them.
But for my part I do love being out in the country. Just look
at that sea for instance, ma'am. It isn't the open sea of course
from here, but just look at——"

And then he stopped, and she saw his hazel eyes fix themselves with a keen look. And she saw Hugo make a slight
movement with his arms as if instinctively he was trying, in
vain of course, to raise himself up. And she looked away to
the left over the iron railing and she saw Peter Kharkoff
walking slowly on to the mole which protected the harbor.

He was alone, and his head was uncovered to the still warm
rays of the declining sun. Some boys were bathing from the
blue and white huts beyond the long and low jetty where the
rowing-boats lay at anchor. As they swam out into the bright
blue sea they called shrilly to one another. The shrill sound
of youth was in their voices and rang up out of the sea as their
small round dark heads crept out in the blue. And presently
Peter Kharkoff paused on the mole and stood still as if
watching them.

When she saw him Imogen was conscious of a violent shock.
She felt tremendously startled and she showed that she was
startled by a bodily demonstration. Before she had time to
try for self-control she had sprung up out of her chair and
gone to the railing. But having got there she realized things
and instinctively began to act. She laid one hand on the railing,
half turned towards the two men behind her and said:

"Just look at those boys swimming out! How I envy them.
Can you see them, Hugo?"

"No," he said.

His eyes were fastened upon her. And Milligan, too, was looking at her with a sort of surprised curiosity. Both of them had evidently been struck by her impulsive movement, and were wondering what was the matter. She did not look again towards the tall figure standing on the mole. She felt painfully self-conscious. She even had a feeling of guilt and did not know how to look natural, how to seem simple and at ease.

"You swim every day now, don't you, Milligan?"

"I do, ma'am."

"Is the sea warm?"

"Quite warm."

"I must have a bathe or two before we close the villa. I love swimming. In London I swim a lot at the Bath Club."

What was she talking about? What had she just said? Her hand clung to the iron railing. She felt two pulses beating as if in her ears.

The gramophone went on huskily shrieking. The fat, soft-looking woman was diligent in putting in disk after disk. And each of the disks meant more ragtime. Imogen began to feel confused, as well as self-conscious. Why was the Jew here? How long had he been in Sainte Maxime? What was he doing here? She had supposed that if he meant to come he would telegraph or write to her. She had imagined him arriving as an invited guest to stay at the villa. It had never occurred to her that he might come without a word and, having come, might not choose to make his arrival known to her immediately. And where was he staying? She wondered. An immense wonder mingled with her self-consciousness. Had he been there, perhaps for some time, without her knowledge? She had never been in Sainte Maxime since her first visit to the Ermitage de Provence with Hugo. Perhaps Peter Kharkoff had been here for some days. But why? What could be his purpose? And again she remembered the strange, prolonged silence in the little room full of books. And again she thought of Peter Kharkoff's peculiar deliberation. It was like a method —that deliberation of his. He had spoken to her about a preparation of the way for him. But it seemed to her that he prepared his own way, made, perhaps, some mysterious thought-process his own herald.

"That gentleman over there seems very much interested in the bathers, doesn't he, ma'am?"

"What gentleman?" she asked, trying to speak unconcernedly.

"On the stone jetty, ma'am."

Milligan pointed, and then Imogen had to look again.

She saw Peter Kharkoff still standing in the same place with uncovered head, his hands clasped behind him. He seemed to be gazing at the boys' heads creeping along the surface of the sea.

"Very remarkable looking, isn't he, ma'am?" Milligan asked.

"Remarkable looking? Is he?" (She stared. The dreadful feeling of self-consciousness was still with her.) "Oh—why, how extraordinary!"

"What's extraordinary?" asked Hugo's strong, gritty voice from the couch.

"Why—it's someone I know! Why it's Mr. Kharkoff!"

The gramophone ceased for a moment, then broke out stridently again. But Imogen did not hear it now, did not know whether it was silent or shrieking. She turned, she had to turn, to Hugo.

"Don't you remember Hugo, I mentioned——"

"Yes, I remember!" he interrupted her.

He was staring up at her now, and the expression in his eyes was like a challenge. She turned her eyes away from his.

"He must have arrived here unexpectedly."

"You didn't know he was here?"

"No, I didn't! Of course not!"

She was strung up and she showed it.

"That's all right," said Hugo.

She saw Milligan's kind face looking puzzled and uncomfortable.

"I must go and tell Mr. Kharkoff we are here. I'll bring him to you, Hugo. I want you to know him."

"Thanks."

There was, she thought, a sort of cold excitement in his voice, and his eyes looked both ardent and somehow hostile.

She hesitated.

"Hugo—you will be—you won't——"

But she couldn't say it. To say it would be so utterly futile. That she should plead Peter Kharkoff's cause to anyone! No; that was impossible.

And without another word she turned away and left the two men.

CHAPTER VII

As IMOGEN walked away from the terrace and crossed the dusty road she was filled with a profound curiosity. A few minutes before she had felt painfully the desertion of the Riviera by all whom she knew. Sainte Maxime had seemed to her a lost place where she lingered in exile. Now suddenly she felt it to be the center of the world.

As she stepped on to the rough paving-stones of the mole she felt the evening sunshine upon her with gratitude. The air was quivering with gold and blue. In the distance she heard the shrill boyish cries coming up from the sea. And the sunshine, the gold and blue, the sounds of youthful humanity were to her strange, beautiful and full of mysterious romance, had something ineffable in them, an appeal to her senses and to her heart which nothing had ever had before. And she felt within her a stir as of hidden forces.

She looked and saw that Peter Kharkoff had turned and was coming towards her. And suddenly it seemed quite simple and natural—this unexpected appearance, the long silence which had preceded it, this encounter by the sea, apparently fortuitous, really perhaps destined. There was nothing strange about it. It was right that he and she should meet thus. They could not have met in any other way. That was how she felt it.

They came together just in front of one of the barges loaded with logs of wood. But no men were working near it at that moment. The loading up had perhaps been finished and the barge was waiting till the time came for it to put out to sea with its burden of stripped trunks. Two men were visible on it standing near one another, dark-eyed, hairy men, with faces burned brown by the sun and wrinkled by sea winds. Speechless, with folded bare arms, they stood leaning against the logs, smoking their pipes and staring calmly before them.

And suddenly everything seemed wonderfully calm to Imogen in the gold and blue of the evening. The church-bell sounded over the water from Saint Tropez, and its deep voice was expressive of the calm of nature in this quiet place and of the calm which had come back to her.

"I was sitting on the terrace and I saw you here, so I came across," she said, holding out her hand to him. He took it gently in his, and let it go without definite pressure.

"When did you come here?" she asked.

"Yesterday," he said.

He looked at her calmly with his large veiled eyes, and she felt that he knew all about her, all that she had felt, her suffering, her impatience, her rebellion, her patience, and her recent fierce revolt and almost despair, since she had last seen him.

"The man I told you about is over there on the terrace of that café," she said. "You had my letter so you know how things are between him and me."

"Yes. I had it. It was very sincere. That letter of yours had truth in it."

Imogen felt an intense sensation of pleasure when he said that. And it was not her greedy vanity that was pleased, but something else, something far away from vanity.

"I tried to be sincere when I was writing," she said, very simply.

"Let us go to your friend," he said.

They walked slowly towards the café, and again Imogen was touched by the romance of the evening. With Peter Kharkoff she felt nature as she had not felt it before, felt it as if she were very near to it, were almost one with it. The boys were swimming back to the bathing-huts, and she felt them not as bathers separate from the sea, but as happy beings belonging to the sea and carrying something of the sea in them. So harmonious did they seem with the sea and in their joy of it.

"It's beautiful here," she said.

"The whole world is full of beauty," he answered.

"Is it? Yes, I suppose it is. But sometimes I feel the ugliness of the world more than the beauty."

"Think of the beauty more and the ugliness less. Then happiness will grow in you. You have often fought against beauty."

"I? How?"

"You have often fought against the beauty you carry within yourself. You have been afraid of it, as if it were a wild beast. You have even wanted to kill it. But you have not been able to, because it is indestructible."

And then they crossed the white road and she saw Hugo and Milligan.

Milligan stood up quickly when they came up, with an instinctive soldierly briskness and alertness. Hugo lay, as he always lay, nearly but not quite flat, looking towards them. As she drew near to him Imogen saw an extraordinary keenness of observation in his eyes. He was intent upon Peter Kharkoff as she had never seen him intent upon a man yet. Behind him the gramophone was still shrieking ragtime. But now, although she heard it, she did not see a vision of niggers leaping and shaking big bodies in the dust.

Afterwards she knew that she had done the usual thing, had "introduced" Hugo to Peter Kharkoff, had said who Milligan was. It had seemed unnecessary, as everything formal, everything of what is called etiquette, seemed unnecessary when Peter Kharkoff was there. But she had done it. And Hugo had muttered something. And Milligan had said, "Good afternoon, sir." And he had given his chair to Peter Kharkoff. And then, because of good manners, he had gone away into the near distance among the palm trees, and had left the three of them together. But before he went Imogen had seen him give Peter Kharkoff a straight, earnest look, and she had made a mental note of it, and had realized that Milligan's opinion of Peter Kharkoff would interest her deeply.

She heard it that night, and other opinions too, her father's and the old lady's. But Hugo's opinion she did not hear.

Peter Kharkoff sat down beside Hugo's couch, and Imogen went into the café to ask the soft, fat woman to stop the activities of the gramophone. Hugo had begged her to do that in a sentence. "Geney, please do stop that cursed thing!" When she was with the woman she thanked her and said that now they had had enough of the melodies from Marseille.

"Certainly, madame!"

And the monster was brought to heel.

"That monsieur, your friend, is staying here," the woman then said, looking out to the terrace from which the sunshine was beginning to travel away.

"Here!" said Imogen, astonished.

"Yes, madame. He must be a Jew, we think. We are not very fond of Jews. They are too powerful in France and have done much harm, we consider. And look at Russia! But we like this monsieur. We find him not like other Jews."

While the woman was speaking Imogen noticed that she kept her eyes fixed upon Peter Kharkoff.

"He is very simple in his tastes, madame. He is quite satisfied with what we have here. Do you know him well?"

"I have met him in England and in Switzerland."

"Ah! He is a traveler. He has seen much. He knows men, and women too. I am sure of that, madame."

There was a strange, dreaming look in her pale-brown eyes. For a moment she looked unusual, interesting even.

Imogen paid her and went back to the terrace.

She found Peter Kharkoff sitting beside Hugo in silence. There was something in his expression, his attitude, that was both intimate and detached. As she looked at him she knew that some of his power came from his absolute lack of self-consciousness. He never surely had in his brain the common, pervasive thought of mankind—"What are you thinking about me? What is your thought of me?"

It seemed to her that he was unselfconscious like an animal and unselfconscious like a god.

As she joined them she looked quickly from one to the other, and she felt that instantly she called up in Hugo a sudden and violent change which she had just, but barely, the time to note. It was a change, she believed, from a calm akin to the calm of the Jew to the reverse of calm—to fever. And it seemed to run all through Hugo. She seemed to notice it even in his outstretched body. It was as if he woke from a dream to reality, as if he were sharply hostile to that reality, even as if the hostility were given additional sharpness by that fact —of the previous dream.

And she knew that she had awakened him, and she thought of herself at that moment as the unintentional enemy of the Jew's power in him.

She spoke. She said something. And Hugo said something. And then Milligan came back from the palm trees, and by his manner and look she knew that he thought it time for Captain Dennistone to be taken home.

"We ought to be going, Milligan?"

"Yes, ma'am, if you're quite ready."

Peter Kharkoff got up.

She looked at him. She wanted to ask him to leave the Ermitage de Provence, to come and stay at the villa. She wanted to say that she had expected him to come there, that her father too had been hoping for him. But she couldn't do it. And in a moment Hugo's couch had been got down into the road by the sea, and was being wheeled away by Milligan in the direction of the villa. And she and Peter Kharkoff were walking behind it. She had not asked him to come with them. Because of his manner his coming had seemed a matter of course. And she knew that he would accompany them as far as the villa.

"My father will be very glad to see you," she said. "He wants to know you. He's not quite an ordinary man though he isn't specially clever. He lives a good deal more than most men in thought. I don't believe he could ever feel lonely. He has no ambition. I think he's a happy man."

"There is a great deal of happiness in the world," said Peter Kharkoff. "I have heard many people deny the possibility of anyone being happy in what they call 'this world.' But they cannot see what is before them. It is almost impossible to be anywhere, and to look about you with clear, *seeing* eyes, and not to see the face of happiness."

"But oh, what a lot of unhappiness there is!" she exclaimed.

At that moment she was thinking of Hugo, of herself linked to his motionless life, of the future.

"What is it that has the greatest effect upon the life of men?" he asked her. She thought for a moment.

"The actions of other men?" she then said.

He said nothing. She felt that he was not satisfied with her remark.

"You don't agree with that," she said. "But surely——"

"It is thought linked with feeling," he said. "You speak of unhappiness. The origin of the unhappiness in the world lies in thought, in the wrong thinking, the evil thinking, of men. You, for instance, think yourself into unhappiness, and your unhappiness reacts upon that man who loves you and makes him unhappy too. The accident which has shattered his physical powers has increased the sensitiveness of his mind. He feels your thoughts quite as definitely as his body feels your touch when you lay your hand upon him. Thought lies behind action like a thing hidden, in ambush. Have you ever even tried deliberately to think rightly, nobly, gloriously?"

"I don't believe I have. I have always considered thought as untrammeled and almost ungovernable. I believe most people consider it—thought-power, I mean—very much as I do."

They walked on a little way in silence. Then she said, "Why do you keep an hour-glass on your table?"

"To remind me that long as the journey seems the journey is not forever."

"You mean the journey of life?"

"No.   I mean something vaster than that."

"What?"

"I mean the journey of mankind upward through the centuries, or through whatever measurement of time you choose to make. It is still the custom to speak in terms of time, so I do it."

"Do you really think mankind is ascending? Do you honestly think that, after all that has happened lately and is happening now, after the war and the peace?"

"Mankind is ascending. The progress may seem very slow to you."

"It does!" said Imogen.

And she was unable to keep a sharp sound of irony out of her voice.

"That does not matter," he said, without irony.

"No! The seeming to me—that's of no consequence except to me. If you only knew how unimportant I feel!"

"That is a lie of the spirit within you then."

"How—a lie?"

"You are important, and secretly you know that, and generally you feel it. It is only at moments that you feel unimportant. The feeling important is the rule with you and with all human beings. And the reason of that is that truth must express itself in you and in all human beings."

How natural it seemed to Imogen to be walking along by the sea edge, on the dusty road in the calm of the approaching evening, and talking with Peter Kharkoff. A very faint sound came from the wheels of Hugo's couch now and then. Milligan had let down the awning. Imogen looked at his straight manly back, covered by a gray jacket. What would Milligan think of the conversation if he had heard it? And Hugo? Suddenly she felt that she and Peter Kharkoff were neglecting the crippled man who was imprisoned in his infirmity. And she made a movement to go to him. But Peter Kharkoff stopped her.

"No. Leave him alone," he said gently. "He needs to be very quiet just now."

"Yes? Does he?"

They were near the gate of the villa garden. Peter Kharkoff turned towards the gulf, and Imogen turned with him. On the blue water only one boat was visible. It was the boat which she had seen before gliding in the distance of the sea, the boat with one white and one orange-colored sail. In the softly shining evening the white sail, the larger, looked ivory pure. The smaller orange-colored sail looked marvelously picturesque and somehow adventurous. The one suggested fairyland, the other argosies of the East, the robustness of the world romantic, the lure of the passionate life. The white sail was the bigger, yet by its vividness the orange-colored sail almost blotted it out.

Milligan wheeled Hugo slowly forward, turned the couch to the right, disappeared with it into the avenue of mimosas. Imogen was alone with Peter Kharkoff beside the sea. She saw that his eyes were fixed upon the sailing-boat, which was tacking, evidently maneuvered by seamen who were making for the harbor of Saint Tropez. She gazed at the boat too. Presently he stretched out his hand.

"Your friend's life seemed like that colored sail out there, didn't it? It was vivid, glowing, full of warmth and color," he said. "And now you think of it as pale, like the white sail which the other almost effaces. But you are wrong in your thought. His life is more vivid now than it was when he was always in movement. The movement of the body is very little compared with the activity of the soul!"

"But there's a saying, 'What the eye does not see the heart does not feel.'"

"Do you think that saying is true?"

"I don't know. Perhaps not."

"It is not true. The heart feels many things which are invisible to the sight. Your heart does about him, and his does about you."

The little sailing-boat had been brought sharply round to the wind. It was heading straight for Saint Tropez.

"In a few minutes it will be safe in harbor," he said.

And in his deep, rather heavy voice she felt safety and harbor. And she had a longing for rest. She knew such a longing wouldn't last. She was far too young, too greedy, too lively and healthy to desire rest as old people often do. But Peter Kharkoff had injected into her an understanding of rest that for the moment brought with it actual longing.

They turned, crossed the road and went into the garden of the villa.

That evening Peter Kharkoff stayed to dine at the villa, and

did not leave it to walk to Sainte Maxime till nearly half past
eleven. When he went Lord Lowrie eagerly accompanied him.

"I like walking at night," he said. "This isn't politeness,
Monsieur Kharkoff. It's a desire for fresh air and some more
of your company."

Imogen saw them start off together. The deep blue darkness
of the starry night took them. She went back to her mother,
who, marvelously, was still up and who did not even look
sleepy.

"Well, old lady, past bedtime, isn't it?"

"Is it?"

"It's nearly half past eleven."

Lady Lowrie looked profoundly astonished. She couldn't
have believed it possible. She had never known the time to go
so fast before. How ugly Imogen's friend, Mr. Kharkoff,
was! But what a remarkable face! She could look at it for
hours without wearying. Why? Because there was so much
meaning, so much goodness and humanity in it. Yes, there
was. A most interesting man and most unusual. Fascinating
even. She was sure all women must find him so. Why had
he never married? For she understood there was no Mrs.
Kharkoff. Perhaps he had never been able to care for a
Jewess, but didn't think it right to marry outside his own
religion. She was sure he had a deep understanding of women.
She was glad Hugo had decided to dine downstairs for once,
though it was of course painful to see him obliged to eat lying
down, and having to be waited on hand and foot, as they say,
though what exactly foot had to do with it, she really didn't
know, and never had known that she could remember.

She wondered what poor Hugo thought of Mr. Kharkoff.
She had seen him looking at Mr. Kharkoff very hard once or
twice. Henry was evidently delighted with their guest. Yes,
yes, it was bedtime. She would make up for being so late
tonight by staying in bed a little later tomorrow. She really
wished that Mr. Kharkoff would come and stay at the villa
as Henry had proposed. But probably he had no dinner-
jacket with him, and that made him shy of accepting. Not
that a dinner-jacket really mattered so very much, though of
course one was accustomed to—— "Good night, dear!" A
muffled kiss, a gazelle-like elongation of the neck, and Lady
Lowrie was in the hands of her astonished maid, Martin.

And then Imogen went up to Hugo's sitting-room, meaning

to bid him a second good night and to—what else? She had the feeling that he hadn't gone to bed yet. And she was right. For when she tapped at the door, immediately she heard his strong voice inside, "Come in!"

She opened the door and went in. She found Hugo lying on his couch near the open window. The door into his bedroom was open too, and she saw a light there and heard someone moving about: Marfield getting things ready for the night.

"Well, Hugo! I've just come in to say good night again." She looked down on him trying to keep the curiosity she was feeling out of her eyes.

"Good night, Geney," he said, looking up at her.

She bent down and took his hand gently. "I hope you're not tired."

"No. Why should I be? What have I done to be tired? What do I ever do?"

"To be sure!" She paused. Then she said, "Good night." She did not bend quite down to kiss him, as she usually did now that they were engaged.

As she was about to go he said abruptly, "I say!"

"Yes?"

"That fellow's a Jew."

"Yes."

"Why didn't you tell me?"

"I thought if I did it might prejudice you against him."

"Did you think I shouldn't find it out?"

"Oh no."

"Why did he come here and not tell you?"

"I don't know."

"It seems a damned odd thing to do, doesn't it?"

"Oh," she said. "So many things seem odd if we are hopelessly conventional. But he isn't conventional. He does things in his own way. And he chose to come like that. Good night. Sleep well." And then she went quickly out of the room.

On the landing she met Milligan who was probably—she didn't know—going up to bed. She stopped. "I've just been in to see Captain Dennistone. Why did he decide to dine downstairs tonight?"

"He didn't say, ma'am, but I think it was because he was interested in that gentleman. And no wonder!"

"Why—no wonder?"

"Oh, he's very remarkable, ma'am."

"D'you think so?"

"I certainly do."

"D'you like him?"

"Well, I can't hardly say I know him, ma'am, can I? But he draws you at first sight. He's the sort of man who would have enormous influence in any hospital. Any nurse could see that."

"Any nurse! That's rather interesting. But why exactly? You see I'm not a nurse and don't quite understand."

"He gives out something. He's got tremendous magnetism, ma'am, believe me."

"I expect you're right. I think so too. Good night, Milligan."

"Good night, ma'am."

And then she went downstairs. She meant to wait up till her father came back. She opened the front door and went out into the drive. Nothing was stirring. It was a very still night but she could just hear the level wash of the sea. The garden was strongly perfumed with night-scented stock. She stood and looked up at the stars.

She didn't often do that, but when she did she usually felt the utter absurdity of the Christian's belief that God is a great Father presiding over the existence of every individual being among the teeming millions of this earth, and perhaps also over innumerable other existences in other wheeling worlds. To-night, however, strangely, she did not feel that. In the presence of the unknowable she seemed conscious of faith. And, stranger still, the stars didn't make her feel unimportant although she felt liberated from egotism. She meant much to Hugo. She meant something—she knew that now—to Peter Kharkoff. And so—it seemed at least to follow—she meant something to God.

She walked slowly down the drive between the silent mimosa trees, now bereft of their yellow tresses, till she came to the gate. Then she stood there waiting.

She didn't think of smoking though of course she had her cigarette-case with her. It was perhaps the urge of her almost perpetual restlessness which made her smoke so much. Smoking was something to do. But she was not restless tonight and so she forgot her cigarettes.

Milligan's words had meant a good deal to her. It was

odd how she wanted people to feel about Peter Kharkoff as she felt. She had had to leave Hugo abruptly just now because he had seemed to be criticizing Peter Kharkoff, and she couldn't bear that. She had been afraid of showing too much, of telling Hugo, perhaps, what she felt about this man who had come to Sainte Maxime for him.

She wondered what was going to happen between her and Hugo. Their relation to each other seemed to be made more complex by the coming into their lives of Peter Kharkoff, and it had been complex enough already. For what she had done, the offering of herself to Hugo, instead of drawing them into a much greater intimacy with each other, had, she thought, created a strange but very definite reserve between them, had created in them a multitude of under things which they felt the imperative need of concealing or trying to conceal from each other. She wished she could know exactly what Hugo's opinion of Peter Kharkoff was. She felt an intense curiosity about that. She knew that Hugo couldn't remain entirely unaffected by Peter Kharkoff's influence. Everyone felt it, even her mother. Milligan felt it strongly and in a peculiar way. She called it to herself a "medical way." And her father?

While she was thinking about her father she saw a dark shadowy figure quite near to her. Then she heard a sound of steps and Lord Lowrie walked briskly up. "Waiting up for me, Imogen?"

"For you and the night, old papa. I'm so glad there isn't a strong moon."

"Why?"

"This deep blue darkness is more to my liking just now. There's something exquisite in mystery. Without mystery what would the world and life be?"

"And what would the human heart be? We shall hear midnight strike in a moment."

"Over the water. I feel the beauty of this place tonight."

"That friend of yours brings out the essence of things. He contains an influence which elicits. I'm sure you feel tonight more keenly than you usually do because he has been here. He has a similar effect upon me."

"Do you like him?"

Before Lord Lowrie replied the bell of Saint Tropez sounded on the other side of the gulf in the first stroke of midnight. They stood silent to listen. And as Imogen listened she thought again of the sand slipping down in Peter Kharkoff's hour-glass, of the advance he had spoken of, and of something else. If what he had said were true, if one could absolutely believe that it was true, then the passing of time must seem a wonderful and beautiful happening. But that strange fear she had had! That, too, was connected with the passing of time.

The voice of the bell ceased, and after a moment Lord Lowrie said, "Do I like him? Like is one of the weakest of words. I really can't dignify it by applying it as an expression of my feelings about Monsieur Kharkoff. There's mystery in that man, and I don't mean the human mystery which belongs to every child of man. Some folk I feel as finite. Although we are all of us pilgrims of Eternity I feel them as having begun at birth and as being certain to finish at death. There's no length to them; no stretching out, back to the dim past, forward to the dim future.

"But when I am with this man, Peter Kharkoff, I feel as if I were with the whole of the past and the whole of the future. It's a sensation I have never had before with any man. He is like continuity imprisoned somehow in the body of a man. No, imprisoned isn't the right word. Let's say—choosing to make its temporary home in a man. Emphatically he is not as I am, not as you are, not as Hugo Dennistone is. And yet he's totally unlike all the so-called exceptional men I've met up to now, the big mediums, the big theosophists. Even in India where I've met some amazing people I've never met his like. And yet he claims to have no peculiar powers. In fact, he lays no claims, is totally without pretension. But his personality—that's a different matter. That claims you silently. He ate meat at dinner. That surprised me."

"Did you think he was sure to be a vegetarian?"

"I suppose I did. I know I was surprised when he accepted mutton. How ridiculous we are! Grotesques, my dear, grotesques!"

"Why d'you say that?"

"I was thinking of my puerile surprise when Monsieur Kharkoff ate mutton. Already I was trying to fasten a label on him. 'You're a remarkable man of a certain type so you've got to be a vegetarian!' When he took mutton it was a smack at my folly. Since then I've done with preconceived ideas. Monsieur Kharkoff stands out alone among men. And I wanted to brigade him with the lentil-eaters and the wearers of flannel next the skin."

"The old lady thinks perhaps he wouldn't stay here because he hasn't brought a dinner-jacket."

Imogen saw her father's eyes twinkle in the darkness. "That's the finest appreciation of character our beloved wife and mother has ever brought off." He put his hand over her arm and they turned in at the gate. They walked up the drive in silence.

When they reached the house Lord Lowrie stopped. "That's an extraordinary man. I know it because since I've been with him the night seems different to me. I look at the night with different eyes, feel it in a different way from my usual, humdrum, stupid old-man way. The darkness is a new darkness to me. Even the stars aren't as they were."

He stood very still, and she stood still with him. Then he said, "He'll be here again tomorrow."

And they went into the house.

CHAPTER VIII

SINCE Peter Kharkoff's arrival at Sainte Maxime Hugo had shut his mind against Imogen. His reserve had increased. But beneath this reserve she believed that great mental activity was going on. And she began to understand that lack of intellectual activity need not mean lack of mental activity. Hugo's brains were certainly not considerable. She thought them almost negligible. But she realized now that his mind could be fiercely alert. In the old days she had often said that though Hugo wasn't "brainy" he was certainly "no fool." But she had never believed that he was capable of the energy of thought which seemed to have taken its rise in his bodily misfortune, but which had surely been greatly increased by the coming into his life of Peter Kharkoff. In spite of Hugo's reserve with her she was increasingly aware of this energy. She felt it, though it was never expressed to her. She seemed often to see it manifested in Hugo's face. That was changing. Now and then she noted a refinement in his look which was

new to her, a sharp clearness of expression which made her
wonder.

Was Peter Kharkoff pouring into Hugo some of his thought-
power? But if so to what would this thought-power lead?
To what would it impel the receiver of it? What would happen because of it? Or would it be spent on the wind?

She couldn't believe that. And Hugo's reserve, combined
with this strongly felt increase of mental activity, awakened in
her a vague sensation of alarm. There were moments when
she even felt like one floating on a stream which was traveling
towards rapids, felt the suck of an energy she could not combat,
though there rose in her the instinct to struggle.

All about her she felt a strange pressure of thought. It
weighed upon her mysteriously. Sometimes it seemed to give
her wings, sometimes to overwhelm and almost to suffocate
her. She felt herself fighting it; she felt herself yielding
to it; she felt like one in a nightmare trying to flee from it
on feet that were rooted to the ground. And then strangely
she was at ease with it, seemed to be breathing it like an atmosphere of which she had need.

She knew where it came from.

At moments she thought that she regretted having summoned
Peter Kharkoff to Sainte Maxime, that it would have been
better for her if she had never seen him, and followed him, and
forced herself upon him as she had done at Drearney. At other
times she felt that the whole thing had been inevitable. It was
difficult now for her to conceive of life not merely without
Peter Kharkoff but without even the knowledge of his existence. For without any apparent effort, without any apparent
desire, he had taken complete possession of her. Her glorious
independence was gone. In looking back upon her life she
could hardly believe that she had ever had it.

The great heat of the year was now coming to the Riviera.
The weather was perpetually fine. One brilliantly sunny day
succeeded another and each one closed in a cloudless night.
The roses were out. The garden was full of flowers. The
sea and the sky were marvelously blue. Little streams still
sang in the woods, making a cool sound in the sultry weather.
Life called you out of doors.

Every day Peter Kharkoff walked over to the villa from
the Ermitage de Provence, where he lived not only without
murmuring but apparently with complete contentment.

"I've never met a man so entirely indifferent not only to luxury but to what most of us think of as ordinary comfort," said Lord Lowrie one day. "And yet he makes no pretense of being an anchorite. There's no pose of the ascetic. It's true that he doesn't drink wine or smoke. But otherwise he's like other men. He doesn't starve. He eats what's put before him. He doesn't seem to attribute any special virtue to abstinence. He never preaches or fulminates against anything. And yet one feels that he has all the virtues, that in him they are great. One at any rate he has in the fullest measure."

"What's that?" asked Imogen quickly.

"Charity. I simply can't imagine him attacking anyone or growing warm in condemnation of anyone. And yet I've never met a man whose good opinion of me I should value so highly as his if I could obtain it. It seems rather weak, but I find myself continually wondering what he thinks of me."

"And haven't you any idea what he thinks, old papa?"

"Nothing evil anyhow. I'm certain of that."

"Don't you——" she hesitated; then, with resolution, she said, "You don't find him indifferent?"

Lord Lowrie also hesitated, seemed to be questioning himself, searching. "Do you?" he asked her at length, looking at her inquisitively.

She returned his gaze steadily. "I have sometimes thought that there's a great indifference in him. What I mean is that the things nearly all of us find a good deal of meaning in don't seem to affect him."

"It's true that there are certain situations common enough in life which I could never imagine him in."

"Such as——"

"I can't conceive of him as a husband, the father of a family."

"Nor I. Still less as a lover," she said, smiling. Her tone as she spoke had been almost satirical and she tried now to force a look of satire into her eyes.

"A lover!" said Lord Lowrie. "No; I can't imagine him as a lover. And yet I'm certain Kharkoff has a power of loving immeasurably greater than most men have."

"What makes you think that?"

"There's an immense humanity in the man. One feels extraordinarily safe and at rest with him. There's a vast silent kindness in him. One thing specially strikes me in him.

I never feel that he is thinking about himself. Hasn't that struck you?"

Imogen thought for a moment. Then she said, "Yes. I believe it has."

"Isn't that rare?"

"I suppose it is."

"Suppose! Come now! You're young, but for your age, you know a good deal about what's called the world. You've met an extraordinary number of people. Of how many men could you say as much?"

"Not of many."

"Could you say it of even one other man?"

"I don't think I could."

"Such an abnormal lack of egotism seems to me to imply a supreme concentration on others, and such a concentration, I think, could hardly come out of anything but love."

"Of humanity!"

"Well—yes." Again Lord Lowrie looked at his tall daughter rather sharply.

"Love of humanity—love of humanity!" she said, half smiling, looking down, and with a curious intonation that gave out a flavor half lightly satirical, half tragic. "And what about individuals, old papa? Can you imagine Monsieur Kharkoff loving an individual, except of course as one of the vast mass called collectively humanity?"

"You mean loving an individual as, for instance, Hugo loves you?"

Imogen looked startled. She moved abruptly. "That's coming down to the concrete with a vengeance. But—very well! I'll give you your comparison, old papa."

"Then—no, I can't."

"Nor I. Monsieur Kharkoff may be many things, but I'm certain that one thing he could never be. He could never be a great lover."

Again she was smiling. And her tone was light. But Lord Lowrie seemed to hear undertones, which were thrilling with a sort of restrained and frail bitterness.

"Perhaps not, perhaps not!" he said. "I don't pretend to fathom such a nature as his, though I'm sure he fathoms my shallows easily enough."

"Do you think that one human being can ever really fathom another human being's nature?" said Imogen.

"If you had asked me that question before Mr. Kharkoff came here I should certainly have answered 'no.'"

"But—now?"

"Since I have known him I shouldn't dare to say 'no,'" said Lord Lowrie.

Imogen was silent. She stood looking down. Her face was grave. She fidgeted with her long hands. Finally she said, "It is impossible that Mr. Kharkoff can be different from all the rest of us. I mean of course in the characteristics which belong to the human species. He may be cleverer, or deeper, or more enlightened than most of us, but he cannot be cleverer, deeper, more enlightened than all other men. Can he?"

"It doesn't seem probable," said Lord Lowrie.

"Probable! What is it—what are you thinking? What do you make of Mr. Kharkoff?"

"What do *you?*" asked her father.

She did not answer.

"What made you so anxious to get him here?" said Lord Lowrie, after waiting for the reply which did not come. "If it was for Hugo Dennistone——"

"It was!"

"Well then, why did you think Mr. Kharkoff could do something for him that no one else could do?"

"I don't exactly know why. I just felt it was so. It seemed to me that it was so. Directly I heard of Hugo's terrible accident I had a longing to call in Mr. Kharkoff." She tried obviously to give a light sound to the familiar phrase so often employed about doctors. But the attempt was a poor, almost a pitiful one.

"As a sort of doctor for the soul?" asked Lord Lowrie.

"I don't know. I was in trouble. It seemed a sort of instinct to seek him out and tell him about it."

"I can understand that. And what's he doing for Hugo?"

"I don't know. I can't make out. Hugo is very reserved with me in spite of—although we are going to be married." She said the last words very slowly.

"It's May now," said Lord Lowrie. "The weather seems hotter every day. Your mother's beginning to talk about London and Lowndes Square."

"Is she?"

"D'you think Hugo likes being here, or d'you think he wants to go North?"

Suddenly, while her father was speaking, Imogen realized things—the closing up of the villa till next winter, the departure for England, the separation—of necessity—from Peter Kharkoff, the arrival in London, the facing of the music.

"I don't know. I haven't asked him. Shall I?"

"I think it would be as well. We could of course keep the villa open later than usual if he wished it. And what about Mr. Kharkoff?"

"How d'you mean, old papa?"

"He says nothing about leaving Sainte Maxime. Will he go when we do? Or having persuaded him to come here do you think we can go off and just leave him here by himself?"

"I suppose if he knew we had to go he would leave either before us, or when we did."

"Well, time's getting on. These matters need thinking about and deciding on."

"Are you in a hurry to go, old papa?"

"I! My dear, I should be perfectly contented to stay here all the summer through. But you could never get on without your usual dose of London. And your mother could never stand the midsummer heat here."

"How do you know I want my usual dose of London?"

"Don't you? If you don't you must have changed very suddenly and very completely."

"Remember," she said in a cold, inflexible voice, "that I am going to alter my life. I am going to marry a cripple. And you mustn't think I shall do it light-heartedly, without understanding what it is going to mean for me." She paused and looked into the distance. "I shan't be able to live exactly as I like any more. If I'm to be Hugo's wife I mustn't, I can't, be the typical wife of these days. It's all very well to be having a magnificent time if your husband's having a magnificent time too, to go your way if he can go his. But there'll be only one way for Hugo. My life isn't going to be at all the life I had imagined, the life I'd looked forward to."

"And you are sure you can face it—go through with it?"

"You think me a selfish beast, I know. But why shouldn't I be able to do what other women have done? Hugo isn't a clever man, but he's fine. What he bears and the way he bears it! I must try to help him." She looked at her father steadily. Then she added, "Father, I think Hugo and I had better be married soon. It's no good waiting. He and I have nothing to wait for. And perhaps when we are actually married he will be happier with me than he is now."

"Do you think he's unhappy as things are? I mean in your engagement?"

"I think it has made him feel his helplessness perhaps even more than he did when we were only pals."

"That's natural enough. Every man in love wants to fascinate the girl he's in love with, to show himself at his best before her."

"Milligan told me once, after we were engaged, that Hugo was going through hell."

"I don't think that's true of him now."

"Peter Kharkoff has made a great difference. I feel that. But I can't quite understand what sort of difference it is." She sighed. Then she said, "There's mystery in this house, old papa." And then she left him.

It was nearly noon, and she believed that Hugo was out in the garden. Now that the heat was great he usually stayed there under the trees till the gong sounded for lunch. She went out of the house to find him.

His couch was not on the terrace near the drawing-room windows, and after looking for it among the palms and on the lower terraces in front of the house she turned and went up behind the house, following a path that led to a gate through which one could pass out into the woods and the scrub where the stream ran singing on its way to the sea. Near this gate, on the left, there was a space sown with grass, bordered with rose-bushes and sheltered by some large umbrella pines. And here she came upon Hugo quite alone. She had expected to find Peter Kharkoff with him, or at any rate Milligan. But she was glad he was alone.

"Where's Milligan?" she said, as she came up to his couch.

"I sent him away. I don't want him always with me."

"And Mr. Kharkoff? Hasn't he been with you?"

"I think he's gone off for a long walk. He went out by that gate. He spent a few minutes with me. But you know how fond he of walking by himself in the woods."

"Yes. He loves solitude." She sat down on a bench by his couch. "I've been having a talk with father," she said. "He wants to know how long you would like to stay on here."

"How long? But I thought the house was to be shut up at the end of this month."

"It needn't be. It could quite well be kept open through June. D'you like being here?"

"Yes."

"What about staying on through June?" As she said the last words she was looking at him, and she knew by his expression that some thought, some vital thought which was perhaps new to him, had suddenly come into his mind.

"I shouldn't mind," he said. His blue eyes were scrutinizing her now and she felt that he was going to say something connected with that new thought. "I think I should like to stay on. But you mustn't, Geney."

"I! Why not? Why should I go away?"

"There's nothing for you to do here."

"Do you want to get rid of me?" she asked.

She felt startled by his look, his manner, his words. She did not understand just what was in his mind.

"I think you ought to go. I think you ought to have a bit of London. It's the season now. Everybody's there. All your pals. You ought to be there too."

So that was it! Hugo wanted to get rid of her for a while. Her mind went to the man in the woods, to Peter Kharkoff. Swiftly she envisaged the two men together in this quiet place without her. And she felt something burn within her. Wasn't it jealousy?

"Well, I might go on ahead of course," she said in a very light and casual tone. "And then when you come in July we could be married, couldn't we? I don't believe in a long engagement. I don't see what we have to wait for. I could have a bit of the London season, as you suggest, and then we could settle down. Was that your idea?"

"Well, I didn't get quite as far as that. But if you would really be ready——"

"I'm ready now!" she said, quickly, decisively.

"Are you?"

He put out a hand towards her. She took it, grasped it, without knowing how strong, how feverish, her pressure of it was. She had a sudden violent impulse to run on the spear of her destiny.

"Why should we wait, Hugo? Why should I go to London at all? Tell me why you want me to go."

"I feel you ought to," he said. And there was, she thought, obstinacy in his voice. "I've been thinking a lot lately," he went on in quiet, level tones. "And I feel you ought to make quite sure that you're really ready to tie yourself up to a log like me."

"I am ready. I have told you. I have asked you. What more can I do?" Without knowing that she did so she spoke with a touch of exasperation. "What's the matter?" she added. "Have you changed? Aren't you satisfied with——"

A squeeze of his hand stopped her.

"Well?" she said.

She felt upset, almost angry, and full of questions and doubts.

"It's like this," he said. "I want you to test yourself. We've always been great pals. You see me lying here like this. You've got a heart. It tells you to stick to me now I'm down. But I want you to think of yourself for a bit. I know you pretty well, Geney. I expect I know your nature as well as any man as ordinary as I am ever could know it. And I want you to be quite sure what you're doing."

"So you think a month on my own in London might bring me to my bearings! Or—or did anyone suggest to you that —that——"

"No—no one," he said firmly.

She sat for a moment in silence. Then she said, "Well, it isn't a bad idea. I'm a restless being of course. And I've been lying low for a good long while. I believe I'll do it, Hugo. I believe I'll be off."

She glanced round at the umbrella pines, at the newly sown grass, shrill with its young green, at the palm trees in the distance, the yellow and blue glimpses of the house among the trees. Just outside, beyond the gate, in the wood and the scrub multitudes of crickets were making their strange creaking noise which sounds like heat made articulate, like heat and summer saying "We are here! You must heed us. You must give yourself up to us!"

She fixed her eyes on the gate by which he, Peter Kharkoff, had passed out into the wood. And she imagined him gone forever, not coming back, taken by the rough overgrown land beyond the carefully planted and tended gardens of her father. Would she want to stay here then? Would she hate the thought of leaving this hermitage then? Even as it was, the words, the mental pressure of Hugo, had caused the restlessness natural to her, the love of life inherent in her, to stir like

living things that had slept and been suddenly disturbed in
their slumber, had pricked them into a sort of irritated activity. She felt distressed, angry, startled by what had just
happened. She even felt—why she didn't know—faintly suspicious, but she knew that Hugo's unexpected suggestion was
one which she was going to act upon. As he had made it she
would go. She would leave him in the villa and she would
plunge once more into the life she knew so well, and had supposed that she loved so much, the life of her London in the
brilliant days of June.

"I shall go! I shall go!" a voice said within her. She
looked again at the small white gate and then at Hugo. "Was
it really your own idea," she said, with a sort of slow reluctance, "that I should go on to London in advance of you,
leaving you here?"

"Yes. It just came to me when you asked about the villa."

"Then it hadn't been in your mind before?"

"Lots of things have been in my mind. How shouldn't they
be?"

"But—lately?"

"How d'you mean, Geney? I don't think I quite understand."

She got up. Her eyes had gone again to the little white
gate. "It's all right, Hugo. Your idea's a good one. I do
want a change. I'm not made for perpetual quiet." Directly
she had said the last words her heart accused her, and she had
an impulse to beg Hugo's pardon. But she checked it, realizing that to do that would only make her unintentional offense
more definite. "And now," she said, "I'm going for a little
stroll in the woods. If I'm late for lunch tell them not to
bother about me. Will you?"

"All right!" he said. There was, she thought, a new look
of tenderness in his eyes as she glanced once more at him
before going away, an almost pitiful look. But why should
Hugo pity anyone, least of all her?"

She went up to the gate and opened it. The wood of it
was hot against her hand, burning hot. She did not look
round again at Hugo, but she felt that he was watching her,
and she felt too that he knew how she was drawn into the
woods and what it was that drew her. She shut the gate behind her and went on. Very soon she was out of sight of the
house.

The narrow rough path wound on through a forest of cork trees interspersed with scrub. In the distance the ground, which rose gradually, occasionally dipping down but always to rise again, was lifted in hills. Always, as Imogen went on slowly, she saw those hills in front of her closing in the horizon. She was moving upwards on a usually gentle incline, but in the distance she was aware of steepness. If she went on much farther she would presently have to climb. And the heat that day was really intense, a burning heat. And the voice of the heat—the eternal creaking noise made by the thousands of crickets—was loud and perpetual in her ears. She could not catch any glimpse of the sea where she was now, but she knew that it was fiercely blue. The sky too was blue without a cloud and looked fierce, she thought, as she glanced up at it. The pressure of heat seemed upon her and another pressure.

She thought of the Paris and London seasons now in the full flow of their restless exuberance. She had drunk deep of the delights and excitements of both. Away from them she could taste them through her imagination. And she did this. And then, as the noise of their tumult died away in her ears, she knew that she was going through a phase more tumultuous than any she had lived through in Paris or London; she knew that the noises of men sink into insignificance when a nature is stirred to the depths and lifts up its voice.

For the deep calm which she had been conscious of before Peter Kharkoff had come to Sainte Maxime, and again on the evening of his arrival, was not with her now. She had felt it gloriously when she had stood with him on the mole of the little harbor. And on the way home she had felt it increasing about her. And later in the deep blue night she had linked it romantically with the wide calm of nature. But now it had gone from her.

She had said to her father, "There's mystery in this house, old papa." And she had not merely said it, she had felt it. And now she was pursuing mystery through the forest of cork trees, through the scrub, through the perpetual music of the crickets. She was going after it into the wilds, leaving houses and the dwellers in them behind her.

Although she didn't know what direction Peter Kharkoff had taken after he had gone out of the garden, although the stretch of woods was vast, she felt sure that presently she would come upon him. She felt that he was not very far away from her and that she was going towards the place where he was.

And before very long she came to it. At a distance, high up in a small clearing of the forest, near to a silver thread of water which flowed down to her and gave its music to her ears, she saw the figure of a man standing motionless. Although she could see no details, only a dark upstanding something which she felt to be a man, she knew at once that she had found Peter Kharkoff.

The figure was standing absolutely still and when she saw it Imogen stood still too. The silence around her was broken only by the murmur of the stream and the unceasing noise made by the crickets. She felt the fierceness of the sun upon her and about her. The blue beyond the still figure on the hill above her was fierce too and quivering with heat. As she looked she had a feeling that the being up there whom she knew to be the Jew, Peter Kharkoff, belonged to nature in a peculiar way as no other man belonged, and the definite knowledge came to her that, from the first time she had seen him, she had set him apart from all other men. Never had she been able to think of him as one of the great crowd of men. He had always seemed to her a being apart from them, superior to, and different from, them.

Now she saw him on a height, and that seemed as it should be. She knew that physically she was going to mount up to him, and to join him on his height, and to stand beside him on it, looking over the prospect he saw. But she had a longing to be able to join him on another height too, and to see what he looked out on from it. She had that longing, but with it there came another longing, intimate, searching and horribly full of sex—the longing to draw him down from his isolation to her, to lure him from his contemplation of the infinite to a narrower contemplation—of her, to force him to concentrate on her. He had taken possession of her because of his difference from all other men. Now she had a terrible longing to force him to become like all other men.

After a long pause she went slowly forward again. And now she felt the heat more. Since Peter Kharkoff's arrival she had continued to paint her face, although she had removed all her "make-up" before she had paid him that visit in Geneva. She did not wish her father and mother and Hugo to notice that she made any change because of the visitor. Now in the heat she hated her paint and felt uncomfortable, unnatural under it. And she realized that she must be looking disgustingly artificial among the cork trees, in the scrub, under the glare of the sun.

As she drew nearer to the figure of the man she saw that she had been right in her conviction. He was Peter Kharkoff, and she saw his large eyes fixed upon her watching her approach.

When she was near him she stopped and called out, "Hugo told me you were somewhere in the woods. I wanted a walk, so I thought I would try to find you." Then, without waiting to hear any answer from him, she went on more quickly and joined him. "I knew I should find you," she said.

He smiled. When he smiled he looked very simple, almost homely. "I was looking at the sea," he said. "I was looking for our boat."

"With the orange and white sails."

"With the white and orange-colored sails—ycs."

"Our boat!" she said.

She stood for a moment looking out over the gulf which was spread below them. Then she sat down on the hot ground with her back against the half-stripped trunk of a cork tree. Peter Kharkoff remained standing. She looked up at him and thought she had never seen him look so tall before. And as she went on looking at him she was struck by his appearance of physical strength. She was struck by his obvious bodily force. There was the curious, blunt, and yet impressively powerful look of a lion in his face. And his body too must be tremendously powerful, she thought. Nearly always she had hitherto seen him, thought of him, as a strongly functioning mind using a body. Now for a moment she saw him only as a body, felt exclusively his physical man.

And the thought came to her—"That man cannot have lived all his life entirely unaffected by women." And the longing, ugly, almost sacrilegious perhaps, but very vital and intense, increased in her, the longing to fasten her girlish charm upon him, to make him feel it and respond to it.

"Aren't you going to sit?" she said, looking up at him, looking along his legs and his body up to his broad chest and shoulders.

He looked down at her. He was not smiling now. There seemed an unusual intentness in his gaze. His large eyes

were widely opened, and the veiled look, so characteristic of
them, had gone out of them. She felt that he was looking
right into her and must be able to see all that was in her.

He did not answer her question with words, but there was
a rock close to him and he sat down on it, and remained
silent. And his silence seemed to press upon her like a
weight, soft and heavy. She felt it like that. But a moment
later she felt it differently, like a wave that was bearing her
away. But there was opposition in her now. The desire to
give herself up to his power was combined with the fighting
desire to make him feel hers. And she struggled against what
she felt as an almost irresistible influence. This man was not
a god and he was not a freak. He must therefore be subject
sometimes to the passions of a man. For such a force as she
and others felt in him could not satisfy itself entirely in
thought-action. There must be moments when he was purely
man, and no man is purely thought.

As all this passed through her mind she met his eyes again,
and he said, "Do you remember our walk by the sea after we
met at Sainte Maxime?"

"Yes, of course I do."

"Do you remember what we spoke about?"

She considered for a moment. Then she said, "About
thought—d'you mean—and its action in the world?"

"Yes."

Suddenly she felt angry. She felt like one in bondage to
thought, not to her thought but to his. And she felt that she
wanted to break out of this bondage and to be free, as she had
surely been free before she had ever met him.

"But life isn't all thought," she said. "One can't always
live in the mind."

As she was speaking she realized that ever since Hugo's
accident, and even before it, ever since she had met Peter
Kharkoff in Drearney, her mental life had been far stronger,
far fiercer, than her physical life. And how she had suffered,
how she was suffering still. And perhaps solely because of
that. And she revolted against the dominion of his mind over
hers. Wasn't she becoming his prisoner? She had a burning
desire to make him hers.

"I've thought too much lately!" she exclaimed. "I'm sick
of thought." She looked up into his eyes with a strong attempt
at defiance, and added, "I'm going away from here almost di-

rectly. I've been talking to Hugo about it in the garden.—
where you left him. I found him there all alone."

"It is good for him to be alone just now."

"Is it? I don't know. I didn't think about that. I went
to ask him whether he liked being here, whether he would like
to stay on through June. He said he would, but that I mustn't
stay. He wants me to go to London, to see my friends, to
have a little life after all this." She made a gesture.

"Do you find it lifeless here?" he said.

"Well, it isn't quite what I've been accustomed to. I'm
rather a restless creature, you know."

"Yes; you are restless."

"Don't forget that I'm still young," she said, rather sharply.
"And it isn't natural for youth to be always sitting still and—
and contemplating eternity."

"I know—I know!" he said.

"I've done my best. I've prepared the way."

"Go to London," he said. "Go back to your friends, your
life there. Why shouldn't you? Don't you consider yourself
free?"

"Yes, of course I am free. But what about you? You
came here because I asked you to come. Will you go away
when I go?"

"If Captain Dennistone is staying on for a while I will stay
on with him."

"In the house?"

"No. I will remain where I am. I like my daily walk by
the sea."

Imogen felt a pang of jealousy. She hated to think of Hugo
and Peter Kharkoff together in the sunshine and the sea-
loneliness without her. And she hated the calmness with
which Peter Kharkoff had received the information about her
impending departure. She had watched him when she had told
him of it and he had not given a sign that he regretted it.
Perhaps he wanted to get rid of her. Perhaps he was looking
forward to being alone with Hugo—Hugo freed from her
perpetual presence. And she remembered that she had thought
of herself as the enemy of the Jew's power in Hugo. And the
jealousy increased in her and became more peculiar. There
seemed to be a double strain in it. She felt jealousy of Peter
Kharkoff with Hugo. But she also felt jealousy of Hugo with
Peter Kharkoff. It seemed absolutely impossible that such a

man as Hugo could ever feel the influence of a man more than
he felt hers.   But if he did?

She knew that she wouldn't like it if Hugo ever came to
prefer the Jew before her.

And as for him—this man sitting on the rock above her
in the sunshine, with his thick hair uncovered to the rays of
the ardent sun—what could she do to destroy the immense indifference in which his kindness surely moved as in an atmosphere?   What could she do to reduce him to the level of a
man who felt women, felt their sex, their charm, their needs?
Humanity!   Love of humanity!   That was all very well.
There was nobility in it, perhaps; there was perhaps even greatness.   But a woman can never be so impersonal as to be satisfied with her inclusion in such a love as that.

There was an anger in Imogen so fierce that she didn't
dare to give it expression.   And she sat for some time in silence.
But in that silence there was no ease, no simplicity.   "Where
are my weapons?" she thought.   And the answer came back,
"With him you have none."

But that assertion within herself must be a lie.   She looked
at Peter Kharkoff.   She stared at him.   It seemed to her that
she summoned all her force of vision and brought it to bear
on him, on this appearance of a man, a Jew-man, sitting
there in the sun close to her.   He was so close to her that she
had only to put out her hand and she could touch him, grasp
him.   She could see the lines on his curiously blunt irregular
face, deep lines, and faint, scarcely perceptible lines spraying
off from near the eyes and the temples.   His heavy eyelids were
lowered above the eyes which were surely quite indifferent to
her girlish charm.   His powerful, unselfconscious hands,
browned by the sun, were laid palm downwards on the warm
rock.   The thick hair rose, with its heavy surge upward, above
his forehead. His obviously strong body was there erect beside
her.   She saw a fly running and pausing on his shoulder.   Apparently he was just a Jew, a foreign Jew of perhaps forty years
old, not handsome, but impressive, striking, obviously intellectual and high-minded, obviously self-possessed without a touch
of ostentation, strong, imbued with a sort of patriarchal kindness, quiet, deep.

But what was he really?   What was his mystery?   Why
did she feel him as a man entirely apart from all the other
men whom she knew, and yet now as a man one with all

other conquering men? Why did he possess her in this seemingly occult way?

She went on staring at his big, strong body and asked herself why it was that she was inhibited from thinking of him as she could have thought of any other obviously fit man. There were men—she knew several—who, frail and weak in body, were brilliant in mind. They looked predominantly mental. One thought of them as minds rather than as bodies, and knew why one did so. But there was nothing ethereal about Peter Kharkoff. He had a body which was surely meant to be used in all the natural physical ways. Such a man, had he lived in another age, might well have been at home among lusty patriarchs, have been the head of a numerous progeny, have calmly governed subservient wives and concubines.

Many women must have felt his influence. Many women must have been strongly attracted by him, have been ready to give themselves to him. He must have had "adventures." He must have had amorous experiences, emotional episodes in his life. She said this to herself and she tried to force herself to look upon Peter Kharkoff as she looked upon other men. She even went further than this and tried to force herself to regard him with the youthful cynicism which she reserved for those who were not frank in their pleasures and their sins, who tried to throw dust in the curious eyes of the world.

She had sex. She had good looks. She had—so she had been told—charm. She had the mysterious something which can lure men. Youth was hers, vitality, swift intelligence. And something else too was hers, something which life had taught her meant a great deal to men, and which must surely mean something to this man, though he had never shown her either the least trace of it in himself or the least recognition of it in her. The summons which she knew so well had never come to her from him. And she had never yet cared to send it to him, either by look, or touch, or word. Something in his atmosphere had seemed to strip her of all grossness, to strip her to purity of thought and of intention whenever she was with him. That was, perhaps, partly why she had named him the Unearthly.

Nevertheless, despite appearances, he might be subject to the attack with a certain weapon. He might be just like the other men who, so varied in brains and attainments, were all one when the senses were in question. She knew how enormously deceptive many people are. She knew how deep and searching is the Jekyll and Hyde story, conceived in a dream perhaps, but rooted in humanity. Nothing of this man's past was open to her. She had never known him in his youth when the blood is hot in the veins. Of his secret life she knew absolutely nothing. He might be a sham. He might be a charlatan. She had named him the Unearthly. But what had she known about him when she had given him the name? Perhaps she and her aunt were merely a couple of silly women, impressed by a striking appearance, a deep voice, an unusual manner, a touch of curious foreign charm to which they were unaccustomed. And perhaps Peter Kharkoff, under the cloak of his seeming indifference to that which is attractive to all normal men and is irresistible to most, was really like the others whom she had known, was really an animal combined with a being not animal, but which cannot escape from his yokefellow while the body which holds them together is endowed with the mystery of life.

"Perhaps I have invented the Unearthly," Imogen said to herself. "A few clever touches such as I know how to give and he may show himself as a mere man, and perhaps as one of the merest of men."

She moved a little closer to Peter Kharkoff. She laid a hand on the warm rock near his.

"How brown your hands are getting!" she said. And she threw into her voice a sound which experience had taught her was seductive to men. "I love the sun color," she added. "I hate the paleness so many people considered good seem to aim at in their lives." Carelessly, as if scarcely aware of what she was doing, she touched the back of his right hand several times with her finger-tips.

"I suppose I'm a pagan," she said, "like so many of the people who live along the shores of the Mediterranean. At Sainte Maxime, when you look at one of those copper-colored sailormen who've knocked about all their lives among the sunlit islands and the ports teeming with careless life—don't you ever wish you were one of them?"

"Never," he said in his deep, quiet voice.

"Do you never wish to be the man you are not?" she asked.

"No, never," he said with great simplicity. His face just

then seemed to her even more enigmatic than usual. His hand still lay palm downward on the rock. It had made no response to hers.

A longing rose in her to stir him, to force him out of his calm, to see him, as she had seen many men, stirred by her, hungry for her and showing their hunger. She wanted just then to mean to him what she had meant to others, to mean more to him than she had meant to them, far more. And a preposterous desire came to her to make him understand that, young though she was, she had conquered a position for herself in a great city, in London. But when she looked at him she simply couldn't put forward any of her minute claims, couldn't tell him that in a certain set she was the fashion, that her remarks were repeated from mouth to mouth, that young men ran after her, that girls thought her wonderful, that clever old men trotted round her, sat in her pocket and made fools of themselves about her. The so-called glories of this world, the prizes men scramble for, the bonbons fashion throws to its pets of the moment—what could they mean to him? Did even she really care for them? The question came up in her mind, perhaps for the first time.

If she could make this man care for her how would it be then?

She imagined herself with him, belonging to him, totally his. Couldn't she forget all the things which collectively had hitherto meant life to her if she were living with him? Or would the spell break at the frosty touch of familiarity? And she remembered women who had made unaccountable marriages, who had linked themselves with men not in their world, who had disappeared with strange men lured by some fascination inexplicable to all those who knew them, following a light unseen by others. She had sometimes wondered about such women, smiled at them, pitied them. Now she felt that she understood them. Half frivolously not long ago she had expressed fear of the power of Israel, a fear that had been, perhaps, obscurely felt by her long before she had met Peter Kharkoff. But then she had been thinking of worldly power used selfishly, ruthlessly, to gain purely material ends. Now she was face to face with the power of Israel. But it was a mysterious force much greater in essence, much more potent and far-reaching than any that glittered before the dazzled eyes of men.

"You come from the North, don't you?" she heard herself saying. She had not expected to say that. She did not know why she had said it.

"Yes," he answered. "I was born in the north of Russia."

"Some people expect a Savior to come from out of the North to heal this groaning world," she said. As she spoke she gazed at him, watching for some change of expression to come into his face and transform it, for some look of consciousness, for some sign—she scarcely knew what. But none came. "Do you think he will ever come?" she asked.

"Do you want him to come?" he said, turning slightly on the rock so that he faced her. "It would be a new sensation, wouldn't it?" The words were, she thought, sarcastic. But there was no sound of sarcasm in the voice which uttered them.

"Are you one of those," he continued, "who are looking outside of themselves for a forcible Savior, for someone who will come like an armed man in the night to save them by force in spite of themselves? If you are I think you will be disappointed. I don't think such a Savior is needed by the world, and I don't think he will come to the world."

He paused, keeping his eyes upon her. Then he leaned towards her and said, "When a doctor is called in by a sick man and finds certain symptoms of disease, what does he do? He uses remedies which he hopes will cause those symptoms to disappear. He uses palliatives. The man has a granulated throat, let us say. The doctor does something to get rid of the granulations. If he succeeds in getting rid of them he is satisfied. But what has caused them? Has he attacked the cause when he burned the throat with his electric wires? No. Because more often than not he does not know what the cause is.

"Now I know a man who is not a doctor, but who effects cures of the body often when doctors have failed. His methods, however, are not theirs. What he tries to do is this. He knows that each man possesses a life-force, which has the power, if fully roused, to throw off disease. So he does not try to get rid of symptoms which are surface indications of disease, but he tries to rouse the life-force into full activity, to induce it to go to work and throw off the disease which has caused the disagreeable or perhaps odious symptoms.

"So with the soul. A man cannot be forcibly saved as it were from outside. He carries his own power of salvation within himself. Each man must save himself. All that a so-called Savior can do is this—find the means to induce the man to do that, wake into activity the force which the spirit possesses but which it is not exercising. Don't you sometimes feel that you carry within you mysterious forces which you have never yet fully used? Don't you sometimes feel weighed down because of the unused powers which are lying inert within you?"

"Perhaps I do. I—I'm not quite sure."

"Forces unused lie heavy on the soul. But forces used seem light in their buoyant strength."

"So a Savior, according to you, is he who has the power to wake up in a mass of men and women the instinct of self-salvation." She was silent. Then she said abruptly, "Are you a Christian?"

"If you mean by that word a lover of Christ, I am," he answered.

She was struck by his substitution of the word "lover" for the generally used word "follower" in such a connection. But he did not say it emotionally.

"I don't think I and my pals are Christians, whatever we may choose to call ourselves," she said. "There's a lot of humbug talked about Christianity. The world's sick, very sick. Can such a world as ours be induced to save itself, do you think? I wonder. Here, with you, one loses that sense of catastrophe which broods just now over all great European cities, which broods over London and Paris for instance. And I hear the same of Berlin, Vienna, and other big towns. I don't know exactly why that is. You carry with you an atmosphere that no one else has. But why are you so far off?"

"Don't trouble about that. I am as near as it is necessary for me to be."

"The fact is," she said with energy, "that your body is sitting here with me near the Mediterranean, but *you* are in many other places. I feel it. I know it. And I suppose others feel and know it. Yes, it must be so." And again there came to her anger, the feeling of defiance, the desire to rebel, and—more than that—to entice, to subjugate.

She put out her hand and clasped his.

"Why can't you be a little more human?" she said. "Why can't you be like other men? They're as God made them and meant them to be. But you seem to stand apart from them all. And that's like a tacit condemnation."

At that moment she had a sort of confused consciousness of sensual and spiritual emotion, apparently blended together, and rising in her like a flood. It was a sensation such as she had never known before. Physical desire was mingled with an aspiration to get beyond and away from physical things, to mount up towards something with which the body could have nothing to do. And the sensation was exquisitely keen. The whole of her thrilled with it. And it increased in her till she felt that she was possessed by it and had lost control of herself.

The desire for the Jew as a man was intertwined with another desire, which might be hysterical but which seemed intimately part of herself, as if it had its source in the foundation of her being, a desire to merge herself with him in a way mysterious and wholly unphysical. But because she was very earthly, a typical product of her era—greedy, restless and perhaps, without being often conscious of it, sad under all her seeming gaiety—the only way to reach that desired spiritual communion seemed to her to lie through the doorway of the physical. It was as if there was a room which she must go through in order to get into a much more beautiful room beyond.

"Can't you and I get a little nearer to each other?" she said.

"Why not?" he said. He fixed his eyes on her and they were penetrating as he added, "Tell me. Just how do you want to draw near?"

"How?" She looked at him and something within her faltered, felt terribly ashamed, even felt afraid. She was certain that he knew exactly that strange compounding of sensations within her, the physical reaching out to him which was mingled with another quite different reaching out. And now she was acutely ashamed of the physical part that had been prompting her and governing her. She tried to summon her normal hardihood. She tried to assert to herself that there was nothing to be ashamed of in physical inclinations, that they were wholly natural, that deprived of them she would be less, not more than a woman. But she continued to feel ashamed. She took away her hand from his. She felt that under her paint she was flushing.

"Tell me," he repeated, but gently.

"In your way, whatever it is," she said. "It is sure to be the best way, better than mine."

Wasn't that abject? She didn't feel it to be so. She was putting herself now definitely into his hands, and a sense of rest came to her. It might only last for a moment, but while it lasted it was exquisite. She had the feeling that, with the words, she was resigning herself to him, was sinking into him. The feeling was akin to what she believed to be the sensation of a woman in love giving herself without any holding back of anything, a sensation which she had hitherto only known in imagination. It was akin to that, but it was not that. For she felt that she had gone beyond what the many women who have known that voluptuous resignation have experienced, that she knew something they did not know, that in purification one could actually feel more acutely than in a combination of mental exaltation with physical ecstasy. And she, in that moment, felt purified. The physical desire had gone from her, and with it all the inevitable uneasiness which physical desire always creates. It was as if, without passing through the room through which so many feet of women have trodden, she had succeeded in gaining the more beautiful room beyond.

The chorus of the crickets was about them. The sun blazed out of a clear heaven. Blue called to blue—from sky to sea. And again, as in the flat of the rue les Bergues, an inevitable moment seemed to have been reached. But in the Jew's flat it was he who had spoken the final sentence. Under this blue sky by the Mediterranean Imogen had spoken it.

Having spoken it, and suffered the immensity of feeling which followed upon it, she got up, and in a moment he and she were going down through the scrub and the forest of cork trees towards the hidden house where Hugo was.

Hugo! Hadn't she forgotten Hugo? Hadn't she, in feeling and thought, been utterly false to Hugo? Strangely enough she didn't feel that she had forgotten, that she had been treacherous.

As they went down through the wood she said to herself, "Somehow it's as if Hugo were in him, and he were in Hugo."

Book Four—The Test

CHAPTER I

ON THE evening of that day Imogen told Harriet to pack up, and told her people that she had decided to start for England on the following afternoon. The abruptness of her decision to go immediately was caused by her desire not to go at all. She hated going, but she felt that her desires and reluctances had nothing to do in the matter. What had she to do in London? Nothing that was of any importance. Yet she must travel there, and alone, leaving her people, Hugo and Peter Kharkoff behind her. Perhaps her father and mother would follow almost immediately. That might be. But Hugo and Peter Kharkoff would probably stay on at Sainte Maxime for at least another month. And even then——

What would happen then?

That question sprang up in her mind when she was saying good-by to Hugo. Her last hurried trip to London had been a journey to him when he was lying in agony and, as she supposed, perhaps not far from death. And now she was about to travel to London away from him.

"Last time I went to old London I went to you," she said.

"Yes, Geney."

"You wanted me then."

"More than you knew."

"And now you're sending me away from you—Oh yes, you are, Hugo. You suggested my going. Don't you think that was a dangerous thing to do?"

"I don't believe we know half our time which are the dangerous things for us in life, and which aren't," he said.

"Perhaps not." She paused, looking down at him. Then she said, "And now? Doesn't your instinct tell you anything?"

"Geney dear, you've had such a devil of a time with me, I feel you ought to have a little bit of freedom."

"But shall I be free?"

At that moment a great sadness, even a sense of desolation, came to her, swept over her. She did not understand it fully. There seemed to be love in it, because it was so intimate, and love is at the bottom of every intimate ache in the soul. She knelt down on the floor, so that she might be close to Hugo on his couch.

"Well, good-by, old boy," she said. "I feel rather bad at leaving you. Don't forget me."

What banal words those were, words said so often in moments of departure. But on her lips they had meaning, they had sincerity. Just then she knew that her connection with Hugo had become closer than she had realized, that pain and tragedy had knit them more tightly together than she had understood till now.

"How could I forget you? Why d'you say that?"

"There are greater things than I. There are irresistible things."

"What d'you mean, Geney?"

She leaned down and kissed him.

"When you come to England we won't wait. We'll be married very soon."

He put an arm round her.

"If only I was like all the other fellows!"

There was a momentary savage sound in his strong voice, and his arm shook against her body.

"Perhaps I shall love you better like this," she murmured.

It was the very first time such a possibility had occurred to her, and even now she did not know whether such a miracle— for wouldn't it be a miracle?—could happen.

"No—you couldn't," he said.

"Can you answer for a woman? How much do you know about a woman?"

"A woman! I think I know something about you, Geney."

She got up.

"Well, I must go. Think of me on my journey to old London."

"Yes, I will."

She went to the door and stood still by it.

"I can't feel London any more. It used to mean so much to me. I thought of it as Life. And now it's grown quite pale, like a thing from which the blood has drained away, the riotous red blood."

"Wait till you get back to it."

She half shut her eyes. She was trying to hear the voices of London. But she couldn't. Instead she heard the creaking noise of the crickets sounding in the heat among the cork trees. And she was looking up at the Jew.

"You think me incapable of change," she said. "But I don't think the same of you."

And then she opened the door and went out, meeting Milligan on the landing.

"Good-by, Milligan," she said, and she held out her hand. "I've got to go to London."

"Right, ma'am."

"Why d'you say that?"

"Beg pardon, ma'am. I only meant——"

"If Captain Dennistone is very dull without me you'd better pack up and follow me."

"Yes, ma'am. Excuse me, but is Mr. Kharkoff going too?"

"No."

"I'm glad of that."

"Why?"

"He's great company for Captain Dennistone. You recollect, ma'am, what I said to you about the influence he would have in hospitals?"

"Yes, I remember."

"I was right, ma'am. Captain Dennistone's a different man since Mr. Kharkoff's been here."

"Different—in what way?"

Milligan wrinkled his forehead.

"I hardly know how to put it, ma'am. But he seems to bear his trouble differently. What I mean is he seems more at home with it like."

Imogen remembered just then the savage sound in Hugo's voice. That seemed to contradict the statement of Milligan, and yet she felt that Milligan had spoken the truth.

"I'm glad if it is so," she said. "I shall see you presently in London."

"Yes, ma'am. Good-by, ma'am, and thank you for all your kindness."

The motorcar stood at the door. The luggage and Harriet had already gone to the station. Imogen said good-by to the old lady, and looked out of the window.

"Is Mr. Kharkoff in the garden?" she asked.

"I think he must be, dear," said Lady Lowrie vaguely. "I fancy I saw him somewhere a few minutes ago."

"Somewhere?"

"It may have been in the garden. Or was it in the house?"

"Father's going to take the station en route to Valescure. If I don't find Mr. Kharkoff, say good-by to him for me, will you?"

"Of course. But surely——"

"There's nothing sure about him when one comes to conventions. Good-by, old lady."

Imogen did not find Peter Kharkoff in the garden, and she got into the motor and told the chauffeur to go to the station. As the car stole down the drive, and turned to the left into the road along the sea, there was a horrible melancholy in her heart, a blackness of melancholy. But almost immediately, looking out of the window, she saw Peter Kharkoff standing hatless by the sea edge. Without any signal from her the chauffeur pulled up.

"I thought I shouldn't see you," she said. "Have I the time——?" She looked quickly at her watch. "Yes. I'll get out for a moment."

She got out of the car and told the chauffeur to go on very slowly for five minutes. "Then wait for me, please."

"Yes, ma'am."

He made the car creep on.

When she was alone with Peter Kharkoff, she said, "Why am I going to London? I keep asking myself that and I don't find any answer except this—that I am obliged to go." She looked at him. "Is that it? Am I obliged?"

"Don't you believe in free will?"

"I don't know. Can thought perhaps *compel?*"

"Suppose it could, wouldn't that be very sad?"

"In what way—sad?"

"What would goodness be if you were compelled to be good? What would self-sacrifice be if you were compelled to sacrifice yourself? What would loving be if you were compelled to love?"

She said nothing for a minute. They walked on slowly, following the creeping car along the white road. At last she said, "Have you read Omar Khayyam? But of course you have."

"Yes, I have."

"You don't agree with him. You don't think we are puppets taken out of a box and put back into our box when the play is over. I'm glad of that. It would be awful to be compelled to be good. And yet sometimes——" She looked at him sideways, and she did not complete the sentence. "Goodness is only beautiful if one can say 'I love goodness. I see the beauty of it. I choose it rather than evil.' If there's no free will there's no real wonder, no real glory in human life. And I feel there is. With you I feel there is. But the wonder and the glory don't lie where I used to think they did. Oh, why am I going away?"

"Perhaps you will know why presently."

"Shall I? I wonder when I shall see you again, and where. It won't be here. It won't be in London. Perhaps it will be in Geneva. If it is, will you take me into your studio in the garden?"

"Yes."

"I want to see what is there. My aunt gave Hugo two books. But I haven't read them. Something has held me back from reading them. Oh, the car has stopped! Well, good-by." She put her hand in his. "I want to thank you for coming, for staying here so long. Milligan told me just now that you have done a great deal for Hugo. I feel that too. He's different. Good-by, good-by."

She took away her hand. They were at the edge of the sea and she looked out over the gulf, perhaps taking farewell of that too.

"Ah, there's our boat!" she said.

Far off in the glittering distance she saw the boat with the white and the orange-colored sails leaving the Gulf of Saint Tropez for the open sea.

"It's going out to sea," said Peter Kharkoff, in his heavy deep voice.

"And I?" she thought. "Where am I going?"

At that moment she compared herself with that little boat. It was setting out into the wider waters. The breeze was driving it on. And was not she, too, setting out on seas uncharted? And what was driving her on away from familiar waters? But nothing surely could compel her, unless it were the little bit of God which was housed within her, the little bit of God which can enable a man to save himself. At that moment she felt intimately conscious as never before of the possession of something precious, something which she had neglected, but which her neglect had never been able to alter. Its shining purity was still unclouded. Its fragrance was unimpaired. Its vitality was as the vitality of the dawn among the peaks of high mountains.

As she got into the waiting motorcar and met the quiet eyes of Peter Kharkoff a sudden flash, which seemed to her like a flash of deep understanding, came to her.

"That's what makes him different from all other men. He's got more of God in him than they have."

The car moved. Peter Kharkoff smiled at her. She did not smile in farewell, but she lifted her hand in a gesture of grave good-by. And as she lost sight of him she murmured to herself:

"And less, much less, of the animal part of man."

CHAPTER II

IN PASSING through Paris Imogen stayed for two days at the British Embassy and visited some dressmakers. On the evenings of her stay she went to the theater. She saw a play called, appropriately enough, "Nudité," on the first evening; on the second she saw a Russian company in Gorki's "Asile de Nuit." In the latter she found something of Peter Kharkoff. She could not have told exactly what it was. But in all the misery and squalor of the play there was a truth, a humanity, a depth, a faithfulness to life, a sincerity, which moved her profoundly. And she felt that if she had seen the play before she had known Peter Kharkoff it would not have moved her in exactly the same way. The play seemed to her to be illumined mysteriously by him, so that she saw it as otherwise she would not have seen it. And in the actors, starkly true to life in their acting, she found something of Peter Kharkoff's large simplicity and totally unselfconscious sincerity.

At the dressmakers' on the contrary she was amazed at the affectation she met with. The artificiality of the manikins came to her like a gust of patchouli smelt in sea air. As she looked at their swaying hips and mincing steps, at their mask-like, staring faces, at their detached, unmeaning gestures, she pitied these human clothes-pegs, and wondered (for the first time) if it were possible for a girl with a brain and a heart to be happy in such a profession.

"But we've got to have clothes!" she thought.

And then a fantastic idea came to her.

"If I had brought Peter Kharkoff with me here! If these painted girls were suddenly confronted with him!"

And she had a sort of half michievous, half genuinely curious longing to summon Peter Kharkoff into that hot and perfumed abode of the vanities, to see what would happen when he came.

Somebody whom she met in Paris, a girl who was what is called "a friend" of hers, gave her a novel to beguile the journey to England.

"It's rather fun. We're all reading it. But if you happen to go into a kindergarten don't leave it there."

When her train glided out of the Gare du Nord Imogen opened this paper-covered book, which, as she saw on the cover, had already been bought by over sixty thousand people. Inside she found a mass of filth, which seemed to make the carriage stink as if the contents of a sewer had been emptied into it. She read for some time, she forced herself to read though she really didn't want to, in spite of the interest in filth so almost universally prevalent in the human species. But presently, moved by an irresistible impulse, she opened the carriage window wide and flung the book out.

"I believe I've hit an unfortunate village with the beastly thing!" she said to herself, as she saw a flying vision of houses. "Can't be helped!"

And then she settled down to think. And presently, while she thought, the stink in the carriage of the book seemed to grow less, to be dying out as the fresh air rushed in.

"What a prude they'd all think me!"

Yes; wouldn't they? But really it had come to this, that she had begun to prefer an untainted atmosphere to the rank effluvia of sewage.

When she saw the cold-looking faces of the Dover Cliffs, the bare downs on their summits, the castle watching among its green lawns over the town and the harbor, she was sharply aware of the journey she had made since she had last been in England, the journey not of the body but of the nature, the mind and soul.

"How different! How different!" she thought.

And in the Pullman car she lived in the heart of change, of vital change.

But it was in Victoria Station that transformation seemed to meet her fairly and squarely, to confront her, like a powerful mist-figure, in the path.

It was a hot, dry evening. In the echoing station, where shadows hovered on the outskirts of the feverish crowds, one seemed to smell the dust outside. The roar of the "season" was audible in the distance. While she waited with Harriet behind the wooden barrier for her registered baggage she listened to it, and it seemed to be meant for her, to be addressing itself to her. In it, mingled together, blending like the various instruments in a large orchestra, she imagined that she heard many voices that were familiar or that had been familiar in her ears, voices of girls whom she called by Christian or pet names, of gay young men who had made love to her, joked with her, chaffed her, danced, hunted, acted with her, of clever women of the world who had helped to teach her the lore of the worldly life which was all of life they knew, of pretty actresses and professional dancers with whom she had trodden daintily the fringes of Bohemia, of brilliant elderly men, politicians, writers, professors, philosophers, preachers, of daring young devils busily engaged in trying to *épater les bourgeois* without being conscious that in doing so they were only imitating men, now silent, of the past, who had long since mingled their dust with the dust of those they had despised in many a crowded cemetery. Canon Barrimore's deep voice! Wasn't that audible among the others? She found herself listening for it, and remembering that evening of destiny when, from the top of the steps beyond the screen of Drearney Cathedral, she had first seen the face of the Jew.

London was calling—calling to her. But she didn't feel any thrill of response within her. The smell of the dust, acrid and dry, was in her nostrils. Beyond the feverish crowd the shadows were assembling. And she felt melancholy and strange as she confronted the falling of night. The great roaring city, despite those many known voices in it, repelled instead of welcoming her. She felt herself an alien in it, oddly small and desolate. It was as if a great coldness had sprung up between London and herself, as sometimes happens between two who have been even unduly intimate and who have many recollections in common. She knew too much about London, and London knew too much about her. That was how she felt it. And there was born in her a curious dread of London such as she had never known before.

She told herself that she was tired by the journey from Paris in the heat, that big stations always have a depressing and devitalizing effect on sensitive people, that Victoria Station was full of hollow echoes and dreary at the best of times. But her feeling of dread, or at any rate of nervous apprehension, persisted when presently she was out of the station driving through the familiar streets towards Lowndes Square. And she found herself longing, almost like a desolate child, for Sainte Maxime, for the palms, the cork trees, the blue and purple waters of the gulf, the boat with the white and orange sails. All that seemed home, and this was not home.

But why was all that home?

The house in Lowndes Square was partially in curl-papers. But servants were there. The window-boxes were full of flowers. Many letters awaited Imogen on the hall table, and she had not been ten minutes in the house before the telephone bell began to sound. Her pals were ringing her up. Their chatter reached her ears through the devilish little instrument which simplifies and complicates life. They were asking her to do this and do that, were proposing pleasures for that very night. "Get into something and come to Molly Lancaster's ball at the Ritz. She's sent you an invitation." "Where are you dining? Come round to Claridge's. We're only half-way through. Going to the Winter Garden afterwards, and then to the ball at Greville House, and anything else that occurs to us." "Is that you, Imogen? Thank the Lord. Box B. at the Gaiety as soon as you've pecked at something, and afterwards come on with us to . . ." etc., etc., etc.

Imogen poured negatives into the telephone, gathered up the letters and notes, and got into the lift. She touched the button and ascended to the third floor. She had ordered dinner to be brought to her sitting-room. Soon after half past eight Henry, who was always on duty in London, brought it in, rolling a table before him. While she ate it Imogen looked through her letters.

She still felt strange and an alien in the great city whose murmur she heard outside. Never before had she felt like this in London, not even when she had come back to be with Hugo after his accident. A dreadful detachment was upon her like a spell, a sense of being supremely separate from London and all its pleasures and activities. She realized that hitherto she had always felt herself to be a part and not an insignificant part of the great whole called London, had identified herself with it instinctively whenever she was in it. London had seemed somehow to belong to her, to have been thoughtfully provided as the wonderful setting in which she was supremely fitted to shine. But—now!

Presently Henry brought coffee and rolled the dinner table away. Imogen was alone in her familiar room. She lit a cigarette.

It was the evening of a Tuesday. She had been in London less than three hours, but already her thoughts turned to Drearney. She had a longing to go there. Perhaps she would run down on Saturday and spend a couple of nights with Aunt Towser and go to the cathedral in the evening. All these letters and notes were a nuisance. A pestilence of invitations had descended upon her. She lay down on her big sofa and looked about the room.

And then Hugo was with her again. It was the last time she had seen him erect, a very male man in health. The last time! And neither of them had had any premonition of what was coming. They had had a sort of row that day. She could hear Hugo's strong, gritty voice saying, "Upon my soul, Geney, you want a damned good bringing to heel." They had parted coldly that day. They hadn't known—they hadn't known! And the next time she had seen Hugo he was a wreck, huddled on a bed in the nursing-home in Bentinck Street, looking up at her with blue eyes which seemed to be saying, "Why? Oh, my God—why?"

Could she ever love him better because he had fallen by the way of life and come into great tribulation? He had said no, that she couldn't. But did men ever know all the possibilities of women? If he was wrong, if it was possible, mightn't they even yet be happy, he and she?

The two short lines showed in her smooth forehead. She smoked a little faster.

She had told Hugo that he thought her incapable of change. Peter Kharkoff didn't think that. The second time she had been with him, in Geneva, he had foreseen, had almost prophesied, change in her. Hadn't he? And she had changed. But how much?

Perhaps that was why she had had to come to London alone, in order that she might learn to know how much she had changed. And it seemed to her that it was so, that she did not know yet the exact meaning or extent of the change in her, but that she would learn that now in London, face to face with the familiar figures whom she would encounter on the morrow and on many morrows. They would not have changed, and their very changelessness would perhaps serve as a measuring-rod to the change in her.

And knowledge too would surely come to her through the absence of the Jew. The conviction came to Imogen that knowledge comes in absence. When Peter Kharkoff had been with her day by day she had felt him like an atmosphere, like a climate, like the face of Nature. Now London would be there to contend with him, to blot him out if it could, blot him out in her.

She would give London the chance. If she did that the test would be an acid test. And she was in the mood for that.

For a moment she thought of putting on an evening gown and going out to join one of the gay parties to which she had been urgently invited. She even got up from the sofa and went towards her bedroom. But a glance into the glass told her that she wasn't looking quite her best. She examined her face curiously, attentively. Had she aged? She was still of course young, quite a girl. And her face was quite young in spite of its paint. But she surely looked older, definitely older, than when she had left London for the Riviera. And her face no longer looked absolutely familiar to her. There was something of novelty in it, "an odd look." She said to herself, "I look odd." The mysterious imprint of new experience had surely been set on her youthful features.

There came to her a longing to get rid of all her make-up, and then to see how she looked, what was underneath. And she went into her bedroom, and there, instead of dressing to go to one of the balls of that night, she removed all the artificial red, white and shadowy blue on her cheeks, lips, neck, and beneath her eyes. When she had done this she felt quite different, younger and calmer. She looked again in the glass. Certainly her face was changed. She was even startled by the amount of expression in it, and by the difference of that expression from her former habitual look of saucy self-possession and semi-satirical humor. Her face, she thought, looked grave and deep. The word came to her—"deep." Her natural complexion was still a very good one despite all the trials and outrages to which she had subjected it. She had a clear white skin.

"Shall I leave it alone?" she asked herself.

Should she face London on the morrow unpainted? It would be a daring thing to do. It would be a return to the Geneva night when she had had the impulse to cleanse herself of artificiality before setting forth on the quest for the Jew. She had never repeated that experiment. And Peter Kharkoff wasn't here.

She washed her face crudely in cold water, dried it, and felt oddly clean. Did she enjoy the feeling? Something seemed missing. It wouldn't be easy to get accustomed to the un-painted face. But several times lately, as on the day when she had followed Peter Kharkoff into the forest of cork trees, she had felt sick of her paint, had felt that it quarreled with Nature, made her look ugly in Nature's bosom. And tonight she had a longing to be quit of all artificiality.

How almost indecently natural those Russian actors in Paris had been! One of them—poor devil!—had been full of lice, in his rôle, and had scratched himself until the whole audience had been made intimately one with his physical misery. Imogen in her stall had had a dreadful desire to scratch, and she had seen people near her moving uneasily, shifting under the spell of that horrible acting. Horrible—yes! But it had been right as no deviation from the natural can ever be right. And the whole audience had instinctively realized the rightness of it.

The removal of her make-up and the washing of her face in cold water seemed to bring Imogen nearer to someone who was now a long way off, and even nearer to Hugo too. And she connected the thought of the marriage decreed with the thought of a new start on a path leading away from all artificiality.

Presently she went back into her sitting-room and examined it with a sort of frigid interest. This was, or had been, her shell, the place into which she retired to curl up now and then for a few minutes, the place, too, into which her intimates, or those whom she chose to honor with a semblance of intimacy, were admitted for confidential talk. It was a pretty enough room. It was harmonious, luxurious, full of interesting things, of variety in harmony, of evidences of what is called culture.

She had taken trouble over it, and people had praised her taste and her cleverness. But a bare room with deal boards, walls of books and an hour-glass meant more to her now than this beautiful room did. As she looked at the various pictures, statuettes, at the etchings, the china, the bibelots which she had collected, at the books in their valuable bindings, many of them inscribed with flattering words to her by their authors, she came face to face with the vanities of her life before she had met the Jew. And she was amazed by the cold sensation of indifference which she now felt towards the elaborate minutiæ formerly given such importance by her.

"I lived in all the little things," she said to herself. "In them and by them."

But would she ever be able to live in them and by them again? And if not, by what was she going to replace them? She would always love sport. But Hugo's horrible accident had turned her mind from all thought of sporting activities, and though she didn't feel, and couldn't imagine, that her natural courage was or could ever be affected by a tragic happening connected with sport, yet hunting would probably never in the future be to her quite what it had been in the past. She must always connect it with Hugo. And Hugo would never give her a lead across country again.

This return to London alone brought to her a feeling of loss. She had recently lost a great deal. Satisfaction in quantities of things had been withdrawn from her. She didn't care for things as she had cared. Apparently she had been robbed of powers of caring which she had hitherto enjoyed. And yet she was still very young.

A fear of emptiness came to her. If life should begin to seem empty to her how awful that would be. And then, seeing hollowness, feeling hollowness, Imogen knew that she was suffering from a tremendous reaction. She had been leaning mentally and perhaps spiritually on another, and now she seemed abandoned to herself, had to stand alone.

A thrill of that old jealousy went through her. She thought of night in the villa, Hugo lying on his couch near the open window through which the faint sound of the sea came in— someone perhaps beside him.

Why had they wished her away?

Or had they both wished her away? She wasn't quite sure about that. Here in London, removed from him, and therefore able, she supposed, to consider him with a certain impartiality, she realized that she wasn't able to read Peter Kharkoff as she could read many other men, that she seldom, or never, knew exactly what he was thinking. She knew now, in London, that she hadn't been able to tell whether he had wished her to leave Sainte Maxime or not. At one time she had believed that it was he who had prompted, not with words but with thought, Hugo to suggest to her that she should go to London while the villa was still open, while he still stayed on there. In the garden she had believed, had felt practically certain, of that. But she wasn't certain now. Peter Kharkoff had seemed satisfied at her going, had shown no desire to prevent her from going. But had he actively wished her to go? She wondered now.

About Hugo she didn't wonder in the same way. Probably in his great generosity he had felt that he must give her another chance. Or perhaps he couldn't bring himself even now to trust in her power of unselfishness; perhaps, though he loved her, even because he loved her, he was afraid of marrying her quickly, felt that he dared not do that without putting her more fully to the test. She had been afraid of her own unselfishness. Perhaps Hugo was afraid of it too, but in a different way. For she had feared its possible strength. He perhaps feared its possible weakness, was seeking to test the unknown ground before he ventured to step on it. Peter Kharkoff would never do a similar thing. He was amazingly free from doubts. Now she came to think about it she knew that she couldn't imagine him having any doubts about her. He just seemed to know— and far more than she knew.

That was another difference between him and other men; that he believed deeply in what they either could not believe in, or could only half believe in with many reservations. Hugo loved her and doubted her. Peter Kharkoff didn't love her but he didn't doubt her. But if he didn't doubt her, couldn't doubt her, did he, perhaps, love her in some strange, far-reaching way, some penetrating and yet impersonal way, glorious, but physically undemanding?

She felt her pulses quicken at the thought, but there was absolutely nothing of sexuality in her excitement. She no longer wanted to draw near to him in that way. That desire had died since their solitary interview in the forest.

Her father had spoken about Peter Kharkoff's possible power of love. And she—she had usually dwelt upon his enormous indifference. Perhaps her father had come nearer to the truth of Peter Kharkoff than she had. Perhaps his detachment from the absorbing excitements of the worldly life, the comparative solitude in which he lived, enabled him to see more clearly than she could into a character that was totally unlike any that she had encountered in her busily frivolous existence.

She wished that she had talked more intimately and often with her father about Peter Kharkoff, the man who believed more in the inner goodness of her than she had even been able to believe herself.

"But if he knew all I've been!" she thought.

And she felt as if her unpainted face was flushing.

Her telephone sounded. She did not answer it. She felt startled and distressed, almost frightened by the sudden, unexpected noise. The bell went on ringing persistently. At last she went to the telephone and took the receiver.

"Imogen—is that you?"

"Yes. Is it you, Lois?"

"No other. You've got to come to number four, Park Street."

"I can't. I'm tired. I'm just going to bed."

"Tired after only the nip over from Paris! I don't believe you. Who's with you? Tell me his name."

"There's nobody."

"Honor?"

"Of course."

"Well, I'll take your word for it, but I'm coming to see."

"I shall be in bed."

"I'm bringing Teddy Basingstoke with me. We'll soon get you up between us. Expect us in ten minutes. Good-by."

The acid test!

Should she submit herself to it at once, that very night? She knew what the evenings at number four, Park Street, were like. For a moment she stood hesitating. Then she went into her bedroom.

"Harriet, get me something to put on, will you? That yellow thing I got in Paris will do. I'm going out in ten minutes."

"Yes, ma'am."

Imogen went over to the mirror on the dressing-table.

"My face!" she thought, startled.

For the moment she had forgotten. Instinctively she

reached out towards the silver boxes that were scattered over the table. But she drew her hand back.

"No, I'll go. But I'll go as I am."

Imogen did not get into bed that night till the dawn of the morrow was breaking. As she looked out for a moment before drawing the dark blind over the window she imagined dawn by the Mediterranean. Then she let down the blind, drew the curtains and got into bed.

Had she enjoyed herself? It seemed to her that she both had and had not. She had plunged again into the atmosphere very natural to her in the past. The time had run by swiftly while she lived in it. Her vanity had been pricked by the joyous reception her friends had given to her. They had made her feel once more that she was very much somebody in their London. She had set herself to shine and had quickly found that the old daring had not become atrophied by lack of use, that her weapons had not rusted because for a time she had laid them away. A certain gaiety had boiled, or perhaps rather had bubbled up in her. Some of the former youthful recklessness and impudent audacity had pushed up in her too, proving to her that what she had thought of as the new Imogen had not entirely displaced the Imogen London knew. She had had a success, a facile success. And she had enjoyed it. And she had despised it. For it had been too easy. Coming back to London after an interval filled with pain and with fascination she felt a new contempt for those who, once a thing is the fashion, bow down to it like mechanical dolls. She was a thing that was still "the fashion," so down went the empty heads, and "Isn't Imogen wonderful?" was still the parrot cry that saluted her ears.

Even her unpainted face had had an immense success. Everybody, of course, had noticed it immediately, and everybody had supposed that she had shown it to make a sensation. She had passed through a tragedy, she had stretched out her hands to the nobilities, she had dedicated her life to a cripple, she was going presently to be married to a man who would have to be wheeled to the altar lying down on a couch, and she was greeting the new and dedicated existence with a sensational ablution which marvelously became her. Like the widow who looks lovelier in weeds than in colors she had made of her sorrow a triumph.

"What a marvelous sense Imogen has of the fitness of things!" had been the comment of a woman whose whole life was an effort to appear to be the possessor of what she called "perfect taste," though in reality she had none at all.

The outside of the cup and platter! All through the night Imogen had been acutely conscious "somewhere inside" that she was back among those who looked upon that, who cared for that, whose thoughts were occupied with that. And underneath the excitement—for actually she had succeeded in feeling new to conventional gaiety—she had been aware of strain, of irritation, and even of resounding emptiness. Nevertheless the time had flown, and some part of her had enjoyed, and some part of her had thrilled to the wonted touches, and some part of her had been coaxed into the purring that is the natural music of egotism.

And something had really happened too.

She had met a new man, a Russian, who, either not knowing about her sacrificial romance with Hugo, or perhaps not caring for such a trifle, had shown with a definiteness which might have seemed blatant if it had not always remained subtly well-bred that she attracted him more than any other woman in that gathering of pretty women, and that he wished and meant to know her well. He was a Count Berazov, who had recently appeared in London from the Argentine. His history was this. Immensely rich, he had been totally ruined by the revolution in Russia. He had escaped and starved in Rome. Then he had found work in a smart hotel as a waiter. An enormously rich widow from Buenos Aires had taken an apartment in the hotel. Berazov had waited upon her in her sitting-room. She had found out who he was, had fallen in love with him, had married him and taken him away to South America.

There, on a country estate of hers, she had died in giving birth to a child by him, and had left him her fortune. The child had died too. Like a dream in the night had slipped by through his life this romance, if for him it had been a romance. After the interlude of sordid poverty, of carrying plates and trays, he was once more rich. After the interval of being possessed by a watchful woman who hungrily adored him, he was once more unattached. After a moment of being the father of a living child, he was once more childless.

Pale, slim, tall, with dark-brown, smooth hair and large, sad, gray eyes, he had an oval clean-shaven face, not handsome but full of refinement and of personality. His hands were the typical hands of the artist. He was unpretentious in manner, very simple and quiet, and ardent in melancholy. His voice was soft and somehow suggested heat. A savor of the barbaric seemed to emanate from him subtly, a something of Asia and the North, but of those Northern regions where though the world is covered with snow the heat of the sun is scorching. Fate for a time had forced him to carry trays. Those long-fingered, narrow hands had doubtless accepted tips. But he had a fascination of genuine culture combined with another less explicable fascination which belongs to many Russians, an allurement deeply physical, suggestive of physical recklessness and bodily daring in wickedness.

Imogen had spent most of the evening with him, and had invited him to visit her the next day in the sacred room on the third floor.

Why?

Something in her, recently subdued, had abruptly sprung to attention at the touch of his long white fingers, at the steady glance of his sad gray eyes. The reckless devil that he surely was, a devil that had rioted in the brilliant days of Russia, and had been ruined, and had suffered hunger, and had worn evening dress in the Roman sunshine while ministering to the appetites of travelers, and had been desperately loved and endowed with riches, and set free by the hand of death, had held out a hand to a devil in her. And her devil had responded. And—an ache had begun in her suddenly. She hated this ache; she feared it. And yet, so contradictory was she, something in her cherished it, and welcomed it and held to it.

After the months of unselfishness, and mental excitement, and ardent debates of the mind, after the strenuous exercise of overthinking, there had come a sudden rebound.

That night she had been secretly the prey of her body.

She slept profoundly. When she awoke the ache was still in her like a new living thing. It persisted. On the very threshold of the test—so she thought of it—she had been met by a stranger in whom was housed a diabolical enticement for her. It was just that—an enticement, a something that beckoned to the senses, a something that called to that in her which she knew to be wild. It seemed to her that the reason of her coming back alone to London was this—that she had had to meet and to know this stranger. If she had not gone to that extremely intimate, and extremely unbuttoned affair in Park Street, she might never have met this man, Berazov. For it seemed that at present he was scarcely going out at all, was avoiding general society. He had only gone to Park Street because he had known the hostess intimately in Paris, and had understood that only a few artists were going to be there. But he had gone and Imogen had gone. And now she felt that it had had to be so.

A peculiar and hideous desire had reared up its head like a serpent's within her. She shrank from it. She felt it to be abominable, a thing to be slain. But it was keen and powerful and would not abandon her. It was this: a desire to be revenged on two men by the Mediterranean. Hugo and Peter Kharkoff had sent her away from them. (For she coupled now closely the one with the other.) They had banished her. Very well, she would run wild in her banishment. She would let herself go. She had not intended to leave them. She had not suggested going. She had not wanted to go. But some mysterious pressure had pushed her away, the united pressure, perhaps, of two minds, one acting on the other.

And she was obscurely jealous, perhaps somewhat as Towser had been jealous of her in Drearney on the night of her interview with the Jew. And that obscure jealousy pushed her now towards Berazov. Whenever she thought of Hugo and Peter Kharkoff together in the peace of Sainte Maxime she had the longing to grasp at some fierce pleasure, to pay herself angrily back for something she was missing.

But she was unhappy in this longing.

In the morning she went out shopping with Lois Tremayne who poured all the gossip of their London into her ears. Afterwards they went to lunch at the Ritz with Lady Tenley, a small, rich American, comfortably separated from an English husband, who oscillated like a pendulum between the Ritz in London and the Ritz in Paris, and whose life was spent in giving parties of all kinds to which everybody invited invariably went. At this particular lunch Imogen met twenty-two people whom she knew. Among them was an old and very famous statesman whom she had been intimate with ever since she was a child, and who had always called her by her Christian name. She sat at lunch between him and a Chilian diplomat, and talked generally to him.

This was the first time she had met him since her engagement to Hugo had been given out, and he spoke about it to her with a sort of gentle surprise.

"You are going to do a great thing, Imogen," he said.

"Great!" she said. "Is it? Oh no, I don't think so."

"Yes, it is—at your age."

He looked at her. Although he was well over seventy his brown eyes were still very bright, and his thin figure was still very upright.

"What was it made you feel you could do it, dear Imogen?"

He spoke in a low voice, which was almost drowned by the uproar of conversation around them.

"I don't quite know. I just felt one evening that I couldn't leave him to face life alone lying always on his back. But sometimes I'm terrified of the future."

"You yielded to the coercion of your best part. When we do that—not too often, eh?—the other part often takes fright. I've known the same thing, the same thing."

He half shut his eyes.

"And what happened in the end?" Imogen asked him, eagerly.

"Generally a compromise, I'm afraid. But, my dear, I've been a politician since I was thirty, and the poison of compromise has got into my blood. By nature you are uncompromising. Stick to the uncompromising." He smiled at her. "It's so much more manly."

"But, Glenn dear, I'm a woman."

"Yes, but never be afraid to be manly. Compromise is really nothing but a diplomatic compounding with the Devil."

"What's that about the Devil?" twittered Lady Tenley's soprano voice on the statesman's other side. "If there's anything new about him I want to hear it too."

And then Imogen began to talk to her Chilian neighbor.

She was home again by half past four. Count Berazov was coming at five. She went up to her sitting-room to wait for him. And to fill up the time she began to write a letter to Hugo.

While she was writing it the obscure sense of injury in her increased. Bending over the paper she was again by the Mediterranean among the palms, the pines and the cork trees. She was with Hugo and Peter Kharkoff in the garden near the gateway to the forest. But they did not see her; they did not feel her presence.

And it seemed to her that Hugo was learning to do without her.

Peter Kharkoff had surely an extraordinary power of absorbing into himself the personalities of others. Whether he used this power deliberately or almost unconsciously she wasn't even now certain. But here in London, separated from the two men who were wound up in her life, she felt him drawing Hugo, the essence of Hugo, towards himself, his essence.

She laid down her pen and sat with her chin in her hand.

Hugo's motive, perhaps not understood by him, in telling her to go to London had surely been this, that he wanted to be left alone with the Jew. And now they were alone together. For the old lady and old papa didn't really count as interruptions. The vital interposition between Hugo and Peter Kharkoff had surely come from herself. She had summoned Peter Kharkoff to Sainte Maxime for Hugo, but she had been intent upon him herself so long as she had been there. What a difference to Hugo her departure must have made! Had he, perhaps, actually been glad when the motorcar had taken her to the station, and the silence of her removal had fallen about the house?

"Count Berazov!" said Henry at the door.

CHAPTER III

THAT first meeting in intimacy—for Imogen always felt a sort of intimacy with those whom she admitted to the room from which she carefully excluded so many people—was the beginning of an episode which was to leave a definite mark on her life. Berazov was not an ordinary man and his life experiences had not been ordinary. He had much more temperament than the average man has. Although he was still comparatively young—only thirty-six—he had touched extremes.

And he carried extremes in him.

There was melancholy in his disposition. But he could at times be riotously even wildly gay. He was tremendously physical, but he had a deep and perfectly natural interest in the things of the mind. He was perverse and simple, complex and childlike. At moments he could be extraordinarily coarse. A peasant could scarcely have been coarser. Yet his habitual atmosphere was full of refinement. The amazing ups and downs of his life seemed to find their reflection in the ups and down of his temperament. He was never uninteresting. He was never a bore. Silent he might be; dull he could not be. He was irreligious and strongly interested in religions, cynical and yet romantic, shocked at nothing, coldly disgusted at some things. Usually he was grave and had a look of intentness, the expression of an investigator, of a pursuer. But there were moments when he fell away into an indifference like the indifference of a dreamer detached from ordinary life. Often very casual he was capable of pertinacity. He had great fascination which never seemed intentional, was often unreliable and always forgiven for that fault because he seemed so totally unconscious of it. He was very human, very easy to get on with, absolutely devoid of affectation or pretension of any kind. Whatever he was doing, however odd or perhaps even outrageous it might be according to the ideas of others, came from him dressed in the garments of sincerity.

He was disarmingly natural. One felt that there were depths in him.

His interest in literature and in the arts was great. He knew instinctively what was valuable and genuine in literature, painting and music, rejected instinctively all that was merely eccentric, manufactured and forced. The naturally bizarre he delighted in and he welcomed all sincere novelty. Music was a passion with him. In his own country, before the revolution, he had been an ardent sportsman.

In that first interview in the upstairs room he told Imogen about his life as a waiter in Rome. She had heard from Lois Tremayne about that episode and frankly asked him about it. He did not turn it into farce, or apologize for it. He just spoke about it as he might have spoken about his life at court, or in the Russian army as an officer. Apparently it had interested him, as well as disgusted and amused him.

"Have you ever been dining in a smart restaurant and heard a crash of glass and crockery?" he asked her presently.

She said that on one occasion she had, in the Palace Hotel at Biarritz.

"What effect did it have upon you?"

"An irresistibly comic effect, like that produced by the noise of a heavy man tumbling upstairs."

"I went through a good deal in Russia. But the tragedy of such a crash as that put Russian horrors into the shade. I caught my foot in a dowager's dress in the restaurant of the Grand Hotel in Rome and fell with a dinner. People laughed. I paid. And I had to face the maître d'hotel partially dressed in hors d'œuvres."

Imogen wanted to laugh but somehow she couldn't. He told her more episodes of a waiter's life, and with a few brief touches sketched for her the psychology of waiters.

"You've probably never thought about them."

"I don't believe I ever have—really."

"Many of them are extraordinarily good judges of human character."

"Are you a good judge?"

"Since I have been a waiter?"

"Yes—if you like."

"Doesn't each one of us think him or herself a good judge? Don't you think you are a good judge?"

"I used to. I'm not sure now."

At that moment she thought of the Unearthly. Berazov looked hard at her as if expecting some explanation of that "now." As none came he went on talking about his life as a waiter. He spoke of the time when he was a "floor waiter," and attended on people in private rooms, and told her with detached calmness and in thoroughly plain language of two or three extremely unsavory episodes.

"What a barbarian he is!" she thought. "To speak like that to me!"

A few minutes later he was discussing a question of art with her and commenting on some of the treasures in her room. He got up from his chair and examined various things minutely. She watched his tall figure moving gently about with an air of being quietly at home, his long fingers carefully, with a delicacy not the least effeminate, touching this thing and that.

"I can't see *you* crashing," she said.

"It was the dowager's dress. She appeared to belong to what they call in Rome the black world. (I heard afterwards that she was the friend of cardinals.) I embroidered her black satin skirt elaborately with mayonnaise of prawns. It really was a masterpiece, but she couldn't see it."

This time Imogen could not help laughing. And he too smiled.

"And then I went to the Argentine," he added.

And suddenly he looked melancholy, almost wistful.

"Your life has been extraordinary," she said, thinking of the sudden return from poverty to riches, of the swift death which followed what to the woman must have been a great romance.

"I sometimes think every life must seem extraordinary at moments to the liver of it. Yours for instance?"

Again she thought of the Unearthly—a Russian too. Yes, her life at this moment seemed to her to be extraordinary. She looked across the room to the writing table on which lay her unfinished letter to Hugo.

"Doesn't it?" he asked in his gentle low voice that suggested heat to her.

"What makes you think so?"

"The waiter's capacity for psychology."

"I believe you knew a great deal about psychology before you became a waiter."

"But ever so much more since then. To be a floor waiter in a great hotel is a marvelous education. You have no idea——" he paused.

She saw in his eyes an intention to force questions from her. She really felt curious, but she was determined not to show it. Her curiosity, she knew, was ugly though she felt it to be natural, even dreadfully human.

"I can imagine that the Argentine was an even greater education," she said.

At that moment her mind went to the woman who was dead and who had borne a child to the man who was now sitting so near her.

"Oh yes," he said. "That too——"

And then he looked absent-minded, even dreamy, and seemed for a moment to forget where he was, and her. And that dreamy forgetfulness fascinated Imogen, and pricked her to restlessness, and brought back the ache in her.

When he had gone she was devoured by restlessness and knew not how to be still.

Presently she remembered her letter to Hugo and went to the writing table to finish it. When she sat down and looked at the half-covered sheet of white paper her life at Sainte Maxime came up before her, her connection with Hugo, her intercourse with the Unearthly. How different she felt here in London. Something of her had surely been laid to sleep out there by the bright blue sea, and something of her had

been roused from sleep. She was conscious today, as perhaps
never before, of two separate strains in her, and had an odd
sense of slipping back from some goal that she had been moving towards. She had subconsciously wanted to reach that
goal. Yet she also wanted, at least now she wanted, to slip
back from it into what uncommonly good people are inclined
to call "the mire." She felt a secret desire and love of sin
in her. (Only none of her set called it, or anything else,
"sin" nowadays.) She also felt a longing for elevation, a
longing to be uplifted above certain desires, and certain wild-
nesses, and certain reckless inclinations.

There was a moment when she seemed to be wishing with
all her strength that she were "all of a piece" as some human
beings, she fancied, perhaps were. When she thought of the
man who had but just left her she felt almost sure that,
various though he was, and perhaps full of complexities, he was
incapable of such opposites as she unfortunately housed within
herself. The touch of barbarism, she believed, protected him
from certain soul troubles. She could imagine him looking on
at himself with quiet cynicism, smiling and saying, "You have
to be so. You are so. And it doesn't matter."

Would the Jew have any effect upon him?

Abruptly she finished her letter to Hugo. When she posted
it—she posted it herself in order to feel its going—she wished
she were going with it. And yet she didn't wish it—because
of Berazov. He excited her. He stung her to perversity.
Always she was conscious of that revengeful desire to pay herself back in London for what she had lost, was losing, in Sainte
Maxime. She even had a desire to injure Peter Kharkoff in
a certain way for letting her go. She could hear his deep voice
saying, "Go to London. Go back to your friends, your life
there. Why shouldn't you? Don't you consider yourself
free?" And then immediately afterwards, he had said that
he would stay on with Hugo.

She felt angry whenever she thought of that. And yet—
would she have Hugo and Peter Kharkoff here in London with
her just now if it were possible? Yesterday, before nightfall,
her answer to that question would surely have been an eager
"yes." But now she had met Berazov.

She could scarcely believe that only yesterday afternoon she
had never seen him, had never even heard of him. Somehow
he meant more to her already than any other man in London.

Again, and more sharply than ever, she was aware of reaction, of rebound. She had been living and sometimes suffering severely in thought. Now she had a longing for action, and even for violent action. A few weeks ahead lay, she supposed, the strange marriage that must radically change her life. But she had a few weeks. Hugo himself had given them to her. It was not she who had snatched at them.

"Don't you consider yourself free?"

Imogen didn't go down to Drearney on the following Saturday. The impulse to do that had died away in her since she had met Berazov. Instead she motored down to Windsor with him, went to Virginia Water and strolled with him in Windsor Park. And in the evening she dined with him in a small and very chic restaurant called—no one knew why—the Tour d'Eméraude.

Imogen had never been accustomed to hide, or to try to hide, what she was doing from her friends, or from those who knew about her and followed her social career from a distance with the respectful wonder and horror peculiar to nobodies. She had no intention of beginning to be secretive now. As to Berazov he was as careless of secrecy as a child though he had none of a child's innocence. The Tour d'Eméraude, very small, was usually packed with the elect. And even on that Saturday it was so packed. Lois Tremayne was there with Teddy Basingstoke. After dinner they were going to motor down into Surrey and spend the "week-end" with a house party near Frensham Ponds. Two or three husbands Imogen knew were there with other people's wives. A famous American dancer, a sort of friend of hers, was dining with lemon-colored Lord Sark who, though over sixty, was still what he called "larky" and always up to something. The pretty room in fact was well supplied with "tongues." Looking round Imogen saw all these people as just merely tongues.

"I'm so glad you like him," Lois Tremayne found an opportunity to whisper to Imogen. "I tried to make him play with me, but he wouldn't. He was waiting for you. He's tremendously attracted by unpainted faces. But then he's an oddity. Did you know it? Was that why you gave up painting?"

Lord Sark gave her his twisted smile and a look of rascally understanding, and the American dancer considered Berazov with an earnest attention which rather suggested the prelude to an organized attack. He seemed totally indifferent to the tongues. That was a peculiarity of his, the power of apparently not noticing, not being at all aware of the negligible, the, to him, uninteresting.

Lois Tremayne's whispered remark made Imogen wonder why exactly it was that Berazov had evidently at first sight taken such a liking to her. She was thoroughly accustomed to men running after her. Her vanity in the past had usually prevented her from asking herself any questions about why they did that. But there was something in Berazov, a peculiar genuineness, a something fastidious, and also a wordly wisdom, divined instinctively by her rather than actually noted, which told her that he was a type of man not easily allured at first sight. Although she knew she was pretty she also knew, though she never mentioned the fact, that many girls were as pretty as, or prettier than, she was. On the first evening of their acquaintance she had had little time to put forth all her powers of attraction. And Peter Kharkoff had made her more doubtful of herself than she had ever been before she met him. Her self-conceit in truth was greatly abated though she tried to conceal that fact. And now she wondered, not perhaps humbly, but with at least a touch of secret humility, why Berazov, who evidently just at present was living a retired, perhaps an exclusive life, had so promptly shown and proved a desire to be intimate with her.

They sat long over dinner. Lois and Teddy Basingstoke had gone off in a two-seater to Surrey. Lord Sark and the dancer followed them. The Tour d'Eméraude was nearly deserted.

"I think I shall have to go," Imogen said.

"Why?"

"We can't sit here forever. The waiters are looking murderous."

Berazov smiled.

"Poor chaps! I have looked like that. I have longed to assassinate!"

"Then you ought to be sympathetic."

"It's quite early, only half past eleven. May I come back and spend a couple of hours in your delightful room?"

"No," said Imogen.

"Come with me to Knightsbridge then. And let us go on talking in my flat."

"But we've been talking since this morning."

"We Russians are never tired of talking—to the right people."

She thought of the long silences of the Unearthly.

"I know a Russian who is very often silent. And his silences are the most interesting silences I know."

Berazov looked at her queerly, not kindly, she thought. There was an almost suspicious sharpness in his eyes for a moment. The dreaminess had faded entirely out of them.

"Well, are we going?" he said.

"Yes."

She got up immediately and let him put her pale-green cloak round her. It was thin and fell over her tall figure to her ankles. They went out to the street and got into a taxicab. Berazov gave Imogen's address to the chauffeur. When they reached Lowndes Square he said:

"You'll let me come in? I frightened you by the two hours. Let us say one. And I'll only talk half the time."

He got out and stood by the door. And she remembered a return home with Hugo after hunting, his request to come in with her. And again her life seemed to her extraordinary. Like Hugo, Berazov was tall. In no other respect had he any resemblance to Hugo. He too was very physical, but not in Hugo's former way. For in his physical attraction there was a subtle something which Hugo had lacked, a suppleness, a delicate fierceness, a suggestion of the unexpected which she had never found in Hugo.

"May I come in?" She was out now on the pavement.

"Yes, of course. Why not?" she said in a rather hard voice. And she put her latch-key into the door.

No one met them in the hall. She had told Henry not to stay up. They got into the narrow lift. As she pressed the button she thought of Sainte Maxime, and a sudden gust of angry sorrow went through her.

"All this is useless!" she thought. "Why am I doing it?"

She looked into Berazov's rather sad gray eyes, looked—so it seemed for an instant—through them into the large veiled eyes of the Jew. And a feeling of desertion came to her.

"Here we are!"

She got out. Berazov followed her into the long, silent room. She had turned on a light at the door.

"I'll come back in a moment."

She went into her bedroom. When she came back she had
sent Harriet to bed.

She lay down on the sofa and Berazov, with a quiet air
of being absolutely but not impertinently at home and at ease,
sat down in a deep armchair near her. He was smoking and
so was she. To her surprise he sat still in silence. For a
minute or two she expected him to speak. Then she became
convinced that his silence was intentional. She could see that
he was not absent minded, had not fallen into one of his waking
dreams. He just chose to be silent. She said nothing, and
went on smoking her cigarette. And she remembered the
silences of the Jew. In them she had felt curiously safe, like
one enclosed happily in protecting arms. In this silence she
felt quite different, fidgety, anxious almost, at any rate not at
ease. She intended to keep quiet so long that Berazov would
be forced to speak, but presently she couldn't bear the curious
strain of his speechless intimacy, and she said:

"So you can match the Russian silence I spoke of with
another!"

"Ah, you are intelligent!" said Berazov, smiling.

"Is that why you wanted to prolong our tremendous
tête-à-tête?"

"Not entirely. But intelligence always makes the wheels
turn smoothly. Creaking wheels—I don't like that."

"Well, I thought I heard creaking wheels in our silence,"
she said.

He stretched out his arm and laid hold of one of her hands.
When he did that she heard the noise of multitudes of crickets,
and she was stretching out to touch the hand of another. He
moved his chair nearer to her sofa.

"Were you comparing it with another silence?"

"But now *you* are being intelligent!"

"Can I help that?"

Her body liked the feel of his hand on hers. His was the
sort of hand that her body liked. And yet something in her,
apparently adverse to the pleasure of the body, wished that
he would take his hand away from hers.

"Let us both give in to our intelligence," she said. "Why
should we struggle against it? Besides it is certain to get the
better of us if we do."

"Well then—that Russian silence you spoke of in the Tour
d'Eméraude interests me."

"Why?"

"An intonation in your voice, a look in your eyes, a movement of your figure when you spoke of it."

"Of my figure?"

"Yes. The figure can express so much with a momentary attitude. It's the whole body's way of speaking."

She felt that Berazov was trying to get upon the track of the Unearthly. Evidently in the restaurant she had shown much more than she had realized she was showing. But did it matter? His long hand was still upon hers. And now it was holding hers closely.

"Why do you bother about me?" she said.

"Don't many men bother about you?"

"Oh! Had you heard about me before you met me?"

"Of course. One knows about London even if one has been a waiter in Rome."

She felt disappointed.

"That sort of social reputation is ridiculous," she said. "It's made by fools, and it's accepted as gospel by fools. And only a fool could value it."

"Then you certainly don't value it."

"Not now."

"If you only knew how wonderful your pronunciation of 'now' is!" He drew his chair forward till it touched her sofa. "It seems to mark some miracle of progress, some leap from the darkness to the light. On your lips it is the most marvelous of words."

She still felt that he was trying to get upon the track of the Unearthly. It was as if he were following a trail— or hardly that; as if he were somehow aware that there was a trail some instinct prompted him to follow, and was casting about in an effort to find it. Should she help him to find it, or should she endeavor to head him off from it into a different direction?

"Why do you look at me like that?" he asked. "Your eyes are suddenly full of secrets."

"You can see secrets?"

"Yes, plainly; as one can see windows. But the rooms are hidden. I should like to see just one of the rooms."

"Which one?"

"I must leave the choice to you. But there's a small window, not on the ground floor. I seem to see a light gleaming

behind it. And I fancy—don't you sometimes in English country houses label the rooms, 'Blue Room,' 'Red Room,' and
so on?"

"Yes."

"I should think on the door of the room behind the lighted
window there must be the label 'Now.'"

So he was still casting about near the trail. She began
to wonder at his subtlety. For surely she had not been so
self-revealing as he chose to imply.

He pressed her hand gently. She wished to get rid of his
hand and she wished not to lose the feeling of it. She looked
down on it. It attracted her. She longed to touch it, to
stroke it with her other hand. And she longed to unclasp
his long fingers and be released.

Where was the Unearthly tonight? She remembered the
light of the lamp shining out dimly to the snow-covered rue
les Bergues. He was surely still up. Perhaps he was out
alone in the night, standing on the deserted mole of the harbor
at Sainte Maxime, looking over the moonlit Gulf of Saint
Tropez. She heard the church-bell sounding across the quiet
sea in the night.

"Now—that's the name of the room."

"You're a Russian, the type of Russian that was chased
out of Russia during the revolution, the Corps-des-Pages,
Russian-Guard type of Russian," she said slowly. "Aren't
you?"

"Yes. I suppose I must acknowledge that I'm a child of
the old régime."

"Tell me—have you any feeling against Israel?"

"The Jews!" And the softness had gone out of his voice.

"Yes, the Jews."

"They're vermin! They're bloodthirsty vermin. They've
ruined my country. They've drowned my country in blood.
Surely—but of course I know that in England you are free
from our Russian prejudices. All Jews love England, I believe. One meets them in society over here. They reach
the highest positions."

"And in the arts?"

"Oh, as executants, as pianists, violinists—but why are we
talking about the Jews?"

"There's a Jew in the room you wanted to see, the room
behind the lighted window."

"A Jew?"

She felt that he had an impulse to take his hand away from hers and that he resisted it.

"Are you one of the multitude that bows down to Israel's power?" he said.

He was looking at her closely, and she noticed a penetrating expression in his eyes. She realized that he could be cruel if his passions were roused.

"But the world will rise up against it presently," he added, not waiting for an answer. "Blood will pay for blood."

"That sort of payment's no use. Until we can get quite away from those ideas the world will remain what it is, a playground for devils."

"Are you an adherent of the gospel of love?" he said with a faint smile. "I mean the love that embraces the ruffian, the street-walker, the verminous beggar in the doss-house with the same ardor you would give to your lover?" She felt a closer pressure of his hand. "Have you been caught in Tolstoy's net, Tolstoy who hated the woman who had borne him enough children to stock a mixed school? If you can love your enemy I contend that you can't love your lover."

"Tolstoy wasn't a Jew."

Berazov leaned towards her.

"Who is this Jew?"

"Why are you interested in him?" Imogen asked, not lightly but with a deep curiosity which she scarcely tried to conceal.

"But am I?"

She didn't answer.

"If I am it is something in you that has made me interested."

Imogen sat up on the sofa. She had finished her cigarette. She didn't light another, perhaps because her right hand was still in bondage.

"It isn't very complimentary to me," she said, in a would-be light tone. "This extraordinary interest you are showing— not in me."

"You are very perverse."

"I don't see how."

"You lure me towards your secrets and then you attack me for showing interest in them. I am interested in them because I am interested in you."

"And why—in me? I'm sure it isn't because of that ridiculous social vogue, or whatever you like to call it, we spoke of."

"No, it isn't because of that. Such things I don't care for."

"Lois Tremayne said you were attracted by unpainted faces."

"That's quite true. I have a prejudice in favor of the natural surface of life. No Frenchman of my class would be able to understand that. Do you understand it?"

"Oh yes—now."

"Again that *now!*"

"I can even appreciate a verminous beggar in a doss-house now."

"What do you mean by that?"

"I saw some Moscow people in Gorki's 'Asile de Nuit' when I was passing through Paris."

"Ah. . . . I understand! The man with the lice. That's great acting. One felt the lice."

"Someone else's. But how many of us feel our own?"

This last remark of Imogen's seemed to strike Berazov more than anything else she had said since they had known each other. He stared at her, and his eyes showed that he was intently interested in her. Suddenly he took away his hand and got up.

"It's odd," he said abruptly. "But I can't understand you. Or is it somebody in you I can't understand?"

He stood looking down at her. His face was very pale and now his eyes were shining.

"Someone else! How could it be someone else?"

"That Russian you spoke of, whose silences are so interesting, what type of man is he?"

"But why should you care to know?"

He moved his shoulders. "He's the Jew, isn't he?"

"Yes."

"A Russian Jew. I have always detested Jews, and naturally Jews have never loved me. In Rome sometimes I had to wait upon them. That was my greatest humiliation. Are you in love with a Russian Jew?"

Imogen felt that she reddened.

"If I were, what has that to do with you?"

"You surely aren't angry at my asking the question! I know you're English, but you can't be conventional English. Why shouldn't I ask and why shouldn't you tell me?"

"Well, I'm not in love with a Jew. Haven't you heard about me?"

"Yes, of course I have. I told you so."

"I meant, heard about what I am going to do?"

"No. Are you going to do something remarkable, something interesting?"

"In a very short time I am going to be married to a man who can't sit up, who is always lying down, who will never be able to do anything active again."

"A poor fellow crippled in the war?"

"Not even that. His condition was caused by an accident in the hunting field."

"And are you going to marry him?"

"Yes."

"Then I suppose you are very fond of him?"

"Yes."

After a pause Berazov said, "Has he anything to do with this Russian Jew?"

"Yes. But why should you think so?"

"I don't know. I just felt that he had."

"They're together now. I left them together on the Riviera when I started for Paris."

There was something in the tone of her voice as she said that which evidently caught and fixed Berazov's attention. He moved and sat down again by the sofa.

"D'you know that there's something very strange about you?" he said. "I felt it at once when you came into that room in Park Street. Of course I had heard about you. And to tell the truth what I had heard hadn't given me the least desire to meet you. But you were quite different from what I had expected. The top part was rather like what I'd heard—yes. But underneath I felt that you were quite different. Your face wasn't painted, and I knew almost at once that you were more genuine, more real, than the other women there. I felt too that you'd been through some vital experience. That's why I wanted so much to know you, really to know you. And, besides, you weren't happy."

"You seem very sure of yourself, very sure that your intuitions are bound to be right," she said, with a touch of defiance.

"Yes, I'm quite sure about that," he said simply.

"Anything else?"

"You allow me? Well, then—this. Don't do anything that your temperament and character don't prompt you to do, out of pity or altruism—anything of that kind."

"I really can't conceive why you are talking to me like this."

"Somehow I feel you are in the toils."

Imogen now felt definitely that she had had to meet Berazov, that she had come to London ignorantly in order that she might meet him, that it was he whom Fate or Chance had selected to provide the acid test she had thought about, that he, a Jew-hater, was beginning to try to combat the Jew's power in her.

"In the toils!" she said, smiling satirically, or trying so to smile. "In what toils?"

"I suppose it's a man. And I'm nearly sure he's been trying to twist you out of your natural shape."

"I don't think you can possibly know what my natural shape is."

He only smiled at this remark.

"As you're so very frank with me," she said, "may I ask you something?"

"Yes—anything."

"You're very cultivated. You know the world very well. But aren't you a barbarian?"

"I expect so. To have a barbarian strain in one brings one very near to nature. And the nearer to nature a man—at any rate a *man*—gets the more comfortable and contented he feels."

"Comfortable and contented!"

"Just now you can't imagine feeling either, can you? You're so angry about something."

This time Imogen was genuinely startled.

"Angry—what about? What is there to be angry about?"

"I don't know. But I feel you are angry, that there is an undercurrent of anger in you. I have felt it all day. It's like a subterranean stream. One can't see it, but one can hear the murmur of it."

"You are abominably intuitive," she said. "Much more so than any man has the right to be."

It was late in the night now. She had forgotten all about the time. A deep interest possessed her. It began to seem to her that, when he had told her to go to London, that she was free, Peter Kharkoff must have foreseen what was waiting for her in London, that he had wished that she should not avoid it but confront it. He had surely not wished her to remain in the quiet and the safety of Sainte Maxime. She had been driven out—so she chose to think of what had happened—for a purpose. And now that purpose was being accomplished.

She had thought of the test as a large one, London against Sainte Maxime, London life against the life in the villa and by the sea, her world against the Jew. And Hugo no doubt had conceived of the test as very ordinary and plain, so far as he had conceived of it at all. (Even now he had no subtleties such as Berazov obviously had.) But the test had been narrowed down. And because of that narrowing down Imogen realized the sharpness of it, and something else too, the curious progress she had made since she had been with Peter Kharkoff. She knew that Berazov had been speaking the truth when he had said why he had at once wanted to know her well. Again the Jew had made use of a human being, in this case herself, as a vehicle. The "vital experience" Berazov had spoken of had been simply the coming of Peter Kharkoff into her life. Berazov had felt Peter Kharkoff in her without knowing, without having the least suspicion, that it was so.

But she knew perfectly well what Berazov would presently want of her, whither his interest in her would certainly lead him, and probably very soon. The large physical indifference in which Peter Kharkoff moved as in an atmosphere was matched in Berazov by a large physical intentness. He was intensely physical and she had known it from the moment she had met him. Any path trodden with him could have but one end. She was as certain of it as if that end had already been reached by her with him. Underneath all the usualness of a clever, imaginative, sensitive and highly cultivated man, crept in hiding the normal animal with all the animal's appetites.

By her feeling with Berazov she was able to measure Peter Kharkoff's amazing immunity from the governing principle in man. She had once wished to discover that principle in him. Now she found herself queerly thinking of it with a curious new contempt in spite of the fascination which at that very moment it was exercising over her. She wanted it, and she wanted it away. She seemed to share it, in her woman's way she did share it, and yet something in her was disgusted by it and longed to avoid it.

"No man on earth would be able to understand me at this moment," she thought. "Except one."

And it was through him, that one, that she had made the progress which now set her at violent odds with herself.

"What are you so angry about?"

"Nothing that you could understand."

"I'll undertake to say that isn't true. I believe I could understand any human emotion if the causes of it were properly put before me. And I'm certain I could understand any emotion of yours explained to me by you."

"Why of mine?"

"Aren't we rather in sympathy one with the other?"

Again he laid his hand over hers.

"We! Better say that bits of us are, perhaps, in a certain sympathy, bits of me with bits of you."

She knew, while she was speaking, that probably side by side with that sympathy lay a possibility of disgust, at any rate in her. About him she couldn't tell that.

"What are you angry about?"

"What does it matter?"

"Mightn't your anger be a friend to me?"

"Perhaps it might."

"Well then it concerns me."

"You said just now I was in the toils."

"Yes."

"Mightn't it be because of being in the toils that I'm angry— if I am angry."

"We'll assume that you are for the sake of argument. Yes, I suppose it might. To be in the toils must be abominable. Then why not break out of them?"

"In order to be taken by others?"

"Is that inevitable?"

She was silent. He held her hand closely and softly.

"Is it?"

"I don't know. But I think it's quite possible to be safer, and even perhaps happier, in what you choose to call the toils, certain toils, than in what I suppose you would call freedom."

"How so?"

"Russians like arguing, I believe."

"They love it—at the right time."

"Then assuming this is the right time, I imagine that many people, caught in the toils of a religion which prohibits many things to them, are happier than many others who have no religion at all."

"We are getting too abstract," he said.

"Not at all. Isn't what I say quite true?"

"I must come away from the abstract. I can't breathe comfortably in its atmosphere. Are *you* in the toils of a religion?"

"No."

"Sure—sure—sure?"

"An incentive to—to goodness"—she looked and felt half ashamed as she said the last word—"needn't be a religion."

"Has God got hold of you?" he said, with sudden brutality.

Imogen felt that she flushed violently all over her face, to her hair, to her neck.

"That's usually the utter ruin of any passionate woman," he added.

Imogen took her hand bruskly away from his.

"Don't speak to me like that!" she exclaimed. "I won't have it."

She felt as if someone had been outraged by that outburst of his, but not necessarily herself.

"Forgive me if I've insulted your feeling for religion. Perhaps you're an ardent Catholic."

"I'm not a Catholic."

"Don't tell me you're an ardent Protestant, for that's a contradiction in terms—to me."

"I'm not. I told you I was not held by any religion."

"Then what's the matter? What have I done? Why are you angry with me?"

He was gazing into the face which she knew flamed with the banner of angry blood, eagerly, with a now bold admiration. And she knew that her sudden fire had lit a fire in him, that her sudden anger had spurred the animal in him.

"I asked you if God had got hold of you. Why should that make you furious?"

"You said more than that. You said——"

She stopped.

"Go on!" he said.

"I shall not. But I won't allow such things to be said to me. And—and—if God had got hold of me I should be more than thankful. How dare you speak with contempt of such a happening as that?"

"I'm sorry," he said, but without either anger or the least touch of genuine contrition. "Somehow I didn't think you had anything of the English Puritan in you. If I had thought

so I would have been more careful. Can't you forgive me?"
This allusion to Puritanism was as wind to the glowing embers
of Imogen's anger. But suddenly some words spoken near the
Rhone on a winter's night sang roughly through her mind.

"You oughtn't to give him that part of humanity as your
tribute. He deserves something better than that."

She was silent for a moment, thinking about those words,
feeling them, letting them sink down into her. In the silence
the flush began to die out of her face, and a curious calmness
invaded her.

"Can't you forgive me?" he repeated.

'I'm not a Puritan. I've nothing of that in me. You
don't understand."

"Then help me. Tell me something more about the two
men you have left together on the Riviera, your crippled lover
and this mysterious Jew."

Subtly, or by mere chance, he had hit upon the very words
to drive out her new calm and revive her strange feeling of
anger. He had led her thought to those two who had sent her
away.

"I can't understand what interest they can possibly have for
you."

"Nor I! And yet I'm interested in them, diabolically interested in them. And it's all your fault."

"Yes," she said. "It must be."

She spoke seriously, even with a deep gravity, and for a
moment, as she looked at him, there was a new unselfcon-
sciousness in her eyes.

"I hate Jews. I think they're the curse of Europe. What
has this Jew got to do with me?" said Berazov.

"Nothing. How could he have anything to do with you?"

"I don't know yet. But I feel that he has, or that, if not,
he may have."

A clock struck in the room.

"It's getting awfully late," Imogen said. "We mustn't
sit up all night here."

"Why shouldn't we if we wish to? What does it matter
if we do?"

"But I don't wish to."

"Has the convention of 'bedtime' got hold of you? Let me
tell you something. I know by the look in your eyes that if
you go to bed now, sending me away like a naughty Russian

boy—though I'm thirty-six—you won't sleep. You'll lie
awake. You'll toss from side to side. You'll count the hours.
You'll be torn by regrets. You'll want to get up, to go out,
to do something wild and impossible. That's my diagnosis."

"Do you want to stay here till breakfast-time tomorrow?"

"Or today. I shouldn't mind. In fact I should like to."

"The servants would probably give warning."

"Are English servants really like that? Unsympathetic
brutes! With all their faults our Russians are far more
human. Nothing surprises a Russian servant."

"Really we must——"

"There's no must in a life that's really worth living. And
—my diagnosis! Wasn't it absolutely correct?"

Imogen looked down.

"Wasn't it?"

"Perhaps it was."

"There are few things so abominable as lying in bed pretending it's sleeping time when your whole brain and nature
are in activity, when——"

"Don't! Don't! Don't!" she said with exasperation.

"It's such sheer waste of time, and all really live people rebel
against waste of time, because all really live people feel how
short their time is."

"I can't sit up with you all night."

"Does the Jew drive you to bed?" said Berazov.

And in his voice was the brutality she had noticed when he
had said, "Has God got hold of you?"

Imogen got up from the sofa swiftly.

"What is it?" he asked, getting up too.

"Do you think women of our time, modern women as they're
called, are slaves?" she said, but not with any fierce anger,
gravely even with a deep and searching seriousness.

"Have you read Nietszche?" he asked.

"Some of him—of course I have."

"Have you read him on women?"

"I don't remember."

"He says that in every woman there is a tyrant and a slave.
I think that is one of the truest and deepest things ever written
about women."

"Perhaps it is. But you evidently believe that in my nature
the slave predominates."

"Why do you think that?"

"You spoke of my being in the toils, of God getting hold of me, of the Jew driving me to bed."

She paused, he didn't say anything, and she went on:

"What I do I do of my free will. But I've noticed that if one does something which another doesn't wish one to do that other usually implies that one is acting under compulsion. I suppose that's a way of trying to save a situation. Isn't that it?"

"Who knows? I don't. And I don't care either. If I've been wrong in thinking I saw the slave in you, prove me wrong. Perhaps you are the exception among women—all tyrant. If it is so you have the power to make a slave of me."

"I may not want to do that even if I have the power."

"Then you aren't woman at all. Is your maid still up?"

"No."

"She was up when we came in."

"Yes."

"Why did you send her to bed?"

"Because I know how Russians talk when once they begin, and I have some consideration for servants. Now you really must go."

Berazov looked hard at her. She did not turn away her eyes from his. He was accustomed to women. He was very intelligent about them. His intelligence didn't desert him now. He knew that this girl longed to give way to him with part of her. He thought it possible that even now he could persuade her to give way. Long experience of society in many places had taught him to believe that conventional morality, though still "received" in public, and occasionally even made much of, was in private looked upon as a negligible bore. A tide of free love was sweeping over the world obliterating many old landmarks. He did not believe that this tall English girl, who had let him come up to the third-floor room next door to her bedroom, who had told her maid to go to bed, would be held back from any strong gratification of the senses by any convention, by any menace of an established religion, by any touch of English Puritanism. Bogeydom, he felt sure, meant very little, or nothing, to her. As to Mrs. Grundy's opinions she had probably never bothered to think about them.

And yet—there was something, which stood between her and him, and which caused him to hesitate. As he looked at her eyes he saw bodily desire in them. He knew that he attracted her tremendously. He knew that she wanted him.

But something told him to wait.

Such caution was against his nature, for he was a man of violent impulses which he seldom troubled to control. But it seemed now to be imposed upon him.

"Good night," she said.

"You won't sleep."

"Perhaps not."

"Nor shall I."

"I can't possibly prescribe for your insomnia. You can take yourself down in the lift, can't you, and let yourself out?"

She had gone to the door and now she opened it. As he joined her by it he said:

"Why are we doing this? What is the reason? I know there is a reason. But what is it?"

She didn't answer, and he took hold of her by the shoulders and began to kiss her. She let him kiss her, and yet, while he was doing it, he knew that that was all he would do, all she would let him do that night. And when he stopped and let her go she went to the lift door and opened it and again said good night.

He got into the lift, touched the button, glided down to the hall and let himself out into the freshness of the dying night. And he knew neither why she had sent him away, nor why he had gone.

"She's an enigma—that girl!" he said to himself. "There is something in her I haven't got at. It must be——"

But he couldn't tell what it was.

Nevertheless, as he walked towards Knightsbridge, he found himself cursing Israel.

CHAPTER IV

WHEN Berazov had gone down in the lift Imogen waited by the door of the lift shaft. She was listening for the sound of a heavy door being shut in the hall below. But it chanced that Berazov let himself out into the night very quietly, and she heard nothing and, hearing nothing, she presently wondered whether he had left the house, or whether, perhaps, he was waiting downstairs because he had noticed the struggling influences warring within her, her cruel indecision.

Directly he had gone she had wanted to call him back, to keep him with her in the solitude of the house whose other inmates would doubtless be unconscious and unheeding for hours. Perhaps he guessed that and meant to come back. She felt sure that he was capable of doing that, or indeed of doing almost anything, however unconventional, if a strong impulse took possession of him. She was surprised now that she had got rid of him so easily—if she had got rid of him. But perhaps he would come back. And she listened eagerly, leaned forward, peered down the lift shaft. But there was no sound below. The cord was motionless. The lift was stationary at the hall level. He must have let himself out quietly and be now on his way home.

Nevertheless she could not lose the idea that perhaps he was still in the house waiting. He had read a part of her too accurately, a part which she hated and now even feared. She knew that. And in those kisses which she hadn't resented he had learned a great deal about her. She wondered what had driven such a man away at such a moment; and wondering and doubting, and still desiring, though she did not acknowledge desire just then to herself, she at last pressed the button, brought the lift up, got into it, and descended to the hall.

The lights were out. Nobody was there. She went into the dining-room, the library, even into the ballroom at the back of the house; she ascended to the first floor, visited the drawing-room, her mother's sitting-room. All were empty. It was evident that Berazov had gone.

When she was certain of that she went back to her sitting-room and shut herself in there.

Berazov's diagnosis! He had understood one side of her horribly well, and that side had been uppermost during his long visit. And yet had it been uppermost? She had sent him away. But afterwards she had gone down to look for him, and she had longed to find him. And even now she was wishing that he hadn't gone, that he was still sitting close to her, that his hand was clasped upon hers, that his lips were pressed against hers.

"What a beast I am!" she thought.

And though she tried to think that all she had been feeling and still felt was quite natural, and therefore not to be condemned, she could not get rid of that sensation of being a beast.

Berazov's brutal questions lingered in her mind. They had struck on her like hammer blows. The directness of them, coming from a stranger, had startled her. But they hadn't seemed to issue from a stranger's lips.

"Has God got hold of you?"

She would never forget those words. It seemed to her now that they had torn away wrappings from something within her, had exposed something of her to herself. That something was surely her conception of the Jew. It had lain in her hitherto closely folded up in mysterious pretenses or cloudy aberrations of the mind. Now it was clear of them. Now it was naked and could be seen just as it was.

She saw Peter Kharkoff at that moment as an exceptional being through whom God had been working to lay hold of her. She felt him as the vehicle through which an energetic power was endeavoring to obtain possession of her. That energetic power was God. So she believed just then. But why such a thing should be, why she should be selected for such a tremendously personal—she felt it to be that—reaching out, she couldn't understand. And now she began to be alarmed, her imagination began to be alarmed. Presently she even began to feel angry and combative. Yes—in spite of her august conception of what was happening to her! In the words of the old statesman whom she had talked with at Lady Tenley's luncheon, feeling an attempt at coercion her "other part" took fright. And feeling frightened she felt angry. For though the coercion seemed to come upon her from outside, a part of herself was undoubtedly at one with it, was joining in it.

She felt hideously two just then. And there seemed actual physical pain as well as mental anguish in the feeling. Perhaps she had never been harmonious. She did not remember, but she doubted whether she had. But now she felt herself to be a violent, a shrieking discord. She had read of course of "conversions." She had even known personally a French actress, charming, popular, young, and free-living to an extent that she had never contemplated as a possibility for herself in her most unregenerate moments, who had suddenly given up the stage, distributed her fortune among the poor, left her lovers without warning or a word of good-by, and disappeared into one of the most severe religious orders. And she had

lightly wondered about these conversions, had wondered much
more definitely about the actress, who had been almost a friend
of hers, and who had never shown to her the least bias towards
religion. And the comfortable word "hysteria" had been present in her mind. These people of violent, inexplicable changes
were "unbalanced," were hysterical. She could never be the
victim of such assaults as those to which they succumbed.

Now she saw the actress, seemed to be staring at her from
the sofa on which she was lying. The actress had been of the
boyish, gamin type, very pretty, very impudent and daring,
always apparently gay and careless hearted. Her influence
upon men had been exceptional, even in Paris, the city of
influential women. That such a being, with those sensual,
knowing eyes, should be happy out of the world, enclosed in
walls beyond the reach of the most hardy and enterprising
lover, bowed perpetually in prayer, fasting, totally deprived
of luxuries, without even the solace of "clothes," seemed incredible. And Imogen looked at the vividly imagined face and
asked of the far-away nature, "Are you happy?" But a cloud
of incense obscured the face and there came no answer to the
question. And Imogen was afraid. The comfortable word,
"hysteria," had lost its solacing influence. It could not account
for all the bizarre changes which make certain lives so inexplicable to the looker-on. And she saw the Jew at work long
before she had known him, saw him for the first time as a symbolical figure. And she felt afraid of him, and she felt anger
and rebellion against him.

A clock presently struck four. She sprang up from the sofa.
Before she went to bed she took a nearly cold bath, and drank
a glass of St. Galmier water. Then she swallowed two tab-
lets of aspirin and lay down and presently slept.

In the morning the peculiar nightmare feeling which had
frightened her was diminished, but she still felt nervous, uncertain and unhappy. Berazov's allusion to her being in the
toils had struck deep into her. She continually thought of
it. She said to herself, "I am free," but she did not feel any
light-hearted sense of freedom. Something was weighing upon
her. Her morale seemed bowed down beneath it. When she
thought of Peter Kharkoff's remark, "Don't you consider yourself free?" it seemed to her that it must have been spoken in
irony. Perhaps he had always looked upon her with irony.
What had been his object in consenting to her journey to

London? For he had consented to it. She knew that, because she knew that if he had said a word in dissuasion she would have stayed at Sainte Maxime. She had wanted that word. She had waited for it. But it had not been spoken. Then why was she in the toils?

She met Berazov again, and again the ache was in her. He fascinated her, and yet she was inclined at moments almost to hate him, because it seemed to her that he was fascinating her past, what she had been but was not entirely now. Formerly he would surely have captured the whole of her. Now that was impossible. But he had a horribly firm hold on a part of her. Very quietly, very unassumingly, he pursued her as men pursue women in a highly artificial and civilized society. Perpetually he showed, but generally with subtlety, that he wanted her.

He did not try to deceive her into believing that he loved her. He was too clever and assumed that she was too clever for that. Such pretenses were not for such people as they were in a sometimes passionate but rarely sentimental world. He did not pretend even to a trivial falling in love. There was a sort of crude sincerity in even his subtlety which won upon her. Sometimes secretly she compared it with the sincerity of the Jew, and then she saw two sincerities: the one of desire, or, to put it more brutally, of lust, the other of purged thought-force. Then she looked upon swamps and mountain peaks. But there was vegetation that grew lush in the swamps, a richness, a denseness of growth and of decay. And the mountain peaks, though marvelously pure and lifted up towards the sun, were terribly bare. And she wondered, almost with torment, why two such contrasts were presented to her as if there were no *via media* in life. Why couldn't she do what she supposed the average woman did, journey along a highway neither very low down nor very high up?

And she felt Berazov and the Jew as extremes. But that was why they interested and fascinated her in strangely different ways. She had never been fond of the ordinary.

Always, in the midst of this part of her life experience, she held to her decision about Hugo. She was very fond of Hugo. In a way she felt that she loved him. She was full of a tenderness of pity for him. She knew or believed she knew that she was going to marry him. This time was an interlude between her former carelessness of a highly successful and pretty girl and her future self-sacrifice as a strangely married woman. And the reason why Hugo played a comparatively shadowy part just now between two immensely vital realities was because of the blow of fate which had stricken him down. That was it. And knowing that that was it, Imogen knew the dreadful importance which wholeness of the body has in this mortal life. She could not think of Hugo as she had once thought of him. He was diminished. He was abated. And yet she had known before she had left the Riviera that in some mysterious way he was increased.

But presently she received a letter from him which changed her outlook, took him out of the shadows.

Hugo had little facility as a writer. His style was abrupt and manly. He was not given to that amplitude of detail which often makes the letters of women so human and charming. But this letter of his struck Imogen as out of the ordinary, as less Hugoesque than the other letters she had had from him, not many.

Dearest Geney,

Glad you got safely to old London. I hope you're enjoying yourself among your pals. But that goes without saying. You couldn't have a bad time in London as long as you've got your health, and thank goodness there's not much the matter with that. Life goes on as usual here. It's hot, but I like the heat. Your mother's beginning to complain of it, and I don't think she'll stick it much longer. Your father doesn't seem to mind it and takes his walks as usual. Milligan bathes twice a day. I must say for him he can swim, though I could do as well in the old days. But all those things—of the body I mean—came easy to me. Not so the mind! I realize now that mentally I was indeed a rotter, and sometimes I wonder how people could have put up with me as they did. But I suppose what they call "a certain liveliness" and an athletic frame cover a multitude of shortcomings in the eyes of the charitable. Unless lots of people are blind. And 'pon my word I often think now they are. I'm sure I was. I see a bit clearer now, though I dare say my sight's still none too good. And, my God, Geney, what a lot there is to see in this old world of ours! But I won't spread myself over that or you'll be bored stiff. Mr. Kharkoff comes over every day. ("Why *mister?*" Imogen asked herself here. It wasn't Hugo's way to give such polite prefixes to men whom he knew, or even to men whom he didn't know.) I see a good bit of him, for now it's so hot he doesn't take such long walks as he used to when you were here. I find him wonderful company. Milligan says he would be a godsend in any hospital and that he's got about five times the

amount of animal magnetism in him that the average man
has. I don't know anything about animal, or any other, magnetism, but Mr. Kharkoff ("Again mister" thought Imogen,
with growing surprise.) though not a sportsman, and though
a Jew, is a very good fellow and has been more than kind
to me, and I should be a cad not to frankly acknowledge it,
as I do now. I don't think I ever let out to you about him
before you went. There are things it's difficult to talk about,
and as I've always been down on Jews—to tell the truth I
still can't abide 'em in the lump—I feel I ought to put it right
now and say that I owe a lot to Mr. Kharkoff. If I'd met
him when I was well I should probably have been a damned
fool and classed him with the crowd you can see along the
front at Brighton on any fine Sunday. But one lives and
learns. And, being a cripple, I've learnt to respect a Jew.
I believe he'll stay on till the villa shuts and I go with the
rest. Then I understand he's going back to Switzerland,
first to Geneva, and then to a place up in the mountains called
Sils-Maria. By what he says it must be a good place and
pretty high up above most things. Not a bad place to be
in—that, I expect. Well, I must stop this screed. I doubt
your getting to the end of it. In old London one hardly has
time to turn round or look at one's letters. Here it's different and I was glad to get yours. London! By Jove, it seems
a long way off, and I've a fancy it'll always seem a long way
off to me—the London I used to know. God bless you, Geney.
Love from

Yr. old Pal
Hugo.

Several things in this letter gave Imogen cause for thought.
And there were things left out which, womanlike, she missed
and wondered about. No longing was expressed for her.
Hugo did not write that the shining coast seemed desolate now
she had gone to England. He wouldn't have put it that
way, but he might have put it in a way of his own. Then
there was no allusion to their eventual marriage, and no hint
was given of where Hugo meant to go when the villa was shut
up. "Go with the rest" was absolutely non-committal.

She read again the passage about Peter Kharkoff's eventual
destination and she became convinced that Hugo's desire was to
go with him to Sils-Maria. "Not a bad place to be in—that,
I expect." Evidently Hugo hadn't grasped the fact that Sils-
Maria was only a couple of hours' walk from St. Moritz on
the road towards Italy. And yet she and he had been at St.
Moritz together. But to them that region "pretty high up
above most things" had meant just one more place of hectic
amusement, of pleasures crowded together.

She shut her eyes and saw a vision of painted girls in bright jerseys rushing over white fields of snow. She had been one of them. And she saw sleigh parties on moonlit nights when you "tucked up" with your particular man and made love through the snow-laden forests. And she saw the crowded ballroom of the Palace Hotel illuminated with colored lights and echoing to the music of jazz. How they had danced and gambled and made what was called love in that place "high up above most things." And two hours' walk away Sils-Maria by its clouded stream had been sleeping in the embrace of the snows.

She remembered it. She had been over there two or three times, though never with Hugo. She had loved its musical name and had been interested in it because Nietzsche had spent summers there and she had read letters of his addressed to friends from "Sils-Maria." And once or twice, even in the midst of the rowdy crowd which had accompanied her there, she had found time to wonder about a life such as Nietzsche's, a life lived in almost absolute loneliness, prisoned—so she had thought of it—in the intellect, independent of all upon which she depended, released entirely from the bondage of pleasure.

And now Peter Kharkoff was going there, and—she knew it—Hugo wanted to go there with him.

"My God, Geney, what a lot there is to see in this old world of ours!"

She leaned over the letter. She brooded over it. And she felt that for Hugo the horizons were widening. A larger vision of the world and of life was opening before him. And again she saw the Jew as a symbolical figure directing Hugo—and how many others?—on the way to a wider world.

But a moment afterwards she saw him, realized him, as a man of exceptional power and concentration who was deliberately withdrawing Hugo, the man who had been hers, from her. And she remembered some words spoken by Hugo and herself just before she had left the villa to take the train to Paris. She had told Hugo not to forget her, and he had replied, "How could I forget you?" And then she had been moved to say—and she knew she had spoken solemnly, "There are greater things than I. There are irresistible things."

And now he wanted to go with the Jew to Sils-Maria. Was the irresistible power at work upon him? She saw Hugo absorbed, drawn away beyond her reach, far beyond, into a distance from which even his love could not travel to her. For a moment her cheeks burned and she was frightened. Then she seemed to recover herself, to be back in the commonplace, and she said to herself, "He would rather go to Sils-Maria with Peter Kharkoff than come to London to me."

She was fastened on the letter now, trying to pierce into it, to pierce down to the under meanings, to those mind processes which throw up apparently casual words as boiling water throws up steam. A cloud—but the water is clear below it.

So Peter Kharkoff was more with Hugo now that she was no longer there. He didn't take such long walks as he used to take when she was living in the villa. Hugo attributed that fact naively to the increase of the heat on the Riviera. She could not accept that explanation. He found Peter Kharkoff "wonderful company." What did they talk about together? She longed to be able from London to overhear one of those long conversations under the palm trees or upon Hugo's balcony at night. Two such strangely different men! What would they talk about, and how did their thoughts come out, in what form travel to each other? She was filled with a burning curiosity. But her curiosity would never be satisfied. She guessed how different must be the talk between two men and a woman from the talk between two men, no woman near. And though Hugo loved her—didn't he?—she knew that something in her, and in his relation to her, would render it impossible for him to talk before her as he might talk with Peter Kharkoff alone. He would be shy of letting loose about serious subjects to her because he believed that she had a very small opinion of his mental capacity.

"I've shut him up with my damned contempt of him!" she said to herself bitterly.

And then she compared that contempt of hers with Peter Kharkoff's deep simplicity, which seemed to hold, to be able to hold, no one in contempt, and something within her fell to crying over the past.

Those widening horizons! Could it be that intercourse with Peter Kharkoff, that the influence of Peter Kharkoff's mind and personality, were teaching Hugo to look not only at the world with different eyes but with different eyes on her? That possibility presented itself to Imogen. Hugo hadn't surely ever been really critical of her in the past. Now and then he had been down upon her when he had been out of temper, when her caprices had momentarily irritated him. But he hadn't been normally critical of her. It occurred to her that intimate intercourse with such a man as Peter Kharkoff might make Hugo look at her with new eyes. He had learned to respect Peter Kharkoff. What did he feel about her, about her character, now? She was accustomed to be everything that Hugo admired, wanted, clung to. But now? Wasn't there a new tone in his letter? Wasn't there a hint of independence or even of withdrawal?

She looked again at the end. "God bless you." A familiar expression enough but Hugo had never before used it to her in a letter. It was not at all what she would have called a Hugoesque phrase. Yet she felt it had been written on that sheet of paper spontaneously, even that it had come from the heart. And suddenly she remembered the pitiful look Hugo had once given her, in the garden at Sainte Maxime just before she had started to search for Peter Kharkoff. That look—this "God bless you!" She couldn't help connecting the look and the words. Did Hugo pity *her?* If he did, if he could, he had been journeying, and he had gone very far.

She knew that there was much to pity in her. But that Hugo should know, or divine that, startled and disquieted her. She realized that Hugo's long worship of her had meant very much to her. The loss of it would be very dreadful to her. And yet she dreaded marriage with Hugo and she was fascinated, enticed by Berazov, was even physically in love with him. And Peter Kharkoff in a strange way obsessed her. Was it possible that at the same time three men could mean simultaneously so much to a woman? Hearing of such a thing she would have disbelieved it. Experiencing it she could only know it to be true.

For a long time she could not put Hugo's letter away. When at last she did so she sat down and wrote an answer to it. In that answer she assumed as a matter of course that when Hugo left Sainte Maxime he would come at once to London to her. She did not ask him to come. She simply wrote as if it was thoroughly understood that he was coming, as if it had been arranged between them definitely that he would come straight to London when he left the Riviera. She could not resist putting into her letter an allusion to Sils-Maria. She wrote:

> You write as if Sils-Maria were some romantic place quite out of the world. But, my dear, it's close to St. Moritz. I've

been over there several times with cheery crowds. Surely
you've been there with me in the old days? It may be "pretty
high up above most things." But it isn't above all the fun of
the fair as we knew it in the good old rowdy Engadine.
What larks I've had there! Your mention of Sils-Maria
brings them all back!

Her mouth was hard as she wrote those words, and there
was a cruel gleam in her eyes. Her sense of injury was growing, had been growing ever since she had first read Hugo's
letter. As she put her letter into an envelop, she thought:
"If Hugo does go with Peter Kharkoff to Sils-Maria instead
of coming to London and me, I've done with it. I've done
with the whole thing. After all I've been through I won't
bear to be treated like that."

When she had sent off the letter, when the activity it had
engendered was at an end, she felt bitter and restless, and also
—a very rare sensation with her—horribly alone, even abandoned. Out of this feeling of being abandoned there rose in
her a desperate mood. Carried away by a flood of egotism she
recounted for her own benefit all she had been through since
Hugo's tragedy, because of it. But her egotism did not stop
there. She dwelt mentally not only upon what she had done,
but also upon what she had been prepared to do. It wasn't a
small thing for such a girl as she was to be ready to give up
her life to a crippled man. And she remembered all her mental
debating, all her reluctance, all the nervous irritation she had
endured because of the expectation of others, her determination not to be driven into self-sacrifice, and then that amazingly sudden yielding to an impulse and rushing on the spear.

She had suffered keenly. Now looking back she believed
that she had suffered even more keenly than had actually been
the case. Her recompense, assumed, never for a moment
doubted, was to be the exclusive love of a man to whom she
would stand in the relation of Providence. She was to possess
absolutely. Nothing less than that had ever been contemplated
by her. Subconsciously she must always have counted upon
that as the reward of her self-sacrifice. Now consciously she
knew that what she had deemed a certainty was perhaps not
certain. And it seemed as if all about her things hitherto
thought absolutely stable were crumbling. She exaggerated the
evil. She felt Hugo escaping from her incited by the Jew.
She sat still and tried to imagine her life without him.

"There are irresistible things."

She had said that, and when she had said it she had been thinking of Peter Kharkoff, of the influence that emanated from him, an influence which she had deliberately brought into Hugo's life. And once she had almost asked Peter Kharkoff whether he was not irresistible, when she had said to him, "Cannot thought perhaps *compel?*" She had not forgotten his answer, nor her amplification of it when she had spoken of the glory of free will. But had she free will and had Hugo free will? She did not ask herself that question about Peter Kharkoff. She could not imagine him governed.

Her letter to Hugo had gone. A process of time must elapse before she knew what effect it would have upon him. Several days probably had to be got through, and meanwhile she would be in uncertainty. He might resist her will. He might follow the inclination she had divined and instead of coming to London go to Switzerland with Milligan to look after him. He might go to Sils-Maria. If he did that what was she going to do?

"If he does that I shall consider myself free," she said to herself. "I shall take it as a definite indication that he doesn't need me, doesn't even want me any more."

And then?

But she could no longer imagine her life without Hugo, unwanted, unneeded by him. Still less could she imagine it without Peter Kharkoff. Nevertheless she felt that if she gave up Hugo she would lose Peter Kharkoff with him. She linked the two men so closely together now in her thought that she could no longer dissociate them. It seemed to her that Peter Kharkoff had transferred himself from her to Hugo. She had suddenly lost the extraordinary feeling which had come upon her when Berazov had said, "Has God got hold of you?" when he had told her that she was in the toils. Then she had been startled, even perhaps alarmed secretly, in spite of her almost angry rejoinder. But now she was afraid of a slipping away of influence, of an indifference that would bring winter about her. There was a worse thing for a woman than being in the toils. There was a worse thing for a woman than being tied to a crippled man who loved her and depended wholly upon her. There was the tragedy of being unwanted, of being out in the open in freedom—alone.

For a moment she felt all the horror of freedom.

CHAPTER V

BERAZOV had become deeply interested in Imogen. Her physical attraction for him had increased since the night when she had tacitly refused herself to him after, as he believed, intending to give way to his desire. (For why had she let him into her house at such an hour of the night, and why had she sent her maid to bed, if she had only meant to have a platonic conversation with him?) But now she interested him in another way, as even an ugly woman, full of subtleties, might have interested him.

His hatred of Jews was one of the most sincere things in him. He had been brought up to hate them by a Jew-hating father. Since the revolution in Russia in which so many Jews were implicated he had detested them more than ever. Now he had a conviction which he could not get rid of. It was this: that a Jew, a Russian Jew, was standing in the way between him and this girl, whom he certainly fascinated, who had encouraged him, but who was, he believed, mysteriously held back from him by some outside influence.

He did not credit Imogen with any innate virtue although he had called her a Puritan, although he had asked her so brutally whether God had got hold of her. He had always been inclined to cynicism about the virtue of women. When quite young he had been one of the most sought-after men in the gayest society of the city then called St. Petersburg. He had also known his Paris, his Riviera. And women had been too kind to leave him shivering before the snows of their purity.

In those days he had had little to do with young unmarried girls. But since the war, and since he had known London well, he had found a new field for amusement, a field in which maidens wandered about with surprising nonchalance. Unmarried Italian girls of good family were, he knew, very carefully looked after. Even when a waiter in Rome he had heard no scandal about them. To French girls of good birth the opportunity for naughtiness still seemed to be gracefully denied. In the Argentine he had been closely bound up with a woman who adored him and had not been able to prospect very far beyond her embracing arms. But in England—he had not yet sampled the United States—the war had evidently brought into being a new race of girls whom he thoroughly appreciated. The genus Chaperon, always a nuisance, had happily in England fallen upon complete disaster. The rout of the boring lady had been as thorough as the rout of his own aristocracy. Her flying skirts were no longer even visible in the distance. She had "ceased upon the midnight" of the ballrooms—whether with or without pain didn't matter at all. And the English girls of the best society—Berazov knew no provincial English girls—had kicked their demureness after her.

Unprintable conversations were now quite common in London, Berazov cheerfully found, between unmarried girls and men. Possibly wrongly in some cases, he judged that unprintable conversation implied unprintable conduct when blinds were drawn close against an eagerly peeping world.

Berazov knew that Imogen was one of the leaders of this, to him, new type of English girl. Before he had met her her social fame had reached him. He had heard of her as a pretty, clever, determined, even daring creature, who always took her own way and who didn't care a damn for the consequences. Absolutely released from prejudices—whatever that may mean; Berazov took it to mean absolutely indifferent to the ten, and any other, commandments—she was currently supposed to have the most wonderful time of any girl in England. Berazov had expected to be amused by her. But he had expected also to find her a mass of vanity and caprice, ruthlessly selfish, probably artificial, certainly egotistic as only a worshiped and fêted girl can be. He had been agreeably surprised. Soon he had discovered that Imogen was as genuine as he was. Her physique and something in her which was manifest to him though perhaps not to everybody had fascinated him at once. But now he was more than fascinated. His brain was interested in Imogen. He was "intrigued" about her.

After that night of conversation with her in the silent house in Lowndes Square, Berazov, who knew many of Imogen's intimates, made discreet inquiries about her in likely quarters. He heard a good deal about Hugo Dennistone. He heard nothing at all about any Russian Jew. The impression he gathered was that Hugo had always been Imogen's special man, and that she meant to stick to him and would undoubtedly marry him. Afterwards—well, probably Hugo, given the conditions, wouldn't be too exigent. And meanwhile Imogen was certainly out for all the fun she could get. Otherwise why should she be in London while Hugo was with her people on the Riviera? Nobody seemed to be aware that there was any Jewish visitor in the villa at Sainte Maxime.

Berazov was very careful in his inquiries. Indeed he so disguised them that they could scarcely be recognized as inquiries at all. But on one occasion, when he introduced the subject of Israel ingeniously into a conversation, he was surprised to hear that Hugo Dennistone hated Jews, would never have anything to do with them, was even notorious for his unreasonable prejudice against them.

"And after all what the devil should we do without them?" said the young man to whom Berazov was talking. "Financially speaking they keep the world going. But money means nothing to Dennistone when it comes to a Jew."

"When it comes to a Jew." It was evident to Berazov that the "set" to which Imogen Lowrie and Hugo Dennistone belonged had no suspicion that any Jew was playing a part in their lives. And yet it certainly was so. For Imogen had been driven—it had seemed to Berazov like that, a driving—to say so to him. She had told him that Dennistone had to do with a Russian Jew, that they were together on the Riviera, that she had left them together when she had started for England. And Berazov had been absolutely aware, while she was speaking and afterwards, that this Jew was an influence, a potent influence, in the girl's life. She had denied that she was in love with this Jew. That denial might be true or untrue. There were, Berazov found reason to believe, different ways of being in love. And this girl, this Imogen Lowrie, was very many sided. But whether she was in love, or not, with this Jew whom nobody seemed to know, Berazov was almost positive that it was his influence which had been upon her when she had denied herself what she had certainly desired, and even greedily.

Imogen had been right. Berazov had learned a great deal about her in those kisses which he had given her and which she had not resisted. But there was a great deal more which he wished to know about her. Her physical desires were, he believed, abnormally strong. But it was evident to him that there was another strength in her and that it was not of the body, and it was in that strength that he seemed to feel this mysterious Jew, of whom he had said when Imogen had asked, "How could he have anything to do with you?" "I don't know yet. But I feel that he has, or that, if not, he may have."

Since that night of frustration Berazov had seen much more of Imogen, and yet he was not really in his opinion more intimate with her. She had not asked him again to her room. They had never again spoken of the Jew. He still knew that she was physically fascinated by him, knew it as if she had bluntly told him so in the undressed language of charming young England. He knew that no man in London attracted her as he did. And yet——

But there the wall rose before him, blank, cold, forbidding. And the days went by quickly. The summer heat must be becoming torrid on the Riviera. He wondered whether this fellow, Dennistone, and the Jew would stay there much longer. It was not likely. And when Dennistone left wouldn't he come to England, to London? If he did, things would surely become more difficult for Imogen Lowrie then. She wouldn't be so free as she was now. Berazov felt irritated by his non-success. And his unsatisfied curiosity also irritated him. He found himself perpetually dwelling on the unsolved mystery attaching to this unusual girl. He longed to penetrate it. And he strangely continued to feel that it had something to do with him. He hated Jews as a race. Now he began to hate an individual Jew, whom he had never seen, whose personality and even whose name were unknown to him, but who was, like himself, a Russian.

From his fragmentary conversation with Imogen he had gathered certain things about this Jew. His intelligence was quick, and he had also more intuition than the average man. He had begun to brood over what he had gathered. His intuition got busily to work upon the scanty material that had been supplied to him.

A man of great silences, and one whose silences were interesting to a clever girl of the ultra-modern type.

"She compared his silences with mine. But mine was not natural, merely *voulu!*"

A man capable of bringing about a great change in a girl of the world, in a girl naturally vain, and full of self-importance, of course cleverly disguised, in a girl not naturally religious, pagan rather, probably by nature and instinct, pleasure-loving, sensual—yes, sensual—courageous, sporting, and also artistic and in some degree cultivated. Therefore a man very far indeed from being stupid or vulgar or in any degree timid.

Different types of the Jews he had disgustedly come across rose at this point before Berazov's eyes, which he had shut in order that they might see the non-present. Which of these types was *his?* There were polished Jews, intellectual, artistic, luxurious, smooth as suéde gloves and sharp as stilettos. And there were Jews of the people, Jews who were food for pogroms, cringing, smiling, hand-rubbing, whispering Jews, with eyes that could see a dropped pin in a Petersburg street. But they were not for her. His mind dismissed them, kicked them out savagely. And he saw other Jews, such as in the past have furnished fit subjects for certain great painters: substantial bankers with powerful heavy faces and thoughtful eyes, rabbis, teachers of their faith, majestic men steeped in religion, and artists streaming with music.

He saw Rubinstein at the piano, a leviathan-Jew able to glorify even Beethoven. He had never really seen Rubinstein, but his mother had described the great genius to him, and he had made a grimace, and had resolved that he would have hated Rubinstein in spite of his music. He saw Einstein, the Jew in science; Spinoza, the Jew in philosophy; Reinhardt, the Jew in the theater. He saw the almost legendary figure of a wax-pale, weary, yet always fantastic man with a greasy lock, Disraeli, the Jew in politics. He saw Meyerbeer, a charlatan of genius.

To what type of talented, gifted, remarkable Jew—for he must be that—did her Jew belong, the Jew who was surely from a distance holding this girl back from pleasant sins she secretly longed to commit?

A man of great silences, a man who held your interest, who gripped you without words, a man who could bring about change in an evasive, a pagan, a very self-consecrated and self-admiring feminine soul.

That word "now." He, Berazov, had fastened upon that word when Imogen had spoken it. She had said that she didn't value her social reputation *now.* And there, in that word, he now definitely felt the Jew. He didn't know why, but so it was. Intuition perhaps? He had spoken, half teasingly, of some miracle of progress, some leap from darkness into light. And then her eyes had been full of secrets. The Jew had put them there, like lamps set in hitherto dark windows. And immediately afterwards, for the first time, she had spoken to him of Israel. And instantly he had connected Israel with change in her, with the miracle of progress expressed in the word *now*. Her face had been very strange when she had asked Berazov why he was interested in the Jew. There had been in it an earnestness almost amounting to awe, something deep and peculiar that had for the moment transformed her. The Jew was in that look. And then she had made that extraordinary remark about the lice. He had said, "One felt the lice." And she had answered, "Someone else's. But how many of us feel our own?"

The Jew was in those words. Hunting, hunting the Jew through that night conversation, through that night interview, Berazov found him everywhere. "How many of us feel our own?" The lice that infect all humanity, the lice that crawl over the fairest bodies, that are hidden on the most honorable men and have their homes on the most beautiful women. He, this Jew, had brought her to see them, to see, to feel, her own lice!

"He must be some remarkable philosopher," Berazov thought, "who has taken possession of her mind, who has made her want to be more purely mental than she naturally is."

He knew from general report of the wonderful Imogen that she had always been very fond of clever and brilliant men, and that many such men, some of them elderly or even old, had been devoted to her. Why should she exclude a brilliant Jew from her intimacy? Berazov made up his mind that Imogen, probably abroad, had fallen in with some remarkable Hebrew of profound learning or exceptional gifts, and had become the victim of his personality, insomuch that from a distance he influenced her. And his influence was antagonistic to any license of the body. Therefore he was probably what is often called a "high-minded" man.

Berazov began to hate him, and in his hatred of him seemed actually to know him.

One afternoon late, he was sitting in the drawing-room of his flat in Knightsbridge thinking about the Jew. And as he often did when giving himself up more or less to his imagination he had shut his eyes. With his eyes shut he was leaning back in a deep armchair and smoking a small pipe filled with a brand of fragrant tobacco which he was very fond of. It was a tobacco which sometimes, so he fancied, had the power to give him dreams. Perhaps he was half dreaming now. The windows of his room, which looked into Hyde Park, were wide open, and he could hear from where he was sitting the hum of the life of the park, the blended noises of many activities, out of which started now and then the sharp notes of the motorcars. As on several previous occasions—for really by now this Jew-business was beginning to obsess Berazov—he was calling up before him imaginatively Jews of differing types, and setting them one by one beside Imogen. And as each one, obedient to his summons, rose up, or as it were dawned upon him from the void, Berazov gazed at him and mutely asked him, "Is it you?"

Presently, while indulging in this quiet orgy of the imagination—his body was very comfortable in the deep armchair, and the delicious cloud of tobacco seemed to close him in from too harsh realities, sharp-edged and blatant—Berazov felt, but always vaguely, as if he were in some sort of communication with Imogen, whom he knew he was going to meet at a certain house that evening. And instead of asking the Jews one by one, "Is it you?" he seemed to be asking her, "Is it he?" And he felt, as Jew after Jew rose up, and he asked, and asked, her "No." "No, it is not he! No, it is not he!" Weary of negatives, he tried presently to rouse himself, like a man resolved on a strong effort, like a man who says to himself, "I *will*." He would summon his enemy, the Jew who stood in his way. He would see him, would know what he was like.

And then a strange thing happened. For there rose up suddenly before Berazov's closed eyes the most famous Jew in the history of the world, a figure hanging on a Cross. And he seemed to feel rather than to hear a voice saying, "They call him the King of the Jews." And he remembered his own words to Imogen, "Has God got hold of you?" and he shuddered and opened his eyes.

What did it mean—the shudder that had gone through him? It had been a shudder in which there had been an intimate thrill, such as he had occasionally felt when he had witnessed a great piece of art in the theater, or heard something wonderful in music, as when he had seen Chaliapin brooding above the world in "Mephistopheles," or listened to the sounds of the bells falling from heaven at the end of the first act of "Parsifal." But also in that shudder there had been a coldness as of fear or even of dread.

He got up, knocked out his pipe, laid it down and went to one of the windows. There he stood for a long time, with his hands thrust into the pockets of his smoking coat, watching the motors whirling by along the broad road, the people strolling on the path railed off beneath the trees.

Berazov had been brought up to believe in the Russian Orthodox Church, and for a long time he had supposed or assumed that he did believe in its teachings. But he had always been a sometimes careless and vehement, a sometimes melancholy and cynical, lover of life. He had not bothered about looking to the Beyond. And since the war and the Russian Revolution he had given little thought and no devotion to religion. Like multitudes of men he had sunk up to his throat in the mess of life, and once there had simply tried first to endure being there, and then eventually not to mind being there. Impossible to extricate oneself, therefore try to be at home and at ease in the mess, as certain reptiles are at ease and at home in noisome swamps.

But now, standing by the window, he did feel the mess like intolerable mud closely embracing him, sticking revoltingly as if to bare limbs which quivered to be away. And a deep melancholy took possession of him. He had been brutally flung out of his natural life. His country had been as it were snatched away from him. He had no hope of ever returning to it. All his posssessions had been confiscated. His houses, his horses, his pictures, his art treasures, his books, even his clothes and hats and boots and shirts had gone into the hands of those whom he hated and despised. He was rich now from a dead woman. He could live again as he had been accustomed to live. But what was the good of it all?

It seemed to him at that moment that he had only one genuine interest in his life—Imogen. Till now he had never felt sentimental about her, but now in his melancholy he did feel sentimental, felt an actual longing, which seemed of more than the flesh, for her. Perhaps that longing was really born out of her resistance to him, perhaps merely out of his melancholy which instinctively sought for some refuge from itself. But the vision of the Jew whom the world, so Berazov thought, seemed almost totally to have forgotten, had irritated that longing till it had become a somber but violent passion. For Berazov felt deeply convinced, mystically convinced, that when he had said to Imogen, "Has God got hold of you?" he had actually struck hard upon the truth. The invisible foe, who sometimes fights by the side of a woman, less often, it seems, by the side of a man, was at war against him. But he resolved that he would shake off the obsession of the Jew. Before him was a plainer issue.

He turned away from the window.

"It's just the ordinary case of a girl who, clever though she is, isn't clever enough to have entirely released herself from absurd scruples," he said to himself. "She may have thought she was free, but someone has been clouding her mind with orthodox teachings. There will always be religious maniacs in our charming madhouse, and always people to think they are sane."

That was what he said to himself. But he had not forgotten the thrill, and he had not shaken off the obsession of the Jew.

CHAPTER VI

ONE of the unwritten rules in the society of London is, "Encourage your friends' love-affairs. Help things on." Since Imogen's meeting with Berazov and obvious interest in him it had been the understood thing that Imogen and he must always be asked everywhere together. Berazov for the moment was Imogen's man. Her tragic marriage would take place very soon. Till it did, it was obviously her friends' business to see that she had a magnificent time. And this interesting and enterprising Russian, so quiet and yet so very capable in all the complicated business of the world, was evidently the man who could help her to have it. So she and Berazov met everywhere. They met on the night after his reverie over Israel, at a small musical party given by Silvia Moray at her minute, but astonishing house in Regent's Park, called by all her friends "the dolls' house."

The Morays were supposed to be very poor. They always said they had nothing. But as they always did everything nobody minded their poverty. As they couldn't afford a decent house they had to put up with Scotborough Lodge, which had at any rate one merit not to be despised in London. It stood in quite a large garden. The poor Morays were absolutely ruined, according to their own account of the matter, by the expenses of the two gardeners. Still, as Silvia said in her melodious soprano, "We get our vegetables for practically nothing, and we can sit out in summer without having to pay those horrid men for green chairs." An obvious advantage! And the smallness of the house didn't matter when, if it began to bulge under the pressure of Silvia's innumerable friends, you could always create a vacuum by stepping out into the garden.

Silvia, so she averred, only gave one party a year. Really she gave dozens, but these dozens didn't count, as they were always arranged on the spur of the moment by telephone, and were never even thought of until after six on the days when they took place. But every June she gave a "party," to which she didn't invite everybody whom she knew, but only those whom she loved, really loved. There were about two hundred and fifty of them. The garden was illuminated in their honor. A supper that had obviously never heard of an English cook was served in a marvelous room brought from somewhere for the occasion and planted on the lawn. And there were entertainments. One year she had Grock; another year Pavlova. On another occasion the chief tennis stars, including a diva from France, played exhibition lawn-tennis by artificial light. This year, the year of Imogen and Berazov, there was music. Arthur Rubinstein played, and an Italian girl from America, with a face like the Madonna and three more notes in her voice than had ever before been found in a human being, sang gloriously.

When Berazov arrived Silvia Moray, who as usual was marvelously white and marvelously thin, as self-possessed as an orchid and as poor as a church mouse, told him at once to look for Imogen in the garden.

"I saw her among the rhododendrons searching for you. Do go and comfort her."

"Comfort her! What's the matter?"

"I don't know. But I thought she was laughing like someone who's had bad news. Isn't the moon behaving pretty? Here comes the Bakewell Group!"

And indeed at this moment the "Bakewell Group," a brother and two enormous sisters, all steady poets, moved solemnly forward in mass formation from the hall of the dolls' house, with an air of impending intellectuality.

"Aren't they darlings? They take themselves seriously, as the Bishop of London does himself. They ought to wear aprons like him. But I believe they hope they're atheists. She's among the rhododendrons still I am almost sure."

Berazov left her and went out through the open windows of the little Chinese drawing-room into the garden.

The night was mercifully warm, even hot, and the moon, as Silvia Moray had said, was "behaving pretty." It helped the illuminations contrived by the hostess, but was too modest to interfere with them, to make them look garish. It had a pleasant round air of superintending the fête without having any desire to "boss" things. A perfectly behaved moon such as one sees too rarely in London! Somewhere, listened to devoutly by as many of those whom Silvia really loved as could get near him, Arthur Rubinstein was playing "Petroushka."

Following his hostess's clue Berazov made his way towards the rhododendrons, which grew in large clumps beyond the lawn and served as a screen to the tennis-courts and the kitchen garden. On the lawn he met many people whom he knew, among them Lois Tremayne with, as usual, Teddy Basingstoke. "Imogen's somewhere by the rhododendrons," said Lois directly she saw Berazov.

"Has she a passion for the shrub?" asked Berazov with his slightly melancholy smile. "Silvia Moray exclaimed 'rhododendrons' at me directly I arrived."

"I don't think her passion is concentrated on any shrub."

"No?"

"No. Imogen's very human, isn't she, Teddy?"

"What d'you mean by that?" asked Mr. Basingstoke, a primrose-colored young giant with a very determined pair of blue eyes and a loud deep bass voice which women found enticing.

"Only that she isn't the sort of girl who gives herself up to dogs and herbaceous borders and all that sort of thing. The rhododendrons are only a passing fancy. And besides she's mitigating them with a canon."

"What's that?" said Berazov.

"A clergyman of sorts. This one's a famous preacher and a great friend of Silvia's. I often wonder whether he lets her share in his collections. She's so dreadfully poor, you know."

The supper room was suddenly lit up and a bugle sounded.

"Just like Bayreuth, isn't it?" said Lois Tremayne. "I do wish I had Silvia's poverty. Are you hungry, Teddy?"

"Well, that bugle seems to have given me a thirst."

"I know. It takes one suddenly with music. The chord of C Major always suggests Cordon Rouge to me. The cocktail chords are different. A Minor makes me long for Martinis, and——"

They moved towards the supper room, and Berazov looked in the direction of the rhododendrons.

The fact just stated by Lois Tremayne that Imogen had chosen a clergyman as her companion at such a very unclerical party had irritated Berazov, who had not recovered from his melancholy mood of the afternoon. What did she want with a clergyman? And had anything unpleasant happened to her? He hadn't forgotten Mrs. Moray's remark about bad news. She had probably been speaking at random. Nevertheless her words had immediately made him think of the Jew. And he had actually felt apprehensive.

One of Silvia Moray's rules at her parties was this: "Give them supper all the time." Now, although it was quite early, people were streaming towards the lighted room on the lawn with an air of definite purpose. The crowd in the garden was thinning out. Berazov could not only see but discern. And now he saw a black coat and a high black silk waistcoat, a round collar, a red face, white hair, and beside all this a tall girl in a frock of gold lace who seemed almost to tower above her strangely chosen companion. And they were near to the rhododendrons.

He went slowly towards them. As he drew near, Imogen, who seemed to be talking earnestly to Canon Barrimore, probably felt his nearness, for she suddenly turned her head, saw him and, as he believed, broke off the conversation, leaving the canon more or less in the air. Berazov judged this to be so by the somewhat startled and inquiring demeanor of the reverend gentleman, which finally developed into something very like bridling as Berazov came up and held out his hand to Imogen. When he did this and met her eyes in the mingled light of the moon and Mrs. Moray's cleverly arranged lanterns, he knew at once that something had happened. His keen, experienced eyes noted unerringly that the girl was strung up, nervy and less self-possessed, less well balanced than usual. There was something slightly shrill in her manner, something delicately haggard in her appearance. And she made the mistake, unusual with her, of forcing her liveliness instead of being entirely natural.

"She's had a blow of some kind," Berazov said to himself.

And instantly, although he hadn't the faintest idea what the nature of the blow was, he had the feeling that this blow had perhaps created his opportunity.

Imogen introduced him of course to Canon Barrimore, with the explanation, "Count Berazov is the Russian friend I was telling you about, who has been out in the Argentine." Then she added, to Berazov, "Canon Barrimore goes into residence this week at Drearney where I have an aunt living. D'you know Drearney Cathedral?"

"No," said Berazov, "but of course I know it's one of the finest cathedrals in England."

"I hope you'll come down and see it," said Canon Barrimore in his powerful voice. "I should be delighted to give you lunch and show you over it."

Apparently he had quite recovered from his short fit of bridling, and was ready to make friends with Berazov.

"I have studied most of your chief writers," he added. "Tolstoy, Dostoevsky, Turgenev of course have been read by every educated man. But I know also the works of Gorky, Kuprin, Merejkowsky, Andreyev, Chekhov, and many others. Tolstoy, great as he was, was wrong, about the moral beauty of your peasants. The revolution has shown that."

He engaged Berazov, evidently with purpose, in a discussion on Russian writers and the Russian situation. Berazov was conscious that he had to do with a clever though slightly self-important ecclesiastic who was bent on keeping himself thoroughly "up to the mark" in all the topics of the day, and who loved to explore any brain that he thought was worth exploration. Imogen meanwhile remained with them looking, Berazov thought, unnaturally eager and intelligent, but as if underneath this too sensitive mask she were horribly distrait and secretly self-absorbed. And occasionally when a reasonable opportunity for laughter was given by one or other of the speakers she, as Silvia Moray had said, laughed like one who has just received bad news.

"When are you coming down to Drearney again, my dear Imogen?" the canon said presently. "We have not seen you there since—let me see, wasn't it in November last?"

"Yes. It was in November."

Something in her tone as she made this commonplace reply gripped Berazov's attention.

"You preached on salvation," she added. "And on the absurdity of mankind crying out for new Saviors."

Canon Barrimore suddenly looked confused, almost ashamed.

"Did I? Yes, I remember—I did."

"A very fine sermon!" said Imogen. She paused, seemed to hesitate, then added, "With a postscript."

"Ha!"

The canon looked more confused, almost guilty. He glanced at Berazov, who wondered what caused his obvious embarrassment.

"There are moments," he said, "when one's confidence in one's own arguments is shaken as if by a breath of—ha—what shall I call it?—skepticism, subtle skepticism, creeping upon one from some unknown mind, with which one is in mysterious contact without being really aware of it. Many public speakers, many preachers would probably know what I mean."

"And this occurred on that occasion?" asked Berazov, looking at Imogen.

"Yes, I—ha—believe it did," said the canon. "I even think I know whose was the mind that affected mine."

Imogen looked startled and tensely inquiring.

"But I may be wrong, I may be wrong. It's only a surmise, only a surmise."

There was a pause. Berazov thought of it as a dead pause. For a brief instant the life seemed to have gone out of them. From the brilliantly lit up and isolated supper room a roar of conversation, confused, hilarious and somewhat vulgar, came to them in the night. Beyond, the curiously small house showed its lighted windows behind beds full of sleeping flowers. A few people were strolling about or standing or sitting in groups lit up by colored lanterns and the moon. Now and then from the music-room of the house came a soprano cry, melodious, round, prolonged. The Italian girl from America was singing to a rapt crowd invisible from the garden. And these three, Imogen, Berazov and Canon Barrimore, stood for a moment like three puppets in the night, still, vacant, as if bowed by some invisible force. To Berazov at that moment their setting seemed unreal, nightmarish, as a country fair might seem at night to a wanderer glimpsing it from afar out of a somber wood.

"And whose mind was it?" said a voice at last.

Berazov was conscious of surprise, of life flowing back upon

them and in them. Imogen had spoken. Canon Barrimore
had shifted his right foot, tucked in his chin, then seemed to
let it go, as if he couldn't bother to control it.

"You wouldn't know," he said. "But I have some reason to
suppose it may have been the mind of a man called Peter
Kharkoff. A Russian, by the way, Count, but not at all of
your caste, if I may use the word. A Russian Jew in fact."

"Yes?" said Berazov.

He was concentrated on Imogen now. She stood quite still
on the grass looking at the canon with deep attention.

"Do you know Mr. Kharkoff?" she said.

"No. I have never met him. Do *you* know him?" said
Canon Barrimore, evidently surprised.

"Yes. He has been staying at Sainte Maxime close to us
this spring. He has often been over to see us. My father is
very interested in him. He is still there. Hugo Dennistone—
he's staying at the villa——"

"I know that," said the canon.

"Hugo has taken a great fancy to him, and is seeing a lot
of him."

"I had no idea you knew him."

"My aunt didn't tell you?"

"I haven't seen her lately."

The canon looked at Berazov.

"I hate Jews," said Berazov, not angrily, with simplicity.
As he spoke his eyes were on Imogen. "I consider that they've
ruined my country," he added.

"But hadn't your country treated them pretty badly?"

"You don't know them as I do."

She looked at him for a moment, and he thought he saw
anger struggling with something else in her eyes. Then she
said, "They are very persistent. I think that's their strength.
They have more persistence than others." She turned again
to the canon. "But do you really believe that Mr. Kharkoff's
mind influenced yours that night in the cathedral?" she said.

"I don't know. It's impossible for me to know. But from
something that Hendry—he's our organist at the cathedral,
Count, a very clever man—said to me about Mr. Kharkoff's
great mental power I think it's just possible. And so you
know this Mr. Kharkoff, Imogen. That's very interesting."

He was evidently going to say something more when Imogen
broke in with, "Mr. Hendry's quite an original, isn't he?"

"Yes. He's sometimes almost embarrassingly unlike the rest of us. But he's clever and very sincere. I believe he's going to spend his holiday this year in Switzerland, either with or near to Mr. Kharkoff."

"He too!" exclaimed Imogen.

"Too!" said the canon. "I don't quite understand."

But she volunteered no explanation, and Berazov came to the rescue.

"Another worshiper!" he said with what seemed to Imogen a bitterness of sarcasm greater than he intended to show.

She had the feeling just then that Berazov was overcome by his own bitterness.

"He seems to have an enormous admiration for this man," said Canon Barrimore. "But Hendry's an enthusiast."

"What about, I wonder?" said Berazov. "What is there to be enthusiastic about in this weary chaos? Surely your friend can scarcely be so very clever if he's enthusiastic in these days."

Canon Barrimore was just opening his capacious orator's mouth to reply to this question when Silvia Moray came up to them slowly over the close-clipped grass, with two-thirds of the "Bakewell Group," Miss Bakewell and Mr. Barrington Bakewell.

"Aren't you hungry, Canon dear?" she said.

"Well, I hardly know. To tell the truth I wasn't thinking of quails or anything of that kind."

"Think of them now with us at a table for four. *You've* been thinking of them for ages, haven't you, Barrington?"

The enormous brother shook back his hair and exposed a long columnar throat to the moon.

"Where are you hiding, so small and frail, bird created for supper, sleek succulent quail?" he murmured.

"Come, Candida!" said Mrs. Moray to the sister who seemed bowed beneath the moon in eternal silence. "And you find a corner with Berazov, Imogen. I know you'd hate a sextet."

She took the canon away without subtlety. That was her way. Her motto, if she had one, was "Be bold, sweet maid, and let who will be subtle." And she had certainly made a success of her life. She had even made a success of her husband, who had something to do with Lipton's, although he was totally inadequate. Someone had called him "two yards and three inches of incapacity." And the description hit him off exactly.

He was a giant without brains. Silvia "ran" him, and apparently loved him.

"Are you hungry?" said Berazov, when they were alone.

"No. I've been dining out at Claridge's. We only finished about an hour ago."

"Let us find some seats. What is behind the rhododendrons?"

"Tennis-courts and vegetables."

"There must be seats by the tennis."

"There are."

They went up a narrow path to the back of the shrubs and came upon some benches facing two grass courts and beyond them Mrs. Moray's famed kitchen garden.

"They look awfully hard," said Imogen, pushing out her unpainted lips.

She was carrying a wrap of white fur over one arm. Now she put it round her shoulders.

"Are you cold?" he said. "It's such an extraordinarily hot night for England."

"I've just come from the Riviera. Don't forget that."

She sat down on a bench, and he sat beside her.

"You don't let me forget it."

"What do you mean?"

"Your mind is perpetually there."

He paused, but she said nothing.

"But I suppose that is natural."

"Why?"

"The man I suppose you love, at any rate the man you're going to marry, is there."

He was watching the girl very narrowly as he said that, and he saw her lips twitch, and two tiny lines appear between her eyebrows.

"Where the heart is there the mind must be also."

"Heart and mind don't always run meekly together in double harness," she said. "Surely you have lived sufficiently to know that. I think they are often in opposition."

"Yours?"

"Mine and other people's. I don't suppose I'm an exception in that matter."

"I don't know that. I think you are exceptional. I think you're a queer one. In Russia, you know, among Russians, scarcely anyone or anything seems queer. Perhaps because

there we are all queer together. But over here I don't think
it is so. And you stand out among the English. Of course
you have the varnish of your world. By merely seeing you,
being with you for five minutes, I could place you. But for
all that I think you're a queer one, and never more so than
tonight. Why don't you paint as all the other girls do?"

"How very abrupt you are!"

"I'm full of questions about you, and about your Jew."

She moved. He thought she was going to say something
angry. He had meant to provoke her, and expected a rebuke
or at least a sharp-edged rejoinder. But she said nothing.

"Do you know," he said after waiting for a moment, "that
several times lately I've been tempted to spend two or three
nights out of London—at Sainte Maxime?"

"Why don't you go there?"

"A man has a natural inclination to see what his enemy is
like."

"Do you think Hugo Dennistone is your enemy?" she said
with a touch of sarcasm.

"I was speaking of this Jew who seems to be about me ever
since I have met you. I'm getting uneasy. It's as if Israel,
whom I have always hated, and who has driven me out into
exile—yes, yes! Israel is at the bottom of every Russian
horror!—it's as if Israel had now resolved to meet me at last
personally in the way, individual to individual, man to man,
and to have it out with me."

"But you are obsessed by this mania of persecution by
Israel!"

"Oh no, I'm not. Your Jew is my enemy."

She shook her head. He was amazed by her self-control,
which seemed, he thought, prompted by something sad which
had softened her strangely.

"He is no man's enemy. He might be the enemy of something *in* you, but never of *you*."

Berazov looked at her for a long time in silence. Again in
that Regent's Park garden he seemed to see the figure of the
greatest of all Jews; again that curious, intimate thrill went
through him. At last he said, "You defend him."

"What against?" she interrupted.

And this time there was a hint of anger in her voice and
manner.

"Let us say then that you speak kindly of him, and yet

you're angry with him. I feel that. He has made you angry, and unhappy. He has dealt you a blow."

"How can you know such a thing as that?"

"Anyhow you've had a blow today." She did not deny it.

"And I feel," he said, after waiting for the words that did not come, "I feel that he has had something to do with the dealing of it."

"I can't understand," she said, gazing at him as if with profound inquiry, "why you are so concentrated on a man you have never seen."

"The reason of that lies in you."

"Yes, it must."

"And now tonight your friend, the preacher, practically tells us that he too has come under the spell."

"He did come under it."

"You know it?"

"I feel certain of it."

"What happened?"

She seemed to hesitate. Then she said, "Why should I tell you?"

"You don't want to tell me?"

"It can't matter either way."

She looked away from him across the tennis-courts. She stared into the night, and he heard her sigh. Her long hands were tightly clasped. They looked strained, tormented.

As she didn't speak he said at last, "Do tell me."

And then, still looking before her into the night, she related to him briefly the curious episode of Canon Barrimore's sermon and its extraordinary conclusion.

"*He* was there," she said when she had finished.

"The Jew?"

"Yes. I saw him that night. I spoke to him that night."

"And you think he influenced the canon?"

"Oh yes. It was his doing."

"But what is the mystery about him? Do you mean to tell me that you think this man is a new Savior—a Jew from Russia?"

"I didn't say that."

"How is he different from the rest of us?"

"You would feel how if you met him."

"But as my meeting him is extremely improbable can't you explain to me how——"

"No, I can't."

"You won't! That's how it is. Perhaps because I'm a Jew-hater?"

"Hugo Dennistone was a Jew-hater till he met Peter Kharkoff. And now——"

A strange look of distress came into her eyes, and she looked at Berazov as if she were asking him a silent question.

"And now!" he repeated. "What has happened?"

"And now he isn't."

"And that makes you sad?"

He felt that she was on the verge of telling him something, of making things clear to him. And he let his arm drop a little on the back of the bench till it rested against her white fur.

"What is it? Has the Jew too much influence over your lover?"

Instead of answering him she said, "Have you ever intended to make a sacrifice, and then realized that perhaps the possibility of your being able to make it was being taken from you?"

"I can't remember that such a thing has ever happened to me."

"Without knowing it almost, a woman can get to love the prospect of sacrifice."

"Yes?"

"And then it hurts not to be able to make it. There's a peculiar pain in being prevented from doing the difficult thing."

"Have you been prevented from making some sacrifice?"

"I'm not sure, but I think it may be so."

"And that's why you are unhappy tonight?"

"I feel awfully lonely," she said.

"That's strange! This afternoon in my flat I felt horribly lonely too. I don't want to spread out my misery, to whine. I have got a great deal. A fortune from a poor woman who cared for me, who is dead because she loved me, dead with our child. Most of my compatriots are terribly poor. They come to me, many of them. It is a procession of misery. I have been like them and now I am rich again. Something to be thankful for. But I felt very lonely this afternoon. You see one has lost Russia! Just suppose you had lost England. And I was thinking over things—thinking over life—and it seemed to me that I was really interested in nothing except *you.*"

"If that's true I pity you. Life is enormously interesting to me now."

"*Now!* Again that fatal word! But you're young, ever so much younger than I am."

"It isn't that."

"Then we are up against the Jew again!" exclaimed Berazov with sudden intense irritation. "At every moment I feel this man in you. I can't get away from him. D'you know, this afternoon in my flat all alone, I was calling up Jews?"

"Calling up Jews?"

"Yes, before my shut eyes. It was because of you that I sent out my summons. I said to myself, 'What is her Jew like? What is his type?'"

"Well?"

"Well, many Jews came."

She turned towards him. Her white fur touched his shoulder as he leaned a little towards her. Her eyes were fixed upon him and looked profoundly interested.

"Jews without names, of different types, varnished and unvarnished, terribly well-dressed—there are some of these here tonight—and ragged, unwashed, filthy. And then dignified Jews with names came."

"What names?"

"Well, I saw Rubinstein, Spinoza, Einstein, Meyerbeer, Reinhardt, Disraeli—your Disraeli."

He paused.

"Yes?" she said.

"That's all."

"No, it isn't. Whom else did you see?"

After what seemed to her a long silence he said:

"At the end I saw the King of the Jews."

He spoke in a low voice. Imogen trembled. A trembling seemed to run all over her and to cease.

"Is your Jew Christlike?" he asked.

"There's nothing conventionally Christlike about him."

"Is he very learned?"

"He may be."

"But it isn't that which has impressed you?"

"Oh no."

"What is it?"

"Telling about such a man wouldn't be any good."

"I feel he's my enemy. But I feel more. I feel he's yours."

"No."

"You say he could be the enemy of something in one, but never the enemy of oneself. I don't believe that. I feel he's troubling you, hurting you. I feel you're restless, unhappy tonight, and all because of him. Isn't it true?"

"Even if it is I shouldn't—I've no right to——"

"I can't think how it is," he interrupted. "You seem to belong to the governing type of women but really you're the slave type."

"It's no use your trying to make me angry."

"What has he done to you?"

"I don't know."

"You're in love with him," said Berazov brutally.

"Perhaps it would be better for me if I were."

"Why?"

"There could be nothing disgusting in any love felt for him. He's released. That's how I feel him. And one would be released in one's love for him."

"Released? From what?"

"From burdens we have to bear."

"We? You and I?"

"Most of us. Almost all of us."

"D'you know what I believe?" Berazov said in a hard voice. "I believe that this Peter Kharkoff is simply a very clever, unscrupulous man who has succeeded in getting a hold over you, in taking you in. In my poor Russia God knows we have fanatical mystics enough, and——"

"It's no use your talking to me like that," she said, interrupting him, but quietly.

"Do you mean to say—you're a clever girl—you have never doubted him?"

"What do you mean exactly by doubting?"

"Have you never thought you might be mistaken in him, that he mightn't be really the man he presented himself as, the man you had supposed him to be?"

"I *know* he is genuine."

Berazov put one arm round her shoulder against the white fur.

"I feel he's persecuting you in some mysterious way. Forget him. You said you felt lonely tonight—as I did this afternoon. I felt horribly lonely and then I thought of you. And I knew that no one could take away the feeling but you."

"What I could give you couldn't take the feeling away."

"How can you know?"

"Because I know just what I have to give you, what sort of thing, and how much."

"Perhaps that is exactly what I want."

"No; it can't be."

"How can you possibly know that?"

"Because I know there are universal truths, truths that cover us all. And you can't be exempt from them. You are under their law like every other man."

"You are talking out of the mouth of the Jew!" exclaimed Berazov.

He took away his arm. There was intense irritation in his look and manner, irritation amounting to acute exasperation.

"Ever since I was a boy I've had to do with women," he said. "But I've never felt with any woman as I do with you. With you I feel as if I were in contact with two natures instead of only with one. I see, feel, understand you as I'm sure you really are. I want you as you really are. I even feel you want me. But—you're all clouded and made extraordinary by someone else. It's as if another mind, another nature had grafted itself somehow upon yours. Why didn't I know you before you met this man? You must have been different then."

"I was," she said, looking down.

She spoke in a voice that seemed dreamy with melancholy. At that moment she was looking back on the gay girl who had traveled down on a night of November to Drearney after a day's hunting with Hugo.

"And weren't you happier, more natural?"

"I believe I thought I was happy. I always seemed to be having what's called a good time. I just did whatever I wanted and didn't care—if that's being happy. As to being natural—well, I lived according to one part of my nature. But I didn't know then what my nature really was. Lots of people are as ignorant as I was then, I think."

"Do you know what your nature really is now?"

"Better than I did then at any rate."

"I wonder if you do," said Berazov.

"I know I do."

"I think you've allowed yourself to be put into a strait waistcoat and that you're trying in vain to be happy in it. But even a lunatic can't be happy in a strait waistcoat. And you're very sane." He paused and then added, morosely, "Too sane! Ah, I would give a great deal to stir you into a little of the madness I have known in women."

"Don't try to do that," she said.

He put his arm behind her again.

"But I have tried—haven't I?—and failed."

"After you had gone that night I went down to see if you were still in the house," she said, speaking with a sort of dogged coldness.

"No!"

"But I did. So now you know what I am."

"And I had gone! What a fool I was!"

"No. You thought I meant it all, and I did mean it."

"But then why——"

"And after I had meant it I went to pieces. There's nothing odd in that. If you know women, as you want me to think you do, you must know how often we crash—after being firm."

"I'm almost afraid of your honesty," he said suspiciously. "Why are you being so honest? *That's* not like woman."

"I feel I want to. What you said about being lonely was honest. And I've learned that sincerity in intercourse makes life worth ten times more than it ever can be when it's plowing its way through insincerity. Why shouldn't you and I be sincere with each other?"

"Well, you're a girl of not much over twenty, I suppose."

"Nearly twenty-two."

"And I'm a man going on for thirty-seven."

"You tried to make me your mistress. That was sincere enough, wasn't it?"

Strangely enough something in Berazov felt shocked when she said that. Was it his breeding? Or what was it? He knew young England's terribly fearless discussion of the un-mentionable. He knew that Imogen had been typical of the particular section of young England which was all of the British nation that he really knew. He himself had treated her with almost brutal frankness very soon after getting to know her. Yet now he felt shocked. And it seemed to him as if she were turning light upon something to which only darkness was appropriate. Her words sounded ugly in his ears.

"You don't like my saying that."

"Why shouldn't you say it? Why shouldn't one say anything?"

"But I see you are hating it. And so am I."

"Then why——?" He threw out his thin hands in a curiously foreign gesture of deprecation.

"Why? Because I have a notion that it's good for us, you and me, to see ourselves as we really are. You tried to make me your mistress. I sent you away. And then I went down to see whether you were still in the house. That's how it was."

"I cannot see the good of discussing that night. It wasn't a pleasant or successful night for me, I can assure you."

"Nor for me. But what are you and I doing now? Where are we heading to? What does our association mean? How do we intend it to develop? What's the good of it?"

"To analyze an intimacy between a woman and a man is the surest way of killing it."

"Are we intimate, you and I? That night, just when we were going into the house, I said to myself, 'All this is useless. Why am I doing it?' That's what I said."

"I have thought, especially since I have had to give up living in Russia, that at moments we Russians are the most sincere people on earth—*at moments*. But I think you are beating us tonight," said Berazov with a plaintiveness that was very nearly boyish. "I feel I can only leave it in your hands, or in the hands of the Jew, whichever it is. I can no longer disentangle the one from the other, you from your Guide, or whatever he is. Women I claim to know. And men I believe I know. But a man confronting me in a woman, a Jew man in a non-Jewish woman—no, that's too much!"

He had drawn a little away from Imogen as if involuntarily, not exactly as if she repelled him, but as if he were chilled by the strange turn she had given to the conversation.

"I told you I felt horribly lonely," he added. "But I would far rather be lonely than have intercourse with someone I can't see, and whom, probably, I never shall see. I wanted you. I want you still, and much more now than on the night you've pulled to pieces and trodden on. But I want you without him—that man. I should hate him if I knew him. And I reject him absolutely in you."

"You wouldn't hate him. And you can't reject him."

"But I say that I do."

"I have wished to. I've meant to. Since I've been back in London I've tried to. But I haven't succeeded."

"Then you acknowledge I was right when I said you were in the toils?"

"Yes."

She said the little word gravely, with a deep significance and gravity.

"Yes, I suppose you were," she added, after an instant. "For I have met someone who has made me feel my own lice. You remember?"

"Yes, I remember."

"I didn't feel them before. I do now. And—I want to get rid of them."

"And does that mean giving up all the pleasures of life?"

"No. But there are things one can't do any more."

"Any more?"

He was looking at her now with an ugly interest which she recognized for what it was.

"And things one has never done, but which one has been tempted to do—one can't do them either."

She laid her hand gently on his arm.

"Berazov, I don't know exactly what you have thought about me. You are Russian and I'm English, and I think perhaps some of us English girls of *now* are deceptive because of our new and to some people, many people perhaps, disgusting frankness. I can't answer for other girls, even of my own set. But—I'm *not,* up till now. D'you understand?"

"Yes."

"When I met you I was miserable and angry. You detected that I was angry. I had a longing to run wild. I wanted to run wild with you. That night I meant to. But I couldn't. I sent you away. Then I went downstairs in hopes of finding you. But you were gone. I know why. You hadn't been allowed to stay."

"You mean that I was a fool to go!"

"No. You had to go. That's how it was."

He looked down at the long, unselfconscious hand lying on the sleeve of his evening coat. And suddenly he felt that he wanted this girl in the real way, not with his body only, like an animal, but with something much more subtle, much more mysterious, much more beautiful even.

"Why are you going to marry this crippled man?" he murmured.

"But perhaps I'm not."

"Not!"

"Probably not."

"But I thought——"

"So did I. But today I had a letter from Sainte Maxime. When he left there he was to come to England, and we were to be married. Well, he wants to go to Switzerland instead."

"With the Jew!" Berazov said sharply.

"Yes."

At this moment the silence in which they had both been forgetting that they were at Silvia Moray's annual "party" was broken by the sound of voices. They heard a man's voice say, "I've had the run of this place and I know where to go. You follow me, Millie, and I'll bring you where there'll be nobody but carrots and turnips. Come on!"

"A kitchen garden?" said a woman's high voice.

There was a laugh. Then the same voice, nearer, said:

"I'll bet you someone's found it out before us. Perhaps my husband!"

Imogen got up and glided softly away to the left. Berazov followed her, quietly as a cat. When they were safely away she whispered to him:

"Other people's lice! And—our own?"

"If you're really free," he said, catching at her hand, "won't you——"

"Hush! Don't say anything more. If you have rejected *him* you have rejected me. Let's go and hear Arthur Rubinstein."

CHAPTER VII

AT THE end of that week Imogen went down to Drearney to stay with her aunt at Ewenden House. Berazov had tried to persuade her to accept an invitation to a house party in Kent in which he was included. But she had gently and obstinately refused. She saw clearly that Berazov was falling in love with her. He had wanted her crudely, as she had wanted him. Now he was beginning to want her in a different and far more mysterious way. This troubled her and also excited her. For she felt as if he were being drawn to her by the attraction not only of herself, but also of another in her. And this other, it seemed to her, was ruthlessly setting her free, or trying to set her free. But perhaps he couldn't. Perhaps that was impossible. Perhaps even he had not the power to release her now. For if she were released how could Berazov feel the Jew in her as he said he did, as she felt that he did?

She was convinced that the very thing against which Berazov railed, the very thing he denounced in her, was the thing that was drawing him on from mere physical lust to something much subtler and deeper.

When she drove up to Ewenden House in the dust of a hot summer afternoon she felt curiously detached and apart from the ordinary in life.

Miss Creswell met her in the hall scented with sweet-peas, gave her an inquiring look and welcomed her warmly.

"I thought you wouldn't come near me till the season was over."

"You might have come up to London to me."

"And interfere with your gaieties? I'm too discreet, Im. When are Minnie and your father coming back? Minnie writes that the heat at Sainte Maxime is terrible. And yet they stay on there."

"I had a telegram just before I left London. They arrive on Tuesday."

"On Tuesday!" She paused. "And Hugo Dennistone? Is he coming with them?"

"They say nothing about it in the telegram."

"But hasn't he——?"

"I'll tell you about it while I'm here. What's the time, Towser?"

"Just after half past three."

"What time's the cathedral service?"

"At four."

"Let's go to it."

"Of course, dear, if you would like to."

"I should. I'll just go to my room for a minute and put on a hat with more of a brim. It's quite tropical here today."

"Yes, isn't it?"

Imogen looked out into the garden which was brilliant with flowers.

"Color—heat—but where's the sound of heat?"

"The sound of heat, Im? What do you mean?"

"Where are the crickets? I miss them."

And then she went upstairs.

The short walk to the cathedral through the town emphasized for Imogen her feeling of detachment. As she looked at the Drearney people, going cheerfully about their business, shopping, gossiping, hurrying off to lawn-tennis, making their way towards tea parties, she felt as if an immeasurable distance lay between her and them. She had always felt thoroughly apart from them, but not as she felt now. Formerly her feeling had been that she belonged to the great, they to the small world. Now she knew the smallness of that world of hers as well as the smallness of theirs. And she wondered at them not as a smart woman wonders at a dowdy, but as one with seeing eyes wonders at the blind. "How can it be dark to you? How can it be possible that what I possess at this moment beside you is out of your reach?" She marveled at their rosy cheerfulness. Some of them greeted her aunt. Some of them just knew her.

"Oh, Miss Lowrie, are you back again? How well you are looking! And how's London?"

"How's London!"

They turned into Cathedral Lane which was full of the sound of bells. Its narrowness seemed to imprison the bells. From the jutting-out windows, over pots of geraniums, two or three old, curious faces peered down.

"There goes Miss Mossop! And there goes Miss Creswell with somebody! I do believe they're going to cathedral. It isn't often she goes on a Saturday."

Peering at life over geranium pots while the wrinkles grow deeper and the hair gets scantier! Imogen looked up and wondered, but not as she used to wonder.

And then they were before the great archway giving access to the precincts, and she met the eyes of her aunt.

"Yes, that's where I followed him. It seems such a long time ago."

"Does it, dear?"

"Centuries. I wonder whether Mr. Hendry will be playing the organ today?"

"Probably. He often plays on a Saturday, I believe. It's a half-holiday, and lots of trippers come over. And he likes them to hear good music."

"Does he bother about trippers?"

"Oh yes. He's tremendously keen on what he calls 'the ordinary man.'"

"I wonder whether anyone is ordinary," murmured Imogen.

And then they went into the nave, and everything changed. They were in the gray world, with its wonderful flavor of age and its tremors from out of the past, with its strange echoes, its shadows and bars of unexpected light, its remoteness, its suggestion of God. And the smell of the past was about them. And the dust of dead centuries seemed to stir and rise up in the jeweled gleams which were shed from old painted windows played upon by the sunshine, of dead centuries sleeping on the breast of Eternity.

And again Imogen wondered whether anyone is ordinary. She knew that she was quivering with life. She felt that she was treading on the edge of events that were going to alter her life. She had a sense of fear and of expectation. And this gray world increased it. The pagan spirit in which she had often rejoiced, or thought that she was rejoicing, was surely fading out of her. She was overwhelmed by a streaming sense of religion.

Heavens! Here was Mr. Swarpes floating forward with benign majesty, the pomade still fresh in his hair! And far away the five-minutes bell was sounding. Mr. Swarpes stood aside in easy majesty, and they went into the carved places of honor. And then Imogen was kneeling down with her eyes against her hands laid on the fat velvet cushion. And the old questions were in her: "What am I? Where am I going? What is my destiny? What is going to happen to me?" Among rings of yellow light edged with blue she saw Hugo lying on his couch under the palm trees. And someone was sitting beside him. She felt the pressure of the Jew's deep silence. Then the sound of the far-off bell ceased, and the whisper of the organ was in her ears. Was Mr. Hendry playing it? She wondered and tried to divine. This was an improvisation, someone expressing his mood in soft music till the procession should come. She heard the far-off beat of its traveling footsteps. She got up. Berazov was sitting opposite to her.

He was with a tall, white-haired woman, whom Imogen didn't know, but whom she guessed instantly to be an American. No doubt they had motored over to Drearney from the house in Kent where Berazov was staying for the week-end; the house she had refused to go to. She felt startled and irritated. Yet Berazov had as much right to be there as she

had. He smiled faintly as she saw him, then looked away.
The organ grew louder. The procession came in, Canon Barrimore at the end of it, with his head held erect and his chin
tucked well in.

"It is Mr. Hendry who is playing!" whispered Miss
Creswell.

"But how do you know?"

"I know his way of playing."

The organ ceased, and the precentor's light tenor voice was
lifted up in the opening words of the service, "When the
wicked man," etc. Imogen saw Canon Barrimore looking at
her from his "return" stall, then looking at Berazov. Mrs.
Barrimore was nearly opposite to her, tall, lean and enigmatic,
with that faint smile which was characteristic of her hover-
ing on her lips. Some trippers in the seats near the painted
tombs between the choir stalls and the altar rails were gazing
up at the pillars, the arches, the colored windows, with eyes
that looked almost stupefied and uncritical. Imogen glanced at
the American woman with Berazov. She looked alert and
full of interest, as if she were taking it all in. When Canon
Barrimore read the lessons sonorously she listened with rapt
attention. Imogen thought, "She is new to English cathedrals.
She is sucking in one more experience." And she was disturbed. The streaming sense of religion had gone from her.
She felt plucking at her the claw-like fingers of the world.
In vain she tried to abstract herself. She could not. When
the anthem was sung she remained seated, sunk deep in her
carven stall. But even then she felt those fingers about her.
And it seemed to her that she was frustrated.

Why had Berazov come? She was resolved not to speak to
him. When the service was over she and her aunt would stay
in their places till the outgoing voluntary was finished, and
then go away by the side door that led into the precincts
opposite to Mr. Hendry's house. By doing that they would
surely avoid Berazov. And when the last Amen was sung
Imogen whispered:

"I want to stay for the voluntary."

Miss Creswell nodded.

That day Hendry played a sonata of Rheinberger. Imogen listened to it with shut eyes, determined not to look at
Berazov, not to give him even a glance of dismissal or farewell. Her mind was busy about Hugo. Nevertheless it

found time to concern itself with Berazov. And always it
seemed to be filled in some mysterious way by the third man,
by Peter Kharkoff. She could not release herself from these
three men. And she was thinking of the organist, too.

"Can't we go to tea at Mr. Hendry's house when it's over?"
she whispered in the last movement of the sonata.

"Do you want to?"

"Yes, very much."

"And what about Canon Barrimore? He's sure to——"

"I want to go to Mr. Hendry's. Let's go out by the side
door. Hush! I must listen."

She turned a little in her stall, always keeping her eyes
closed.

When the last chord was struck, filled the choir with sound,
ceased, she opened her eyes.

Berazov was gone.

"Let us catch Hendry as he goes out," said Imogen, getting up.

"Very well. We'll try to if you like. But he may be going
somewhere. He mayn't want us."

"If we come across him I'll make him want us."

When they came out of the choir on the top of the steps
leading down to the nave Imogen at once saw Berazov with
his white-haired companion lingering by the tomb of a bishop
near the second pulpit. Berazov was looking towards her, was
evidently on the lookout for her.

"Come on, Towser!" she said abruptly. "We'll go by the
side door. And—lucky!—there's Hendry!"

At that moment the organist, in a Norfolk jacket and gray
flannel trousers, his ardent hair sticking up on his head in
energetic confusion, came hurrying along behind the screen
that shut in the right-hand side of the choir. He saw them
and stopped, but like a man who meant to go on again in
an instant.

"Hullo!" he said. "Good afternoon."

He looked at Imogen with his acute, clever eyes, and she
saw an expression of surprise come into his face. No doubt
he had noticed the absence of paint from it.

"What was that you played?" she asked.

"Rheinberger. Like him?"

"Yes. But he's made me thirsty. May we come to tea
with you?"

Mr. Hendry looked rather embarrassed.

"I should be delighted of course."

"But you're busy," interposed Miss Creswell sensitively. 'You've got something to do."

"Oh, as to that I've always got something to do, but——"

"You've met Mr. Kharkoff," said Imogen. "I've been seeing him at Sainte Maxime. I thought I should like to speak to you about him."

"I'll give you tea with pleasure. I oughtn't to, because, to tell the truth, I've got a sort of engagement. But I'll let it go. Do come on please!"

His manner was amazingly offhand, though not the least rude, because it was so perfectly natural. Imogen rather liked it. He strode on with his loose-limbed, careless walk, with them beside him, crossed the grass and came to his gate.

"Here we are. Do come in. Oh, there's the canon with a couple of friends!"

"Don't wait for them!" Imogen whispered to him. "Come, Aunt Annie!"

And she hurried into the garden, followed by her aunt and the organist, both looking surprised.

"I'm afraid Canon Barrimore will think you rather rude, Im," said Miss Creswell gently. "He's so fond of you, and he saw you in cathedral."

"I can see him tomorrow. But I'm not in the mood for strangers after the Rheinberger."

Hendry looked pleased.

"I say strangers," Imogen added after a moment of apparent hesitation. "But I know one of them."

"The good-looking woman with white hair?" said her aunt.

"No, the man. He's a Russian. I've met him in London."

She turned to Hendry who was just stretching out his long fingers to ring the drawing-room bell.

"An interesting man," she continued. "A thorough man of the world. Not like our friend, Mr.—I mean Peter Kharkoff."

Hendry looked eager. But before he could say anything his parlor-maid opened the door.

"Tea for three, Lucy, please. And be as quick as you can."

"Yes, sir."

"And——"

"Sir?"

Hendry looked at his two guests with a sort of boyish, half-shy whimsicality.

"Shall we have it in here?"

"Just as you like," said Miss Creswell.

"The fact is I *loathe* this room."

Lucy, standing at the door, looked as if something had bitten her.

"Can't help it, Lucy! I do. Still it's the drawing room, I suppose, so shall we——"

"I hate it too," said Imogen.

"That's good!" he cried, smiling. "Tea in the muddle, Lucy."

As they crossed the little hall he said in his high-pitched energetic voice,

"That room's cold even in summer. But the muddle keeps this one cozy and warm at all times. I've no taste in arranging a house. I just know what I hate and what I like. Let me move some of that music for you."

Bending he hastily picked up some manuscripts and scores out of the chairs and threw them on tables.

"I've got a bad habit of filling the chairs," he said. "That's better. Do please sit down."

Miss Creswell obeyed, but Imogen remained standing. As she looked round the untidy room she was thinking of a room in Geneva; as she looked at the writing table covered with music sheets, pamphlets, letters and newspapers, she was thinking of a bare table on which stood an hour-glass and a lamp that shone out into snowbound darkness. In this room of a worker, so different from Peter Kharkoff's, she nevertheless felt Peter Kharkoff as she had not felt him since she had come back to England.

"This man works," she thought. "And *he* thinks. And he has thought here."

And then she remembered the books which she hadn't read, and the figure carved in wood which she hadn't seen, and the studio in the derelict garden. He worked too. But she had, perhaps, only seen his thought-room.

Her aunt and the organist were talking. Perhaps they had seen that she was for the moment absorbed in thought. Lucy, still looking as if she had been bitten, brought in the tea, and Imogen sat down in a well-worn armchair and was ministered to by her host in rather an awkward, slap-dash way.

She realized that he was what is sometimes called an "original," also that he was a clever, shyish gentleman, intellectual and cultivated, but not at all a man of the world. In everything he was the antithesis of Berazov, but she felt attracted by his obvious genuineness. And there was something in his searching, and yet sometimes shy, or at any rate conscious, glance which interested her and made her feel sympathetic towards him. He was, she felt sure, much more than a capable organist, even than an accomplished musician.

"You know Peter Kharkoff," she said presently, with bluntness, realizing that with this man no preparing of the ground was necessary. "My aunt told me so."

"I've met him once," said Hendry. "That's all."

Imogen looked at him earnestly.

"It was enough?" she said.

"Enough to go on with. Enough to—well, one can tell the sort of thing a dish is by one taste, what a book must be by two or three pages, can't one? And so with music. A few bars of Beethoven are enough in a way. But one wants more. One can judge by very little, but that very little gives one a jolly big longing for the whole."

"His whole! You'll never have that."

"Perhaps not. And yet one might in a way."

"What way?"

"I think great men have a power of giving themselves sometimes in concentrated form, in the round as it were. Little men haven't. The world in one action, one sentence—can't a great man sometimes give that? His world, I mean, himself."

He leaned forward. His upspringing hair shook and his eyes glowed.

"I'll give you an instance of a great man giving you the whole in a sentence."

"Do."

"Christ, when he said, 'Father, forgive them for they know not what they do.'"

"That's true," said Miss Creswell.

"Yes," said Imogen, looking down.

There was a silence. Then she said, "Do you think Peter Kharkoff a great man?"

"I do."

"But in what way is he great?"

"Well, I felt the universal in him as I've never felt it in any man before. And I felt truth in him as I've never felt it in any other man."

"And—that's all?"

"Isn't it enough?"

"You've never read any books which might be by him?"

"No. Oh, by the way!"

He jerked out the words with almost startling energy.

"What is it?" asked Miss Creswell.

He turned sharply to her.

"You told me your niece had once seen an extraordinary bust in wood, called 'Pure thought divorced from emotion.'"

"I did," said Imogen. "It was carved by a Swiss who——"

"No, it wasn't!"

"But he told me——"

"A lie. That's nothing unusual."

"How do you know it was a lie?"

"Peter Kharkoff carved that bust. I wrote to him about it. (I write to him sometimes.) He used to know your Swiss, found talent in him, and gave him the bust—I think because he wanted to fan the talent into inspiration. Kharkoff likes to help things along. The result in this particular instance was a damnable lie."

"How absolutely disgusting! But when he knew—when Peter Kharkoff knew?"

"He didn't make any comment to me about the fellow's conduct."

"The bust was by him! How extraordinary! Once I thought it was like him. I don't mean physically."

"I know exactly what you mean," Hendry said.

"But I was wrong."

"Yes?"

"His thought is pure, purer than the thought of anyone else I have ever known. But I'm quite sure now that it's not divorced from emotion. Oh no! But I've got to think that three-fourths, perhaps, of the average person's emotion is just sentimentality."

"True! True! True!" cried Hendry. "And so we lose touch with the genuine thing, because we're forever playing about with what is at any rate half false, half gimcrack, half——"

He broke off. Then abruptly he exclaimed:

"I hate sugar, but not the sweetness that comes out of flowers. There's all the difference. That man must feel tremendously, under his power of thought. I say!"

"Yes?" said Imogen.

"I am going to spend my holiday with him."

"In Switzerland?"

"Yes; in Sils-Maria, where Nietzsche used to write. Grand work his, wasn't it? I've fed on it. But it isn't enough. Not by far."

"When are you going?"

"August. I'm an organist, you see. All the ordinary blokes take their holiday in August. So I have to. Schoolmasters, organists, bank clerks, curates, off we all go in August. And I'm going there."

His eyes shone, and he looked like an enthusiastic and clever boy.

"Sils-Maria!" he repeated.

Imogen turned towards her aunt, who, as in the room with the hour-glass, had been merely a listener to a conversation which interested her profoundly.

"I think Hugo is going there too," she said.

"To Sils? But I thought——"

"He seems to have no wish to come back to London."

The two women looked at each other for a moment in silence. In that silence Imogen of course read the thought that was in her aunt's mind.

"If you go to Sils-Maria," she said to Hendry, "probably you'll meet Captain Dennistone. You know about his accident."

"Yes, poor chap!"

"If he is there be as nice to him as you can."

"By Jove, I will, Miss Lowrie. You may depend upon that. But——" he hesitated.

"Yes?" she said.

"But won't you be there?"

"I? Oh no! Why should I?"

"It's only that I thought—I understand that——"

He glanced at Miss Creswell and back to Imogen, got very red, and then said:

"Well, I wish you were to be there. And I'm sure others will wish it too."

"I don't think so," said Imogen.

She sent a glance to her aunt, and Towser got up.

"We mustn't keep you any longer, Mr. Hendry. Thank you for letting us come in."

"I'm glad you came."

He looked hard at Imogen with his rather piercing yet somehow shy eyes.

"I've enjoyed it. We all three know Peter Kharkoff. We all three think much the same of him, I suppose. Doesn't it somehow seem to"—he reddened again—"to bring us together?"

"But I'm sure he doesn't want disciples," said Imogen.

"No. He doesn't seek anything of that kind. But he doesn't reject us."

"Not you. For you are going to Sils-Maria. Good-by."

Hendry seized rather than took Imogen's hand.

"Good-by. I admire you most tremendously for what you've done. You know what I mean. Good-by, Miss Creswell. I'll let you out. I won't ring for Lucy. She's upset—about the drawing-room, you know. She thinks it's fine."

With a jerk he had the front door open and let them out.

"Shall you be at cathedral tomorrow?" he asked.

His eyes were on Imogen.

"In the evening I probably shall," she answered.

"I'll fish out something fine to play for you. D'you like Bach?"

"Is there anyone who cares for music and doesn't like Bach?"

"The sentiment there isn't sentimentality, eh? Good-by."

He stood at his door with his enthusiastic hair sticking up, to watch them leave him.

"That's a genuine chap!" said Imogen. "Genuine to the core. One could even tell that by his ridiculous hair. Every separate hair seems to say, 'This is how I am. I can't help it. Take me, or leave me. I've got to be like this.' There's something almost comic in his sincerity. And—and something pathetic too. *He'll* never be a man of the world."

"No indeed!"

"What diversity there is in human nature, Towser. Think of those four men: Peter Kharkoff, Hugo, Hendry and Berazov! But I forgot. You don't know Berazov, the Russian who sat opposite to us in the cathedral today. Now he is a man of the world to his long finger-tips. He——"

She broke off. A large motor had just glided up beside them and stopped.

"Miss Lowrie!"

Imogen saw Berazov's large melancholy eyes, and the hand which had held hers pulling back the catch of the motor's door.

"I couldn't go without greeting you."

He was out, standing beside them. She introduced him to her aunt. He, in turn, said:

"Mrs. Burnse-Laman would so like to know you—both. May I——"

And then the handsome, white-haired head of the American appeared leaning out from the motor.

"Of course we saw you in the cathedral," said Berazov when the introductions had been made. "We motored over from Auderley Castle."

"And had tea with that delightful Canon Barrimore," said Mrs. Burnse-Laman from the motor. "He was very distressed, Miss Lowrie, that you chose the organist instead of him as your host for tea. He hinted that you had been guilty of lese-majesty."

Without waiting for a reply, in a high clear voice, very self-possessed and *mondaine,* a voice that to Imogen suggested American life in Paris, she engaged Miss Creswell in quite an ardent conversation about English cathedrals and English cathedral life, always leaning politely out of the motor.

"Will you be in London on Monday?" asked Berazov.

"Yes."

"Let me see you. Let's dine together—at the Tour d'Eméraude. Shall we?"

"I believe I'm engaged to ever so many things."

"Break your engagements."

"I don't see why I should."

"Will you meet me on Monday?"

"I don't really think I can."

"If you don't, if you refuse, d'you know what I shall do?"

"Haven't an idea."

"I shall take the night train to Paris and Sainte Maxime."

"Don't be absurd."

"I shall do it."

"My people leave the villa on Sunday."

"I'm not going to see your people."

"You may not see—anyone."

"I'll take my chance of that."

She looked into his large gray eyes.

"I believe you would."

"Dine with me on Monday."

"Perhaps I will."

"I'll fetch you at eight."

"—religion in a sort of green drowsiness of dreaming. That is how it seems to me, straight from Paris."

"Oh, I hope it's awake."

"No, no! Take away the drowsiness from these marvelous old places and all the charm would go with it. My esthetic sense—ah, we must go! Yes. It's a long way to Auderley Castle. Good-by. Good-by. Lese-majesty, Miss Lowrie! You must make it up with that dear, clever canon. He was really like a lover deprived. Wasn't he, Count? Good-by!"

"Good-by!" said Berazov.

He shut the door, leaned back. The motor glided away, turned to the left through the archway and vanished.

CHAPTER VIII

IMOGEN was not much given to confidences of any importance. But before she left Drearney on the Monday for London she allowed Towser to see at any rate a little into her heart. She told her nothing about Berazov, did not seem to have him in her mind. And Miss Creswell, perhaps naturally, asked no questions about him. But they discussed Imogen's connection with Hugo, and Imogen allowed her aunt to know how disturbed she was about Hugo's desire and intention—for it seemed to be not less than that—to go from Sainte Maxime to Switzerland instead of coming to London and her.

To Miss Creswell this reluctance on Hugo's part to come to England seemed very strange, but she would not allow for a moment that it proved that his love for Imogen was diminished.

"It must be," the girl said with obstinacy. "I judge by facts. A man who loves a girl always wants to be with her or at any rate near her. You know that as well as I do, Towser."

"I *know* Hugo Dennistone is deeply in love with you," said Miss Creswell.

"Men are far more mysterious than we women generally think them. Hugo—yes, even old Hugo is mysterious. I didn't think a time could ever come when I should say that of him with conviction. But it's true. You say you know Hugo loves me. Well, it was he who sent me away from Sainte Maxime."

"Sent you away?"

"Yes. He wanted me to go and that was enough for me. I went. I left him with Peter Kharkoff. And now he doesn't want to come back to me."

"Perhaps he dreads coming back to England where he knows so many people. Perhaps it's on account of his condition. A crippled man might wish to hide himself."

"Hugo isn't like that. He's essentially brave."

"Of course I know that. But he may have become very sensitive."

"He has. He's far more sensitive than he used to be, or seem. But a man of Hugo's type wouldn't shrink from facing his friends in England as a cripple by the side of a girl he loved."

"Can there be another reason?"

"What reason?"

"Suppose he thought, has come to think, that you don't love him?"

"I asked him to marry me. *I* asked *him.*"

"Yes? But even so—do you love him, Im?"

"I care very much for Hugo."

"I'm sure you do, but still——"

"I have a feeling for Hugo I have for no one else, could never have for anyone else. He's the man who has always cared for me, and he's stricken, helpless. Should I be a woman if I hadn't a deep feeling for him?"

"No; you must care for him."

"I do. And now he doesn't want to come to me. He prefers to go to Switzerland and to be with Peter Kharkoff."

"You don't mean to say you are jealous of Mr. Kharkoff?"

"If I were I don't think it would be strange. Do you?"

"But d'you think that Mr. Kharkoff is influencing Hugo against you?"

"I don't believe Hugo would ever have wished me to leave

the villa before he did if Peter Kharkoff hadn't been there.
I know he wouldn't. And of course it's obvious that he is
going to Switzerland—for he will go, I know it—because of
Peter Kharkoff. There's no other reason. I see quite clearly
into this matter."

"Then, if you do see clearly, why is Mr. Kharkoff trying
to take Hugo Dennistone away from you?"

"I couldn't tell you that."

"Then you don't see clearly."

"Not into Peter Kharkoff—no. My faculties are too limited
for that. And so are everyone else's. The question is now—
what am I going to do?"

Miss Creswell looked at her niece rather anxiously.

"This is an opportunity for freeing myself," Imogen continued. "When I left the villa I told Hugo I wished our
marriage to take place as soon as possible. I said there was
nothing to wait for. And there isn't. Hugo's condition will
never change. He will always be as he is now. I told him
that as soon as he followed me to London I was ready to marry
him. And now he's going to Switzerland."

Miss Creswell laid a hand on one of Imogen's.

"Dear Im, I'm afraid this is hurting you very much."

"Well, it isn't very pleasant, is it? You are ready to devote
your life to a man—and then he doesn't want you."

"That is what I don't believe, what I will never believe,"
said Miss Creswell with decision. "I am positive Hugo
Dennistone adores you."

"This is a very odd way of showing it."

"But you yourself say that men are mysterious. Then there
may be something hidden in all this."

"When I asked Hugo to marry me he didn't say no. He
wanted me. No man ever wanted a woman more than he
wanted me then. But then he had never seen Peter Kharkoff."

"Im—tell me—what do you think has happened?"

"I don't know. I have thought, and thought about it, but
I don't know."

"And what will you do?"

"One of two things, Towser. At least I believe so. I
shall either give up the whole thing—and if I do it will be a
real giving up, drastic, old Towser; a thorough giving up not
only of Hugo, but of Hugo's Influence and Guide, of Peter
Kharkoff—or else I shall go out to Switzerland and play my

own hand. One or the other of these two things I shall do.
You may be sure of that. And now let's talk of something
else. I wonder what Mr. Hendry will play for us tonight."

He played for them Bach's great Fugue in C Minor. Afterwards Imogen thanked him. They all went to supper at the
Barrimores' house, where Imogen was forgiven for her lese-
majesty, perhaps partly because she was genuinely enthusiastic
about the canon's sermon, which had had no postscript this
time.

Early on the Monday morning she went back to London.

When she was in London and had driven to Lowndes
Square she found the servants preparing for the arrival of her
father and mother. On the morrow they would be there.
She would be once more en famille.

Meanwhile there was Berazov to deal with.

She resolved that she would spend the evening of that day
with him. She believed that if she put him off, refused to
see him, to be with him, he would do what he had threatened
to do. She wasn't afraid about that. Why should she be?
If Berazov chose to seek Peter Kharkoff in Sainte Maxime
that didn't concern her. Indeed, when she thought about
it, she found herself wishing that Berazov, the Jew-hater,
could confront the Jew who so strangely interested him.
But she felt that she must see him, that she had to see
him. She hadn't decided which of the two things she was
going to do. Until she saw Berazov again she felt that she
couldn't decide. He had pushed himself into her life. He
had thrust in—she felt that now—farther than she had
realized. If Hugo wouldn't have her, wouldn't allow her to
sacrifice herself, if Peter Kharkoff withdrew himself from her,
taking Hugo with him, she must have something. And she
knew that Berazov was beginning to love her. She must see
him that night.

The organist came up before her. Why was that? She
didn't know. What had he to do with all this?

It occurred to her that if she decided to go out to Switzerland she would meet him there. But surely she wouldn't go.
Since she was sixteen she was accustomed to be pursued.
Always people had come trailing after her. Was she now
to be the pursuer? And then she remembered her former
journey to Switzerland, when she had gone to Geneva. Hadn't
that been a pursuit? When she thought of that she felt that

she couldn't make a second journey to Switzerland. That would be too humiliating. And they wouldn't want her. She had no reason to think they would want her.

And yet was it possible that Hugo had got beyond wanting her? She thought of the look in his eyes, the touch of his hands, the trembling of his poor body against hers. How he must have changed if he didn't want her any longer.

But—there are irresistible things! She had said that, and when she had said it she had felt that it was true. She had forgotten free will then. She did not think of it now. It seemed to her that if Peter Kharkoff chose he could take Hugo away from her. Whether he really wished to do that she didn't know. Why he should wish to do it she could not imagine. But she could not deny his power, for the most real and intimate part of her asserted it.

She broke her engagements for that evening. When eight o'clock struck she was simply dressed in one of her plainest frocks and waiting for Berazov.

As soon as the bell sounded and Henry brought him in she said, "I'm coming out to dine with you. But don't let us go to the Tour d'Eméraude."

"Anywhere you like," he said, taking her hand very gently and holding it.

"Let's go to some out-of-the-way place where we shan't know anyone."

"But certainly. Shall we dine quietly at Victoria Station, or at the Euston Hotel, or at one of the Lyons Restaurants? Isn't there a peaceful little place called the Corner Cottage? What about that?"

"I never heard of it. No; not any of those."

"Chelsea? Soho? Simpson's in the Strand? The Monico? Odennino's? I am ready for anything."

"There's an out-of-the-way hole in Chelsea. We might perhaps go there. It's called the Black Cat. Do you know it?"

"No."

"In a corner just by a stable yard. It's almost in the stable-yard, not very far from the river. Plane Tree Corner, they call it."

" 'The Black Cat, Plane Tree Corner, Chelsea'! It smiles on me. Let's go there."

She looked at him, seemed to hesitate, then said, "Yes; we will."

She put on a thin dark cloak. She was wearing a dark little hat that came down rather low on her forehead.

"You've got a taxi?"

"Yes."

As they started she thought, "I wonder whether I shall ever go out anywhere with this man again."

It was an odd thought. Something cold, almost sinister about it; no intimacy in it, no warmth, no kindness even. And the expression "this man" was an ugly one. Yet that was how she put it in her thought. And then immediately she wondered—what did such a thought mean? Why had it come to her? There was a strange dreariness about it.

Henry opened the hall door.

"Why——" she said, surprised. "It's raining!"

"Yes. It began half an hour ago," said Berazov.

Henry opened an umbrella. She walked under it to the cab. As she got in she felt as if she were going out to spend the evening with a stranger. Everything about her seemed peculiar, the summer night, the rain, the cab, Henry with the umbrella, Berazov getting in after her.

"Tell him, will you? The Black Cat, Plane Tree Corner, Erlie Street, Chelsea," she said in a low voice.

Berazov leaned out and gave the direction.

"Does he know it?"

"Yes, I think so."

As they drove off she saw Henry looking at her with steady, civil, but surely wondering eyes.

In the cab they were silent. It seemed to Imogen that Berazov took his silence from her, that he had to take it. He had meant to talk. It would have been natural to talk. But she infected him with silence. And so they drove on through the wet warm streets, and the summer breathed on them sadly, and gave to them and the city its tears.

They soon came into Chelsea. The chauffeur took a round-about way and drove them along by the river. Berazov was sitting on Imogen's left, and she saw him staring out of the window on that side. She saw part of his right cheek, his ear, his neck, some thick hair below the edge of his black soft hat. All that she saw looked to her melancholy. Why was he staring out at the river and the falling rain? She felt sorry for him and for herself. Both of them were lonely creatures. Although he was very rich he had lost a great

deal, almost everything. And it seemed to her that evening
that she had very little. Her impudent joy of life was gone,
her immense self-satisfaction, her young carelessness, her sense
of her power.

Drawing out the catalogue of the lost she went beyond her
sense of power, and came back to it. Hugo's last letter had
been a terrible blow, although she had—hadn't she?—been
expecting it. It had been a blow under which she was quivering still. That no doubt was why she was feeling so melancholy now, and why everything looked strange to her, as
things look in the light and darkness of storm. But she must
react against the blow. She must come to some decision.
And this man sitting beside her could perhaps help her to
decide. But could he? She knew that she had infected him
with her mood, that he had come that evening feeling pleased,
even perhaps triumphant, because she had broken her engagements for him, had yielded beneath the pressure of his wish.
But now he was silent, distrait, melancholy. Her mood had
overcome his.

"He's weak!" she thought. "There is weakness in him."

She looked beyond him out of the window and saw a bridge
spanning the dark, rain-washed river.

"He's gone too far," she said.

Berazov started.

"Please tell him to go back a little way, and then to the
left, and then I'll direct him."

Berazov leaned out and spoke to the man. They went
back. Then Imogen told him. Almost directly they drew
up at a small black and white corner house, above the narrow
door of which was a black cat carved in wood with an arched
back and a lifted tail.

It was pouring rain now.

Imogen hurried into the house while Berazov was paying
the chauffeur.

The restaurant was on the first floor at the top of a narrow
staircase, and consisted of two moderate-sized rooms. Probably these rooms had once been a double drawing-room. Now
they were decorated in black and white. On the walls were
panels of white with black borders. And in each panel appeared a black cat, fierce, sly, amorous, surreptitious, seductive, spitting or purring. There were deep black settees with
cushions along the walls with dinner tables in front of them.

The electric lamps were hidden under white silk shades with black trimmings. The woman servants were dressed in black and white.

When Imogen and Berazov came in, there were only three people dining; a short, fat, determined-looking girl, with jet-black clubbed hair cut in a dense fringe across her forehead, who was accompanied by a pale anemic young man, with fluffy brown hair, a mustache and a tiny fan-shaped beard, and a very old lady in green, on whose touzled old head was a hat trimmed amazingly with a stuffed parrot.

As Imogen and Berazov passed her she was picking at a sardine, holding a fork in bony fingers covered with diamond rings. The anemic man was whispering to his determined companion who was eating white soup. The rain could be heard behind windows covered with thin black silk curtains.

"A funny little place!" said Berazov. "I suppose it has heard of Montmartre. Is it run by a Frenchman?"

"He calls himself a Roumanian."

They sat down side by side on one of the black settees and ordered dinner. And still Imogen felt that everything was peculiar. She had dined at the "Black Cat" several times with various people, but she had never been aware of its atmosphere as she was aware of it now. In its black and white coquetry there was something spurious and sad. The couple opposite were like whispering phantoms in a not strong dream. The old woman with the parrot in her hat was a tragic grotesque.

"What is the matter?" said Berazov in his soft, warm voice.

"You feel things are wrong tonight, out of gear?"

"How can I help feeling them so when you are like this? Shall we have champagne?"

"Oh yes, do let us!" she said.

Anything to carry them a little way from this weighing melancholy. He looked at the wine list and ordered something. Then he laid the list down and said again:

"What is the matter?"

Imogen looked at her soup plate.

"I scarcely know. Why didn't I let you go tonight?"

"To Sainte Maxime?"

"Yes. You would have gone?"

"Oh yes, if you had refused. I had made up my mind."

"And when you had got there?"

"I should have found out your Jew."

"And then?"

"What then wouldn't have depended only on me."

"No. How would it have been?"

She wondered—intensely. Peter Kharkoff would have overcome Berazov's Jew-hatred. That was all she knew.

"You should know better than I can, knowing him."

"Yes. But what do we know?"

"Damnably little," said Berazov moodily.

He looked across the room at the old lady with the parrot.

"I don't want to be the male counterpart of that old specter some day," he said. "Eating alone in a restaurant on a night of rain."

He shivered, and she realized how slim he was. And she wondered about his health.

"A stuffed parrot for one's company!" he added. "How awful!"

"You will always be able to find someone to be with," she said.

"Someone! What is the good of that? I have been with *someone* and felt desperate because of the loneliness."

She felt sure he was thinking of his dead wife, and probably of his life with her in South America.

"Yes, please open the champagne," he said to the golden-haired girl who was waiting on them, and who looked like an artist's model.

"Do you ever feel lonely?" he said, turning to Imogen.

"Yes," she said.

It struck her that she had never known a feeling of real loneliness, the stricken feeling, before she had met the Unearthly. He had subtly deprived her of the immense self-confidence which till then had buoyed her up almost as if on wings. He had made her feel dependent. And with this feeling of dependence the lonely feeling had come.

"Do you feel lonely tonight?" he persisted.

"Yes."

"I am glad. When one feels lonely," he continued, "it is nearly always as if one were the only creature in all the world cursed by that misery."

"Look at those two," Imogen said in a very low voice. "They are quarreling!"

The man with the tiny fan-shaped beard and the fat girl

with clubbed hair were evidently involved in a serious difference of opinion on the settee opposite. The girl, frowning heavily, was gesticulating with both her large-fingered hands, which she was thrusting forward towards the man's face, while she belabored him with words spoken in a hoarse voice of the streets. He, flushed and evidently agitated, pushed his tiny beard out and up towards her face as if hypnotized by her anger. He placed a pale hand on her leg. She slapped it with a "Take it away!"

"Ladybird!" he ejaculated in a voice rising towards soprano heights.

"I forbid you to call me that!" she responded. "I'm sick of you and your nonsense. Pay the bill. That's all you're good for. I'm going."

"But we haven't——"

"I'm—going!"

She got up. He pulled her down by her rose-colored skirt. She grunted, as if the sudden pull and the sitting down had half choked her. A sharp "Hush!" came from him. She stared across the room at Imogen and Berazov. The conversation declined into a muddle of violent whispering. Across an omelette aux fines herbes the old lady with the stuffed parrot looked on with an eager interest in which deep experience sat enthroned. Two young men in evening dress came in with an air of slightly self-conscious hauteur. The man with the tiny fan of hair cried "Please!" to a waitress, and ordered half a bottle of champagne, *Gout Américain.* The old lady with the parrot ordered a Kirsch.

"Loneliness would be better than that, don't you think?" said Imogen.

But he didn't agree with her, or didn't choose to agree, and they began to discuss human relations. Berazov asserted that many people enjoy a quarrel because it leads eventually to an amorous reconciliation.

"Those two will be all the happier tonight," he said, looking across the room at the pale man, who was anxiously pouring champagne into the fat girl's glass. "Because they have had a row. Even the average fool, without being aware of it, gets sick of going always on the level."

"How extraordinary well you speak English," she said.

"I was brought up as a child to speak it by English nurses and governesses."

They ate. They drank champagne. They talked. It seemed that their weight of melancholy was lifting. Imogen realized that it was far easier for her to talk with Berazov than with Hugo crippled. Compared with Berazov Hugo was slow. But how genuine he was, how tremendously real. If only he were a whole man! There would surely have been no difficulties between them then. They would have married and lived a great life together, a life in which sport would have predominated. And they would have had remarkable children.

This thought of children brought with it a horrible insight, seemed to uncover a knowledge that had, perhaps for long, lain hidden in some secret place of her. In one way she shrank from Hugo now. And it was just in that way that she was drawn towards Berazov. Could Hugo have divined that dim repugnance on her part? Could that have anything to do with this strange withdrawal which was causing her so much pain? But, if it were so, then perhaps the influence of the Unearthly had not been upon him when he had sent her away.

"What are you thinking about?" said Berazov with a touch of irritation. "You look at me. You talk to me. You drink champagne with me. But—where are you?"

"Here," she said, forcing herself to smile.

"You are considering something, weighing something up. Even when we were starting to come here, just when we were going out of your house, I noticed it. You gave me such a look. It was as cold as the north wind over the Steppes."

She remembered her thought about "this man."

"I'm sorry," she said.

"You've made me care for you, really care. You understand? Really!"

"You didn't care really that night."

"No."

He glanced at the golden-haired waitress, who was a little way off, standing against the black and white wall in a quiet, graceful pose.

"I'm sure she has sat to painters," he said.

"What made you look at her just then?" she asked, as he looked again at her.

"I don't know."

"I do."

She felt an abrupt disgust, even a sensation of revolt. But it was not only against something in him. It was also against something in herself and in the greater number of those whom she knew.

"What was it?"

"Something I sometimes hate."

"I know. But can you get beyond it?"

"Could you get beyond it in caring for me?"

"Yes, now," he said, lowering his voice. "Something in you—I don't know what—seems to be leading me away from the mere physical desire I had for you to something strangely different. I am speaking sincerely."

"Yes."

"Are you—are you disgusted? I don't mean——"

"Don't explain, because I understand."

"Then why do you look at me like that?"

"How?"

"As if you were asking endless questions about me and yourself."

"Perhaps I am."

"What has happened since we were at Silvia Moray's?"

"How can you tell that anything special has happened?"

"By you. By your atmosphere—whatever you choose to call it."

He poured some more champagne into her glass. On the other side of the room the two quarreling lovers were now dreadfully reconciled, and the fat girl had lifted her right hand to toy with the tiny fan of hair on her pale cavalier's weak chin. The old lady with the parrot was inflexibly disputing her bill with the waitress. The two young men were eating their dinner coldly and sharing a bottle of Medoc. Imogen looked at them all and then again at Berazov. She had an odd longing to be very sincere with him. Tonight she was able to pity him, and she liked him better than she had ever liked him before, despite the fact, or perhaps because of the fact, which he had acknowledged and which she felt, that his desire for her had undergone a definite change.

"Can't you tell me what has happened?" he asked, still in the very low voice.

"Well, you know that I considered myself engaged to Hugo Dennistone."

"Yes. Everyone seems to know that."

"I've had a letter from him. I don't think he's coming back to London to marry me."

Berazov sat looking at her in silence.

"Evidently he doesn't want to come to London."

"He wants you to go out to him?"

"Oh no! He doesn't suggest that. He seems quite satisfied to be without me. I think he will go to Switzerland. In
fact I'm sure he will."

"All alone?"

"I don't think he'll go alone."

After a pause Berazov said, "And you? Will you go to
Switzerland?"

"I? Without being asked? My dear Berazov, do you
really think I'm the type of girl who pursues a man with an
affection he doesn't want? I believe since the war which has
brought about such a dearth of men it's considered quite the
natural thing for women to chase after men. But I haven't
got the habit of doing that. No. I—I consider that my engagement to Hugo Dennistone is at an end."

"You are free?"

"Oh, as to that——" she said bitterly.

She broke off abruptly.

The old lady had at last settled her bill. Now she got up
with her head on one side, and went away, walking feebly.

"She's going back to her loneliness," said Imogen.

At that moment the sense of her own loneliness overwhelmed her.

"What is freedom?" she said desperately to Berazov.
"What that old woman's got? I'm not sure that I care about
freedom. But if it's forced upon me—what you call freedom
—I may as well try to get something out of it. This is the
last night I shall be alone in the house except for the servants."

"Yes?" he said.

Her voice had been ugly and hard. Her face seemed to
him ugly as she continued, "My people are coming back tomorrow. Let's go back after dinner, shall we?"

"Yes—yes," said Berazov.

He answered quickly, but she thought she detected a look
of hesitation, of reluctance, in his face.

"Give me some more champagne, will you?" she said.

He filled her glass. The fat girl and the man with the fan-
shaped beard got up and went out. The girl was holding his
arm.

"They're off to their complete reconciliation," she said.

"Yes," said Berazov again.

"How dull you are!" she exclaimed, with a sudden fierce irritation which amazed herself. "Do I bore you? Or do I horrify you? Or what is it?"

He didn't answer.

"Don't you want to come back with me?"

At that moment she felt like a girl of the street, who had accosted a man and been brutally thrown off.

"Of course I do."

But she didn't believe him. She felt sure he was lying. Nevertheless she got up.

"Let us go," she said.

Berazov signed to the golden-haired girl, who brought him the bill. He paid it and helped Imogen to put on her cloak. She was very pale now. She looked round the room.

"I shall never come here again," she said. "Never!"

"But why not?"

"All these black cats! It's like a room in a nightmare! And the rain always pouring down! Come along!"

Berazov followed her down the narrow stairs to the door giving on the street corner by the stable yard. The night was dark. The rain was very heavy. No cab was in sight. They stood waiting in the shelter of the doorway, over which there jutted out a protection of wood like an eyebrow. Berazov took hold of Imogen's arm.

"If you will marry me," he said. "I want you. But I want *you* now, not merely your sensuality. Do you understand?"

"Oh yes. I understand."

"Well?"

"I'm afraid I could only give you what you call my sensuality."

"Are you sure?"

"No. I'm not sure of anything tonight."

"Git you a kib, gen'leman?" said a hoarse voice at Berazov's elbow.

He started violently.

"Who's—?" He looked, and saw a thin youth, miserably clad and soaked with rain.

"Yes. Bring us a cab and I'll give you a shilling."

"Right, gen'leman!"

The night bird was gone. Berazov and Imogen stood to-

gether in silence waiting. The youth was away for a long
time, and all that time Imogen was giving herself up to the
darkness, and to the sound of rain which seemed to blot out
life with all its multitudinous sounds from her. She felt
secluded out of life. Did that French actress whom she had
known feel like that within the enclosed silence of her nunnery? Perhaps she had chosen well. Perhaps it was best to
be absolutely drastic in life, to give yourself whole either to
the world with all its pleasures, or to the other world with all
its promises. Imogen felt just then as if she had been more
complete before she had known Peter Kharkoff than she was
now. For there had been a completeness, a finish, in her
then absolute worldliness. Then she had lived whole-heartedly.
All her offerings had been laid on the altar of self. Now
wasn't she a sort of hybrid? She had tried for self-sacrifice.
But perhaps the trial had been half-hearted. For something
within her had held back. She hadn't loved Hugo enough to
be unselfish without feeling the burden. And then she had
tried for the joy of the senses—with Berazov. And again
she had been half-hearted. At the critical moment she had
once more held back. She had infected Hugo mysteriously
with doubt of her bona fides in unselfishness, with doubt of
her capacity for sacrifice and her capacity for love. And then
she had infected Berazov mysteriously with doubt of her bona
fides in desire, with doubt of her capacity for purely sensual
enjoyment and careless physical passion. The one man had
had doubts of her nobility, the other of her degradation.

What was she then?

It seemed to her at that moment that she was unable to give
herself wholly either to the splendor or to the squalor of life.
She saw herself miserably paddling in the shallows. Yet the
voice of the deep was in her ears. A frightful sensation of
feebleness and smallness overcame her.

Two lights shone through the rain. A taxicab came up, the
pale youth running beside it.

" 'Ere you are, gen'leman!"

Berazov put a shilling into the dirty hand held out to
receive it.

They drove to Lowndes Square in silence. When the cab
drew up before Lord Lowrie's door Berazov got out and was
going to pay the cabman. But Imogen stopped him.

"No. You must take him on."

Henry opened the hall door.

"But——"

"You mustn't come in.   What would be the use?"

She fancied that a look of relief went over his face.

Without another word she ran into the house through the rain, and Henry shut the hall door behind her.

Book Five—The Voice of the Deep

CHAPTER I

IN THE month of July in that year Hugo Dennistone and
Milligan arrived at the station of St. Moritz by an afternoon
train and were driven in a special carriage along the lake of
Silvaplana to the village of Sils-Maria, where they put up at
the Hotel Alpenrose, the last house in the village. Marfield,
Hugo's man, had been sent by his master to England for his
annual holiday. Peter Kharkoff had gone to Geneva.

Milligan couldn't fully understand "Mr. Hugo," as he now
always called his employer. Once he had thought he understood Mr. Hugo pretty well. But now he didn't know what
to make of him. And the situation they were in puzzled him.

Why had Miss Lowrie, the damned fine kid whom he so
ardently admired, gone off to London alone? And why, when
the villa at last was shut up, had Mr. Hugo decided to come
to Switzerland instead of joining her in London? There
was no talk of her coming out presently to join them. Indeed
there was scarcely any talk of her at all. She seemed to have
faded out of the picture.

Milligan thought it all over again and again in that wonderful air of the Engadine, which has something pitiless in its
purity.

Could Miss Lowrie have repented of her bargain? Could
she have sheered off after getting back to England and plung-
ing once more into London life? He didn't want to think
that. She was too fine surely to let a crippled man down
after promising to stick to him. Then was it Mr. Hugo's
doing? Had he drawn away from Miss Lowrie, deliberately,
without Miss Lowrie's wishing it, even against her will? Had
he "given up" Miss Lowrie? But he had been so mad keen
about her; and what had he to put in her place?

Mr. Kharkoff! Milligan considered the Jew. He had been

very glad—for his patient's sake—that Mr. Kharkoff was to
stay on in Sainte Maxime when Miss Lowrie went. His
alert nurse's instinct told him that Mr. Kharkoff was doing
his patient good. That remarkable man was surely, by some
mysterious means, drawing the sting from the tragedy of
Mr. Hugo. He seemed to be a medicine-man to the soul.
His influence was beneficent, almost as definitely beneficent
as can be the influence of a powerful drug, such as morphia,
over a body in torture. But the influence of a drug eventually
fades away; Mr. Kharkoff's surely remained. It was with
Mr. Hugo now, Milligan believed; indeed he felt sure of that.

Had Mr. Kharkoff somehow succeeded in taking Miss Lowrie's place? That a man of Milligan's type could even consider such a question was proof of the tremendous impression
made upon him by the Jew. Normally he would have considered that a man's "girl" must stand for practically everything to him. But the power—Milligan still called it "animal magnetism"—that emanated from Peter Kharkoff had a
curious enveloping quality. Even a girl's influence over her
lover might, Milligan felt, be affected by it, be perhaps diminished by it. Yet why should Mr. Kharkoff wish to counter-
act the influence of Miss Lowrie upon her lover, when he
was such a friend of Miss Lowrie's?

Thinking over this Milligan had a moment of wonder and
ugly doubt. Could Mr. Kharkoff be sweet on Miss Lowrie
himself? It was possible. Miss Lowrie was a splendid girl,
and Mr. Kharkoff was a strong, powerful man. But somehow—Milligan didn't know exactly why—it was difficult to
think of Mr. Kharkoff as in love with anyone. He wasn't
like ordinary men. He seemed free from their preoccupations.
He wasn't exactly up in the clouds, but he was surely very
intellectual. And—another thing—Milligan felt that he was
very straight. He could surely never try to substitute himself for Mr. Hugo by underhand methods. Milligan could
not doubt that he was a good friend of Mr. Hugo. And
Mr. Hugo held to him tremendously. There was no doubt
about that. Mr. Kharkoff was in Geneva now, but he was
very soon coming to Sils-Maria, and Mr. Hugo had taken
a sudden fancy to go there, knowing that he would have Mr.
Kharkoff's company there.

Yes—but had he forgotten Miss Lowrie?

Puzzling over it all Milligan presently got down to physical

things. His long experience of them suggested to him possibilities, even perhaps probabilities, which troubled him. He
knew a great deal about Mr. Hugo but there were things
which he didn't know. And now, in Switzerland, he wondered whether the body, the care of which was his particular
métier, had asserted itself at the expense of the heart and
soul—what Milligan called "the rest of it." It might be so,
and if it were so that would perhaps explain this separation
of Mr. Hugo from the beautiful girl in London. But then—
did she know? Had Mr. Hugo written to her, explained
things?

Milligan was not an inquisitive fellow. With his patients
he was always quite wonderfully discreet, and he carefully
avoided asking them unnecessary questions. He did not depart
from the rule he had made for himself now. He kept his
own counsel. But he watched Mr. Hugo closely without
seeming to. He turned things over in his mind. He even
went further; he pondered them in his heart.

He had never been in Switzerland before, though the war
had taken him as far afield as Serbia. The journey up the
world from Zurich had impressed him tremendously. Then
had come the drive from St. Moritz, and the settling down in
the quiet hotel with the white walls and the green shutters,
with the arcade and the small rough garden dotted with shining red seats. Beyond the low garden wall stretched a great
open space, like a vast green, unfenced lawn. This lay between the big lake of Sils and the smaller lake of Silvaplana
away on the right, and was faced by a wall of mountains
lightly powdered with fresh snow. For the summer had so
far been cold and rather severe among the heights, and the
snow lay lower down on the mountains than was usual at that
season of the year.

Milligan was deeply interested in everything that had to
do with bodily health and hygienic conditions. A new climate
was a fascinating study to him. And the climate of the
Upper Engadine seemed to him the most marked, the most
individual that he had ever been in.

"I've never struck anything quite like this before, sir," he
remarked to Mr. Hugo. "It seems somehow to take you
right out of yourself."

He saw a pair of bright blue eyes look at him with what
seemed a flicker of quite unusual interest.

"What do you mean exactly by that, Milligan?"

"I scarcely know how to say, sir. Don't you feel it though? There's something—it's as if you weren't quite yourself. It isn't exactly like being light-headed and yet in a way it's almost like that. It's a kind of getting away from everything sort of a feeling, even getting away from yourself."

"I know," said Hugo in his strong, gritty voice.

He was silent for a minute after he had said that. Milligan thought his voice had sounded quite solemn and somehow impressive in the brief remark.

"We have got away from things down below," Hugo added presently.

"That's true, sir. They say you have to get acclimatized up here, and that it takes time, in some cases as long as a month or six weeks. It's the height up of course."

"Yes. It's the height up. We have got to get accustomed to it."

Again Milligan noticed a curiously impressive tone in the very masculine voice, which somehow came rather startlingly from the supine frame. And now the very masculine blue eyes, eyes of a sportsman and a soldier, were looking away across the grass from which the hay had been gathered, towards the range of near mountains which closed in the view opposite, just beyond the highroad. The sun was shining that day, though there were clouds in the sky, and a pure, very cool and light wind came to them from the Maloja beyond which lay Italy. Milligan had wheeled the crippled man's couch far out into the midst of the plain.

They were alone on the roof of the world. Behind them, unseen by them, lay the small village, far enough away for its sounds to be beyond the reach of their ears. The cry of its waters was inaudible to them. But they could just hear the voice of the trout stream in front of them, clear, shallow, lively, flowing swiftly over its bed of polished stones.

"You wouldn't know how high up it was, sir, would you, except for the feel of the wind and seeing the snow so low down?" said Milligan. "Being surrounded as we are by mountains, I mean."

"I think I should. When I shut my eyes I can feel I'm far up."

As he spoke Hugo shut his eyes. Lying on his back, and now perfectly still, he looked like a man asleep in the vastness

of nature, placed out there in the midst of the great stretch
of grass, girdled by waters and guarded by mountains, that
he might sleep in tranquillity under the blue and white sky.
It seemed even as if the wind went over him carefully, lest
it might wake him. And Milligan, watching from his little
camp chair, had a thought not of sleep but of death. He had
seen many people die, both in and away from war. Sentimentality about either life or death was not characteristic of
him. Yet now as he looked at "Mr. Hugo" the thought came
to him, "Why isn't he let to die?" He had become very much
attached to Hugo. In consequence of that feeling of attach-
ment, for himself he couldn't wish Hugo to die. But now,
seeing the closed eyelids, the long motionless body, the
smoothed-out look of the bronzed forehead, he thought how
much better it would be for that quiet man if he were dead,
unless he was going to have the girl who had gone to London,
to comfort him in his married life. And yet what sort of
life would it be for a fine girl like that to be tied to a man who,
however male in nature, couldn't do anything active, almost
anything that the average man could do? And it wasn't even
the war that had brought him to that. If it had been——

"What are you thinking about, Milligan?"

Hugo had opened his eyes. They were looking at Milligan.
His voice sounded semi-suspicious, and Milligan felt himself
redden.

"I really couldn't say, sir. Nothing in particular. I
couldn't call myself a great thinker at any time, I'm afraid."

"No?"

"No, sir. Though of course as to that we all of us must
think. We can't help ourselves, can we?"

"Up here I seem to be able to think damned clearly."

"That's the air, sir."

"And the silence, and being away from everything. Just
now I was thinking of the war."

"Were you, sir?"

"Yes. Sometimes in the war I felt I'd give all I had and
more for a week of complete silence and nothing doing."

"I expect most of us felt like that at times, sir."

"I should say so. And I was thinking that now I've got
more than the week. Funny the contrasts in a chap's life—
isn't it?"

"Would you wish to go back, sir?"

"How d'you mean, go back?"

"Be as you were, sir, and the war still on?"

There was a long pause. To Milligan it seemed very long. At last Hugo said:

"Be as I was—no! But I should have before we were at Sainte Maxime."

And somehow Milligan knew that Mr. Hugo had turned his meaning, had turned it away from the body.

Hugo said nothing more till he asked Milligan to move his couch and let him have a good look at the lake of Sils before going back to the village. Milligan got up, folded the camp chair and obeyed.

"Thanks. Tilt it up a bit, will you please?"

Milligan tilted the head of the couch up so that the prostrate man could look out the more easily over the distant lake to Maloja.

"Am I too heavy to hold up for a minute or two?"

"Good Lord, sir, no. My arms are like iron. I could hold you for half an hour without feeling it."

"You're infernally strong, I know."

"Pretty well for that, sir. Why, when I was no more than sixteen——"

And then Milligan remembered himself and "dried up." He knew Mr. Hugo didn't want any of his gassing just then.

Holding up the end of the couch easily, and bracing his arms against it, he too looked out towards Italy, a land he had never seen. Beyond the many shades of green and of yellow in the rough lawn he saw the blue lake. (For it was blue that day.) Its wooded shores looked soft, even gentle. In the distance the water glittered in sunshine. Far off, at the end of the lake, stood a dusky palace at the opening of the pass leading to the southern lands, where olive and orange trees show their silver and gold, and the larches and stone pines are not. A barrier of noble mountains, dark but with blue in their darkness, closed in the view. Nearer, the snow powdered over the mountain tops above the ardently climbing fir trees, which seemed to aspire like living things, hinted at chastity in nature, suggested a possibility of mounting above the hugger-mugger of life into a region more serene, more pure.

"The hugger-mugger of life." That was how Hugo thought of it just then. He had not thought of it so when he was up to the neck in it. His eyes turned again to the lake, and he saw a lift of steel color in the water, rising in the wake of a motor-boat heading for the Maloja and traveling fast.

"D'you remember that boat we used to see on the Gulf of Saint Tropez, Milligan?"

"To be sure I do, sir, the one Miss Lowrie was so fond of."

"Was she? It wouldn't do here."

"No? Why not, sir?"

"It belongs to the South, to the sea—to the world we've got away from. You're right. One does feel tremendously different up here."

"We aren't fully acclimatized yet, sir. That's how it is."

"Ah! You think that's it, do you?"

"Don't you, sir? And I shouldn't wonder if, when we go down again, we feel half stifled at first in the climate down below."

"When we go down?" said Hugo, with what Milligan thought of as a curious vagueness.

"Yes, sir."

Hugo looked again towards the lake and the far-off mountains. The motor-boat had disappeared.

"I can imagine people coming up here to me. But somehow I can't think of going down to them, Milligan."

"Well, but sir——"

"It all seems far away—down there."

He made a slight gesture with his right hand, lifting it very little. And that gesture too seemed to Milligan vague.

"Let me down. Even your arms must be getting tired of my weight. Take me back to the village, will you? By Jove! That *is* a view! I wouldn't exchange this for the South."

He sighed deeply, and it was a long-drawn sigh, whether of vague melancholy, or of contentment, or perhaps of longing, Milligan couldn't tell—in spite of those last words. Milligan let the head of the couch gently down to the grass, and turned it round towards the village. But presently he turned it at right angles to get on the road.

As they drew near to the village he said, "When will Mr. Kharkoff be coming, sir, do you think?"

"The beginning of August, I believe. He's taken two rooms in a chalet somewhere above the village. He was there last year. I wish I knew where it is."

"We might go up the village tomorrow and find out."

"I don't know the name."

"I can easily ask, sir."

And on the morrow, which chanced to be a Sunday, early in the afternoon Milligan pushed Hugo's couch through a narrow lane between some rather tall houses towards the stream and the steep road mounting up to the Waldhaus.

"Where are we going?" asked Hugo.

"I've found out where Mr. Kharkoff stays when he comes here, sir. I thought you might like to see it."

"But it's somewhere on the top of the hill. You can't take me up there."

"I don't need to, sir. Not but what I could easy enough. We can see the house from below."

"That's good. I should like to have a look at it."

The sound of an accordion came to them from some hidden place near the white church with its blue-faced clock. It mingled with the sound of the stream that hurries along at the edge of the village. The Sunday holiday was being enjoyed by the peasants, who were making merry after the midday meal. Two or three heavy, men's voices broke out in a song which sounded solemnly cheerful. Milligan wheeled the couch by a garden with bushes, amongst which some children with straw-colored hair and water-pale eyes were playing. The bell of the church sounded. A wolf-dog, smelling along the gutter, looked at them for a moment with glassily shining eyes, strangely unlike the children's, and went on its way. The noise of the stream grew louder. They emerged into an open space, crossed it, and gained the farther side of the village, at the foot of the steep road up to the Waldhaus, and close to the edge of the fast-running, clouded stream which fills Sils-Maria with music.

Here Milligan stopped. "There it is, sir! See? Right up there on the edge of the precipice."

Hugo stared up. Far above them on a height covered thickly with fir trees, with a sheer drop of gray rock beneath it, stood a wooden chalet of the type one sees almost everywhere in Switzerland. Only a part of it was visible from below—deep-brown wood, small windows, a jutting roof, a strong foundation of stone. The stream curved at the base of the precipice, and was fringed by smooth green lawns on its farther side. A glimpse of the village could doubtless be seen from the chalet, which was nevertheless totally removed from the small hubbub of life at the foot of the Waldhaus height.

But Hugo did not think of any eyes, least of all Peter Kharkoff's, peering down upon the village from the windows of the chalet. For his gaze was held by a ridge of deep green, by a great cloud of dark trees in the near distance, beyond and facing the chalet and set apparently right against the snow-fields of a mountain which closed in the view. It was as if the massed phalanx of trees were pressed against the still, white breast of the snow. And the snow was not light, a mere powder recently fallen, but deep and flawless, a snow that never melted, that perhaps had never been trodden.

"That's his place!" Hugo muttered. "That's the place for him right enough." And he lay there for a long time in silence, looking from the snows to the chalet, then back again to the snows. "I wish we were living up there, Milligan," he said at last.

"Do you, sir? But we might get into difficulties up there—with the walks, I mean. It might be all up and down. Here we are nicely on the level."

"Nicely on the level—are we?"

"Surely, sir. Why——"

Milligan stopped, for at this moment a tall, thin priest, perhaps forty years old, holding in one hand a small book bound in black, strode across the road with an air of somber purpose and stopped near them at the edge of the stream. He glanced at them, then looked away up the road towards the Waldhaus, down which at that moment a large limousine car came creeping slowly, as if with precaution. It drew up beside them gently, the door was opened, and a tall woman in deep mourning got out and shook hands with the priest who took off his hat. Then she turned towards the limousine, and Milligan, and even Hugo—for the door was wide open—could see inside a young man, terribly pale, lying stretched out at full length on a species of litter. Putting her head inside the car the woman evidently said something to him. Then she drew back, and without another word walked quickly away into the village and disappeared in the direction of the church. Meanwhile the priest took her place in the car and shut the door behind him. And Milligan saw him bend over the young man, open his little book, and begin to read in a murmur.

"What's he doing?" asked Hugo.

"Saying prayers, I should think, sir," almost whispered Milligan. "Can't you hear him?"

The low and rapid murmur of the priest's voice reached them faintly for a moment in spite of the noise of the stream.

"It's evidently an R. C. padre, sir." Hugo nodded.

"Poor young fellow!" Milligan added.

"D'you think he's very bad?"

"Didn't you see him, sir?"

"Just a glimpse."

"That's a dying man, sir. I couldn't say what is the matter with him. But he's a dying man. I should only give him a very few days."

"Really?"

"I suppose the padre's trying to give him some comfort before he goes."

"That's it, no doubt. I think I'd rather listen to the stream and look at the snow up there."

"Would you, sir? But we—you and me—may easily be good for another forty years or so yet."

"Don't you believe it, Milligan."

"But really, sir——"

Hugo lifted a hand. Milligan was silent. In the pause they both heard the murmur of the priest's voice in the limousine. Hugo's masculine, and always healthy-looking face, with its strong darkness of suppressed hair and its densely thick eyebrows, set in a stern intent look. He seemed to be listening, but his eyes were fixed not on the car beside him but on the snow far above him. Milligan said nothing more.

Presently the tall woman in mourning came back. Hugo felt sure she had been praying. She looked desperately unhappy. She glanced swiftly into the motor, then drew back a little and stood waiting. And then, evidently for the first time, her dark eyes looked down upon Hugo stretched on his couch by the stream with Milligan standing beside him.

Seeing him she moved as if startled, and an expression which seemed mingled of solicitude and something like fear came into her face. Then she seemed to recover herself, to get a hold on herself again. A flush covered her pale cheeks. She came slowly up to Hugo's couch.

"Pardon!" she said in French. "I was startled. I thought —another lying so, close to *him!* For a moment I—forgive me, monsieur!" She gazed down at Hugo. Then she said with a sort of only half-suppressed fury, *"Encore la guerre! Encore la maudite guerre!"*

"Mais non, madame——" Hugo began.

But before he could say anything more the limousine door was opened, and the tall priest stepped out. The woman at once turned round to him. For a moment they spoke together in muffled voices. Then she got quickly into the limousine and shut the door behind her. Instantly the car moved on into the village and disappeared. The priest stood for a moment looking after it. Then he turned round, looked at Hugo and Milligan and lifted his hat.

"You are staying here, monsieur?" he said, speaking to Hugo.

"Yes, Padre."

"Can I do anything for you?"

Hugo looked again at the chalet and the snows and moved his head.

"No, thank you, Padre."

"Bien, bien!" said the priest.

But he still lingered, and his eyes followed Hugo's to the snows, and then to the chalet perched above the precipice.

"Do you live up there, monsieur?" he began.

"No.   We're at the Hotel Alpenrose.   But I've a friend coming to that chalet almost directly."

"Ah!" said the priest.   "May I ask his name?"

"Peter Kharkoff."

A strange expression came into the priest's thin, rather long face, an expression that softened it, gave it even something of the look of a child.

"Peter Kharkoff!   He was here last summer.   I know him. He spoke to all the village people.   We aren't very many. He never came to mass, but sometimes he went into the church.   I think he is a nature-worshiper.   Anyhow he is a good man.   In fact there are not many men like him."

"None," said Hugo.

"No?   Perhaps you are right.   I used sometimes to think——" He broke off.   Into his rather narrow gray eyes there came a deeply meditative expression.   Then he lifted his head and seemed to make an effort.   "I am glad he is coming back.   I am glad he likes our village.   You are fortunate to have him for a friend.   Good-by, monsieur."

He took off his hat again and walked slowly away.

CHAPTER II

AFTER the evening spent at the Black Cat Imogen resolved to have nothing more to do with Berazov. Secretly she was ashamed to meet him again. She felt that she had humiliated herself before him, had been tacitly rejected by him.

It was useless for her to recall that it was she who had told Berazov that he mustn't come into the house after they had driven to Lowndes Square that night, that she had sent him away. The fact was—and she was sure they both knew it—that Berazov had not really wished to come in, that a strange reluctance had taken possession of him. That reluctance had been born out of a new feeling for her, a much deeper feeling than he had had before. She appreciated that. She even valued that feeling in him. Yet, nevertheless, she felt injured and ashamed. It was awful to have sunk so low as she had. She burned with resentment against the man who knew that she could stoop down to the gutter, who had seen her stooping down. And she loathed herself for what she had done. It was as if the devil had driven her on. And that Berazov should have been the means of stopping her on the path she was trying to tread made her at moments almost hate him.

Nevertheless, she was thankful that her abominable impulse had been checked, though she could not think of the man who had checked it without feeling a heat of irresistible indignation. Vanity and pride writhed together within her. She could not be reasonable. And in her unreason and anger she felt strangely young.

On the following morning, before the coming of her parents, she sent a note to Berazov telling him, without any explanation, that she did not wish to meet him again. She asked him not to reply to the note.

He did not reply. That surprised her. She had not perhaps expected this obedience. A strange cold seemed to gather about her. It was not dissipated by the arrival of her mother and father.

Her mother was vague and muddled as usual, very tired from the heat, somewhat confused at exchanging the calm of the villa for the bustle of London. But Lord Lowrie looked well, clear, and, Imogen fancied, unusually observant. After his wife had gone up to her room and her maid, he took Imogen into his special room at the back of the house to "give her the news." At least so he said. But she had immediately the feeling that he wanted to do more than that. However, he began by describing the life at the villa since she had left it, while she listened, feigning a light interest combined with an equally light indifference.

"And what have you been doing?" he said, after a few sentences.

Imogen was not prepared for the question. She had expected more information from him. Really she had been deeply interested in what he was saying, had been longing for a full narrative of events. And now she was brought up short with this question.

"I!" she said.

"Yes. We old fogies have been idling in the sunshine, while Hugo lay in his chair doing nothing, unable to do anything, poor fellow. You've been up to the neck in all sorts of things, I suppose."

She was silent.

"Had a good time?" asked her father.

It seemed to her that there was a great curiosity at the back of his casual words. With lightning-like rapidity she considered whether to be sincere or insincere. With her mother she would almost certainly have been the latter. But somehow she couldn't be insincere with her father. There was a good deal of sympathy between them, and it governed her now. Besides, she had a great longing to release herself to someone. "No," she said.

"How was that? Didn't your innumerable friends rally round you?"

"Innumerable friends! Oh yes—they did." She wanted to tell him that it had seemed to her, that it seemed to her now, as if all the interest of life had been left behind by her when she had driven down between the mimosas on her way to the station of Sainte Maxime. She couldn't quite do that. But she could express her strange new weariness of London. And she added, "I've been trying to pick up the threads. But, for the present at any rate, I feel I'm through with old London." She looked steadily at her father. "Hugo seems to be feeling as I do. Doesn't he?"

"Hugo! That's different. What could he do here now?"

"He could be with me."

"Perhaps he'll turn up presently."

"Presently? When? Do you mean sometime in the autumn?"

"Well—yes. I suppose that's about it."

"Old papa, that will be too late."

"I don't quite understand the situation, I confess, Imogen. Have you and Hugo decided to break things off?"

"We haven't decided together on anything. Hugo doesn't want to come back. That's how it is. Another influence has displaced mine."

"Another influence! You mean Peter Kharkoff's?"

"Of course I do."

Lord Lowrie was silent. He was sitting near a writing table, and now he stretched out a hand and began moving things gently about on it. While he did this he lowered his eyebrows.

"Isn't it so?" said Imogen. "Why should Hugo choose to go to Switzerland when he knows I have been expecting him here? Peter Kharkoff is going to Switzerland. That's the reason."

"Yes, it must be."

"Don't you think I can consider myself free now?" she asked.

"Tell me—I've never quite understood matters—would you feel very thankful to be free?"

He was surprised to see tears come into his daughter's eyes. "I don't know," she said. "But just now I feel most awfully left."

She got up from the sofa she was sitting on. While speaking she had been encompassed by a dreadful dry feeling of loneliness. The future seemed abruptly to have been taken from her. It was as if hitherto she had always possessed a future and had lived happy in that possession, always conscious of it without being aware that she was. Now she hadn't it any longer, and she was aghast. And there was fear in her heart.

She looked out of the window. Behind the house there was a narrow terrace of stone, with two seats on it and some green tubs holding flowering shrubs. Beyond was a carved stone parapet. Imogen stared at this empty stone terrace and, for the first time perhaps in her life, she mentally contemplated an empty, cold life, realized or seemed to realize just what it would be. She turned round.

"I suppose I was fonder of old Hugo than I knew I was," she said. "When I said I would marry him I did feel I was making a sacrifice. What's the good of pretending? In a way I dreaded marrying him, dreaded the life I should have with him. But now I know that I had always relied on him. It had never occurred to me that he could want to get out of it. I've had a shock. That's the truth. But I shall get over it, old papa. You can be sure of that."

"Then you're going to give Hugo up?"

"I consider that he's giving me up."

After a silence Lord Lowrie said slowly, "What does Peter Kharkoff count for in all this?"

"What do you mean exactly by that?"

"You spoke of his influence with Hugo having swallowed up yours."

"Isn't it pretty obvious that it has?"

"When you asked him to come to us was it for Hugo you wanted him?"

"Yes. At least I believed so at the time."

"Then you thought he could do something for Hugo."

"Yes."

"I'm wondering what. I'm wondering whether perhaps he hasn't done it, or whether he isn't in process of doing it."

Imogen looked at her father but said nothing.

"Instead of kicking against the pricks wouldn't it be better, wiser, to leave it to him?" said Lord Lowrie.

"What else am I doing?" said Imogen.

"Yes—but with trust instead of in anger!"

"Oh—am *I* to give up my whole personality too?" she exclaimed.

"Any social celebrity you have attained hasn't been gained by doing that, my dear."

"I hate all that social nonsense!" said Imogen. "I am sick of it. It means nothing to me now. But when it comes to the man one is engaged to——"

"Tell me! D'you care enough for Hugo to wish for his happiness before all things? He's been through a lot you know."

"I want poor Hugo to be happy."

"Then don't worry! Just leave things alone. He's safer than he's been since his accident. If he goes to Switzerland be sure it's the best thing he could do." He saw questions in her eyes. "No, I can't answer you. What—how much—can we understand? But sometimes if only we have enough confidence to rest on the wave, not to struggle, it will carry us in to the shore."

"So you want me to do nothing, just to let Hugo slip away from me without a word, without explanation?"

"I should do nothing."

"And what am I? Engaged to him still, or not?"

"Just leave it. That's my advice."

"And what am I going to do? How am I going to spend my time?"

"You never seem to have any difficulty in deciding what to do."

"You're speaking of my life as it was!" she said desperately. And then she went out of the room.

When she was alone she was more conscious than ever before of the absorbing influence of the Unearthly, and she had a strange sense as of a Power taking quiet, but inexorable possession of those who came within its radius. Her father, she realized, was one of them, Hugo another. Milligan in his different way had immediately felt the influence. Her aunt, the organist, Canon Barrimore—each of these had been affected by it. Madame Coiret too! And—Berazov? Perhaps his was the strangest case of all. For he had only been reached through her. Unconsciously she had conveyed to him a weapon which later he had been obliged to turn against herself, or perhaps truer to say against something in her, the ugliest part.

And she remembered standing by the Gulf of Saint Tropez on the morning of her departure, and, with Peter Kharkoff, watching their boat setting sail for the open sea. Silently then she had compared herself to that little boat, driven on by the wind towards the wider waters, compelled to the sea. And she had been intimately conscious of the possession of something precious, something which she had neglected but which had remained absolutely unaltered by her neglect. The vitality of it, the secret intense vitality—she had felt it then. Hadn't she thought of it as the radium of the soul? She had carried it away with her from the shore of that blue and purple sea. She had brought it to England, to London.

And then she had tried to smother it in dust, to trample it down, to get rid of it perhaps. And Berazov had checked her hand—hadn't he?

And now Hugo—her father——

She must let Hugo go. She saw him putting out to sea, sailing away from her to far-distant horizons. Her father had really only advised her to do what she had already known she must do. Or—was that true? She remembered her remark to her aunt about either giving up drastically, or going out to Switzerland to play her own hand.

Dared she to go out to Switzerland? If she didn't do that what lay before her? What was there for her to do? Berazov had been a great distraction. He had given her moments of concentration which had brought with them forgetfulness. For when the senses rear their heads there are things that crouch down and seem to die. But he was of no use to her really. And she had felt that again and again. The life that formerly had satisfied her, or had given to her sensations which had combined in a clever simulation of satisfaction, now presented itself to her as a thing intolerably arid. An immense change must certainly have operated in her. She thought again of her former acquaintance, the French actress, who had stepped from the stage into the nunnery, and now she could almost understand her.

Anything can happen in a human being. The great light shines in the way and conversion is accomplished, or a Thais beckons from Alexandria and the holy man is lured to his doom, and goes out eventually from the woman who has given herself to God through him, blaspheming.

Through him! The irony of it! And the irony of Berazov coming within the orbit of Peter Kharkoff's strange influence through her! But he had come within it, and she had even told him so. She had told him so when she had said, "You were gone. I know why. *You hadn't been allowed to stay.*"

But Peter Kharkoff had said to her, "What would goodness be if you were compelled to be good?"

He had implied the existence of the power of choice. Well then she could choose now. What was she going to do? Was she going to give up Hugo—that is to let him go without attempting a protest, or an effort to keep him—and to give up, with him, the man whom she had brought deliberately into his life, and who had apparently drawn him away from her? Or was she going to pocket her pride, to outrage her vanity, and to follow, like a dog, after the steps of the master?

She could not decide what to do. Meanwhile she drifted on,

remaining in London. Her father had spoken of having confidence, of resting, not struggling, of being carried in to the shore. Often she wished she could take his advice. Often she thought of Peter Kharkoff's large simplicity, of his atmosphere of deep calm, and wondered why she could not do that. But he was not there beside her. And she was young. And her youth seemed to prevent her from having complete trust at a distance. But one thing she did; she tried not to struggle. She aimed at resignation. But she felt very unhappy. And sometimes it seemed to her that she was like one suspended between earth and heaven.

Always the thought of Hugo was with her, and with it the thought of the Unearthly. She had stopped writing to Hugo. Presently he wrote to her, a short letter from Switzerland. When she saw the address, Hotel Alpenrose, Sils-Maria, Engadine, a thrill went through her, and she had a great longing to be there. The words seemed to pull at her. She felt oddly lured by them, lured by their purity. (For they seemed to her pure, pellucid, like the silver rills of Switzerland that run through the grasses, singing in undertones.) She ached to be away, near the snows, high up where the fir trees climb among the rocks, and waterfalls like white tresses hang down the mountainsides.

In his letter Hugo made no mention of Peter Kharkoff. He wrote briefly of his quiet life with Milligan, and sent her affectionate messages. She was very conscious of affection in his letter, though he made no allusion to coming back eventually, gave no hint that he wished her to travel to him. Pondering over the letter she gained the conviction that Hugo didn't wish for her in Switzerland, but that his affection for her was still very deep. Surely he was holding it in check. But why? And why did he avoid any mention of Peter Kharkoff? Was there a spell upon him? She felt mystery in his letter.

The last days of July slipped away. Imogen had been invited to a big house party for Goodwood. She refused it. The London season was over. She had been asked to stay on a yacht for Cowes. She refused that too. Pals of hers said, "Come to Deauville—to Venice." She did not even hesitate to consider their propositions. She knew she couldn't go. Even the Lido with its life in the sea didn't tempt her. Yet she had nothing to do. Her existence seemed to be in abeyance. Yet often she felt excited, even feverish. And she was horribly restless despite her effort after resignation.

Of course there was plenty of gossip going on about her engagement to Hugo Dennistone and his non-appearance in England. People had had no scruple in plying her with questions about him. When was he coming? How was he? Where was he? She answered that he had gone to the Engadine for the sake of his health. They could get nothing more out of her. But all her special friends realized that something was "up" between her and Hugo. And, remembering Berazov, they suspected that she was wavering in her resolve to give up her life to a powerless man.

Yet Berazov for some time had not been seen with her though he had not left London. Since Silvia Moray's party he had ceased from going about. Had he quarreled with Imogen? Or were they seeing each other secretly? Or— what? The season ended before the mystery could be solved. And then Goodwood, Cowes, Deauville, Venice, Scotland put other ideas into curious heads, other preoccupations into frivolous hearts. In the late autumn, when the little season began, it would be possible to gather up the threads of Imogen's affairs. Meanwhile, as for some unknown reason she wouldn't do anything—"any damned thing" as Lois Tremayne put it to Teddy Basingstoke—there was nothing for it but to let her alone. Many of her friends felt pretty sure that she was arranging something with Berazov and did not want anyone to know. As for Hugo Dennistone, perhaps after all she couldn't bring herself up to the scratch, perhaps she was giving him the chuck. They would know soon. That was certain. But now for flight! And they dispersed gaily to the four winds. And August stole upon the town.

Suddenly—the day after bank holiday—Imogen jumped into a cab, drove to Victoria Station, and took a ticket for Drearney. She hadn't sent any message to her aunt to say she was coming. She felt sure she would find Towser there. But when she arrived at Drearney station, just after twelve o'clock, she was surprised to find herself in the midst of tremendous bustle. Everywhere flags were flying. Charabancs full of trippers were crowding into the town. A band was playing on the Dane. Excursion trains were letting loose people from the nearest seaside towns. Flies innumerable were gathering up eager parties and driving away in clouds of white dust.

"What on earth's going on?" Imogen asked of a porter.

"It's Drearney week, ma'am. Didn't you know it?"

Drearney cricket week! Imogen's spirits fell. Why hadn't she remembered that the first week of August was always kept by Drearney as a high sporting and theatrical festival? Her aunt always entertained for the week. She knew that there were lunch parties every day at Ewenden House for "county" friends who had driven in. The house too was probably full of visitors staying for the week. Cricket, amateur theatricals, county balls, illuminations, concerts sped the summer days and nights on their way.

"Damn it!" Imogen muttered. "Why didn't I remember?"

"Carriage, ma'am?"

She shook her head, and walked out into the open space in front of the station. What should she do? There wasn't a train back to London till three o'clock. She wouldn't go to Ewenden House. She was resolved upon that. She couldn't face a lunch party in her present mood. She couldn't talk cricket with a lot of county people whom she probably wouldn't know. Yet she walked towards the town, and presently, through a narrow alley, came into the High Street.

This was beflagged from end to end, and decorated with hundreds of strings of fairy lamps, and crowded with carriages, motorcars and people.

Imogen looked at it with profound distaste. In that moment she felt half afraid in some curious, but very intimate way, of the joyful town. Just in front of her across the street was the narrow mouth of Cathedral Lane, spanned by a flutter of flags. The cathedral close lay beyond. She hesitated for a moment. Then she crossed the street quickly, dodging the traffic, and made her way down the lane towards the old archway through which she could see a glimpse of the precincts. The cathedral towers rose above it in the blue. For Drearney was not disappointed of its proverbial fine weather for the week.

As she passed beneath the projecting upper stories of the ancient houses she met Miss Prowse, the precentor's sister, carrying a string bag full of miscellanies. Miss Prowse stared, bowed, hesitated. Imogen saw that she was longing to speak, to inquire, to find out, but walked on swiftly, realizing the turned head, the eager, popping eyes which were pursuing her.

She had made up her mind what she was going to do. She

was going to the organist's house to find out whether he had
started on his holiday, whether he had already departed to
Switzerland. Probably he had gone on the first of the month,
like so many of the "ordinary blokes" among whom he had
classed himself. She was trying to make up her mind that it
would be so. But she was hoping secretly, though hardly
allowing this to herself, that he might still be there. Perhaps
the "week" would have kept him.

When she got to his gate she looked quickly at the small
dark-brown house, and saw that the blinds were up and the
windows were open. Her hope grew. But perhaps he had
"let" for the week. She opened the gate and walked up the
garden path, and immediately heard an energetic cry, "Hallo,
Miss Lowrie!"

At the window of the room on the right she saw the lean
figure, the eager eyes, the leaping hair that had amused and
interested her, and immediately she had a great feeling of
gladness.

"Coming!" Hendry cried.

And then he was at the door in knickerbockers, a Norfolk
jacket, a soft collar and dull-red tie, dressed, she felt certain,
for a journey.

"You're going?" she said, as he clasped her hand with his
long thin fingers.

"Starting this evening for London. I cross tomorrow. But
do come in."

"Yes. I want to for a minute."

He led the way to his sitting-room which was in a really
dreadful muddle.

"I'm clearing out things," he said apologetically. "You've
come to your aunt for the week?"

"Oh no! I only came down this morning. I'm going back
this afternoon. I'd forgotten that there was a week. I haven't
seen my aunt."

He looked very happy, but a little surprised.

"It's most awfully good of you to let me see you," he said.

She saw bright inquiry in his holiday eyes. He was sitting
on the window-seat with his back to the garden. She had sat
down on the chair with the wooden back at his writing table.

"I thought I might catch you before you started for Switzerland," she said.

"You aren't coming out?"

She didn't answer for a moment. The sight of this man in his holiday suit—she thought of it as that—with the eager light of anticipation in his clever but now boyish eyes had waked in her an intense desire to be off and away to the green lawns and the streams at the foot of the mountains, to breathe in the pure and purifying air that seems cleansed by the snows, to be close to nature, to be away from crowds, far away—but not alone. Not the old desire for St. Moritz was upon her just then. Surely she had shed that self which had formerly traveled up the world in pursuit of new forms of gaiety, new forms of violent excitement, which had led the painted life in the snows. Now she longed for a new Switzerland.

His searching and yet shy eyes were upon hers trying surely to read her, but not with a hard curiosity, rather with a quick sympathy.

"I don't know," at last she answered. "I hadn't intended to go."

"No?"

"But seeing you on the verge—I seem to see a shadowy knapsack on your shoulders——"

"Ah!"

"It tempts me."

"Captain Dennistone's there, isn't he?"

"Yes, at the Hotel Alpenrose."

"Jolly name!"

"Where will you be?"

"Oh, I must look for a cheap place. Peter Kharkoff will be in rooms in a chalet above the village. I may go there if he doesn't mind. But I expect he'd rather be alone."

"Anyhow, go to the Alpenrose and introduce yourself to Captain Dennistone. Say I told you to. Will you?"

"I promise."

"And will you do something for me?"

"Anything I can," he said eagerly.

"Write to me—here's my address—and tell me how Captain Dennistone seems, how he is getting on, will you?"

"I'll write directly I know."

Imogen got up.

"Oh, but you're not going!" he said.

"Yes, I must."

"But can't I give you lunch? There isn't much in the house I'm afraid, but——"

"No, thanks. Go on with your preparations. You'll have a glorious holiday. I feel that."

"You are kind to care whether I do or not."

"You deserve it. You've earned it. It must be splendid to earn, to have earned one's joy. Write to me as soon as you can."

"It's the first thing I shall do when I know."

And only a few days later a letter, written in a small, clear and surprisingly delicate handwriting, was brought to Imogen in London.

She didn't open it at once. She kept it in her hand and went slowly up to her sitting room. There she sat down, and still held it for a time unopened. She had an odd, unreasonable feeling that what this envelop held would decide, perhaps would fatally decide, her action in the immediate future, would decide her to sacrifice her pride and go out to Hugo, or to stay in England and give him up. (For she still held to her decision to do one of these two things.) And she hesitated to read the hidden writing. For it seemed to her that the step she would take—in whichever direction it was—would be of tremendous importance.

At last, however, she tore the thin envelop and read what was in it.

> Hotel Alpenrose
> Sils-Maria
> August 7th.

Dear Miss Lowrie:

I'm staying here after all. Found I could make a price that wouldn't break me. It's marvelous here, grand, uplifting. The weather's good and bad. It varies from day to day. But I don't seem to care. The scenery is so sublime, and the air makes me want to run and leap and sing, and in fact generally make a fool of myself. Peter Kharkoff is here in the chalet. It's high up, much higher than this, and his windows look right on the snows. I'm with him every day.

Now as to what I promised you. I have got to know Captain Dennistone and his attendant, Milligan. Directly I saw the former I did what you asked me to do, went up and introduced myself, and said I'd been with you just before I left Drearney. You asked me to let you know how he seems, and how he's getting along. He looks in a way well. He's got a splendid color, and if he wasn't always lying down, and you weren't closely observant, you might think he was in perfect health. But there's something—it hardly seems physical—which sets me wondering. He's an awfully masculine fellow, isn't he? Anyone can see that. And yet there's something about him that I've never noticed before in that type of man, the soldier and sporting type. (He is that, isn't he? Of course there's nothing whatever of the artist about him.) It's something spiritual, something at times almost ethereal. I've talked to him. But he never shows it in what he says— at any rate he never does to me. No, it's in his look sometimes, in his manner, in his atmosphere. (I rather hate that expression, because it's so often used by affected fools. But I don't quite know how else to put it.) He seems—away. You'll say that doesn't mean bad health. Perhaps not. But in a man of that type it sets me thinking, wondering, looking ahead. Such detachment isn't ordinary, and it must mean something. What—I leave to you. I wouldn't say he's unhappy, but his happiness—if it is that—is absolutely out of the ordinary. Not the happiness of his type. Something austere about it as if—as if—no, I can't express myself. But I may be wrong, all wrong. There are overtones in him. There's music it wants a marvelous ear to catch, music that seems to be on the way to vast distances. Where's he traveling? I keep asking myself that. Are you coming out? I haven't said a word as to that. But you would find it very wonderful here. One may not climb. (I do—a little.) But without climbing one often feels on the peaks. You see Peter Kharkoff is here.

Hubert Hendry.

When Imogen had finished reading the letter she read it again. She sat over it for some time, reading now here, now there, giving herself to impressions, then trying, she thought, to withdraw herself from them. Finally she got up and went to the nearest telegraph office. From there she sent the following telegram to Milligan. "How is Captain Dennistone please wire Imogen Lowrie"—and her address.

Coming out of the telegraph office she found herself face to face with Berazov, whom she had not seen since the night of their dinner in Chelsea.

He stopped, took off his hat and said, "When are you going to Switzerland?"

Imogen felt that the startled blood rose and flamed in her cheeks.

"What do you mean? I never said I was going."

"No. But I feel you will." He was looking at her with a sort of hard earnestness. His large, sad gray eyes seemed energetically trying to read all the secrets of her, and not to care whether she resented that or not.

"You will go," he said.

And when he said that Imogen knew he was stating a fact. She knew that she would go, that she must go. When she had sent the telegram to Milligan she had supposed that on his answer would depend her action. If he telegraphed reassuring news of Hugo's condition she had said to herself that she would let her pride have its way. If not she would go. But now she knew that in any case she must go. Simply—she couldn't keep away.

"Perhaps I may," she said. "London's very dull now."

"Won't you tell me where exactly you are going? Switzerland's a small country, still——"

"Why should I tell you?"

"I might come there."

"Why?"

"I think I ought to know my enemy." He smiled as he said that. "I have had intercourse with him through you. I should like to meet him face to face."

While he spoke Imogen felt that it was inevitable, that it was all inevitable. She must go out to Sils-Maria. Berazov and Peter Kharkoff must meet. It had to be. And why should she be afraid of it? She was not wont to have fear as her companion.

"If I go—Sils-Maria in the Engadine, not far from St. Moritz," she said. "But I don't say that I am going."

"D'you try to deceive yourself?"

"Good-by," she said gently.

She met his glance, not with defiance but with firmness. He had humiliated her but in doing so he had saved her from a much greater, a much more intimate humiliation. She ought to be grateful to him. For a moment she saw the Jew in him, and a voice seemed to say, "That night I was there."

She held out her hand.

"I still care," he said. "In the second way."

"I can't. I shall never be able to."

"No. I don't believe you will. You're meant for someone else, perhaps."

She thought of Hugo. She remembered the night when she had seemed to see an hour-glass on her table in the villa. And the sands were running out very fast. For whom was she meant if not for Hugo?

"Good-by," she said again.

And then she went on her way.

CHAPTER III

IMOGEN said good-by to her mother and father and traveled out to Switzerland alone. She didn't take her maid with her. She felt that to be afflicted with a maid on such an errand as hers would be intolerable. When she told her father what she was going to do he didn't seem surprised, didn't raise any objection to her going. The complete unconventionality of such an expedition was of course obvious, and he did just mention it. But when Imogen said, "I can't help it, old papa. A chaperon would drive me mad, I'm going to a region where chaperons couldn't draw breath," he only said, "But people are sent up there for breathing purposes, aren't they?" and began speaking of Hugo.

Imogen knew that her father would have considered her wiser if she had followed his advice, if she had trusted, been quiet, let things take their course, given herself to the wave in fact. But she couldn't do that. The lure that drew her away from England was irresistible. She felt starving for the heights. London was abominable to her. Although she supposed that the power of choice must be hers she felt compelled to get away from it, compelled to go to the place where two men were, Hugo and Peter Kharkoff. No other place seemed really to exist in her mind except the village of Sils-Maria. Perpetually she saw it before her, heard its winds and its waters, breathed imaginatively the air that had traveled over the snows to it.

When she left London her thankfulness was like a prayer. She slept at Zurich in the Hotel Savoy, and dined alone in the raised part of the restaurant. Immediately below the steps three musicians played, a violinist, a pianist and a 'cellist. She dined very late, and there were only three people in that part of the restaurant, a woman and two men. One of the men, a fat, fair young man with a Jewish face and a very commercial body, was obviously the giver of the feast, and must have been "out" to do business with the other man, a thin American with gigantic spectacles, who was the husband, Imogen felt sure, of the woman. He plied his companions with champagne and was in frequent colloquy with the young Italian violinist, whom he induced to play certain languishing tunes. Later came fox-trots, and springing up with astonishing

lightness he persuaded the woman to dance with him in the
narrow space between the tables, while the American husband
looked on gravely through his spectacles. A strong scent from
the woman bathed Imogen when the dancers came near to her,
and made her long to be away from all cities.

As she ate alone she felt excited and even nervous. It was
a rare thing for her to feel nervous. She was conscious of
humiliation. Perhaps for the first time in her life she was
deliberately going to be with those who possibly did not want
her. (For it had come to that. She no longer knew whether
Hugo wanted her.) She was "pushing herself in," and was
not sure of her welcome. No word had gone before her. Her
arrival was unexpected. She was giving herself the chance of
seeing whether Hugo cared or not. For by coming upon him
unexpectedly she would surely be able to convince herself of his
exact feeling towards her. He would be startled and must
convey what he felt to her. What she was going to do she
had to do. But she realized thoroughly that she was humbling
herself in doing it. And that realization and her doubts caused
her to feel "strung up," excited, nervous, not sure of herself.

Pop went another champagne cork from the neighboring
table. The Italian violinist, who walked about while he played
and was usually close to Imogen, gave his soul in a tango.
And again the fat, fair Jew with an eye to business lured
"madam" from the table, while the grave husband was left
with the champagne. It was obvious that the Jew believed it
necessary to fascinate the wife in order to have "a soft job"
with the husband. And Imogen saw that the lady was falling
under his spell. She drooped and languished in his enfolding
arms. (He wasn't at all a dancer à la mode. In his eagerness
for business he gripped his partner most unfashionably.) Her
pale eyes blinked as she entered the world of dreams. Once
more her scent flowed over Imogen. The violinist played at
her, joining the Jew in his little plot. And the husband rather
furtively filled his glass again, and sipped, musing through his
spectacles.

And Imogen thought with disgust of the world in which
everyone is hunting his sordid interests. "And I? Am I a
huntress?" she asked herself, as she paid her bill and got up
to go.

As she went out she saw the violinist staring at her over
his fiddle and she knew exactly what he was thinking about.

On the following morning she took the express to Coire. There she changed and got into the train for St. Moritz, almost submerged in an ocean of traveling Jews. For all Israel seemed on the way to the Peaks. She couldn't see a single Christian face in the train till a Swiss came to puncture her ticket, and the faces she saw repelled her. In not one of them did she find any indication of lofty thinking, of strong imagination, of idealism, of any interior beauty shining unselfconsciously through the envelop of the flesh. And she wondered why all these dark and apparently eager people, swarthy and dressed up rather than well dressed, were making their way up the world into one of the purest realms of Nature.

She tried to forget them. She looked out of the windows as the long train, rounding curve after curve, moved slowly onward and upward. She saw streams sunk deep down in ravines, whose sides were rocky or covered with brushwood, bushes and fir trees, waterfalls leaping from precipices into waiting pools far below, little wooden bridges spanning the streams, great slopes of emerald green, smooth shaven as carefully kept garden lawns in England, dark pine woods in whose aisles a mysterious twilight reigned, rocky and snow-covered peaks lifted between green and blue.

The sky was without a cloud, but pale. There seemed to be some white in its blueness, as if some of the snow had filtered into it and remained. At each curve of the line new peaks appeared, new stretches of park-like country, new forests. And above all this grandeur of nature, save the actual peaks, were two men, two of those tiny beings who creep on the breast of Nature carrying marvelous possibilities, carrying passions, glory and tears, the here and the hereafter, within them. And she was going to them.

She forgot the eager Jews who with glittering eyes were appraising the panorama, for which they had paid at a station or an agency, and which was now being duly unrolled before them. She was drawn away from the train into another world.

When the train drew up in the familiar station of St. Moritz her nervous feeling returned. She felt doubtful and very lonely. Porters from the St. Moritz hotels were waiting; from the Kulm, the Palace, the Carlton, the Grand. For a moment Imogen hesitated as she looked at them. Should she, as usual, stay in St. Moritz and, from there, as if casually, visit Sils-Maria? Should she "save her face" by doing that?

"Palace, madame?" said a huge, rosy-faced hotel porter, holding out a great arm towards the little jewel-case she was carrying.

She half stretched out her hand to him, then drew it back. Then she turned to the railway porter who was helping her.

"I want a carriage, please. I'm going to Sils-Maria. Here's my luggage ticket."

Soon she was ensconced in a big landau drawn by two fat white horses. Some of her luggage—she hadn't brought very much—was corded on the back. The rest was put on the box, and bestowed on the seat opposite to her.

"The Waldhaus, Sils-Maria," she said to the driver.

At that moment she had made up her mind not to stay at the Alpenrose Hotel. A strange feeling that was like shyness prompted her.

She saw the huge hotels staring down on her from the height above the St. Moritz Lake, the omnibuses full of happy Jews mounting towards them. And she too must go into St. Moritz, pass through it to gain the serener country beyond and the road to Maloja.

As she drove through the village, crowded with women and girls in "jumpers," with men elaborately got up to look as sporting and adventurous as possible, her nervous or shy feeling increased. Soon the houses were left behind, and the high road mounting among trees drew away towards the Maloja. The huge Suvretta House, with its hooded head staring out towards the lake of Silvaplana, appeared on the right backed by sloping green hills. A tennis tournament was going on just in front of it. Umpires were calling the score. Ball boys were running to and fro jerkily. Perched high up on lofty benches under the long lines of windows women in light dresses and men in flannels were watching. The afternoon wind, not very strong now for the day was already waning, traveled up the long valley from the pass of the Maloja.

The white horses trotted slowly on their substantial feet. The coachman's fat back looked comfortable and sleepy. As Imogen glanced at it she couldn't help thinking, "Your life— and mine!" And her complexity troubled and perplexed her. If only she could smooth her life out, get rid of the tortuous wrinkles, be simpler, more childlike, more trusting.

Nature was calm and spacious about her. The wind that ruffled the waters of the lake, along whose edge the horses were

trotting now, was pure. Not far off was the man who, sometimes when she was with him, had given to her a wonderful
feeling of peace, of safety, of simplicity. Would she have that
feeling again with him? Would he welcome her? Or would
he be indifferent to her? Did he know occultly that she was
coming, was now on the way? When she thought about that
it seemed to her that he surely must know. But Hugo could
not know unless Hendry, the organist, had told him that possibly she might come out. But Hendry would not have said
anything. And, even if he had, Hugo would have no idea when
she was coming.

Although really the white horses were moving along by the
water deliberately, it seemed to Imogen presently that they
were going very fast, were carrying her very swiftly to Sils-
Maria. If she should not be wanted there? If her company
wasn't desired? How horrible that would be. Nothing of
course would be said. Nothing would be intentionally shown.
But she would know. She would know at once. She felt that
one glance at Hugo would tell her. She knew him so well.
She could read him. Peter Kharkoff she didn't pretend to
read. But he could not mind her coming. Such a trifle could
not affect him whom nothing surely could ever move to irritation, still less to anger.

The carriage was now drawing near to a small promontory,
a slight pushing forward of the land into the Silvaplana Lake.
Evening was at hand. The wind was rapidly failing. The
waters of the lake were sinking into sleep. Seated in the
corner of the left side of the carriage Imogen, looking out over
the indented shore and the now almost quiet waters, perceived
this promontory, and on it, at the farthest point, relieved
against the softening light, the solitary figure of a man. He
was standing absolutely still, leaning, she thought, slightly forward as if gazing down into the water. Tall, dominating, his
figure stood out with a strange arresting power in this lonely
place, seemed to people the landscape, to fill it with brooding
life. And she remembered the bust she had seen in the studio
of the Swiss sculptor, "Pure thought divorced from emotion."
Although she could not see this man's face something in his
attitude, in the downward droop of his head, in the fixed gaze,
divined not actually noted by her, recalled the impression she
had received from the bust, an impression of depths upon depths
of thought, of a strength, a force of pure thinking which could

surely accomplish great marvels, could surely bring about what it wished. And she knew at once that it was thus, by the lake of Silvaplana in this lonely place, that she had to meet Peter Kharkoff again.

She called to the coachman. He turned on his box and looked down at her with cold, shallow blue eyes. She asked him to stop. Calmly he pulled up his white horses. She opened the carriage door and got out. The lake shore was not fenced off from the highway. She stepped onto the springy turf and went towards the man by the water. She did not hesitate. She had to go. She did not fear to disturb him.

As she approached Peter Kharkoff over the grass she remembered the longing that had seized her in the wood above the Gulf of St. Tropez, when she had seen him standing above her on the height looking over the sea, a longing, full of sex, to draw him down to her, to force him to concentrate on her, to force him to become like all other men. She had no feeling of that kind now. Rather did she wish to travel into his dream of the world and of life, if it were a dream, to give herself up to his conception of the scheme which she couldn't understand, to trust herself to his knowledge, to leave her fate in his hands.

How futile really had been her attempt at rebellion when she had traveled to London, when she had plunged once more into the old life which had once sufficed her, when she had encountered Berazov. She had thought she could be again as she had been, only with even less reserve, with an impudence of the body added to match her impudence of the mind. But it had not been possible. She had thought to rebel against Peter Kharkoff. But now she knew that the rebellion, if she had carried it out, would have been not only against him but against herself. To do what she had intended to do, what part of her had certainly wanted to do, she would have had to defy, to overcome herself. It had seemed, at the end, as if Berazov had prevented her from doing that. She had even thought so. But it could not really have been so. The guiding, the restraining hand must surely have been far off.

She had left Sainte Maxime, but she had not been able to escape from the will and the influence there. She knew that now, and a feeling of simplicity, of childishness, came to her.

She went up to Peter Kharkoff, stood beside him, and said, "I have come. I don't know whether I am wanted, but I had to come."

He didn't seem startled, though she had come up over the grass with a light, soft tread. He turned and at once held out his large hand. And then the mystic sense that had dominated her for a moment died away. And she felt his humanity, felt she was with a good friend, with one who was very understanding, and of whom it was impossible to be afraid.

"Did you think I should come?" she asked him.

"I knew we should meet again, and before very long," he said. "Are you going to Sils-Maria?"

"Yes. There's my carriage." She pointed to the white horses. "Hugo wouldn't come to England to me," she added. "So I have come out to him. He doesn't know. I haven't told him. I thought I would give him a surprise."

As she spoke she was watching him closely. For now, already, her suspicious instinct of a woman was awake. She couldn't help its awakening in spite of her deep-down trust in him, a trust that seemed absolutely inevitable. For hadn't the power of this man overcome her power over her crippled lover? And, if so, hadn't that power been used with deliberate intention?

"Shall I drive to the village with you?" was all he said in answer to her statement.

"I wish you would. But perhaps you meant to stay out a long time, didn't you?"

"I wasn't thinking about time."

"I wonder what you were thinking about. I am always wondering about that when I am near you."

"Let us go to the carriage," he said. "I dare say you are tired after your journey. But in this air you won't feel tired very long."

"No. It's wonderful."

"It's the air people need," he said simply.

And when he said that she felt that he must know what she needed far better than she knew it herself.

They got into the big carriage. The big coachman cracked his whip. The fat white horses trotted, bearing them on into the breast of the evening. And Imogen knew again the blessed difference between doubt and complete rest of mind, measured by her present peace her immediately preceding torture of nervousness and apprehension. Though she did what human beings often do, tried to keep hold of her suspicions, her unrest, tried to retain her malady, she sank into calm irresistible.

The wind now died completely away. The lake of Silvaplana was left behind. The green plain spread before them with the village of Sils in the distance. A silver trout stream kept them company on the left of the carriage. In the distance, beyond Maloja, the mountains lifted their mysterious heads, a grand company of sentinels. And Imogen remembered her former visits to this region, and knew that she had never really seen it, had never at all fully realized its majesty and purity before, had never allowed herself to come under its influence or to comprehend its significance. For she had always carried with her an opposing influence and had given herself to that.

"I've been here before," she said. "In the winter. But I've never realized what it was, because I've always been with a crowd. Why do most of us herd together like animals?"

"Don't you think it may be because most people are afraid of life?" he said.

"And they feel safer in company than alone?"

"The world is full of fear. That is why courage is made such a virtue. If men could rid themselves of fear think how the glory of life would be increased."

"Yes. It would be wonderful."

"Fear is at the root of almost all the evils that humanity suffers from. It is the subtlest of all the poisons. And its face is so ugly that nothing horrifies humanity so much as to be forced to look on fear. To see fear naked is to see perhaps the most terrible thing in the world."

"But how is it possible to cast out fear?"

"Think courageously. Make a habit of thinking courageously. Whenever a fear comes to you refuse it lodging. Be pitiless to it. Don't let it stay with you even for a moment."

"But you speak as if we had only to will—to do."

"Try to will what is fine, and see if it isn't so."

"Do you think we can conquer our natures?"

"The greatest mistake a human being can make is to think that his nature is evil. It is not. And everyone has had moments when he has known that it is not, has not merely thought—but known."

He turned slightly and looked at Imogen with his large and heavy eyes. "Haven't you ever struggled to overcome the good in you and failed?" he asked her.

The question seemed to pierce to the roots of her. All her

recent life in London seemed to rise up before her clamoring an affirmative to his question. It was as if she were enabled in some extraordinary and inexplicable way to see it for a moment whole, all its events grouped together and set before her simultaneously.

"Goodness is not always so easy to drive out as many people suppose," he said after a moment. "And its power of endurance is marvelous. There's a great obstinacy of goodness in this world. You have felt it."

"Yes," she said, thinking of herself.

"One often hears of men being conquered by the evil that is in them. But very little is said of the other victory, the victory of the good."

"But isn't either the result of compulsion?" she couldn't help saying, remembering a conversation she had had with him at Sainte Maxime.

"No. There is something inside a man which can choose and does choose. And that's his great mystery—that something."

"The most awful thing is to be half-hearted, I think. There was a moment in London when I felt *you* had made me half-hearted. It seemed to me as if you had come into my life and pulled me to pieces, turned me into a sort of hybrid, incapable of either forceful goodness or forceful"—she couldn't say evil even now; something of modernity in her, of her epoch, prevented that. And she hesitated for a word—"forceful selfishness, egotism. Do I mean that? Perhaps. It seemed to me that I used to be at any rate all of a piece, and that now I was unraveled. That is how I felt it."

"Do you feel that now?"

"I don't know."

The carriage turned to the left. They were near to Sils. They were skirting the vast lawn to which Milligan sometimes wheeled Hugo Dennistone. Beyond lay the long lake of Sils, calm in the evening light, untroubled by any traffic. Far off the Maloja Hotel stood up like a dark palace between the lake verge and the dusky mountains. The typical music of Switzerland, the music of swaying cow-bells, chimed through the evening with the chime of the stream. And a strangely intimate calm descended on Imogen's spirit. She looked towards the houses of Sils-Maria and she had a feeling of home-coming, as if this was the place she was meant for; as

if here she could be freely herself, as if here she must know
what herself really was. She heard herself sigh.

Then she said, going back to the last words of their conversation, "Perhaps that's not true. Perhaps this evening I
don't feel so incomplete. But I'm with you. D'you know I
think I must be a very weak vessel? Perhaps most women are.
I feel, when I'm with you, that you are thinking for me and
that I am somehow one with your thought for me."

"You are learning to be your true self," he said in his slow,
deep voice. "What does it matter who gives the lesson? The
teacher counts for less than the scholar. And now you have
the will to learn how to live." A moment after he said,
"Where are you going to stay?"

"At the Waldhaus. Where is the Alpenrose?"

"There!" He pointed. "At the edge of the village."

"Hugo's there."

"Yes."

She thought when he said that there was something absolutely impersonal in the sound of his voice. And that imper-
sonality challenged her.

"D'you think he'll be glad to see me?" she asked. "He
isn't expecting me. D'you think it will be a happy surprise
for him?"

"You are the one on earth whom he cares for," said Peter
Kharkoff.

To her surprise Imogen felt that there were tears in her
eyes, that they were welling up and threatening to fall over
the lids of her eyes and down her cheeks.

"Am I?" she murmured. "I wasn't sure. At least I had
a sort of doubt in England. But I've been—I've been trying
to forget him there, to forget him and—and many things. But
it was of no use. I couldn't—I couldn't."

They were in the village now, close to the place where Hugo
on his couch had lain beside the limousine in which the priest
had murmured prayers to the dying man. And a breath of
pure cold came to them from the snow-field upon which the
windows of the chalet above the precipice looked out.

"I'll leave you here," said Peter Kharkoff, "and walk home."
She called to the coachman to stop his horses.

"You won't tell him I've come?" she asked, as he got out.
"I don't wish him to know before I see him."

"I won't tell him."

As the white horses strained at their collars to mount the hill, she gave him a last intent, earnest look. And just at that moment she remembered that she had another friend in the village, the organist.

CHAPTER IV

IMOGEN took two rooms with a terrace in the Waldhaus. They were at the end of a corridor. The terrace commanded a view of woods and mountains. After she had unpacked and arranged her things she wrapped a fur round her and went out bareheaded to watch the falling of night. The sky was quite clear. There would be stars presently. In the air there was now a touch of almost wintry coldness. Everything was very still. The afternoon wind had died completely away.

The terrace was fairly large. Imogen could take a few steps on it. She walked slowly and softly up and down, turning and turning almost like an animal in its cage. But she did not feel caged. On the contrary she had a great sense of freedom upon this height alone, in a silence which seemed very wonderful to her. Now and then she stopped and stood very still. The darkness was gathering in the undulating woods all about the Waldhaus, was creeping over the plain between the two lakes. As she watched she felt as if she could hear the oncoming footsteps of night. She saw a few lights below. Their significance increased as the darkness became slowly more definite. At last it was night.

She went in and rang her sitting-room bell; when a waiter came she asked for some food. In a few minutes he brought it in on a tray, laid a small table quickly and arranged it. Imogen shut the terrace window and sat down.

Now she began to feel rather tired and also rather strange. The air on this height was getting hold of her, was beginning to exercise influence over her. She drank a glass of red wine and some soup, ate some mutton, quickly peeled a peach, then ordered a cup of black coffee. When the waiter brought it she asked him where exactly the Hotel Alpenrose was. She had not quite "placed" it in her mind when Peter Kharkoff had pointed it out from the carriage. She had seen several houses, had not been sure which it was.

The waiter explained carefully. She thanked him and drank the coffee. Then she went into her bedroom and dressed for going out in a short fur coat and a cap and thick walking shoes. Oddly enough, now she had a feeling as if it were winter. For in spite of the stillness directly she opened the window she felt a breathing of cold. She took up a walking stick, left the bedroom and went down the long empty corridor. After descending the staircase she came into the hall and saw that it was crowded with people sitting about, drinking coffee and beer, playing bridge, patience and chess, or talking busily in loud voices. She heard nothing but German.

As she crossed the end of the hall to go out a distant band began playing Wagner's "Träume." A big boy in uniform standing beside the revolving door stared at her as he gave it a mechanical push to let her through. She came out on to the space in front of the hotel, turned to the left among the trees, then struck into the sharply curving road that led down abruptly into the village immediately below. She walked fast. She had made up her mind what she was going to do, and she wanted to do it quickly, not to give herself time to think about it too much, to call up imaginations about it, or to feel nervous as to its outcome. She remembered Peter Kharkoff's words to her in the carriage that afternoon about fear. She felt, distinctly felt, fears, like living things, trying to approach her, to stay with her, to possess her, but she seemed to herself to resist them tensely, like one making a physical effort. Henceforth she must have nothing to do with fear. Formerly she had often secretly prided herself on her courage. Now she knew that, though physically she had plenty of courage, she was not immune from the shadowy but often terrific fears of the mind and soul.

She descended into the village. The lighted windows gleamed upon the dark. A few people were hanging about. She heard voices coming to her through the enveloping voice of the stream. Some tourists in front of a hotel stared at her inquisitively as she passed them, and made some remarks in German. She went down a dark lane between dwelling houses. A dog barked at her from behind a wall. She heard a shutter let down somewhere. Slowly she filled her lungs with the extraordinary air. She had an odd, perhaps morbid, longing to increase the feeling of strangeness which she had been conscious of now for some time, and which she knew must come at least partly from the peculiar quality of the air in this valley. She felt at the same time herself and not fully herself. It was as if something were overcoming a part of her, and the part not attacked missed an habitual companion. She felt incomplete, and there was a lightness in her head which seemed to have something to do with the darkness, what exactly she didn't know.

The village of Sils-Maria is very small, and Imogen was soon at the edge of it and had come to the Alpenrose Hotel, whose many windows were lighted up. She was about to go in when she heard close by a steady tramp of feet near to her and coming towards her. Without knowing why, she hesitated and listened. Then she saw the figure of a man coming from the darkness into the yellow gleam before the hotel. It was Hendry, hatless, in a rough knickerbocker suit, gray stockings, thick square-toed boots, a flannel shirt unbuttoned at the neck, without a necktie, bronzed, and carrying a big gnarled stick with an iron point. As he came near to her she noticed an inward look in his steady eyes and realized that he hadn't yet seen her. And she had a brief instant of keen contemplation of him, saw him as a completely solitary individual alone in the night with his cargo of thoughts and dreams and aspirations, saw him as she had never yet seen him. Then his face changed. He had seen her, and the sight of her drew him away abruptly from his own mystery, simplified his expression quite marvelously, brought out of the almost stern thinking man the eager boyishness of him.

"By Jove!" He changed the stick quickly to his left hand and held out his right. "Funny I didn't feel it! No, not even when I was coming up. I mean feel that you were here. I've been for a longish tramp down the Maloja. Started very early this morning." He was still holding her hand and looking enthusiastically at her. "I had an idea you might come. But I never expected you tonight." He let go her hand. "You're staying here! That's splendid!"

"No. I'm at the Waldhaus."

"Oh!"

"I've come out to see Hugo Dennistone. Don't let us go in for a minute—unless you're awfully tired and hungry," she added, with a quick thought for him.

"I'm tremendously hungry. But that can wait."

She moved a few steps away from the hotel, he with her.

"I had your letter. And Milligan sent me a telegram. He said Captain Dennistone was well. By that he meant of course just as usual. What do you think—really?"

"Well, you see I never saw him till I met him here."

"I know. Since you wrote have you seen more of him?"

"Not very much. I don't think he cares for company particularly, except for Peter Kharkoff's."

"I met Mr. Kharkoff coming here. He drove part of the way with me. Is he often with Hugo Dennistone?"

"He sees him every day, I believe."

"Your letter was rather strange. It gave me the impression——" She hesitated. What exactly was the impression his letter had conveyed to her? "Can you tell me exactly what you feel about Hugo Dennistone? I mean about his general condition?"

Hendry looked, she thought, slightly embarrassed, not quite so natural as usual. "He doesn't look ill," he said.

"No. I gathered that from your letter."

"I scarcely know how to put it, really. Perhaps you know, as I do, impressions which one has and which one can hardly define. It's awfully difficult. Dennistone's so tremendously masculine, but—there seems to me to be something almost mystical hanging about him, an indefinable something."

"And that makes you think, or feel—what?"

Again Hendry looked embarrassed.

"You don't want to tell me?"

He looked at her, as if making an effort.

"I don't think I do," he said. "Besides, what would be the use? An impression of mine couldn't mean much to you. And —aren't you going to see for yourself?"

"Yes. I am, of course." But she still seemed to hesitate. "Has he got a sitting-room?" she asked.

"Yes. I believe they turned the bedroom next to his into one for him. I've never been in it. He's never asked me. I just see him now and then downstairs or in the garden."

"Do you like him?"

"Yes. I think he's a fine chap. But I expect he was much easier to get on intimate terms with before his accident than he is now."

"Or—before he met Peter Kharkoff," Imogen said slowly.

He looked at her but said nothing. She could see his eyes shining with inquiry in the semi-darkness.

"Well, I must go in and try to see him," she said, when she knew he wasn't going to make any rejoinder to her last remark.

She looked round at the night. The stars were out now. It was clear and cool, almost cold. She could feel the solitude of the valley, the solitude of the two lakes, one on either hand of them, the solitude of the heights and the snows.

"You've had a wonderful day. I'm sure of that," she said. "I can see it in your face. What a beast I've been to keep you when you're famishing. But I've always been selfish." As she spoke she moved towards the hotel.

"I'm quite enjoying your selfishness tonight," he said. "But I am frightfully hungry, and longing for beer too. Prosaic, isn't it?"

"I envy you," she said. And she said it in a way that made him know she meant it. They went into the hall together. "Good night," she said.

"But shan't I see you when you come down?"

"I don't know. I don't know how long I shall stay."

"If it's late mayn't I walk back with you to the Waldhaus? Not that there's the slightest danger here."

"Of course not. Besides, I 'm sure you're dog-tired. If I don't stay long perhaps I'll look in on you in the dining-room. But I can't tell—yet."

And then she turned to the concierge of the hotel, and as Hendry went off he heard her asking whether she could go up and see Captain Dennistone. But he didn't hear the concierge's answer. It was, "I'll send up and see, ma'am."

And the concierge was about to summon a boy when Imogen said, "Look here! I'm a very old friend of Captain Dennistone's and I want to give him a surprise. He doesn't know I'm here. Just tell me the number of his sitting-room and let me go up." As she spoke she put a five-franc note into the man's hand. "It's all right. You've seen me with that gentleman, Mr. Hendry. And I'm a friend of Mr. Peter Kharkoff too."

"Indeed, ma'am. Well, it's number eleven on the first floor."

Imogen turned away and began to go slowly up the staircase. On it she met a young, very dark waiter who looked at her with inquisitive black eyes. When she reached the corridor on the first floor it was deserted. She soon found number eleven, and stood outside the door looking up at it. Now that she was there, now that she had arrived at her destination, she hesitated to knock, to go in. Her long connection with the man beyond that door, with Hugo, oppressed her, troubled her obscurely. She remembered their active and wild youth together, their careless gaiety, their joyous arrogance, which had surely come from the pride of the body—and all that seemed very distant and very long ago. The hand of Fate seemed to have lengthened things out, to have changed Time's values.

And what was there to come? With what intention, what resolve had she come out to Switzerland and made her way now in the night to this closed door? She didn't know. She hadn't decided. But she now felt that what she had done in the body ought to be linked with some definite resolve of the mind, that she ought to go into the room behind that closed door with an intention to excuse her abrupt and unexpected coming. But wouldn't love be excuse enough? Wasn't love in fact excuse enough for almost anything? And when love was combined with pity what need of questions? Surely the reason stood plain. Nevertheless she felt doubtful, like one who hadn't enough faith in her own bona fides. Hugo's strange and unexplained withdrawal had shaken her confidence and her self-confidence.

Was she in conflict with the Unearthly?

She heard a voice and saw the dark young waiter with the inquisitive eyes coming towards her with a tray. Then quickly she stretched out her hand to the door of number eleven and knocked on it.

"Entrez!" cried a voice within.

The young waiter went by, staring with Italian eyes.

Imogen put her hand on the door.

"Entrez!" called the voice again.

Then she opened the door and went in, filled with an anxious curiosity.

She saw a bedroom turned into a sitting-room, clean, trim, banal. Two or three armchairs, a writing table, a screen, a center table had been brought in to suggest a "salon." A wardrobe remained showing that the room was usually a bedroom. There was a badly arranged vase of flowers on the table in the middle of the room. Lying beside it were a copy of the Morning Post and a copy of The Field. There were also three books with library tickets pasted on them. At the end of the room a window was wide open to the night, showing a bit of the sky with its stars. In front of it was Hugo's couch, arranged so that his feet pointed towards the window as he lay. A rug was drawn over him up to his chest. His arms lay outside it. As Imogen came in she looked at the back of his head. He seemed to her to be staring out at the stars. He was alone.

When she had come into the room she paused for a moment by the door.

"Qui est là?" said Hugo. And she saw him move as if he wished to look round.

She shut the door softly. "It's I—Imogen!" she said.

And she went up at once to the couch and stood by it looking down at the prostrate man. He looked up at her in silence. He was evidently very much startled. She could see that clearly. And for a moment it seemed to her that she could only see that—his amazement, could not penetrate through it or discover what lay beneath it. And she felt that it was not a quite normal shock of surprise at a totally unexpected happening that for a moment held him in a sort of paralysis, but something sharper, stronger.

The thought in her mind was, "From where and what have I recalled him?"

He had been looking at the stars; lying there alone in the cool night air looking at the stars. And perhaps he had been traveling among them, voyaging from star to star of that glittering company. She was sure he had been very far off. And she was quite sure of something else—that he had not been thinking of her.

"Geney!" he said at last. And he put out a hand.

She bent down and took it, drew up a chair and sat down by his couch.

There was still a faintly startled expression on his face, and she noticed that he had reddened. There had been a movement of the responsive blood, attacked by the mind. His blue eyes looked half bewildered, like a child's. She could not take her eyes from his face.

"You weren't expecting me! You didn't think I should come!" Before he had time to answer she added, "What were you thinking about when I came in?"

She was suddenly filled with a profound curiosity about that. He didn't answer and still looked half bewildered, and she said, "You were not thinking about me."

As she knew this and stated it, bitterness welled up in her, as if it had been gathered at the sources of her being and now abruptly flooded her. She felt that this man, though inert, tied to his couch, was nevertheless escaping from her—or was at the least intending to escape. She felt herself the huntress—evaded. Something in him was swerving away from her; and she had thought him so absolutely hers.

And then she remembered Peter Kharkoff's words to her that day, words which had brought sudden tears to her eyes. "You are the one on earth that he cares for."

If that were true what was the explanation of Hugo's strange attitude towards her? She felt jealous of the power which she divined in him, the power to travel to regions which were unknown to her. Suddenly she felt sure that Peter Kharkoff had enabled Hugo to go beyond any place that she was able to gain. While she had been in London, miserably trying to excite and to content herself with things physical, Hugo had been initiated.

She stared at him. There was something blank in her gaze. She repeated to herself, "Initiated—initiated." And she felt outside. But there was a fighting spirit in her, and it came uppermost in her now.

"I think you've been forgetting me lately," she said. "But I've been remembering you. At first I thought you were coming to London. I expected you. I thought it was arranged between us that you'd follow me. When I found you didn't intend to come I hesitated for a while. I didn't quite know what to do. Then I felt that I must come out to you. Whether you wanted me or not I felt I must come. I arrived by the afternoon train. Peter Kharkoff drove part of the way with me here. I'm staying at the Waldhaus."

"At the Waldhaus!" he repeated. "Are you there?" And his voice sounded surprised. It seemed as if the mere fact that she had put up at the Waldhaus astonished him.

"Well, I had to go somewhere," she said. "And I didn't know whether you would care to have me in the Alpenrose. That's what it has come to, Hugo. I don't know. I'm in the dark. I hardly thought that things could ever be like this between *us*. In the old days we were more open-hearted to each other."

"In the old days—" he said. He broke off and lay looking at her. And then there came upon her a strange feeling about him. It was the feeling that he was far away from her. It was a feeling of distance. "We can't go back to them," he said.

"No, of course not. But we can go on to new days that will be different, quite different, but that surely needn't be unhappy."

She tried to speak firmly, but nevertheless there was something faltering in her voice, in her manner as she said those words. There was—she knew it—no real conviction in them. Something in Hugo's bright blue eyes, which were fixed upon her, took away from her all her normal, hardy self-confidence. There was a very soft look in them, and a great earnestness, but they seemed to be considering her with a scrutiny to which she was quite unaccustomed from Hugo.

No longer did he accept her simply, with a great masculine simplicity, as Imogen Lowrie, the girl he admired and loved and wanted, the human creature of a different sex to whom his sex instinctively clung, the woman who could enable him to fulfil himself—his destiny. She knew that. She knew that he was considering her in some surely profound way, not coldly, but from a standpoint of which she knew nothing. And she felt small, doubtful, ignorant and strangely humble. Formerly she had—wasn't it so?—looked down on Hugo from altitudes of the assured and self-confident mind. Now, not her mind but something else—her spirit perhaps—felt itself inferior to his. She realized that he had knowledge which she hadn't acquired, and she realized too that it was knowledge tremendously worth while.

"I want to make you happy," she said.

"You've been wonderfully good to me, Geney," he said. "And it's been all the more wonderful because sometimes you've had such a struggle over it."

"A struggle!" she said. She felt as if her face were scarlet. The skin of her face tingled. She felt unveiled, exposed, found out, felt as if a harsh white light had suddenly been turned upon all the most secret places of her. "How can you say that? It's not true!" she said, bowed beneath the stark truth of it. She got up. "I—I think that's the most cruel thing that's ever been said to me," she exclaimed.

"Geney dear——"

"You send me away from you. You make me go to London. You try to force me back into a way of life that I had practically done with. And you stay—you stay—in the atmosphere I had begun to be happy and at peace in. And then, instead of coming to me in London where you knew I was waiting for you, you come up here to stay for an indefinite time—without me. And when I can't stand it, and follow you here, you tell me I have had—I've had to struggle to be good to you. You may have learned many things since we were together. You have. I feel that. I don't know what they are. But you've learned a very ordinary thing too—how to be cruel."

"Geney dear, I didn't mean to be cruel. I was really thinking how wonderfully unselfish you have been. I was——"

"What did you mean by a struggle? How could you know there was any struggle? How? How?" She still had the horrible feeling of a woman come upon when she was naked, without protection or hiding-place. And his remark had startled her dreadfully, had revealed to her a man far more subtle and secretly observant than she had supposed Hugo to be.

"If you say there wasn't——" he began.

"I have said so!" she said, trying to speak with assertive conviction, and looking at him with the hard, steady eyes of a determined person telling a lie and resolved to stick to it whether it carried out its task of convincing or not.

"Oh—Geney!" was all he said. And it was he who looked down, almost as if ashamed, while she still stood there, near the open window, staring at him with ugly determination.

"I know what it is," she said after a terrible pause in which she felt devastated by a strange angry excitement and by thrills of a subtle fear. "I know what it is. You have been seeing me lately not with your own eyes but with the eyes of another. That's it! And you've been thinking about me not with your own but with another's mind. I'm not surprised, not really a bit surprised. When I was in London I thought how it would be—might be. I thought—I had a feeling that you were beginning to criticize me, to weigh me up, to get on the track of my faults. I know I have plenty, but I thought there was one man who accepted me as I was—with them, with all of them. I thought you did. Oh, he's been my enemy! All the time he's been my enemy. I brought him to you because there was something—I thought he could help you perhaps in your trouble. And now he's made you see me with cruel eyes."

"No, Geney, there's no cruelty in him. And he couldn't teach another man to be cruel."

"Then why did he take you away from me?"

"But he hasn't."

"Then why did you come here, instead of following me to London?"

"Geney, don't stand there." He lifted a hand. "Come and sit here by me."

There was no anger in his voice or manner, no agitation in his eyes. Only a great seriousness showed in him. And this seriousness, at the basis of which there must surely be calm, made Imogen feel inferior to him. Again she thought, "He's initiated, and I'm not."

"Come—Geney."

She came over and sat down again close to him. "Well?" she said. And she lit a cigarette. She was making a great effort to recover her usual self-possession, to conceal from him the fact that she was still seething with excitement. Always, in their former relations with each other, she had secretly felt herself to be superior to Hugo. This new and growing feeling of inferiority disturbed her horribly. "Why did you come here?"

"I felt I had to. I felt I needed to think things out more thoroughly than I'd been able to do. It's awfully difficult to explain. I felt I had to be quiet a little longer."

"And my being with you prevented you from being quiet!"

"Yes—perhaps. Anyhow, I knew London was impossible for me."

"But why not ask me—tell me? Why not explain things?"

"I didn't see quite how I could make you understand."

"I know. You thought that, being what I was, I was incapable of understanding certain things, things that *you* could understand."

"I've been through a lot that you haven't been through," he said simply. "I've had a chance to think given me that you and most others haven't had. I used always to be doing things. Now I'm always thinking things."

"And feeling things?" she said, fixing her eyes on him.

"Yes. When I look back I know I scarcely thought at all in the old days. It's different now. You shouldn't expect me to be the same."

"And you shouldn't go on thinking that I am the same.

Your accident hasn't happened to me. But it's altered me."
Her eyes had an inward look in them now, and she added,
"It seems to have altered all the values for me—your accident." She was looking back on the old world—of hers and
his. And it seemed to be lying in shadow, like some strange
and abandoned derelict. "And yet you go on thinking that I'm
essentially unchanged, that all the change is in you."

He was silent.

"Isn't what I say true?" she asked.

"I don't say you haven't changed. But think how young
you are, Geney—and nearly all your life before you. You
have moments of thinking you'll never want to be as you
were. I know that. But there's no force upon you. On me
there is. I *can't* be as I was. My life as it was has been
ripped away from me. I've *got* to be different."

"In the body—yes. But I wasn't thinking about the body."

"It has a say, Geney. It has a tremendous say in this life
of ours. Don't make any mistake. Mine used to seem to be
me. Now it's just my prison. That's the difference, Geney,
old girl. But yours still seems to be *you,* doesn't it?"

"Perhaps. Partly, not wholly. But in a way I suppose it
does."

She looked down at her body. She tried to consider it
coldly as a shell. But she couldn't. He was right. It did
seem to be herself, because all of it was vitalized by the powerful spirit of energetic life which she felt permeating it, pulsing
all through her.

"I can't help that," she said. "There are things I can't help.
But I'm not all helpless. You talk of my being young. After
all that's happened lately, I sometimes don't feel young at all.
You sent me off from Sainte Maxime almost as a baby is sent
off to the nursery to play with its toys."

"But you didn't play?"

"Perhaps I tried to play. I did try to play. You did a
dangerous thing when you sent me away." She frowned. She
was staring now into vacancy. "You stayed in safety, and sent
me away into danger. I think—I think it was selfish of you—
both."

She paused, waited and then said, with her eyes on him:

"Were you happy without me? *You,* I mean?"

"I was learning to be more at home with things than I'd
ever been since the accident."

"At home with things?"

"It seemed rather like making peace with my fate, Geney. I hadn't been able to do that before."

"And have you made peace with it?"

He seemed to hesitate for an instant. Then he said, "Something very like that, I think."

She had a feeling of sudden cold. "And am I to be left outside of it—this peace?" she said. "Don't you want to take me into it?" And again she was painfully conscious of a great distance between her and this man who had loved her, who perhaps loved her still, but in a way that was strange, that she hadn't learned to understand. "Do you want to keep me outside of everything?" The cold feeling was increasing upon her, a feeling of being shut out.

"What have I done to earn all this?" she went on. "I've puzzled over it. I've lain awake at night in London and thought and thought—why. I've lain awake till I've heard the sparrows. But no answer has come. No one seems to believe in me. There was a man in London. He wanted me, and I thought I wanted him—in a way. But he couldn't believe in my beastliness. And you can't believe in my other sincerity— such a different sincerity! There's so much more of me in it! And so you send me away, and try to keep me away. If only you could really believe in me do you know what would happen? I should be what you believed."

Just then it was as if illumination came to her. Hesitation left her, and those fears—couldn't she hear their retreating steps? She leaned towards him as he lay looking up at her.

"I was angry just now. You hurt me. But what you said was true. I have had to struggle. I didn't want you to know it. I hated you knowing it. And I felt you knew it through him, Peter Kharkoff. It seemed to me that he had given me away to you. And that startled me. But the struggle's over now. Since I've been in London this time I've learned a great deal about myself. I want to marry you, old boy. When I'm out of your life I feel out in the cold. It's a dreadful feeling. Do let me come really into your life, and try to make it better. That's my only way to happiness. I'm certain of that. Perhaps whatever we do we're being selfish, trying to satisfy some interior need. It may be so. Anyhow I believe I'm being selfish now. Because I feel a tremendous need to be in your life, such as I've never felt before."

There was an intense scrutiny in his eyes as he lay looking at her when she had finished speaking. She felt that with the whole of his mind he was considering something.

"Why don't you speak? What are you thinking about?" she said.

"Suppose things were with me just as they are now, Geney," he said, "only that we, you and I, had never come across Peter Kharkoff, how would it be then?"

"How? What do you mean, Hugo?"

"Are you sure that the struggle would be over then? Suppose I had been up here alone with Milligan, and we had never so much as heard of Peter Kharkoff?"

"Yes?"

"Would you have felt that you *must* come out to me then? Does he stand for nothing in all this?"

She didn't answer him.

"He's up there in the chalet near the Waldhaus. Suppose he wasn't. Suppose you didn't know there was such a man in the world?"

"What is it you want to imply?"

"I'm only asking you. Marriage with a fellow in my condition for a girl like you is such a tremendous undertaking. There's only one thing could make it a success, only one thing. And that thing would have to be stripped of every influence, even of his influence."

"Yes, of course. I understand. I know what you mean." She got up from her chair uneasily. "There it is again!" she exclaimed. "Your eternal doubt of me!"

She went to the open window, turned her back on him and looked out. This place without Peter Kharkoff, without the knowledge that he was near, without knowledge of his existence? Hugo and she alone here? Hugo's strange questioning made her realize how the Jew had become a dweller in their two lives, how he had influenced them, how their lives embraced him, or he embraced their lives. Even in thought she could not disentangle their lives from him, and therefore she could not answer Hugo's questions. It was impossible for her to imagine her existence ignorant of the fact that Peter Kharkoff was.

Standing there, looking out into the night, she tried to do that. But she simply couldn't. It seemed as impossible for her not to know that he was, as not to know that there were stars. She looked at them, then at the night leaning over the plain between the two lakes, hidden from her eyes now. The strange, wonderful air which seemed to have changed her, to have detached her from her quite usual personality, to have set her floating—something like that; she didn't know exactly how to put it to herself, but she was definitely aware of feeling physically as well as mentally unusual—came to her, bathed her, made of her a possession. And she remembered the words, "It's the air people need."

He knew what they needed, what she, what Hugo needed. But why should he know that? Why had he entered into their lives as no other man had done, as, she felt, no other man could have done? What was the peculiar quality in him which permeated others, stealing through them as that wonderful air stole across the grass, stole through the pine trees, that high air, bringing healing and strength, altering, subduing, vitalizing? What was his secret? Did Hugo know? Was that why he seemed to her almost mystically changed? Was that why he had made such a peculiar impression upon Hendry, the organist? Had Hugo learned it after she had left him by the Gulf of Saint Tropez? Had he been learning it while she had been fiercely trying to console herself with husks in London? She turned round, but still stayed by the window. "Hugo," she said. "What's the secret of this man? What's the secret of Peter Kharkoff? Do you know it?"

She could see by his eyes that he was startled by her question. She didn't wait for him to answer then, but added, "You want to know from me whether my feeling for you is stripped of every influence, even of *his*. Wasn't that it?"

"Yes."

"How could it be, since I know him? It seems to me that his influence permeates me. He may not want it to; he may not try to make it do that; but it does, it must. That day, when I heard of your accident, I went to him. I had to go to him, to take your case to him. Why was that? And later on, when we were still at the villa, I had to try to bring him to you. What did I expect of him? And what has he done? What *is* he? Do you know? Have you found out?"

"He's never told me. He never assumes anything. I mean never assumes to be different from the rest of us."

"But he *is* different."

"Yes."

"Do you think——" She stopped. Then she said, "What do you think?"

"He's much better than the rest of us."

"Yes?"

"He seems to *know*. He does know."

"What?"

"What we don't know, the meaning of it all—why."

"But how can that be?"

"I couldn't tell you."

"Do you think—does he seem to you Christlike?"

"No. Somehow he doesn't."

"But then—what?"

"Don't ask me, Geney. I couldn't explain. He's more like my idea—no, it's no use. I can't explain." For a moment he looked restless, almost agitated.

"From time to time in the world's history exceptional men have come upon the earth," Imogen said slowly. "I suppose they had some special task to carry out."

"I dare say."

"Has he?"

"The world's in an awful muddle since the war, isn't it?"

"Yes. And almost everyone's a pessimist."

"He isn't."

"No. That alone makes him seem wonderful to me."

"He believes in human nature," said Hugo very simply. "He believes in us, in all of us. That's helped me a lot."

"Then if he believes, and has helped you by believing, why can't you believe? Why can't you believe in me? You must. You shall."

A sudden desperate determination had come to her, a sort of passion for sacrifice, combined with a longing to be within the circle of safety which surely surrounded him. Since she had seen Hugo again a sense of loneliness had increased upon her and now began to overwhelm her. He was, she felt, in spite of his helplessness, the martyrdom of his body, somewhere, in some state, some place even, where something in her desired to be. She must join him there. An intense longing for dedication swept her. At that moment she felt like a devotee.

"Take me into your life," she said. "Really into your life. You say I've had to struggle to—to—I'm not struggling now. All I want, all I care for now is to be your wife, to take care of you, make things better for you, be one with you."

She got up from her chair and kneeled down beside his couch. At that moment she forgot everything in the tremendous and strange desire to sink herself in—what? She said to herself—in Hugo. She probably believed that it was in Hugo. As she took his hands in hers she probably believed that she was concentrated on Hugo.

"He says you do care about me. He told me today that you care for me. Then what is there to keep us apart any longer?"

"Geney! Bend down a little more."

"Yes? Yes?"

She bent down. He whispered something into her ear.

When he had ceased there was a moment of absolute silence. Then she said, "I don't care. I don't care. We are going to be married. It's meant that we should be married."

But she had become very pale.

CHAPTER V

It was late when the door of number eleven opened and Imogen came out. Milligan met her in the corridor and greeted her without surprise. He had been told by the dark young waiter that a young lady was with Captain Dennistone and had guessed at once who she was. He was pleased, even delighted, and showed it in his usual unselfconscious way.

"Very glad to see you, ma'am. I'm sure your coming will cheer Mr. Hugo up."

"But do you think he needed that?" she asked.

"I don't know. We all did our best for him, and I will say he seemed rather happy here—in a way. But still now it will be very different."

"It's all decided, Milligan. We're going to be married very soon."

"That's good news, ma'am. Splendid news."

"Good night, Milligan."

"Good night, ma'am."

She was gone. It struck Milligan that she wanted to get away from him. There was something rather strange about her. Wasn't there? She had looked excited, strained even. And there had been something troublingly self-conscious in her eyes which had made Milligan feel for once almost awkward.

He stood still for a moment in the corridor after she had disappeared in the direction of the staircase. Then he looked at his silver watch. It was twenty minutes to midnight. He had been waiting for a long time for his employer's interview with the "young lady" to be over. He put his watch back and went into Mr. Hugo's room.

Meanwhile Imogen went down the staircase quickly. She did not realize the hour. She had no idea how long she had been with Hugo. The thought of time had never been in her mind since she had been in that upstairs room, and it was not with her now. She felt like one who had gained a victory, but not easily. And wasn't it a double victory, won over another and also over herself? At last surely she was shaking herself free from that horrible hybrid something, from that mixed personality which had caused those whom she knew best to doubt her, to withhold all real confidence from her, and which had also tortured herself. Now she had definitely cast in her lot with the better part of her. And she had done it not carelessly, not at haphazard, but with intense resolution, and knowing fully at what cost. She thrilled with the excitement of endeavor followed by accomplishment.

When she came into the hall it was dimly lit and only the night porter was there. Then, and only then, she realized how late it was. "Good night," she said to the man.

He came to let her out. The hotel was locked up. When he had unfastened the door he wished her good night in broken English and stood for a moment watching her go into the dimness of the night thickly powdered with stars but moonless. And just before she faded out of his sight he saw a dark figure approach her and as it were melt with hers into the void. He stepped outside, stood there and listened. But he could hear nothing, no footfalls, no voices. And after a long pause he went back into the hotel and shut and locked the door behind him.

The dark figure was Hendry's. Imogen saw him without surprise. She had not been thinking of him. She had totally forgotten him. But now his joining her in the darkness seemed quite natural.

"May I walk back with you?" he said.

"Yes. Oh, but——" she suddenly remembered. "You've been walking all day. Didn't you tell me—the Maloja? You must be tired out."

"No, I'm not."

"Besides—what time is it?"

"Nearly midnight. What does that matter? It's all the more reason really for someone to walk back with you."

"Is it?" she said vaguely. And they walked on together in silence.

The village was asleep. No light showed in its darkness. The absolute soundlessness let through to them—so it seemed—the voice of the stream which flowed beneath the precipice of rock at the edge of the village.

"How strange the water sounds in the night!" said Imogen. "Like Nature happy in being left to herself. Nature must surely be happiest when men are subdued by sleep. Let us go to the edge of the stream just for a moment."

"Yes."

"It's this way."

They stopped where Hugo had lain on his wheeled couch and heard the faint murmur of the priest's voice to the dying man in the limousine. Imogen listened, looked down on the water which sounded loud in the night. Then, without knowing why, she looked up, and away; far above her in the darkness, she saw the steady gleam of a solitary light. Hendry saw her look at it for a long time, and her young face seemed to him to be stern in its earnestness.

At last she said, "That isn't the Waldhaus. Who lives up there? Someone is awake."

"That's where Peter Kharkoff lives."

She said nothing, but continued to look up at the light. And in that moment a great peace flowed into her heart. The trouble of the world seemed to fade, to diminish, finally to be no more. Someone was watching over all things, was watching over her, keeping her safe. She had a sense of quietly resigning herself into hands that could not let her fall into any abyss of sorrow, of shame, of sin. And she felt whole, not divided. She felt complete.

When at last she withdrew her eyes from the light and spoke again she said, "Hugo Dennistone and I are going to be married almost directly. We arranged it tonight. I think I can make him happy. At any rate I'm going to try. And I shall put my heart into it. He's fine, isn't he? Don't you think?"

"I'm sure he is."

"And I'm sure you know what is fine and what isn't," she said. "I'll go up to the Waldhaus alone. It's close by. And you must go home and sleep." She held out her hand to him.

"But shall I leave you here?"

"Yes, please. Good night. Thank you for coming with me."

He left her with the stream—and the light.

Imogen stayed where she was for some time, ten minutes or more. She heard the church clock chime in the dark. She drank in the cold pure air from the snow-field not so very far away. Another air, she fancied, came up to her from the ruffled surface of the swiftly flowing stream at her feet, a softer, more delicate air, intimate and insinuating. It seemed to be whispering to her secrets of Nature. She felt very near to Nature just then in the night.

Often she gazed up at the little light far away on the hilltop. And she remembered the light shining out on the snow in Geneva. And she had a longing to climb up to that height, to go to a door and knock, and to tell Peter Kharkoff what she had done that night. She had convinced Hugo of the genuineness of her love. She had made him accept her. She had truly dedicated her life at last. She would be a childless wife. But she would surround a crippled man with her love. And she would strike a great blow against something in her nature which she had mentally indulged to a point almost of lasciviousness, though she had, by chance as it seemed, stopped short there, avoided the physical completion of the thought-process.

Did Peter Kharkoff know? And if he did, wouldn't he believe that now at last she knew how to live? She couldn't help, in spite of her love for Hugo, feeling about her a sort of glory of self-sacrifice. For she was an ardent girl and she was dedicating herself to sterility. She thought of the French actress. Hugo must be her nunnery. She had a longing to enter in. There surely she would find peace and contentment. She would cast off the exasperating longings of the flesh. She would give herself to the spirit. With her purity she would match the different purity of Nature, the purity she was feeling, was drinking in, was giving herself to now, alone in the night.

She was gazing down at the stream when suddenly she was conscious that something had happened, something which made the night different. She looked up towards the precipice. The light on its summit had disappeared.

CHAPTER VI

WHEN Imogen was at last once more in her room at the Waldhaus she could not go to bed. Perhaps she was tired. She was probably very tired. But there seemed to be no power of sleep in her, and she felt no desire for sleep. She could not bear the thought of leaving the night and Nature outside, of shutting out those two marvelous companions. And she went out on to her terrace and sat there till the night was beginning to fail, and the peculiar chill precedent to dawn crept up through the forest trees that surrounded the Waldhaus. Then she got up, went to the parapet and stood looking down into the dimness, in which presently she fancied she could discern a faint hint of grayness, wavering, indistinct, surreptitious, day stealing among the trees, as yet timid and shy, and unsure of his welcome.

She was not ready for him yet, could not hold out her hands to him. She longed to retain the night with its high thoughts, and its vaporous dreams which seemed full of legend, with its ideals which mounted quite easily towards the stars. And she went in from the terrace, drew the shutters and kept darkness with her. As soon as she was inside the house and had done that, she knew that she was tired, even very tired. And she went to her bedroom, undressed quickly, got into bed and very soon slept.

Just before she fell asleep she had the thought, "At last it is decided! At last I am on the threshold of my real life."

And she didn't feel afraid of it any more.

She slept profoundly. Layers and layers of sleep surely covered her, and beneath them, dreamless, she was almost as one dead.

She was awakened, long before she had finished with sleep, by a knocking on the door of her bedroom. She sat up bewildered. The knocking went on and seemed to her to get louder and louder. At first she didn't realize things, and imagined she was in Lowndes Square and that her maid was outside. Knowing she hadn't had enough sleep she was angry, and called out something. (She never knew what.) But the knocking persisted, and seemed at last to knock her brutally into the knowledge of where she was and of the happening of the previous night.

"Switzerland—Sils-Maria—Hugo—the Waldhaus!" Yes, now she knew, now she realized! But why this knocking?

"Yes! Yes!" she called out. And she got quickly out of bed, put on a dressing gown and went to the door.

"What is it? What's the matter? What do you want?" she called out in French. A voice answered in French:

"Madame, a gentleman has come. He wishes to see you."

"A gentleman! I can't see anyone. I was asleep. You've waked me up. Please go away."

"But, madame, it is important."

"Who's speaking?"

"The concierge, madame. The gentleman will wait till you can see him."

Could it be Berazov? She felt angry, indignant. "Who is it?" she said, close to the door.

"Madame?"

She unlocked the door and opened it slightly. "What is the gentleman's name?" she said. "Have you got a card?"

"No, madame," said the concierge in English. "He hasn't got one. But his name is Hendree and he knows madame. He is staying——"

"Mr. Hendry!" interrupted Imogen, astonished.

"Yes, madame."

"What time is it?"

"A little after eight o'clock, madame."

"Mr. Hendry here!"

She didn't speak for a moment. The man and she stood on either side of the partially closed door in silence. Then she said, "I'll come down as soon as I'm dressed. Please tell him."

And she shut the door. She didn't lock it. She didn't think of locking it again, but, having shut it, she stood still for a moment in the dark room. What could have brought Hendry to the Waldhaus at such an hour, have led him to insist on seeing her when he must have known she was likely to be still asleep?

They had parted so late by the stream, scarcely eight hours ago. And even then she hadn't gone home. He had left her standing by the water. And he had had a tremendous walk, had been out all day in that air which brings strength, but which also brings sleep to a man. He wouldn't have waked so early unless someone had roused him. He must have been roused as she had been. Why?

Suddenly she felt full of dread. To combat her dread she began quickly to do things, to make her toilet. And while she was doing that she tried not to think. She tried to concentrate entirely on the ordinary things, the things she did every morning. Presently she was putting on a gown. And just at that moment she knew that her dread had been growing all the time she had been washing and dressing, and that it was now taking entire possession of her. She was horribly frightened.

When her gown was on she was ready to go down to see why the organist had come, but she felt as if she couldn't bring herself to do that. Like one who, fearing to be found the victim of some awful disease, dreads to visit a specialist, the man who can find out, she longed to delay, to preserve for still a little while the ignorance which was torturing her, but which might nevertheless be a better condition than hers would be when she knew. And she moved aimlessly about the room, stood still, moved again, again stood still. A sickness of dread was with her. She had never felt anything at all like it before. The physical and the mental joined hands in it. She was positive now that Hendry had come with some frightful news.

But she didn't whisper a name. She tried not to admit a name into her mind.

At last she felt that there was nothing for it but to face the fact, whatever it might be. And she opened the door to go down. She saw a corridor with boots outside doors. The sun was shining outside. A waiter came carrying a tray laden with coffee, milk, rolls, butter, honey. He knocked at a door. If the knocking on her door had meant that! She went down the corridor slowly and came to the lift shaft. She pressed the bell. Directly she had pressed it she wished she hadn't. The lift traveled so fast. She would rather go down by the staircase. And she was just moving away when the lift appeared smoothly, and the boy in it opened the cage door. He held it, smiling, and she had to get in. Instantly he shut the door, touched something—with incredible swiftness she felt—and the lift glided down and was on the hall level. Then he opened the door, and she stepped out to meet the fact.

She did not see Hendry and went towards the bureau. A man in livery came to her. She thought he looked at her with almost eager curiosity.

"Where's——" she began.

"The gentleman is over there, madame."

And then she saw the figure of a man standing near a window at the end of the large and otherwise empty hall. It was Hendry. He was standing still with his back towards her, apparently looking out of the window. He hadn't seen her yet, hadn't felt her approach. She stood for an instant and stared down the hall at him. He knew—the fact. As she stared at him she was trying to get at it. And strangely it seemed to her that she did get at it. But she refused it. She said to herself, "No, it isn't that! It can't be that! One can't find out a thing by looking. One can't see into another's mind. No—no—no!" And then Hendry turned round sharply and saw her. And so she had to go to him.

"Good morning," she said, as she came up to him. "I'm sorry I had to keep you waiting. But when you came I was fast asleep. What is it?"

Hendry's face was much bronzed by air and sun. Even his forehead was brown. For he hadn't worn a hat since he had been in the Engadine. But in spite of the color burnt into his face she had the feeling that he was pale. It was like that. She seemed to feel pallor in him. His rather sharply cut, intellectual features looked knife-like and pinched. And his eyes only met hers for an instant. Then, as if afraid of piercing deep into something they shouldn't see, they looked away. And even when he spoke they didn't look at her. He forced them to look away, though it was almost impossible to him to speak to anyone without keeping his eyes on the person spoken to. Imogen thought in the brief moment of their meeting hers she had detected an expression that was like an expression of guilt in them. But how could that be?

"What is it?" she said again, trying to speak in a light commonplace voice.

"Sorry to disturb you, but I had to come! I hate to—I'm sorry it's fallen to me to—oh, what's the good of all that? We've got to bear things in life. Whatever comes along for us we've just got to bear it. I've come because there's trouble down at the Alpenrose."

"Trouble? What trouble?"

"Hugo Dennistone is dead. This morning when Milligan went in to him he found him dead." He was still looking down. His usually energetic, rather high-pitched voice sounded colorless.

After a long pause Imogen said, "I believe I knew it was that. I believe I knew directly they told me you were here."

Then he looked at her. "You expected——"

"Oh no!"

She sat down heavily on something. She didn't know whether it was a chair, sofa, what it was.

"Oh no! It was only when they told me you were here— so early. But why should he die? Why should Hugo die? He wasn't ill. He was crippled, but he wasn't ill. He looked wonderfully well. You seemed to think—when you wrote to me in London did you think he was going to die?" Why was she talking—talking? Why was she sitting there and talking? She didn't know. "Did you?"

"I didn't think anything. But I did have a feeling that he was much nearer to the other side than all of us round him were."

"Ah!" She sat for a minute. Then she said, "Why did he die? What made Hugo die?"

"He needn't have died," said Hendry.

"Needn't have died? What do you mean?"

"I mean that it seems—Milligan thinks he chose to die."

"Chose! But how can we—but we can't——"

She stopped. She hadn't understood, but now she grasped the meaning of his words, and sat very still, bowed under the weight of it and trying, but numbly, to realize all it implied. For she felt that this act, of which he had just told her, had been prompted by something not at all ordinary, by something with which she was intimately connected, in which she had even played a definite part. Behind Hugo's terrible act she detected, as if hiding in shadow furtively, another act that perhaps had prompted it. And with that act she was concerned.

Last night! What had this death got to do with last night? Hugo had told her something. He had confessed a secret that was very hard for a man to tell. Could it be that afterwards, in the night, when she had left him alone, the bitterness of that manly confession had tormented him, had finally driven him beyond sanity, had prompted him to end his difficult life? But she had received his confession with eager tenderness. She hadn't hesitated—not even for an instant. She was certain of that. Her "I don't care!" had come at once, and it had been desperately genuine. For she had realized in that moment the

possibilities of self-sacrifice opening out before her, and she had
rushed to seize them, to hug them to her.

She saw Hendry looking at her with terribly seeing eyes.
Could he read her? Had Milligan——

"Tell me how it was!" she said. And she composed herself
to listen, mechanically. She had to hear it. She had to know.
It was best to get it over.

"When Milligan went into Dennistone's room this morning
he found him dead."

"Why was Hugo dead?"

"He had taken an overdose of morphia in the form of pills.
It seems that after his accident, at the time when he suffered
acute pain, he was allowed morphia."

"Yes, I know."

"He must have kept some with him. Milligan didn't know
it. Perhaps his servant knew. But he is in England."

"Yes."

Hendry didn't say anything more. At last Imogen asked,
"Is that all?"

"Yes."

"He was just found dead? No writing—no message—
nothing?"

"No. Nothing has been found."

After another long pause Imogen said, "I suppose this seems
to you like the action of a coward. But Hugo was not a
coward. He didn't know how to be a coward. It's impossible that he should have ended his life because of fear, because
of *himself*." While she was speaking she seemed to be feeling
her way towards the truth of this matter, or at least to be
trying to feel her way.

"I knew him so little," said Hendry. "But to me he seemed
a fine type of fellow. He reminded me of a splendid tree that
had been felled and was lying on the ground."

"Yes. He was like that." She sat for some minutes in
silence. Hendry could see in her eyes that she was thinking
deeply. And he felt that there was in her a great pain of the
mind. She was in travail with thought. He knew that just
then he was forgotten. If he got up quietly, if he went away,
would she know? He doubted it. She wasn't looking at him.
He didn't think she would know. At last she came back—it
was like that, like a coming back—looked again at him, and
said, "Does Peter Kharkoff know?"

"No. He can't. No one's been to tell him. We thought of you first."

Imogen got up. "I'm going to tell him."

"Now?"

"Yes."

"Shall I come with you?"

"No, please. I must go alone. How does one go? Please tell me and I'll find the way. It isn't very far, is it?"

"No."

"We'll go out and then you can tell me."

He followed her across the hall and out into the open space before the hotel. It was a perfect morning, crystal clear and very still. The air had a marvelous element of lightness, of purified thinness in it. Hendry thought of how a lark must feel as it rises; and the tune of Schubert's "Hark, Hark, the Lark!" went through his mind. Every day, almost every hour, some music of another's or of his own, went singing through his mind that was a home of melody. At Heaven's gate! A conventional phrase! Yet it was difficult for the most enlightened man not to fall at moments into those old beliefs, not to see at moments those pictures of the imagination. Up in the blue! It ought to be somewhere there! Absurd! But that air made him think of the Courts of Heaven. And what was she thinking of? He could not tell. Her face was very pale. Her features looked stern, almost austere. She must be shaken to the depths. But she looked simply like a very grave, rather cold girl, with a woman's expression, self-controlled, but with some suggested intensity, held in leash, yet formidable somehow.

They were deep in the wood out of sight of the Waldhaus. She stopped. "Aren't we quite near it now—the chalet?" she said. "Surely we must be."

"Yes. You can see the snows." She looked through the trees and saw a gleam of white dazzling in the sunshine. "His windows look on them. You have only to follow the path."

"Good-by then. I'll come down presently—to see *him.*"

"Yes."

He stood where he was. She walked slowly on, followed a turn of the path, disappeared among the trees.

"What is she going to do?" he asked himself, as he turned to go down to the Alpenrose, to the dead man whom he had scarcely known, yet whom he felt fiercely through her.

It seemed to him that she was bracing herself up to some

stern encounter, that she had some purpose in view so definite, so strong, that it enabled her for the time to rise above the tremendous shock he had just inflicted on her. She was instinct with purpose. That was what had made her look formidable to him.

As he went down among the trees to the village he wondered about Imogen. How much had she loved the man who was dead? Surely very much. But if he had loved her what could have driven him to this tragic act on the eve almost of their marriage? And now, without doing the natural thing, which would surely have been to go at once to the Alpenrose where her lover lay dead, she was going with that austere face, those fixed, unwavering eyes, to tell Peter Kharkoff what had been done in the night.

Would Peter Kharkoff be able to help her? It seemed to Hendry that through his mere personality, the strength and the calm of it, he could help anyone, in any trouble however acute and tremendous it might be. But the girl's face had not been like the face of one seeking for consolation. There had been, he thought, nothing wistful in it. He could not "see" the meeting of those two in the chalet opposite to the snow-field.

A few minutes, a few turns of the winding path, and Imogen stood before the chalet on the edge of the precipice. There was silence all about it. No one was visible. It might have been untenanted. But there were geraniums in the window-boxes; the shutters were fastened back against the walls; some of the windows were open. And the entrance door stood open too. The morning sunshine bathed the cozy, intimate-looking dwelling and glittered on the snow-field, from which it was separated by the valley in which the stream ran lifting up its voice. Imogen could hear it where she was standing, and its distant music seemed to add to the peace of this happy solitude.

She waited for a moment, listening to the stream, looking at the pale glitter of the snow. Then she went up to the open door and knocked on it with her knuckles. In a minute a door opened at the end of an uncarpeted passage with a polished wooden floor, and an elderly Swiss woman appeared, with a sturdy figure and a serious rosy face, out of which looked a pair of pale-blue eyes set in a network of tiny and shallow wrinkles.

"Good morning. Herr Peter Kharkoff lives here, I believe."

"Yes, mistress."

"Is he in?"

"Yes."

"Can I see him?"

"I dare say you can. I'll go and see."

She turned round and mounted a flight of narrow uncarpeted stairs, leaving Imogen standing in the entrance. How ordinary it all was; this clean, commonplace Swiss dwelling, this sturdy, unromantic countrywoman, the geraniums in their boxes, the clean, shining wooden floor which looked as if it had just been scoured, the smell of coffee which came from the kitchen! But to Imogen it was not ordinary. Nothing seemed ordinary to her that morning. She was laboring under the power of the fact. But no longer was she travailing with thought. On the contrary thought seemed to have stopped dead in her mind. She was aware of things in a strange mechanical way, but this awareness did not seem to be connected with thought about them. She was aware of the sound of the stream far below her, of the sunshine, of the snow and its glitter, of the shine of the wood in the chalet passage, of the geraniums pink and red in their boxes—and of the fact that Hugo was dead. But she was not now conscious of using her mind in connection with those facts. They were— and she was. And that was all.

Peter Kharkoff was in this house. She was going to see him. She had come there through the wood to see him, as once she had gone through the snow with her aunt to the rue les Bergues to see him. He had received her then. He would receive her now. In a minute that broad, rosy-faced woman would return and ask her to come in. Ah! already she was calling from the head of the narrow stairs, "Please to come up!"

Imogen went to the staircase. She saw the woman standing above her and looking down calmly. She went up the stairs. On the left she saw a door standing open. "Is that it?"

"Yes, mistress."

She walked through the door and was confronted by Peter Kharkoff. He was standing by a table in the small, bare and very clean room, a room that looked as if it had just been scrubbed. It had two rather small, square windows. Both of them stood wide open showing the snow-field opposite, a dazzle of white. The room was full of the sunshine of early morning, and of the cool, almost cold freshness of early morning air.

On the table were some books and manuscripts, a few letters, a cup half full of black coffee, and the hour-glass which Imogen had seen in the rue les Bergues. In it the sands were running. When she saw them she remembered her imagination—or hallucination—in the villa at Sainte Maxime at night. That had been a premonition of this end. And she remembered, too, the boat pulling out to sea, leaving the land-locked harbor of Saint Tropez for the wide blue of the Mediterranean. And she felt—perhaps for the first time, really, in the depths of her—that Hugo was gone.

The Swiss woman shut the door behind her. She heard Peter Kharkoff's deep, rather low voice saying "Good morning." She did not give him the conventional answering greeting. She was looking at him to see if he knew. She had woven so many imaginations and fancies about this man; she had had such strange and tremendous thoughts about him; he had, perhaps often unintentionally, made her feel so much, that now she had the almost cold desire to bring him really to the test; and it seemed as if the possibility of doing that had been put in her power. She searched him with her eyes, and while she did so everything that she had felt and known and wondered about and suspected in connection with Peter Kharkoff, the Jew, the Unearthly, seemed to come back upon her, to bathe her like a tide.

"Do you know?" That was the silent question she was asking him then. "Do you know what has happened in the night at the Alpenrose Hotel?"

And, with that, there was in her another question. "Did you intend it to happen?"

And a last question—"Did you bring it about?"

She looked steadily at Peter Kharkoff. There was even a hard, piercing expression in her eyes, the physical manifestation of the determination that was in her mind, to find out, to come to a conclusion, to know whether this man was her friend or her enemy. For since she had known the fact of Hugo's death the faint fear or suspicion of enmity, a sort of hag of the mind, had begun to haunt her again.

"What has happened?" she heard his voice say. And his eyes were on hers.

"Don't you know?"

He went on looking at her, and she felt that, without intending to, she was giving him knowledge, that what she knew was slipping out of her into him, as water can slip from one vessel into another.

"I didn't know when you came into the room," he said. "But——" He paused; then he said, "Hugo Dennistone—he is dead?"

"Yes. He's dead. He chose to die. He needn't have died, but he chose to die. Why was that?"

"He opened the door with his own hand and passed through of his own will?"

"Yes."

A clouded, almost a stern expression transformed Peter Kharkoff's face, and Imogen realized that she had never before seen him look angry or unhappy. And even now, while she looked, his expression changed, seemed to unfold into calmness and serenity again.

"May I sit down?" she said. "There are things I want to say to you."

He put a chair for her near one of the windows facing the view. As she sat down on it the pure glitter of the snow was in her eyes and all the pale shining of morning. She turned the chair sideways. She wanted to look not at the morning but at him.

He was standing. It seemed that he didn't intend to sit down. But there was nothing restless in his attitude. It seemed natural to him to be on his feet. The sunshine fell on him, showed the gray threads in his thick hair, the many lines on his powerful face.

"Hugo was very fond of you, I suppose," she said.

"We understood one another," he answered.

"After I had gone. After Hugo had sent me away."

"We saw more of each other then."

"It seems to me—it has seemed to me for a long time—that Hugo wanted me to leave him so that he might draw nearer to you. And I was in the way."

"There are regions beyond human life on earth, and the earthly desires of human beings. Sometimes events make human beings realize that and long for them. Why did you wish me to come to Sainte Maxime?"

"I could hardly say. I had a feeling that you could help Hugo more than anyone else."

"And perhaps I was able to."

"But you took him away from me!"

That was the accusation by which Imogen felt possessed. And it was gathering strength. For now Hugo was gone from her forever, and with him was gone the great opportunity she had tried to grasp, had believed she had grasped on the previous evening, the opportunity for an extreme of self-sacrifice.

"And now——" She stopped. After an instant she went on. "Did you think I couldn't do anything for him? Or did you think I should do him harm? Did you think I didn't love him enough?"

"If you asked me to come to your lover wasn't it—think back!—wasn't it because you felt that you couldn't do nearly enough for him?"

"Perhaps it was."

"And now, do you feel that you could have done enough, that a man's need is limited to the love and self-sacrifice of a woman whom he loves? Do you feel that?"

Imogen didn't answer.

"Can't you reach out to the other needs, to the needs beyond? Don't you instinctively realize them? Haven't you got them yourself? Hasn't everyone got them—the needs with which our companions have nothing to do, in which we are solitary, mysterious and intense?"

"Have you got them?"

"Yes," he said earnestly.

And at that moment Imogen felt a sudden great sense of relief and of a nearness to him such as she had never felt before.

"But if a woman couldn't satisfy such needs as you speak of, Hugo's needs, how could a man?" she asked.

"No man could satisfy them. But it might be possible for someone, man or woman, to show the way towards the ultimate possibility of satisfaction."

"And you did that." Before he could answer she added, "I could never have done that. I am too much of an egotist."

And again she saw her own egotism. It rose in front of her like a specter with cold attentive eyes, forever on the watch to satisfy its eternally greedy appetite.

"That's the great difference between you and the rest of us, perhaps," she said. "You don't seem to be thinking of yourself. And we can so seldom think *really* of anyone else. Even last night——"

"Yes?" he said.

But she seemed to be brooding deeply and not to hear him.

Her head sank down a little, as if bowed by the weight of her thought. Her hands lay in her lap. On her right cheek the sunshine fell. The left cheek was in shadow. Her eyes were looking down. Peter Kharkoff could see only the lids of them.

"Did Hugo wish not to marry me?" she said, at last looking up.

"He never spoke to me about that."

"I had a feeling, a very strong feeling when I was away from him, that he was turning away from me, was withdrawing himself from me. I had the conviction almost that it was through your influence that he was doing that. Was it? Didn't you wish us to be married?"

"I didn't come to Sainte Maxime, when you asked me to, with any wish for or against any such thing as that. It couldn't be so. When you asked me to come I know you never thought that if I did come such details would be any concern of mine."

"No; that's quite true."

"You wanted me to help the man who loved you to get beyond the tragedy of his life. That was how I saw it."

"And that was how it was."

"Clinging solely to an earthly love, to any earthly love, wouldn't have brought that about."

Suddenly Imogen's love and wish for self-sacrifice seemed to her very small, yet it was not because there had been any irony or the least touch of contempt in his quiet voice. Rather it was that something in his personality, voice and speech, again as so often before seemed to enlarge the horizons. A sense of vastness came to her from him, and made things that had seemed to her of the most vital and transcendent importance shrink in value, diminish, lose their force and grow pale. She realized that though she had felt at times almost powerless in the face of Hugo's catastrophe, and though she had begged Peter Kharkoff to come and help her, she must really all the time have been thinking of herself as Hugo's sheet-anchor, as the one thing to which he clung and could cling, as the one hope of his heart, as the last and only desire of his now nearly impotent life. Till she had been—so it had seemed—pushed out of his life for a time, she had really always regarded herself as the one essential thing that could make or unmake Hugo's destiny in regard to happiness.

And now she heard this voice sweeping away, like a wind,

earthly love, her love, her poor, vain, fragile love, full of
doubts, of denials, of egotism, even of pride in its own so-named
self-sacrifice. And she realized the smallness of the world in
which she had been living—herself its center—and something
at least of the domain which lay beyond it.

"And so you took away Hugo's hands from mine?" she said
at last. "You showed him the way of release?"

"You are making a mistake," Peter Kharkoff said.

He drew up a chair and sat down near Imogen, and he
looked out to the snow-field opposite to the window. For a
moment he was silent. She watched his face and she felt that
he was far away from her just then. And yet she felt also as
if something of her was with him in the distance, was ranging
with him among the regions beyond.

Still looking at the snows he presently said, "It is a very
common mistake. You think the greater cannot contain the less,
whereas it does. Your lover never traveled away from his love
for you, although he traveled, although he went very far. In
all his traveling he carried his love for you with him. But it
changed."

"It changed?"

"Yes. Because he came at last to the place where a man has
to cast off the last rags of his selfishness."

He was still looking at the snows, and now she looked with
him. They seemed so close that she imagined that a fly
crawling over them would be visible to her. And yet there
was a far-away look about them too, a white remoteness, an
unearthliness like the unearthliness of a vision. And she felt
fully for the first time the awe of the snows and the immense
lure of the peaks. And she knew that in human nature, which
loves to wallow, there is nevertheless rooted the strange contradiction, the impulse to mount.

Yes, the impulse of the Alpine climber is an impulse of all
humanity, felt perhaps only in very rare moments by the
greater part of humanity, but felt at some moment of life by
everyone. The thrill of it was in her now, seemed to tremble,
to vibrate like the string of an instrument of music. And she
remembered the feeling that had come upon her when she had
been alone with Hugo the night before in his little room with
its window open to the stars, the feeling that he had been in
some place she had never been in, that he had gained some
knowledge she was ignorant of, that he had attained to an

insight that was not hers, that he was initiated and that she was not. And now Peter Kharkoff had told her why Hugo had made this impression upon her, why he was changed.

And yet he had done this awful thing. He had taken his fate into his own hands, had, if a man can, snatched his destiny from the keeping of his Creator and dealt with it brutally himself. Was that the act of a completely unselfish man?

"Did he reach that place?" she heard herself asking.

"Do you doubt it?"

"But he didn't leave things in—but he ended his own life! Poor—poor Hugo!"

"And don't you know why?"

"I!" she said, startled. "How should I know? How can I know?"

He sat looking at her now in silence. And as a few minutes before she had felt that she was giving him knowledge, now she felt that she was silently receiving knowledge from him. But she tried to push the knowledge away, to get rid of it out of her mind. Her mind tried to refuse it harborage.

"You haven't told me what happened last night," Peter Kharkoff said. "But I suppose you visited your lover. I suppose you let him know you were here."

"Yes. I went to him rather late. I spent a long time with him. I came here because of him. Naturally, I went to see him."

"And do you tell me you still don't know why he has done this?" he asked gently.

But in his gentleness she felt a spear point that pierced her. And it was the exquisitely sharp spear point of truth. Useless to try to evade that! She must suffer one of those wounds which are the healing of the nations. But the suffering was intense, so intense that she could scarcely keep from crying out under it.

"How can I know what was in his mind? How can I know?" she said desperately.

"Love is very full of knowledge which it has never been told by any lips. All we are is known to the Unseen because of that. Didn't you love Hugo Dennistone enough to know—why?"

"Do you mean—was it because——"

She broke off. She couldn't ask the question. She was still trying uselessly to refuse the truth, was still trying to shrink away from the spear point. She got up from her chair, went to the window, stood by it and looked out upon the snow. And as she looked at its flawless whiteness she seemed to feel the redness of the blood flowing from the wound he had made. And she imagined her blood falling upon the snow and abolishing its whiteness.

"It was his way of proving how much he loved you," Peter Kharkoff's voice said behind her. "He couldn't be selfish any more and so he couldn't accept your sacrifice. But you were determined to make it. That was why you came here. And of course he knew that."

"Yes, he knew it. I told him. But I didn't call it a sacrifice."

As she said the last words she realized, almost with a sense of irony, that that fact hadn't mattered. For Hugo had attained to a terribly complete knowledge of her. Still haunted by this ugly and dreadful sense of irony—like a thing laughing dryly in darkness—she turned by the window and faced him. There was something she wanted to know.

"You say he did it for me. Do you defend it? Do you justify such an act as that—a man's taking his own life?"

"No. He took the wrong way. But it seemed to him the only way. You must have made him think it was by the ardor of your determination to give up what *you* were never meant to give up."

"Why shouldn't I——"

"You are a *woman*. You were not created to be a saint. You haven't the stuff of a saint in you. And if you tried to be one the world wouldn't be the better for it. He knew that. And by his death he has saved you from a shattering moral failure."

After a moment, during which she stood perfectly still with her eyes upon him, he added, "His way wasn't the right way. But he hadn't a great brain. I think he'll be forgiven for that because he had something which reaches out much farther into the invisible, because he had a great heart."

"Yes," she said in a low voice. "I know Hugo will be forgiven."

And it was then that she shed her first tears for the death of the man who had loved her.

CHAPTER VII

IMOGEN sat alone upon her little terrace looking down on the woods round the Waldhaus. She wore a plain black dress, her mourning for the man who was dead. That morning, in wind and rain, Hugo's body had been lowered into the ground of the small cemetery of Sils-Maria. (At the inquiry which had been held as to the cause, or causes, of death it had been ascertained officially that Hugo had brought about his own end. There had been no doubt about that. He had chosen to die. It was supposed by the Swiss officials who had been concerned in the inquiry that his mind had become unhinged through stress caused by his physical condition of impotence, that he had been unable to bear any longer his life of complete inertia.)

Imogen, Milligan, and a handful of Hugo's relatives, his mother, two sisters, and a brother, who had traveled out from England on receiving the news of the death, had been in the churchyard. And two men had also come there, but had stayed a little way off, had kept in the background, and had gone away together directly the short ceremony came to an end, Peter Kharkoff and Hendry, the organist. Imogen had not spoken to them, but she had known they were there, she had been glad they were there.

When all was over she had said good-by to Hugo's people, who were staying at St. Moritz and who intended to leave the next day. She had not suggested seeing more of them, and they, intensely reserved in their grief and horror, had evidently been relieved to see the last of her. She had gone away with Milligan, had accompanied him to the Alpenrose, had gone upstairs and taken a last look round the room in which she had found Hugo on the night of their final interview.

Milligan was going to pack up the things which had belonged to Hugo, and to take them to St. Moritz to his relatives. On the morrow he would be gone. He had promised to "call up" and see Imogen before starting. They liked each other. She was touched by his genuine distress at the loss of "Mr. Hugo," and by his evident genuine feeling for her. He didn't understand the reason for Hugo's tragic action. He had not expected it. In his opinion Mr. Hugo had been "the last man" likely to do such a thing. And so he had told Imogen. She had not explained matters. It was impossible to do that even to clear the memory of the dead. There are some things that can't be explained. They are too personal, too close to the heart of things, of a too desperate intimacy to be stripped by words and given naked to minds unfitted to comprehend them. Peter Kharkoff and Imogen knew; to them knowledge of this happening's cause must inevitably be limited. The world seldom understands. It was impossible that it could understand now. But Imogen understood. Sometimes her mind seemed actually to ache with the subtle pain of understanding.

Now it was afternoon. Down in the village the church clock had just struck five. The weather had cleared. The wind had gone down. But it was colder than usual in summer even up on the roof of the world. And this summer coldness, under a now bright sky, seemed to inject a peculiarity into the atmosphere, a something not quite normal, that accorded with this day of Imogen's life, a day that must forever stand out in the procession of the days of her life, a day that could never be forgotten by her, or be confused in her mind with any other day.

This was the day of Hugo's definite departure out of her life. So long as his body had been above ground she had been able still to feel something of nearness, of bodily nearness to him. But with the falling of the earth upon his coffin that feeling had left her. Then, at that moment, they had been severed totally the one from the other. And she had felt completely the meaning of what he had done. So much did the body, the things of the body, still mean to her.

Now that the brief funeral was over, that the ceremony which had as it were made this day abnormal to her was at an end, she had the feeling that a whole epoch was finished for her, that a great "Finis" had been written across the sky. The ignorance of her youth had died with Hugo. She could never be spiritually ignorant any more. Her spirit had received education. Feeling that, realizing that, she felt also, vaguely as yet, the necessity that lay upon her of making a great effort after readjustment. She felt not only that she must presently embark upon a new type of life but that she must be new in it. She could not be just the old Imogen living in a somewhat new way. That was impossible. Destiny had been too drastic with her for that. Fate had cut too deep. She knew that her soul had been scored. The writing upon her of circumstance was indelible. She would not forget. She would not rebound. She would never again be exactly as she had been. She was absolutely sure of that.

Since her ·interview in the chalet with Peter Kharkoff she had had a new conception of love, a new conception of life. She felt that for long he had been perhaps leading her towards them, these new conceptions. Now she had reached them, had taken hold of them, had made them part of her. The suicide of Hugo and Peter Kharkoff's explanation of it, which she knew to be the true one, had made her understand for the first time the inner meaning of unselfishness. Hence her new conception of life. Because of Peter Kharkoff the wand of Hugo's complete self-abnegation had touched her and she felt as if, from the dry rod that she herself had been, pale flowers were springing. She had begged Peter Kharkoff to come to the Riviera to help Hugo. Now it seemed to her that he had used Hugo as a means to force her out of her blindness, out of her dark ignorance of life. And in the process had come about the destruction of Hugo. She saw now. But Hugo was dead. She understood now. But he was dead. It was as if he had been offered up as a sacrifice for her. But surely she wasn't worth it.

She missed him. She knew that she would miss him far more. In the beginning of a loss one doesn't know its cruelty, just as in the beginning of a night one doesn't plumb the depths of its darkness. The midnight of her loss was not upon her yet. But already, since the burial, she saw her life like a tree stripped of its leaves. And there was an emptiness in the valley before her. Hugo crippled had filled up her life as Hugo whole had never been able to do. For Hugo whole had only brought her pleasures, the shared pastimes of the body, gaiety, laughter, the half-hidden desires of the flesh—to be satisfied presently. But Hugo crippled—what had he not brought her?

Sitting there alone, out in the almost cold air of the now waning afternoon, she tried to catalogue his gifts. But she could not. They were perhaps too many and too strange. And today she was not in possession of her usual bold coolness of mind. That coolness too had surely been an attribute of her ignorance.

Henceforth she would have to do without Hugo. All the reason for the intense mental activity that had been hers since the announcement of his accident had reached her in Geneva had disappeared with him. For months her mind had been painfully and ceaselessly busy about him, wavering, debating, deciding, rescinding decisions, coming to them again, trembling on verges, leaping over, lost in abysses, scaling heights. The terrible fierce vitality of the mind! The agonies of the hidden thing! And all the time this end in the distance had been coming nearer and nearer. And at last had come her journey to Switzerland, her desperate hunt after self-sacrifice, which had led to this sudden death and to the saying of those words which she felt were branded upon her:

"You haven't the stuff of a saint in you. . . . By his death he has saved you from a shattering moral failure."

What terrible words those were! And yet she hadn't resented them because she had felt at once that they were profoundly true. She hadn't resented them but they had surely swept away the last tattered remnants of her self-satisfaction. Even her moral vanity lay dead, the most intimate vanity by far possessed by the human being.

Peter Kharkoff for all his gentleness knew how to apply the scourge. And he had applied it to her.

She wondered where he was at that moment, what he was doing, what he was thinking, whether he was thinking of Hugo, of her. She had lost the sense which had formerly sometimes tortured her, the sense of his great indifference. He was certainly not indifferent. But whereas the thoughts of most people range within a strictly limited circle, are often feebly concerned with a few individuals, his surely had no limit. She felt that humanity was his field. But she was able to feel also now that Hugo had meant much to him, and that she meant something, definitely something. Hendry too—he had surely a very strong feeling for Hendry.

But she felt that Hendry was not typical but exceptional. There was something rare in Hendry. He had called himself one of the ordinary blokes, but he wasn't ordinary. Even his attitude towards his art, towards music, showed that. She wondered whether Hendry would ever shine out from the crowd as a great musician. She felt that it was possible. He had such enthusiasm, such sincerity. He was exceptional, but she was not. And for years she had thought herself exceptional, a wonder-girl, a being apart from the herd of fashionable girls, one fitted by her gifts and her nature to impose her will on the multitude, to make those around her yield to, and follow her whims. And the end of it all was the suicide of her lover and those terrible words of Peter Kharkoff.

What was going to happen now?

She could not see any future. But she had the feeling very definitely that she wouldn't die young, that her earthly future would be a long one. Perhaps as Hugo had proved himself in dying she would have to prove herself in living. What he had summed up in one act she might be destined to convey in a long series of acts. She hoped she would be able to convey something fine, not a cheap merchandise of the soul. Hugo had saved her from a great moral failure. She owed it to him to use her salvation by doing, by being—especially by being—something worth while. Only in that way could she prove that his love hadn't been all in vain. She owed Hugo a gift.

It was strange the difference that she felt between Hugo's knowledge of her on the night of their last interview and Peter Kharkoff's knowledge of her expressed with such tremendous plainness during her morning visit to the chalet. The thought of what Hugo had known caused her even now a pain that was linked with shame, the sort of pain that stirs the difficult blood and makes the eyes reluctant to perform their office. It was dreadful to her to think of what Hugo had known. But she did not mind Peter Kharkoff knowing the same thing. It seemed right that he should know it, right and inevitable. She shrank in spirit from the dead man's knowledge; in Peter Kharkoff's she rested.

Why was that?

Asking herself that question now she became aware of something, she became aware that her feeling for, or her conception of, Peter Kharkoff had subtly changed since she had come out to Switzerland. Or had both changed, feeling and conception?

Ever since the night when she had arrived at Drearney and found her aunt so strangely under the spell of the stranger, the unknown Jew, she had been haunted by thoughts, imaginations, sometimes by wild and almost portentous fancies, that she had never dared to express quite plainly, that she had never even dared to formulate quite definitely to herself. The prophecy of a Savior coming out of the North to heal the stricken world had not been laughed at by her in spite of her impudent modernity. She remembered that she had shivered as she had repeated the words of her aunt just before going to bed. And she had said, "How cold that sounds!"

At that moment certainly a strange feeling of awe had come upon her, mingled with a sensation of presage. On the following day she had gone out alone in the twilight, "to get a breath of air." Really she had been driven out—to search. Then had followed the service in the cathedral with Canon Barrimore's strange outbreak. (From him it had come like that.) And she had known that the stranger was near by, somewhere in the great church. And then she had seen him, and followed him, and been alone with him in the night. And ever since then her life had been changed.

It had been changed because really, in spite of her strong spirit of independence, in spite of the wilfulness that pushed her to attempted rebellion, Peter Kharkoff had taken possession of it. He had not seemed to desire to take possession of it, or to make any effort after possession. But so it had been. And the full knowledge of that extraordinary fact, the absolutely full knowledge, had come to her in London through Berazov's perception of it, through a mere hazard acquaintance's perception of it. When Berazov had felt Peter Kharkoff in her, then, and only then, had she fully understood the empire his character, his personality, had obtained over hers. And still she had fought against it, almost with venom.

And then Berazov had joined the enemy against her—or rather had joined the friend for her. It seemed incredible that Peter Kharkoff, a man on the Riviera, should have been able to influence the events of her life through a Russian in London whom he had doubtless never seen or heard of. And yet she was convinced that it had been so. And she was equally convinced that out of her had issued the influence which had returned to her from Berazov, made as it were visible to her nature by him. In her it had not been potent enough. But when it had acted upon her through another she had been forced to recognize it, she had been persuaded to yield to it.

That had been almost like magic. And she knew that there had been moments when in her thoughts of Peter Kharkoff she had connected him with what is often called the miraculous, but what would be better named the uncomprehended. Those words "a Savior from the North" had suggested the miraculous to her imagination. Then had come the happening in Drearney Cathedral which had been quite extraordinary.

Her evening interview with Peter Kharkoff, despite his simplicity, even his homeliness, had deepened the impression which had been prepared for by Miss Creswell. She had named Peter Kharkoff the Unearthly. And ever since then she had thought of him as a being apart, had connected him in her mind with all the strangeness which surrounds the human life as darkness surrounds a lamp set out of doors in the night. She had not felt afraid of him. But she had wondered about him as men wonder about the unknown.

To Imogen Peter Kharkoff had been the one man to whom she felt tremendously inferior, the one man of whom she could never think with her native satire of a spoiled and self-satisfied girl, the one man who carried with him an atmosphere which suggested to her vast possibilities, hidden powers and the mystery of the unknown, the one man at whose feet she felt that she could sit like a child. All this he still was to her. And yet now she knew that since the death of Hugo a great change had been brought about by one word and by his way of saying it. At their interview in the chalet, when she had told him of Hugo's death and the way of it, he had asked her whether she didn't feel those needs of the human spirit with which our companions have nothing to do, in which we are solitary, mysterious and intense. And she had said, "Have you got them?" His answer had been, "Yes."

He had said it with intense earnestness. He had given her the impression then that those needs were perhaps greater in him than in any other man, or, if not that, were felt by him with a sharper consciousness of them than any other man had. And at that moment she had felt a nearness to him such as she had •never felt before. For in these shared needs there was a great companionship. She was thankful he felt them, because they emphasized his humanity though they stripped him of the magical atmosphere her imagination had woven about him like a garment.

And so now she was able to rest in his knowledge of her. He too was under the Law. And sometimes she had been inclined to think—but she would not formulate that thought.

She heard bells sounding thinly below among the trees. She listened. They were not cow-bells but bells on the necks of horses. They came to her ears more distinctly, bells on the necks of horses climbing the steep road from the village to the Waldhaus. They had disturbed her reverie. Now she felt suddenly restless. And she got up and went to the railing of the terrace. And then again the sense of emptiness came to her. She looked over the railing to the trees, among which somewhere the bells still sounded, and she thought of her comrade and lover down there in the cemetery. She would always be drawn back to Sils-Maria. Wherever she went, whatever happened to her, she would have to come back to the little village among the heights. Till now she had not thought of going away.

The bells were passing now among the trees on the left. Presently they died away.

The brightness had gone out of the evening sky. The chill in the air grew more definite. And a feeling of helplessness came to Imogen. It was intensified by the knowledge that very soon she would have to go away, to leave Hugo in his tomb by the stream, to leave the man who had brought her to a knowledge of herself. She would have to go away and to begin again. How difficult it would be! Hitherto as a rule she had dealt with life confidently. She wouldn't be able to do that now. She had felt herself to be a young expert. Really she had been numbered among the profoundly ignorant. Now she was full of the timidity of knowledge. Love had taught her to be humble. It was extraordinary that Hugo, whose brain she had been inclined to despise, had been able to give her such an unforgetable lesson.

Hugo! She saw him before her in the evening in the pride of his manly strength. In her ears was the sound of his strong, intensely masculine, rather rough voice. His bright blue eyes looked into hers. Always at the back of her mind had been the certainty that some day she would marry him. Their physical union had seemed to her somehow inevitable. And now her latest memory of him was of a man all mind and spirit, in the body incapable.

Hugo—Hugo!

She strained her eyes towards the village below. It was as if she were trying to see the patch of earth underneath which he was lying.

A tap on the door behind drew her attention back into the sitting-room. *"Entrez!"* she called.

A page boy opened the door and came through the room to her carrying a card. She took it and read, "Comte Serge Berazov."

She held the card and stared at the words while the page boy stood waiting. And in her ears was the sound of bells on the necks of horses. "Where is this gentleman?" she said at last.

"Downstairs, madame. He has just arrived. He has taken a room in the hotel. He wishes to know if he can see madame."

"Yes. You can bring him up."

The boy went away. Imogen stayed on the terrace. So those bells had been on the horses bringing him here!

There was another tap on the door. It was opened and she saw Berazov crossing the room. Her first thought was, "He looks conventional." She saw him just then as a polished man of the world, a cosmopolitan, the kind of rich man who has known all the pleasures of society, who has penetrated all the secrets of luxury—saw his varnish. But he had suffered, had been horribly poor, had been a servant. And he had known the meaning of physical danger.

"Are you afraid of the cold out here?" was her greeting to him. She had a strong disinclination to go into the house, to be with him between the four walls of her sitting-room.

He came out on the terrace and took her hand.

"No."

"We're having a bad summer."

She saw him looking at her dress. But though it was black there was nothing to indicate mourning. Nevertheless his look made her wonder whether he had seen in the papers the news of Hugo's suicide. Or perhaps he always looked at what a woman had on. Not many men do; but there are some who do. And he was fastidious, critical. He might be one of them.

"Did you think I should come?" he asked. And he turned his large, rather melancholy eyes from her gown to her face.

"I don't know. I haven't been thinking about that—lately. But at first I thought it was quite possible."

"And then you forgot about it?"

"Yes."

He looked out to the woods, now gathering the dusk into their arms. All the brightness had gone out of the sky. Dark gray clouds were coming from the mountains beyond the plain between the two lakes. An invisible hand seemed to be stealthily drawing them over the sky.

"Are you one of those who forget easily?" he said.

"I don't know. Perhaps I used to be. I may not be now."

"Now—now!" he said. And she remembered their night interview in her room.

He had spoken savagely. She felt that when he had come into the room, onto the terrace, his nerves had been on edge, that he was a prey to nervous irritation. She had seen the varnish only for an instant. Now she felt that beneath it there was a—cultured—barbarian.

"By God, I wish I had met you before you had been taken hold of and changed!" he said. And again he stared into the woods, seemed to sweep the horizon with his gaze. "Where is he?" he asked. "He's here, of course."

For an instant she was deceived and thought he meant Hugo.

"I can feel him here," he added, before she could speak.

And then at once she realized her mistake. Hugo didn't exist. Berazov didn't know that probably. In any case he wasn't concerned with Hugo; whether he knew or not, Hugo didn't exist for him but was blotted out by another. His mind was too full to hold Hugo living or dead.

"Peter Kharkoff is here," she said. "He lives not far off in a chalet at the edge of the woods."

"I must see him," said Berazov, still with the savage sound in his voice. There was, as Imogen noted now, a sort of passionate gloom in his face.

"What's the matter?" she asked him. She hadn't forgotten her grief. But she had to take notice of his extraordinary mood.

"Don't you want me to stay?" he asked. "You haven't asked me to sit down. Are you disgusted at my arrival?"

She was on the point of telling him of Hugo's suicide, and burial that day. She was quite sure now that he didn't know. If he had known, unconventional as he often was, surely he would have left her alone that day. He would have sent up a note of sympathy perhaps. But he wouldn't have asked to see her. He would have waited for a summons from her.

"What is it?" he asked, noticing something strange in her eyes.

"Do sit down." But even now she didn't suggest going indoors. There were chairs on the terrace. She sat down on one of them. He sat down too. As he did that he coughed in such a way that she realized he had a cold. "Don't you want a coat?"

"It doesn't matter."

"Do go and fetch it. I've got a fur on so—do fetch your coat."

"Would you mind if we went indoors?"

"I'd rather stay out. But you must have your coat."

He frowned. "I had to do without a coat altogether at one time."

"I'll get you a rug."

And before he could stop her she was indoors, went into her bedroom and came back with a rug. "Here—put it over your knees."

He laughed. "Thanks! How absurd all this is! Why don't you go indoors with me?"

"I don't want to," she said with obstinacy. "If you're afraid to stay out, we can meet tomorrow."

"Why not tonight at dinner?"

"I'm not going down to dinner."

"You're angry with me for coming."

His assumption that her attention was fastened on him astonished her. He didn't understand where she was. That was natural enough. But it was difficult to realize that her brain and heart condition was totally uncomprehended by this subtle man who in London had almost shown divination when with her. She longed to tell him that when she had run in out of the rain that night in Lowndes Square, leaving him on the doorstep, she had in truth gone out of his life. The test had been accomplished. She couldn't! And she had even made him reluctant, had turned him, at any rate for the moment, into a protector of the virtue of woman.

"I'm not angry," she said gently. "You practically told me you were coming. But I hadn't expected you tonight. I was thinking of other things."

"I believe you'd entirely forgotten me. I know you had. I made such an utter fool of myself in London that you had every right to. Since you went away I have realized my folly. The spell"—again he spoke with savage irony—"has snapped and I've got back to sanity." When he said that Imogen realized exactly why she hadn't wished to go with him into the sitting-room. "Do you understand what I mean by that?"

"Yes," she said bluntly. She couldn't fence and pretend with him or with any man that evening.

He seemed startled by her merciless way of saying that word.

"You do! And you? What has happened to you since that night at the Black Cat? We met once since in the street, but you didn't tell me, and I couldn't feel then how it was with you. What has happened to you? I feel"—he hesitated with his eyes fixed upon her—"I feel—I begin to feel"—again he hesitated and again he looked at her dress—"that something tremendous has happened."

She got up, and again stood by the parapet of the terrace. The screen of dark gray clouds had now been drawn over the whole of their sky, and night was coming on. "Yes, something has happened," she said.

"What is it?"

"I came out here to join Hugo Dennistone, to whom I had been engaged, as you know. I arrived in the late afternoon, as you have. In the evening after dinner I went down to the Alpenrose Hotel where he was staying to see him. I saw him and was with him for a long while. We decided we would be married very soon. I left him. During that night he committed suicide. He was buried today in the cemetery down there."

She pointed, and as she did so she looked down towards the place where the village lay by the stream. When she dropped her hand he had got up and was standing close to her.

"I've been in Paris. I haven't looked at the English papers. I didn't know."

"No—of course!"

"I shouldn't have attempted to see you. I am very sorry." There was a startled and, she thought, a shocked expression on his face. "Do please forgive me. I'll go at once. And I've been talking about myself!" He added something, rather a long sentence, evidently said to himself, in Russian. It sounded to her strangely plaintive, liquid with plaintiveness.

"Never mind," she said. "After all life goes on. And I chose to see you."

"Why was that?"

"I hardly know." She was silent, as if considering. "It may have been that I have a feeling I must wind things up. You know, as one does before one starts on a journey."

"Wind things up?"

"Yes. We aren't going to be friends, Berazov. You and I couldn't be friends. And the rest—that's quite over."

"Why did you refuse to go with me into the room there?"

"Because I didn't trust you. And after what has happened down there I couldn't take even a chance. Not today!"

"I'm sorry." He stood there looking downcast as a boy might. There was something extraordinarily simple and human in his attitude, in his manner. He even seemed to her very young just then. And he had asked no questions about the tragedy. She couldn't explain it to him. She had to leave him under a wrong impression of her humiliation. But there was absolutely nothing in his demeanor, or in his eyes, that showed any suspicion of humiliation on his part. He might have a barbarian in him, but she was thankful to him at that moment for being a gentleman.

"Well—" he said, after a pause. She thought he was going. But he checked the movement and said, "One thing more. Can you tell me the way to where *he* lives?"

"I'll take you there," she said, moved by a sudden strong impulse which she couldn't have explained. "Go and get your coat. I'll join you in the hall."

He went into the sitting-room, crossed it and went out, shutting the door. Then she went to her bedroom, put on a hat, took her walking stick and came out into the corridor.

Winding things up! What had brought that phrase to her lips? She had to start again. She had to readjust herself to utterly new conditions. She had to leave things behind. And she knew that she and Berazov could never be friends. After what had happened that was impossible. Besides he was unstable, fascinating but unstable. He had proved that just now when he had said savagely that the "spell" was broken. She knew exactly what that had meant. He had gone back to his original desire, perhaps even intention, concerning herself. Such a man couldn't be a friend to a girl of her type, a girl who hadn't the stuff of a saint in her. She must leave Berazov behind, with so much else. But before doing that she would take him to see his "enemy."

When she went down she found him waiting in the hall for her with his overcoat on and a stick in his hand. He was carrying a soft black hat with a rather wide brim. When he put it on it made him look older and picturesque. They went out together into the woods.

At first they walked along the narrow path in silence. Berazov had a deep look of melancholy on his pale face and seemed to be absorbed in thought. Now she felt strongly the foreignness of him and was no longer aware of the varnish. She felt him as just a human being, but as a human being of a different race from hers, full of contrasts that could never be her contrasts, full of moods that she couldn't fully understand. She was still aware of his physical fascination, but she was no longer subject to it as she had been in London. It seemed to her that Hugo dead conquered that subjection in her, made her safe from it out of his grave. The thought of physical contact with Berazov was even repulsive to her. And yet—she did not exactly know why—she had never liked him more, in a simple, human, undemanding way. And even in her grief, her stillness of grief beginning, she felt deeply sorry for him. There was something so tremendously solitary in the man.

"We aren't far off now," she said, at last breaking their long silence.

"Peter Kharkoff!" he said.

She heard him sigh, and it seemed to her that he walked more slowly, with a dragging step, not like a tired, but like a reluctant man.

"You do wish to see him?" she said.

"Of course! Why not?"

She looked at him. "I was only wondering." He stood still. "It's true! I do feel suddenly a sort of hesitation." He looked at her with eyes that were very sincere. "I'm almost afraid," he said, very simply.

She had stopped too. "Why?"

"I can't tell you. But something in you impresses me with the power of this man. It's as if you were heavy with him. I have felt it all the time among the trees. Perhaps—perhaps I had better not see him."

She felt now that he was mystically afraid.

"Are the snows near?" he added in a low voice. "I seem to feel them."

"His windows look out on them, his open windows."

Berazov shivered.

"I don't know what to do."

Now she felt or seemed to feel all the indecision of his variable nature, gathered together and oppressing him.

"We must go on," she said firmly. "He drew you here, not I."

"No, it was you. I came because I couldn't keep away from you."

She moved her head. "No."

"If that is so then you came here not for the man who is dead but for *him*."

"They seemed almost to be joined together," she said.

He looked at her intently, but he didn't say anything. She walked on and he followed her. It was like an obedience, but not to her. That was how she felt it. A turn of the path brought them in sight of the chalet. The windows were dark, but a faint light shone out through the open door from the kitchen at the end of the passage.

"Is that where he's living?" asked Berazov.

"Yes. There is a servant. There may be other people in the house too. I don't know. But he lives alone."

"You know we have lots of local saints in Russia," he said slowly. "They claim healing powers, as John of Cronstadt and Rasputin did. They are great"—he smiled—"at driving out the evil from those who are possessed by demons. Now, although I'm Russian, I don't believe in all that sort of thing. Education, knowledge of the world, take you beyond belief in such nonsense. I'm a skeptic."

"If you are a skeptic—whatever that means, I don't quite know—why are you afraid of going with me into that chalet? Isn't it because you feel that you might come out believing?"

"Believing? In what?"

"It might even be in yourself."

A pale irony seemed to her to gleam out of his face. "Do you believe in yourself?" he said.

"Yes. I think I do. I do—now. Or at least I'm beginning to."

"Didn't you before you ever met *him?*"

"I had only self-confidence then," she said. "Then I hadn't seen the man with the lice."

"Ah! That night! I went away cursing Israel. And yet—there was a power upon me. D'you know why I hesitate now?"

"Why is it?"

"It's because I know my own Russian-ness. Almost every Russian has mysticism in his psyche. I might be taken hold of as even you could never be. You don't know what extremes Russians are capable of. And to fall at the feet of a Jew!" He was strangely agitated.

She put her hand on his arm. "Perhaps you think I am

curious to see," she said. "I'm not. Go in alone. Just tell him I brought you here."

"But what will you do?"

"You'll find me somewhere about here when you come out. If you don't see me give me a call."

"Yes?" He stood as if in hesitation for a moment. Then he turned and walked away. She saw the light in the passage obscured as he stood before the doorway of the chalet. A moment later he went into the house.

Imogen stood still for a moment after Berazov had gone into the chalet. Then she began to walk up and down in the gathering darkness. She had not forgotten Berazov. The impulse she had had to bring him to Peter Kharkoff had been genuine and strong, and had surely sprung from a feeling of sympathy for him. Nevertheless, she had not mentally followed him into the chalet, was not now mentally there with him. She knew positively that the short relationship between Berazov and herself had nearly run its course. It would leave its mark upon her, a mark that would never be effaced. But she knew that he was going to vanish out of her life. She knew that it was not meant that he and she should be more closely knitted together. They had met on the way. He had done something for her. She had now done something for him. There it would surely end.

Strangely enough she was not even curious as to what was going on within that house on the edge of the precipice, the bulk of whose darkness she saw as she came to it again and again in her pacing walk. The dead man had hold of her. Through him she had felt with the greatest intimacy the influence which had brought her to a new understanding of life. Through him she still felt it. It was as if he had flung away his life in order that she might be forced to see the true meanings behind the so often deceptive appearances. In her future, however long, Hugo would always have his share. Berazov was only an incident in her life. He expressed for her one side of life in a sharp-edged way, and because of that, and of the test she had been enabled to make through him, he stood out from the crowd of men she had known. But much of him was cloudy to her, like muddy water. For a moment she had felt him intensely, when he had—hadn't he?—thrown her off on that night of rain in London. If he had held on that course possibly he might have won his way into a lasting intimacy with her. But now he had told her that the spell was broken. And in doing so he had inadvertently given her the measure of his shifting nature. He was an "interesting" man. Hugo had scarcely been that. But Peter Kharkoff and Hugo between them had taught her that the value of a man's heart is greater than the value of his brain. And now she was walking with Hugo.

She did not know for how long she had been doing sentinel duty in that lonely place when she became aware that with the oncoming of night there was another oncoming—of cold. She stood still. Yes, it had become strangely cold. There was a sharp breath in the air. The night was going to be a very dark one.

The muffling up of the sky which she had noticed from the terrace at the Waldhaus must have been thorough. There would be no starshine. It was difficult to believe that this was an August night. Actually she began to feel that there was snow in the air. It was surely not the presence of the snow-field not far off that she felt, but the coming of snow.

That was not impossible. She knew that occasionally in August a fall of snow takes place at St. Moritz; and if in St. Moritz, then here too.

She was at the edge of the wood very near to the narrow path which led down to the Waldhaus. She glanced at the beginning of the path which almost immediately vanished in darkness. And then she realized the oddness of her situation, waiting out there in the night for a man whose connection with her life she felt to be already practically closed. The night was forbidding, she thought. There was no wind, no breeze even that was perceptible to her. But the stillness was menacing because of the cold in it, because of the dense character of the darkness, like a heavy cloak, which enfolded without giving shelter.

Now she began to think about the two men who were together in the chalet close by, and began to wonder what was happening between them. The Jew-hater was confronting the Jew; the Russian aristocrat was confronting the Russian Jew. It must surely be a strange interview. Hugo had not let her mind dwell on it till now. From his grave he had held her in a grip that she couldn't escape from.

She turned, looked towards the chalet and listened. She could still see the one ray of light that came through the doorway on the ground floor, but while she was gazing at it a shadow obscured it, she heard a faint noise, and saw blackness where the golden yellow had been. Someone had come down the passage and had shut the house door against the night. She wondered whether a key had been turned, a bolt drawn. She had not heard. But perhaps she had been a little too far away. Now that the door was shut she felt lonely and she began to wonder about the time.

While she had walked up and down she had been so absorbed in thought that she had forgotten the passing of time, and now she had no idea what time it was. She had not brought a watch with her. It might be getting quite late. She might have been walking to and fro for an hour or more. The shutting of the chalet door suggested to her that the woman of the house was shutting it up for the night. Was it possible that Berazov was no longer with Peter Kharkoff? When walking up and down Imogen had several times gone a good distance beyond the chalet on either side. Berazov might have come out and gone away into the wood without seeing her. She had told him to give her a call. But perhaps he had forgotten to do so. Or, not seeing her immediately, he might have thought that she had got tired of waiting and had gone back to the hotel, and he might, as he supposed, have followed her. And then the woman of the house, knowing he had gone, might have shut up the house for the night.

Would it be better to go away?

While she was standing at the edge of the wood and considering what to do, she felt something like a very light, soft touch on her face. It came again—and again. She put up her hand and found that her cheek was damp. Then she saw in the darkness faintly that snowflakes were falling over her and all about her. The darkness was full of the white falling morsels. She looked down and could see them melting about her feet. Down there in the village they must be falling on Hugo's grave.

The snow seemed to gather strength, as a wind may gather strength in the darkness. She felt it all about her like a presence. Its softness seemed to have pressure. She was conscious of the growing whiteness of the world. This deed would be done in the night, and in the morning man would wake up to change. Winter would seem to have come, to have made its way into the heart of summer. Nature would be under a spell, all its wayward colors concealed, as if stricken to purity, as if forced to play the saint and the virgin.

She had thought to be the snow-maiden. She had resolved to dedicate herself to the whiteness of an enforced virginity. And she had been driven away with a flaming sword as unfit. And now she stood alone in the darkness, and the snow was falling upon her as if in irony. The irony of the snow was tremendous about her. And with each touch of the cold whiteness on her cheek she seemed to hear Hugo saying:

"You were not meant to be white. You don't know yourself. If I had lived you must have been the victim of a shattering moral failure. Therefore I had to die. I had to give you back to the life you were meant for, the life fulfilled with a man not stricken as I am stricken."

What could the night of his death have been like to him? She had walked with Hendry to the stream at the edge of the village, and he had left her there, and then, presently, she had ascended the hill, and had gone in and slept. And Hugo, alone, had been playing out the secret drama of his end. When had he made up his mind not to live? At what hour of the night? Or perhaps in the dawn? And had he acted on a sudden irresistible impulse? Or had cold reason prompted him? Of one thing she was sure. He must have realized that she had absolutely made up her mind to dedicate herself to him, that nothing he could do would prevent her from sacrificing herself. And as she knew, couldn't help knowing, that he loved her he had had no effective weapon to fight her off with. And so he had chosen to die because he had foreseen disaster if he lived.

It was dreadful to have been so well known, so much better than she had known herself. But she could not deny that Hugo and Peter Kharkoff had known, did know, the truth of her. She had wanted to be much more than she was able to be. She had wanted to be wonderful and she was only an ordinary woman. And so Hugo had died and had left her to give herself eventually to another man.

It should not be to Berazov. Her spirit and flesh revolted from that idea.

The snow was dense now. She could not stay where she was. She must either go to the chalet, or she must go back to the Waldhaus. After some minutes of hesitation she decided to go to the chalet and she went to the shut door and knocked.

No one came. She knocked gently again, then sought for and presently found a bell. She pushed it, and heard it ringing somewhere inside. Then she heard steps in the passage, the door was opened and the woman of the house stood before her peering out into the darkness and the snow. On seeing Imogen she looked surprised.

"Good evening, mistress," she said. "Do you want to see Mr. Kharkoff?"

"I wanted to know whether a gentleman who called some time ago is still here. He came with me. I brought him. I've been waiting for him outside."

"He is still here, mistress." (She held up one hand.)

"Don't you hear him?"

"Hear——"

"Listen now!"

Imogen listened, and immediately distinguished above-stairs the sound of a voice. It was rather high pitched, and, from where she was, sounded emotional. It went on and on. Nothing interrupted it. She had an impression of a fierce, emotional outpouring. She did not hear any words definitely. If that had been possible she would not have listened.

"What time is it, please?" she said to the woman.

The woman drew out from some hidden pocket near her middle a large silver watch. "It's just on nine."

"Nine?"

"Yes, mistress."

After a pause, filled up by that high-pitched, emotional voice above-stairs, Imogen said, "When my—when that gentleman leaves Mr. Kharkoff will you please tell him that I have gone back to the Waldhaus?"

"Yes, mistress."

"Thank you. Good night."

"Good night, mistress."

"Look at the snow!"

"Aie! It's a strange night of summer to be sure!"

Still the voice went on speaking rapidly on that upper floor. As Imogen turned away into the night, gave herself to the snow and the darkness, she had the conviction that Berazov was emptying himself, was pouring out all the contents of his nature and personality at the feet of his "enemy," the Jew.

She crossed the little open bit at the back of the chalet, already lightly covered with a tattered mantle of white, found the track that led down towards the Waldhaus, and entered the almost black darkness of the woods. She was obliged to walk cautiously and her progress was slow. But presently she saw at some distance before her, and lower down than she was, the lights of the great hotel. She went on towards them, and when she wasn't far from them she saw between her and them a darkness approaching her. It came up to her, moved aside and was just going to pass her, when she stopped.

"Mr. Hendry!"

"What? It's you, out in all this snow!"

"I've been up to the chalet."

"I'm going there now." He took hold of her hand gently. "I was there today—down there by the church."

"I know."

"I feel it's all right with him." He didn't press her hand, but just held it with his musical hand. And she felt a great sense of friendship coming to her from him.

"There's someone up at the chalet," she said. "A man I know. He arrived today. I took him there. I didn't go in."

"Shall I walk as far as the Waldhaus with you?"

"Yes, do."

They walked in silence till they came into the winding road that leads to the space before the hotel. There they stood in the falling snow and she asked him, "When are you going back to Drearney?"

"I've only got ten days more. Then the holiday time of us ordinary blokes is over, you know, and we have to get back into harness."

"Do you mind?"

"Well, I revel in my life here. I feel it's cleaning me out, getting rid of a lot of dust and dirt that was lying about in the corners, you know. But I've got to get on with my work. I think I shall be ready to begin again when the time comes."

"And I shall have to begin again."

"Yes," he said gently. "That'll be more difficult, I'm afraid."

"It will be difficult, very difficult. Have you ever felt as if a whole life had come to an end for you, and that you must start on another and quite a new sort of life?"

"No, never."

"I do. You see I've been told the truth, the absolute truth about myself, and I've been unable not to believe it. Some-

times I think we are told truths about ourselves which don't
affect us because we don't believe them. But I know now that
I must try to content myself with being a good deal less than
I had thought I could be."

"Ah—I know!" he exclaimed. And an inward look came
into his keen eyes. "Some people can breathe comfortably on
the heights and some just can't. And those who can't must stay
a bit lower down."

"Yes. I'm one of them."

"Anyhow," he said, like a boy, "you're true blue. I'm
certain of that." An extraordinary look of warm, understanding kindness, even tenderness, came into his eyes as he stood
looking at her. "True blue! And that's what matters."

"But he said to me once that this air is the air people need."

"Then some day——" he said. And when he said that she
felt the beginning of a great hope in her heart.

A quick step sounded beyond them. Imogen looked round
and saw Berazov.

"Well, I'll be off!" said Hendry. "Good night."

"Good night." As he went away he passed Berazov, and
Imogen saw Berazov give him a long look.

"Why did you wait?" said Berazov as he came up. "In all
this snow! And it's so late! I forgot. I forgot everything."

He was very pale and looked, she thought, exhausted. Yet
he had been walking fast. She had noticed the swiftness of
his steps.

"I forgot about the time, too, till just before it began to
snow."

"May I come up to your sitting-room just for a minute?
I won't stay."

"Yes, come."

They went up in the lift. When they were in her room
Berazov said, "I have confessed myself to a Jew!"

He began to walk up and down the room. She noticed now
that there was perspiration on his pale face. She felt that he
was exhausted. Yet it was obvious that he was terribly excited.
"D'you know your Bible well?" he said, stopping before her.

"No; not very well."

"There's a sentence in it that comes to me—*He told me all
things that ever I did*. Do you remember it?"

"Yes. But I can't remember in what connection. Didn't a
woman say it? Yes—surely."

"Perhaps. I don't know. But I know this; I told that man all things that ever I did. I emptied myself. I had to empty myself. It was like a seizure. I told him, and yet I felt that it was unnecessary, I felt that he knew already. And now I'm empty. There's nothing in me. There's nothing left. I've got rid of it all. Let him bear it, if he can. If he doesn't want to, if he isn't fit to—up to it, as you English say—then he shouldn't be as he is." Suddenly he stretched out his hand and gripped her shoulder with it. "I told him about *us* in London," he said. "D'you mind?"

"No!"

"You don't hate me for that?"

"No."

"I told him what I said to you about God and the Jew. I couldn't help it. I had to. It was *he* who was there with you. But you know that of course."

She didn't say anything.

"I told him of my Jew-hatred—everything. And now it's gone. Everything's gone out of me. I couldn't hate now." He was still holding her shoulder. But she was sure that he didn't know he was holding it. *"Le panier est vide!"* he said, breaking into French.

He was staring at Imogen. But she wasn't at all sure that he saw her. There was something visionary in his eyes.

"Tolstoy wrote a thing called 'The Kingdom of God is within you,'" he said. "I've met so-called saints in Russia. I've met healers, mystics by the dozen, dirty wanderers, some of them impressive, some of them with hypnotic powers as Rasputin had, some of them all charlatan, making money in the name of God." (He crossed himself.) "This man, this Jew, doesn't belong to that tribe, or to any tribe. I'll tell you how it is with him." (He lowered his voice.) "There's more of the Kingdom of God housed within him than there is in any other man I have ever met. He may not know it. But I know it. He's got more than his share."

A shiver ran through his body. And then he spoke for two or three minutes in Russian. Imogen did not know what he was saying, but to her it sounded like a prayer. He stopped speaking, looked down, and then turned to go out of the room. But at the door he stopped abruptly and turned round.

"That man I met tonight, just when I was coming up to you, was the man you were with that day I came over to

Drearney, the man you went to have tea with, instead of
coming to Canon Barrimore's—wasn't he?"

"Yes," she said.

"Some day—it may be a long time yet, a very long time, but
some day you will marry that man."

He turned and went out of the room.

On the next morning the world was covered with summer
snow, and Berazov had gone.

CHAPTER VIII

NOT many days later, but when September had come in and
the time of the vintage was not very far off, Imogen arrived
alone at Geneva and put up once more at the Hotel les Bergues
on the edge of the Rhône. She had managed to secure a back
room from Sils-Maria, although the hotel was crowded. For
the Assembly of the League of Nations was taking place, and
busy men from the near countries and the ends of the earth
were gathered together to promote the cult of the olive-branch.
The bustle in the sunlit streets was considerable. Secretaries
ran to and fro. Carefully dressed delegates with dispatch cases
under their arms passed solemnly across the bridge by the
island in shining motor-cars. Smart women had gathered in
throngs to look down from the galleries of the bare hall
devoted to the meetings of the League upon the important
peacemakers sitting in lines below. Geneva was vivid, was
genuinely alive. The great fountain played by the lakeside,
the steamers were decorated with flags, the townspeople looked
almost frisky. And no voice cried above the various tumult of
the town, "Is it peace?" Here man was at least making his
effort, and no rooms had been solicitously reserved for the
ironic.

Imogen arrived late in the evening. She was only going to
stay for two nights. Then she would travel back to England
to begin again.

On the following day in the afternoon she set out on the
errand which had brought her to Geneva. But on the way
she deviated from the direct route to her destination, and after
crossing the river she went first to the book-shop of Madame
Coiret. She found many people there intent on the buying of

magazines and books. The assistants were all hard at work, and she saw Madame Coiret in the distance, surrounded by a group of earnest American tourists, and evidently being bombarded with questions. She lingered in the shop glancing at a book here and there, and gradually edging her way towards the proprietress. An assistant at last got free and came up to her.

"What can I do for you, madame?"

"I know Madame Coiret. When she's at liberty I want to speak to her for a moment, please."

Evidently hearing her name mentioned Madame Coiret looked round with her earnest eyes. For a moment she did not seem to recognize Imogen. Then she smiled faintly and bowed. A moment later she extricated herself from the maze of horn spectacles and came up to Imogen.

"I think you came to see me once at night with Mademoiselle Creswell."

"My aunt—yes."

Madame Coiret held out her hand gravely.

"Have you time? Can I speak to you for a minute? Of course I see you're very busy."

"Yes. I mustn't go far. I fear I can't ask you upstairs. But please come in here." And she led Imogen to a small book-room at the back of the big shop and shut the door behind them.

"There are so many here for the Assembly, and others who come because they think there is something to see. Monsieur Paderewski for instance is here for them to stare at. Betweenwhiles some of them drop in to buy books and ask for information about various things."

"I'm only here till tomorrow. Then I'm going to England."

"Do please sit down."

Imogen took a chair, by a table covered with books, in the sunshine coming from a window that looked out towards the river. Madame Coiret politely took another chair.

"After what happened that night, madame, I thought I should like just to see you in passing through. I scarcely could tell you why, apart from my gratitude to you for—no, that's not quite true."

She paused. Madame Coiret waited with her eyes fixed on Imogen's face.

"I saw Peter Kharkoff that night. And since then I have got to know him much better. When I was in great trouble he came to me on the Riviera. I have seen him in the Engadine too, at Sils-Maria. I wanted to tell you that he has changed all my views of life."

"I am not surprised," said Madame Coiret.

"Do you remember my telling you that night about an accident to a man who wanted to marry me?"

"Yes."

"He is dead."

"I am very sorry."

"The accident didn't kill him. He committed suicide at Sils-Maria while I was there quite recently. We were going to be married."

"How terrible!"

"Yes. He did it on account of me. And Peter Kharkoff has made me understand exactly why. And through that understanding I've come to a real knowledge of myself, and of some, at least, of the meaning of life. I felt I should like to tell you. And now I mustn't keep you. I'm going to the rue les Bergues. Peter Kharkoff is expecting me. He has promised to take me into his studio, to show me a statue in wood there carved by him. It's a statue of Christ. Perhaps you have seen it."

"I have seen it once," said Madame Coiret.

"I came here to see it and him once more. Then I shall go back to England and start again."

Madame Coiret stretched out a thin, dry hand and touched Imogen's right hand which was resting on the table among the books.

"I'm glad you are going to see it," she said. "You are young. All those who are young can help with the future, if only they can be brought to understand what is necessary in life, if life is to be made better, not only for a few of us, but for the race. And it's really so simple. It's so simple. But somehow men and women find it up to now so very difficult, often I suppose so impossible to—to—how can I say?—to work out in practice." She took away her hand and added, "If, as you say, Monsieur Kharkoff has changed all your views of life *you* might try."

She did not explain exactly what she meant. Imogen was left to guess at that or to inquire into the matter. But she did not inquire. She felt that probably Madame Coiret was going to say something more, or that, if she did not, light would come to her presently in Peter Kharkoff's studio. From Madame Coiret she gathered that the wooden statue might convey the hidden meaning to her. Of course already she could guess at it. The words "compassion," "pity," "love" came up in her mind as she sat in the sunshine among the books waiting for more.

"It's very strange to me," Madame Coiret said, after a rather long pause which she had evidently filled up with thought. "The difficulty people often seem to have in giving way to their good impulses. Many resist them and are certainly ashamed of them. The fact is, perhaps, that we have an inclination to hide the part of us which lies deepest and which is most essential in us. Do you know"—here she seemed to Imogen to be making a conscious effort, and a very faint flush came into her face—"that my husband carefully concealed his affection for me. He came of a Geneva family, and was sternly religious, if you can understand that. His atmosphere was harsh. I was not exactly afraid of him, but I often felt ill at ease with him. And often I thought I irked him. It was only when he was dying that I discovered that I meant much more to him than anything else in the world. He was in great pain, and it seemed that he had to tell me. The pain seemed to tear the avowal out of him. I remember he said, 'Now I'm going I can't help telling you——' We ought to show those qualities and feelings which *must* shine out in the farther regions much more than we do. But I think goodness is terribly shy in many people. And shyness makes people seem often the reverse of what they are. I want to take as my motto, 'Uncover your good.' But somehow——"

At this moment there was a sharp tap on the door. Madame Coiret called *"Entrez!"*

The door was opened and an assistant appeared. *"Pardon, madame, mais une dame Américaine——"*

"Je viens." Imogen got up with Madame Coiret. "I'm so sorry to have to——"

"It's all right. Thank you for seeing me. Good-by."

"Good-by."

Imogen bent forward.

"May I?" She gently kissed one of the still slightly flushed cheeks. "It is difficult. But I shall remember your motto."

A sudden light shone in the bookseller's grave dark eyes. "Be one of the young who help with the future." She touched Imogen's right shoulder, smiling now. "My English isn't so bad," she said in English. "Put your shoulder to the wheel —eh?"

And then they went into the shop.

Imogen walked to the rue les Bergues. When she came to the beginning of it she was surprised to find it very different from her remembrance of it. All the trees were of course in full leaf now. There were flowers in the gardens. The sunshine was strong that day, and the mellowness of the first days of September seemed to breathe out of the warm earth, and to lift itself up to her and to bathe her in subtle fragrance. When she came to the gate of number seven Peter Kharkoff was standing there waiting for her with uncovered head.

"Am I late?" she said. "I went in on the way to see Madame Coiret."

He opened the gate and they shook hands. As they did so she looked at him with a woman's all-seeing eyes, and instantly she remembered the wooden bust she had seen in the Swiss sculptor's house, "Pure thought divorced from emotion." She felt that thought, deep, steady, prolonged and purposeful, played a great part in the life of this man; she felt that in him the use of the mind was a religion; she felt too that he had just recently been dedicating himself to an intense ardor of thought. But she could no longer think of him as one given over to pure thought devoid of emotion. It seemed to her that now she had learned to read him aright. And she knew that even if—and she did not know that—his aim were to extricate his thought from the labyrinth of feeling, nevertheless the prompting motive at the back of it was controlled emotion. The great indifference she had once attributed to him was a myth. He felt; and more deeply than any other man she had ever known.

"If you are late I didn't know it," he said in his deep voice.

She noticed now that he had a key in his hand and she looked towards the studio.

"You are going to keep your promise?"

"Yes."

As they went down the rough garden path bordered with straggling rose bushes she felt a great longing for Hugo to be with her to share this experience.

Peter Kharkoff put the key into the door, turned it, opened the door and let her into the studio. A thick blind was drawn over the north light in it. As she went in she saw in the twilight of it a large dim something at the farther end of the room. She stopped and stood still. Behind her she heard Peter Kharkoff shutting the door. Then he went over to the wall, found a cord and pulled at it. The heavy blind crept away from the glass of the light. The afternoon sunshine came in.

The studio was very bare. It looked like a workshop, not like a room that was used both as a room for working in and for sitting in or entertaining people in as many studios do. There were no ornaments, no curios. Round three sides ran a very broad wooden shelf. Standing on this there were a few busts in wood. The only furniture in the room was three chairs with straw bottoms. Imogen stretched out a hand, pulled forward one of these chairs and sat down on it opposite to a large wooden statue, but not near to it. She felt that she must see it from a distance. As soon as she had sat down Peter Kharkoff walked past her, and, crossing the floor, went out through a small doorway just beyond the statue into a farther room which she had not noticed before. His steps died away. She was alone in the studio.

She did not know what she had expected to see. In truth she had never identified, or even tried to identify, Peter Kharkoff with the work which she knew he sometimes did, work of writing, of carving. She had felt him always as a great personality, never as an artist, although she had known for some time that she had long ago seen, and been deeply impressed by, something that had been conceived in his mind and wrought by his hands. She did not know what she had expected to see. But directly she looked at the wooden figure standing on its platform near the end of the big room she knew that she had not anticipated seeing anything at all like it. And she knew also that her idea about the possible personality and appearance of Christ, despite her supposed modernity, her supposed emancipation from all prejudices and preconceived ideas in art, must have been always strictly conventional. Once she had said to her aunt that directly the word 'Savior' was mentioned five people out of six thought of long fair hair, white robes, white hands, slow movements, conventional gestures of blessing, emaciation, vegetarianism and beards. She had spoken frivolously in her still frivolous period, a period that already seemed to her very far away. But she now knew that she herself must have been numbered among the five people she had secretly laughed at. Certainly she had never dreamed of a Christ like this.

She saw a young man, or rather the dawning of a young man—it seemed to her at first like that—not fully released as it were from the material, the mass of material, that the sculptor had chosen to work on. He seemed to be on the point of emerging from it full of vigorous power. His limbs—the part of them, that is, which the sculptor had chosen so far to show—were those of a swift, not of a heavy, athlete. His body looked light and active, yet very strong and entirely unafraid. Moreover it had, Imogen felt, a marvelously cheerful look, a radiance of eager life about it, keen, absolutely unconventional. There was nothing there to demand pity, to claim affection because of a presage of suffering. No clothing was suggested. Yet somehow there was no marked suggestion of nudity either. As Imogen sat and gazed she simply felt that she was confronted by life housed in the human male body, by intense life, absolutely courageous, absolutely free from any doubt as to its mission in the world. That was her first impression. And its mission was surely to spread hope, confidence in the future, joyous confidence untouched by the faintest suspicion of doubt. This was indeed a son of the morning, she thought. But a Christ! No, surely not a Christ!

That was her first impression. But as she continued to look, giving herself or trying to give herself up wholly to this wrought conception of Peter Kharkoff, she began to feel that her conventionality was getting in her way, was trying to blind her to his meaning. She was still lingering with the Christs of Italian painters, with Holman Hunt's "Light of the World" and "The Shadow of Death," with how many other Christs which, en masse, have stamped a convention upon the minds of men. She must escape from them. And she continued to sit and to gaze at the statue, trying to be quite unbiased. And gradually, as she sat there in the absolute silence, she seemed to herself to be coming to an understanding of what Peter Kharkoff had meant to convey in this work of his. It was surely not a representation of Christ, the son of Mary, but an embodiment of—what?

The face of the statue was crude and looked unfinished, and

was crowned with a suggestion of rough, strong hair. It reminded Imogen faintly of the face of the Sphinx. It reminded her too of the face of a wonderful young Russian peasant. It was beardless. And that seemed to her, though she did not know why, right. The face had to be beardless. And as the face of the Sphinx suggests not a personality but rather a conception, a conception of Eternity, so this face of Peter Kharkoff's Christ suggested to Imogen now not a holy person but a conception of affection. And this affection was not a pitiful love, but a strong, warm, all-embracing affection, robust as the mountains, wide as the sea or the firmament. And there was a mighty eagerness in it, an eagerness that lifted up the heart, that called forth an answering eagerness.

Imogen began to smile as she looked. But tears came with the smile. And she thought, "Why is the world afraid? Why am I afraid?" And then all fear went away from her. Looking still, she soon entirely lost the young Russian peasant. He seemed to fade away in the statue, leaving only the conception of robust, unfaltering, wide-spreading and confident love. And Imogen felt sure that this Christ was Peter Kharkoff's conception of the love of God for man, shown to man in the likeness of man.

What had perhaps puzzled her when she first looked at the statue, what even now made her wonder, was the absence of pity from this conception. For there was no pity in this Christ.

She heard the steps of Peter Kharkoff returning, she saw his tall figure and powerful face in the doorway, crowned with the thick slab of upstanding hair. And then she remembered that once she had thought him indifferent. Was that because he never showed any conventional pity for suffering? Now she had the conviction that his apparent lack of pity came from his absolute certainty of what the end would be, of the ultimate destination of man. This conviction came to her suddenly as she saw him coming towards her. And she rejoiced in his lack of pity, or perhaps, better to say, in his lack of all expression of pity. And now it inspired her with a marvelous feeling of courage.

He who sees the goal and sees that it is glorious has no need to weep over the perils of the way.

She got up from her chair. She said nothing about the statue. She just joined Peter Kharkoff, and they went out together from the studio into the afternoon sunshine.

Before she parted from him that day, when the evening was falling, she said to him, "You are my friend now. I know that. Or—no—you have always been my best friend. But I used to be half afraid of you, I think. I wove strange fancies about you. Did you know it?"

"Yes. I knew it."

"I had a name for you. I called you 'The Unearthly.'"

He looked down steadily at her with penetrating eyes, and for a moment there was silence. Then he said, "You gave that name to me? And why not to yourself?"

"To myself!" she said, wondering.

"Haven't you and I, and all of us, those needs, those yearnings we once spoke of together, yearnings in which we go out from our comrades, our friends, even from those who love us, and are alone and mysterious? We spoke of them, you and I. Don't you remember?"

"Yes, I remember."

"Don't we all share those needs, those yearnings, in spite of our loneliness in them?"

"Yes, I believe we do."

He looked away from her for a moment as one who looks to a far horizon. Then he said in a low, withdrawn voice:

"The truth is this, surely, my friend and comrade: every one of us is unearthly."

THE END.